MOON OF ICE

BRAD LINAWEAVER
MOON OF ICE

54,008

ARBOR HOUSE | William Morrow   New York

Library of Congress Cataloging in Publication Data

Linaweaver, Brad, 1952–
Moon of ice / Brad Linaweaver.
    p.   cm.
ISBN 0-87795-945-5
I. Title.
PS3562.I4715M6   1988   87-27210
813'.54—dc19   CIP

Manufactured in the United States of America
Published in Canada by Fitzhenry & Whiteside, Ltd.
10 9 8 7 6 5 4 3 2 1

Moon of Ice appeared as a novella, "Moon of Ice," in *Amazing,* © 1982,
and in *Hitler Victorious,* © 1986.

To the Mad Gang, my old group of friends,
with a special nod to Bill Ritch.

To three editors who helped my story through
its gestation: Elinor Mavor the first time out,
Gregory Benford the second time, and David
Hartwell for making the novel possible.

To my agent, Cherry Weiner, and my wife, Cari.

And finally to the Sense of Wonder that makes our
field notable.

ACKNOWLEDGMENTS

With a book as controversial as this may prove to be, acknowledgments should come with a disclaimer. Everyone listed below either contributed encouragement or suggestions (and in some cases both). When they see this page, they will also be encountering the final form of the novel for the first time. Omitted are names more prominently displayed in the dedication. Wendayne and Forrest J Ackerman, Robert Adams, Clifton Amsbury, Jimmy Arthur, Isaac Asimov, Robert Bloch, Berl Boykin, Ray Bradbury, David Brin, William F. Buckley, Jr., John F. Carr, Joe Celko, Gordon B. Chamberlain, Chauntecleer Michael, Comrade Wally, Marion Crowder, Earl Davis, Martin H. Greenberg, Paul Greiman, Craig Halstead, Big Lee Haslup, Robert A. Heinlein, Gail Higgins, Arthur Hlavaty, Phil Klass (William Tenn), Victor Koman, Samuel Edward Konkin III, Kerry Kyle, Robert LeFevre, Rebecca Leggett (Aunt Becky), June and Melville Linaweaver (my parents), David T. Lindsay, Alex Lucyshyn, Sandi March, Dr. Bill Martin, Michael Medved, Chesley V. Morton, André Norton, Alex Nunan, Michael Ogden, Gerald W. Page, Jerry Pournelle, Dr. Steven S. Riley, Leland Sapiro, J. Neil Schulman, Cary Ser, Michael Shaara, Robert Shea, Joe D. Siclari, Charles T. Smith, L. Neil Smith, Norman Spinrad, Mark Stanfill, Edie Stern, James L. Sutherland, Wilson "Bob" Tucker, Dr. James Whittemore, Warren Williams, Robert Anton Wilson, and Zolton Zucco, Jr.

PROLOGUE

He who controls the past controls information.
He who controls information controls decisions.
He who controls decisions controls the future.

—George Orwell, *1984*

They took him out under the stars of Burgundy, and they laid him upon the damp grass. The women had implements of marking, and these they used to write a secret language upon his forehead. Behind them stood the flagellomaniac, his muscles grown hard and lean from the use of his whip—and trembling in anticipation should need arise to punish the chosen one.

"Behold the heavens, behold the eternal enemy," intoned an elderly man, his voice muffled by the deerskin hood he wore. "Tell us what you see."

The chosen one did not hesitate: "Above is an eternity of ice."

"Tell us the answer to our dilemma," demanded the voice.

"Only through fire do we hold back the ice; only the flame melts the dagger that would freeze our souls."

The whip cracked through the still, summer air, leaving a red welt above the right pectoral muscle of the chosen one—who felt the pain as an electric shock, followed by a dull ache. A sudden tightening in the stomach made him glad that he had only eaten a plain potato before the ceremony. Through gritted teeth, he corrected his error: "The dagger would freeze the Folk Spirit that underlies the Aryan Soul, and we who are of the *Völk* must stand as one."

The man in the deerskin hood took no notice of the interruption, but he continued in the same even tone of voice. "What is that?" he asked, as he pointed to a bright dot of light in the east.

"The space station."

"What does it portend?"

"It is an assault on the Eternal Ice; it would bring on us a judgment that might quench the flame."

1

"What must be done?"

"The station must fall. It must burn. It must be given to the flame."

The man in the hood nodded to the women, and the younger came forward carrying a small, black cylinder. "Are you prepared to receive the vision?" she asked.

"I am."

The cylinder had a small suction cup on one end, and by this means was it attached to a spot on the chosen one's forehead that had been marked with a polygon. Immediately the night sky above the chosen one disappeared, to be replaced by roiling clouds at midday . . . but it was a darksome daylight that gave the impression of night.

He got to his feet, but with some difficulty because of heavy armor that he now wore. He could smell his own sweat and cursed the strain on his legs. But there was no more pain from the welt; it was as if he had never been whipped.

In his hand was a weapon unlike any he had ever seen. Four oddly shaped blades rotated slowly above a handgrip that seemed almost an extension of his mailed fist. Somewhere deep inside, there was knowledge whispering to the chosen one: "This weapon is of the people and of the soil; it is the *Völk* weapon. It can only serve if you obey!"

Behind him was a great throng of beautiful women and handsome youths. They all looked to him. Then they looked beyond, and he felt a compulsion to follow their gaze. What he saw made him tremble.

Giants loomed on the horizon, dark as the hills whence they came. They had sloping features and little pig's eyes that glittered with a deep malice. And they were on the march. Raising his weapon, the chosen one sought to engage the foe, but again his secret voice spoke to him: "There can be no defense unless the Folk Spirit is pure. One there is among you who corrupts the rest."

Yes, it was true—he could find one who didn't belong. The face did not have the fine features of its companions, nor was it bestial like the giants. The face was an unnatural amalgam of the attractive and the repulsive. And the owner of that face knew he was found out the moment the chosen one caught his glance.

Now did the blades of the weapon begin to spin, faster and faster, until they were a blur of motion. The weapon pulled his arm toward

2

the fleeing form of the enemy . . . and then, despite the weight of the armor, he was flying, lightly and quickly and with joy. He marveled at the surgical precision by which the traitor's head was separated from his ungainly body.

Although the blades still spun madly, he could see a stain of red to mark their work. And now the weapon lifted him straight up into the purple vault of the heavens . . . and he felt himself thrown at the bovine faces of the giants, so brutish that they did not even show surprise. Expressionless they had lived; expressionless they died.

When the sanguinary work was finished, the chosen one stood in a lake of blood. The people cheered and loved him. He was complete. Then did the people point to the sky, where far away to the east glimmered a sickly, yellow light. There would he attend to his most important task.

The blades were at rest. Gazing at them, he was grateful that so long as he wielded such a weapon, nothing could withstand his might. Not even the stars were safe from the man who held the shining power of the Swastika.

CHAPTER ONE

In the twentieth century there will be an extraordinary
nation. . . . And that nation will be called Europe.

—Victor Hugo,
Preface to *Paris-Guide*

New York

"You're damned lucky, young man, that you're not speaking German today!" The speaker was an elderly man. Although dressed conservatively, there was something incongruous about the delicate rose tattooed on his left cheek—a concession, no doubt, to popular taste, an eccentricity of the professional reactionary.

"Excuse me, sir, but I *do* speak German, along with Japanese, Russian, Yiddish, and, of course, the King's English, not to mention American." Alan Whittmore was used to this sort of abuse and had gotten to the point where he had a number of set answers. As editor of the latest incarnation of *The American Mercury,* it was par for the course.

A new voice joined the chorus: "Your hero Mencken would have sold us down the river, you dead-ed. If it hadn't been for FDR, God bless 'im, we'd be a German colony today, all rightso." The speaker was a Townie, dressed in camo jungle gear and wearing a pink top hat. Judging from the glazed condition of his eyes, he was high on Speck, but that in no way diminished his desire to participate. "Trouble with you dead-eds is you got no grip on harsh realities, dig?"

"Pardon me, but I'd very much enjoy having my lunch in peace. If you wish to engage in badinage, you'll have to be civil, or we'll continue the discussion outside, once we find a witness—perhaps this gentleman who was here first—and I claim first choice of weapons." If he read his man right, that would be the end of it.

"Dampen down," said the Townie, retreating those few crucial steps, before departing altogether, leaving the floor to the old man.

"Do I know you?" asked Whittmore, affecting a smile.

"I'm Dr. Evans. Why don't you ever publish my letters to the editor?"

So that was it! Whittmore's memory was suitably jogged. "You are premature, sir. Your most recent missive has been selected to lead off next issue. I must say that you put the Revisionist case as well as can be expected. As you are familiar with my editorials, you know that I'm sticking with the majority view on this issue. I still believe it was for the best that Roosevelt was impeached. But please join me."

"Thank you," said Evans, settling himself with great care into the seat opposite.

"Health troubles?" asked Whittmore politely.

"Bursitis. Made the mistake of trying the Manchurian method, but now it's worse. My wife warned me against Chinese superstitions, but I didn't listen. God rest her, I've been falling apart since she passed away."

"Perhaps you will allow me to minister to your needs. A drink?"

"A Berlin Blockbuster if you please."

"You won't even know you have any pain after that." Opportunities such as this should not be wasted. It was all too easy to become complacent in one's weltanschauung. Opposing views could be made into a tonic, provided they came in a polite package.

"Sorry about the kid," said Evans, noting that the Townie had merged with his gang, now congregated about the blind man's bluff game. Their occasional shouted imprecations were their sole contribution to the serious matter of barroom debate. "He seems erudite for a young hoodlum. Followed me over. He probably recognized your picture from the papers."

"I've been getting a lot of publicity since Hilda Goebbels signed with me."

A nude waitress glided over on roller skates, flashing a wide grin at them and depositing the drink for Evans, without losing either momentum or a drop of the amber liquid. "I always tip her extravagantly," Alan explained.

"I'm not from the boonies, even if this is my first trip to New York." It was common knowledge, even in Idaho (the good doctor's address, as Whittmore recalled), that in cosmopolitan places the bigger the tip, the less attire was worn by the waiter or waitress who was out to cultivate repeat business. A whole industry had cropped up, producing apparel that could be quickly donned or shed as custom dictated.

"You're here about your book," said Whittmore. Once his memory had been triggered, he was good at detail.

"Thank you for remembering my letter. Vineyard Publishing has agreed to bring it out, even though my thesis is unpopular."

"More power to you, then. Perhaps you don't know this, but I first came to H. L. Mencken's attention in a fight against local censorship. If he hadn't given himself one last editorial fling in the sixties, I doubt I'd hold the position I do today. Anyway, I live by Voltaire's maxim about defending to the death an opponent's right to be heard."

"I know, I know." Evans sounded irritated. "You people use the First Amendment, and the Fourth as well, to undermine any hope for social justice." Evans took his stand: "I am not a Libertarian."

"Obviously the case, but do you have a label you wear in public, other than the one on your suit?"

"Sir, I fought in the Second World War."

"So did my father, and he became a Libertarian."

"Well then, I used to be a New Dealer, but today I think of myself as a traditionalist conservative."

"At least you've remained consistent over the years. But tell me, do you begrudge us our success?"

The old man had been around. He knew when to make a tactical retreat. "I would never dream of interfering with free speech."

"Good man! We'll radicalize you yet."

Evans was having none of it: "Not so long as there is the social injustice of the flat tax, sir." Half the Berlin Blockbuster was gone, apparently inhaled. Whittmore noticed that the more the man drank, the more he peppered his conversation with "sirs" . . . as though he had at some time ingested Boswell's *Life of Johnson,* surely the final word in terminal pomposity. Worse than that, the old man was adopting an annoying familiarity: "Listen here, young fella, you've been decent to me and I want to return the favor. There's a change of mood in the country. This business of normalizing relations with the Greater Reich is not going over. The American people won't stand for it."

A number of quips, courtesy of Mencken's influence, flitted through Whittmore's mind, but he restrained himself. The old man saw himself as a conduit through which flowed the popular will; and if what he had to say just happened to contradict the latest TVotes poll, Whittmore was not about to disabuse him of his notion. The teenage Alan had elected to be a high-church agnostic rather than a fire-and-brimstone atheist. When people claimed to know either the will of God or the will of the people, Whittmore might first think of Adolf Hitler as the patent model for such absurdity, but that was no reason for being insensitive to the vigorously self-deluded. And so: "Perhaps they are not sure what they want. It is not the American government that is having relations with anyone. Remember that as we limit the power of our own state, private individuals are free to deal with whomever they please. If one American corporation finds itself fighting a skirmish with Nazis in South America on Monday, that's no reason another outfit may not open shop in Europe on Tuesday. The National Socialists have so bungled Europe's economy that they have no choice but to let in entrepreneurs."

Dr. Evans was shaking his head, presenting himself with a problem as he was trying to swallow the last of his drink simultaneously. "We're doomed, doomed. Cultural exchanges are bad enough, but the trading of technology will do us in. You speak of opening markets, but all I see is a black abyss."

"A line from your book?"

"A new dawn is coming. The nuclear stalemate won't last forever. I tell you that the Nazis are evil and must be destroyed." Here was a man for whom the war had never ended. Perhaps he was one of those oddballs who continued to refer to sauerkraut as liberty cabbage.

There was no levity in Whittmore's voice as he said, "I agree that the Nazis are evil, but no more so than the Communists they tried and executed at the war crimes trials."

"Ha, you opposed those trials in one of your first editorials, sir!"

What an inconvenience! Here was Whittmore, minding his own business, having a peaceful lunch at Oscar's, when out of nowhere materialized a loyal reader of his words. "Yes, I did, but only because of a moral insight that I cannot claim to be original with me: two wrongs don't make a right."

It went on in this vein for some time. At one point, Evans went so far as to argue that Lord Halifax was innocent of having contributed to the distrust and paranoia that made World War II inevitable. Whittmore told him that his opinion was shockingly unin-formed. Then the dialogue degenerated into the sort of rhetoric one hears on a school playground: of the "is so/is not" variety. By some miracle of grace, they managed to avoid the topic of Pearl Harbor. Even so, there was no longer communication worth the name. They were bouncing slogans off each other, and Whittmore didn't even have a drink of his own.

"One day America will pay for its treatment of Roosevelt, our last great president!" declaimed Evans, his face positively livid with pas-sion.

Wittmore's response was equally windy: "Dewey and Taft helped undo the damage; and those who followed put America back on the road to sanity." Although Evans would grant a kind word for the last Republican presidents, he had nothing but scorn for those who had followed, and their parties, from the America Firsters to the Liberty party. Whittmore got Evans to admit that he saw no value in any of the presidents who had served since the failure of the military coup in 1952. That there had been a proliferation of new political parties did not seem to him an acceptable outcome; he would have preferred a return to the old two-party monopoly, a return to "normalcy," and two chickens in the imaginary pot of the Good Old Days.

"It's true that I was taken in by the scare stories of a Nazi sneak attack," said Evans, "but the conspirators would never have gone to such lengths if the first Liberty party president, crazy Rothbard, hadn't driven them to it. It's a wonder we weren't invaded!"

"The defense of the country was never in doubt—and this was proved by the calm response of those generals who remained loyal to the president while keeping an eagle eye, if you will, on how thoroughly bogged down were the Berlin boys in their latest recon-quest of the glorious Russian steppes. Were you one of the public-spirited fellows looking for Nazis under every bed back then?"

"Please don't accuse me of Roggeism, sir. If I worried about guilt by association I wouldn't be here with you."

"My apologies, then. But I thought that careless fraternization was still cause for alarm in the Bipartisan party."

"What makes you think I'm a member?"

"Well, aren't you?" Whittmore prided himself on his political instincts. The small, ineffectual party gave disaffected Republicans and Democrats of yore a place to congregate. This fellow was made to order as a BP delegate.

"Very well, I am. Where else is a patriot to go these days? You say that the defense of the country was never in doubt. I beg to differ. There is more to defense than just keeping the enemy out. Football coaches tell us that the best defense is a good offense, therefore the righteous must be offensive in nature. Uh, that is, I mean to suggest that our foreign policy was activist during the war. We knew what we wanted. The worst thing that could have happened was the conflict ending in stalemate. Everything had been arranged for Total Victory. Now we are passive and weak."

"Now we are safe and strong, but only after a general housecleaning. Not all the power addicts were on the Axis side. We fixed that."

"But surely you don't think that the fire at the State Department was a good thing. Think of what we lost!"

"Accidents will happen."

"Well, no matter what you say, isolationism will destroy us in the end. There is no neutrality in this world."

"Nonintervention opens doors that an empire would close."

And so forth. They had raised their voices, a mistake in a restaurant flooded with Townies who were already bored with their game—a banal use of computer graphics and a cattle prod that could only engage the attention of mental children for a brief period—and were attracted to the sound of anger as if they were lawyers. The intellectual of the gang came skipping back, his top hat tilting ludicrously, as if a chimney in an earthquake. The rumbling of violence was in his manner, and his compatriots were close behind. Evans began to tremble, no doubt unused to the ways of Town No. #1.

"I hate to be surrounded before dessert," said Whittmore.

"Still want to rip and roar outside, Herr Editor? You goddamn kraut lover. Bet you're a Slav lover, too. Let's go for broke, hey?"

The machine pistol in Whittmore's pocket was useless inside a place this crowded. He wasn't going to spend the rest of his life in insurance litigation. Trouble was that bums like this had no family ties any longer, and what passed for a community among them was not exactly awash in funds.

Whittmore's half-million-dollar insurance policy against assassination would mean that Uni-Life would receive one of their more expensive Hunt-and-Destroy licenses. Well, solvency was every

9

American's docket. He'd be doing both Uni-Life and himself a favor if he could maneuver the Townies outside.

"Hold it!" Everyone in the restaurant knew the owner's voice. Oscar sounded like he was speaking from inside an echo chamber. He was as heavily built as his place. He'd made a name for himself as far back as the Detroit race riots. He was probably not much younger than Evans; but you'd never believe it to look at the condition of his muscles. "Townies, I wants a word with you."

"Ho, ho, Mistuh Sleep-and-Eat, you run the biz, but you're no scholar. Bad grammar equals big bucks, hey?" The intellectual was at it again. Alan could tell from the expression on Oscar's face that he was not inclined to dispute the Townie at the verbal level. Too bad, thought the editor; because the proprietor could express better than anybody the feeling during the times of trouble that the NRA really stood for the Negro Replacement Act. Well, the Townies were about to experience removal for reasons no man of goodwill could question.

A bald girl, who couldn't have been any older than fifteen, shrieked at her ostensible leader: "You gootch! You gettin' us in dutch with a nigger bruiser!"

"I've got no Chinese down my back, bitch!" was his witty reply. "Just for that, you don't get any fluid tonight."

Unconcerned with domestic quarrels among the emotionally handicapped, Oscar headed straight for his target and lifted the Townie by the lapels of his camo jacket. "Now lissen here, dirt-boy. I gots nothing against your money. Anytime your money wants to come into my joint, it's welcome. I has a kid studyin' to be an aerospace engineer and every cent I can spare goes to him in Florida. But when you mess with other customers, mebbe they won't let their money come visitin' next time."

The logic of the argument was entirely lost on the Townie, whose mental equipment was otherwise engaged, to wit: "You're tearin' the suit, coon." Among his other virtues, Oscar inspired loyalty in his staff. Waitresses, clothed and otherwise, began skating over, each holding the most lethal weapon known to the strip: razor sharp serving trays. In an amazing display of extrapolative ability, the gang broke into its constituent parts . . . and each and every mother's son and daughter of them ran for their lives. Chastened from his lack of

10

moral support, the Townie dangling from Oscar's large, black hand attempted to be diplomatic: "Lookie here, uh, innkeeper. We were just fraggin' around, joshin' don't you know. Jeepers creepers, there's no need to wad your panties."

"Oscar," said Whittmore quietly. "I have a theory I've been wanting to put to the test."

"What is it, Mr. Whittmore?"

"I believe that the harder you shake this kid, the more English words will pour out."

Oscar had a disarming chuckle that he now enjoyed to the limit. "I has been feeling scientific lately."

The experiment began: "Now wait a mo', you gribbin' "—SHAKE —"Uh, er, we can glom"—SHAKE—"Damn your blitzkriegin' "— SHAKE—"OK, OK, stop, will you?" Oscar stopped. "What do you want me to do?" asked the Townie.

"I understood what he said," said Evans, getting into the spirit of the moment. It took but another moment to convince the young man to deposit his remaining gold notes on the table as restitution for any mental cruelty that Whittmore had suffered. Then the Townie left, swaying as if he were an uptown socialite. Whittmore convinced Oscar to take a sizable tip from the windfall, and the proprietor joked that he wouldn't disrobe in gratitude.

Dr. Evans never did regain his belligerency of tone, but surprised Alan with: "You would have made a good New Dealer."

"God, you must simply love nostalgia! I guess you mean it as a compliment, in which case thanks."

Evans didn't seem to hear. He was looking at the door where the Townie had departed the premises. "I hate listening to a punk like that pretend at patriotism. If Oscar hadn't done it, I would have laid hands on the bum for ignorantly employing the term 'jeepers creepers.'"

"I'm afraid I don't understand."

"As I mentioned earlier, I served in the Pacific. We set up signs in the jungle with an arrow pointing one way for clear paths the jeeps could use, and another arrow pointing where the creeping vines made egress impossible."

"I've heard that phrase for years, but I had no idea what it meant."

They began walking to the door, and Whittmore offered the old

11

man a ride in the cab. "No, thank you," he replied, "but I would like to ask you one last question. Are you really going to bring out those books by Hilda Goebbels?"

"I'm on my way to see her right now."

"It won't be good for your country."

The presumption of the man was too much. Whittmore might never be gracious to a stranger again. "What the hell do you mean by that?" As he asked the question, he felt a drop of rain sting his ear.

"Why give that person an American audience?"

"Stop right there!" They had reached the curb. "I don't like what you're implying. Nobody in the world is a more devout anti-Nazi than Hilda Goebbels."

"That's what she *wants* us to believe. But when you consider all the things her father did—"

"Part of what we know against her father is thanks to her! And she's about to release even more information. She's a hero to the European underground. America is lucky to receive her."

"Blood is thicker than water."

It started to rain in earnest. For one crazy moment, Whittmore watched drops splash about the rose on Dr. Evans's face, anticipating that the tattoo would wash away.

"You've asked me a lot of questions. Let me ask you another. What is the main thing you hate about the Nazis?"

Dr. Evans didn't hesitate: "They're bigots."

CHAPTER TWO

And many more Destructions played
In this ghastly masquerade,
All disguised, even to the eyes,
Like bishops, lawyers, peers or spies.

—Percy Bysshe Shelley,
The Mask of Anarchy

It was raining hard, and Whittmore was glad that he had hailed a Frontier Hugger, a cab line renowned for all-terrain wheels. He was going uptown on a street with as many craters as the surface of the moon. He didn't like it, but he wouldn't buy it.

Betting pools were still giving best odds against anyone taking on the responsibility of the unowned thoroughfares. Meanwhile, people lived by the slogan "If you can't make the road for the wheels, make the wheels for the roads." It was an obvious market solution.

As one of the curses of being an editor, Whittmore had a good memory for statistics. There had been 900,000 miles of highway in 1940. The plans for expansion had been on a monumental scale that, quite predictably, took no cognizance of local economies. The New Dealers had drawn a number of faulty parallels between the building of the railroads and the haphazard construction of these superhighways; and they had planned their projects to go on and on, once the troublesome matter of World War II had achieved its industrial objectives.

The irony was that all their dreams had come true, but on another continent, and thanks to another kind of public works project. Hitler had kept his promise about the autobahns for the Greater Reich. Today, superhighways stretched the length of Europe and even penetrated into the dismal Russian east, where none had ever dreamed a road could find its way. And yet the markets did not exist to support the maintenance of these vast ribbons of transport (and the

13

promises that the roads would bring commerce in their wake had hardly lived up to the rosy projections).

Albert Speer had devised variations on every technical solution imaginable, but there were never enough marks to cover the costs. His successor, Frack, was enamored of the notion that roads could be constructed in sections, and as one piece wore out, it could be replaced by another in stock. The transport difficulties were incredible: guerrilla action soon concentrated on intercepting the giant trucks bringing the new sections and wearing out the road they traversed. Use of railroads led to even more problems. And so the National Socialists further bankrupted the Reich. In keeping with Hitler's approach to other problems, his last official order had been to start work on the greatest autobahn in the world. Half finished, overrun with weeds, the remains of this project reached half the length of Africa.

Whittmore felt a small satisfaction to know that some locally maintained U.S. roads were superior to anything in Europe today, which proud thought neatly coincided with a jarring bump beneath him. Never one to discount an omen, Whittmore amended his position by picturing vast tracts of land that had never been graced with an American highway system. Critics of the market continually complained about wasted space and went so far as to suggest that if the city owned the road Whittmore was even now enjoying it would no longer be a surrealistic study in potholes and jagged buckling. Whittmore could not help but imagine a worse scenario: a situation in which tolls were paid on a daily basis . . . and the roads remained in a state of disrepair. A student of borough politics, he was always willing to assume the worst.

A question that had been nagging at him recently was the old thorny riddle of causation: did people determine the objects they made and used, or did the articles determine the inclinations of the people so completely that "choice" was largely illusory? Did the road taken have to determine the outcome, when there were so many stopping places along the way? Surely all decisions resided in the individual ego, but then, there were so many egos to consider. Although an adherent to the Great Man Theory of History in his writings, Whittmore was coming to sorrowful conclusions about the ponderous weight of events in their cumulative power.

On the spur of the moment, Whittmore asked the cabbie: "What do you think of German roads?"

The man, a chunky Russian in his mid-forties, grinned and said, "I've never driven them, but I can tell you plenty about Hong Kong. You don't get around there without a 'copter."

Well, if one had the stomach for it, that was probably the best way to travel. Still, Whittmore preferred wheels, even on his last trip to New Berlin. They drove like maniacs over there, as if worried they would lose their statistical distinction for highest automobile casualties in the world.

A particularly nasty bump brought Whittmore firmly back to the realities of Manhattan. His head had struck the ceiling. Such was his vanity that his primary concern was that he not appear disheveled before the woman he had wanted to meet for years: Hilda Goebbels. When she had telephoned the day before to say that she would be waiting for him in the penthouse of a swank hotel, he had felt his pulse quicken in excitement, as if he had just been granted an interview with Mata Hari in one of his favorite novels. The comparison was not inappropriate. Hilda was a remarkable woman who had lived dangerously and won battles. Her life was like something out of a romantic fantasy. Bred to be one of the aristocracy of the New Order, she had finally balked at being a Nazi Aryan princess. But it was a perilous journey to go from being a youthful rebel to underground revolutionary. Along the way, many rumors had attached themselves to her name, the worst being the charge Whittmore had just rebuffed from Dr. Evans.

Other rumors had less the ring of a charge in open court than the confidential whisper of gossip in a closed bedroom. Was it true that she had had a lesbian relationship with a young Jewess? Was it true that Hitler had once tried to seduce her? Was it true that she had killed her own brother, and this after an incestuous relationship? That which titillated sold copy, but Whittmore disliked pandering to it, especially when he thought of the "Wowsers"—Mencken's invaluable label—who would buy every detestable excess of the libeler's art, linger over every libidinous passage, then mount the public rostrum to declaim against the very thing that engaged their attention.

There was one rumor about Hilda Goebbels that fascinated Whittmore, but it was an entirely different sort of thing from the gossip mongers. If untrue, it was nonetheless born of high regard for the woman, even if it had an almost comic book quality to it. The suggestion was that she had helped to prevent World War III by thwarting a conspiracy of the SS.

No matter how fantastic the claim, if she was the subject of it the story was worth investigating. Whittmore knew for a fact that although not a scientist herself, she had helped advance the cause of medicine. She had done this by smuggling important papers about genetic research out of the Reich and into British hands. Although ostensibly allied with Europe in Mosley's postwar Fascist government, a sizable portion of the populous British Isles maintained economic ties with their North American cousins. Alfred Rosenberg could complain all he wanted to about the so-called "brain drain" (as it was vulgarly described in what remained of London), but German discoveries, and the discoverers themselves, often found their way to American shores. In this instance, Hilda had been the transmission belt for what, one expert told Whittmore, was the most important theoretical work and experimental records since entering the atomic age.

The woman could have had American citizenship right then, with ribbons on it, but she chose to travel the world sans any citizenship for nearly half a decade. She had written that, as an anarchist, she saw no reason to give her sanction to any state, even one as freedom loving as the American Republic. It was hard sometimes for Whittmore, a professional advocate of limited government, to realize just how deep ran Hilda's aversion to any form of the state; but, then, she had been born into the heart of Nazism.

Well, she would make a lot of people happy by her symbolic cooperation. Bio-Cure Industries was throwing a big party for her next week, and she had accepted their invitation, with the one proviso that she not be asked to say their advertising logo for the cameras: "Splice genes and live longer."

Since the death of her father, the notorious propaganda minister and all-around bureaucrat of the Greater Reich, Hilda had gone to elaborate lengths to secure his private papers. The cost had been high, in life as well as money, but she had achieved her purpose. Now, five years after the death of Joseph Goebbels, his apostate daughter was about to release the final entries of his world-famous

16

diary, material that had been suppressed in Germany and all its colonies. That Alan Whittmore had become involved with the release of this material still seemed unreal to him. Hilda was going to sign an exclusive contract for both the diary entries and her own autobiography with the youthful editor who was bouncing in the back seat of a New York cab while dreaming of sitting at the wheel, if only briefly, of history's engine.

Yes, it was the biggest break Alan had had since coming to Mencken's attention in the twilight of the grand old man's life. Thank God that his father had lived to see that much. And thank God that the elder Mencken, failing badly in his sixties, had consented to try a new treatment that not only added years to his life, but gave him the stamina to return to editing for one last fling. According to legend, Mencken had had only one quibble before undergoing therapy: he wanted a written assurance that what he was about to receive was in no way a disguised form of chiropractic procedure! Whittmore doubted the veracity of the story, but he enjoyed telling it anyway. Sometimes the instinct of the journalist got in the way of the would-be historian.

There would be no room for that sort of thing with the Goebbels manuscripts. Every expert in the world (no matter his field!) would be out to challenge every line of what was printed. He'd read somewhere that paranoia was the condition of having *all* the facts. If there was any virtue to be had from the nervous habit of glancing over one's shoulder, now was the time to cultivate it!

Partly as a joke to himself, but more in the manner of a dare, Alan turned around and looked through the back window of the cab. The car immediately behind was a very well-maintained specimen of a Horch limousine. At first he was seized with admiration for the quality of maintenance on the antique, the make of which he estimated to be 1936. The rain was beading on the glossy wax finish, and as the car swayed on the unnaturally large wheels required for travel in New York City, it gave the impression of a ship at sea, weathering the storm in all its black majesty. The second feeling he had was a gentle self-mockery. The small ripple of paranoia could become a tidal wave that would engulf the last of his good sense if he didn't get hold of himself. *Just a coincidence,* he told himself, *that a sinister vehicle should be available on cue.* The damned car did give a first impression of being a hearse.

There was really no escape from worry. Those without money worried how to get it; those with it worried how to keep it; and nobody but nobody thought he had adequate security, the magic word that all too often was synonymous with power. How much of the madness in the world was the result of governmental worries? Many had thought the solution was to find the state a good therapist. Hilda was one of those who preferred giving the state over to the service represented by hearses. As for Alan, he was content with the state as an invalid, and a strong Bill of Rights as the eternal nurse-maid.

Still, there were problems. Remove America's Secret Service, and watch foreign agents rush to fill the vacuum. Put some kind of Secret Service back in place—as one of the functions of a limited govern-ment—and everyone began to worry that it would be a shadow government working to return the superstate. Keep secrets from Americans, so that German intelligence would not receive bonuses from the free press across the Atlantic, and everyone would begin to suspect collusion between America's Secret Service and the Nazis. And the worst of it was that whoever was spying for whatever purpose, Alan worried that they would be sure to keep an eye on him. This business with Hilda would probably make his career, but at the price of an ulcer.

It was simply too much to believe, however, that an enemy would be trailing him in a vehicle as suspicious as the anomaly closing in on his rear. No, it was probably some little old European lady who didn't trust any technological development that had come from the war or its aftermath. Sure, that was it.

No sooner did he have the thought than it became an obsession. He had to see the owner of the car!

At four in the afternoon, the traffic was nothing short of hideous in those areas reserved for private vehicles. Most inhabitants had the sense to use the extensive mass transit available in the prime business areas. As half the city streets had been sold to private owners, pedes-trians had a variety of routes from which to choose, many of which took them through quaint and colorful bazaars, where they could buy anything from a drug to a gun. The Bronx had become some-thing that had to be seen to be believed. Out of a sense of history, and an unwillingness to fix something that isn't broken, the original names for streets and avenues had been retained regardless of the new zoning for pedestrians and vehicles. New York was proud to boast one of the cleanest environments of any large metropolis in the world. Unfortunately, it also had an unacceptably high crime rate. Why, only last year there had been over one hundred murders. That might not seem like a lot by New Berlin standards, but it wouldn't do for an American.

A heterogeneous population was not the ideal mixture for tranquillity, but it did make for progress. The ideal was to allow the diverse population to move at its own varying speeds, in time with a cacophony of different drummers. Ahead, he saw that even in the rain, a goodly number of cyclists enjoyed themselves on the Oakes Bikeway, a ribbon of genteel transport arching over the motorized vehicles below as it linked First with 125th Street.

Alas, the publishing industry, preferring nostalgia and tension, operated very much out of prewar New York, and Alan Whittmore had long ago gotten over the feelings of claustrophobia he'd had when he first came to town. He'd almost come to the point where tobacco smoke in close, unventilated rooms no longer put him off, but he would never really be comfortable with the rocking motion of riding on these moon-cratered streets. He wished to hell someone would buy them! Neighborhood cooperatives owned the majority of streets, with legal control over how much traffic, and of what kind, they would allow. Business areas were paid for by businessmen, and maximum traffic was to be found there. But there were the awkward areas, the limbo regions, that provided a turf over which city government could battle. Human nature being what it is, and even more so with public servants, the residue of the old bureaucracy, smaller but still fat, was not about to cooperate with itself and set one price for all. So the battle continued, and every week there was a new proposal for how to remove the unpopular presence of local government.

Although he only had a short distance to go, it would take a long time to traverse it. At last they came to a traffic light where the taxi would turn right. Perhaps they would lose the "hearse" here. The rain was letting up and he had a clearer view of it. The chauffeur could be seen past the slow movement of his windshield wiper. He was a big man in an outfit as anachronistic as the vehicle he drove. An old-fashioned touring cap and bug-eyed goggles made it impossible to see anything about his face other than that he was young and bearded. More than ever, Whittmore wanted to see the person in the back seat.

The light turned. They turned. The limo turned with them. Now it was a straight shot to the Isabel Paterson Hotel. He hoped he could determine whether or not he was being pursued. As the cab neared its destination and began to slow, the hearse slowed as well, but its left-turn signal was on and it was evident that the driver wished to pass a suddenly relieved young editor. Whittmore was clambering out of the cab and reaching for his wallet when the Horch glided past and he tried to catch a glimpse of the vehicle's owner. His relief burst like a bubble in a storm.

The man in the back seat had a face that would have attracted attention under any circumstances. His head was very large, and a shock of white hair extended from his scalp as if it were electricity crackling about a rheostat. His features were as angular as if they had been those of a statue; his nose was sharp as a beak, his chin as square as a building stone, his forehead as high as if he had no hair at all. These features would have surprised Alan in and of themselves, but what was unbearable was that the head was turned toward the curb. The man looked straight at Alan Whittmore . . . and he grinned. Then the long, black car pulled away and rejoined the flow of traffic. Alan continued to stare at the place where the man had been; he listened to the gentle slapping of the rain against the hotel canopy behind him. He was afraid.

"Something wrong?" asked the cabbie, still waiting for his money.

Alan said nothing as he paid, turning away before the cabbie could negotiate for some of the change that was surely too much to be an intended tip. He didn't hear another word because he was falling, falling into the face of the stranger.

CHAPTER THREE

And ye fathers, provoke not your children to wrath.

—Ephesians 6:4

There was a carnival going on inside the hotel. At least that was the impression Whittmore received as he stepped into the lobby. Balloons and posters adorned the marble-and-wood interior with which the Paterson Hotel impressed first-time guests. The largest sign read WILD EAST CONVENTION 1975/REGISTRATION. An emaciated individual was wearing a T-shirt with the legend MUTANTS FIND ADVENTURE EAST OF THE URALS. This, Whittmore concluded, must be a science fiction fan. The culture shock of stepping into a different universe was sufficient to temporarily diminish his fear of the man outside.

Yet he couldn't help but wonder what Hilda was doing at this hotel. Surely she wasn't part of the convention! A sudden fit of dizziness seized him, and he had to sit down. As no chair was available, he found an unoccupied spot on a raised portico in the center of the lobby on which perched a statue of the American Entrepreneur, whose granite face seemed to consider Alan with a most disapproving expression. No, no, this wouldn't do at all. It made him think of the man with the white hair again. Alan got to his feet so quickly that he accidentally jostled a teenage-girl who was dressed—if that was the word for it—in some ill-fitting pieces of silver suggesting a harem girl's costume. "Excuse me," he muttered to her disappearing back. She had not seemed to notice.

The brief interlude had helped return Alan's composure. He would think about the man later; now he must concern himself with the Goebbels manuscripts.

An officious-looking man at the desk had all the information Alan required: "Miss Goebbels left word that she would be detained but that you should wait in her suite." Normally, he would be annoyed at her lack of punctuality, but now he was grateful for the time alone.

21

With the power of self-delusion most effectively employed by professional wordsmiths, he would soon have himself convinced that the man in the hearse didn't mean him any harm.

The elevator ride was uneventful.

After tipping the porter who had shown him to the room, Alan allowed himself the pleasure of a sense of proprietorship in the elegant surroundings. Whatever scent was being used gave the impression of fresh air.

And it was soothing to walk on the snow white carpet that was just plush enough to maximize comfort without turning into a trek through a dessert topping. Across this sea of carpet was a heavy rosewood table on which, propped up against a lamp in the shape of the Statue of Liberty, was a note obviously intended for him. As he went over to the table, he saw multiple versions of himself in the various mirrors set at strategic points about the suite.

"Dear Alan," the note began, "I have taken precautions with the final entries of my father's diaries for reasons that will become apparent when you read them. It is my sincere hope that these extraordinary steps will prove unnecessary. Will be with you as soon as possible. Please have anything in the bar, but I ask you not to use room service. The other manuscript is here." She had signed it with her initials.

Here was an opportunity to have that drink he'd needed so badly in the company of Evans, a thirst made all the more acute by the taxi ride. Running a thumb over the width of the manuscript on the table, he estimated the quantity and type of alcohol most suited to the job at hand. An inventory of the bar gave him a warm feeling about Hilda's acculturation to the American Way of Life—all his favorites were lined up, generously full bottles awaiting his inspection. Settling on a golden-hued tequila and bright green lime, he apologized to the shade of Mencken, who never approved of mixing his booze with his work, and settled into the couch by the large picture window. The feeling of unease dissipated with the first swallow of tangy, watery fire. With manuscript on his lap, he began to read the lady's memoirs:

NOTES TOWARD AN AUTOBIOGRAPHY
BY HILDA GOEBBELS
WRITTEN SOMEWHERE IN THE PACIFIC
MARCH 1970

I am no longer a European. Is this the sole requirement to become an American? I have no certainties about what to do any longer. Only yesterday I was calling myself an anarchist as a positive statement. Today it is only a negation, a way of saying that I deny the state, but what good is that if I do not know what I affirm?

They tell me that Father is dying. I wish that I could celebrate, but even this news holds no pleasure for me. Even here, cradled in the swell of open sea, I cannot escape gossip. They say that he is turning back to the Catholic church. Oh, the poor fools. The one honor I must grant my father is that he left himself no avenues of escape. He who did so much to build a hell on earth will take his medicine without begging for nectar. He took what he wanted from the Roman church—certain structures of authority—and left whatever humanity there was behind. He was a true materialist, the man who always chooses the worst and leaves the rest.

A Puerto Rican woman leaves me Catholic tracts to read. Initially she spoke to me in a rather dreadful Low German—heaven knows where she picked it up—but when I responded in passable Spanish, we got on. Her name is Maria, and I am polite to her, even though she thinks that my lack of grief for my dying parent is deeply sinful, and she peppers her speech with the German word *Sündig!* to make sure that I am not misinterpreting her strong disapproval of my indifferent attitude. What she cannot understand is that I rejected all forms of authority long ago save for the proposition of natural law.

I have learned a lot, perhaps too much, in these last few years. It amuses me that people on the outside ever thought that the Nazis wanted chaos. Their crime was the crime of authority, of order. The chaos came when others strove to be free. If there is a natural order, then leave it alone. I don't know that there is, but I do know that order cannot be imposed. If the Christians are right, then I'm sure that many Nazis are even now discovering that the Devil has some real potential for establishing new orders.

One would think that as my father nears death, I would frequently see him in my mind. I do at times; his flat, large features, high forehead and pinched mouth, gave an impression of a mummy suffering from acromegaly. But I can never retain his image for long. Even in death, his position is usurped. I see Hitler more often. Alas, in this I regret to say that I am my father's daughter.

Father lived in Hitler's shadow in life. Why should the death of either of them change anything? Memory is my curse. If I could expunge either recollection, I would rather lose my times with "Uncle Adolf" than those spent with my twisted father.

When I was a child, I played in Hitler's sight. When I was older, I dined with him, . . . often listening to him tell me stories about our earlier times together. Memory is insanity. Oh, to drive it away! He never tired of telling everyone about the occasion when, as an impressionable six-year-old, I had placed all my stuffed dogs outside my bedroom to guard me. An SS man had been telling me blood-curdling fairy tales about witches and ogres and other denizens of the mysterious Northern Lands. I was always able to take a hint. Uncle Adolf couldn't stop laughing over my practical response to our mythic heritage. I think what really won him over was that I trusted dogs. He often said that he only trusted dogs and the SS; and both served the same function for him.

The only forgiveness I can spare my father is that we shared the same experience of the Fuehrer Principle in action. Those who cluck their tongues about easy resistance and automatic revolution do not know what an intimate relationship with a dictator is like. Just as those who were never in a concentration camp, Axis or Allied, cannot really share in the communion of anguish. Even so, I believe that the camps provide me with an invaluable metaphor. Being in a room with Hitler was the most refined version of a concentration camp.

They say that power corrupts. An American thinker has said that immunity corrupts. In the end, I think it is hatred that corrupts. Hitler cared more for his hate than his power. With the power of empire in his hands, he laid waste whole peoples.

The most love I ever received from my father was the evening he came home and announced to the entire household that I was Hitler's favorite. This could not have come at a worse time. I had only recently made the most dangerous discovery an adolescent girl can make: I was a tease. A young girl's vanity is as cruel to others as it is satisfying to herself. My father and I became collaborators in that moment. In plotting our campaigns to keep this special favoritism alive, I had my first real understanding of how my father thought.

I doubt that anyone else was more qualified for the role of Reichspropagandaminister than he. The Greater Reich deserved Paul Joseph Goebbels.

I was only fourteen when I was invited to dinner with Hitler and his personal filmmaker, Leni Riefenstahl. It was but a few weeks before I was to leave for Bavaria. Mother had been describing the beauties of Pathfinder's Youth Camp for years, and I was at last to begin attendance. I had been dreaming of forests and streams and mountains, and suddenly I was at dinner with the Fuehrer, and he was suggesting that I star in a movie about a young girl's odyssey to the mountaintop. Classmates had been teasing me that sooner or later my father would put me in a movie. (Father's penchant for arranging screen tests whenever he had a new mistress was Europe's most open scandal, so a nod in the direction of his family might not be judged as entirely inappropriate.) I had not expected to receive such an offer from the Fuehrer himself.

Riefenstahl said very little at first, but Hitler eventually ran down, and she took over. The story would be similar to her 1932 picture *Das blaue Licht* (The Blue Light). The high, cold mountaintop would represent the ideal to which my character would aspire. The crass villagers would interfere, out of a misguided desire to protect me. The paradox would be that only by leaving them and standing atop the mountain, alone, could I best serve them, and so serve the race. The film would end with a festival, the Fest der Völker, and the common people would be reunited with the soil. Hitler and Riefenstahl looked at me as though I were the prize jewel in someone else's collection.

It must have appeared that I was committing a crime against the state, the felony of an anticlimax. I wanted to know if the filming would interfere with summer camp. Hitler was uncharacteristically concise: "You can't do both." Hoping to make the best of a bad situation, I asked what mountain I would be climbing for the film. I regretted asking because no sooner were the words out of my mouth, than Hitler began to laugh. I positively detested his laugh. Then he began talking and talking and talking. He spent at least a quarter hour on the theme of "life as art" before explaining that my scenes would be done in a studio of UFA. The actual mountain scenes, what few there were, would be done by a second unit, and a double would be used.

So that was my choice: a real mountain or an illusion. It never occurred to me that I should doubt my freedom to choose in the matter. Children of the privileged escape the daily bludgeoning in a tyranny, and thereby increase their risk. It was not until much later that I realized how remarkable it was that I survived my caprice. I turned down the offer without considering for a moment that it might be a command!

One of the perplexities of Hitler was that he would, on rare occasions, make a thoroughly pathetic attempt at persuasion. Such was my favored position—at that moment—that I received the treatment. Not all the scenes would be shot in the studio, he announced airily. There would be some on-location work for me. I would be allowed to deliver a stirring monologue in the reconstruction of his birthplace in the little town of Branau, *the* tourist attraction of what had been Austria. And if that special honor weren't enough, I'd even attend the premiere of the film in the biggest cinema palace in Vienna, the city that Hitler would never forget, and never leave alone. He could not resist boasting again of how thoroughly he had expunged the city of the pernicious influence of Sigmund Freud; and I could not resist thinking that in the fullness of time, that lovely city might be free of Hitler's influence.

When I persisted in my refusal, he became himself again. Gone was the benign facade of Uncle Adolf as a shadow crossed his face. For the first time, I really noticed his eyes. The young invariably depend on a certain amount of diplomacy from their elders. I was quickly disabused of this notion. He stood, while pointing a trembling finger at me, and I half expected a lightning bolt to leap the distance between us. He shouted that I lacked my father's will, and that any other young girl would leap at the opportunity to be a film star, and that were it not for my family, I'd end up some little linen weaver or glovemaker. As suddenly as the storm had arisen, it passed. He stood as stock still as if he were one of his statues by Arno Brecker, but without the heroic physique and poise that the sculptor was always considerate enough to add. If Hitler could be frightening in one of his rages, he was positively unnerving when he was silent in anger. It seemed to me at such times that there was a frightful vacuum at the center of the man, and if one weren't careful, one could be drawn into that vacancy.

The truth was that there was a surprising amount of leeway

granted those in his private circle, provided one did not commit the unforgivable faux paus of expressing a pro-Jewish sentiment. And I suppose that my youth was a contributing factor to the granting of latitude; that, and the importance of my father to the Fuehrer. Hitler even made light of the fact that Father had never completely gotten over the way Leni was granted complete independence of his office as national minister for propaganda and the enlightenment of the people . . . and this during the period of severest censorship. Perhaps, Hitler suggested, I was helping Daddy to pay off an old score.

At the time, such considerations were the furthest thing from my mind. I was a willful teenager, enjoying the adolescent pleasure of recalcitrance. (Thank God my life took a turning before I became a useless coquette.) Hitler resumed his seat, his damaged arm shaking slightly—always an ominous sign. He changed the subject again. I can't remember how the conversation ended, except that the ruler of Europe had retreated into a dull bourgeoise rambling, his idea of "petit talk."

Leni, who had not moved since the outburst—perhaps she too was unconsciously posing for one of Brecker's statues—returned to the living. I doubt very much that she had ever been enthusiastic about using me in the film anyway. The young actress she finally selected bore a striking resemblance to herself.

There was one unexpected bonus. Hitler had been too angry to entertain us with one of his impressions. He loved to do them. Mussolini still topped the list, a dubious honor that Il Duce's death had done nothing to alleviate. Friends had told me that Hitler had even perfected an impression of my father by lowering his voice to Dr. Goebbels's deep bass resonances (voted most sexy voice in a poll of German fraus) and mimicking the bouncing stride that Father used to compensate for his clubfoot. I was spared ever witnessing this particular horror. I wonder why Father never consented to having an operation to correct his deformity. During the war he frequently alluded to his plans in that regard, but added that personal indulgences would have to wait until victory was ours. His master never waited when it came to amusements.

A week later, Hitler would send a bouquet of flowers, the closest he ever came to civility with anyone, but I was no longer one of his favorites. Mother took this surprisingly well. My siblings did not care. Father's silences were eloquent.

27

CHAPTER FOUR

Cesare! Do you hear me? It is I calling you: I, Caligari, your master. Awaken for a brief while from your dark night.

—Robert Wiene,
The Cabinet of Dr. Caligari

NOTES TOWARD AN AUTOBIOGRAPHY

So I attended the youth camp. It was just outside Bamberg, interestingly enough. This was the place where Hitler had first won over Father—who up to that point had been aligned with Gregor Strasser. Father always knew when to alter his plans, something I've yet to learn, and pray I never shall.

When addressing us in formation, our troop leader, Herr Juergen, spoke with Prussian precision; but at rest, he would lapse into the friendly cadences of the Bavarian country folk. The first day, he told us about the tradition of the *Wandervoegel,* various back-to-nature youth groups of the prewar period. It was one of those clear and sunny days when you could actually see the color of the leaves and the stones and each blade of grass. There was a fresh pine smell in the air, and in the distance you could make out the snowcapped mountains as if they were made of fine crystal. We were standing in the courtyard of a well-maintained castle, a museum piece. The setting and the mood were perfect to reminisce about simpler times and easy choices. Alas, the sermon ended with the requisite dosage of propaganda. He told us that today's sense of discipline added a dimension that had been missing from the anarchic days of the 1920s. That phrase would come back to me many times . . . as I searched for an unregulated life of my own.

One thing you have to grant to the National Socialist life-style: they have more ways of reminding you of your duty than can ever be enumerated. Good old Juergen planned our schedules with care and maneuvered us where we could see the mountain from which Hitler had directed some of the war's most dangerous campaigns: high above the rocks and scars of snow lurked the gray fortress of Barbarossa. I trained myself to ignore it whenever the mountain came into view.

I have pleasant memories of that summer: the sound of running water in the clear mountain streams, the fresh aroma and satisfying flavor of cabbage and sausage, the mildly erotic pleasures of sleeping half nude on the porch of a cottage with four other girls from my troop. (Naturally they wouldn't let us live in the castle.) There was much singing, and even the tone-deaf were made to sound better through the acoustical perfection of our natural opera house. The trees were beautiful.

Father didn't believe in beauty, unless he could make a sexual object of it. I knew that much even then. If he had been there, he would have been pleased at what I found my second week: an unfortunate buck had gotten his antlers tangled in the low branches of an Aspen. There the poor animal would starve to death if no one freed him. "There's the beauty of nature for you," I could imagine my father saying. "All that lives is awaiting death."

The animal was terrified. The more it attempted to free itself, the more completely was it entrapped. None of us were tempted to draw near, at first, as the danger outweighed our charitable impulses. But at last I could stand it no longer and began slowly to descend the hill. I had no idea what to do, but I felt that I must act regardless.

It was late in the afternoon, the time of day when clouds have an unreal look. This was not good for shooting. Suddenly there was the sharp explosion of rifle fire, from somewhere behind and to the left of me. The buck fell dead, still attached to the tree as if he were crucified, as a number of squirrels—silent during the deer's struggles—set up a clattering of discontent.

And so I met my first lover. His name was Gunther. As he walked toward us, his eyes went straight to mine, despite the more attractive—I thought—Irena standing beside me. Throughout the skinning and gutting of the animal, he kept up a mildly ironic commentary about young women thinking themselves huntresses rather than hearth keepers. The humor would have been more to the point had any of us been carrying weapons. Gunther was a fairly simple lad, and once he fixed upon a witty observation, the facts couldn't be allowed to interfere. I was less interested in what he was saying than that he kept sneaking glances at me the whole time.

He was from Burgundy. That probably explained his interest in the occult, a subject that meant nothing to me then, but would one day make a ruin of my life. As for the moment, I was trying to remind him of the few weak double entendres that had begun our conversation, but it was too late: he had focused his mind upon Thanatos, and Eros would simply have to wait.

He began telling us how anyone who had ever set foot in Bavaria should be interested in the secret lodges of the Illuminati. Then he announced that the number 23 was of overwhelming importance to me. I would make a crucial life decision when I reached that age . . . and did I know that the year 1923 was one of the worst dates of the Depression? (The Burgundian manner of thinking was maddeningly associational, and this was my first contact with it. At the time, my sole concern was that the crazy brain was inside a magnificent, muscled body that had attracted my attention by sending a bullet whizzing past my head.)

No, I admitted that I didn't know much about dates, except the kind you eat . . . and did he have plans for supper? The ploy failed, as he continued to intrigue us (he thought) with his odd litany. He must have dragged out a dozen of his examples, but the ones I remember were: Did I also know that the year 1923 marked the failure of the original Putsch, costing many young Nazis their lives? Was I aware that the French army humiliated the Fatherland by occupying the Ruhr in that year, on the pretext of default in payments on the odious war debt? *And most astounding of all,* he assured me, it was none other than Article 231 of the Versailles Treaty that placed all the blame for the First World War on Germany, and what did I think about that?

The other girls were suffering from a severe attack of the giggles, but I seized my chance to make a conquest. With all the sincerity at my command, I assured him that what he had been saying was of the greatest possible interest to me, and I would very much enjoy learning more. Perhaps he was not as naive as I thought him at first, but I have since revised my opinion through vanity. I was more attractive than I thought I was, and his unspoken agenda was most likely the same as mine. Teenage girls never recognize their own beauty.

We eventually worked our way deeper into the woods. The giggling was louder than ever, but we soon put the other girls at a satisfactory distance; and I made sure that we were alone before I asked him some questions. Had he ever been kissed by a girl before he kissed her? Had he ever had a girl adopt a posture that she usually reserved for saying her prayers for a less spiritual purpose? After I had kissed him and then knelt to answer the second question, he was eager to continue the instruction along any lines I thought fruitful. And it was a pure delight to see that his face was blushing a red every bit as bright as other parts of him.

Birth control was readily available for someone of my class. (The National Socialists had a use for orphans of the right racial stock, and the way to get them was through the lower classes of our supposedly classless, socialist paradise.) I assured Gunther that he need not worry about precautions because I was using the recently developed Pill (originally intended for biological control of officially designated "inferior races"). It was my first time for many experiences. Pine needles are more uncomfortable than penetration of the hymen. As for Gunther's technique, the best that could be said was that it was there. Still, the novelty of the first time makes up for a lack of finesse, and Gunther's passion was real. I quickly climaxed. The manner in which he kept kneading my nipples made me wonder if he was looking for a secret switch that he could turn on. When his hands crept lower, he did better. For my part, I drove him wild by the simple expedient of biting his ear. He was enamored of my teeth.

When it was over, I knew more about sex, but it would take many years before I would know anything about love. The reward of the moment was that Gunther invited me to attend The Harvest Festival with him in Burgundy come autumn. Maybe it was because I'd had arguments with my younger brother, Helmuth, about Burgundy, but I quickly agreed to attend. I thought that if it turned out to be as ridiculous as I'd heard, I could talk Helmuth out of wasting his college years there. If it turned out to be better, I'd be fair about it: I'd simply avoid bringing up the subject again. Admissions of error are not meant for kid brothers.

31

That evening, back at the cottage, Irena crept into bed with me so that I could whisper all the details to her about *l'amour*. Descriptions soon proved inspirational, and before I knew it, Irena was under the covers, doing for me what I had done for Gunther. I was fond of symmetry and noted that the day's triangle had consisted of one blonde, Irena, one brunet, Gunther, and myself as the redhead. All in all, it had been an educational twenty-four hours.

Nothing else that happened at Pathfinder's Youth Camp proved as interesting (not even my first attempts to climb the scenery); and it only took one day in Burgundy to overwhelm every other experience up to then. Sex is only so remarkable a discovery; but insanity encourages one to sit up and take notice. Gunther had arranged my schedule so that I wouldn't miss an annual event of the small country. As I had told Helmuth many times, Burgundy would have its silly side because it was managed by the SS. As a kid brother is wont to do, he promptly informed to Mother. This told me more about Helmuth than it did anything else. Now I was about to find out firsthand the meaning of a Burgundian ceremony.

The entire population had turned out (with rare exceptions for the ill and elderly) to join hands in a line of people of such length that it extended past the borders. Neighboring provinces of the Greater Reich were eager, if not happy, to cooperate with the SS. The only visitors who were allowed to participate were citizens—or their children—from the Greater Reich with membership in the Party. When I asked if I could merely be a spectator, the answer was a firm no. Not really aware of what was to happen, I joined hands with Gunther and the rest of Burgundy.

I looked down at my feet, where rust-colored leaves were blanketing the ground. I saw an ant bravely carrying a dead beetle three times its size across the rough surface of a large, triangular stone. The ant could have gone around the rock.

Strategically placed on small platforms were senior officials of Burgundy whose hands were apparently viewed as less crucial to the effort than their voices giving us instruction. They all had portable microphones, and loud voices to boot. At first, the exercise seemed routine (except for the hand-holding stunt) and political. It was very much a Hitler Youth kind of affair. We were told by our speaker how the Fuehrer had not yet finished teaching the enemies of the Reich their lesson. How dare Frenchmen still hold resentment against us when they had treated us so badly in the past? How dare they condemn our racial policies after the way they had exploited Africans . . . and besides, we had taught them a thing or two about anti-Semitism, for which they should be grateful. I assumed that the tirade began with the French because we were so near to them in Burgundy. The incredible hypocrisy was that he criticized them for importing colored troops to fight in the war, Berbers, Moroccans, Senegalese, and Bantu warriors. Was I the only person on line able to recognize the discrepancy between crying crocodile tears over French behavior in Africa, immediately followed by a conventional racist harangue? The frightening answer was that I could by no means be unique in this.

Then he branched out to other nationalities. How dare Englishmen look down their long noses at our policies after the way they had treated the people of Ireland and India and so on? At the end of each little performance, the crowd would murmur assent. By the time he got to the ongoing difficulties in Russia—a new kind of weapon, the hydrogen bomb, had recently been tested on a large Slavic population in the east—the murmur of the crowd had become as loud as the sea at high tide. We were sure teaching the enemies of the Greater Reich a lesson, all right. Talk of America brought shouts of rage from some and silence from others. Talk of the Orient brought a number of hisses from those who wished to show off that they were cosmopolitan.

He got around to the Jews. Needless to say, the reaction was more negative than even the Slavs had inspired. The problem was that I had begun to wonder about the Jews. Why was it, I found myself wondering, if the Jews have been removed from the Fatherland and its territories, they continued to pose the greatest threat? It seemed that the more we were harangued to thank the Fuehrer for saving us from them, the more we were told to be on guard against them every single day. The seed of doubt had also been planted by the inexplicable behavior of my father whenever the subject was raised. He seemed coldly cynical about most of the Reich's enemies; but the mere suggestion of Jewish influence made him positively unhinged.

As I stood there, huddling in my sweater, feeling my hands become sweatier with every passing second of the enforced togetherness, I thought back to some pictures I'd seen at Pathfinder's Camp.

33

One girl had smuggled some photographs into the cottage. They were nothing that we hadn't seen before—pitiful victims of the great upheaval, sacrifices in the name of a unified Europe. Every German coffee table had picture books of victims: victims of the saturation bombing thanks to the Americans and the British, victims of Russian sadism during the most dangerous stretch of the war, victims who had been proud Germans in the Sudetenland. These we had seen many times. Then, too, there were the books of Stalin's victims among his own people, endless pictures of starving Ukrainians from the mass slaughter of 1932 and 1933, carefully compiled during the war crimes trials, which Hitler had used to build up morale among the subject peoples (those who had survived both the Swastika and the Hammer-and-Sickle) and to create new National Socialisms with enough sense to take their cues from German managers. Every German child grew up with images of scorched earth and wasted bodies along with his daily milk.

But I had never seen pictures of such mind-numbing atrocity as these that now passed before my eyes at summer camp. The pornographic secret of our cottage was that these were victims of Germany. I'd seen something like the radiation victims before. The government was frank about the Bomb. Whenever they released data about the atomic weapons used at the close of hostilities, the reports were accompanied with statistical projections of what German losses would have been without the weapons that, everyone agrees, saved Hitler's regime. No, the pictures that I could not stomach, that burned into my mind forever, were of children who had been operated on with a skill twisted to diabolical purpose. They were no longer human, but enough remained of the original shape to be recognized. I believe that I screamed. There is also the troubling recollection that I was the only one who cried out. Worst of all, I remember someone laughing.

There were other pictures, final statements on the art of brutality. The starved. The beaten. The diseased. These were dreadful to see, but the torture suffered by the poor wretches had not altered their human forms. Even those who were more bone than flesh at least still possessed the dignity of human bone. None presented the pure vision of the pit that blasted me from the half dozen medical photographs. The other pictures had been labeled from a number of diverse back-

34

grounds, a last epitaph of identity for anonymous ciphers en route to a mass grave. But all the pictures of teratological nightmare were clearly labeled as Jews. Attempts had been made to render the children subhuman or nonhuman.

The face I could not forget was of a boy who could not be more than a year old. His arms and legs were indistinguishable lumps of unarticulated flesh, useless appendages on a torso that had been rendered scaly by either chemical means or radiation. To think about it was to endure a physical pain. Gazing at me was a face defined by a child's skull (the only recognizably human element) but wearing the wrinkles and sagging flesh of an ancient Methuselah. The pictures I had seen of Gandhi, taken the last year of his life, were youthful by comparison.

I could not entirely credit what I had seen at Pathfinder's Youth Camp, and yet something deep in me knew that it was true. If I had showed the evidence to my father, I'm certain he would have denied its authenticity. He would have said it was a result of trick photography and nothing of the sort had ever been done by Nazis. Perhaps I dreaded that such a statement from my father *would* remove all doubt. I had not trusted him since the time I overheard him with one of his mistresses, bragging over how simple it was to deceive Magda Goebbels.

Standing in an open field, a small link in a human chain, I listened to a Burgundian exhorting us to join in a prayer against every Jew still alive in the world . . . and I was haunted by the face. I had been turning against the official line on anti-Semitism for some time, but I could not remember the turning point. Perhaps I had never been a racist, but with that protective self-delusion enjoyed by the young, had never allowed myself to really think about a doctrine so important to National Socialism. It had been best not to think at all.

A year earlier, I had begun collecting copies of books that Father had ordered burned in the fire that proved so newsworthy. My original motivation had been no more than a childish prank. The first book I had found on the list was by Moses Mendelssohn, a Jew who had been known as the German Socrates. The book was too adult to interest me then, and this was the case for most of them. When I finally got around to reading these books, I had a far better sense of what the Fatherland had lost; but nothing else would ever carry the shock of recognition that was mine upon seeing the child of the damned. It was a kind of intellectual cheating to put too much stock in the respective talents of those who had been banned and burned and murdered. A pragmatic weighing of the scales smacked too much of the way my father approached things, aside from the Jewish question, to which he had only emotional and violent answers. Only with age did I come to realize that the face haunting me cried out for all innocents butchered and forgotten, made into bloody statistics for whatever reason.

On that chill afternoon in Burgundy, I did not analyze my reaction; I merely lived it, and found myself helpless. Rage turned to fire in my veins as the spokesman, spitting out words from a pinched face sporting a pathetic duplicate of Hitler's moustache, explained the scientific basis for what we were doing. It seemed that we were standing so that we were aligned with the magnetic poles, or some such nonsense, and that a psychic cone of energy would be generated, causing distress to Orthodox, Conservative, and Reform Judaism without discrimination. That the procedure was total nonsense didn't matter. It was detestable. I wanted no part of it. Hand to hand, and hate to hate, I tried to break free of the line.

Gunther, sensing that I was pulling away, squeezed my hand so hard that it hurt. As ill fortune would have it, the man on the other side was, if anything, even more robust and indifferent than my oafish boyfriend. And so my rebellion remained largely an intellectual effort. For what it was worth, I prayed for a boomerang effect.

The most ridiculous moment came when the crowd began to hum. It sounded as if a swarm of bees had gone quite mad. At the conclusion of this, the damage was supposed to be done. The most distasteful moment came when our speaker, and his comrades obviously, called for a moment of silence in memory of Reinhard Heydrich. Accordingly, I sneezed. There were undeniable advantages to being the daughter of Dr. Paul Joseph Goebbels.

After a ritual summoning of the Overman within each and every one of us—the one moment I felt in touch with my own ego—the ceremony concluded with singing the anthem for the Greater Reich. This I was willing to do. I was still very young. I enjoyed hearing about the glory of our nation, from the shining Baltic to the shining North Sea on one side; and from the shining Aegean to the shining Adriatic on the other; and nowhere was a drop of industrial pollution envisioned as marring those vast shields of open sea. (Perhaps the anthem was only appropriate in Burgundy, with their strict prohibitions on industry within the borders.)

Later I would discover that Leni had been shooting one of her documentaries that very day. I escaped being captured on her film by no more than two kilometers. Given the way I already felt about it, I counted myself lucky not to be part of the record. Father would later complain that Leni knew I was in attendance and deliberately snubbed me by not hunting the line for my beaming countenance. Thank you, Leni!

I would not make love to Gunther again, although it took a while for him to take the hint. When I went to bed that night, happily alone, I resolved to leave the next morning. Let no one doubt the woman's prerogative! An offhand comment at breakfast was sufficiently intriguing to overcome the revulsion I also felt. There was to be one more event before I'd leave this land of malevolent wonders. They were to hold a trial.

The defendants were animals. It was alleged that two goats and a pig had committed high crimes against duly constituted authority. The prosecutor was known simply as Ernest. He made a far more vivid impression than the defense, a harmless old woman who, I'm sure, was there solely as a formality. At first, I was convinced that the whole affair was a joke. But as the proceedings were cranked through the legal machine, and nobody made light of anything, I accepted the improbable reality. By an effort of will to make Nietzsche proud, I resisted laughing.

The goats had gotten loose from their owner and eaten a neighbor's beans. The pig, a fat old sow, was not guilty of trespass, but had violated Racial Law by attacking a hapless child who had fallen in the family's pigsty. Ernest reminded the good people present that Burgundy had restored medieval law as an antidote to the decadent modern ideas of criminal responsibility. The majesty of the law, so went the argument, was to ignore motives on the part of the transgressor and to remember that punishment was not for the criminal's benefit. The only reason to whip or torture or electrocute or gas or behead or shoot or fine or imprison someone was as an object lesson for the community. The opinion of the criminal mattered not in the least. Now, if even the modern-thinking judges in Munich and Hamburg and New Berlin recognized this principle to the extent of punishing the mentally defective and the insane, then all that the people of Burgundy were doing was extending the point to include animals.

The terrifying part was that I started to enjoy the logic of stupidity. The kids with whom I attended school saw nothing wrong with placing an idiot in the stocks. They'd be the first to throw rotten vegetables at the drooling target. Yet they'd laugh at the goats and pig being publicly berated. One made about as much sense as the other. Adolf Hitler had called for the New Man. Predictably, he received something as old as the blood on a caveman's spear.

When the trial was over, the goats and pig were executed. A giant of a man, wielding an axe so big that I was afraid he'd give himself a hernia despite his size, beheaded the animals. I deduced that the animals would be eaten. If the Burgundians didn't show some sense now, how could they exist at all? Sure enough, a feast was given, and lamb and pork were on the menu. Maybe this was the way officials redistributed the meat.

The barbecue went late into the night. Gunther made one last great attempt to win back my affections, but I wouldn't forgive him for what he had done on the line. My hand still ached. When he suggested that I would have gotten into serious trouble if I'd broken away, I reminded him, in my haughtiest tone, just who I was, and what I could get away with. Whatever doubts I secretly entertained contributed to a performance so self-righteous and overbearing that he pulled away from me as if I'd slapped him. One thing you can say for Nazis: they know how to be subordinate.

Gunther no longer interested me, but I was of interest to the Burgundian judge, Ernest. He took me aside to inquire about the health of my parents and provide me with an opportunity to question the events of the afternoon. I wouldn't take the bait. When someone wants to tell me something, I wait for them to do it. He finally relented and said the last thing I ever expected to hear in Burgundy.

"We are not so eccentric as we seem," he began. "We know that we exist on the sufferance of the Greater Reich and the goodwill of the Fuehrer. The technological achievements of Germany are the envy of the world. Only American industry is any match for it. Without the modern German military, we'd be in no position to indulge ourselves here. I myself served with a panzer division, so I know what I'm talking about."

"Why tell me?" I asked him, with no attempt at being polite.

"You look on us with modern eyes, and in those eyes I see the same intelligence that has made your father one of the most important men in the world. A day is coming when we must all remember that National Socialism is the glue that holds us together, no matter whatever differences we might have."

And with a sly wink, as though I were privy to some dirty little secret, he departed.

CHAPTER FIVE

To all doubts and questions, the new man of the first
German empire has only one answer: Nevertheless, I will!

—Alfred Rosenberg,
The Myth of the Twentieth Century

My years of schooling were not easy for any of us. I kept getting into trouble and was sent to one institution after another. By the time I was a seasoned college student, confused and uncertain about my future, Mother began threatening to take three of her children with her on a trip to see the world. The honor fell to the three eldest: my older sister, Helga; my younger brother, Helmuth; and myself square in the middle. The younger girls, Holde and Hedda, were spared. As I write these words, I am overwhelmed by my family's lack of imagination, in this case the fixation on the letter "H"! The personality of the Fuehrer touches us even in our sleep.

Father enthusiastically supported the expedition. The other children would be looked after by the staff in the villa at Schwanenwerder on the Wannsee. This would leave him free to have an open-door policy for his mistresses at his favorite house near the Brandenburg Gate in New Berlin. Despite his contributions to reshaping the city, he still preferred those sections retaining the flavor of the original Berlin.

I was in hot water with Mother from the beginning. As she was planning her itinerary, I asked that we visit the one region she abhorred above all others. "No," I remember her saying, "we will not step foot in the Wild East, as you young people call it. Didn't we have enough of that in the war? Never, never!" There was no use pointing out that the Fuehrer's policy was to relocate as many German farmers as possible in the Ukraine, and that the Party's slogan remained "Push Eastward." But despite the hot-blooded rhetoric, the reality was that the lines were stabilized at the Urals. Beyond that was no-man's-land. After serving the required duty in one of the

40

military branches, young men had several options. The most daring chose to prove their mettle in the frontier beyond the Urals, where brigandage was a way of life, and where the motley bands of Russians and Mongols and Chinese and Arabs and Jews and Koreans and God knows who else had no use whatsoever for the Greater Reich and its racial theories.

Screaming and kicking every step of the way, Alfred Rosenberg had had to accept the idea of a free region, an area of containment that could be used as a testing ground for people and weapons, but would not be intended for conquest and colonization. He created the *cordon sanitairé* that he had planned, but his hopes for a chain of border states, and a Caucasian federation, underwent modifications. He had learned from his previous mistakes, for there was no doubt that he was among the Party leaders who had guided the Fuehrer on a suicidal course when German divisions first rolled onto the Russian steppes. The peasants were eager to greet us as liberators. Millions were ready to join us in a war against Stalin. The practical voices of Germany called for an alliance with these people; but the mad heart of Nazism could not modify itself.

Reality had its say, and in a few years the Reich itself faced certain destruction at the hands of an enemy that should have been turned to our service instead. If we had not been granted a nuclear sword with which to lop off those hands, well, Frau Magda would not be planning a pleasure junket one fine spring day in the late 1950s.

Mother was not alone in her phobias. There were times when Hitler still winced to see a snowfall. Himmler was bothered by nearly everything. The untroubled Nazi was the anomaly. Father and Goering, different in so many ways, commanded respect by collecting artworks by their enemies. Bad associations meant nothing to them.

As a headstrong young woman, I positively lusted after the disreputable. Naturally I was excited about visiting the newly formed American Republic; but nothing could compare to the salutary chaos of the Wild East. Rosenberg's Cultural Bureaus were satisfied to leave unconquered a region that could not organize itself into an effective resistance . . . and every school child thanked God for the allure and romance of a place free of law.

Mother only wanted to travel to safe places, and it had taken a bit of doing to convince her that she wouldn't be raped in the Americas.

I knew next to nothing about South America, but I'd been reading up on the United States. The very thing that made Mother afraid to travel there was, in fact, the reason we'd be let in the country.

"They have abolished most of their laws," she said in her most worried tone. "They were a frontier society already. They'll be turning back into the Wild West if they're not careful."

"Mother, it's because they've opened their borders that we can go."

"They let anyone in now, just anyone," she answered. "Think of all our enemies. Think of all the Jews who live in America. And they allow any kind of perverted sex there. I'm sure that they all have diseases. It's dangerous to touch a Negro, and they have so many." I remember taking her hand and calmly saying that we wouldn't visit the U.S. until the last leg of the trip, and we wouldn't go then unless she really wanted it. And the whole time, I was seized by the most unbearable contempt. Hitler especially admired my mother because she came from one of the better families. Here was the Fuehrer, enemy of the aristocracy . . . and a sycophant for any compliment from the class he had sworn to overturn. Worse for me was the spectacle of my mother babbling like some uncultured fishwife, afraid of anything and everything. There was nothing aristocratic about the woman.

At any rate, we reached a compromise. I promised not to press about the Wild East if she promised that when we went to France, we would avoid all things Burgundian. She couldn't understand why I hadn't enjoyed my time there and insisted on showing me the beautiful pictorial spread the quaint little country had received in *Signal,* the magazine for the masses if there ever was one. I responded by thrusting one of my lurid paperback novels at her detailing the thrills to be had on the windswept plains of Upper Mongolia. She knew when to surrender. Helmuth listened to the exchange in stony silence, no doubt plotting my downfall. He was in every way his father's son.

The trip began with a lengthy circuit of the empire. We used plane, train, and hired car. We visited France and Spain; then Italy, Yugoslavia, Rumania, Bulgaria, Greece, Turkey, and Iran. We spent a day in Afghanistan, then a week in India. Before leaving Calcutta, I made one last attempt to persuade Mother to come at least within the

periphery of my beloved Wild East, by visiting our furthermost
outpost within China at Manchoukuo, but that was too close to the
American/Japanese zone for her, and as there was currently an
altercation between an American corporation and an SS expedition-
ary force, she may have had a point.

We could have made plans to cross the Pacific and visit the U.S.
beginning with California, but Mother was terrified of the thought.
She was absolutely convinced that all the craziest people in the world
were congregated in Los Angeles, and that we'd never get out alive.
We stuck to the original travel plan, which entailed a boring trek
back across Europe, and also meant that we'd only be seeing the East
Coast of the U.S. on this trip.

So we concluded the European part of our adventures with stops
at Lithuania, Latvia, Estonia, Finland, Sweden, and Norway. We
saw dozens of cathedrals. We saw no dwellings of the working class.
We passed by many cemeteries. There was a rumor that subject
countries had the highest rate of suicide in the world. Whatever the
truth of that, everywhere we went we saw different peoples being
Germanized, and therefore discovering a new reason to hate Germans. At least I enjoyed my time in our Swedish hotel. We had the
cutest maid, and she was broadminded.

We took a boat to England and spent a murky day there before
embarking on the long voyage to South America. I made a wager
with Helmuth that Helga would be seasick first. He bet on Mother.
I won. In retrospect, it disturbs me that the few occasions when I had
a rapport with my brother was when we were indulging our mali-
cious streaks.

The crossing was dull. Helmuth and I played a game of planning
a route that would be the perfect nightmare vacation for Mother. The
largest portion of the trip would be a pictorial journey through the
Middle East, where a series of small wars had turned most of that
inhospitable region into a free-fire zone, from Morocco to Indonesia.
(Hitler had no end of fun supporting first one side, then the other.)
When we presented her with the fruits of our labors, she sighed and
shook her head. Helga said that we were horrid.

I was glad that I'd brought my books and tapes on English. My
instructors had given me highest marks, but Konrad Obernitz had
complained that I'd have trouble with those American cowboys

because I had no aptitude for the vernacular. He suggested that I had a certain priggishness that biased me in favor of a more stilted speech than was popular in the States. He was one to talk, frequently insisting that his charges address him as "Herr Doktor Doktor Obernitz," the kind of top-heavy formality that is the curse of the German mind.

Formality was the least of our concerns when we arrived in Pernambuco to pick up our interpreter, Señor Alfredo. I'd been brushing up on my Spanish, but one exposure to the rapid-fire conversation of the locals—the verbal equivalent of a machine gun—and I longed for Europe, where the various populations diligently pursue a mastery of German. Señor Alfredo was a good interpreter, but he frequently had a repellent odor of cheap rum and cheaper cigars. Mother promised to buy him a box of the very best Cuban cigars if he acquitted himself professionally. He was deeply moved that she would offer him the flattery of a bribe. I remember that he was short and easily excited, that his white Panama suits were invariably soiled within an hour of his donning them, and that after informing me that my Spanish was awful, he afforded me an opportunity to practice English. He spoke English at half-speed. Helmuth hated him, which was another point in Alfredo's favor.

From Pernambuco, we traveled south until we arrived in Buenes Aires. Mother was especially gratified. There were quite a few Germans living in Argentina, engaging in what—our consulate would tell anyone who asked—was a friendly competition with North American businesses over markets. For the Monroe Doctrine, it was *In pace requiescat!*

Old friends of the family appeared in frightening profusion. As it rained for several days, we had to make the most of our situation. I was persuaded to wear my least favorite dress and play the hostess. We were cornered in a hotel that had never heard of modern air ventilation, and I teased Helmuth about how his Burgundian heroes should experience such heat and humidity so that they would better appreciate unadorned nature. Helga wouldn't join in our games. Her complexion was as pallid as it had been aboard ship.

Before leaving Argentina, we were exposed to a Brazilian businessman who was in town to "purchase supplies," but I had my doubts. I had acquired a knack for ferreting out people with an eye open to political contacts, the men who need influence to compensate for a lack of ability. This remarkably obese creature boasted that he was half German, and we should be proud of the practical reforms he had implemented in his company. His favorite German word was *Pflicht,* his gospel the duty of work. That his primary exertion was navigating his bulk through doors and up stairs I had no doubt.

Mother later told me that she couldn't stand him, especially when he leeringly told us about how he made female applicants raise their skirts so that he could see if their underskirts were clean and pressed. "Lots of these girls would take their clothes off to get a job, if you know what I mean. I just wanted to see who was really neat and who was dirty. You never can tell with them." He launched into a tirade against the racial hodgepodge that is Latin America. Mother listened. The price of being a Nazi. When we were alone and she complained, I hoped that she shared my revulsion over how the man was treating his employees. I should have known better. She only resented his indelicacy in discussing such things in front of fine German ladies.

We took a newly opened train line cross-continent and concluded our excursion among the Latins in Chile. The Pacific looked just the same as the Atlantic, although I found myself thinking of California again. I did so much want to see Hollywood. In the absence of show people and movie moguls who didn't have to take any heed of Father's aesthetic and political theories whatsoever, I settled for plain and unobtrusive reality to satisfy my taste for the unusual. The Indians lived in shacks and lean-to's that seemed insubstantial indeed against the relentless salt breezes blowing in from the sea. Perhaps as a statement about modernity, they would relieve themselves in unexpected places, such as the middle of railroad tracks. They had turned their poverty into an art. Only now, as I recollect those empty days of spoiled voyeurism, am I revolted at the young woman who observed the misery and wonder of those lives as something for her entertainment.

In our brief circuit of the Greater Reich, we had been surprised and amused by some of the folk customs that stubbornly resisted change, despite hygienic measures enforced by one of National Socialism's new departments. But our modesty and inhibitions were really put to the test by the outdoor urinals of Chile. A tiny partition

45

was barely adequate to cover the genital region, and the rest of you was free to commune with the open sky. None of us availed ourselves of this rare opportunity, except Helmuth, who timed his release to coincide with a procession of nuns that passed close by.

We stayed in a private home atop a cliff, receiving a refreshing cool breeze from the ocean. Helga and I enjoyed standing on a small, elegant patio that overlooked the surf leaving white lace patterns on the rocks below. Helga's health greatly improved. Our host was an Italian engineer who insisted on taking us, our very first night, to a German-owned restaurant specializing in steak Tartar. So I had my taste of the Wild East after all, but in the Southern Hemisphere!

The owner of the establishment was as jolly a fat man as the Brazilian had been grim, and he oversaw the serving of his favorite dish. They brought a huge platter with a mound of raw, red meat in the middle. Quantities of the finest sirloin had been finely ground no less than three times, until all the gristle was dissolved into paste. Surrounding the meat was a circle of raw eggs, peppers, and onions.

Mother beheld the vision and announced her decision: "Never!" It was left to the next generation to uphold the family honor, but I would require liquid encouragement. Alfredo warned us off any drink laced with absinthe, a drug, he assured everyone, that was causing considerable mischief throughout the continent. As the sun follows the moon, the dinner party's discussion quickly degenerated into praise for the firm antidrug policy of National Socialist Europe (when in doubt, they eliminate the addict . . . provided he's not an official), and a forlorn hope that similarly progressive measures could be applied to the backward societies of South America. I said nothing. I did not dare let myself begin. At the suggestion from Helmuth that everyone might be forced to take urine tests to determine drug levels, I could only think that if the Nazis can't get your blood, they go after your piss.

Having settled on a potent, dark German beer, I screwed up my courage to try the steak Tartar. Selecting a piece of white bread, I put a dab of the red paste on it, as a painter might prepare his palette, carefully placed the concoction in my mouth, and hurriedly washed it down with cold beer. By the third time around, I realized that the flavor wasn't all that bad and ate more honest portions.

There had been moments of the vacation when I could temporarily forget who I was. That night, in that restaurant on a hill, I was at peace. Yet even brief moments of respite, half a world away from the iron eagle's claws, were not to last. It was as if none of us had any reality independent of the Fuehrer. Mother wouldn't eat the meal, but her comment was as predictable as I was weary of hearing the same old anecdotes: "Hitler is a strict vegetarian. Normally I differ with him on that. He's very tolerant. But seeing this uncooked meat, well, I'd rather be a vegetarian than eat it."

With no consideration that everyone else was dining on the subject of her ire, she was off and running. The shark-fin soup they brought her didn't even slow her down. As she told her interminable stories of Hitler's likes and dislikes, Helmuth and I exchanged glances. He had rubbed blood from the dish on his forehead and made an upside down triangle, which we both knew was the symbol for water among the ancients. Cute. My brother had his own inimitable way of fighting boredom. I passed him the water, and we waited for Mother to notice. Helga finally drew our antics to her attention. "Helmuth!" she cried, and there was a collective sigh of relief round the table as Magda Goebbels picked a new subject.

The New England writer Edgar Allan Poe has written about the imp of the perverse, an uncontrollable desire to perpetrate something precisely because one feels it is imprudent to do so. At that moment, I had no reason in the world to make trouble, but I did.

"When it comes to uncooked flesh, I prefer sushi to steak Tartar," I said, a trivial matter to most of the assemblage, but not to a Goebbels. Father had recently launched a series of advertisements against the Japanese dish, ostensibly for health reasons, but most informed Europeans knew that the fight was over symbolism, his guiding light in all things. The Party's current line was that the former ally must never be forgiven for the treasonable behavior of allowing itself to be conquered instead of being reduced to heroic ashes. As relations between Americans and Japanese steadily improved, the Reich suffered an increasing degree of amnesia. Since no one had responded to my endorsement for raw fish, I was foolish enough to continue. I mentioned Father's wartime articles trumpeting the astounding news that the Japanese were the Oriental analog to Aryans. This embarrassing moment in the development of Nazi

47

ideology was not considered polite dinner conversation anywhere in the Reich. It didn't go over too well in Chile either.

Helga tensed up, Helmuth grinned, and I knew that I had done it. Mother had one of her "heart palpitations," and we had to make our apologies. Alfredo, ever the diplomat, attempted to save the evening, but the damage was done. Our Italian host and we returned to the villa, Mother exhausting the theme of a daughter's faithlessness every kilometer of the drive.

I wept . . . but they were tears of hatred instead of remorse. As even Rommel appreciated strategic retreats, I moved back into my shell. It was after midnight, and everyone had gone to bed except Alfredo and myself. He was a gregarious man. We sat on the patio under a gibbous moon, and we talked until dawn.

In two days, the Goebbels clan would board an experimental rocket plane and fly to our next port of call in Miami, Florida. Father's lust for publicity followed us everywhere, and this stunt was already being referred to as the Pogo Stick. It was unlikely that I would see Alfredo again, but I promised him that I wouldn't let Mother forget to mail him a box of the best Havana cigars.

"*Grácias, Señorita,*" he answered, then returned to English. "Latin America lacks unity. Is this good? Is this bad? For years and years, our politicians were bound by one passion: resentment over imperialism from the north. The only good *Yanquis* were nineteenth-century gentlemen who had opposed their country's lording it over her southern cousins—men like Godkin and Carnegie and Sumner. Their voices were drowned out by our would-be saviors. They would amputate our limbs before gangrene set in. We could not explain to the *Norteamericános* as they sawed and chopped that we had no infection and required no treatment."

He lit one of his noxious cigars, but was thoughtful enough to sit downwind. As the smoke was dissipated on the night air, he asked: "Are you familiar with *Luftverkehrsnetz Der Vereinigten Staaten Sud-Amerikas Hauptlinien?*" I shook my head. "British intelligence concocted a phony map of a proposed plan Hitler had for conquering our beautiful continent. This piece of paper was used for the propaganda purposes you'd expect. It's a funny thing, but very few of us ever believed it. The United States, now there it was believed. I have a copy of the map on my wall at home. It is an inspiration to me."

He puffed. I thought. Then, pointing the cigar at me, forgetting for the moment my aversion to smoke, he said, "When I began my career, I noticed that the officials who were most easily bribed by the *Yanquis* were the ones who resented it so strongly, and yet bribery is a way of life here. This was a mystery to me. But now it is different. Since the U.S.A. has forsworn imperialism, the money flows in different channels. Before the war, Chile did about the same amount of business with the United States as it did with the Axis. Many other countries here did more business with Hitler than they did with Roosevelt. Now here is only the one empire, the unity of Europe. North America has been, how do you say it, Balkanized? But they are still rich, as we are still poor. Which way do we turn? Europe offers certainties. To the north, there are corporations warring among themselves. Dealing with one may mean wealth, another may mean worse poverty."

"Take the chance," I told him instantly. "Choose profits."

"You say this, you of all people?"

The conversation was frank, as befitted our mutual trust. "The certainty offered by the Nazis will end in slavery for your continent," I said.

"Germans treat us as fairly as anybody. They have yet to send the marines."

"I've recently toured the part of the world where Germany has 'sent the marines.' They never leave. Besides, don't you trust the changes in the United States? Would you put on a new yoke the moment an old one is removed?"

The moment he laughed, I knew that I'd been right about him. "Many think as you do, but I never expected to hear such words from a child of the elite. You must receive underground newspapers in Germany. You take a risk with me. I wouldn't have been hired as your guide if I didn't have a minimal Party association."

"I wasn't born today. Membership alone doesn't prove much in this world." I had gotten to the point where I could tell true believers from people in search of a job. I wasn't naive enough to believe Alfredo's name had been drawn out of a hat. He was an honest cynic. He told me how in his youth he had been a Marxist and spoken of classes. Today, he could parrot a very similar rhetoric, only now the magic word was race instead of class. But he thought all of it was nonsense. What he believed in was the holy trinity: the U.S. gold dollar, the German mark, and the Swiss franc. He lacked the moral courage to publicly witness to this faith. I certainly had no right to condemn him. I'd yet to discover individualism myself.

Pulling out his wallet, he peeled off two soggy bills. They were American twenties. "One is counterfeit. Can you tell which?" I couldn't. "It doesn't matter in the least. They are both believed here. New dollars, old dollars, on the gold standard, off the gold standard . . . if it's U.S. money, it will buy more than this will." He showed me the *escudo,* Chile's national currency. "Now this is just a piece of paper. It's all in the mind."

He explained how smuggling was the heart of business throughout the continent. It was called *Negotio.* The customs agents were a special breed of barefoot officialdom, too corrupt to be corrupted. "We will deal with anyone," he concluded proudly.

"Watch out for strings attached to German goods," I replied.

Patting me on the arm, he said, "What a traitor you are. Let's be friends for life."

I left Chile thinking that they might not have the political freedom that existed to the north, but compared to what I considered normal, I had felt the bracing wind of freedom among its rocky crags. I would have preferred joining Alfredo in his friend's sailplane. They were going to glide on the thermals outside Santiago, as I was thrown into the sky at a greater velocity, a speed precluding languid contemplation of the scenery.

As Mother had intended, we were behind schedule and could spend no time to speak of in the dreaded American Republic. She was afraid of assassination. My head was still spinning from the descent of the rocket plane as Mother booked passage on a ship to take us from Florida within the week.

I wouldn't come. She was at the end of her rope, because instead of arguing, she gave me funds for a few days. I stayed nearly two months, working at odd jobs, and saw a good portion of the American South. I did not loudly advertise my name.

In Boca Raton, I got something of a tan, improved my accent, and did my first work as a waitress. In Tampa, I became accomplished at hitchhiking and explained to one overly friendly Greek that I had received basic training in martial arts. Not everything that Father insisted upon was a bad idea. In Jacksonville, I did have to render unconscious a pimple-faced young man who wore a Swastika around his neck. If he was counting on the medallion to improve his chances as a rapist, he was in the wrong line of endeavor.

I saw a jazz festival in New Orleans and touched many black bodies without contracting diseases. I hope that I didn't give them anything. One young man touched me in a most direct and satisfying way. He was graceful, and he knew all my secret places. I loved his dark skin and his laughter and the gin and tonic on his breath. I remember the scent of his cologne. Black is beautiful.

There were odd pleasures to be found in many places. In a small town with the unlikely name of Toomsooba, I saw that a recent German horror film had arrived on American shores: *They Saved Stalin's Brain.* There was no censorship, but the American distributor had given it a classification of "R" for racist content. My favorite scene was when the Russian mad scientist pauses in his evil scheme so that he may salute a picture of Josef Stalin hanging on the wall. The audience howled with laughter. The dubbing was perfectly terrible.

By late summer, I was in Atlanta, Georgia, the site of Mother's favorite film. But then, the Fuehrer liked *Gone with the Wind,* so as the night must follow the day . . . Atlanta made a strong impression on me. Since the wrenching changes in American life were recent history, I was sensitive to incongruities. Atlanta was a hotbed of contradictions.

For the first time since leaving Burgundy, I encountered a follower of the Nordic cult! That the Burgundian religion could take root in America seemed impossible. A woman activist in the Liberty party who had penetrated my disguise (such as it was) cheerfully explained. The crazy young man dressed in ritual cloak and carrying a copy of a book by Professor Karl Haushofer was viewed as a harmless eccentric. If he did any violence to his neighbors because he didn't like their race or religion, then he would be punished for violating a fellow human being's rights. He would have to pay restitution, or work it off, until his debt was paid.

Knowing the pernicious doctrines of the cult all too well, I asked what would be done should the fanatic murder someone. As no amount of restitution could replace a life, the murderer would forfeit his own life. Justice would be the coin of the realm. All that sounded pretty good, but I was shocked that Americans could hold ideas inimical to their own interests. The woman from the Liberty party assured me that there was nothing uncommon about it in the least. The solution had been to remove the structures of local government that allowed one group to enforce its standards on another. The law was simple: thou shalt not initiate force or fraud.

Given my skeptical nature, I immediately wondered if a centralized government didn't pose a greater threat to freedom than the power of local authority. But the idea was an embryo then. Compared to Europe, I had discovered the promised land. In Atlanta, Georgia, there was practical freedom in an ordered, social context.

The most dramatic proof was that in a city dominated by Baptists of every hue, none of their views on alcohol or sex or observance of the Sabbath carried the weight of law. Only in America could such a miracle obtain! Protestants and Catholics, Jews and Muslims, atheists and agnostics—they all lived in peace. The lady told me that when immigrants went into the melting pot, all that was boiled away was the hate. "Of course, confidentially," she added, "we do have strife with a sect of primitive Baptists who believe in holding your head under water until you agree with them. We do the best we can."

Freedom of religion and freedom from religion was something I had never seen in practice. (With all his power, Father still kept the fact of his atheism largely a private matter.) I met a Buddhist who was very quiet. I met a Hindu who was quite noisy. I met a practitioner of Haitian Voodoo who promised to use his spells only for good. I even met a large, raw-boned woman dressed in more black leather and silver than an SS Gruppenfuehrer. She was a member of an all-woman, lesbian motorcycle gang of Orthodox Wiccans. They called themselves the Mothers. She inspired me to consider a strictly heterosexual life-style.

Although there were problems in such a diverse population, by and large they were good neighbors. I was stunned. According to the theories of Adolf Hitler, these people should have slaughtered one another. The conflicts between their values were beyond anything ever dreamed of in the Weimar Republic. If that German house could not stand under its stresses, what gave the American house its firm foundation? Throughout all the years of my education, I had been repeatedly exposed to Rosenberg's doctrine of polylogism, the notion that different peoples had different truths. Aryan logic was not the same as other logics, and so it had no choice but to conquer anything that was different. When I became hungry for freedom, I didn't know it, but I also acquired an appetite for One Logic for All.

Encountering a carnival of tolerance and freedom should have been the purest delight, and evidence that there might be one truth under which all men could live. On one level, I was exalted. But although I'd been rejecting the Nazi philosophy, I had to admit that experiencing living proof of one's wildest speculations is unsettling.

CHAPTER SIX

The legitimate powers of government extend only to such acts as are injurious to others. But it does me no injury for my neighbor to say there are twenty gods, or no God. It neither picks my pocket nor breaks my leg.

—Thomas Jefferson,
Notes on Virginia

The one-way ticket to New Berlin reposed in my pocket, as if it were a poisonous beetle I dare not touch. Why was I returning home? I'd saved my money and bought the fare. It was not a command performance, a summons sent by special messenger. I had chosen to leave a place that promised much, only to return to a continent of extinguished hopes. It was not that I missed my advantages; I was certain of that. I had to return to Europe as an enemy, but I didn't know how I would translate raging emotions into practical action.

Late summer was a grand time to wander in the woods, and I spent my last night so occupied. Wrestling with ambivalence did not compare to the pleasure of turning white sneakers red with Georgia clay. I heard singing and followed it to a clearing. The music was coming from beyond a lake. Vagrant night breezes picked up the notes and carried them over a generous tangle of trees to my ears. How relaxing to bathe in the church music and not have to analyze the content.

It was probably some evening gathering of Baptists, heartily singing their simple hymns, seeking to overcome their equally simple conception of evil with the common goodness in their laborer's traditions. The high notes were charming—the product of children searching for an elusive quality at the top of the scale. Bearing down with only an occasional false note, the organist made the best of a limited talent; and I could imagine a ramshackle wooden building as a perfect setting for the harmless performance. The hymn was every bit as clean as the Burgundian ceremony had been filthy.

A sudden caress on the face reminded me that I was still in America, tasting the subtle breezes for which her Deep South is famous. I was safe temporarily from the dark world of *Mein Kampf.* The breeze was warm and soft, and it brought a gift: an assortment of fireflies, winking their small, phosphorescent bodies in mimicry of the cold, white stars above. Holding out a hand, I saw one of the tiny creatures alight on my palm. I barely felt it. I was happy.

I went home on the largest passenger jet in the world at that time, the Hindenburg. (Germans believe if at first you go up in flames, then try, try again.) My firm resolution was to return one day and see all of America, especially the Statue of Liberty and Hollywood Boulevard. In my satchel, I carried a treasure trove of books, new titles to circulate among comrades in the Reading League. Thanks to my rating, I'd be passed through customs without the books being confiscated. Looking back, I understand that Father could have removed my classification so as to teach me a lesson. Then again, he preferred finesse where his family was concerned.

Among the books were works by the Jewish anarchist Emma Goldman. Her autobiographical *My Disillusionment with Russia* closely paralleled my own growing disenchantment with Germany, but she had lived her ideas, while I had done nothing, for good or ill. The light she had shone upon Moscow and Lenin cast shadows of discontent across the years and over New Berlin and the elderly Hitler. The similarities were pins to prick the conscience.

On the flight, I carried the day's edition of the *New York Times* with a feature story on two new appointees to the American Supreme Court, one a distinguished lay Catholic, the other a philosopher who had written a formidable essay on atheism. Such a development would have been unthinkable in the Protestant America of only a few years earlier; and the name of a brilliant Jewish legal mind was being bandied about as a possible later appointment. (Eight years later, she would indeed assume her seat on the bench.) The reaction in Europe was exactly what should have been expected. Father had already broadcast his opinion that the Americans were deliberately tweaking the nose of Nazi opinion, as if the domestic affairs of America should take heed of a foreign power's obsessions before managing its own house.

The judges who had been confirmed in their august positions were both adherents of Natural Law and interpreted the Constitution in terms of the nonaggression principle. They both read the First Amendment as an unequivocal statement against censorship, prompting the Catholic justice to say, "Religious convictions should not be confused with secular law. For example, the Index of banned books is for the faithful. It is not a matter for the statute books." These words demonstrated as well as anything that the United States had undergone a second revolution. Father took this as a personal slight, so committed was he to the Nazis as revolutionists, while plutocratic Americans were supposed to behave, well, properly.

There was a serious difference between the justices over abortion. One saw the fetus as a citizen. National Socialist judges never had to concern themselves over such troublesome distinctions. The Reich's policy was spelled out: Aryan abortions were discouraged; non-Aryan abortions were encouraged, outside of meeting the quota for slave labor in restricted industries.

The story devoted a paragraph to Father's outburst. I knew that he had a personal motive in objecting to the Supreme Court news. He was already using his considerable influence to insert anti-Catholic scenes in a new string of musicals being produced at UFA. (The additional footage was altered to Anglican clergy for pictures exported to the British protectorate.) I knew what had triggered this activity. The Vatican had finally gotten around to excommunicating Father, along with Hitler and Goering on the same day. Now it was one thing to put *The Myth of the Twentieth Century* on the Index in the prewar period. It was quite another to take the moral high ground in Nazi Europe.

Most of the world had nearly forgotten that these candidates for the anti-Christ (should the office be open) were still on the membership rolls of the competing firm. Cynical practitioners of Realpolitik, Nazi leaders undermined the churches while maintaining outward decorum for the *Völk* who, theoretician Rosenberg knew better than anyone, could not be weaned from their superstitions overnight. Excommunication was a symbolic rebuke, meaning nothing to Party ideologues on the personal level. But that Rome should take an action against secular power—this called for more than a symbolic response. At the very least, Bormann's campaign against the churches would be reinvigorated. On the other hand, Hitler had sworn not to make Napoleon's errors with the Holy See. Well, I had problems of my own.

Fortunate was the child who escaped *Pimpfe,* being trapped in the Hitler Youth, or the League of German Girls. These officially approved groups had the good equipment and the good field trips, but what a price one paid to enjoy them. Shortly after the Jewish youth organizations were terminated, the remaining non-Nazi gatherings discovered that they weren't allowed to do much of anything. Kids will go where the action is, even Lutherans.

Father used to brag how he had adopted certain methods of the Jesuits for application in the *Kinder-Land-Verschicküng* camps and used the techniques to turn young Catholics against their own religion. I had seen how effective this could be. In no time at all, boys and girls who had been eating fish on Friday were singing, "Der Papst ist tot" (The Pope is dead).

If certain political difficulties didn't preclude a direct strike on the Vatican, it would have been reduced to rubble long ago. I thought everyone in the world was aware of the situation. Yet while I'd been in Georgia, I'd encountered, as part of the crazy quilt of beliefs promulgated there, a fundamentalist "Friend of Jesus" who went around babbling that the Vatican was secretly cooperating with New Berlin. He paid no heed to my assurances that a fruitful dialogue between the two parties was improbable. This person, who seemed more wild-eyed than the displaced Burgundian had been, solemnly intoned that we were in End Times. Hitler was the Beast foretold in Revelations because he had destroyed Russia and set in place a European hegemony. The sadly named "Friend of Jesus" said that Rome was the Great Whore that would serve the Swastika and all its works. When he spoke, there was spittle on his chin afterward. The world is full of lunatics. I grow weary in the recounting.

Caring not for the company of the mad was no mood in which to greet Father. He took me aback by ascertaining the day of my return (I must have been recognized the instant I went through security), and in an action without precedence, he was waiting for me. He'd only just returned from a fact-finding mission in Bohemia and Moravia, whichever facts were certain not to include the name of Czechoslovakia. His talent for euphemism was perfect.

How I longed to ask if he'd run out of girl friends in town! But I wasn't suicidal enough to do that. I'd voluntarily returned to the web. I stepped with caution, and for good reason. It was a long way from the International Desk at New Berlin's busiest airfield to the intimate discomforts of home.

When Papa was sweet, I tasted the bitter flavor of terror. Taking me by the arm, he led me to his Volkswagen touring car, and drove us to a café on the Wilhelmstrasse. En route, he chatted idly about the weather and dropped the hint that I had a treat in store if I was a good girl. We arrived. The proprietor fell over himself providing us with top service. The propaganda minister is a walking advertisement, after all. Father waited until we were seated in the privacy of a corner that had been reserved for him outside, before letting the axe fall.

"Your mother and I have had a long talk," he began, adding cream to his coffee with slow deliberation. "She told me about your idiotic remarks. What do you have to say for yourself?"

I believe that I prayed . . . prayed that nothing of my conversation with Alfredo was known to him. I operated on the assumption that that encounter had not been compromised. "She was upset when I told the truth."

"The truth! What do you know about truth? You're a young pup, playing at being the radical, lacking appreciation for the privileges you enjoy in the New Order. You're not a child any longer. What will you do with your life? You're not married, and not likely to be at this rate. You don't have a career. You majored in chemistry, but you've done nothing with it . . . and believe me when I say that the Reich can always use chemists. You're a dilettante, and that's something to your credit because it's kept you out of worse trouble. Listen, Hilda, it's about time that you grew up. There's no free sauerkraut in this world. Socialism is not for children who play but for adults who serve and die, if need be. Now hop to it." Then, without even waiting for my response, he turned his attention to the nut mousse with plums.

I was trembling with rage, but I couldn't show it, not to him. "How am I to grow up?" I asked, barely above a whisper.

"We'll begin with your treatment of your mother. How dare you have a fit of temper in public? You didn't used to be like this."

"When was this?"

"Helmuth and Helga were there, my dear. They saw it all."

"But it was Mother who became angry and—"

"We needn't focus on details. I'm speaking of a general pattern.

You have been sarcastic to your mother; you were even abusive! And then this nonsense about remaining in the United States to see the sights. You've caused me no end of embarrassment."

He was holding his anger in check, and a small voice in me shrilled that my rage was but a spark against the red furnace burning in his breast. Watching his cruel mouth, I was afraid. A bad father would make a most formidable enemy even without the force of an empire behind him.

"These are difficult times," he said, "and our faith is sorely tested. We must extend the defense perimeter. We continue to deport enemies of the Reich from liberated territories. The number of our People's Courts expand without an upper limit. We must put enemies on trial. We must make an object lesson of them. We will not forget our foes. They shall never be forgiven. Do you hear me?"

He paused, and he was trembling. Absently swirling ice cubes in my punch, I waited for the storm to pass. Suddenly he spoke in a perfectly calm voice: "What if you had been kidnapped?"

"The thought never occurred to me."

"Don't you read the papers? Acts of terror are committed against us by Jewish pirates the world over. You could have been held for ransom."

"Why didn't you send SS men to bring me back?"

His eyes narrowed. "You were watched."

I gasped, then spoke without thinking: "I don't believe you."

Three beefy men walked by, unattractive in ill-fitting suits. They had Gestapo written all over them. One whistled at a pretty fraulein crossing the street. A blackbird flew overhead, screeching at other birds that were out of sight. These things happened as Father and I stared at each other, absorbed by the ticking from an ornate grandfather clock just inside the door of the café.

"Let's be off," he said, smiling. "Time for your surprise."

One thought welled up to drown out the rest: say nothing more, *Dummköpf!* We drove in silence, except when he told me how he'd let his chauffeur go and that he rarely used the Mercedes-Benz any longer. The People's Car was good enough for him. Symbols. Always symbols. I noticed that he had added steel sheets to bulletproof his connection to the *Völk.* And he'd kept his car phone.

They were waiting for us at the very exclusive Otto Skorzeny Aerodrome and did everything but roll out the red carpet. Father loved his perks. They brought out one of Goering's helium planes. When I'm nervous, I get the hiccups. I probably always will. That afternoon, I had them with a vengeance. The tear-shaped aeroplane was not a mode of transportation I was inclined to try. Besides, I'd just spent most of the day in flight anyway. The conclusion was never in question: I would have to fly in the damned thing.

Maybe I was prejudiced against it because it was one of the Reich marshal's brainchildren. This was, after all, the same man who had conceived the notion to build railroad engines out of concrete when Germany was desperate for resources late in the war. Next to that, even Himmler's plan to use dandelions for fuel seemed worthy of investigation. The nastiest military jokes are at Goering's expense to this day, largely because of his poor performance on air defense, but there was plenty of blame to go around. As for his oddball ideas, most never got off the drawing board, except as punch lines, but the helium plane was a notable exception.

They poured water down me until the hiccups were gone, and then I had my revenge. They had to wait while I repaired to the Ladies' Room. Then my time ran out. Boarding the plane, I caught the eye of the pilot, who was having difficulty squeezing his six-foot frame into the cockpit. Father and I were the only passengers.

The helium plane operates on the principle of a zeppelin and mainly was used for reconnaissance. When the pilot is over a promising spot, he redistributes the gas in the ample wings, and the aircraft descends as a leaf drifts earthward. Today this marvel of German aeronautical prowess is virtually discontinued, replaced by a new family of autogyros.

Goering's toy certainly satisfied Father's purposes. "We'll enjoy a tour of the backyard, eh, daughter?" he asked. "You've grown up with this glory, but have you ever really seen it?" He was up to his old tricks and was going to give the show full production values. The opening chords of Wagner's *Parsifal* were piped through the speaker, as we rose above the clouds. No wonder he had been interested in the weather. Lights! Camera! Action!

"We're going to remake *Triumph of the Will,*" he said casually. "The new capital demands it."

"With or without Leni?" I asked. The imp of the perverse would have its way.

He was terse. "That hasn't been decided." He was expansive.

"Today is for you. Drink in the experience. Rediscover your heritage."

The sunlight playing off the clouds created a jewel-box effect, a dance of colors to draw me out of myself and whisper that the works of man are ephemeral. Ghosts of the past and ghosts of the future descended with us through the eternal clouds to the vast marble mausoleum that was the giant city still under construction, and already cracking at the seams.

We came in over one of the completed sections. The wide plateau of the South Station slowly crept beneath us . . . and the monstrous cavern that was the Arch of Triumph loomed ahead. Beyond that stretched the dry riverbed of concrete that was the Grand Boulevard. Work crews were busily engaged planting one of the numerous rows of trees that would grow on the banks overlooking the vehicles that would drift by in the current.

"Notice the shadows reaching out to embrace our neighbors," said Father. He did not even sound sarcastic.

The music was inspiring, lifting me higher and higher, swelling chords that rose to challenge the gods, but the helium plane was descending with every note. The afternoon sun put the city in the best light. But the imposing structures were dead things, designed as showpieces the functions of which could not be divined. We veered off for a close view of Goering's Palace (how Hitler had spoiled that man). This building was a perfect example of architectural window dressing. Father agreed that the Graeco-Roman motifs had been overdone, what with statues of charioteers frozen in motion, as if wishing to stampede and escape from the forest of Doric columns.

Directly across from the palace, an equally imposing and Romanesque edifice was still under construction: the Soldier's Hall. The sun glinted off more gilded pomp and grandiose colonnades. Steel girders crisscrossing next to the ancient world's splendor increased the feeling of weirdness. Small, black shapes scuttled like beetles along the lengthy base of the memorial. The Volkswagen was everywhere.

"To the heart of New Berlin!" declaimed the minister of propaganda and gauleiter of the city. His face was flushed with excitement and I wondered if he might have an orgasm. The helium plane rose several meters before the pilot kicked in the propellers, and we flew toward the recently finished Great Hall, the world's most expensive building, guaranteed never to pay for itself. The dome was

27,468,000 cubic yards and had a space reserved at the top that has since been filled by an iron eagle. "The Fuehrer will hold a world's fair when the work is finished," crowed Papa. I wondered how the Nazis would persuade the world to attend.

We were losing daylight by the time we banked for a final run past Hitler's Palace and the Mussolini Monument. Offices of the Reich protectors were to be found in these echoing, empty halls. The functionaries of command increased as the locusts of the Bible, each hoping that one day supreme power might be his. But Hitler lived on.

"Do you see that?" asked the extension of the Fuehrer's will who thought himself the creator of the Fuehrer. He was pointing to an ugly modern building in the distance, curiously out of place beside a gargoyle- and goddess-festooned Opera House on one side and a row of forlorn private shops on the other (the latter a concession to business amidst a jungle of public works). "I hope that you won't force me to show you the inside."

"I don't understand."

"You're looking at an insane asylum. After all, one doesn't place a beloved member of the household in a work camp. It just isn't done." He was to be commended for his candor. Day after day of suspicion without an object is tiresome. Conversations become ballets of indecision. At least Father had the virtue of detesting ambiguity.

"You would do that?" I asked. Why was it that as he threatened me, I fixated on his hair? The dye he was using was a little too black, as if it were shoe polish. When the war ended victoriously, his hair had begun turning white.

"I love you, Hilda. I care what happens to you. Now, I'm the first to admit that certain offspring of other officials are far more spoiled than you. I've always encouraged you to listen to the blood. Aryan youth of the highest caste should have the freedom to discover their duty for themselves. I've encouraged this in you. I'd hate to think that I went too far. How much longer will you be irresponsible? Don't you realize that you are part of a noble community?"

Hovering above the gray cinder block of a National Socialist madhouse, I was sane enough to discover my civic pride and to sense that patriotism is a requirement of mental health. "I never thought of it that way," I lied, hoping that he would stop. Hope springs eternal.

Who should have known better than I that Father could match his hero's penchant for long-windedness?

And so he elaborated. It seemed that Mother had learned of my sexual egalitarianism. I couldn't believe that he would have the gall to lecture me about sex, he the great Casanova. I had not reckoned with the man who claimed to be the Voice of the People, working tirelessly to learn public sentiment, and at the same time writing: "A government derived from the people must never tolerate a go-between 'twixt it and the people." Hitler was his god, but hypocrisy ranked only a little further down in the pantheon. He excoriated my sexual behavior as if he were a celibate monk. But as he continued, I was relieved to note that my lesbian encounters were not mentioned. Either he was deliberately avoiding the topic, or else he didn't know. Homosexual activity could still earn the practitioner a pink triangle and free lodging in a concentration camp; although everyone knew that exceptions were made. At any rate, my boyfriends were sufficient to his purpose.

He had me all right, and he wasn't about to let it end. Not he! "Did you know that more people died during the war from disease than from the bombings, and that's including the atomic bombs? Now don't get smart and factor in postatomic diseases. You know very well what I mean. The old-fashioned germs killed us. Don't you think sexual transmission was a big help to the Grim Reaper?"

"Father, do you want me to answer or only listen?" If he wouldn't be sarcastic, then I would.

"Listen, naturally." He could be honest when he wished. Although I did not use it then, hanging in space and fearing accidents, I would in the next few weeks drop snippets of information leading him to an inescapable conclusion: I'd been compiling my own file about Father's indiscretions that not only matched, but probably surpassed, similar efforts by intelligence agents. Hitler had, as a useful quirk, a bourgeoise obsession with propriety—the attitude that a sadistic concentration camp commandant was a moral man if he didn't cheat on his wife. Then there were other secrets that Father had been careless in keeping from my eyes. He had enough skeletons in his closet to fill a cemetery.

Sons and daughters generally strive to make a good impression on their parents. I won Father's respect by responding to his threat in a likewise brutal fashion. I suppose that it was a rite of passage. I

wasn't proud, only relieved. My motive had been survival, not an-
gling for a berth in the family business.

We didn't speak to each other again that day. Too much had been
said. He instructed the pilot to take us home. The sun was setting
and we were bathed in red light that looked like blood. The city was
also crimson. Recalling my impressions today, I believed that New
Berlin was probably the greatest city on earth . . . but it hadn't been
designed for human beings. The scale was actually malignant. Surely
the staggering sum of 25 billion Reichsmarks could have been better
spent.

My room had not been touched, and I gratefully locked the door
so that he wouldn't see me cry. For a moment, I was so afraid that
I couldn't even hear. I bit my tongue, tasted blood, and moaned.
Moaning was good. It brought back the sound.

I was Papa's little girl again. He had primed me for nightmare, and
the years of adolescence and young adulthood were stripped away,
leaving me a doll dressed in bright peasant apron, a jewel in my
parents' collection of pretty things. I was so weary that I collapsed
on my bed. No tears came, but I did dream.

Childhood is when you store up all your real demons. Adult fears
never replace them, but only result in their retrieval. I didn't dream
of straitjackets and padded rooms and creative surgery. Far worse,
I slid back in time.

When I was a girl, I barely escaped incineration in the Allied fire
storm of Hamburg, the damned summer of 1943. That his own
daughter should survive a tragedy that staggered the imagination
was not considered acceptable propaganda that season, so Father
buried the fact that I was ever there. But Hitler may have considered
my survival further proof that the Goebbels family had been selected
for a divine mission.

Hamburg was the fuel of my bad dreams ever after. I remember
people caught in asphalt that had been suddenly rendered into a
primordial tar pit by the intense heat. They could do nothing but
stand and scream as a curtain of fire closed in, burning them as black
as the asphalt. I remember a pregnant woman, running through the
rubble, every inch of her a living torch. I will not allow myself to
remember the children.

By some miracle, I was pulled into one of the shelters that did not
become a tomb of living corpses, flesh roasting, lungs full of carbon

monoxide. The weather must have been in an RAF uniform that night, the way the wind conspired to spread the fire storm to the broadest possible number of victims. The firefighters could do nothing against the phosphorus bombs and the tornadoes of flame.

I was glad to have survived afterward, but at the time I was too horrified to care; I only wanted to be spared further horror, which awaited me up above, amidst the steaming wreckage. A screaming man was carrying a suitcase, begging someone to tell him what to do. As he stumbled, the case fell to the ground, disgorging its contents—a shriveled brown mummy that had been his wife. I saw her face and wanted to rip my eyes out. Long afterward, when I was shown the face of the Jewish child, victim of SS scientific research, I would relive the full meaning of the Hamburg wife.

That choking night in Hamburg, I lost my belief in God. Today, I shake my head at the simplicity of youth. I pray to no deity for reasons of the intellect, but I have learned that terror does nothing to disprove God. All religions accept the reality of man's inhumanity to man. That is their starting place. It is possible that someone in Hamburg was converted to religion by encountering a brimstone punishment worthy of the Devil.

Although I reject the supernatural, my dreams take no heed of my conviction. The torments of Hamburg coalesced, that long ago summer, into one image I refer to as the Asphalt Man. Trepidation at entering an asylum was the trigger to bring back my childhood phantom in full force. I had thought myself rid of the thing, but I learned that nightmares are never banished. They are only endured.

Even now, safe on this ship on a calm Pacific, bound for Tahiti, the tall, black figure with the burning red eyes returns to haunt me. The dream has changed again, but the Asphalt Man remains. I know why the particulars are different. Burgundy is the reason . . . Burgundy and Father's dying.

CHAPTER SEVEN

Freedom is always the freedom of those who think differently.

—Rosa Luxemburg,
Letters from Prison

New York

Here the typed pages of English were interrupted by handwritten sheets in German, in the immediate tense. Alan Whittmore read several paragraphs of the new material before he realized that he had shifted languages.

The body is burning. Enshrined at the summit of the pyre, lit by the flame of the acolytes, it darkens and smokes and gives off a popping sound. The stench is terrible.

For this is a Viking's funeral, replete with the lowing sound of great horns carved from whalebone. The men blowing into the long horns appear to be northern fighting men from the twelfth century: a procession of horned helmets, leather stockings, coarse boots, and dried leather tunics. The men holding torches around the pyre are similarly attired, but the rest of the company are outfitted in twentieth-century military uniforms.

Rising from the pyre is a black monolith sweating blood, the Asphalt Man. With the advent of such a terrifying apparition, violence explodes onto the gathering. Beyond the cordon of modern soldiers and ancient warriors, a troop of guerrillas make an attack. Shouts! Gunfire! The concussion of grenades! There used to be a wall to the courtyard, but it disappears into a jagged ditch of red and brown . . . and not all the red is from the soil.

I am one of the attackers, irresistibly drawn to the funeral fire, and the demon hanging above it. My weapon is a Mauser, from the firm that also manufactures adding machines. I increase my score by taking aim at the largest of the enemy, a giant blond man who is rushing toward me. His weapon is a battleaxe, and idly wondering if brandishing such a weapon might give him a hernia, I pull the trigger. One burst and his midsection is wreathed in a garland of blood and human pulp. Into the wine of his own bowels he collapses.

The defenders have hand grenades, too. One detonates nearby, and there is a pink ball of chaos in my head and spots before my eyes as I go down. I am fortunate. I only lose a tooth. Stumbling to my feet, half running, howling, I am an animal, a wolf ravening to kill. The Asphalt Man wears a crown of flame and nods approval to each and every one of us, raving and bleeding for his amusement.

I am first to the pyre, and pull the pin on my grenade. The burning corpse is nearly consumed, and the sour odor of roasting flesh has been diminished by the charred gunpowder smell that permeates the air. But the dark shadow, ascended from the pyre, mocks me to destroy destruction. I throw the grenade up high, so that it arcs down to the top of the pyre, where it will touch the charred remains of the corpse before going off. There is maniacal laughter. It is mine.

The explosion does nothing to the Asphalt Man but make him bigger and blacker. The battle still rages. Fire raging in my veins, I rejoin the melee.

There is someone I must find: a crippled man; a man responsible, in part, for the current fighting—and for long decades of dying before this day. Seeing him, my heart leaps with joy. He is lying on the ground near a broken radio, and I pray that he is not dead, as I wish very much to kill him myself.

I rush to greet my father.

The handwritten passage broke off, but Whittmore did not return to the manuscript. He stopped reading if only to catch his breath. There was something almost indecent about personal confessions. He'd not expected so much personal torment in Hilda Goebbels's writing. It made him uncomfortable.

The phone rang. He didn't answer it at first. The etiquette of the situation was elusive; but the phone kept ringing. "Well, I'm a voyeur anyway," he muttered and went over to answer the call. Lifting the receiver, virtually convinced that it must be Hilda inquiring after him, he felt like an idiot for not answering sooner.

"Hello," he said. There was dead silence on the line. "Hello?" No words, no breathing, no clicks or static. Just silence. Then, adding insult to presumption, the other, if there were another, hung up. "You gootch!" said Whittmore to the dial tone, employing a Townie profanity. He slammed down the phone. To hell with etiquette.

He hadn't taken two steps when he heard a key turning in the lock. Now surely this was his writer at last. A smile of welcome froze on his face as the door opened, and framed in the doorway was a gaunt man with hair white as the carpet neatly combed atop a skull-like face with Mandarin cheekbones.

One second is a long time, if in that brief instant one has the illusion of complete recall. Alan's déjà vu was painful: he saw the man from the limousine entering the room. His life didn't flash before his eyes, but a catalogue of unpleasant deaths flashed by.

The next second made all the difference. It was not the stranger from the limousine, but a man to whom he had once been introduced at the Waldorf-Astoria: Harold Baerwald, author of a series of books under the pseudonym of H. Freedman. Following him into the room, tightly clasping a brown packet, was their hostess: Hilda Goebbels.

She did not show her age, but at a glance could be mistaken for her teenage self. She was one of those lucky women who as they approach middle age seem to have a second lease on youth. Alan knew that she had had a child once, but the revealing dress—transparent down the side—revealed no stretch marks; but, then, New York sold a lot of body makeup. Her hair was long and red, as she had worn it in youth, although it had lost some of its luster. This was not a woman who would use hair dye—no chip off the old block. She had a good face with large eyes under arched eyebrows, and a strong chin, which he liked in a woman. Her cheekbones were high, but nowhere as pronounced as those of the elderly man at her side. The nose was turned up slightly, giving her expression a challenging, or haughty, aspect. But the mouth was well proportioned, the upper lip slightly extended, giving her smile a V at the center. He caught himself staring at the mouth that had kissed and tasted so many.

"I see you've made yourself at home, Alan. I remembered that you like tequila." The voice sounded deeper than it had when he spoke to her over the phone. Her eyes were on his.

"I'm sorry. It's only that I'd been reading about how you lost a tooth. Oh, but that was a dream, wasn't it?"

"So you do read German! That dream corresponds to an event, all right." Grinning, she showed Exhibit A. "Top row," she said. "Can you tell?"

He took a quick inventory. "No," he admitted.

"Good. The dentist earned his marks. Although I should say gold. By that point, I only traded on the black market."

"Hilda has one problem in an otherwise idyllic existence," said Baerwald. "She expends considerable energy in becoming famous; but then hopes to keep her economic transactions private."

"Bad habits are hard to break, Harry," said Hilda. "Over there it was survival; but here it isn't really necessary. America is land of the brave and home of the free."

"Well, that's land of the free and home of the brave, but close enough," said Alan.

"Forgive me. I was thinking in terms of cause and effect. And I hope that my bad manners haven't caused you gentlemen distress. I haven't introduced you."

"Haven't we met before?" Baerwald quizzed Whittmore.

"I'm flattered that you remember." They shook hands. "It was that fund raiser for world peace."

"Ah, yes. I'm always willing to lend my efforts to voluntary charity for immigrants. Very soon now I'll finish my study of why the Wagner-Rogers Bill was defeated in 1939. America must never close her doors to refugees again."

"The door is open, but they make their own beds," said Hilda. "We saw some newcomers living in a packing crate on the way over."

Alan sighed and repeated a phrase that had become a litany for him: "I'm afraid that laissez-faire capitalism has not made everyone rich."

Baerwald cleared his throat and spoke too loudly for close quarters: "No, but it hasn't sent anyone to concentration camps either! There are worse fates than being a beggar."

Hilda and Alan exchanged knowing glances. They were both junior to this elderly but vigorous gentleman in the never-ending struggle for liberty. He had been a "U-boat," the term given to Jews who continued to live, hidden, in Berlin under the very nose of Dr. Paul Joseph Goebbels at the height of World War II. He had remained "at large" long after his lover and friends had been taken; and after the last member of his family, an older brother named Herman, had disappeared into the chaos of the New Order. The Gestapo caught him on the Potsdamer Chaussee Strass in 1944, but only because he had put himself at risk to pass crucial information to a double agent working against the National Socialists. The information concerned a certain Dr. Richard Dietrich, who was supposedly nearing completion on one of the many secret weapons Hitler kept promising to use when he tired of being "Mr. Nice Guy" (a U.S. army joke of the time).

The agent made certain that he was not taken alive, but Baerwald was arrested. When it was determined that he was a Jew, a debate ensued. After all, there was a clearly delimited set of procedures for dealing with a spy, and another for dealing with a Jew. Here was the kind of case to give bureaucrats endless headaches. As Baerwald could not be divided in two (both components remaining alive, of course), there was nothing to do but trust that the SS would employ their typically subtle measures to insure the optimum quantity of Nazi justice. Baerwald was first sent to Sachsenhausen, a camp in the Berlin area that had been the dock for "U-boats" before. There Baerwald received serious beatings. His wrists retained scars from occasions when his arms had been handcuffed behind him as a preliminary to hanging him from a hook, a procedure sufficient in itself to cause blackout without the beatings on which the guards never stinted.

He had been scheduled to be sent to the east, where, it was intimated, he would enjoy the hospitality of either Auschwitz or Majdanek. Of dark rumors there was no end. Even after the tortures he had endured, he could not quite bring himself to believe that human beings were capable of the evil described in frightened whispers. He only knew that his lover had been sent far away in the east to a place called Treblinka, and he'd heard nothing from her since.

Harold Baerwald never learned the truth about Auschwitz one way or the other, because he didn't arrive at his destination. In the month of July in the year 1944, the world entered the atomic age. Two human consequences were that, first, Baerwald escaped his captors, and second, Hitler's regime survived. In the chaos that ensued from the ultimate Vengeance Weapons, a train carrying prisoners east was derailed. Baerwald crawled from the wreckage and saw the sun come out at night.

A week later he was suffering the hell of radiation sickness, but he was at sea and making light of the fact that he hadn't gotten his sea legs. They loved him. A boatload of refugees, they bound each other's wounds, succored the sick and dying. They had so little—a few bandages, some quinine water—and yet there was a deep cheerfulness on that ship. To witness genuine goodwill at the rim of doom was more glorious than anything else in his life. Alive or dead, what mattered was that he was free. And so, surviving his illness, he became H. Freedman, and wrote wonderful books telling everyone that nothing is more important than liberty.

He had taken it on himself to nurse a dying man whose pride it was that he had escaped from Buchenwald. They had formed a pact that should Baerwald survive, he would tell the man's story. The testament became *To Live in Hell,* and its most famous line was "Hier ist kein warum." This was the motto of the camps: There is no why here. The rules changed on a daily basis. One group of inmates would be given a task that another group would be told to undo. Tortures were calculated to increase a sense of uncertainty; this was more highly prized than pain. The man said that he had begun his imprisonment under the cruel tutelage of SA guards. He thought that nothing could be worse until his jeering tormentors were replaced by young, emotionless robots of the SS. The original system appeared utopian in contrast to the new. Madness had become the order of the day, but it was scientifically applied. What preserved this one victim's sanity was his realization that nothing is done without a purpose. He had a revelation in fact: obviously Heinrich Himmler had the task of determining if the perfect slave could be created, provided that the experiment received an unlimited supply of human material. The orders were insane on the surface, but underneath they were a test of both SS robots and the prisoners who were to be made into robots. For the will of Adolf Hitler to be supreme, all other wills had to die.

Baerwald never forgot that the most wicked crimes of the Nazis were against the people they left alive. To enslave a man's soul is worse than to kill his body. As for the latter, they even took the intimacy out of murder. While others wept, Baerwald decided to understand; at all costs he would understand. The voice of H. Freedman was the perfect antidote to the voice of *Mein Kampf* . . . because Freedman did not speak in the language of fear.

Alan Whittmore was familiar with this man's works, and he was honored to be in his company. He felt a bit ashamed that his first reaction to the old man in the doorway had been one of stark terror. Hilda noticed Alan's consternation. "Excuse me, is something wrong?" she asked.

"I guess my paranoia is showing," he answered lamely.

"Oh, I thought that was your tie!" she replied.

They all laughed and there was a lessening of tension. Alan's tie looked as if it were a section of wallpaper with the color of a blue-green organic soup that had spawned various forms of protozoa passing themselves off as designs. The thing had been a gift from his mother-in-law, a woman who had never reconciled herself to freedom for pornographers and would have her revenge on the crazed freethinker her daughter had been so foolish as to marry.

"Your expression was murderous when I first saw you," said Baerwald. "I thought you might be a reviewer."

"Let's apply our critical faculties to food," said Hilda. "I've made special arrangements to have a number of dishes sent up." Alan was less impressed by the generosity than he was by the strangeness of her insistence. It had stopped raining. Later in the evening would be an ideal time to patronize one of the better restaurants. She wouldn't have it; and yet she had also asked that he not use room service earlier. Was it that she had deep-seated authoritarian tendencies that she could not relinquish?

Hilda played bartender. With a second drink expanding the warmth in his chest, Alan Whittmore relaxed into the technical side of his craft. To his first question, Hilda answered: "The difficulty with translating German into English is that German is a more precise language. English is for poets but German is for technical manuals. Ambiguity is alien to the Teutonic mind."

"Hold on," said Baerwald in a jovial tone, "I thought French was the language of poets."

"No, it's the language of diplomats and lovers, which is much the same thing actually. It is especially well equipped for accepting terms of surrender."

"There are times when you sound just like your father," said Baerwald.

"God help me, I know it."

Alan hoped to keep the conversation lighthearted, despite the tremendous odds against. He interjected with, "How about puns? I imagine they give translators quite a headache."

Hilda brightened at the question. "Sometimes we can find an adequate substitute, close enough in meaning and still retaining the flavor of the original. I always hate it when I must sacrifice word play in a translation." Her eyes wandered to the packet she had placed on the table beside her manuscript. "Some things cannot be sacrificed," she said in a lower voice. Then, changing tone yet again, she asked: "How far did you get in your reading?"

"I've only just begun, but I'm fascinated with it so far. I must admit that the stuff on Burgundy is hard to believe. I knew that they were crazy but—"

"They are not insane," Hilda interrupted. "We would be better off if they were, uh, crazy. You, and your fellow Americans, have no inkling how nearly you came to total destruction."

"Well, nuclear stalemate works. I haven't noticed any new world wars lately. Some say you helped maintain the balance at a critical juncture. I'm hoping you might go public."

"Alan, I'm not talking about the Reich or its missiles. I'm talking about Burgundy and a worse weapon than all the hydrogen bombs in the world." It was certainly turning into a day of surprises for the editor of *The American Mercury*. Visions of canceled subscriptions began to dance before his eyes, and he forgot to blink as Hilda continued: "The data on genetics that I sold to scientists over here was not acquired cheaply. Until now, I've kept secret my information about an insidious conspiracy. The data was the only good thing that came of a scheme to commit the Final Crime. Now I have a document to support my accusation."

"You're talking about the Burgundians?" asked Alan. "A handful of religious fanatics who don't enjoy living in modern times . . ."

"To these people, any date with A.D. after it is modern times," said Hilda. "Despite that, they could tolerate progressive views up until the ninth century, when, according to their shamans and historians, everything went to hell. A few years ago, they decided to correct history's mistake. They were stopped. But they will try again. The next time, they must be defeated forever."

Here was a strange turn of events, all right. Alan Whittmore was not happy. Could it be that this fabulous woman was herself suffering from a mental aberration? He suddenly felt guilty about neglecting his wife lately. At least she lived in the same universe as he. His brief editorial career had been devoted to combating hysteria and panic;

and now Hilda Goebbels, daughter of the Great Liar himself, was carrying on in so eccentric a fashion that she cast doubt on her considerable virtues. The situation was untenable.

No, he berated himself—he must not think that way. Had he not been in the grip of fear because of an unfriendly glare from a decrepit gentleman riding around in an antique automobile? Who was he to judge this woman for overheated rhetoric? He owed it to her to suspend judgment until she'd made her case.

While these thoughts were racing through his mind, Hilda was opening the package on the table. She brought its contents over to him, a musty old volume of Houston Stewart Chamberlain's *Foundations of the Nineteenth Century*. Flipping open the cover, he saw that the inside had been hollowed out, and reposing at the center was a diary. He didn't have to open the book-within-a-book to know its author. This was the reason he was here.

"If a ponderous, fat book had to be gutted," said Hilda, "I could think of none more deserving than a tract by an Englishman that laid the basis for Nazi racial theories."

"But why have you gone to such lengths?" asked Alan.

"After you've read it, you'll understand," said Baerwald. "But do you really want to know? Ignorance has its compensations."

"I get the impression you two are playing mind games with me, and I don't like it."

"Please believe me, Alan. We don't mean to annoy you. We want you to know what you are getting yourself involved with. Borrowing from your popular culture, it's as if you have the *Necronomicon* in your hands."

"The what?"

"Forgive me, I'm referring to an imaginary tome of evil from the American fantasist H. P. Lovecraft. He was a prewar writer, and there is quite an audience for his stories back home, among those who can get the books, of course."

Alan shook his head. "You know more about my own country's entertainers than I do. I'm afraid I have little time for fiction. I stick to facts." As if on cue, three sets of eyes turned to the little diary. "This is factual, right?" he asked.

"Unfortunately," said Hilda. She disappeared into the bedroom and moved some furniture about before returning with another typed manuscript, her translation of the small volume Alan had opened.

He had immediately recognized her father's handwriting, thanks to earlier research.

Dinner had not yet arrived. The appetizer would be a big lie or a disturbing truth from the inventor of modern propaganda. The Goebbels technique was practiced worldwide, selling everything from soap to the first space platform. Words from the source had to be treated with the greatest of caution. But if Alan Whittmore was to publish these words, it was about time he read them.

CHAPTER EIGHT

If you gaze long into an abyss, the abyss will gaze back into you.

—Friedrich Nietzsche,
Beyond Good and Evil

ENTRIES FROM THE DIARY OF DR. PAUL JOSEPH GOEBBELS, NEW BERLIN APRIL 1965/TRANSLATED INTO ENGLISH BY HILDA GOEBBELS

Today I attended the state funeral for Adolf Hitler. They asked me to give the eulogy. It wouldn't have been so bothersome except that Himmler pulled himself out of his thankful retirement at Wewelsburg to advise me on all the things I mustn't say. The old fool still believes that we are laying the foundation for a religion. Acquainted as he is with my natural skepticism, he never ceases to worry that I will say something in public not meant for the consumption of the masses. It is a pointless worry on his part; not even early senility should enable him to forget that I am the propaganda expert. Still, I do not question his insistence that he is in rapport with what the masses feel most deeply, with the caveat that such exercises in telepathy only produce results when both sides are apathetic.

I suppose that I was the last member of the entourage to see Hitler alive. Albert Speer had just left, openly anxious to get back to his work with the von Braun team. In his declining years he has taken to involving himself full time with the space program. This question of whether the Americans or we will reach the moon first seems a negligible concern. I am convinced by our military experts that the space program that really matters is in terms of orbiting platforms for the purpose of global intimidation. Such a measure seems entirely justified if we are to give the Fuehrer his thousand-year Reich (or something even close).

The Fuehrer had recently returned from his estate on the island of San Michele. When he was certain that the end was approaching, he wanted to finish his life either in Berchtesgaden or the city that so uniquely belonged to him . . . and to me. My heart leapt with joy when he chose the latter, and once again infused the capital with his presence.

We spoke of Himmler's plans to make him an SS saint. "How many centuries will it be," he asked in a surprisingly firm voice, "before they forget I was a man of flesh and blood?"

"Can an Aryan be any other?" I responded dryly, and he smiled as he is wont to do at my more jestful moments.

"The spirit of Aryanism is another matter," he said. "The same as destiny or any other workable myth."

"Himmler would ritualize these myths into a new reality," I pointed out.

"Of course," Hitler agreed. "That has always been *his* purpose. You and I are realists. We make use of what is available." He reflected for a moment and then continued: "The war was a cultural one. If you ask the man in the street what I really stood for, he would not come near the truth. Nor should he!"

I smiled. I'm sure he took that as a sign of assent. This duality of Hitler's, with its concern for exact hierarchies to replace the old social order—and what is true for the *Völk* is not always true for us—seemed to me another workable myth, often contrary to our stated purposes. I would never admit that to him. In his own way, he was quite the boneheaded philosopher.

"*Mein Führer,*" I began, entirely a formality under the circumstances, but I could tell that he was pleased I had used the address, "the Americans love to make fun of your most famous statement about the Reich that will last one thousand years, as though what we've accomplished is an immutable status quo."

He laughed. "I love those Americans. I really do. They believe their own democratic propaganda . . . so obviously what we tell our people must be what we believe! American credulity is downright refreshing at times, especially after dealing with Russians."

On the subject of Russians, Hitler and I did not always agree. I had thought there could be points of contact between us ideologically, and possibilities for a united front against the capitalist West. In short order I learned that Hitler was indistinguishable from Rosenberg when it came to fearing pan-Slavism, of which the USSR was the latest variant. Once again history proved the Fuehrer correct. Our officials in the east often complain that there is no Russian word for saying "this minute." The closest they come is *seichas,* for "this hour." These are the people who had intended to let the Russian winter defeat us, as it had Napoleon. They almost got away with it; but German dynamism prevailed, and our fire melted the ice. They suffered a worse Stalingrad than we had. Hitler had told me personally that the Russians did not deserve as great a leader as Stalin.

There was no point in resurrecting the old debate at this late date. Before he died, I desperately wished to ask him some questions that had been haunting me. I could see that his condition was deteriorating. This would be my last opportunity.

The conversation rambled on a bit, and we again amused ourselves over how Franklin Delano Roosevelt had plagiarized National Socialism's Twenty-five Points when he issued his own list of economic rights for domestic consumption. Even more astounding was that a member of his class would issue to the world, as part of his "Four Freedoms" nonsense, a socialist plank for freedom from want. How fortunate for us that when FDR borrowed other of our policies, he fell flat on his face. He didn't understand Keynes as well as we did! War will always be the most effective method for disposing of surplus production, although infinitely more hazardous in a nuclear age. In those blissful days before we lived under the shadow of the mushroom cloud, we counted on numerous battlefield opportunities to use up weapons. FDR understood this as well. No Party member was more surprised than I when a corrupt American plutocrat used our approach to armaments production, quickly outstripping us because of the unlimited resources he could draw on. It was our time of gravest peril, and all because FDR had figured out that the only way a capitalist democracy can achieve full employment is with the timely assistance of a war.

Taking stock of his enemies was a favorite pastime of Adolf Hitler's, and the entry under "R" had never been closed; in fact, after the death of a foe, he redoubled his acquisition of embarrassing facts. Hitler and Roosevelt had come to power the same year—1933. They both took their countries off the gold standard that year. They both prepared for a future that would demolish the old certitudes. But let's face it, Adolf Hitler was simply better at the game. As a special treat, I'd brought to the sickroom a clipping from a long-ago February, one month before the American leader took office, when the stodgy business magazine *Barron's* forgot itself and published a piece worthy of me. In fact, I have a copy of it in my desk, and upon returning home, I underlined the passage Hitler liked best: "Of course we all realize that dictatorships and even semi-dictatorships are quite contrary to the spirit of American institutions and all that. And yet—well, a genial and light-hearted dictator might be a relief from the pompous futility of such a Congress as we have recently had." Exactly my sentiments when writing about the timid Weimar politicians in the old Reichstag.

Hitler brightened at the clipping. "Those were the days! I had some grudging respect for Roosevelt at first, but I never dreamed he'd become such a threat to us. Too bad we weren't in a position to put him on trial for his violation of international laws and treaties. Why, he nearly broke as many of them as I did!" We both laughed at that. "The Lend-Lease Act! The Neutrality Act! One bad joke after another! And the old hypocrite telling his mongrel citizens they wouldn't have to send their boys to die in the war when he was already fighting us at sea."

"Pearl Harbor was the culmination," I said, "his back door to reach us."

Hitler summed up: "Roosevelt fell under the influence of the madman Churchill, but that dated back to the correspondence between them when they were naval officials in the Great War, and they pulled their Lusitania stunt! The second time around, Churchill had Roosevelt sinking our ships to prove his neutrality. To that, I say, 'Remember the Bismarck!' "

"Fortunately, our greatest enemy in America was impeached," I said. The last thing we'd needed was a competing empire builder with the resources of the North American continent. I still fondly recalled the afternoon the American Congress was presented with evidence that FDR was a traitor on the Pearl Harbor question. The administration had done about what I would do in their shoes—find a scapegoat. Admiral Kimmel and General Short were to be crucified, but the ploy backfired when, during the course of the war, Dewey revealed his information that the Japanese purple code had been broken antecedent to the attack; and this information, of more than casual interest to the men in command at Pearl Harbor, was not passed on. The public outcry had been furious. We could not fathom how Americans could be so upset over sacrificing the lives of servicemen to achieve a foreign policy objective (that is why you have a service in the first place), but their sentimentality was FDR's undoing.

"I've never understood why President Dewey didn't follow Roosevelt's lead, *domestically,*" Hitler went on. "They remained in the war, after all. My God, the man even released Japanese-Americans from those concentration camps and insisted on restitution payments! And this during the worst fighting in the Pacific!"

The propaganda possibilities had not escaped me when FDR signed the order for the "relocation camps" on February 19, 1942. Here was a man who adopted the pose of Christian self-righteousness when condemning us for doing the same kind of thing. His was the country that had helped forge the chains of Versailles and held us down with immigration barriers and tariffs, then bleated about free trade. Into the greatest plutocracy in the world—of the banks, for the banks, and by the banks—came a rich man's son astride his silver wheelchair, dedicated to socializing America through the means of our destruction. Then everything fell apart for him. Everything. "The salvation of the Nisei was largely the influence of Vice President Taft," I reminded Hitler. His remarkable memory had lapses, but these were rare.

"When this Robert Taft became president," he said, "I ceased understanding American foreign policy altogether. And when their two big parties lost so much power that they had to merge into one . . . what was it called?"

"The Bipartisan party was what remained of the coalition between Democrats and Republicans favoring an interventionist foreign policy."

"Right, the ones who understood the world. After America had a virtual civil war in the fifties, and the two major parties became— I'll remember these—the America First group and the Liberty party, I lost all track of what they were doing over there."

"There were some self-proclaimed National Socialists in the America First party, but they never amounted to much; and all the elections have been won by the Liberty party, which keeps receiving defections from America First."

"Ridiculous. I've said again and again that National Socialism is not for export. That eccentric Mosley character in Britain thinks he's me! At least he has the proper racist views."

"The Liberty party in America condemns all forms of racism. Combine that with their open borders today and—"

"Crazy Americans! They are the most unpredictable people on earth. They pay for their soft hearts with racial pollution."

We moved into small talk, gossiping about various wives, when that old perceptiveness of the Fuehrer touched me once again. He could tell that I wasn't speaking my mind. "Joseph, you and I were brothers in Munich," he said. "I am on my deathbed. Surely you can't be hesitant to ask *anything*. Let there be no secrets between us. And it's a funny thing about my age, but I find that at my advanced age, events from the early days are clear while more recent developments are foggy. You speak about anything you like. I would talk in my remaining hours."

And how he could talk. I remember one dinner party for which an invitation was extended to my two eldest daughters, Helga and Hilda. Hitler entertained us with a brilliant monologue on why he hated modern architecture anywhere except factories. He illustrated many of his points about the dehumanizing aspect of industrial-style living compartments with references to the film *Metropolis*. Yet despite her fondness for the cinema, Hilda would not be brought out by his entreaties. I joked that she was mesmerized by the gorgeous chandelier Hitler had recently installed in that dining room, but the social strain was not diminished. Everyone else enjoyed the evening immensely.

On this solemn occasion, I asked if he had believed his last speech of encouragement in the final days of the war when it had seemed certain that we would be annihilated. Despite his words of stern optimism, there was quite literally no way of his knowing that our scientists had at that moment solved the shape-charge problem. Thanks to Otto Hahn and Werner Heisenberg working together, we had developed the atomic bomb first. Different departments had been stupidly fighting over limited supplies of uranium and heavy water. Speer took care of that, and then everything began moving in our direction. After the first plutonium came from a German atomic pile, it was a certain principle that we would win.

I shudder to think what the world might be like if we hadn't won the race. A series of fortuitous developments saved our bacon, from acquiring Norway's heavy water supply to persuading the SS to stay the hell out of it and stop throwing roadblocks in the way of "Jewish physics." Then there was the case of Carl von Weizsäcker. The first year of the war was also the year he had shown how stars generate energy by making helium from hydrogen fusion. He was a natural choice to work on the atomic bomb project, but it came out that he was keeping work from the Party and interfering with the morale of his team. Through a fluke, I was personally involved with putting a stop to that; and his work was reintegrated with the rest of the project.

Looking back, I view that period as miraculous. If Speer and I had not convinced the army and air force to cease their rivalry for funds, we never would have developed the V-3 in time to deliver those lovely new bombs. The marriage made in heaven was between the flying bomb and the rocket, and their progeny was larger and faster, with a guidance system worth the name. In the beginning, there had been so many problems with the V-1 that engineers began calling it the *Versager* weapon, for failure. The Party did not approve of humor of that sort, and the men were reminded that V-weapons meant *Vergeltungswaffe* for retaliation and final vengeance. They caught on.

Once the bombs had been used, the military problem of how to turn the chaos back into tactical advantages was handled by Otto Skorzeny and his newly formed Werewolf detachments. What mattered most of all was that we saved industrial production in the Ruhr, without which we might as well have begun learning Russian and English. My job was to downplay the effects of radiation and poison in the blighted areas. Pamphlets did the job pretty well, except for the poor wretches who went blind.

In the small hours of the morning, one cannot help but wonder how things might have been different. We'd been granted one reprieve when the cross-Channel invasion was delayed in 1943. But 1944 was the real turning point of the war. Hitler hesitated to actually use the nuclear devices, deeply fearful of radiation hazards to our side as well as the enemy. If it had not been for the assassination attempt of July 20, he might not have found the resolve to issue the all-important order: destroy Patton and his Third Army before they become operational, before they invade Europe like a cancer. What a glorious time that was for all of us, as well as my own career. (Helping to round up the conspirators and being assigned the highest post of my life was a personal Valhalla.) For the Russians, there were to be many bombs, and many German deaths among them. It was a small price to stop Marxism cold. Even our concentration camps in the east received a final termination order in the form of the by now familiar mushroom clouds.

If the damned Allies had agreed to negotiate, all that misery could have been avoided. Killing was dictated by history. Hitler fulfilled Destiny. He never forgave the West for forcing him into a two-front war, when he, the chosen one, was their best protection against the Slavic hordes.

How he'd wanted the British Empire on our side. How he'd punished them for their folly. A remaining V-3 had delivered the Bomb on London, fulfilling a political prophecy of the Fuehrer's, and incidentally solving the Rudolf Hess problem. He had regretted that; but the premier war criminal of our time, Winston Churchill, had left him no alternative. They started unrestricted bombing of civilians; well, we finished it. Besides, it made up for the failure of Operation Sea Lion. The operation that finally put the British in our hands was dubbed King's Crown.

Just in case the British didn't learn their lesson amidst the fallout and ashes, we augmented their education at the war crimes trials. This was a pretty piece of irony, as the Allies were first to announce their intention of putting on a show trial at the conclusion of hostilities. Of course they waited until Total Victory seemed a certainty before taking the moral high ground. I would have suggested that they had been corrupted by alliance with Stalin and his kangaroo courts, except that the world was not about to forget our exercise in Realpolitik for the 1939 pact. We beat the Allies to that particular association.

The trials provided an invaluable opportunity. All grown-ups knew that Russia, Great Britain, and Germany had played fast and loose with the rhetorical drivel about recognizing the rights of smaller countries. The prime example was that the English encouraged Poland to be intransigent while never intending to come to her defense. Stalin and Hitler obliged by partitioning the upstart country. The trials were a chance to doctor the record. Everything we said about the British and the Russians was more or less true. The fun came with absolving ourselves of guilt, a new spin on the Great Lie. What with our selecting the judges and announcing that the court would not be bound by technical rules of evidence, the outcome was never in doubt. Hitler boasted: "These trials will be the extension of war by other means." Peacetime has its compensations.

On the largest scale, the impact came from trying the Russians. We hardly brought up Soviet treatment of our POWs. The political aim was to have decisions of the court reinforce our policies in the east. For example, we were able to prove that the head of the NKVD, Yezhov, killed more people than Himmler (although the direct comparison could not be publicly drawn). Dredging up Stalin's mass murder of seven million Ukrainians and three million others of his countrymen helped divert attention from our own activities, while winning the tacit support of the very people we were returning to the status of serfs, where the Bolsheviks had put them originally! A good day's work. Hitler had enough respect for Stalin that he was pleased the Georgian tyrant had not lived to see trial. Unlike leaders of the West, the Iron Man of Russia was at least a fellow ideologue. This was the grand fellow who had said that the undesirable classes do not liquidate themselves. We envied his slave-labor camp system, the longest stretch of such progressive activity that had ever been constructed, but now unfortunately beyond our reach because the camps were east of the Urals in the area that had fallen outside the warm embrace of civilization.

The most enjoyable aspect of the trials was seeing Winston Churchill in the dock at Nuremberg, a pleasure we would have been denied had he been in London when the bomb dropped. He was a broken man, mumbling that the upper crust had let him down and wishing that he'd been at his lodgings when "Jerry's banger" went off, as he put it. I was disappointed that he wouldn't give us his famous "V" sign for posterity. He was never the statesman that Chamberlain was.

Hitler had made it abundantly clear that war would mean the end of the British Empire. Churchill promised his people blood, sweat, and tears . . . and that's what they got. But the Fuehrer had his magnanimous side. Broadcasting to the survivors, he said that as the BBC had had the uncommon decency to pay royalties whenever it used excerpts from *Mein Kampf* during the war, he'd take that into consideration when calculating reparations payments.

My ministry played an important role at the trials, thanks in part to cooperation by Gauleiter Hölz of Nuremberg. What a field day for dirty tricks! For one thing, we would read Russian defendants a document written in Russian, get them to verify its authenticity, and then with sleight of hand, present the court with an altered version in German that the defendants didn't understand. It was a regular cabaret! One defiant fellow, about to join Churchill on the British execution block (segregation in all things), asked how we could accuse him of crimes against humanity when we had atomized his family; thus he demonstrated a fundamental inability to come to grips with the realities of the modern era. No one whom we executed was taught a lesson. That's old-fashioned, egotistical thinking. The lesson was for the survivors.

Conspiracy theorists continue to believe that perfidious Albion secretly runs the world, and I must admit that far too many members of the British ruling class survived to do business with unidealistic Germans. But when history gave us the opportunity, we struck a blow that will never be forgotten. And the power that made it possible was technology.

Standing in a heated room, where a sick man wiped his forehead with a handkerchief, I listened to Adolf Hitler, the man who had wielded the weapons of superscience, admit: "I had reached the point where I said we would recover at the last second with a secret weapon of invincible might . . . *without believing it at all!* It was pure rhetoric. I had lost hope long ago. The timing on that last speech could not have been better. Fate *was* on our side."

So at last I knew. Right doesn't guarantee might. How had Hitler found the courage to fill us all with hope when there was no reason for anything but despair? Could he really foretell the future? It was more congenial for me to conclude that he had bluffed us all again. As he had begun, so did he end: the living embodiment of *will.* There was a kind of energy emanating from those blue eyes of his that held millions of people in thrall. I couldn't help noticing that his bathrobe was the same shade of blue.

It was an honor to have been present at so many historic moments by his side. I remembered his exaltation at the films of nuclear destruction. He hadn't been that excited, I'm told, since he was convinced of the claim for von Braun's rockets at Kummersdorf. At each report of radiation dangers, he had the more feverishly buried himself in the *Führerbunker,* despite assurances by every expert that Berlin was safe from fallout. Never have I known a man more concerned for his health, more worried about the least bit of a sore throat after a grueling harangue of a speech. And the absurd lengths he went to for his diet, limited even by vegetarian standards. Yet his precautions had brought him to this date, to see himself master of all Europe, holding a glass of distilled water with which to drink his toast. Who was in a position to criticize *him?*

He had a way of making me feel like a giant. "I should have listened to you so much earlier," he now told me, "when you called for totalization of war on the home front. I was too soft on Germany's womanhood. Why didn't I listen to you?" Once he complimented a subordinate, he was prone to continue, even referring to so ancient a matter as the work I had done to secure his German citizenship when he was still on the records as an Austrian. Then his sense of humor made a surprise appearance. "It was an inspiration, the way you pushed that morale-boosting joke: 'If you think the war is bad, wait until you see the peace, should we lose.' " I remembered how I'd kept American hate propaganda against Germany read on the nightly broadcasts so the people would not consider surrender to enemies willing to exterminate them right down to baby-in-arms. But Hitler was already on to other things, such as my handling of the foreign press during *Kristallnact,* and finally concluding with his favorite of all my gimmicks: "Your idea to use the same railway carriage from the shameful surrender of 1918, to receive France's surrender in 1940, was the most splendid moment of the war." His pleasure was contagious.

"You understand the power of symbols, Joseph. What is true is never as important as what people believe. Consider this: there is no European continent because Asia is part of the same land mass. Old Haushofer had a traitorous swine for a son, but his real child was the geopolitical theory he bequeathed to the Reich. *He drew our map.* I'm not talking about some puny, overintellectualized concept, but a picture that is real because we made it so. Today the swastika flies from the summit of Mount Elbrus, the highest mountain in the Greater Reich, to the hundreds of fortresses at sea level that protect the Atlantic shoreline. But the soil is no different than if the Allies had won. What has been saved is our blood; and that gives the land its meaning. The last mind to shape this dumb, blind world was Napoleon; but he failed because he was not a German.

"Now consider this: before me, it was a commonplace for European statesmen to downplay figures on armaments production. The game was to keep the enemy in the dark about your strength. Do you remember before the war, when I announced that we had spent ninety thousand million marks on rearmament?" I nodded. "Did you believe the figure when you were using it in your broadcasts?"

"I didn't give it much thought."

"It was a lie. Between the time we took power, and up to 1938, we had spent that amount on everything, domestic and military expenditures combined. By March of 1939, the rearmament came to no more than forty thousand million marks. Why did I do this? While the British and the French were busily at work, violating the military requirements of the Versailles Treaty that applied to them, I was pretending that we had an unbeatable military machine when we had no such thing. After Munich, I was convinced we would achieve our aims with no more than a small war here and there. The saner heads in Great Britain followed a similar course in the beginning. I never doubted the Englishman's willingness to fight for Poland . . . right down to the last Pole. I did not believe we could win a full-scale war."

This came as a considerable shock. Although pleased that he was confiding in me, I was also flustered. "Then forgive my asking, but how did we survive?"

"Our enemies outnumbered us, and outproduced us, but I was counting on one other thing they had in great quantity: stupidity. At least the Russians had courage; which is more than I can say for Americans." Back to FDR, always back to him. "The only battles they won against our brave soldiers were when they outnumbered us two to one!"

"You said they had some good generals."

"Yes. Patton was a great general, but what could he do with men like that? I respected him sufficiently to award him an iron cross . . . painted on the side of the nuclear bomb that ended his career."

I was strangely disoriented, in large part because I had thought I could keep track of what was factual and what fanciful in my propaganda. Now I learned that I was mistaken. The personal excesses of Goering had galled me when I was calling for the public to make sacrifices; but to learn that austerity measures had never been what I thought they were was unsettling.

Hitler's head for figures churned out the answer: "Our slogan was *'Guns before butter,'* but I didn't dare implement what the people

87

would never tolerate. At the close of the First World War, when I returned home to see a collapsing army, and society collapsing along with it, I knew that the future belonged to me.

"I had grasped my historic mission as long ago as 1909, when I was starving in Vienna. The war was a godsend, a golden opportunity to test myself. I survived the rigors of the trenches, volunteering for the dangerous duty of a messenger. Twenty thousand men died in one day. It was dirty and horrible and indecent. Even before the armistice, I suspected that we would be stabbed in the back; but I fought on. I had to be a messenger, so that I could climb out of the living grave and face death in the open. I was only alive then. Had Destiny really chosen me to build the future? If so, I would survive. It was in my stars.

"No-man's-land was to be preferred over days condemned to a prison made of vertical walls of stinking mud, with a few soakaways for the rain as a break in the monotony. We lived with rats. Years later, when I sent my enemies to concentration camps, I remembered the zombies of the trenches. Payment was made in full! I remember seeing a few shells shining wetly after a rain, and then my sight was stolen from me; I, the Leader of the future, was blinded by gas. While I suffered the agonies of the damned, I knew that providence would restore my sight."

It occurred to me that war was Hitler's natural environment, because it offered him the perfect balance between chaos and order. I really didn't like war myself. It was better when enemies didn't put up a fight.

Hitler was breathing deeply, and he paused in his harangue long enough to take a deep draught of water at his bedside, before continuing: "I tell you all this because I want you to understand that peace was worse." His voice was rising, and his face was flushed, but I didn't want to call the nurse. "The Great Inflation made me long for the trenches. What could be more disgusting than to see pure Aryan stock starving in the streets? You remember, I know. Before the war, the mark was trading at 4.2 to the American dollar. The soldiers returned to a weakened mark, where the figure was several times greater, the 'fortunes' of war. Now I ask you, what economist who wasn't dead drunk would dream that by 1923, the mark would be trading at the insane figure of 4.2 billion to the Versailles-stained

American dollar? To think we Nazis were told we railed against imaginary enemies!"

"I remember."

"The people could not be made to suffer more than they had already, not if we wanted their support! We couldn't free them of Jewish capital while their bellies were empty. National Socialism had to work from the start. I had seen the failures of Marxism. They socialized the factories and farms, but the people starved. In Germany, we socialized the people. Then we had *Völk* factories and *Völk* farms, and the people ate, but on our terms! Private ownership is just another symbol, Joseph. Feed the people, then tell them what to do; and eliminate the troublemakers. Speak to them in their thousands, but do so at night, when their bellies are full and their bodies are tired, and they'd rather be making love. You see, I had to fool the other countries about rearmament. The only way was to talk sacrifice but give bread."

As had happened so many times in the past, his explanation was like a flood of light, illuminating the dark corners of my mind. He was right. He was our beacon. Propping himself up slightly in bed, a gleam of joy in his eyes, he looked like a little boy again. If he had been well, he would have been pacing by then. "I'll tell you something about my thousand years. Himmler invests it with the mysticism you'd expect. Ever notice how Jews, Muslims, Christians, and our very own pagans have a predilection for millennia? The number works a magic spell on them."

"Pundits in America observe that also. They say the number is merely good psychology and point to the longevity of the ancient empires of China, Rome and Egypt for similar numerical records. They say that Germany will never hold out that long."

"It won't," said Hitler, matter-of-fact.

"What do you mean?" I asked, suddenly not sure of the direction in which he was moving. I suspected it had to do with the cultural theories, but of his grandest dreams for the future Hitler had always been reticent . . . even with me.

"It will take at least that long," he said, "for the New Culture to take root on earth. For the New Europe to be what I have foreseen."

"If von Braun has his way, we'll be long gone from earth by then. At least he seems to plan passage for many Germans on his spaceships."

89

"Germans!" spat out Hitler. "What do I care about Germans or von Braun's space armada? Let the technical side of Europe spread its power in any direction it chooses. Speer will be *their* god. He is the best of that collection. But let the other side determine the values, man. The values, the spiritual essence. Let them move through the galaxy for all I care, so long as they look homeward to me for the guiding cultural principles. Europe will be the eternal monument to that vision. I speak of a Reich lasting a thousand years? It will take that long to finish the first phase; and then comes something that will last for the rest of eternity."

The fire was returning. His voice was its old, strong, hypnotic self. His body quivered with the glory of his personal vision, externalized for the whole of mankind to touch, to worship . . . or to fear. I bowed my head in the presence of the greatest man in history.

He fell back for a minute, exhausted, lost in the phantasms behind his occluded eyes. Looking at the weary remains of this once human dynamo, I was sympathetic, almost sentimental, and said: "Remember when we first met through our anti-Semitic activities? It was an immediate bond between us."

He chuckled. "Oh, for the early days of the Party again. At the beginning you thought me too bourgeois."

He was dying in front of me, but his mind was as alert as ever. "Few people understand why we singled out the Jew, even with all the Nazi literature available," I continued.

He took a deep breath. "I was going to turn all of Europe into a canvas on which I'd paint the future of humanity. The Jew would have been my severest and most obstinate critic." The Fuehrer always had a gift for the apt metaphor. "Your propaganda helped keep the populace inflamed. That anger was fuel for the task at hand."

What more could be said about the Hebrew pestilence? We extracted some pleasure from contemplation of the Irgun, the sad and sorry attempt by Zionists to do a Jewish version of the Brown Shirts (or, some said, the model was Italy's Black Shirts). Whatever the cross-pollination, it was appropriate that the Irgun and the greatest failure of National Socialism should join one another in the void. (It remains a mystery how Ernst Röhm could have been such a *Dummkopf* as to think Hitler would replace the cream of the German army with a bunch of fuck-ups from the *Sturmabteilung*. Never did a man deserve death more than Röhm.)

"The Jews were useful in one regard," said Hitler. "They provided us with the means to demonstrate the hypocrisy of the so-called 'Free World'! What year was the Evian Conference? It was just on the tip of my tongue."

"Nineteen thirty-eight."

"Correct. We couldn't give the precious Jews away at that conference. The same countries that would later cry crocodile tears never raised a finger to take them."

We had discussed on previous occasions the fundamental nature of the Judeao-Christian ethic, and how the Christian was a spiritual Semite (as any pope would observe, notwithstanding Alfred Rosenberg's weird Gnostic position, which nobody really understands). The Jew was an easy scapegoat. There was such a fine old tradition behind it. But once the Jew was for all practical purposes removed from Europe, there remained the vast mass of conventional Christians, many Germans among them. Hitler had promised strong measures in confidential statements to high officials of the SS. Martin Bormann had been the most ardent advocate of the *Kirchenkampf,* the campaign against the churches. In the ensuing years of peace and the nuclear stalemate with the United States, little had come of it. I brought up the subject again.

"It will take generations," he answered. "The Jew is only the first step. And please remember that Christianity will by no means be the last obstacle, either. Our ultimate enemy is an idea dominant in the United States. Their love of the individual is more dangerous to us than mystical egalitarianism. The decadent idea of complete freedom will be more difficult to handle than all the religions and other imperial governments put together." He lapsed back into silence, but only for a moment. "We are the last bastion of true Western civilization. Today's America is one step away from anarchy. They would sacrifice the state to the individual! But Soviet communism—despite an ideology—was little better. Its state was all muscles and no brain. It forbade them to get the optimum use from their best people. Ah, only in the German Empire, and especially here in New Berlin, do we see the ideal at work. The state uses most individuals as the stupid sheep they were meant to be. More important is that the superior individual is allowed to use the state."

"Like most of the gauleiters?" I asked, again in a puckish mood.

His laugh was loud and healthy. "Good God," he said. "Nothing's perfect . . . except the SS, and the work you did in Berlin."

I did not have the heart to tell him that I thought he had been proved soundly mistaken on his predictions for the United States. How could this be, when he was right about everything else? With the nuclear stalemate and the end of the war—America having used its atomic bombs in the Orient, and demonstrating to the world a resolve to match ours—the isolationist forces had had a resurgence because of the incredible possibilities for defense represented by ownership of these weapons. In the blink of an eye, it seemed, they had moved the country back to the foreign policy it held before the Spanish-American War. Hitler had predicted grim consequences for that country's economy. The reverse unobligingly came true. This was in part because the new isolationists didn't believe in economic isolation by any means; they freed American corporations to protect their own interests.

The latest reports I had seen demonstrated that the American Republic was thriving, even as our economy was badly suffering from numerous entanglements that go hand in gauntlet with an imperial foreign policy. We had quite simply overextended ourselves. New Berlin, after all, is modeled on the old Rome to which all roads led . . . and like the Roman Empire, we were having trouble financing the operation and keeping the population amused. There are times when I miss our old slogan "Gold or blood?"

Although as dedicated a National Socialist as ever, I must admit that America does not have our problems. What it has is an abundance of goods, a willingness to do business in gold (our stockpile of which increased markedly after the war), and paper guarantees that we would not interfere in their hemisphere. Diplomats have to do something. All adults understand that Latin America is fair game, especially the U.S. soft drink companies that put together fierce mercenary armies south of the border.

I preferred contemplation of the home front. There is, of course, no censorship for the upper strata of Nazi Germany. The friends and families of high Reich officialdom can openly read or see anything they can get their hands on. I still have trouble with this modification in our policy. At least I keep cherished memories of 1933, when I personally gave the order to burn the books at the Franz Joseph Platz outside Berlin University. I never enjoyed myself more than in the period when I perfected an acid rhetoric as editor of *Der Angriff,* which more often than not inspired the destruction of writings inimical to our point of view. It was a pleasure putting troublesome editors in the camps. Those days seem far away now in these becalmed days. Many enjoy *All Quiet on the Western Front* without the extra added attraction of rats in the aisles, a little stunt of mine when we didn't want the film undermining morale before the war. I miss the good old days and the rowdy boys who used to work with me. In these timid times, simple intimidation keeps most editors in line.

Hitler would not have minded a hearty exchange on the subject of censorship. He enjoys any topic that relates at some point to the arts. He would have certainly preferred such a discussion to arguing about capitalist policy in America. I didn't pursue either. I am satisfied to leave to these diary pages my conclusion that running an empire is more expensive than having a fat republic, sitting back, and collecting profits. The British used to understand. If they hadn't forgotten, we probably wouldn't be where we are today.

Ironically, Hitler has spent most of his retirement (although he holds the title of supreme leader for life and can overrule the bureaucracy when he chooses) neglecting the areas of his political and military genius and concentrating on his cultural theories. He became a correspondent with the woman who chairs the anthropology department at New Berlin University (no hearth and home for her) and behaved almost as though he were jealous of her job. Lucky for her that he didn't stage a Putsch! Besides, she was a fully accredited Nazi.

I think that Eva took it quite well. *Kinder, Küche, Kirche!*

As I stood in Hitler's sickroom, watching the man to whom I had devoted my life waning before me, I felt an odd ambivalence. On the one hand, I was sorry to see him go. On the other hand, I felt a kind of release. It was as though when he died, I would at last begin my true retirement. The other years of supposed resignation from public duties did not count. Truly, Adolf Hitler had been at the very center of my life.

There were tears in his eyes as he recalled the happiest moment of his life: "To return to Linz in Austria where I had been nothing as a youth; to walk the streets and possess the power of the Hohenzollern kings, and look into the faces of the people who were entirely mine to do with as I pleased; to return to the Fatherland the treasure of the Hapsburg emperors and place the regalia in its sacred place in Nuremberg, where the symbols of German authority will rest for a thousand years, casting their light upon all judgments pronounced in that place . . . I experienced an ecstasy transcending the human dimension. The reoccupation of the Rhineland, the return of Danzig, the conquest of France, the conquest of England, even the defeat of Stalin himself, all these were glories, but none to compare with that day." It was apotheosis! I was complete and made to take my leave.

I wish that he had not made his parting comment. "Herr Reichspropagandaminister," he said, and the returned formality made me uncharacteristically adopt a military posture, "I want to remind you of one thing. Shortly before his death, Goering agreed with me that our greatest coup was the secrecy with which we handled the Jewish policy. The atom bombing of camps was a bonus. Despite the passage of time, I believe this secret should be preserved. There may come a day when no official in the German government knows of it. Only the hierarchy of the SS will preserve the knowledge in their initiatory rites."

"Our enemies continue to speak of it, *mein Führer*. Certain Jewish organizations throughout the unliberated world continue to mourn the lost millions every year. At least Stalin receives his share of blame."

"Propaganda is one thing. Proof is another. You know this as well as anyone. I'd like your agreement that the program should remain a secret. As for Stalin's death camps, talk that up forever."

I was taken aback that he would even speak of it. "Without question, I agree." I remembered how we had exploited in our propaganda the Russian massacre of Poles at Katyn. The evidence was solid . . . and there is such a thing as world opinion. I could see his point. At this late date there was little advantage in admitting our vigorous policy for the Jews. The world situation had changed since the war.

Nevertheless, his request seemed peculiar and unnecessary. In the light of later events I cannot help but wonder whether or not Hitler really was psychic. Could he have known of the personal disaster that would soon engulf members of my family?"

(*NOTE FROM HILDA: I would have been really surprised if Hitler didn't know that most of the finance capital he railed against all his life was controlled then, as it is now, largely by Anglo-Saxon Protestants.*)

CHAPTER NINE

Without the Leader the whole National Socialist movement would be unthinkable.

—Dr. Joseph Goebbels,
My Part in Germany's Fight

The conversation kept running through my mind on the way to the funeral. As we traveled under Speer's Arch of Triumph, I marveled for, I suppose, the hundredth time at his architectural genius. Germany would be paying for this city for the next fifty years, but it was worth it. Besides, we had to do something with all that Russian gold! What is gold, in the end, but a down payment on the future, be it the greatest city in the world or buying products from America?

The procession moved at a snail's pace, and considering the distance we had to cover I felt it might be the middle of the night by the time we arrived at the Great Hall. The day lasted long enough, as it turned out.

The streets were thronged with sobbing people, Hitler's beloved *Völk*. The Swastika flew from every window, and it was evident 'hat many were homemade. When I thought to conceive a poetic image to describe the thousands of fluttering black shapes, all I could think of was a myriad of spiders. *Leave poetry to those more qualified,* I thought—*copywriting is never an ode.*

Finally we were moving down the great avenue between Goering's Palace and the Soldier's Hall. Unbidden, I remembered the day I spent taking Hilda on a tour of the final construction work. Despite her sarcasm, I could tell she was impressed. Who wouldn't be? The endless vertical lines of these towering structures remind me of Speer's ice cathedral lighting effects at Nuremberg. Nothing he has done in concrete has ever matched what he did with pure light.

God, what a lot of white marble! The glare hurts my eyes sometimes. When I think of how we denuded Italy of its marble to accomplish all this, I recognize Il Duce's one invaluable contribution to the Greater Reich.

Everywhere you turn in New Berlin, there are statues of heroes and horses, horses and heroes. And flags, flags, flags. Sometimes I become a little bored with our glorious Third Reich. Perhaps success must lead to excess. But it keeps beer and cheese on the table, as Magda would say. Speer was the architect, and Hitler the inspiration, but I too am an author of what towers about me. I helped to build New Berlin with my ideas as surely as the workmen did with the sweat of their brows and stones from the quarries. And Hitler, dear, sweet Hitler—he ate up inferior little countries and spat out the mortar of this metropolis. Never has a man been more the father of a city. "We'll make buildings that haven't been seen in four thousand years," he said before the war; and some wits suggest that the war was solely for the purpose of keeping his promise.

The automobiles had to drive slowly to keep pace with the horses in the lead, pulling the funeral caisson of the Fuehrer. I was thankful when we reached our destination.

It took a while to seat the officialdom. As I was in the lead group, and seated first, I had to wait interminably while everyone else ponderously filed in. The hall holds 150,000. Speer saw to that, complaining every step of the way. I had to sit still and watch what seemed like the whole German nation enter and take seats.

Many spoke ahead of me. After all, when I was finished with the official eulogy, there would be nothing left but to take him down and pop him in the vault. When Norway's grand old man, Vikdun Quisling, rose to say a few words, I was delighted that he only took a minute. Really amazing. He praised Hitler as the destroyer of the Versailles penalties, and that was pretty much it.

The only moment of interest came when a representative of the sovereign nation of Burgundy stood in full SS regalia. A hush fell over the audience. Most Germans have never felt overly secure at the thought of a nation given exclusively to the SS . . . and outside the jurisdiction of German law. I'm not very happy about it myself; but it was one of the wartime promises Hitler made that he kept to the letter. The country was carved out of France (which I'm sure never noticed—all they ever cared about was Paris, anyway).

The SS man spoke of blood and iron. He reminded us that the war had not ended all that long ago, although many Germans would like to forget that and merely wallow in the proceeds from the adventure. This feudalist was also the only speaker at the funeral to raise the old specter of the International Zionist Conspiracy, which I thought was a justifiable piece of nostalgia, considering the moment. As he droned on in a somewhat monotonous voice, I thought about Hitler's comment regarding secret death camps. Of course, there are still Jews in the world, and Jewish organizations across the Atlantic worth reckoning with, and a group trying to reestablish Israel—so far unsuccessfully—and understandably no people would rather see us destroyed. What I think is worth emphasizing is that the Jew is hardly the only enemy of the Nazi.

By the time he was finished, the crowd was seething in that old, pleasing, violent way . . . and I noticed that many of them restrained themselves with good Prussian discipline from cheering and applauding the speaker (not entirely proper at a funeral). We weren't holding an Irish wake! But if they had broken protocol, I would have gladly joined in.

Even eternity must end, and I had my turn standing at the microphone to make my oration. I was surrounded by television cameras. How things have changed since the relatively simple days of radio. I often miss sending out Party exhortations and edicts over the crackling static of the old *Völksempfanger*. The television picture is more intrusive, but paradoxically it is easier to ignore. The spoken word allows the listener to maintain the illusion of independent thought; but an endless stream of pictures tends to deaden the mind, thereby losing the real power of images—their immediacy. One newsreel in a public theater had more impact than ten television reports today.

My ardent supporters were probably disappointed that I did not give a more rousing speech. I was the greatest orator of them all, even better than Hitler (if I may say so). My radio speeches are universally acclaimed as having been the instrumental factor in upholding German morale. I was more than just the minister of propaganda. I was the soul of National Socialism.

Toward the end of the war, I made the greatest speech of my career at the Sportpalast, and this in the face of total disaster. I had no more believed that we could win than Hitler had when he made his final boast about a mysterious secret weapon still later in the darkest of dark hours. My friends were astonished that after such an emotional speech, I could sit back and dispassionately evaluate the effect I had had upon my listeners.

Alas for the nostalgia buffs, there was no fire and fury in my words that day. I was economical of phrase. I listed his most noteworthy achievements; I made an objective statement about his sure and certain place in history; I told the mourners that they were privileged to have lived in the time of this man. That sort of thing.

Finishing on a quiet note, and heeding what he had told me at our last meeting, I said: "This man was a symbol. He was an inspiration. He took up a sword against the enemies of a noble ideal that had almost vanished. He fought small and mean notions of man's destiny. Adolf Hitler restored the beliefs of our strong ancestors. Adolf Hitler restored the sanctity of our"—and I used the loaded term—"race." (I could feel the stirring in the crowd. It works every time.) "Adolf Hitler is gone. But what he accomplished will never die . . . *if*"—I gave them my best stare—"you work to make sure that his world is your world."

I was finished. The last echoes of my voice died, to be replaced by the strains of *Die Walküre* from the Berlin Philharmonic.

On the way to the vault, I found myself thinking about numerous matters, none of them having directly to do with Hitler. I thought of Speer and the space program; I philosophized that Jewry is an *idea;* I reveled in the undying pleasure that England had become the Reich's "Ireland"; I briefly ran an inventory of my mistresses, my children, my wife; I wondered what it would be like to live in America, with a color television and bomb shelter in every home. (A recent piece in the *New Berlin Review of Books* convinced me that our enemy managed to put out a cheaper color set because they hadn't followed our line of research, vis-à-vis mass-produced microbes and X rays.)

The coffin was deposited in the vault, behind a bulletproof sheet of glass. His waxen-skinned image would remain there indefinitely, preserved for the future. His last request had been that he be dressed in the military jacket he had sworn not to remove until the war was won. As he had in life, so did he in death forbid smoking in his presence; even more important now that he was combustible. I went home, then blissfully to bed and sleep.

October 1965

Last night, I dreamed that I was eighteen years old again. I remembered a Jewish teacher I had at the time, a pleasant and competent fellow. What I remember best about him was his sardonic sense of humor.

Odd how after all this time I still think about Jews. I have written that they were the inventor of the lie. I used that device to powerful effect in my propaganda. (Hitler claimed to have made this historical "discovery.")

My so-called retirement keeps me busier than ever. The number of books on which I'm currently engaged is monumental. I shudder to think of all the unfinished works I shall leave behind at my death. The publisher called the other day to tell me that the Goebbels war memoirs are going into their ninth printing. That is certainly gratifying. They sell quite well all over the world. Even enemies pick up phrases from my books, such as the term I used to describe Bolshevik might as "the iron curtain." This label is now applied to us! The imagination atrophies under representative government, and they have to steal ideas from me.

My daughter Hilda has wasted her studies to become a chemist. She won't have anything to do with industrial firms, but then she veered toward medical research originally. All that money down the drain!

(NOTE FROM HILDA: *When it sunk in just how restricted National Socialist medicine was, I lost interest. Research was slanted toward the homeopathic school because Hitler was convinced that those kind of treatments were keeping him alive. Surely I was the fluke of the Goebbels family, born with a Western outlook; and so my natural pragmatism led me in the direction of allopathic techniques. I just wasn't cut out to be a Nazi.*)

Saints preserve us, as my old nursemaid used to say, Hilda wants to be a writer. Yet another person to sit around and play with words while neglecting the world of action. If her letters are any sign, I have no doubt that she might succeed on her own merits. There's the rub. The worst part is that her political views become more dangerous all the time, and I fear she would be in grave trouble by now were it not for her prominent name. The German Freedom League, of which she is a conspicuous member, is composed of sons and daughters of approved families and so enjoys immunity from prosecution. At least they are not rabble-rousers (not that I would mind if they had the correct ideology). We accommodate their iconoclasm for now, but we may be embracing a risk.

It was not too many years after victory before the charter was passed allowing "freedom of thought" for the elite of our citizenry. I initially opposed the move. It was as if all the incendiary titles I had personally ordered reduced to bland ashes were to be resurrected, as the Phoenix flying home to roost. One title had been given a clean bill of health during the war, however—Einstein's *The Foundations of the General Theory of Relativity*. We had to admit a mistake there. Other books I never expected to see in the possession of Reich citizens (albeit the elite) were works by Tucholsky and Ossietzky, plays by Bertolt Brecht, novels by Thomas Mann and Jaroslav Hasek and Ernest Hemingway. We have a long way to go before achieving genuine socialism. As for the moment, only the masses are protected from cultural decadence.

Hitler was surprisingly indifferent to the measure. After the war, he was a tired man, willing to leave administration to Party functionaries and the extension of ideology to the SS. He became frankly indolent in his new life-style. Censorship is a full-time job! It even wore me out. Anyway, it doesn't seem to matter now. "Freedom of thought" for the properly indoctrinated Aryan appears harmless enough. So long as he benefits from the privilege of real personal power at a fairly early age, the zealous desire for reform is quickly sublimated into the necessities of intelligent and disciplined management. And we can always rely on the people's sense of taboos, a stronger force than state censorship when you get right down to it.

(*NOTE FROM HILDA: It is just a little ludicrous that if Party officials and their families could read and see what they wanted—with myself as the prime example—Father took this as a lessening of censorship. As he wrote the above words, he was involved with trying to suppress, at all social levels, a play that made fun of the Party, and himself in the bargain: a satire by an anonymous author, about which more anon.*)

100

Friday's *New Berlin Post* arrived with my letter in answer to a question frequently raised by the new crop of young Nazis, not the least of whom is my own son, Helmuth, currently under apprenticeship in Burgundy. I love him dearly, but what a bother he is sometimes. What a family! Those six kids were more trouble than the French underground. At least Harald, from Magda's previous marriage, is a placid bureaucrat . . . but I digress.

These youngsters ask why we didn't launch an A-bomb attack on New York City when we had the bomb first. If only they would read more! The explanation is self-evident to anyone acquainted with the facts. Today's youth has grown up surrounded by a phalanx of missiles tipped with H-bomb calling cards. They have no notion of how close we were to defeat. The Allies had thorough aerial reconnaissance of Peenemünde. The V-3 was only finished in the nick of time. As for the rest, the physicists were not able to provide us with a limitless supply of A-bombs. There wasn't even time to test one. I explained how we used all the bombs against the invading armies except for one that we fired at London, praying that a sympathetic Valkyrie would help guide it on its course so that it would come somewhere near the target. The result was more than we anticipated.

The letter covered all this and also went into considerable detail concerning the technical details prohibiting a strike on New York. One notion had been to launch a rocket from the mountains near Traunstein, but it didn't come off, and new hopes were pinned on a long-range bomber that had been developed. It was ready within a month of our turning back the invasion. But there were no more A-bombs to be deployed at that moment, curse the luck! After we had suffered the Allied fire storms, it had become Hitler's obsession to take revenge on New York and turn its man-made canyons into Dante's Inferno. He thought the new weapon was his opportunity, but he had to be reminded by Speer (the usual recipient of thankless tasks) that the atomic pantry was bare. Besides, intelligence reported that America's Manhattan Project was about to bear its fiery fruit. That's when the negotiations began. We much preferred the Americans teaching Japan (loyal ally though it had been) a lesson rather than adding to the radiation and fallout levels on our shores. We'd had enough of their obliteration bombing already, thank you very much, and had done enough damage to the countryside with our own V-3s.

The war had reached a true stalemate, our U-boats against their aircraft carriers; and each side's bombers against the others. One plan was to deliver an atomic rocket from a submarine against New York . . . but by then both sides were suing for peace, and the Citadel of Evil was spared. I still believe we made the best policy under the circumstances. We had so many spies in the woodwork, it's a wonder we got off as well as we did.

What would the young critics prefer? Nuclear annihilation? They may not appreciate that we live in an age of détente, but such are the cruel realities. The postwar policy is one of latent crisis. We never intended to subjugate decadent America anyway. Ours was a European vision. Dominating the world is fine, but actually trying to administer the entire planet would be clearly self-defeating. Nobody could be that crazy . . . except for a Bolshevik, perhaps.

Facts have a tendency to show through the haze of even the best propaganda, no matter how effectively the myth would screen off unpleasantries. So it is that my daughter, the idealist of the German Freedom League, is not critical of the Russian policy. Why should it be otherwise? She worries about freedom for citizens and gives the idea of freedom for a serf the same analysis the Russian serf gives it: which is to say, none at all. Here is one of the few areas where I heartily agree with the late Alfred Rosenberg.

(NOTE FROM HILDA: It is typical of my father to blacken my name by assuming the best about me, in his terms. By this point in my life, I'd come to doubt nearly everything I'd been taught about the Russians as a people. Emma Goldman's testimony had persuaded me that the Soviet system was, in essentials, our system wearing a different face. It was Hitler who learned from Lenin; and it was Lenin who said, "It is nonsense to make any pretense of reconciling the State and liberty." Father is honest in his diary pages, if nowhere else, and his hopeful comment about my sharing at least one of his prejudices may be taken at face value. Before he took me for the ride in Goering's helium plane for the purpose of threatening me with commitment to an asylum, I'd wised up about what I dared say to him. When I was a naive adolescent, I had stupidly thought I might reform Papa!!!!! Maybe I was insane.)

Once again *mein Führer* calls me. I was so certain all that was over. They want me at the official opening of the Hitler Memorial at the museum. His paintings will be there, along with his architectural sketches. (His most accomplished canvas depicts a field in which office buildings, before the Great War, have been stacked sideways as if so much cordwood. The color yellow pervades the picture. I particularly like the sketch he did of the Spear of Longinus, a key item of the Hapsburg imperial treasure. It is the earliest drawing.) They will display his stuffed shepherd dogs and complete collection of Busby Berkeley movies. Ah well, I will have to go.

Before departing, there is time to shower, have some tea, and listen to Beethoven's *Pastorale.*

December 1965

I loathe Christmas. I'm always stuck with doing the shopping! It is not that I mind being with my family, but the rest of it is so commercialized, or else syrupy with contemptible Christian sentiments. Now if they could restore the vigor of the original Roman holiday. Perhaps I should speak to Himmler. . . . What am I saying? Never Himmler! Too bad Rosenberg isn't around.

Helga, my eldest daughter, visited us for a week. She is a geneticist, currently working on a paper to show the limitations of our eugenic policies and to demonstrate the possibilities opened up by genetic engineering. All this is over my head. DNA, RNA, microbiology, and *literal* supermen in the end? When Hitler said to let the technical side move in any direction it chooses, he was not saying much. There seems no way to stop it.

There is an old man in the neighborhood who belongs to the Nordic cult, body and soul. He and I spoke last week, all the time watching youngsters ice skating under a startlingly blue afternoon sky. There was an almost fairy-tale-like quality about the scene, as the old fellow told me in no uncertain terms that this science business is so much fertilizer. "The only great scientist I've ever seen was Hörbiger," he announced proudly. "He was more than a scientist. He was of the true blood and held the true historical vision." All this was said while he poked at me with a rolled up copy of the *Key to World Events* magazine.

I didn't have the heart to tell him that the manner in which Hanns

Hörbiger was more than a scientist was in his mysticism. He was useful to us, in his day, as one of Himmler's prophets. But the man's cosmogony was utterly discredited by our scientists. Speer's technical Germany has a low tolerance for hoaxes.

This old man would hear none of it at any rate. He would believe every sacred pronouncement until his tottering frame decayed into a useful commodity. "When I look up at the moon," he told me in a confidential whisper, "I know what I am seeing." *Green cheese,* I thought to myself, but I was aware of what was coming next.

"You believe that the moon is made of ice?" I asked him.

"It is the truth," he announced gravely, suddenly affronted as though my tone had given me away. Like all zealots, he was persistent, and before I could make good my escape, he had challenged me on the Articles of Faith—among which I recall such gems as that the Milky Way is a shroud of ice sustained in helium, and not a multitude of stars, no matter what the telescopes show; that sunspots are caused from blocks of ice impacting on the solar surface; and to bring it all home, that ice blocks falling into the atmosphere are the cause of our worst hailstorms. "Hörbiger proved his theory," he said with finality.

Hörbiger said it, I thought to myself. So that's all you need for "proof." I left the eccentric to his idle speculations on the meaning of the universe, and his final cry of, "Down with astronomical orthodoxy!" I had to get back to one of my books. It had been languishing in the typewriter far too long.

Frau Goebbels was in a sufficiently charitable mood come Christmas to invite the entire neighborhood over. I felt that I was about to live through another endless procession of representatives of the German nation—all the pomp of a funeral without any fun. The old eccentric was invited as well. I was just as happy that he did not come. Arguing with kooks is not my favorite pastime.

Magda put herself in a Party frame of mind, and there was nothing to be done about it except bite the bullet. My home was occupied by a ragtag folk band. They were off key. Worse, most of the selections were of their own composition, except that the lead song had been suggested by Magda herself and so was politically correct. It was in memory of the six million unemployed of 1932, the year before we took power and set things to rights. My wife throws around numbers with a vigor to match her husband! Symbols and numbers guide us, each and every one. She also coerced me into joining in with the Netherland Hymn of Thanksgiving, a blessedly traditional number, after which the singers stopped howling and started eating.

Speer and his wife dropped by. Who would have thought that an architect could become so effective a minister of armaments, a post he has never relinquished, although much of the work had to be delegated to competent subordinates, leaving him with the freedom to design the dream city of the Reich. His ministry is even more important in peace than it was during the war. This I consider to be an important innovation. Between industrial requirements on the one hand, and concentration camps on the other, National Socialism has no unemployment problem. Nor is the enemy imaginary. Our policies guarantee a steady supply of implacable foes. Eternal vigilance is the price of empire.

Mostly Speer wanted to talk about von Braun and the moon project. Since we had put up the first satellite, the Americans were working around the clock to beat us to Luna and restore their international prestige. As far as I was concerned, propaganda would play the deciding role on world opinion (as always). This was an area in which America had always struck me as deficient because of the absence of one clear position.

I listened politely to his worries, largely of a technical nature, and finally pointed out that the United States wouldn't be in the position it currently held if so many of our rocketry people hadn't defected. "It seems to be a race between their German scientists and ours," I said with a hearty chuckle.

Speer was not amused, but replied with surprising coldness that Germany would be better off if we hadn't lost so many Jewish geniuses when Hitler came to power. "It was as if we cut away a lobe of the nation's brain," he said. To my horror, he launched into a tirade, in my home, about how Hitler's policy for Italy had driven away those Jewish physicists who were at the cutting edge of developing an atomic bomb in the late 1930s, thereby losing us an atomic monopoly. After uttering an oath against the SS (and glancing over his shoulder, I noticed), he began dropping forbidden names in mixed company: Fermi, Segré, Rossi, and Pontecorvo. Was it up to me to remind Speer of Party discipline? The line was that Italians were anti-Semitic by nature, the same as the French. All we did was to help them live up to their potential. I remembered that Hitler once

105

told me the best way he handled the Reich's organizational genius was to bang his fist on the table and boom, "Speer, don't you realize that . . . " followed by whatever was useful at the moment. But I wasn't the Fuehrer.

When I swallowed hard on my brandy, he must have seen the consternation on my face, because he was immediately trying to smooth things over. He is no idealist, but one hell of an expert in his field. I look upon him as a well-kept piece of machinery. I hope no harm ever comes to it, no matter how the tongue may wag. (And he will always have high marks in my book for turning down the honorary rank of SS Oberstgruppenfuehrer. Anything to offend Himmler!)

Speer always seems to have up-to-date information on all sorts of interesting subjects. He had just learned that an investigation of many years had been dropped with regard to a missing German geneticist, Richard Dietrich. Since this reputedly brilliant scientist had vanished only a few years after the conclusion of the war, the authorities supposed he had either defected to the Americans in secret or been kidnapped. After two decades of fruitless inquiry, a department decides to cut off funds for the search. I'll wager that a few detectives had been making a lucrative career out of the job. Too bad for them.

Magda and I spent part of the holidays returning to my birthplace on the Rhineland. It's good to see the old homestead from time to time. I'm happy it hasn't been turned into a damned shrine, as happened with Hitler's childhood home. Looking at reminders of the past in a dry, flaky snowfall—brittle, yet seemingly endless, much as time itself—I couldn't help but wonder what the future holds. Space travel. Genetic engineering. Ah, I am an old man. I feel it in my bones.

CHAPTER TEN

But the state tells lies in all the tongues of good and evil; and whatever it says it lies—and whatever it has it has stolen. Everything about it is false; it bites with stolen teeth, and bites easily.

—Friedrich Nietzsche,
Thus Spoke Zarathustra

March 1966
What kind of retirement is this, anyway? I'm on another publicity junket. Go east, young man; go east. The son of Otto Saur will meet me at the monument-on-treads, as we call it, that stands against the remaining Slavic menace. At the height of his surrealist period, Hitler ordered the construction of a supertank. Poor Speer had only just convinced the Fuehrer that a proposed 180-ton tank was impractical because six Tiger tanks could be manufactured for the same expenditure. I'd loved to have seen Speer's face when Hitler and Saur presented the supertank proposal: a 1,500-ton monster, armed with mortars having an 80-centimeter caliber, not to mention a couple of long-barreled cannon; and to run the thing, an estimated 10,000-horsepower motor.

This mad dream was in 1943, the same year that Hitler finally gave full support to the rocket program and other state-of-the-art technology. I suspect that someone had been feeding him on H. G. Wells again. After all, Churchill was reputed to have originated the concept of the tank; but Wells had written about it many years earlier in a story entitled "The Land Ironclads." The Fuehrer's logic was that if Wells predicted the first tank, and was proven right, then perhaps his predictions of supertanks would come true as well. Only this time, Hitler insisted, Germany would win the race. (When he was a journalist during the Great War, Wells had predicted that future tanks would weigh thousands of tons, running on caterpillar tracks that would permanently damage the soil.) Speer used his considerable powers of persuasion to veto the project, and he threw around budgets and timetables until the matter was shelved.

So the behemoth was not on the schedule for 1944. Instead, the monster was built in 1948, at the tail end of what some have called World War II and a half. We were going solo with the Russians, pushing deeper into their territory, astounded that Marxists kept popping up when we had expected a purely ethnic foe by then. Resource management was at an all-time high, and my propaganda hammered away at the theme. Conservation was so important that we were building *Monte Klamotten* in all our bombed cities, mountains formed of the debris. Waste not, want not. Yet while Germany was discovering new dimensions of frugality, Hitler built his supertank. It was transported in sections by train, and by the time it was assembled, the eastern battlefield in which it was to be deployed had been pacified. So there it stood, and stands, and will probably rust . . . unless we spend the outrageous sum necessary to bring it home for a war museum.

Magda seems pleased that I am leaving. I'll lay odds she has a tryst planned with Karl Hanke, the gauleiter of Silesia. I should complain? She's had the same boring affair for years and years, while I have sown my seed far and wide. Her peccadillo keeps her satisfied and out of my hair when the restless spirit moves me. If it had not been for Hitler forbidding it, we probably would have divorced; but now we are used to each other. She is a most presentable wife and mother; while passion does not interfere with duty.

The children take after their mother when it comes to sex, all except Hilda that is. My stunning, redheaded daughter has my blood and a roving eye. When I saw her dressed in her first evening gown, and her bare shoulder was white against black velvet, I remember thinking at the time . . . no, that will be enough of that.

I go to see the iron leviathan.

Picking up where I left off, with the tank, Commissioner Koch and I contrived a number of photo opportunities. Actually, the monster is good for propaganda. Rumor has it that not even partisans wish to see it destroyed. The thing has never been used in battle, and it is something to show one's children.

Koch and I trust each other because of a number of past considerations. We spoke frankly about the Rosenberg affair. Officially, when

Alfred (Koch prefers to use the informal "Du" when speaking of fellow officials) was at the summit of his power as commissioner for the entire East European regions, he was assassinated by a Marxist revolutionary group. Everybody in the know draws the conclusion that Heinrich did his rival in, and that the reason had unsurprisingly to do with Burgundy. The incidental beneficiary was Koch, who was promoted from gauleiter for the Ukraine to Rosenberg's successor. Koch's record was first rate. He had made invaluable contributions in neutralizing trouble emanating from the North Caucuses and Volga Tartar areas; and he was gifted at handling our fool of a foreign minister, Ribbentrop.

"Over Christmas, Speer was telling me how Rosenberg helped smuggle Ukrainian quartz past the Ministry of Armaments to the SS, and in the middle of the war yet!" I said.

"Himmler isn't famous for gratitude" was Koch's wry understatement. "He's a hypocrite, too. I was shocked when I learned he was using several thousand Jews as slave labor in his SS factories when they were slated for termination. He said one thing in his Posen speech and then faltered in execution."

We had returned to his office, and I was fingering the bishop of his ivory chess set. How much did our lives resemble those pieces restricted to sixty-four squares. Maneuver and outmaneuver; and one serious mistake took you off the board. Himmler was a serious rival. "He's even worse when it comes to matters of faith," I said with feeling. "Rosenberg found that out the hard way. You're certainly right about his hypocrisy. It burns me up the way Himmler controls the best quartz mining in your area, uses his monopoly to stick his nose in the technological progress of the Reich, and then plows the profits into Burgundy where they sit around on their fat asses and bemoan modern life."

"They've got the tourist trade, so what do they care? Heinrich is a rich man. He gets more than his fair share of manganese, lead, zinc, coal—"

"Stop, stop. It makes me sick just thinking about it."

"That's the SS for you." As soon as he said it, we glanced around. It's habit forming.

"Well, they provided me with excellent bodyguards during the war," I said.

"They are the best bodyguards for sure," he agreed. Order was restored.

Koch kept my tour brief. I owe him one. (Next winter I'm putting my foot down. Magda and I will vacation in Vienna, where Wagner so often took his ease.) An unusual sight he saved for last, the corpse of a Waffen soldier who had suffered a peculiar mutilation. Branded across the width of the man's considerable chest was a huge Swastika that had been altered to include a hammer at one point and a sickle at another. Koch was visibly bothered.

"Not all our difficulties are with Bolsheviks. They continually reduce their numbers by trying each other as Trotskyists, you know. The ethnic and nationalist identities reassert themselves and are the real problem."

"They could be National Socialists in their own right," I said with a smile, but Koch's face clouded over. Not everyone appreciates my sense of humor. Time to change the subject. "Uh, who leaves this gruesome signature on our stalwart lads?"

The commissioner was a policeman at heart. "We chased down several false leads. Our first surmise was a Baltic outfit that hates both socialisms; and I can't begin to calculate how many Ukrainians escaped east, cursing Bolsheviks and Nazis with equal passion. Now we are convinced it's a band of renegade Germans."

"What!"

"The Wild East is to blame. Once a German has tasted freedom, watch out. A number of missing persons sneak across the border regularly, and they've all taken the name Schmidt. They're reported to have a leader named Neil, but as they're obviously a gang of deranged anarchists, that's probably untrue."

"Have you caught any?"

"Yes, but they blow up."

"Oh."

The responsibilities of authority weigh heavily on all of us. That's why I would make one last stop, when I wished to head straight home instead.

I have seen the *Europa*. The captain graciously altered course to take me part of the way home. Too bad neither Roosevelt nor Churchill lived to see Hitler's poetic answer to their all too long mastery of the sea. The world's largest vessel of war is 2.5 kilometers in length, and everything but its atomic motor, engine room, bridge, and crew's quarters is made of ice. I understand that an American Admiral Heinlein wondered "how an ice cube over a mile long will stay in one piece." Funny. Those were my sentiments as well when I first heard about it. But as *mein Führer* so often said, where there is a *will,* there is a way.

Like the supertank, the supership was built in sections. The most important ingredient was sawdust added to the water in the molds. The ice blocks were rendered more stable in this fashion. Although its use is primarily restricted to the North Atlantic, water loss in warmer climates is minimal because of the impurities in the ice and the absurd size of a vessel that would have been christened the *Hörbiger* if there was any justice. Goering used his influence to have the greatest battleship of all time named the *Europa* and donated an excellent reproduction of the painting by the same name, a startling nude that was one of the prizes of his art collection. It's a wonder she doesn't catch cold.

Of course, it's warm enough where she is. But I caught a chill on deck that I'm certain will get worse. I hate northern climates. I was not meant to be a Viking! The captain was a tough old sea dog who probably never had a sick day in his life. He also had the virtues we cultivate in National Socialist man, with as firm a grasp of geopolitical theory as the latitude and longitude on his nautical charts. Every man should have a dream. His was the conquest of Canada. He was especially taken by the vision of the uranium and nickel such an enterprise would add to the Reich. He'd even worked out a tentative plan that involved landing in the Maritimes and sending the men up the St. Lawrence River valley. As much as I hate to burst a good man's balloon, I reminded him of the nuclear realities, and how North America might talk a lot about peace and neutrality in foreign policy, but they did so under their nuclear hat with a brim wide enough to accommodate friends to the north. Splitting the atom has done more to dampen the high spirits of fighting men than anything else in memory.

It was beautiful on the *Europa.* I remember smart uniforms, black against the white expanse of the ship. Even our enemies must admit that we have the best uniforms. There was a bronze sunset right out of the *Eddas.* This quite remarkable ship has never been in a battle,

111

another similarity to its spiritual cousin, the supertank. Deterrence is better than war; and awe is a deterrent.

I shall open a medium's parlor. I predicted a cold, and now I have one. These words are being written with a pencil on a pad as I lay flat on my back. If I choke in my own fluids, let my last will and testament show that I am of sound mind and leave everything to neofascist movements abroad. We are the wave of the future, and every country that tries freedom will sooner or later learn its lesson. Even in lunatic America there are voices grown weary of the irrational life that denies the need for order. These voices call for "getting tough" and "cracking down" and "ending permissiveness." The irony is that some who upheld "law and order" in the old United States also opposed the inevitable steps the country took toward socialism. When will they learn that "law and order" and socialism are corollaries? Capitalism is the enemy of both.

The subject is on my mind because as I am stuck in bed, I've had the chance to catch up on correspondence. A number of letters from the states were waiting for me. The very freedom touted in America provides a chance for subversion that we dare not ignore. So far, we haven't made a dent, but we will keep trying.

When the Roosevelt administration ignored the Bill of Rights and launched its sedition trials, they were acting as realists. Now the Bill is used as a hammer to prevent a powerful executive from taking care of its enemies. Hitler said they had become more helpless than Weimar was at its worse. Still, a number of names came to my attention when John Rogge went after his list of fifth columnists. Alas, the ones who were genuinely sympathetic to us were hopeless boobs we couldn't use; and the able ones were staunch nationalists we couldn't turn to our purposes, although some did have fascistic ideas but of the home-grown variety. One such individual who interested me was Lawrence Dennis, who was later to run for president on the America First ticket, but who lost to a libertarian in that wild and woolly country.

Dennis would never respond to my letters. I wonder if George Viereck had still been in business if he might have made a difference. No matter. Dennis had done such an excellent job of indicting old-style American imperialism that I happily used his material. You can't copyright history, and we use anything we want from other countries without paying royalties anyway. There are reasons to be a socialist. The main sticking point with my anti-American propaganda used to be that we did all the same things. Today, there is even less reason to rail against American imperialism because they have given it up. Well, I never let details get in the way of a good campaign.

As soon as I recover, I will get to work on my hundredth anti-American program. This one won't require any lies, only a selective use of facts. The notion that only dictatorships start wars is so pervasive that even now we have trouble with it. And I can't write any more with this pencil.

I can breathe again. To work, to work!

Although the list Dennis compiled is common knowledge in his country, I like to give him credit. *Signal* magazine will carry a cover story on the wars in which peace-loving America has found itself embroiled. If it is so peace loving, how did it get in so many? It angers me that they got out of the Big War without their continent receiving so much as a scratch, just as they had in the previous world cataclysm.

Here is the Dennis list, from his international best-seller *The Dynamics of War and Revolution,* although maybe the first entry shouldn't be included, as it was their revolution. I have no problem including their domestic quarrels, however, as once the revolution was won, it was time to live the peace-loving stereotype they've been shoving down the throats of Europe ever since. And their Civil War led to what our historians refer to gaggingly as the Prussianization of America. Something else I like about the list is that a mere ceasefire does not indicate the end of hostilities when other military-political factors are taken into account.

War of the Revolution	1775 to 1784
Wyoming Valley Disturbances and Shays's Rebellion	1782 to 1787
Northwest Indian Wars and Whiskey Insurrection	1790 to 1795
War with France	1789 to 1800
War with Tripoli	1801 to 1805
Northwest Indian Wars	1811 to 1813
War with Great Britain	1812 to 1815
War with Algiers	1815

Seminole Indian Wars	1817 to 1818
Yellowstone Expedition	1819
Blackfeet Indian Wars	1823
LeFevre Indian War	1827
Sac and Fox War	1831
Black Hawk War	1832
Nullification Troubles in South Caribbean	1832 to 1833
Cherokee and Pawnee Disturbances	1833 to 1839
Seminole Indian War	1835 to 1842
War with Mexico	1846 to 1848
Indian Wars (Sioux, Comanche, Navaho, etc.)	1848 to 1861
Civil War	1861 to 1866
Indian Wars	1865 to 1890
Sioux Indian War	1890 to 1891
Apache and Bannock Indian Troubles	1892 to 1896
Spanish-American War	1898 to 1899
Philippine Insurrection	1899 to 1903
Boxer Expedition	1900 to 1901
Cuban Pacification	1906 to 1909
First Nicaragua Expedition	1912 to 1925
Vera Cruz Expedition	1914
First Haiti Expedition	1915
Punitive Expedition into Mexico	1916 to 1917
Dominican Expedition	1916
The World War	1917 to 1921
Second Haiti Expedition	1919 to 1920
Second Nicaragua Expedition	1926 to 1932

All this before they entered the Big One, for a second crack at us. No doubt their previous warfare was done to extend democracy and make the world safe for large investors everywhere. Of course, if *Signal* ran a chart like this about the Fatherland I'd have the editor's head. The issue is not war, or the grievances on either side. The issue is propaganda. I wish I had seen this data before Hitler died. I would have asked him if he had been familiar with it when he spoke of America's military unpreparedness and lack of martial will. Was he being disingenuous or did he really believe what he said? Apparently America has been the first warrior nation in history unwilling to admit what it is. And now it has finally given up direct warfare, settling instead for economic weapons when it wants something. But that means its actions are finally in line with its propaganda! All this is giving me a headache.

I'm sufficiently recovered to return to the office. First, I must attend to a matter that irritates the hell out of me. Young hoodlums have been spray painting the Star of David on the walls of my ministry. They probably think this vandalism very funny, but I'm not laughing. What's more, it's a sure bet that they are Aryan teenagers. When actual Jewish subversion takes place, it is always serious; not childish pranks.

The press is very good about handling sordid details of this kind. We have the most responsible reporters in the world. They follow orders. Any publicity would only encourage similar vandalism, so as the walls are wiped clean so are the memories of anyone in the vicinity.

Speer's comments about the Jews haunt me. How can someone as intelligent as he is continue to miss the point of our anti-Semitic policy? Destroying their power in Europe does not mean smooth sailing henceforth. Every step we take in the Middle East runs afoul of their schemes. Although we have some small Arab nations allied with us (and a few even attempting a modified National Socialism of their own, but not making a lot of progress because of religious objections inherent in Islam), the majority of Arabs don't like us. Hitler worked out a brilliant strategy for playing Arab factions against one another, when the Jewish wild card came into the picture.

A dozen of our soldiers were recently killed by an operation handled by Jews and Arabs working together! This is intolerable. Although publicly I have to defend our policy in all things, I feel that we have never taken a right step when it comes to the Middle East. One would think that between our synthetic fuels on the one hand, and nuclear power on the other, we wouldn't need Arab oil in the first place. Let the region dry up and blow away! The curse of an industrial empire is that its appetite for energy is insatiable. We need everything, and then some.

Part of the Middle Eastern problem we brought on ourselves back in the 1930s, when we hadn't decided on a final solution to the Jewish problem and were floundering around with one hair-brained scheme after another. Nothing came of the Madagascar Plan, but we actually went through with the initial phase of the Palestine Plan. Very few citizens of the Reich are aware that we moved sixty thousand Jews and a sizable sum of money to Palestine, if the Zionists would provide a market for goods when the rest of the world was threatening us with a stringent boycott because of our Jewish policy! I didn't think it would work; our being in bed, so to speak, with Jewish Palestine. Today we spill German blood into the desert sands whenever the fruit of earlier policies chokes us. An industrial application of murder proved a far more expeditious approach. Go east, young man . . .

One lesson is clear as Hitler's moustache: the Third Reich was the only political force in the world that could drive Jews and Arabs into an alliance. Everybody hates us.

CHAPTER ELEVEN

*The magnificent possibilities of the school as an
instrument of propaganda had been perceived very early;
Alexander Hamilton, who never missed the boat on a chance
of this kind, expounded them in 1800. . . . When the Church
became weak and the centralised, nationalist-imperialist
State grew strong, the State began to do its own dirty
work; and with the schools, press, cinema and radio under
its control, this work is now child's play.*

—Albert Jay Nock,
The Memoirs of a Superfluous Man

Who knows in this crazy world?

—Bela Lugosi as a Nazi plastic surgeon in
Black Dragons (Monogram, 1942)

It was good to spend an entire day at the old office in the Wilhelm-platz. Work keeps me fit. No more colds this year! Restoration work on this fine, white palace goes on steadily, and I don't even want to know which wall was defaced. I have kept the office in its original condition, mindful that they sell postcards in the kiosk out front showing this most public of my inner sanctums, with its marble writing desk next to the huge globe of the world; and both overseen by a colorful portrait of Frederick the Great, who seems to glare at a recent addition to the desk: a terminal hooked up to the latest state-of-the-art liquid-helium-cooled analog computer.

The Propaganda Ministry extends throughout the city, and its departments have multiplied since the days I managed press, film, radio, propaganda, and theater from this one office. Television is a separate division. It receives the most direct control over content. We don't worry all that much about looser standards applied to the other media. The common sense of the *Völk* insures that dangerous ideas will not go unpunished. I think my primary task is to reinforce the people's habits—a reason to keep up the *Der Juden Verbotten* signs in areas that have not seen a Jew in years. Elections serve the same purpose. Once the Party has selected its candidates, it is crucial to get out the vote.

Fresh flowers had been placed in the vase standing on my heavy walnut bookcase, and their petals were a vivid purple in the early morning sunlight. Feeling a decade younger, I was eager to write. Two editorials had been waiting for completion while I galavanted about the continent. Later in the day I was to have a visitor, so the Op Ed pieces had to be disposed of quickly. Here the word processor is a real help, although I refuse to use it for personal writing, or when I prepare a speech. (If I didn't use different-color inks for my speeches, setting off key words and phrases for emphasis, I wouldn't be able to rehearse properly.)

Sitting at the terminal, I finished off the vital plea for a tougher policy on the "pirates," my term for faceless cowards who use bombs against defenseless citizens of the Reich. Some of these vermin can be traced back to the Resistance, but the rest are young guerrillas, gifted in the arts of terror and largely financed with gold from hither and yon. Of late there has been a rash of bombs aboard passenger aircraft (shades of the Hindenburg). My suggestion for how to stop the problem is taken from America, whence many of the pirates originate. There private airlines employ stricter security measures than we do—right down to body searches. The customers voluntarily accept the inconvenience because they are paying for safety. Now if we can only persuade our prudish citizens to disrobe! Not even Leni Riefenstahl's films, reveling in naked young bodies, have made a dent in the taciturn German character. Today's Americans are more playful, and more casual about nudity, the lucky bastards.

More pleasurable was dashing off a piece on the admirable Otto Skorzeny. He has said that nothing but death will persuade him to retire. A recent close shave suggests that a real hero will be among us for some time to come. The information has been declassified, and I was the first to describe how Skorzeny landed a new kind of jet fighter in a dead-stick glide when it would have been safer for him, once the engine failed, to jettison the external fuel tanks. He was over New Berlin at the time and refused to put civilians at risk. What a pilot! I concluded the paean by reminding my loyal readers that Otto is the same daredevil today that he was back in the war, when he used a glider to rescue Mussolini from the supposedly impregnable fortress in which the Allies had imprisoned Il Duce. I kick myself because the first popular movie to depict that aerial feat was American, for God's sake; and they showed their own soldiers using Otto's method for an imaginary mission against Germans!!! What nerve.

With the writing out of the way, I was ready to greet my young guest, who appeared promptly at noon: a new movie director named Stefan Schellenberg. He has made a big splash with his movie *Pflichterfullung im Lichte des Heiligen Gral* (Fulfillment of Duty in the Light of the Holy Grail). The picture had taken in so much at the box office that he was planning a sequel with the same hero, the irrepressible Professor von Moltke (named after the World War I army chief who spent much of his free time on the Grail mystery). As preparations for the remake of Riefenstahl's *Triumph des Willens* (Triumph of the Will) were nearly completed, all that was needed was the director, and I believed this man to be the one.

No sooner was the Holy Grail movie in release than I received a stormy letter from Himmler. It seems that arcane secrets of the Ahnenerbe, the SS occult bureau, had been splashed across the movie screens of Europe—and worse, that the Grail movie was becoming an international hit. This latter development surprised even me. The picture was being touted in America as a nonpolitical entertainment. They have to say that in Britain, but America??? After five viewings, and reading a cross-section of reviews, I had been forced to revise one of my theories of propaganda. Naturally, I sent for the cinema wunderkind who was responsible for the turmoil.

As for Himmler's nonsense, I am utterly fed up with the occult. When Hitler brought the Spear of Longinus to Nuremberg, along with the other Hapsburg treasures, our mystics went off the deep end. The debate between Rosenberg and Himmler flared to new heights in the Thule group. An adherent of Wagner's theory of the Aryan Christ, Rosenberg saw the Grail in a Gnostic light, and the spear that pierced the side of Christ as a totem for those of the pure blood, the same as the holy chalice would be. Himmler was of the old school. As a hard-nosed pagan, he believed the Grail legend to have been perverted by the Semitic superstition of Christianity; and that the spear wielded by the Germanic Longinus had a different significance, albeit possessing magical power for those of the pure blood still seeking the legendary Book of the Aryans or the Aryan

Stone. This endless bickering over fantasy was serious business in Burgundy, but it must not be allowed to interfere with decisions of the Greater Reich. Stefan's film had been viewed as harmless, and even constructive, by some true believers; but what counted with me was that the certificate had been issued by inhabitants of the planet Earth.

Stefan was not overly articulate and I wondered if the most effective passages in his work were less a result of conscious design than a byproduct of his *Kultur.* Was this young man the end product of our state indoctrination in the classroom and cinema? He seemed unconcerned with my criticisms of inconsistencies and holes in the plot you could run a panzer division through. At first I mistakenly thought his behavior in my presence showed his mettle, but that wasn't it. His lack of fear was less a result of courage than an inability to face reality.

As my students are taught every day, the objective of propaganda is to repeat a message so often, and in such a variety of guises, that it becomes part and parcel of the common wisdom. Every prejudice of the people can be turned to the advantage of the Party, and a feeling of virtuousness is to be preferred over an honest conviction. The leitmotif of effective propaganda is to strip the enemy of humanity, so that the mere sight of his face, his accent, his symbols, will inspire immediate loathing. Love of country has limitations, but hatred of the enemy is sublime and forever.

The Grail movie employed the techniques of emotional engineering with sufficient aplomb to merit qualified praise from my ministry, and an invitation extended to its director. As per my request, he had brought a copy of the script so that I could go through it with him, pointing to the parts that worked, and the lapses as well.

First, we have the hero, a man who is an intellectual when teaching archaeology at New Berlin University. The rest of the year, he dons workingman's clothes and goes adventuring in the wilds on the lookout for archeological finds. While having these adventures, he suddenly becomes the ideal of the Workingman, a beer hall brawler able to hold his own with the best of them. The obliteration of class lines is especially to be commended. The fight scenes are carefully staged to maximize visceral responses from the audience at the same time that they overwhelm objections by the sheer speed with which everything transpires.

Stereotypes absolutely dominate the film. The setting is before the war, but after we have taken power. Our hero is looking for the Grail—the Aryan Stone in this story—reputed to be somewhere in Iceland. A troop of British soldiers has been dispatched to the same area by the king of England. The monarch hopes that by obtaining this stone, he will be invincible in war. The soldiers represent such a collection of dunderheads that they never manage to kill even one of the hero's sidekicks, much less impede his progress. They are mainly good at killing each other off through clumsiness. Another incredible touch is that although most of these soldiers would be recruited from the working class, Schellenberg has all of them speaking with upper-class accents. The audience hates them from the word go.

Whenever characters from different ethnic groups aid the hero, they are portrayed in a positive, proletarian light. When these same types aid the British, they become racial caricatures that appeal to every deep-seated feeling of disgust. So far, so good. But here the problem begins.

I pointed out to my young guest that films by Leni and myself handled matters with more finesse than was to be found in his work. For other examples of better filmmakers, I referred to three directors who work in Hollywood: Alfred Hitchcock, Orson Welles, and the traitor Fritz Lang. (I'll never forgive myself for letting Lang escape Germany with the first sound Mabuse film under his arm. To think he turned down my generous offer of the top job in the industry!) An adult thriller, I told Stefan, achieves its effect through a close study of human moods and a cumulative buildup of sinister detail. The Grail picture completely obliterates anything resembling human character. I was in the middle of complaining about his abdication of directorial control through cheap manipulations (as mummies are discovered in the Temple of Thor, a scream is dubbed on the soundtrack to cue the audience to yelp) when I noticed that he was sucking on a lollipop that he must have brought with him. I suddenly needed a drink.

Hoping that a compliment might facilitate communication, I praised the portrayal of the Jewish villain in the picture—as sadistic a torturer as the imagination can conceive, yet he never so much as musses the hair on the heroine's head. The plot won't allow him even temporary satisfactions. (If it had been a film submitted to me, as they all used to be excepting Leni's work, I'd have had the villain do one or two nasty things before the hero thwarts his schemes.)

Come to think of it, just why was this film such a success? If the hero is being chased by the British, the terrain magically alters so that his pursuers will drive off a cliff, even though we were in flat country a moment before. Should the good Herr Doktor Moltke hold on to the outside of an airplane—where the air pressure would sweep him off—the audience cannot be bothered with unfulfilled expectations. Hold on he does, for hours.

The climax is either too clever or too stupid for me to appreciate. A glowing figure rises from the magic stone. Is it the Spirit of Arya or the Gnostic Christ of Manichaeanism? "SS," as we call Stefan around the ministry, doesn't say. He at least has the sense to avoid that quarrel. It suffices that the supernatural visitation disintegrates the remaining British (traitors to their race) while the German hero and heroine not only emerge unscathed, but are even released of their bonds. (Once again, if it had been my story, I'd have had them escape under their own steam.)

Asking "SS" if he didn't see the hidden agenda of his film only resulted in another blank stare and his crunching on the remains of his candy. He is not the only one who didn't see it. Were the hero an independent, egotistical type (suggested by the performance), he would keep the Aryan Stone hidden for his own uses; or, to simplify his life, he would bury it deep in the ground and deny having found it. At the beginning of the story, he denies the supernatural, but he can no longer hold to such comforting beliefs. He does the patriotic thing and turns the stone over to the Fuehrer. Was this a sly calculation on Schellenberg's part to avoid trouble with a certificate, in which case he must not be quite the dolt I see in my office? If "SS" is implying that we won the war for reasons other than Hitler's military genius, then it is a harmless enough conceit in this childlike context. Nobody in the audience is thinking by the time the end credits roll.

When I had finished my analysis, "SS" was completely unmoved. Curiously, he wanted to know if I believed in the Holy Grail, with a special emphasis placed on the Spear of Longinus (an item that doesn't appear in his movie). Dismissing his question with a scornful laugh, I moved the conversation back to business. Was this man to walk in Riefenstahl's footsteps or not?

Showing him that part of my private film collection kept at Wilhelmplatz, I offered to screen my favorite anti-Nazi picture, Hitchcock's *Foreign Correspondent*. Schellenberg had the right content, but he needed to work on technique. He declined my offer! "You haven't mastered the tricks of plotting," I told him. "Your story doesn't show the villainy of Moltke's adversaries."

At last he showed passion about his work: "They're bad guys. The audience knows who they are. I don't have to prove anything."

His uncertainty unnerved me. It might even presage a shift in ministry policy. The crudest race-hate propaganda we had churned out in the old days, such as *The Eternal Jew,* had sought to win over opinion. One last time, I tried to make the case for subtlety. Back in 1941, I had had a brainstorm about one of our British internees we had taken when advancing into Belgium the year before: the famous P. G. Wodehouse. Now there was a nonpolitical entertainer. His quaint, Edwardian view of the world provided me with an opportunity to apply the theory of context management.

Other hard workers in the ministry wondered if I had gone off my head when I had Wodehouse moved to the Aldon Hotel in Berlin, where I offered him the opportunity to do uncensored broadcasts. I knew my man. His commentary was the same lightly humorous material it always was, including a good-natured jesting at the foibles of the powerful, and a jovial uncertainty about the outcome of the war. I had correctly gauged the response of my opposite number in London, who did the anonymous "Cassandra" broadcasts, a more cowardly operation than I would stoop to. Soon all of Wodehouse's home country was howling for the blood of the collaborator. The same writer who had slightly kidded the privileged class was now served on a platter to the British public by members of that class . . . as an example of the privileged class! A double-twist with a back flip worth ten points out of ten. The furor served the purposes of *mein Führer.*

"Wodehouse's content didn't matter," I told Schellenberg. "Context was everything. Does this teach you something you can use?"

"SS" was having none of it. "That's ancient history," he said. "What does it have to do with movies?"

I gave up trying to communicate with him after that. He was an overgrown child, product of Nazi schools and media. I made him. With a good scriptwriter to guide him, he could do the job I wanted, and that would be that. As Hitler's health had deteriorated, plans to recreate the Nuremberg rally and another film had waned. Riefenstahl's original was safe in that regard (although I'm considering the possibility of artificially adding color to her precious little masterpiece). The new picture would be more in the manner of a sequel, while using the same title. Schellenberg would have to travel the length and breadth of the Reich for years to get his film in the can. Whereas Riefenstahl used fifty cameras, I'd allot hundreds to this picture. Progress.

Meanwhile, my young technician had become entranced with lobby cards and stills I kept with my foreign film collection. When he casually passed over some excellent shots of the most glamorous actress of them all, Greta Garbo, it confirmed my worst suspicions about his lack of taste. Then my heart stopped as he began pawing at the film cans. "You have a title I've never heard of," he said petulantly. What kind of creature was he? The source of his irritation, instead of healthy curiosity, was an uncut copy of James Whale's *The Road Back,* a brilliant interpretation of yet another load of pacifistic drivel from the author of *All Quiet on the Western Front.*

"I keep trophies," I told him. "In 1936, our consul in Los Angeles threatened Universal Studios with a German boycott of all their films if they didn't reedit *Road* to suit us. Can you believe that the craven studio heads caved in? Whale was a good director, even if he was an Englishman, same as Hitchcock. He didn't do valuable work after that. To top it off, only a few years later they were grinding out the same war propaganda as all the other studios.

"Like these?" asked Schellenberg, pointing to a tower of film cans from Warner Brothers, the studio that borrowed so many of my techniques.

"Especially those," I answered. Wartime America was willing to learn from me. One of the movies suggested that Warner Brothers didn't mind the idea of a *Kristallnact* if it was directed against Germans in New York instead of Jews in Berlin. Someday I'll make a film of that memorable evening, sparing no detail—the *ping, ping* of violin strings breaking as a music shop burned, and the broken glass from the store windows, glittering like ice under the stars. This kid could probably make a good movie about *Kristallnact* that he wouldn't understand himself.

There was a certain charm about his childlike acquisitiveness as he hinted he'd like to have a memento or two for his collection, in return for which I could have whatever I desired in the way of props or stills from the Grail movie. I didn't mind indulging him, although I was surprised that he mainly wanted American stuff. He didn't gravitate to the Germans of Hollywood, but went after straight Americana. I let him have some Captain Midnight knickknacks. (I enjoyed finding out that this estimable hero of American radio commanded his own SS: the Secret Squadron.) In a fit of generosity, I threw in a one-sheet from *Enemy of Women,* a curiosity released by Monogram Studios that had undergone a sudden title change when the direction of the war shifted in our favor. It was now simply *The Goebbels Story.* I had shown a subtitled print to friends. It was quite hilarious in places, but I was rather taken with the performance by Paul Andor, a better version of me than the one turned out factory-style by Martin Kosleck in productions for the major studios. It was not surprising that I couldn't rouse interest in Stefan for low-budget productions of the Monogram sort, even when I mentioned a legendary secret weapon, or "bomb," they had produced starring the comic strip character Snuffy Smith that went by the improbable designation of *Hillbilly Blitzkrieg.* Stefan collected unusual *objets de nostalgie,* but my desire to track down this film was too much for him.

To get rid of him, in a manner of speaking, I let him have publicity shots from a sampling of American war films I had utilized to prove a degree of racism in their cinema equal to ours, albeit against different targets. But I would not surrender my copy of *Air Fighters Comics* where the cover depicts the intrepid Airboy exterminating a Japanese pilot who must have been a ghoul or vampire considering the size of his fangs, spattered with his own life's blood. (How ironic that our earlier ally—intrepid Samurai I had portrayed as *Herrenvölk*—is today a lackey of Western imperialism.) When Julius Streicher was publishing his gallery of monstrous faces to represent the Jews, he hadn't thought to give them fangs. Live and learn.

Schellenberg was so put out that I wouldn't part with my American comic book that I gave him a consolation prize: a good reproduction of the December 12, 1942, issue of *Collier's,* which presented the "Japs" as a race of bats. Our former partner in the Axis has become so cooperative with their former enemies that I may employ the bat image myself if this keeps up.

True to form, "SS" had no capacity for gratitude. I didn't expect otherwise. But as he was leaving, he had the impudence to ask, "Herr Doktor Goebbels, do you share a dual citizenship between the Reich and Burgundy?"

"Certainly not!" I answered immediately. "Why do you ask that?"

"Oh, just curious," he said. "Let's do lunch sometime and discuss the remake."

He departed and I reflected on what is wrong with today's youth. They have known too much peace. A year on the eastern front would have done wonders for this lad. And as for Burgundy, I was beginning to resent the very name. I longed for the good old days when the religious problem consisted of dueling with conventional Christians in the Centre party.

CHAPTER TWELVE

No happiness without order, no order without authority, no authority without unity.

—Bulwer Lytton,
The Coming Race

May 1966

I have been invited to Burgundy. Helmuth has passed his initiation and is now a fully accredited member of the Death's Head SS, on his way to joining the inner circle of the Thule eccentrics. Oh, well. Naturally he is in a celebratory mood and wants his father to witness the victory. I am proud, of course, but just a little wary of what his future holds in store. I remain the convinced ideologue and critical of the bourgeois frame of mind. (Our revolution was against that sort of sentimentality.) But I don't mind some bourgeois comforts. My son will live a hard and austere life that I hope will not prove too much for him. Then again, he's not a decadent Schellenberg, and my boy ought to make me proud once he's been steeled in the furnace.

No sooner had I been sent the invitation than I also received a telegram from my daughter, Hilda, whom I had not seen since the Yuletide, when she stopped over for Christmas dinner. Who was it who once said to talk as a radical but dine with the establishment? Somehow she has learned of the invitation from Helmuth and insists that I must see her before leaving on the trip. She tells me that I am in danger! The message was clouded in mystery because she did not offer a hint of a reason. Nevertheless I agreed to meet her at the proposed rendezvous because it was conveniently on the way. And I am always worried that Hilda will find herself imprisoned or worse for going too far with her unrealistic views.

The same evening I was cleaning out a desk when I came across a letter she had written when she was seventeen years old—from the summer of 1952. I had the urge to read it again:

Dear Father,

I appreciated your last letter and its frankness, although I don't understand what you want me to do. Why have you not been able to think of anything to say to me for nearly a year? I know that you and Mother have found me to be your most difficult daughter. I remember when I was younger that Helga, Holde, and Hedda never gave Mother trouble about their clothes. I didn't object to the dresses she put on me, but could I help it if they tore when I played? I asked for more casual attire suited to climbing trees and hiking and playing soccer.

Ever since Heide died in that automobile accident, Mother has become very protective of her daughters. Only Helmuth escaped that sort of overwhelming protectiveness, and that's just because he's a boy.

At first I wasn't sure that I wanted to be sent to this private school, but a few weeks here convinced me that you had made the right decision. The mountains give you room to stretch your legs. The horses they let us ride are magnificent. Wolfgang is mine and he is the fastest.

Soon I will be ready to take my examinations for the university. Your concern that I do well runs through your entire letter. Now we have something to talk about again. It is too late to change anything. I'm sure I'll do fine. I've been studying chemistry every chance, and I love it.

My only complaint is that the library is much too small. My favorite book is the unexpurgated Nietzsche, where he talks about the things the Party forbade as subjects for public discussion. At first I was surprised to discover how pro-Jewish he was, not to mention pro-freedom. The more I read of him, the more I agree with what he has to say.

One lucky development was a box of new books that had been confiscated from unauthorized people (what you would call the wrong type for intellectual endeavor, Father). Suddenly I had in front of me an orgy of exciting reading material. I especially enjoyed the Kafka . . . but I'm not sure why. Have you read his story "An Old Manuscript"? Wasn't it among the titles you burned? There is something very disturbing about it.

My biggest surprise is a book by that American writer of German background, H. L. Mencken. I've seen a few quotes from him before, but it was always his criticisms of, wait a minute while I look it up,

Germanaphobia in the United States. I had no idea how many other things he'd written about. His book is very funny. They should teach us more about the Roaring Twenties and Prohibition and gangsters. What made me think of you, Papa, was that Herr Mencken wrote that folk art does not come from the people at all. How could anyone think that, even a famous man like he is? Do you think you should send him one of your books about the creative spirit of the *Völk*? He probably doesn't have the facts. He says that ballads do not come from a nation's community but from individual poets who did the songs originally for the royalty in castles, and that the songs sort of trickled down to the people afterward. Silly, isn't it?

Some students here want to form a club. They are in correspondence with others of our peer group who are allowed to read the old forbidden books. We have not decided on what we would call the organization. We are playing with the idea of the German Reading League. Other names may occur to us later.

Another reason I like it better in the country than in the city is that there are not as many rules out here. Oh, the school has its curfews, but they don't really pay much attention, and we can do as we please most of the time. Only one of the teachers doesn't like me and she called me a little reprobate. I suspect she might make trouble for me except that everyone knows that you're my father. That always helps.

I was becoming interested in a boy named Franz, but it came to the dean's attention and she told me that he was not from a good enough family for me to pursue the friendship. We ignored the advice, but within a month Franz had left without saying a word. I know that you are against the old class boundaries, Father, but believe it when I say that they are still around. The people must not know that Hitler socialized them.

Now that I think about it, there are more rules out here than I first realized. Why must there be so many rules? Why can't I just be me without causing so much trouble?

I don't want to end this letter with a question. I hope that Mother and you are happy. You should probably take that vacation you keep telling everyone will be any year now. I want to get those postcards from Hong Kong!

Love, Hilda

(NOTE FROM HILDA: *It is a wonder that I have seen so many birthdays. How could I have been so dense as to write this letter to my father? I didn't have the brains of an eel after it's been in the soup. I suppose that he loved me in his own twisted way. It helped that I was still sufficiently brainwashed that I would believe his propaganda over a thinker of Mencken's caliber in a matter of historical fact.*)

I sat at the desk in my den and thought about a red-haired little girl who had played in this very room when she was happy and content. I had to admit that she was my favorite and always had been. Where had I gone wrong? How had her healthy radicalism become channeled in such an unproductive direction? There was more to it than the books. It was something in her. I eagerly anticipated our reunion.

On a Wednesday morning I boarded a luxury train; the power of the rocket engines is deliberately held down so that passengers may enjoy the scenery instead of merely rushing through. Hilda would be waiting for me in a French hamlet directly in line with my final destination. I took along a manuscript—work, always work—this diary, and, for relaxation, a mystery novel by an Englishman. What is it about the British that makes this genre uniquely their own?

Speaking of books, I noticed a rotund gentleman—very much the Goering type—reading a copy of my prewar novel, *Michael*. I congratulated him on his excellent taste and he recognized me immediately. As I was autographing his copy, he asked if I was doing any new novels. I explained that I found plays and movie scripts a more comfortable form in which to work and suggested he catch my filmed sequel to *The Wanderer* when it was released. The director was no less than Leni Riefenstahl, irony of ironies.

Other Party leaders may grouch about the lack of privacy, but I've never minded that my name is a household word. It makes of me a toastmaster much in demand. The most requested lecture topic remains my best film, *Kolberg*, my answer to *Gone with the Wind*.

I contemplated the numerous ways in which my wife's social calendar would keep her occupied in my absence. Since the children have grown up and left home, she seems more active than before. It's amazing the number of things she can find to do in a day. I would have liked to attend the Richard Strauss concert, but duty calls.

The food on the train was quite good. The wine was only adequate, however. I had high hopes that the French hamlet live up to its reputation for prime vintages.

The porter looked Jewish and probably is. There are people of Jewish ancestry living in Europe. We couldn't get them all. It doesn't matter, so long as the practicing Jew is forever removed. God, we made the blood flow to cleanse this soil. Of course I'm speaking figuratively. But what could one *do* with Jews, Gypsies, partisans of all kinds, homosexuals, the feebleminded, race mixers, and all the rest? Sometimes when I'm at a dull party, I imagine various conceited people wearing the patches we used on internees: brown triangles for wine-guzzling Gypsies, pink triangles for prancing queers (the SA fags were the worst), and yellow stars for the supreme enemy, the children of Abraham. Next December I'll use the designs for Christmas ornaments.

We reached the station at dusk and my daughter was there. She is such a lovely child, except that she is no child any longer! I can see why she has so many admirers. Too many. I have spoken to her about this. She had the temerity to throw my own affairs back in my teeth. If it had been anyone other than Hilda, I would not have given in to the sensitive side of my nature.

Hedonism is bad enough, but her political activities (if they deserve such a label) are becoming dangerous. When an ambitious young assistant charged her with actual treason, and couldn't back up his ludicrous charge, I had him sent away for a long vacation. If I thought for a minute she was being pulled into the noxious underground, I would take steps. She has gone to the brink, but not taken the plunge.

(*NOTE FROM HILDA: I was already a member of the underground. Only a highly professional organization could keep this a secret from the Nazi state. Any doubts I'd had about its efficacy were soon dispelled.*)

Her folly has not made her any the less attractive. She has the classic features. On her thirtieth birthday I once again brought up the subject of why she had never married. I wouldn't mind her having lovers if there was a husband in the picture. That she may never reproduce vexes me greatly. As always her deep-throated laugh mocks my concern.

A few seconds after I disembarked she was pulling at my sleeve and rushing me to a cab. I had never seen her looking so agitated. We virtually ran through the lobby of the hotel, and I felt as though I were under some kind of house arrest as she bustled me up to my room and bolted the door behind us.

It was the most old-fashioned room I'd occupied in years, with quaint round mirrors and overstuffed furniture. The setting was inappropriate for the virulent exchange that began with: "Father, I have terrible news." The melodramatic derring-do was a trifle annoying, and she was gasping her words while she was out of breath. Leave intrigues to the young, I always say . . . suddenly remembering in that case my daughter qualified for numerous adventures. If only she would leave me out of it!

"Darling," I said, "I am worn out from my trip and in want of a bath. Surely your message can wait until I've changed. Over dinner we may—"

"No," she announced sternly. "It can't wait."

"Very well," I said, recognizing that my ploy had failed miserably and surrendering to her—shall we say—blitzkrieg. "Tell me," I said as I sat in a chair.

"You must not go to Burgundy," she began, and then paused as though anticipating an outburst from me. I am a master at that game. I told her to get on with it.

"Father, you may think me mad, but I must tell you!" *A chip off the old block,* I thought. I nodded assent, if only to get it over. She was pacing as she spoke, and I thought it unfortunate that Hitler could not be with us to evaluate her performance. "First of all, the German Freedom League has learned something that could have dire consequences for the future of our country." It sounded like one of my press releases. "Think whatever you will of the league, but facts are facts. We have uncovered the most diabolical secret."

"Which is?" I prompted her, expecting something anticlimatic.

"I am sure that you have not the slightest inkling of this, but during the war millions of Jews were put to death in horrible ways. What we thought were concentration camps suffering from typhus infections and lacking supplies were in reality death camps at which was carried out a systematic program of *genocide.*" I could not believe that she had used Raphael Lemkin's smear word. The United

Nations effort was long defunct, but we were saddled with the rhetorical baggage to this day.

The stunned expression on my face was no act. Hilda interpreted it as befitted her love for me—she took it, if you will, at face value.

"I can see that you're shocked," she said. "Even though you staged those public demonstrations against the Jews and made blood-curdling threats, I realize you meant to force the Party's emigration policy through. I detest that policy, but it wasn't murder."

"Dear," I said, keeping my voice as calm as possible, "have you been reading philo-Semitic tracts? What you are telling me is nothing more than thoroughly discredited Allied propaganda. We shot Jewish partisans, but there's no evidence of systematic—"

"There is now," she said, and I believe that my jaw dropped at the revelation. She went on, oblivious to my horror: "The records that were kept for those camps are forgeries. They must have thought the real records would all be destroyed by the atomic bombs, but a separate set of documents, detailing the genocide, has been uncovered by the league."

What a damnably stupid German thing to do. To keep multiple copies of *everything*. This matter would have to be suppressed. The only positive side to this turn of events was that I could be certain Hilda was not in the underground. She would never bring the matter to my attention.

(NOTE FROM HILDA: *We were both pawns in someone else's game, but he'd never be able to face that.*)

Hope springs eternal, and I took a stab at shifting her attention from the latest obsession. "Hilda, you persist in using the term *genocide*. Aren't you aware that Lemkin, the man who originated the word, meant it to describe any loss of national or ethnic identity as the result of a planned move? By that standard, genocide goes on in the United States on an almost daily basis, to the extent that people lose their cultural identity in the so-called melting pot. Likewise, anyone we allow to be Germanized, because we find them racially acceptable, is a victim of genocide if he loses his small, ethnic identification."

"Father, you always do this to me. You change the subject, or you go off on a tangent. I don't care about the word. I'm talking about mass murder; the loss of identity through the loss of life, as a planned move."

"Oh." This definitely meant trouble. It was as if my daughter disappeared from the room at that second. I could see her, but she had become indistinct, unreal. A far more solid form came between us, the image of the man who had been my life. It was as if the ghost of Adolf Hitler stood before me then, in our common distress, in our common deed. I could hear his voice and remember my promise to him. Oh, God, was it to be Hilda who would provide the test? I really had not the least desire to see her eliminated. I liked her. There must be some alternative.

As she continued, I realized she was on at least one wrong track, and I eagerly grasped at that. She had gotten the idea that Field Marshal Erwin Rommel was persuaded to take his own life because he had come across evidence of the mass murders and intended to go public. It remains a state secret that the hero of the North African campaigns was implicated in the assassination attempt against the Fuehrer in the army bomb plot. After the fates decreed that the Leader of the Fatherland would survive the bombing of his head-quarters at Wolfsschanze, we had our work cut out for us—and something to take our minds off the Allied invasion. Rommel was a reasonable man. He cared about his family. He took his poison like a good boy. The Rommel problem had absolutely nothing to do with the murder of Jews. Without going into details, I swore on our family honor that I knew Rommel's death to be in no way connected to the issue Hilda had raised. This gave her pause. I think she believed me.

(NOTE FROM HILDA: *I did. But not until reading these pages have I known the truth about Rommel. That he would join in a plot to kill Hitler only raises him in my estimation.*)

What I said next was not entirely in keeping with my feigned ignorance, and if she had been less upset she might have noticed the implications of my question: "Hilda, how many people have you informed?"

She answered without hesitation. "Only members of the league, and now you."

I heaved a sigh of relief and asked, "Don't you think it would be a good idea to keep this extreme theory to yourself?"

"It's no theory. It's a fact. And I have no intention of taking out an advertisement. It would make me a target for those lunatics in the SS."

So that was the Burgundy connection! I still didn't see why I should be in any danger during my trip. Even if I were innocent of the truth—which every relevant SS official knew to be absurd, since I was an architect of our policy—my sheer prominence would keep me safe from harm in Burgundy.

Testing the hypothesis, I asked Hilda what this fancy of hers had to do with my visit. "Only everything," she answered.

"Are you afraid that they will suspect I've learned of this so-called secret, which is nothing more than patent nonsense to begin with?"

She surprised me by answering, "No." There was an executioner's silence.

"What then?" I asked.

"It is not a crime of the past that endangers you," came the sound of her voice in portentous tones, "but a crime of the future."

"You should have been the poet of the family."

"If you go to Burgundy, you risk your life. They are planning an action so stupendous that it will make World War II and the concentration camps, on both the Allied and Axis sides, seem like nothing but a prelude. The Reich itself will be attacked, and you will be one of the first victims!"

Never have I felt more acutely the pain of a father for his offspring. I could not help but conclude that my youngest daughter's mind had only a tenuous connection to reality. Her reactionary politics must be to blame. On the other hand, I regarded Hilda with genuine affection. She seemed concerned for my welfare in a manner that I supposed would not apply to a stranger. The decadent creed she had embraced had not led to disaffection from her father.

I thought back to the grand old days of intrigue within the Party and the period in the war years when I referred most often to that wise advice of Machiavelli: "Cruelties should be committed all at once, as in that way each separate one is less felt, and gives less offense." We had come perilously close to *Götterdammerung* then, but in the end our policy proved sound. I was beyond all that. The

135

state was secure, Europe was secure . . . and the only conceivable threat to my safety would come from foreign sources. Yet here was Hilda, her face a mixture of concern and anger and—perhaps love? She was telling me to beware the Burgundians. I was no cheerleader in their camp, but the idea that they were plotting against the Reich itself was too fantastic to credit.

They had invited me to one of the conferences to decide the formation of the new nation. Those were hectic times in the postwar period. As gauleiter of Berlin (one of the Fuehrer's few appointments of a district leader with which I fully concurred), I had been primarily concerned with Speer's work to build New Berlin. The film industry was flowering under my personal supervision, I was busy writing my memoirs, and I was involved heavily with diplomatic projects. I hadn't really given Burgundy much thought. I knew that it had been a country in medieval times, and I had read a little about the Duchy of Burgundy. The country had traded in grain, wines, and finished wool.

They announced at the conference that the historical Burgundy would be restored, encompassing the area to the south of Champagne, east of Burbonais, and north and west of Savoy. There was some debate on whether or not to restore the original place-names or else borrow from Wagner to create a series of new ones. In the end, the latter camp won out. The capital was named Tarnhelm, after the magic helmet in the *Nibelungenlied* that could change the wearer into a variety of shapes.

Hitler did not officially single out any of the departments that made up the SS: Waffen, Death's Head, or the General SS. We in his entourage realized, however, that the gift was to those members of the inner circle who had been most intimately involved with both the ideological and practical side of the exterminations; which meant that, in practical fact, Burgundy was a country for the Death's Head SS, or Himmler's black order. The true believers! Given the Reich's policy of secrecy, there was no need to blatantly advertise the reasons for the gift. Himmler, as Reichsfuehrer of the SS and Hitler's adviser on racial matters, was naturally instrumental in this transfer of power to the new nation. His rival, Rosenberg, met his death . . . and this set a precedent for future fun and games. As far back as the nuclear destruction of the concentration camps, I believe that

Himmler had been eliminating opposition within his own organization; although I haven't figured out how he managed to have his chosen elite safely away when the bombs dropped, and his least favorite SS men on duty.

The officials who would oversee the creation of Burgundy were carefully selected. Their mission was to make certain that Burgundy became a unique nation in all of Europe, devoted to certain chivalric values of the past, and the formation of pure Aryan specimens. It was nothing more than the logical extension of our propaganda, the secularizing of the myths and legends with which we kept the people fed during the dark days of lost hope. The final result was a picturesque fairy tale kingdom that made its money almost entirely out of the tourist trade. It takes a lot of money to run socialism. America boasts of its amusement parks, but it has nothing to match this.

(My first contact with the atmosphere of unreality pervading the make-believe country was when a minor official approached me with a request that I use my ministry to hoist the U.S.A. on its own petard. The scheme was that since Americans are committed to the sanctity of property rights, I should take steps to register the Swastika as a trademark. Then Burgundy and the Reich would split the loot. Wonderful. It would take another world war to collect the first pfennig. Still, there was a nutty appeal to the idea. The little man was half British, and that probably explains it.)

Hilda interrupted my reverie by asking in a voice that bordered on presumption, "What are you going to do?"

"Unless you make sense, I will continue on my journey to Tarnhelm and see Helmuth." He was living at the headquarters of the SS leaders, territory that was closed off to outsiders, even during the tourist season. Yet it was by no means unusual for occasional visitors from New Berlin to be invited there. My daughter's melodramatics had not yet given cause to worry. All I could think of was how I'd like to get my hands around the throat of whoever put these idiotic notions into her pretty head.

She was visibly distressed, but in control. She tossed her hair back and said, "I am not sure that the proof I have to offer will be sufficient to convince you."

"Aren't you getting ahead of yourself?" I asked. "You haven't made a concrete accusation about this plot. Drop the pose. Tell me what you think constitutes the danger."

"They think you're a traitor," she said.

"What?" I was astounded to hear such words from anyone for any reason. "To Germany?"

"No," she answered. "To the true Nazi ideal."

I laughed. "That's the craziest thing I've ever heard. I'm one of the key—"

"You don't understand," she interrupted. "I'm talking about the religion."

"Oh, Hilda, is that all? You and your group have stumbled upon some threatening comments from occultists, I take it."

Now it was her turn to be surprised. She sat upon the bed. "Yes," she answered. "But then you know?"

"Not the specifics. They change their game every few months. Who has time to keep up? Let me tell you something. The leaders of the SS have always had ties to an occult group called the Thule Society, but there is nothing surprising about that. It is a purely academic exercise in playing with the occult, dear girl, the same as the British equivalent—the Golden Dawn. Certainly you are aware that many prominent Englishmen belonged to that club!

"These people are harmless eccentrics. Our movement made use of the type without stepping on pet beliefs. It's the same as dealing with any religious person whom you want on your side. If you receive cooperation, it won't be through insulting his spiritual convictions."

"What about the messages we intercepted?" she went on. "The threatening tone, the almost deranged—"

"It's how they entertain themselves!" I insisted. "Listen, you're familiar with Hörbiger, aren't you?" She nodded. "Burgundians believe that stuff, even after the launching of von Braun's satellite, which in no way disturbed the eternal ice, as that old fool predicted! His followers don't care about facts. They believe the moon in our sky is the fourth moon this planet has had, that it is made of ice like the other three, that all of the cosmos is an eternal struggle between fire and ice. To tell you the truth, our Fuehrer toyed with those ideas in the old days. The Burgundians no more want to give up their sacred ideas merely because modern science has exploded them than fundamentalist Baptists in America want to listen to Darwin."

"I know," she said. "You are acting as though they aren't dangerous."

"They're an irritation, but that's all."

"Soon Helmuth will be accepted into the inner circle."

"Why not? He's been working for that ever since he was a teenager."

"But the inner circle," she repeated with added emphasis.

"So he'll be a Hitler Youth for the rest of his life. He'll never grow up."

"You don't understand."

"I'm tired of this conversation," I told her bluntly. "Do you remember several years ago when your brother went on that pilgrimage to Lower Saxony to one of Himmler's shrines? You were terribly upset, but you didn't have a shred of reason why he shouldn't have gone. You had nightmares. Your mother and I wondered if it was because as a little girl you were frightened by Wagner."

"Now I have reasons."

"Mysterious, threatening messages! The Thule Society! It should be taken with a grain of salt. I saw Adolf Hitler once listen to a harangue from an especially unrealistic believer in the Nordic cult, bow solemnly when the man was finished, enter his private office—where I accompanied him—and break out in laughter that would wake the dead. He didn't want to offend the fellow. The man was a good Nazi, at least."

My daughter was fishing around in her purse as I told her these things. She passed me a piece of paper when I was finished. I unfolded it and read:

JOSEPH GOEBBELS MUST ARRIVE ON SCHEDULE.
THE RITUAL CANNOT BE RESCHEDULED.
DEATH TO TRAITORS IN HIGH PLACES.

"What is this?" I asked. I was becoming angry.

"A member of the Freedom League intercepted a message from Burgundy to someone in New Berlin. It was coded, but we were able to break it."

"To whom was the message addressed?"

"Heinrich Himmler."

Suddenly I felt very, very cold. I had never trusted *der treue*

Heinrich. Admittedly, I didn't trust anything that came from the German Freedom League, with an oxymoron for a title. Nevertheless something in me was clawing at the pit of my stomach, telling me that maybe, just maybe, there was danger. Crazy as Himmler had been during the war years, he had become worse in peacetime. At least he was competent regarding his industrial empire.

"How do I know that this message is genuine?" I asked.

"You don't" she answered. "It was a risk bringing you these, if that helps you to believe."

"I was going to ask why the Burgundians haven't stopped you."

"They don't know the league broke their code; and the league doesn't know I'm here either. They hate you as much as Himmler."

I felt the blood rush to my face, and I jumped to my feet so abruptly that it put an insupportable strain on my club foot. I had to grab for a nearby lamp to keep from stumbling. "Why," I virtually hissed, "do you belong to that despicable bunch of bums and poseurs?"

Standing also, and grabbing her purse, Hilda fended off my ire. "Father, I am leaving. You may do with this information as you wish. I will offer one last suggestion. Why don't you take another comfortable passenger train back to New Berlin, and call Tarnhelm to say that you will be one day late? See what their reaction is. You didn't manage to attend my college graduation and I'm none the worse for it. Would it matter so much to my brother were you to help him celebrate after the ceremony?"

She turned to go. "Wait," I said. "I'm sorry I spoke so harshly. You mean well, but you've been misled by this damnable league. I see now that we in the government have been too lenient with all of you. I'll call for an investigation at the first opportunity."

Her laughter was not the response I had intended. There was no fear in it. "So I'm to feel guilty over betraying my friends to you. Father, the league is the least of your problems."

"Censorship is the answer. It always worked before, and it—"

"You're losing your touch." She reached into her purse again, and I began seeing that black bag as a Pandora's box. Out came a folded booklet that I recognized. The sight of it made me want to throw up. "You've been trying to ban this play all over the Reich. Thousands of copies are available on the black market, in at least a dozen languages. Every time you destroy one, two more take its place. I was a child on your knee when you told me the story of the Hydra."

Shoving the cursed pages into my hands, she stormed out the door. I watched the closed door for several minutes, not moving, not really thinking. Then I remembered to take my bath. As I luxuriated in the hot water, I watched the crumpled wad of paper that had been the play lying beside the tub, surrounded by steam as if a boulder in the pit of hell. I reflected that a parent can't be too careful about the fairy tales he reads to his children.

CHAPTER THIRTEEN

I am a horse for single harness, not cut out for tandem or team work. I have never belonged wholeheartedly to country or state, to my circle of friends, or even to my own family. These ties have always been accompanied by a vague aloofness, and the wish to withdraw into myself increases with the years.

—Albert Einstein,
Living Philosophies

Last Act, Scene Two, from
Looking for the Jews
by
Anonymous

Forbidden for display or presentation in the Greater Reich, or its territories. English-language version by Hilda Goebbels; puns and slang adapted to colloquial American usage.

SCENE: the Reich Chancellery

The curtain rises on ADOLF HITLER *pacing in his office. He is highly agitated and keeps referring to documents on his desk. This desk is twice normal size and he has the appearance of a child in his father's study as he reaches across for papers. Sitting to the rear center is* MARTIN BORMANN, *busily taking notes. Three of Hitler's aides enter from stage left. They are* DR. JOSEPH GOEBBELS, JULIUS STREICHER, *and* RUDOLF HESS.

STREICHER: *Mein Führer,* now that we've grabbed Germany, we are ready to implement some final solutions, you bet.

GOEBBELS: We'd like to begin with Berlin.

HESS: Why is Bormann staring at me? He gives me the creeps.

142

HITLER: You haven't saluted yet, and you have the creepiest eyebrows of anyone in the room.

(Everyone, including Bormann, who jumps to his feet, gives the Nazi salute)

HESS *(Grumbling):* Speer never salutes, or hardly ever.

HITLER *(Shrieking at the top of his voice):* He's an artist, an ahrrrrr-teeeeeeest, the same as myself! He's not to be judged by the philistine standards of the street rabble.

GOEBBELS: Very interesting that you should employ that particular biblical reference when one considers that—

HITLER: Shut up!

GOEBBELS: *Jawohl.*

(Streicher begins laughing at Goebbels, but a dirty look from Hitler puts an end to that)

HITLER: When I speak of street rabble, I'm talking about you *(He points to Streicher, who stands at attention)*; and you *(He turns around to address Bormann, who continues taking notes)*; but I'm not referring to the good doctor, who is my intellectual. *(Goebbels bows in appreciation)* But enough small talk.

HESS: What about me? You're always forgetting me.

HITLER: You're rabble, too.

HESS: Thank you, oh, thank you.

HITLER: What's the status report on rooting out "the Chosen People"?

GOEBBELS: Chosen for what?

HITLER: Exactly.

STREICHER: Are you talking about the Jews, boss?

HITLER: Yeah, dose guys.

GOEBBELS: The Hebrews are an insidious lot, to be sure. But they won't hide for long. We will put a crown of thorns on their

143

heads, but it will be fashioned from barbed wire. They have infested Berlin long enough, like rats.

HESS: I'll be rat back!

(Hess begins to exit)

HITLER: Halt! Where are you going? I haven't given you leave.

HESS: *Mein Führer,* we have a surprise for you.

(Goebbels and Streicher nod; Bormann takes notes)

HITLER: All right, then, but hurry back.

(Hess exits stage right)

BORMANN *(Half muttering):* He's probably going to defecate.

HITLER: What's that? What's that? I haven't given him authorization to take such steps on his own. There could be international repercussions if Hess takes it on himself to—

GOEBBELS: He's not going to leave the building, *mein Führer.* We've been hoping you would clarify our policy about detecting the Jews; and the surprise has to do with that. Although I always know 'em when I see 'em, less expert National Socialists could do with some guidelines.

HITLER: I've been working on that for weeks, Doc. First, we gotta introduce the public, bless their pointy little heads, to arithmetical reasoning.

STREICHER: Say what?

HITLER: The moral premise of our movement, you dummy cop! We National Socialists believe in what's good for the nation, right?

EVERYONE *(Including Hess from off stage):* Right!

STREICHER: You've made Germany feel good about itself again.

HITLER: And that means the greatest good for the greatest number within the nation, right?

EVERYONE: Right!

HITLER: And that means it is all right to sacrifice a minority for the good of the majority, right?

EVERYONE: You said it!

GOEBBELS: It's kosher. *(Withering in dirty looks from the rest)* Sorry about that, chief.

HITLER: If we accept the premise that the good of the majority takes precedence, then the next step is to select a proper minority to sacrifice. Here the Jew is perfect for the role.

GOEBBELS: The people are getting the drift, but guidelines would still be a real help.

HITLER: Very well. It is crucially important to recognize that there is no such thing as the individual Jew. When I was fourteen years old, I met my first Jew at the *Realschule,* a fellow schoolmate. I was only mildly suspicious of him at first, but I felt a disagreeable sensation that could not be ignored. It was not until I was a young man, bumming around Vienna, that I understood the Jew at last.

(The others exchange glances; they have heard it all before)

HITLER: I was already indignant at the Viennese press for its weak-kneed cosmopolitanism when I encountered the germ that had so infected the city that the press could be nothing other than rotten. The boy in Linz had looked nothing like this: a dark creature in a long caftan, with a long nose and black curls, and giving off a most peculiar odor. Then and there I knew the enemy I would fight forevermore.

GOEBBELS: They are not always so obliging as to appear in costume.

HITLER: That is unimportant. The creature I saw was but one tentacle on the octopus. The Jew has no individual ego. He is only part of a whole. He is the Displaced Person of the Universe. He has no soul. He's a real meanie, I'm telling you.

GOEBBELS: But isn't that the virtue we encourage in our own *Völk,* to submit the ego to the greater whole, the "I" to the "thou"? Oops. *(Goebbels realizes that he's gone too far)*

145

HITLER *(Jumping up and down):* Doesn't count! Doesn't count! Besides, I said the Jew has no ego *to* submit. The German has an ego that we have to beat out of him.

GOEBBELS: But some of the trouble I've had has been with Jewish individualists. Oops. *(Goebbels ducks as Hitler throws papers)*

HITLER *(Jumping up and down)*: There is no Jewish individual! He doesn't exist!

GOEBBELS: May I ask a hypothetical question? It's purely hypothetical. Would the Jew be tolerable if he had his own land? Zionism is a kind of *Völk* conception, and I'm wondering—in terms of an intellectual problem—if the Jews could be lived with if they were segregated on their own soil instead of in ghettos. I bring this up as an academic . . . uh . . . what I mean to say is . . .

(There is dead silence for several beats as Hitler stares at Goebbels)

HITLER: What's up your fundament, Doc? Don't you like your job? You've got good pay, plenty of perks. You are one of the most ardent anti-Semites I know, so why provoke me with these decadent musings?

GOEBBELS: The problem is purely technical, *mein Führer.* We need guidelines to find the Jews, and then we'll kill 'em.

(Hess enters stage right, waving a copy of Julius Streicher's newspaper, Der Stürmer, *and followed by a tall, young blond man)*

HESS: Oh, savior of Germany, we received thousands of applications for an advertisement we ran—

STREICHER: It was my idea!

HESS: —to find an official Heroic Hebrew Hunter. Here stands the winner before you, a real *Mensch* named Olaf Mann.

MANN *(Saluting Hitler):* Seig Heil.

STREICHER: He awaits your command.

HITLER: Get out there and round up those children of Abraham, *mach schnell!* Never forget that they can't be baptized out of their natural condition, which is to be born three ways.

MANN: Three ways?

HITLER: Religiously, ethnically, and *(Shouts)* racially.

MANN: Does every Jew have these characteristics?

STREICHER: He wants to avoid error, *mein Führer.* He couldn't find anyone who looks like the cartoons I publish in my paper.

HITLER *(Ignoring Streicher):* Yes, they have all three, especially the ones who deny it. You must be a fanatic to seek them out and penetrate any disguise. Have you any experience for the job?

MANN *(Pulling out a long list that falls to the floor):* On the first day of the contest, I went to a synagogue. It was easy to find one by following a trail of burning books and broken glass.

BORMANN *(From the back):* Further proof that the Jew is sloppy and slovenly.

GOEBBELS: You can take the ghetto out of the Jew, but you can't make him a German.

HITLER: Silence! *(There is silence)* Speak! *(They all begin to chatter)* No, no, no, no, no, no, no, no, no . . . or, *Nein!* Only Mann is to speak. The rest of you shut up!

(From off stage a VOICE *begins declaiming):* "There must be a chemistry of the immaterial, there must be combinations of the insubstantial, out of which sprang the material—"

HITLER: Not Thomas Mann!

GOEBBELS: We destroy the words, but they echo in the vaulted chambers of our despair.

BORMANN: Please don't repeat that.

HITLER *(Testily):* Is everybody finished? I will hear Olaf.

MANN: So I entered the synagogue, and some were dressed in funny costumes, and some were dressed as Germans. I asked,

"Are there any Jews in here?" The rabbi said, "Maybe." So I asked how I could tell, and the rabbi said I should find out if they live by the Talmud, because being Jewish means being religious. So I started to take down the names of everyone in the synagogue and a young man dressed in the same street clothes I was wearing—

HESS: How did you both fit in one suit? *(Laughs idiotically)*

MANN *(Ignoring the interruption):* —came over and said not to include him because he didn't believe in God. "Being Jewish is cultural," he said. He was there for the music.

HITLER: Don't be deceived. The Jews are a race.

MANN: How do I find the Jews when they're not in costume?

HITLER: By descent, and the first wisecrack will lead straight to a concentration camp. A single grandparent marks a person with the star of David. *(He calls off stage)* Attention! Play some Wagner. I need inspiration.

(The music begins)

STREICHER: Didn't Richard Wagner have a Jewish relation somewhere?

(The music stops)

HITLER: Doesn't count, doesn't count! He has special dispensation. He's the soul of Germany. He's dead. And most important, he was anti-Semitic.

STREICHER: I meant to say: wasn't Wagner a genius?

MANN: One drop of Jewish blood makes a Jew, then?

HITLER: By Odin, you've got it, I think you've really got it . . .

STREICHER: One drop, unless he's the leader of the Aryans.

HITLER: What did you say?

STREICHER *(Nervously):* Unless he can escape the leader of the Aryans.

MANN: Is a Jew always swarthy?

HITLER: Not always.

MANN: Does he always have a long nose?

HITLER: No.

MANN: Does he always have shifty eyes?

HITLER: No.

MANN: The same color hair?

HITLER: No.

MANN: The same bone structure?

HITLER: No.

MANN: *Then how do I tell?*

HESS: He's good at making money.

MANN: Are all rich people Jews?

HITLER: Certainly not. We socialists have many millionaire friends who are true-blue Aryans.

(Goebbels, Hess, Streicher, and Bormann rise, begin to chant, and do a choreographed dance step)

EVERYONE: Give us K and R and U and P and P. Waddaya got? Krupp. Three cheers for Krupp! Give us F and A and R and B and E and N. Waddaya got? Farben. Three cheers for Farben!

GOEBBELS: And let's not forget our friends on Wall Street. Oops.

(Silence)

HITLER: You are too enlightened, Herr Doktor Goebbels. *(Hitler walks over and puts his arm around Goebbels)* But I love this guy.

MANN: Excuse me, *mein Führer,* but you answered all my questions in the negative. If the Jews are a race, how am I to find them?

HITLER: If? Did you say if?

149

MANN: I do not mean to give offense, but I need a method by which to find the Jewish race.

HITLER: It's very simple. You have to trust to the blood. Over a period of many years, I have developed an invaluable method. I *sense* the presence of Jews. Once I was eating in a restaurant that served good, honest German food; and yet, I felt a strange disquiet.

STREICHER: Quiet! He wants us to be quiet! *(No one pays him any attention)*

HITLER: The waitress was a blond girl with a voluptuous figure and soft, rounded features, and full, pouting lips—

GOEBBELS: Yeah, yeah.

HITLER: —but despite the gorgeous appearance of Aryan womanhood, my sixth sense tingled at her approach. Even the wallpaper bothered me. It was necessary to use the power of my will!

BORMANN: Oy vey.

HITLER *(Addressing the back of the room)*: What was that?

BORMANN: OK, as they say in America.

HITLER: I stared at that wallpaper, waiting, waiting, waiting . . .

GOEBBELS: Waiting for the Jews! That would be a good title for a play.

HITLER: I'm staring at the wallpaper, see, and I realized what was pissing me off. The design was a variation on the Star of David! I'd thought they were meaningless triangles at first.

GOEBBELS: Were there eyes in them?

HITLER: You're cruisin' for a bruisin', Doc. After I penetrated the secret of the wallpaper, I invaded the kitchen and found the waitress eating a bowl of matzoh ball soup.

(Everyone gasps)

STREICHER: What a man!

150

MANN: How can I, a mere German, match your powers?

GOEBBELS: You could start by being born Austrian. Oops.

HITLER *(Ignoring Goebbels):* You must develop your faculties. You must act without thinking. When your blood tingles, you will be in the presence of the enemy, the corrupter of Aryan womanhood, the defiler of Aryan children.

MANN: What are the signs?

HITLER: You will feel that something unclean is near, a hater of the Natural Man. All that is honest in you will be repelled by the scheming mentality of the profiteer on human misery. When everything in you cries out that you are in the presence of Evil, it is then that you must do your duty and strike down the vermin.

MANN: I obey. *(So saying, Olaf Mann pulls out a nine-millimeter pistol and shoots Adolf Hitler dead. The others are aghast. Bormann throws down his notepad and joins the others at front center)*

GOEBBELS *(Shouting):* He has stopped the heart of Germany. Strike him down! Strike him down! *(Streicher raises a fist against Mann)*

MANN *(Leveling his gun on the others):* I was only following orders. I will now look for more Jews, and I will do my duty. Are any of you Jewish? *(Streicher lowers his fist)*

(Goebbels, Bormann, Streicher, and Hess are as rigid as statues. Silence. Mann exits, stage anywhere)
CURTAIN

CHAPTER FOURTEEN

I have seen the man of the future; he is cruel; I am frightened by him.

—Adolf Hitler to Hermann Rauschning,
Table Talk

THE DIARY OF DR. GOEBBELS

I felt better after the bath, and still better after destroying the copy of *Looking for the Jews* page by insidious page. My anger against Hilda was so intense that it burned itself out. The rational part of my mind had set up a persistent whispering: So what if your daughter is seriously disturbed, if there is the slightest possibility of danger to you? Survival must be paramount at all times. There were grounds for an investigation of more than just the German Freedom League.

A half hour later I was back at the railroad station, boarding an even slower passenger train back to New Berlin. I love this sort of travel. The rocket engines were held down to their minimum output. The straining hum they made only accentuated the fact of the violent power at our command. Trains are the most human form of mass transportation.

With my state of mind in such turmoil I could not do any serious work. I decided to relax and resumed reading the English mystery novel. I had narrowed it down to three suspects, members of the aristocracy, naturally—all highly offensive people. The servant I had ruled out as much too obvious. As is typical of the form, a few key sentences give up the solution if you know what they are. I had just passed over what I took to be such a phrase and returned to it. Looking up from my book to contemplate the puzzle, I noticed that the woman sitting across from me was also reading a book, a French title that seemed vaguely familiar: *Le Théosophisme, histoire d'une pseudo-religion* by René Guénon.

Returning to the mystery, I suddenly noticed that the train was slowing down. There was no reason for it, as we were far from the next stop. Glancing out the window, I saw nothing but wooded landscape under a starry night sky. A tall man up the aisle was addressing the porter. His rather lengthy monologue boiled down to an elementary question: Why was there a delay? The poor official was shaking his head in bewilderment and indicated that he would move forward to make inquiries. That's when I noticed the gas.

It was yellow. It was seeping in from the air conditioning system. Like everyone else, I started to rise in hope of finding a means of egress. Already I was coughing. As I turned to the window, with the idea of releasing the emergency lock, I slipped down into the cushions. I seemed to be falling as consciousness fled. The last thing I remember was seriously regretting that I had not sampled a glass of wine from that hamlet.

I must have dreamed. I was standing alone in the middle of a great lake, frozen over in the dead of winter. I was not dressed for the weather but had on only my Party uniform. As I looked down at the icy expanse at my feet, I noticed that my boots were freshly shined, the luster already becoming covered by flakes of snow.

A drumming comes from within the black shroud of night and it has a fearful rhythm. I heard the sound of hoofbeats echoing hollowly on the ice and saw emerging from the darkness a small army on horseback. I recognized them. They were the Teutonic Knights. The dark armor, the stern faces, the great, black horses, the bright lances and swords and shields—they could be nothing else.

They did not appear to be friendly. I started walking away from them. The sound of their approach was a thunder pounding at my brain. I cursed my lameness, cursed my inability to fly, suddenly found myself suspended in the air, and then I had fallen on the ice, skinning my knees. Struggling to turn over, I heard a blood-curdling yell and they were all around me. There was a whooshing of blades in the still, icy air. I was screaming. Then I was trying to reason with them.

"I helped Germany win the war. . . . I believe in the Aryan race. . . . I helped destroy the Jews. . . . " But it was to no avail. They were killing me. The swords plunged in deeply.

I awakened aboard a small jet flying in the early dawn. For a moment I thought I was tied to my seat. When I glanced to see what kind of cords bound my arms, I saw that I was mistaken. The feeling of constriction I attributed to the effects of the gas. Painfully I lifted a hand . . . then with increased anguish I raised my head, noticing that the compartment was empty except for me. The door to the cockpit was closed.

The most difficult task that confronted me next was turning my head to the left so that I could have a better view of our location. A dozen tiny needles pricked at the muscles in my neck, but I succeeded. I was placed near the wing and could see a good portion of the countryside unfolding like a map beneath it. We were over a run-down railroad station. One last bit of track snaked on beyond it for about half a mile—we seemed to be flying parallel to it—when it suddenly stopped, blocked off by a tremendous oak tree, the size of which was noticeable from even a great height.

I knew where we were immediately. We had just flown over the eastern border of Burgundy.

Attempting to relax my muscles, I leaned back, very slowly, into the seat, but met with little success. I'd never been so sore in all my life. I was terribly thirsty. Assuming that I'd have a serious dizzy spell if I stood, I called out instead: "Steward!" No sooner was the word out of my mouth than a young, blond man in a spotless white jacket appeared. He passed me a small, fancy menu.

"What would you like?"

"An explanation."

"I'm afraid that is not on this menu. I'm sure you will find what you seek when we reach our destination. In the meantime, would you care to dine?"

"No," I said, relapsing into the depths of my seat, terribly tired again.

"Some coffee?" asked the persistent steward.

I assented to this. It was very good coffee and I was soon feeling better. Looking out the window again, I observed that we were over a lake. There was a long ship plying the clear, blue water—its brightly painted dragon's head glaring at the horizon. My son had written me about the Viking Club when he first took up residence in Burgundy. This had to be one of their outings.

Thirty minutes and two cups of coffee later, the intercom announced that we would be landing at Tarnhelm. From the air the view was excellent: several monasteries—now devoted to SS training camps—were situated near the village that housed the Russian serfs. Beyond that was another lake, and then came the imposing castle in which I knew I would find my son.

There was a narrow landing strip within the castle grounds, and the pilot was every bit the professional. We hadn't been down longer than five minutes when who should enter the plane but Helmuth! But something was wrong. He had blond hair and blue eyes. The only trouble was that my son did not have blond hair and blue eyes! Of course I knew that hair could be dyed, but somehow it appeared to be quite authentic. As for the eyes, I could think of no explanation but contact lenses. Helmuth had also lost weight and never appeared more muscular or healthy than he did now.

There I was, trapped within an enigma—angry, bewildered, unsettled. And yet my first words were "Helmuth, what's happened to you?"

"This is real blond hair," he said proudly. "The eye color is real as well. I regret that I am not of the true genotype, any more than you are. I was given a hormone treatment to change the color of my hair. A special radiation treatment took care of the eyes."

As he was saying this, he was helping me to my feet, as I was still groggy. "Why?" I asked him. He would say no more about it.

The sun hurt my eyes as we exited down the ramp from the plane. Two tall young men—also blond haired and blue eyed—joined my son and helped to usher me inside the castle. They were dressed in Bavarian hunting gear, with large knives strapped on at their waists. Their clothes had the smell of freshest leather.

We had entered from the courtyard of the inner bailey. The hall we traversed was covered in plush red carpet and was illuminated by torches burning in the walls; this cast a weird lighting effect over the numerous suits of armor standing there. I could not help but think of the medieval castles Speer drew for his children every Christmas.

It was a long trek before we reached a stone staircase that I was not happy about ascending. I was not completely recovered from the effects of the gas and wished we could pause. My club foot was giving me considerable difficulty. I did not want to show weakness to these men, and I had not forgotten that my sturdy son was right behind me. I took those steps without slowing down the pace.

We finally emerged on a floor that was awash in light from fluorescent tubes. A closed-circuit television console dominated the center of the room, with pictures of all the other floors of the castle, from the keep to the highest tower. There was also a portrait of Meister Eckhart. I hated everything I'd learned about this bald fanatic who thought himself a German Aleister Crowley. The only good he ever did was to introduce Rosenberg and Hess to Hitler. The evil, little eyes of the portrait regarded me with equal disdain, and added to the sordid effect was a third eye painted on his forehead.

"Wait here," Helmuth announced, and before I could make any protestations he and the other two had left the way we had come, with the door locked behind them. The room seemed to be a kind of museum for ornate Bavarian pipes and the most elaborate beer steins of Europe. Someone was living well.

I went over to a large picture window and surveyed my position from the new vantage point. Below was another courtyard. In one corner was what could be nothing else but an unused funeral pyre! Its height was staggering. There was nobody upon it. Along the wall that ran from the pyre to the other end of the compound were letters inscribed of a size easy to read even from such a distance. It was a familiar quotation: ANY DESCRIPTION OF ORGANIZATION, MISSION, AND STRUCTURE OF THE SS CANNOT BE UNDERSTOOD UNLESS ONE TRIES TO CONCEIVE IT INWARDLY WITH ONE'S BLOOD AND HEART. IT CANNOT BE EXPLAINED WHY WE CONTAIN SO MUCH STRENGTH THOUGH WE NUMBER SO FEW. Underneath the tirade in equally large letters was the name of its author: HEINRICH HIMMLER.

"A statement that you know well," came a low voice behind me, and I turned to face Kurt Kaufmann, the most important man in Burgundy. I had met him a few times socially in New Berlin.

Smiling in as engaging a manner as I could (under the circumstances), I said, "Kurt," employing the informal mode of address, "I haven't a clue why you have seemingly kidnapped me, but there will be hell to pay."

He bowed. "What you fail to appreciate, Herr Doktor Goebbels, is that I will receive that payment."

I studied his face—the bushy blond hair and beard, and of course the bright blue eyes. The monocle he wore over one of them seemed quite superfluous. I knew that he had 20/20 vision.

"I have no idea what you are talking about."

"You lack ideas, it is true," he answered. "Of facts you do not lack. We knew your daughter contacted you."

Even at the time this dialogue seemed overly melodramatic.

Nevertheless it was happening *to me*. At the mention of Hilda, I failed to mask my feelings. Kaufmann must have noticed an expression of consternation on my face. There are occasions I wish we could wear masks every day of our lives. This whole affair was turning into a hideous game that I feared I was losing.

I parried with: "My daughter's association with a degenerate aesthetic group is well known." There was no reason to mince words with him. "I was attempting to dissuade her from a suicidal course, but I resent your spying on a personal family matter that in no way concerns you."

The ploy failed miserably. "We bugged the room," he said softly.

"How dare you spy on *me,* you parasite. Have you any idea of the danger?"

"Yes," he said. "You don't."

I made to comment, but he raised a hand to silence me. "Do not continue. Soon you will have more answers than you desire. Now I suggest you follow me."

The room had many doors. We exited through one at the opposite end from my original point of entry. I was walking down another hall. This one, however, was lit by electricity. We entered a large room that didn't have a stick of furniture, but in which a number of young men (where were the women?) sat in a semicircle on rugs. They wore simple robes made of some coarse fabric. Their heads were shaved.

Kaufmann held a finger to his lips, but he needn't have bothered. I wasn't about to say anything in there. Not a muscle moved or eye flickered as we passed the boys. I noticed that they were entranced by a single apple that had been cut in half and set out before them. I had a hunch that this was not a cafeteria. As we reentered the hallway, Kaufmann anticipated my question. "They're initiates recently returned from India," he volunteered.

"Did Helmuth do this? He didn't answer letters from home for several months."

"I can't tell you that."

"Can you tell me what they are doing, or is that a state secret, too?"

His smile was unfriendly. "It won't hurt to tell you that. They are contemplating Vril power."

"Thanks for clearing it up, Kurt."

We returned to civilization-as-I-know-it and entered an elevator.

157

The contrast between modern technology and Burgundian simplicity was becoming more jarring all the time. Like most Germans who had visited the country, I had only experienced it as a tourist. The reports I had received on their training operations were not as detailed as I would have liked but certainly gave no hint of dire conspiracy against the Fatherland. The thought was too fantastic to credit. Even now I hoped for a denouement more in keeping with the known facts. Could the entire thing be an elaborate practical joke? Who would run the risk of such folly?

The elevator doors opened and we were looking out onto the battlements of the castle. Following Kaufmann onto the walk, I noticed that the view was utterly magnificent. To the left I saw imported Russian serfs working in the fields; to the right I saw young Burgundians doing calisthenics in the warm morning air. At last there were some girls, but there was another item that gave me pause. I was used to observing many blond heads in the SS. Yet suddenly there was nothing but that predictable homogeneity. Something was going on in Burgundy.

We observed the young bodies gyrating and perspiring in the bright sunlight. Beyond them, a group of young men were outfitted in chain mail shirts and helmets. They were having at one another with the most intensive swordplay I had ever witnessed.

"Isn't that a bit dangerous?" I asked Kaufmann, gesturing at the fencing.

"What do you mean?" he replied, as one of the men ran his sword through the chest of another. The blood spurted out in a fountain as the body slumped to the ground. I was aghast, and Kaufmann's voice seemed far away as I dimly heard it say: "Did you notice that the loser did not scream? We teach discipline here." It occurred to me that the fellow might have simply died too quickly to express an opinion; it also was worth considering that if the Burgundians were this wasteful of men, the Reich proper had nothing to worry about.

Kaufmann was probably a sadist. He was certainly amused by my sickened reaction. "Dr. Goebbels, do you remember the *Kirchenkampf*?"

I recovered my composure. "The campaign against the churches? What about it?"

"Martin Bormann was disappointed in its failure," he said.

"No more than I. The war years allowed little time for less important matters. You should know that the economic policies we established after the war helped to undermine the strength of the churches. They have never been weaker. European cinema constantly makes fun of them."

"That's not good enough," said Kaufmann evenly. "They exist. The gods of the Germanic tribes are not fools—their indignation is as severe as ever." I stared at this man with amazement as he continued to preach: "The gods watched Roman missionaries build early Christian churches on the sacred sites in the hope that the common people would continue climbing the same hills they had always used for worship . . . only now the people would pay homage to a false god!"

"The masses are not easily cured of the addiction," I pointed out.

"You compare religion to a drug?"

"It was one of the few wise statements of Marx," I said, with a deliberate edge to my voice. Kaufmann's face quickly darkened into a scowl. "Not all religions are the same," I concluded in an ameliorative tone. I had no desire to argue with him about the two faiths of Burgundy. So far as I was concerned, the remnants of Rosenberg's Gnostics and Himmler's majority of pagans could hold hands and jump down the nearest live volcano.

"Words are toys to you," he said. "Let me tell you a story about yourself, Herr Goebbels. You have always prided yourself on being the true radical of the Nazi Party. You hammered that home at every opportunity. Nobody hated the bourgeoise more than Goebbels. Nobody was more ardent about burning books than Goebbels. As Reichspropagandaminister you brilliantly staged the demonstrations against the Jews."

Now the man was making sense. I volunteered another item to his admirable list: "I hear some young men humming the Horst Wessel song down there." They were even in key. Manufacturing a martyr to give the Party its anthem was still one of my favorites. My influence remained on the Germanic world, including Burgundy. But how quickly they forget.

Kaufmann had been surveying rows of men doing pushups . . . as well as the removal of the corpse from the tourney field. Now his stony face turned in my direction, breaking into an unpleasant smile. I preferred his frown. "You misunderstand the direction of my comments, Herr Doktor. I will clarify. I was told a story about you once.

159

I was only a simple soldier at the time, freezing my ass off on the Russian front, but the story made an indelible impression. You were at a party, showing off for your friends by making four brief political speeches: the first presented the case for the restoration of the monarchy; the second sung the praises of the Weimar Republic; the third proved how communism could be successfully adopted by the German Reich; the fourth was in favor of National Socialism, at last. How relieved they were. How tempted they had been to agree with each of the other three speeches."

I could not believe what I was hearing. How could this dull oaf be in charge of anything but a petty bureaucratic department? Had he no sense of humor, no irony? "I was demonstrating the power of propaganda," I told him.

"If you're so wonderful at propaganda, then why does the rest of the world believe decades after our victory that we were the sole cause of World War II? They seem to think that Europe was Little Red Riding Hood, happily minding her own business, when the German wolf pounced on the innocent Fraulein and dragged her into the black forest, where he devoured her piece by piece."

As he went into meticulous detail about the failings of my control over newspapers, magazines, television, cabaret shows, and apparently his own son's term papers, I had the sinking feeling I only suffer when confronted by an unpleasant fact. There is nothing worse than when a religious fanatic makes sense. You know it's only temporary. Bereft of rational coordinates, he sails on a sea of confusion where the only safe haven is supernatural revelation. I had never approved of the attempt to justify our prejudices on mystical grounds when the best course of action lay in scientific research. Burgundians gave racism a bad name. Hitler in this, as so many other things, was willing to let everyone follow their own stars, so long as conclusions corresponded to the pronouncements of *Mein Kampf.* That was politics.

My failure to shift world opinion was cause for distress. When America turned against FDR, I had thought we had a chance to win favorable opinion there, despite our incompetent bunds of the 1930s. I misjudged the American character. They condemned us more than ever. The collapsing prospects of the New Deal did nothing to help our image; it merely implicated us along with all the other wartime leaders. What was needed was a whitewash, which I did my best to provide. The outcome was never in doubt: only the Reich and its satellites accept the Party outlook. Independent historians across the Atlantic remain my curse, especially a bastard named Barnes.

Believing that one should always give the Devil his due, I granted Kaufmann a fraction of his complaint, to which he answered: "When Schopenhauer said that human life must be some kind of mistake, he pointed the way for our mission: to correct the error with Aryan magick!" I lost my self-control. Kaufmann was exactly what Schopenhauer had in mind when he cried his lamentations into the void. I laughed in my kidnapper's face.

"In what do you believe, if not the race?" he asked sharply.

"This is preposterous," I nearly shouted. "Are you impuning—"

"It is not necessary to answer," he said consolingly. "I'm aware that you have only believed in one thing in your life: a man, not an idea. With Hitler dead, what is left for you?"

"This is insane," I replied, not liking the shrill sound of my own voice in my ears. "When I was made Reich Director for Total War, I demonstrated my genius for understanding and operating the mechanisms of a dictatorship. I was crucial to the war effort then. Hitler chose me, damn you."

"Yes, he did. We have never forgotten. But what you are incapable of appreciating, because your spirit eye is forever closed, is that Hitler was more than a man. He was a living part of an idea. He did not always recognize his own importance. He was chosen by the Vril Society, chosen, damn *you*, by the sacred order of the Luminous Lodge, the purest, finest product of the believers in the Thule. Adolf Hitler was the medium. The society used him accordingly. He was the focal point. Behind him were powerful magicians. He used words of power to control a nation, and then more, much more. The great work has only begun. Soon it will be time for the second step. Only the true man deserves *lebensraum.*"

Kaufmann was working himself up, I could see that. He stood close to me and said, "You are a political animal, Goebbels. You believe that politics is an end in itself. The truth is that governments are nothing in the face of destiny. We are near the cleansing of the world. You should be proud. Your son will play an important part. The finest jest is that modern scientific method will also have a role, as will traitors from the big city."

One last time I appealed to reason: "If there is a traitor to National

Socialism, my friend, it's you. The movement is political. What do you think geopolitics means? You wouldn't be playing these games if the Reich couldn't afford to indulge you, and after my report, you'll be on an austerity budget."

A flash of metal in his hand caused me to jump, but it wasn't a weapon. He held a coin under my nose. "This is one of the German gold coins minted before 1914. They are all in our possession now. Burgundy has never been off the gold standard, and we have other sources of income. Soon money won't matter to the Reich anyway."

"What do you mean by that?"

"You'll find out. Your movement may be political, but ours has never been. No one in Burgundy is accepted until he has been in touch with the Race Memory in the Akashic Record and has been initiated into the secrets of the Eternal Man. This we call being 'twice born'!"

"Why tell me? I don't care."

"Soon that won't matter either." He turned to go. I had no recourse but to follow him. There was nowhere else but straight down to sudden death. As we reentered the elevator, he spat out, "Don't try anything. One kick in the knee can be an initiation all by itself."

Adrenaline pumping through me, thanks to his stupidity of putting me on guard, I forced another question: "Have I been brought here to witness an honor bestowed on my son?"

"In part. But we will bestow an even greater honor on you, one you won't live to regret. You saw the decoded message."

That was enough. There could no longer be any doubt. I was trapped amidst madmen. Having determined a course of action, I feigned an attack of pain in my club foot and crouched at the same time. When Kaufmann instinctively made to offer aid, I struck wildly, almost blindly. I tried to knee him in the groin but—failing that—brought my fist down on the back of his neck. The fool went out like a light, falling hard on his face. I congratulated myself on such prowess for an old man.

No sooner had the body slumped to the floor than the elevator came to a stop and the doors opened automatically. I jumped out into the hall. Standing there was a naked seven-foot-giant who reached down and lifted me into the air. He was laughing. His voice sounded like a tuba.

"They call me Thor," he said. I struggled. He held.

Then I heard the voice of my son: "That, Father, is what we call a true Aryan."

I was carried like so much baggage down the hall, hearing voices distantly talking about Kaufmann. I was tossed onto the hard floor of a brightly lit room and the door was slammed behind me. A muscle had been pulled in my back and I lay there, gasping in pain like a fish out of water. I could see that I was in some sort of laboratory. In a corner was a wildly humming machine, the purpose of which I could not begin to guess. A young woman was standing over me, wearing a white lab smock. I could not help but notice two things about her straight away: she was a brunette, and she was holding a sword at my throat.

CHAPTER FIFTEEN

As I look back, the entire affair has an air of unreality about it. Events were becoming more unlikely in direct proportion to the speed with which they occurred. It had all the logic of a dream.

The room in which I had been unceremoniously dumped had an antiseptic hospital smell that reintroduced a modicum of reality to my beleaguered senses. As I lay on the floor, under the sword held by such an unlikely guardian (I had always supported military service for women, but when encountering the real thing I found it a bit difficult to take seriously), I took an inventory of my pains. The backache was subsiding so long as I did not move . . . but I was becoming aware that the hand with which I had dispatched Kaufmann felt like a hot balloon of agony, expanding without an upper limit. My vision was blurred and I shook my head trying to clear it. Dimly I heard voices in the background, and then a particularly resonant one was near at hand, speaking with complete authority: "Oh, don't be ridiculous. Help him up."

The woman put down the sword and was suddenly assisted by a young Japanese girl gingerly lifting me off the floor and propelling me in the direction of a nearby chair. Still I did not see the author of that powerful voice.

Then I was sitting down and the females were moving away. He was standing there, his hands on his hips, looking at me with the sort of analytical probing I always respect. At first I didn't recognize him,

164

but had instead the eerie feeling that I was in one of my own movies. No, that wasn't it exactly. It was someone else's movie.

The face made me think of something too ridiculous to credit, and then I knew who it really was: Professor Dietrich, the missing geneticist. I examined him more closely. The first impression had been more correct than I thought. The man hardly resembled the photographs of his youth. His hair had turned white and he had let it grow. Seeing him in person, I could not help noticing how angular were his features . . . how much like the face of the late actor Rudolf Klein-Rogge in the role of Dr. Mabuse, Fritz Lang's character, who had become the symbol of a superscientific, scheming Germany to the rest of the world. Although the later films were banned for the average German, the American-made series (Mabuse's second life, you could say) had become so popular throughout the world that Reich officials considered it a mark of distinction to own copies of all twenty. We still preferred the original series where Mabuse was obviously Jewish, and screenwriter Thea von Harbou wrote in the spirit of that perception; but Fritz Lang had not seen it that way when he refused to alter *The Testament of Dr. Mabuse* to depict a Fuehrer hero defeating the mastermind in the last reel. Lang thought Mabuse a perfect symbol for Hitler himself! Artists live in a dream world. But I digress from the living fantasy that breathed in the laboratory of a Burgundian castle.

Since the death of Klein-Rogge (so many are gone), other actors had taken over the part, but always the producers looked for that same startling visage. This man Dietrich was meant for the role, but he was most certainly not interested in auditioning for photoplays when he was already the star of something real.

"What are you staring at?" he asked. I told him. He nodded. "You chose the right profession," he continued. "You have a cinematic imagination. I am flattered by the comparison."

"May I ask you what exactly is happening here?"

"Much. Not all of it is necessary. This show they are putting on for your benefit is pointless."

I was becoming comfortable in the chair, and my back had momentarily ceased to annoy me. I hoped that I would not have to move for yet another guided tour of something I wasn't sure I wanted to see. My curiosity had no physical component at present. To my

165

relief, Dietrich pulled up a chair, sat down across from me, and set me at ease with:

"I expect that Kaufmann meant to introduce you to Thor when the doors to the lift opened, and then enjoy your startled expression as you were escorted down the hall to my humble quarters. They didn't think you'd improvise on the set. They're amateurs and you are the professional when it comes to lights-camera-action. Bravo!"

"Thor . . ." I began lamely, but could think of nothing to say.

"He's not overly intelligent. I'm impressed that he finished his scene with such dispatch. I apologize for my assistant. She had been watching on one of our monitors—where would we be without television, eh?—and must have come to the conclusion that you are a dangerous fellow. In person, I mean. We are all acquainted with what you can do in an official capacity."

It was a relief to talk to such an obviously cultured man. As a sense of ease returned, I took in my surroundings. The size of the laboratory was tremendous. It was like being in a scientific warehouse. Although lacking technical training myself, it seemed to my layman's eye that there was a lack of systematic arrangement: materials were jumbled together in a downright sloppy fashion, even assuming a good reason for the close proximity of totally different apparatuses. Nevertheless I realized that I was out of my depth and might be having nothing more than an aesthetic response.

"They closed the file on you," I said. "They think you've been kidnapped by American agents."

"That was the cover story."

"Then you were kidnapped by Burgundians?"

"A reasonable deduction, but wrong. I volunteered."

"For what?"

"Dr. Goebbels, I said that you have a cinematic imagination. That's good. It may help you to appreciate the teacher." He snapped his fingers and the Japanese girl was by his side so swiftly that I didn't see where she had come from. She was holding a small plastic box. Opening it, he showed me the interior: two cylinders resided there, each with a tiny suction cup on the end. He took one out. "Examine this," he said, passing it to me.

"One of your inventions?" I asked, noticing that it was as light in my palm as if it were made of tissue paper. But I could tell that whatever the material was, it was sturdy.

"A colleague came up with that. It's an application of one of my discoveries. He was a good man, but he's dead now. Politics." He retrieved the cylinder, did something with the untipped end, then stood. "It doesn't hurt," he said. "If you will cooperate, I promise a cinematic experience unlike anything you've sampled before."

There was no point in resisting. They had me. Whatever their purpose, I was in no position to oppose it. Nor is there any denying that my curiosity was aroused by this seeming toy.

Dietrich leaned forward, saying, "Allow me to connect this to your brain and you will enjoy a unique production of the Burgundian Propaganda Ministry, if you will—the story of my life."

Without further ado, he pressed the delicate suction cup against the center of my forehead. There was a tingling sensation and then my sight began to dim! I knew that my eyes were still open and I had not lost consciousness. For a moment I feared that I was going blind.

There were new images. I began to dream while wide awake, except that these were not my dreams. They were someone else's.

I was someone else!

I was Dietrich . . . as a child.

I was buttoning my collar on a cold day in February before going to school. The face that looked back from the mirror held a cherubic—almost beautiful—aspect. I was happy.

As I skipped down cobbled German streets it suddenly struck me with solemn force that I was a Sephardic Jew.

My parents had been strict, Orthodox, and humorless. An industrial accident had taken them from me. I was not to be alone for long. An uncle in Spain sent for me and I became part of his household. He was living as a Gentile (not without difficulty) but was able to take a child from a practicing Jewish family into his home.

It did not take more than a few days at school for the beatings to begin, whereupon they increased in ferocity. There was a bubbling fountain within easy distance of the schoolyard where I could wash away the blood.

One day I watched the water turn crimson over the rippling reflection of my scarred visage. I decided that whatever it was a Jew was supposed to be, I didn't qualify. I had the same color blood as my classmates, after all. Therefore I could not be a real Jew.

Announcing this revelation at school the next day nearly got me killed for my trouble. One particularly stupid lad was so distressed

167

by my logic that he expressed his displeasure with a critique made up of a two-by-four. Yet somehow in all this pain and anguish—as I fled for my life—I did not think to condemn the attackers. I concluded that surely the Jew must be a monstrous creature indeed to inspire such a display. Cursing the memory of my parents, I felt certain that through a happy fluke I was not really of their flesh and blood.

Amazingly, I became an anti-Semite. I took a Star of David to the playground and in full view of my classmates destroyed it. A picture of a rabbi I also burned. Some were not impressed by this display, but others restrained them from resuming the beatings. For the first time I knew security in that schoolyard. None of them became any friendlier; they did not know how to take it.

Suddenly the pictures of Dietrich's early life disappeared into a swirling darkness. I was confused, disoriented.

Time had passed. Now I was Dietrich as a young man back in Germany, dedicating myself to a life's work in genetic research. With a meticulously worked out family background, fraudulent in every detail, I joined the Nazi Party on the eve of its coming to power—I did this not so much out of vanity as from a pragmatic reading of the zeitgeist. I entertained my new "friends" with a little-known quotation from the canon of Karl Marx, circa 1844: "Once society has succeeded in abolishing the empirical essence of Judaism—huckstering and its preconditions—the Jew will have become impossible."

The National Socialists were developing their biological theories at the time. To say the basis of their programs was at best pseudo-scientific would be to compliment it. At best, the only science involved was terminology borrowed from the field of eugenics.

I was doing real research, however, despite the limitations I faced due to Party funding and propaganda requirements. My work involved negative eugenics, the study of how to eliminate defective genes from the gene pool through selective breeding. Assuming an entire society could be turned into a laboratory, defective genes could be eliminated in one generation, although the problem might still crop up from time to time because of recessive genes (easily handled).

In deciding to breed something out of the population, the door was opened as to what to breed *for,* or positive eugenics. Now, so long as we were restricting ourselves to a question of one genetic disease, we could do something. But even then there were limitations. What if some invaluable genius had a genetic disability? Would you dismiss the possibility of his having intelligent offspring because of one risk?

It wasn't until 1943 that Hitler began releasing sufficient funds for all the scientific projects. If the A-bomb failed, a biological weapon was to be the fallback; and I was assigned to lead a team working in that area. In a rare moment of clarity, Hitler insisted that we fly in separate planes to avoid losing all of us in one accident. It would have been easier to disappear if my plane had gone down, but I didn't think of departure until I was interrogated about samples of my work that were being smuggled out of Germany by a spy, a Jew who would soon be sent to a concentration camp. The thought that I shouldn't have to put up with the inconvenience (they had the temerity to send Gestapo men who wouldn't even be allowed inside an SS camp) grew over the years, until it flowered into a mania with me. I would go into business for myself.

Whenever I was engaged in a fruitful line of inquiry, the deranged, mystical ideas of the Nazis would intrude, and complications would set in. They wanted to breed for qualities that in many cases fell outside the province of real genetics—because they fell outside reality in the first place. An example was the request, passed on by Himmler himself, that we develop a revenge weapon to deploy if Germany lost the war. They wanted a virus that would be spread sexually, but only applying to miscegenation!

During this period in my life, I made another discovery. I was no longer a racist. My anti-Semitism vanished as in a vagrant breeze. I had learned that there was no scientific basis for it. The sincere Nazi belief that the Jew is a creature outside of nature was so much rot. As for the cultural-mystical ideas revolving around the Jew, the more I learned of how my patrons perceived these matters, the more convinced I became that Hitler's movement appealed to the irrational. (An ironic note was that many European Jews were not Semitic, but that is beside the point. The Nazis had little concern with, say, Arabs. It was the European Jew they were after, for whatever reasons were handy.)

Although I had come full circle on the question of racism, something else had happened to me in the interim. My hatred for one group of humanity had *not* vanished. My view of the common heritage of Homo sapiens led me to despise all of the human race. The implications escaped me at the time, but this was the pivotal moment of my life.

Even at the peak of their popularity, the world of genetics was only slightly influenced by Nazi thinking. Scientists are scientists first, ideologues second, if at all. To the extent that most scientists have a philosophy, it is a general sort of positive humanism: so it was with my teacher in genetics, a brilliant man—who happened to fit the Aryan stereotype coincidentally—and his collaborator, a Jew who was open about his family background, unlike me.

They were the first to discover the structure of DNA. No, they are not in the history books. By then Hitler had come to power. The Nazis destroyed many of their papers when they were adjudged enemies of the state—for political improprieties having nothing to do with the research. But I was never found guilty of harboring traitorous notions; and my Gentile pedigree continued to withstand the scrutiny of morons.

Long before the world heard of it, I continued this work with DNA. Publishing my findings was the last thing I wanted to do. I had other ideas. By giving the Nazis gobbledygook to make their fanciful policies sound good, I remained unmolested. There would be a place for me in the New Order. I remembered when Einstein said that should his theory of relativity prove untrue, the French would declare him a German, and the Germans call him a Jew. At least I was certain of my place in advance.

The National Socialists and their Third Reich gave me what I needed: unlimited human material. What good is a theory if you can't test it? What I needed most was the supply of pregnant women in a steady stream from the concentration camps. I injected a clone of naughty genes into the livers of the fetuses. The data on synthetic viruses was invaluable and the monster children provided amusement for the more decadent members of the SS.

(NOTE FROM HILDA: *So here is the one responsible for the twisted forms of the wretched children that have haunted my every night since first seeing the photographs in Burgundy.*)

And yet, all my progress left me curiously unsatisfied. It was as if I had the largest jigsaw puzzle in the world, with the central piece missing. And then one day I realized that that piece was not to be found in biology.

Through the haze of Dietrich's memories, I retained my identity; I could reflect on what I was assimilating directly from a pattern taken from another mind. I was impressed that such a man existed, working in secret for decades on what had only recently riveted the world's attention. Only last year had a news story dealt with microbiologists doing gene splicing. Yet he had done the same sort of experimentation years earlier. Even while respecting his achievements, the relish with which he described the unsavory aspects made me a little ill. And then
. . .

What had been a trickle suddenly turned into a torrent of concepts and formulae beyond my comprehension. I felt the strain. With quivering fingers I reached for the cylinder and . . . the images stopped; the words stopped; the kaleidoscope exploding inside my head stopped; the pressure stopped . . .

"You have not finished the program, Dr. Goebbels," said Dietrich. "It was at least another ten minutes before the 'reel change.'" He was holding the other cylinder in his hand, tossing it lightly into the air and catching it as though it were of no importance.

"It's too much," I gasped, "to take in all at once. Hold on, I've remembered something: Thor in the hallway. Is it possible?" I thought back over what I had experienced. Dietrich had left simple eugenic breeding programs far behind. His search was for the chemical mysteries of life itself, like some sort of mad alchemist seeking the knowledge of a Frankenstein. "Did you . . . " I paused, hardly knowing how to phrase it. "Did you create Thor?"

"Don't I wish," he said, almost playfully. "Have you the slightest understanding of what that would entail? To find the genetic formula for human beings would require a language I do not possess."

"A language?"

"You'd have to break the code, be able to read the hieroglyphic wonders of not just one, but millions of genes. It's all there, in the chromosomes, but I haven't been able to find it yet. No one has." He put his face near to mine, grinning, eyes wide and staring. "But I will be the first. Nobody can beat me to it, because only I can do it; and I'm almost there!"

For a moment I thought I was again in the presence of Hitler. This man was certainly a visionary. Moreover, he was dangerous in a fashion beyond any politician. Having caught his breath, he wiped his head with a red handkerchief and said, "I'll admit I did something for that young man, or to him, but it's peripheral to what we really do here. Thor used to be a mere six feet tall. I injected a growth hormone extracted from the pituitary gland in corpses, of which articles we have no shortage in Burgundy."

"Why are you here?" I asked.

"They finance me well. See the requirements," he said, pointing at what he told me was an atmosphere chamber. "The work is expensive. Do you know how to invade the hidden territory of life itself? With radiation and poison to break down the structures and begin anew. To build! I can never live long enough, never receive enough sponsorship. It is the work of many lifetimes. If only I had more subtle tools . . ."

Before I lost him to a scientist's reverie, I changed the subject: "My son's hair and eyes have changed."

"That's nothing but cosmetics," he said disdainfully.

"The SS wants you to do that?"

"It is considered a mark of distinction. My beautician there"—he pointed at the pretty Japanese girl—"provides this minor and unimportant service."

Only a few blond-haired, blue-eyed people were working in the laboratory. I asked why everyone had not undergone the treatment. The reason was because the few I had just seen were authentic members of that genotype. Dietrich was blunt: "We don't play SS games in here."

Although I did not want to leave my chair, he insisted on taking me on a guided tour of his workshop, treating the technicians as no more than expensive equipment. I wondered how Speer would react to all this. The place was even larger than I had first thought. I wondered what Helga would make of it all, cramped in her small cubbyhole at the university.

The seemingly endless stroll activated my pains again. He noticed my distress and suggested we sit down again. "Did I really share in your memories?" I asked him when I had regained my composure.

"A carefully edited production, but yes."

"How is it done?"

"Electromagnetic waves can cause hallucinations. These I control by a process that is tedious but highly effective."

"I thought your area was genetics."

"Molecular biology, Goebbels, is the marriage of earthly salts with the blood of the *Völk*. It is not my field; it is only a means to an end. I have no field. Listen, little man, the arbitrary divisions thrown up between mathematics and science and engineering are devices by which to create specialized fools who wouldn't know the truth if it swallowed them whole. Western science doesn't believe in anything unless it is explained in terms of the atom; National Socialist science doesn't believe in anything unless it is traced to the cell. Yet despite these mental straitjackets, both sides depend on both atom and cell for their very survival. We've reached a day when physicists can't talk to chemists, mathematicians won't talk to anyone, and engineers are deaf. Unlike them, I am interested in the Truth . . . because I have a use for it."

This was all Greek to me, but he spoke so forcefully that he made a deep impression on my admittedly phenomenal memory. Anger over my abduction shrank in this man's presence. Kaufmann was merely an enemy, but Dietrich was a creature from another world. He had my full attention as he described the workings of the remarkable information tube. The device was a propagandist's dream come true. He told how the idea traced back to an inventor named Tesla, a contemporary of Edison's, who had constructed huge coils for storing electromagnetic energy. When he stuck his head in one of them, he'd seen strange lights and colors; he concluded that the coil's field was interfering with his own brain's energy. Dietrich's teaching devices had been developed along these lines, augmented by his own discoveries. Then and there, I decided if I got out alive from Burgundy, I would steal at least one of the micro-Tesla coils.

The politics of Burgundy took on a new meaning. "Despite what you've told me about your, I suppose it could be called a sinecure," I said, "I don't see how a man like you can function in Burgundy."

He did not take offense. "They are innocents in search of an imaginary past. I'm good with children. They think that state-of-the-art science is the discovery of the four elements: fire, earth, air, and water. I simply told them that my genetic work is based on the four bases of life: adenine, cytosine, guanine, and thymine. I'm a wizard to them."

"You said that you'd almost discovered the secret of life. I'm not trained in medicine, but I could try to understand." My curiosity was reborn with a passion.

"There you go again, compartmentalizing your thinking. Haven't you been paying attention? My work with electromagnetism had a more important application than motion picture toys. There is a uniform force. Magnetism, electricity, and gravity are manifestations of this one force! My breakthrough came on the day I discovered that nucleic acids are magnetic. Think of RNA as a gauleiter, passing orders from a Fuehrer nucleus to the peasant ribosomes. Can you grasp that?"

"Yes."

"Good. To break into this process is the next step. The body is a battlefield anyway, so there is room for an interloper to take the high ground. If I can demagnetize and then remagnetize a human being, I can eliminate disease by ordering the diseased cells to become normal cells. Or I can do the reverse. Once again, the difficulty lies with instrumentalities. Imagine that you erase a magnetic tape and begin tabula rasa. You could record anything, Goebbels . . . anything! The future of computers does not lie with dead matter but with organisms I will breed myself . . . for company."

It was all very interesting as he described the myriad possibilities of the Superman. I found it more congenial to picture gods and monsters than to think through the meaning of his favorite topic, to which he returned repeatedly: "Einstein gave physicists a fourth dimension to play with after what he did with time," he said. "More recently, a mathematician living in Königsberg, the city of Immanuel Kant, came up with a fifth dimension, the equations for which make gravity look like . . . guess what?"

I could catch on to a popular term: "Electromagnetism?"

"Exactly! You may understand what I am doing, in the limited time remaining to you." It was the sort of offhand comment to freeze the blood of Surtur, but he paid no heed and continued explaining his weltanschauung—he even had a kind word for the SS project during the war that had done research on whether positively and negatively charged ions in the atmosphere could affect morale; the finding was that positive ions made people irritable and depressed.

"Not everything they did was insane, like looking for entrances to the hollow earth," he said, "but most of the time they accomplish nothing of value. What can you expect when they run off to monasteries in Tibet and Druidic sites in Ireland and buried caves in Iceland, searching for archaeological evidence of the origins of the Aryan race. Boys will be boys."

Then he was back on track with science. He claimed that people had no justification to live unless they advanced the cause of knowledge. He scorned the conservative Babbitts—that invaluable American phrase—who exhausted themselves worrying that their children might not turn out to be perfect reproductions of their useless, bloodless selves. "I've never believed in Natural Rights," he said, "and I know you don't either, if your propaganda against the republic across the sea is any indication." I nodded vigorously, as if I were back in school. "What is a right? Can you weigh it, measure it, taste it?"

"It's probably not even electromagnetic," I added.

"Very good! Why should anyone respect the rights of others if they don't exist? It's another religion, and I don't believe in spooks. Americans wallow in ethical abstractions and it impedes their scientific progress. Soon that won't matter anymore, nothing will; but I'm getting ahead of myself." No sooner were these words out of his mouth than he began spinning around as if a whirling dervish. He came to a stop before a most startled guest. "I made a pun. You see, I have a doppelgänger, but it's only in my mind." He suddenly grinned, and I noticed that one of his teeth was pointed.

"Pardon, what did you say?"

"Oh, nothing important. It's only that my mind is so powerful that it projects another me on an external wavelength."

This was one day I should have stayed in bed. "I thought you didn't believe in spooks," I said.

"I don't."

"Does anyone else see this other . . . you?"

"Sometimes."

"That sounds like a spook."

"Energy is not supernatural," he said, then changed the subject . . . in a manner of speaking. "Dr. Goebbels, if I were to live forever, would that make me God in a nonsupernatural sense?"

"Why are you making fun of me?"

"If I can perform miracles, I'll achieve immortality. Now a second question: If I were the only living ego, would that make me God?"

I was no longer at ease in his company, not the least little bit. I wished that I'd listened to Hilda. Was there no way out? I had to play for time. "Are you sure you're not religious?" I asked.

"You answer my questions with questions of your own, thus demonstrating an unacceptable independence of mind. Perhaps you'd like to sample the contents of the other cylinder?" He'd slyly kept it on his person. As one who had served Adolf Hitler, I recognized a command when it came in the guise of a query. I agreed.

CHAPTER SIXTEEN

Again ye come, ye hovering Forms!
I find you as early to my clouded sight ye shone!
Shall I attempt, this once, to seize and bind you?
Still o'er my heart is that illusion thrown?
Ye crowd more near! Well then, be power assigned you
To sway me from your misty, shadowy zone!
My bosom thrills, by youthful passion shaken
That magic breezes round your march awaken.

—Goethe,
Faust

I attached this cylinder by myself and . . .

I did not know who I was.

In vain I searched for the identity into which I had been plunged. What there was of me seemed to be a disembodied consciousness floating high above the European continent. It was like seeing in all directions at once. The moon above was very large, very near the earth—it was made of ice.

Hörbiger's *Welteislehre!* It was a projection of one of his prophesies, when the moon would fall toward the earth, causing great upheavals in the crust—and working bizarre mutations on the life of the planet. The oceans would rise and there would be a new Flood, but the *Übermenschen* would survive, reveling in their giant bodies, which could become lighter than air at will. Finally, the descending moon would disintegrate, leaving an ice ring of immense proportions surrounding the planet. Then the True Reich would flourish, bathed in the godly light of cosmic rays. Yet all this was not merely a vision of the future; it was also a vision into the antediluvian past. Ours was the fourth moon.

There was a panorama unfolding like the worm Ouroboros: ancient epochs and the far future were melded together in an unbreak-

177

able circle. The world and civilization I knew were nothing but passing aberrations in the history of the globe.

Mankind was fifteen million years old. It had achieved triumphs in the past and degenerated since. Modern man was engaging in the worst kind of self-flattery when he saw himself as a risen ape. He was a dreadfully Fallen Being, but not in the Christian sense believed by Catholics and Protestants; nor in the more outré interpretation of the murdered and martyred Cathars and Albigensians whose travails in European history had contributed to Alfred Rosenberg's Nazi version of Gnosticism. None of these beliefs were drawn from the racial template that could only be divined by the spirit eye of the awakened Aryan. This same spirit sight revealed that astrology was a pathetic remnant of the Great Truth: WHAT OCCURS IN THE SKY DETERMINES LIFE ON EARTH.

I saw ancient Atlantis, not the one spoken of by Plato, but from a time before Homo sapiens. The first Atlantis was inhabited by great giants who preceded man and taught the human race all its important knowledge: I beheld Prometheus as real. Then did I see that the pantheon of Nordic gods had a basis in this revelation. Fabled Asgard was not a myth, but a legend—a vague race memory of the giant cities that once thrived on a terrifyingly ancient earth. And the most powerful of these was Thule, almost forgotten when the first Atlantis was young.

The capital of the first Atlantis had a library the size of New Berlin. Many kilometers of books were devoted to the study of the mysteries of Thule. In the first building that had existed on the planet earth, long before the first ice age drove more advanced hominids south, where they defeated lesser hominids, there stood a calendar that was the Vril Time Lens. It did not record time. It created time. From this came Destiny. The Atlantidean library had pictures of this first building on the island of Thule. Viewed from above, it had six sections, and each was a polygon. One five-sided structure was attached to a larger six-sided structure, which in turn was attached to another six-sided structure a farther distance away. Below, the pattern was repeated with the remaining three structures. Strange lights and gossamer threads connected these structures to one another, but there was a shifting, shimmering quality. Then I intuited what I was seeing, and the words of Dietrich echoed somewhere that I could hear. I was looking at the four bases of life; below glistened the adenine-thymine and guanine-cytosine base pairs of DNA. From this came the double helix. Were the lights and threads the hydrogen bonds? Knowledge flowed into my mind's eye. The Thule beings had planned the future down to the smallest detail. They had written it upon the structure of life, and in the glowing symbols of their calendar.

Man first came into existence because of the descent of an ice moon. Without such events, all life would be puny and weak. An ice moon created the gigantic, rainbow-hued dinosaurs; and another gave birth to the King of Fear, with his many-colored fingers and burning eyes.

When Atlantis sank beneath the waves, the survivors sailed to the Himalayas. At that time, Tibet was at sea level. The cataclysm that reduced Atlantis to a legend—and changed the rotation of the earth in the process—raised Tibet 13,000 feet above sea level. So that untold generations later, earnest young men of the SS could make pilgrimages to lonely monasteries in search of lost Arya.

Most startling of all was the tapestry flickering in myriad colors to depict the final destiny of the Aryan race. There would be a period before the giants, when all of Homo sapiens would perish but for the Aryans. Most of these idealized Viking types would happily prepare, not for their transformation, but for their extermination at the hands of the fortunate few to undergo the godding passage. The ultimate *Übermensch* was not "human" other than for superficial appearance. The human race—as I knew it—was only a means to an end. The Aryan was closest to True Men, but when mutations caused by the descending moon brought back the giants (not merely creation, but a rebirth of specific consciousnesses), then the remaining Aryans could join all the other races of man in their proper place: oblivion. The masters, the gods, would have returned. They would cherish this new world, which was also the old world; and they would perform the rites on the way to the next apocalypse, the *Ragnarök,* when the cycle would start again—for the ice ring would fall, and the earth would be torn.

These images burned into my brain: gargantuan cities with spires threatening the stars; science utterly replaced by a functional magick that was the central power of these psychokinetic supermen who needed little else; everything vast, endless, bright . . . so bright that it blinded my sight and mind and filled my soul with the terror of infinity.

Suddenly I had a body. It was a very old one. I was the senior Druid of my tribe. They were depending on me to acquire enlightenment through attainment of the Holy Grail and a means for combating the pale new religion sweeping the world.

Before me was the Well of Kunneware. Above the well was a globe. This represented the sun, and in its center burned the Swastika. Fire will melt the ice. Coiled on top of the globe was the Dragon Father from which all lesser dragons are the shadows: Nidhögg, Fafnir, Midgardsörmr. The only parts of the earth-serpent that weren't dark green consisted of the red spots of its eyes and mouth, yellow projections of its teeth and claws, and a mud-brown under-skin that was visible as it lifted its unbearably long neck to reach down where it could gnaw at the vitals of the world, eating from the roots of Yggdrasil, the tree of life.

As I neared the Dragon, the heat increased, and it became so humid that my white robes felt as if they were a second layer of skin on my wrinkled body. My brain was turned into a ball of cloying cotton and my eyes were two raw oysters, stinging as if they were full of sand that would never turn to pearls.

Fire and ice. Everything is fire and ice. Only a pact with the fire can withstand the blind forces of the ice.

When I was at the limit of my endurance, and felt the last of my strength draining into the Druid staff I carried, the Dragon consented to produce the Book of the Aryans, written on scrolls made from the hides of monsters that lived beyond the stars. Two secrets were revealed unto me.

The first was that not all the giants produced by the moons of ice were on the side of True Man. During the deluges, races were corrupted, and the Anti-Man was spawned. They had their giants as well. The enemy came in all sizes, and some were terrible monsters; but every last one of them, from the most common to the most frightening, shared one power in common. They could create nothing of their own, but only drain strength from the Aryan race. In the future, the enemy would become so populous as to threaten Aryan man with destruction before he fulfilled his earthly destiny. Yet armed with knowledge, Aryan heroes could defeat the enemy.

The second secret was the means to control reincarnation. The Aryans would have to draw upon heroes of the past in times of dire peril. The parasites challenged the nobility of the dust; so the dust would be raised against them.

Looking to my staff, I saw a pale oval begin to form at the top. The oval became a skull and then was clothed in flesh. The Dragon's eyes were glowing from within the sockets of the skull, and then the flesh took on features, solidifying into the face of the blond giant who had held in his powerful arms some other version of myself in a place I could only dimly glimpse in the far future.

The whole man appeared where my staff had been. He was proud and strong in the glare of the Swastika sun. He climbed up high, reaching the back of the Dragon. Suddenly he was holding something bright in his hand: Siegfried's sword. Then the Dragon Father unfolded his wings and rose into the air. The shadow of the sword held aloft and the leviathan's wings outspread made a three-taloned claw racing along the ground. Cities of normal men and women were waiting, like so much wheat in the wind. Rituals had to be performed.

They flew through space and time, and I was disembodied again, a witness to the wreck and ruin of a modern metropolis. It was New Berlin.

I was screaming, I was screaming, I was screaming.

Dietrich had ripped the device from my perspiring forehead. "This is madness," I said, putting my head in my hands. "It can't be really true. The SS religion . . . no!"

"*Es walten die Übel!*" was his reply.

"I deny these phantoms," I choked out. "I don't believe that the evils hold sway, except in fever dreams."

Much to my surprise, he put a comforting hand on my shoulder. "Of course it is not true," he said. There were tears in my eyes, the pearls from my hallucination, and my expression must have been a mask of confusion. He went on: "What you have seen is no more true than one of your motion pictures, or a typical release from the Ministry of Propaganda. It is more convincing, I'll grant you. Just as the first micro-Tesla coil allowed you to peer into the contents of one mind, this other has provided you with a composite picture of what a certain group believes; a collaborative effort, you could say."

"Religious fanatics of the SS," I muttered. "And it's full of contradictions."

"You recognize that, do you? I expected you to be an intelligent man."

"It's wrong from the start. Hörbiger's cosmogony isn't accepted by any educated person."

"I quite agree about that, but it's not with the peculiar astral theories that the vision contradicts itself, but the predestined racialism."

"Well, yes, but if you reject Hörbiger, the rest falls apart. Wernher von Braun did a devastating piece against the cosmic ice beliefs in an issue of *Signal* magazine that I cherish. Imagine anyone believing in four moons of ice, or that space is full of hydrogen."

Dietrich smiled. "Actually, there is a goodly amount of hydrogen in outer space," he said. "It's not a perfect vacuum by any means. This discovery in no way supports the Hörbigerians, who made so many wild guesses that some were bound to come true. On the other hand, the scientific establishment hasn't exactly fallen over itself giving credit to their opponents for getting something right. Scientists are only human; all too human."

This mild rebuke taught me one lesson: don't try to show off a layman's knowledge of popular science around the genuine article.

"Hörbiger is a crackpot, though," said Dietrich. "Small wonder he is popular in a place like this. As for the SS fantasy in toto, you should be the last person to forget the theatrical side. They have a colorful prediction and a hypothetical history. Their faith draws on deep, imaginative sources—a well from which you have drawn yourself, if I recall samples of your work with any degree of accuracy. Now I admit that the SS cylinder is not as worthwhile as my autobiography. Still, there is something I've been wondering, and you might be able to help. You knew Hitler intimately. Did he believe this stuff?"

The question took me completely off guard. Unconsciously, I had been wrestling with that very conjecture. "Hitler told different people what they wanted to hear," I began. "When he was with laborers, he talked socialism. When he was with bankers, it was money. Put him with a philosopher and he could quote Kant. But he preferred being with the military because he carried so much relevant information in his head that he could always beat them to the facts at hand.

He spent less time with the occult crowd as the years wore on, but he could quote chapter and verse when he wanted to. In his youth, I think he believed parts of this vision to which I've been subjected. I would guess that skepticism increased with age and experience. At least one part of his faith received a hammer blow at Stalingrad. Hörbiger had predicted a mild winter, the feebleminded old goat. No, in the end Hitler only trusted in blood and iron."

"And anti-Semitism."

"That goes without saying. When his friend Henriette von Schirach committed the blunder of defending the Jews in his presence, she was asked to leave the Berghof, never to return. To this day, I'm involved with finding ways to penalize upper-class families that allowed their daughters to marry the money lenders to extricate themselves from debt. The Fuehrer never compromised on that."

"You mentioned friends. I didn't think Hitler had friends."

The man had a point. "To the extent that he did, I was a friend. So was Speer."

"You say that as a boast. Please remember this conversation of ours when you learn what they have planned for you."

"You won't tell me?"

"That's not my department."

"May I ask what they plan for you?"

Richard Dietrich stood and put his hands behind his back. He was appearing to be more like Dr. Mabuse all the time. His voice sounded different somehow, as though he were addressing a large audience: "They have hired me to perform a genetic task. While I'm working on their project, I have the means to finish a job of my own. An ideal arrangement. Which do you want to hear about first?"

"You can tell me?"

"Dr. Goebbels, I will tell you anything you'd like to know that doesn't touch on the surprise they've planned for you. I gave my word on that."

"What is the personal project?"

"I would have expected you to ask for the other first, but even I am not always right. Very simply, I intend to make myself immortal. I thought I'd already suggested as much to you. At the very least, I'd like to live, oh, a thousand years. Can't remember where I picked up that number, but I got it somewhere close to home."

"You're joking."

"The punch line is real."

"What about the other project?"

"A minor operation, really. In this laboratory a virus is being developed that will spare only blond, blue-eyed men and women. Yes, Dr. Goebbels, the virus would kill you—with your dark hair and brown eyes—and myself, as readily as, say, my Japanese assistant. It means that your son would die also, because his current appearance is, after all, only skin deep. It means that most members of the Nazi Party would perish as not being 'racially' fit by this standard.

"I am speaking of the most comprehensive mass murder of all time. A large proportion of the populations in Sweden and Denmark and Iceland will survive. Too bad for the SS that virtually all those people think that extermination of the human condition, or most of it at any rate, is evil. You are aware that much of the world's folk have rather strict ethical systems built into their quaint little cultures. They probably believe in Natural Rights, too. That sort of thing gave the Nazis a difficult time at first, didn't it?"

It was becoming more difficult to understand him because someone was giggling in the room. But I made out that he had considered using sexual transmission as a mechanism for spreading the Final Plague and had referred back to earlier research done during the war on the biological revenge weapon. "Sex would take too long, but that's what they say makes for the best relationships, isn't it? Mustn't rush the orgasm. The mass murder must be hurried through, however. And we can't let the celibate people have a free ride to life and liberty. So I've decided that an airborne virus is best; and it's even quicker than dumping the bug in the water supply. We'll explode virus bombs in ten strategic places across the planet, and even get the Eskimos, because this little critter survives just fine in the cold."

The giggling was getting on my nerves. Dietrich continued: "It will take about one more week to get the bugs out of the thing. Right now it's harmless. Think of that—harmless, and in one place. If only the world knew, eh? Well, that's life . . . in a manner of speaking."

Yes, he was Mabuse, all right. That's who he was. But it was so blasted difficult making out what he was saying over that giggling; only now it had become a deranged laughing. Then I recognized the voice.

I was hysterical. I'd never had the experience before. Part of me wanted to analyze the disturbance, but the rest of me was too occupied with screaming laughter to cooperate. What was left of my concentration was directed at trying to stop the crazy sounds coming out of my chest and throat and mouth.

Suddenly I was surprised to find myself on the floor. Hands were pulling me down and the professor was putting a hypodermic needle in my arm. As the darkness claimed me, I wondered why there were no accompanying pictures. Didn't this cylinder touching my flesh have a story to tell?

CHAPTER SEVENTEEN

Sentence first—verdict afterwards."

—Lewis Carroll,
Alice's Adventures in Wonderland

"Treason!" shouted his Majesty King Pest the First.
"Treason!" said the little man with the gout.
"Treason!" screamed the Arch Duchess Ana-Pest.
"Treason!" muttered the gentleman with his jaws tied up.
"Treason!" growled he of the coffin.
"Treason! Treason!" shrieked her Majesty of the mouth.

—Edgar Allan Poe,
King Pest

It felt as though I had been asleep for many days, but I came to my wits a few minutes later, according to my watch at least. I was lying on a cot and *he* was standing over me. I doubted that there had ever been a man named Richard Dietrich. "Goebbels, I thought you were made of sterner stuff," came the grim voice of Dr. Mabuse.

"You are . . . evil," I told him hoarsely.

"That's unfair. What in my conduct strikes you as unseemly?"

"You said you had been anti-Semitic. Then you told me that you had rejected racism. Now you are part of a plot that takes racism farther than anything I've ever heard of!"

"You've been out of touch."

"The whole mess is a shambles of contradictions."

"No, if you are talking about the SS beliefs, that's one thing; but my position is perfectly consistent. I expected more from a thoughtful Nazi. My sponsors want a project carried out for racist reasons. I do not believe in their theories, religion, or pride. This pure blond race they worship has never existed, in fact; it was a climatological adaptation in northern Europe, never as widely distributed as Nazis think. It was a trait in a larger population group. I don't believe in

186

SS myths about lost colonies from Atlantis or spirit guidance from Thule. Blond hair is blond hair, that's all. My involvement in the project is for other reasons."

A voice in my head was telling me that a man of ability should not do such things. Desperately, I appealed to his mind: "There can be no other reason, Herr Doktor."

"You forget what you have learned. Remember that I came to hate the human race. This does not mean that I gave up reason or started engaging in wishful thinking. If the Burgundians enable me to wipe out most of humanity, with themselves exempt from the holocaust, I'll go along with it. The piper calls the tune."

"You couldn't carry on your work. How will you be immortal if you're dead?"

Sometimes one has the certainty of having been led down a primrose path, with the gate being locked against any hope of retreat, only *after* the graveyard sound of the latch snapping shut. Knowledge has a habit of arriving too late. Such was the emotion that held me in an iron grip as soon as those words escaped my lips. Dr. Mabuse could never be a fool. It was impossible. Even as he spoke, I could anticipate the words: "Oh, I *am* sorry. I forgot to tell you that a few people outside the fortunate category may be saved. I can make them immune. In this sense, I'll be a Noah, collecting specimens for a specialist's ark. Anyone I consider worthy I will claim."

"Why do you hate the human race?" I asked him.

"To think that a Nazi has the gall to ask that question. Why do you hate the Jews?" he shot back. "They think they are the Chosen People. You fellows think you are the Chosen People. My Japanese assistant over there believes herself to be of the Chosen People. Find the group, any group, and I'll show you a majority within that group saying the same. Tribes in Africa believe only themselves to be human. The British were born to rule; only the French have culture; the Chinese live in the only civilization, and everyone else is a barbarian. The American Indian, what's left of him, is the dying ember of the Chosen People. I ask myself why this is the case. I think back to my own flirtation with racism. Can it be that human beings are born racist, that racial prejudice is in the genes? If this is so, why do we babble about improving the lot of man? Why do the most racist people in the world howl about their love of democracy and drool over the nobility of the Common Man? Humans are killer apes. The only equality they accept is to be found in the grave. Very well. I am God. I am going to correct my mistake and give the people equality. World socialism at last! The fraternity of ghosts. They expect no less of their deity. The religions of man only worship a being with the power and the will to slaughter man. My virus will be the Flood of the twentieth century. Of course, God is supposed to create life as well as destroy it; but I will be doing that too."

Never have I experienced such dread as I felt at that moment. It just wasn't fair. I could not think, I could barely breathe, as he continued: "I know what you advocated during World War II, Goebbels. The difference between us is that I've set my sights higher. So what if Germany and the Greater Reich is annihilated? By what right can a Nazi criticize me? And we have agreed that human beings do not have rights."

In desperation, I tried again: "Why do it at all? You won't have destroyed all mankind. Burgundy will remain."

"Then Burgundy and I will play a game with each other," he said.

In a moment of careless familiarity, I asked, "What in God's name are you talking about?"

Another voice entered the conversation: "In Odin's name . . ." It was Kurt Kaufmann walking over to join us. I was pleased that he had a bandage on his head, and his face was drained of color. I wanted to strike him again! He made me think of Himmler at his worst. Looking back, I wonder why at no time I ever thought to use violence against Dr. Mabuse. I was afraid of him, as a child is afraid of the dark.

It is certainly understandable that expedient agreement is possible between two parties having nothing in common but one equally desired objective. There was the pact between Germany and Russia early in the war, for instance. The current case was different in one important respect: I doubted this particular alliance would last long enough to satisfy either party. I was certain that this was the Achilles' heel.

A comic opera kingdom with a mad scientist! If Hilda had known the details, why had she not told me more? I suspect she was guessing at much of the terrible truth herself. The knight in armor and the man in the laboratory: the two simply didn't mix. Since the founding of Burgundy, there had been an antiscience, antitechnology attitude at work.

Even French critics, who never had good things to say about the Reich, managed to praise Burgundy for its lack of modern technique. (The French could never be made to shut up altogether, so we allowed them to talk about nearly everything except practical politics. The skeptics and cynics among them could be counted on to come up with a rationale for their place in postwar Europe, stinging though it was to their pride. What else could they do but make sauces?)

Here was the most advanced geneticist in the world making common cause with a nation devoted to the destruction of science, and nearly everything else. That the Burgundians trusted his motives was peculiar; that he could go along with them was even more bizarre.

I had never met a scientist remotely like this man. The ones who had any philosophy at all belonged to the humanist tradition and believed that genetic engineering would improve the life of human beings. They were naive healers, but indispensable to the Reich—as they are indispensable to modern civilization everywhere.

To what universe did Mabuse belong? And what was this game he intended to play with Burgundy? Apparently, he would use the building blocks of life to create something nonhuman. Despite his jeers at the SS religion, he was counting on it in at least one respect: his creatures might very well be mistaken by a good Burgundian as the New Men or *Übermenschen,* and viewed as an object of worship. He already had blueprints from which to design new life, as witness the images from the SS dream. Where the rest of mankind would oppose these new beings, the Burgundians—trained from birth in religious acceptance of superior beings in human form—would present no obstacle. By the time he succeeded, Europe would belong to Burgundy. And as for men like Kaufmann, they had to believe that wicked science had produced at least one genius who was the vehicle of higher mysteries: a puppet of Destiny. Mabuse could play along with this, because in his solipsistic mania, it didn't matter. Furthermore, his creations would probably not have minds of their own. His would be the only ego when the game was finished.

I looked into the faces of these two men, such different faces, such different minds. There was something familiar there—a fervor, a wild devotion to the Cause, and a lust to practice sacrificial rites. As minister of propaganda, it had been the look I had sought to inculcate in the population with regard to the Jews.

It was evident that I had not been made privy to their machinations carelessly. Either I would be allowed to join them or I would die. As for the possibility of the former, I did not consider it likely. Perhaps the forebodings engendered in me by Hilda were partly to blame, but in fact I knew that I could not be party to such a scheme against the Fatherland. Could I convince them that I would be loyal? No, I didn't believe it. Could I have persuaded them if I had inured myself against shock and displayed naught but enthusiasm for their enterprise? I doubted it. And I was too worn out to try.

The question remained why I had been chosen for dubious honors. The message that Hilda had shown me was rife with unpleasant implications. I took a gamble by sitting up, pointing at Mabuse, and shouting to Kaufmann: "This man is a Jew!"

I could tell that that was a mistake by the exchange of expressions between the two. Of course they had to know. No one could keep a secret in the SS's own country. If they overlooked Dr. Mabuse's ideas and profession, they could overlook anything. This was one occasion when traditional Jew-baiting would not help a Nazi! I didn't like the situation. I didn't want to be on the receiving end.

The voice of Mabuse spoke to me, but the words appeared to be for Kaufmann's benefit: "As I'm not supposed to have a soul, I choose to live forever. You see, Goebbels, everything fits. It's too bad that you will not be around to work with the new entertainment technology. I was hoping we could transfer your memories of the affair with Lida Barova. As she was your most famous scandal, it would have made for a good show. We could have sold the first ticket to your wife. I do know a lot about you, more than you dream. I know that your favorite offspring is not the right genotype to survive. Poor Hilda. How's this for a magnanimous offer: we'll have the last act of your career put on film by Stefan Schellenberg, then transferred to one of our little cylinders. Oh, I forgot; he's making a documentary about Hamburg right now, and he's not slated to survive the virus."

Each word had the force of a blow. Why should Mabuse hate me? Kaufmann grinned stupidly and nodded so vigorously that I half expected to see his head fall to the ground trailing bandages.

Hatred tends to trigger my political instincts, and I struck with: "So even Heinrich Himmler doesn't receive any respect from you, not to mention the insult to the Fuehrer."

190

For a brief, blessed moment I saw that Kaufmann was discomfited, but Mabuse came to his rescue: "Hitler is beyond Burgundian reproaches; and Himmler's day is long past. This is for your benefit."

Kaufmann was back in control of himself. "It is time to face your Destiny, Paul Joseph Goebbels. Don't keep your son waiting."

I had enough wit to say, "It is a son's duty to wait for his father."

Kaufmann was oblivious: "He is with the honor guard. Come." Mabuse helped me off the cot, and then we were marching down the corridor. I was dizzy on my feet, my hand hurt, and my head was thick with pain. So many random thoughts swirling in my mind, easily displaced by immediate concern for my future welfare . . .

Efficiency was not the hallmark of my captors. After Kaufmann's experience in the elevator, I expected that he would not take my acquiescence for granted, and yet he had not unholstered his gun, and there were no extra men with him. If he thought my spirit was broken, I would disabuse him of the notion.

Otto Skorzeny probably wouldn't have been overly impressed with my making a break for stairs leading down into a basement. The off chance that going below might lead me to an exit instead of a cul-de-sac seemed worth taking at the time. I should have realized it was a bad idea when Kaufmann made no immediate motions to prevent me.

As I reached bottom, the footsteps of the scientist and the knight were audible at the top of the stairs, coming slowly and deliberately. I was blocked by an ugly green door limned in the light of one dirty bulb hanging above. It was locked, but there was a key hanging in plain view on the wall; not exactly a maximum security arrangement.

"I wouldn't advise opening the door," Mabuse's voice languidly drifted down, as I did precisely that. Taking two steps inside, I realized that the room had no light but the dim illumination streaming in from behind, throwing my shadow across a completely empty cubicle apparently constructed of plastic. I was standing at the edge of a step. The floor was lower. As I leaned over, the hair on my arms and head began to stand up and my skin tingled all over, as if receiving a charge of static electricity.

Human instincts do exist. Without evidence, I was aware that something was alive in that seemingly empty room. There was no sound, no movement, no odor—not a solitary stimulus but the creeping electrical current. But the fear that began as a bad taste was not electrical, it was horrible; it drove any semblance of rationality from me. I dropped the key, but it made no sound when it struck the floor. Kaufmann's beefy hand was on my shoulder, pulling me roughly backward, as the floor ate the key.

For the first time, I heard the edge of panic in Mabuse's voice as he said, "Get that door shut." A blue-green mass ballooned up in dreadful silence as the door blocked it from my view.

"The cell is a difficult study," said Mabuse as we returned to the laboratory. "The best electron microscopes have limitations. Using magnetic fields to reduce the effect of gravity—all the same thing, remember?—I grew a mutated cell to a size where even the twelve blind men could gather useful data. I'll have to make a new key, though."

My spirit to resist had received another crushing blow. Predictably, it was then, when it was no longer necessary, that Kaufmann leveled his Pistole .08 (the nine-millimeter Luger) at my midsection. I anticipated his warning, word for word: "No more tricks, Goebbels." At least some portion of the universe continued to make sense.

It was late afternoon as we entered the courtyard I had noticed earlier from Kaufmann's office. The large funeral pyre was still there, unused. Except that now there was a bier next to it. We were too far away to see whose body was on it, but with every step, we drew nearer to death.

A door beside the pyre opened and a line of young men emerged, dressed in black SS regalia. In the lead was my son. They proceeded remorselessly in our direction. Helmuth gave Kaufmann the Nazi salute. He answered with the same. Quite obviously, I was in no mood to reciprocate.

"Father," said Helmuth gravely, "I have been granted the privilege of guiding you to repentance." Had he no feelings for me any longer? Was this the lad I had taken to the Bayreuth Festival and whose eyes had mirrored the firelight? He had loved me once. I searched for a break in his emotionless demeanor through which might peek the little boy I'd reared to manhood. I prayed for a sign that he did not hate me, or at the very least that he was ill at ease with his treatment of his father. Perhaps I make too much of it now, but he had acquired a nervous tick that was out of character. Although it was a temperate day and Helmuth was tolerant of a wide range of temperatures, he would take off his jacket as if he were too hot, and then, a moment later, he would put it on again as if he had felt a chill. A disapproving glance from his squad leader put an end to my son's audition to be a quick-change artist. With the cold eye of scrutiny upon him, as the Pole Star gazes down on lonely mariners, he became implacable once again. Magda and I had trained our children to show no mercy where duty was concerned.

Helmuth shoved me, the cruelest blow of all. He was performing for the audience. "You will approach the body," he said. Such was the formality of his tone that I hesitated to intercede with a fatherly appeal. His expression was blank to my humanity. I did as ordered.

Not for a moment did I suspect the identity of the body. Yet as I gazed at that familiar, waxen face, I knew that it fit the Burgundian pattern. It had to be his body. Once more I stood before Adolf Hitler!

"It was an outrage," said Kaufmann, "to preserve his body as though he were Lenin. His soul belongs in Valhalla. We intend to send it there today." My mouth was open with a question that would not be voiced as I turned to Kaufmann. He bowed solemnly. "Yes, Herr Goebbels. You were one of his most loyal deputies. You will accompany him."

There are occasions when no amount of resolve to be honorable and brave will suffice; I made to run yet again, but many strong hands were on me in an instant. Helmuth placed his hand on my shoulder. "Don't make it worse," he whispered. "This must be. Preserve your dignity. I want to be proud of you." Well, that was something.

There was nothing to do; nothing but contemplate a terrible death. I struggled in vain, doing my best to ignore the existence of Helmuth. It was no surprise that he had been selected. It made perfect sense in the demented scheme of things.

Other men began to appear, and it was all I could do to keep from laughing. They were decked out as if performers in a Wagnerian opera. They must have gotten the attire from the Burgundian Museum. Some of the huskiest representatives of the Age of Heroes brought out an entirely modern aluminum ramp. Two of these began to carry Hitler's body up the incline, while Helmuth remained behind, no doubt with the intention of escorting me up that unwelcome path.

One of the antiquarians seemed as old as his costume, a Methuse-

lah with a long white beard (the spitting image of Hörbiger, or the
Druid I had imagined myself to be in the vision). He tottered over
to us, carrying a spear in his gnarled hands. I recognized the artifact
immediately: it was the Spear of Longinus that Hitler had placed at
Nuremberg to cast an aura of ancient authority over the political
trials we held there. I couldn't imagine how they had spirited Hitler's
body away from one city and the spear from another, when both were
on public display! The two possessions of the German people were
reunited as a young SS man took the spear to the top of the pyre and
laid it across Hitler's cadaver.

"The manner of your death will remain a state secret of Burgundy," said Kaufmann. "We received good publicity from your
ministry when we executed those two French snoopers for trespass-
ing: Louis Pauwels and Jacques Bergier. This is different. It wouldn't
go over nearly so well, and . . ." He stared off into space. "I keep
forgetting that soon publicity won't matter any more. The true Aryans who survive the virus will be given one chance to join us. If they
refuse, they die."

"All this talk of death is depressing our guest," said Mabuse.
"Let's cheer him up, shall we?"

"Don't do me any favors!" I nearly shrieked.

"A last request, eh? But there I go again. You may be amused to
learn that they gave you a trial along the lines of the people's courts
you so ardently defend in your propaganda. As the verdict was
known in advance, it wasn't necessary for you to attend."

My options were being reduced to nothing. Even facing death, I
could not entirely surrender. The years I had spent perfecting the art
of propaganda had taught me that no situation is so hopeless that
nothing may be salvaged from it. I reviewed the facts: despite their
temporary agreement, Kaufmann and Mabuse were really working
at cross-purposes. Nothing had altered my earlier resolve to exploit
those differences and sow dissension in their ranks. Mabuse held the
trump card, so I directed the ploy at Kaufmann.

"I suppose I'm free to talk," I said to Kaufmann's back as he
watched the red ball of the sun beyond the castle walls. The sky was
streaked with orange and gold, the thin strands of cumulus clouds
that seemed so reassuringly distant. There were a million other
places I could have been at that moment, but for a vile twist of fate.
There had to be some way to escape!

No one answered my query and I continued: "You're not a geneticist, are you Kaufmann? How would you know if you can trust Dietrich?" He was Dietrich to them, but to me he would always be Mabuse. "What if he was lying? What if his process can't be made specific enough to exclude any group from the virus?"

Mabuse smiled as Kaufmann, not bothering to turn around, answered: "For insurance's sake, he will immunize everyone in Burgundy as well as his assistants. If something goes wrong, it will be a shame to lose all those excellent Aryan specimens elsewhere in the world."

"Nothing will go wrong," said Mabuse.

I wouldn't give up that easily: "What if he injects you with poison when the time comes? It would be like a repetition of the Black Plague that ravaged Burgundy in 1348."

"I applaud your inventive suggestion and admirable interest in history," said Mabuse.

"We have faith" was Kaufmann's astounding reply.

"A faith I will reward," boomed out Mabuse's monster voice. "They are not stupid, Goebbels. Some true believers have medical training adequate to detect the wrong stuff in the hypodermic. And I play fair."

One last time I appealed to my son: "Do you trust this?"

"I am here," he answered in a low voice. "I have taken the oath."

"It's no good," taunted Mabuse. "Stop trying to save yourself."

This plan of mine to sow dissension was getting nowhere fast. I even tried to resurrect the old travails between Rosenberg's splinter group and Himmler's pagan mainstream. Kaufmann said, "We've forgiven the Gnostics. They were misled. It's a tragedy that a great man like Rosenberg had to die. His book *Der Mythus des 20. Jahrhunderts* remains our racial bible. We ignore the silly parts."

They had Hitler's body at the top of the ramp. The SS men stood at attention. Everyone was waiting. The sun seemed to pause in its descent. Time itself was waiting. What had been written for me on the calendar of Thule? I was delirious.

"Father," said Helmuth, "Germany has become decadent. It has forgotten its ideals. That my sister Hilda is allowed to live is proof enough. Look at you. You're not the man you were in the good old days."

"Son," I said, my voice trembling, "what is happening in Burgundy is not the same thing."

"Oh, yes, it is," said Dr. Mabuse.

Kaufmann strolled over to where I was standing and craned his neck for a better view of the men at the top of the ramp with the worldly remains of Adolf Hitler. He said, "We in the Death's Head SS were reliable killers during the war. Jews, Gypsies, Serbs, Czechs, Poles, and so many others fell by the sword, even when it exacted a heavy price from other elements of the war program. Speer always wanting his slave labor for industrial requirements. Accountants always counting pfennigs. The mass murder was for its own sake, a promise of better things to come!

"After the war, only Burgundy seemed to care any longer. Rulings that came out of New Berlin were despicable, weakening the censorship laws and not strictly enforcing the racial standards. Do you know that a taint of Jewishness is considered to be sexually arousing in Germany's more decadent cabarets of today? Hamburg is the worst. *Ent judeng* is a joke. Even the euthanasia policy for old and unfit citizens was never more than words on paper after the Catholics and Lutherans interfered. The Party was corrupted from within. It let the dream die."

The kind of hatred motivating this Burgundian leader was no stranger to me. Never in my worst nightmares did it occur to me that I could be a victim of this kind of thinking.

The men who had placed Hitler's body on top of the ramp had returned to the ground. All eyes were on me. My life hung on the moment. Talk, I thought, talk like you never have before.

"Germany is not as bad as all that! At least we defend our colonies, which is more than the British ever did with theirs." They weren't buying it. I tried something else: "We still have guts. Look at how the Reich kidnaps British war criminals from Australia. The Aussies yammer about how we are violating their territorial sovereignty, but that doesn't stop brave German commandos." One guard warmed to me a bit, but the rest were statues. Think, Goebbels, think! "We haven't lost our nerve. When Hitler came to power with the *Machtübernahme* he laid out the plans for our future, and we have kept faith with that."

"You've grown soft," said Kaufmann. "Why did you stop showing the executions of the traitors in the army bomb plot?"

196

"Wait a minute! I was the one who first suggested we put those films in public theaters. But Hitler said it was a bad idea after we won to subject the public to material as gruesome as that. When the Allies were endangering the soil of the Fatherland, showing a wavering German a shot of a general strangling to death on a piano wire had justification. We were scaring the masses into standing firm. But why show that in peacetime?"

"We have always been at war," said Kaufmann.

"Peace ended with the First World War," added Mabuse helpfully.

"There are alive in Europe today Germans who surrendered with the Sixth Army at Stalingrad," said Kaufmann. "Why are they allowed to live?"

"You should have asked Hitler that! The amnesty was his idea, not mine. He said we'd made enough object lessons by the time he signed the order. Why are you putting all this on me?"

"You are here," said Mabuse. "Some fun, eh?"

Kaufmann made a chopping motion with his hand. "It is time," mourned Helmuth's voice in my ear. Other young SS men surrounded me, Helmuth holding my arm. We began to walk.

Kaufmann's last words to me were: "The Reich is so softhearted that it allows Protestants to have *Busstag,* their Day of Repentance. I offer the same favor to you."

SS men had appeared around the dry pyramid of kindling wood and straw. They were holding burning torches. Kaufmann gestured and they set the pyre aflame. The crackling and popping sounds plucked at my nerves as whitish smoke slowly rose. It would take a few minutes before the flame reached the apex to consume Hitler's body . . . and whatever else was near. My only consolation was that they had not used lighter fluid—dreadful modern stuff—to hasten the inferno.

Somewhere in the blazing doom Odin and Thor and Freyja were waiting. I was in no hurry to greet them.

For the first time in my life, I wondered at how the SA must have felt when the SS burst in on them, barking guns ripping out their lives in bloody ruins. Perhaps I should have thought of Magda, but I did not. Instead all my whimsies were directed to miracles and last-minute salvations. How I had preached hope in the final hours of the war before our luck had turned. I had fed Hitler on stories of Frederick the Great's diplomatic coup in the face of a military debacle. I compared our acquisition of the atomic bomb to the remarkable change in fortunes for the House of Brandenburg. Now I found myself pleading with the cruel fates for a personal victory of the same sort.

I was at the top of the ramp. Helmuth's hands were set firmly against my back. To him had fallen the task of consigning his father's living body to the flames. They must have considered him an adept pupil to entrust him with so severe a task. As his muscles tensed, he leaned close enough to whisper in my ear: "Now you can serve Adolf Hitler for eternity. You always loved him best."

CHAPTER EIGHTEEN

*If Governments, as Mr. Burke asserts, are not founded on
the Rights of Man, and are founded on any rights at all,
they consequently must be founded on the right of
something that is not man. What then is that something?*

—Thomas Paine,
The Rights of Man

What Was Meant to Be the Last Day of My Life

So completely absorbed was I in thoughts of a sudden reprieve that
I barely noticed the distant explosion. Someone behind me said,
"What was that?" I heard Kaufmann calling from the ground, but
his words were lost in a louder explosion that occurred nearby. Then
Mabuse was shouting that he was feeling a reduction in his personal
magnetic charge, and this would only occur if a large number of
enemies were near.

A manic voice called out: "We must finish the rite!" It was Helmuth. He pushed me into empty space. I fell on Hitler's corpse and
grabbed at the torso to keep from falling into an opening beneath
which raged the impersonal executioner.

"Too soon," said one of the refugees from the opera. "The fire isn't
high enough, Helmuth. You'll have to shoot him or . . ."

Already I was rolling onto the other side of Hitler's body as I
heard a gunshot. Out of the corner of my eye I could see my son
clutching his stomach as he fell into the red flames.

Shouts. Gunfire. More explosions. An army was clambering over
the wall of the courtyard. A helicopter was zooming in overhead. My
first thought was that it must be the German army come to save me.
I was too delighted to care how that was possible.

The conflagration below was growing hotly near. Smoke filling my
eyes and lungs was about to choke me to death. I was contemplating
a jump from the top—a risky proposition at best—when I was given

a better chance by a break in the billowing fumes. The men had cleared the ramp for being ill protected against artillery.

Once again I threw myself over Hitler's body and hit the metal ramp with a thud. What kept me from falling off was the body of a dead SS man, whose leg I was able to grasp as I started to bounce back. Then I lifted myself and ran as swiftly as I could, tripping a quarter of the way from the ground and rolling bruisedly the rest of the way. The whizzing bullets missed me. I lay hugging the dirt for fear of being shot if I rose.

Even from that limited position I could evaluate certain aspects of the encounter. The Burgundians had temporarily given up their penchant for fighting with swords and were making do with machine guns instead. (The one exception was Thor, who ran forward in a berserker rage, wielding an axe. The bullets tore him to ribbons.) The battle was going badly for them.

Although I searched the grounds for Mabuse, I saw him nowhere. I did have the pleasure of watching Kaufmann's head explode like a rotten apple. I trust that he appreciated the release of Vril power.

Then I heard the greatest explosion of my life. It was as if the castle had been converted into one of von Braun's rockets as a sheet of flame erupted from underneath it and the whole building quaked with the vibrations. The laboratory must have been destroyed instantly.

"It's Goebbels," a voice sang out. "Is he alive?"

"If he is, we'll soon remedy that."

"No," said the first voice. "Let's find out."

Rough hands turned me over . . . and I expected to look once more into faces of SS men. These were young men, all right, but there was something disturbingly familiar about them. I realized that they might be Jews! The thought, even then, that my life had been saved by Jews was too much to bear. But those faces were like the faces that I've thought about too many times to count.

"Blindfold him," one said. It was done, and I was being pushed through the courtyard blind, the noises of battle echoing all around. Once we stopped and crouched behind something. There was an exchange of shots. Then we were running and I was pulled into a conveyance of some sort. The whirring sound identified it instantly as a helicopter revving up; and we were off the ground, and we were flying away from that damned castle. A thin, high whistling sound went by—someone must have still been firing at us. And then the fighting faded away in the distance.

Within the hour we had landed. I was still blindfolded. Low voices were speaking in German. Suddenly I heard a scrap of Russian. This in turn was followed by a comment in Yiddish; and there was a sentence in what I took to be Hebrew. The different conversations were interrupted by a deep voice speaking in French announcing the arrival of an important person. After a few more whisperings—in German again—my blindfold was removed.

Standing in front of me was Hilda, dressed in battle fatigues that fit her very snugly. "Tell me what has happened," I said, adding as an afterthought, "if you will."

"Father, you have been rescued from Burgundy by a military operation of combined forces."

"You were incidental," added a lean, dark-haired man by her side.

"Allow me to introduce this officer," she said, putting her hand on his arm. "We won't use names, but this man is with the Zionist Liberation Army. My involvement was sponsored by the guerrilla arm of the German Freedom League. Since your abduction, the rest of the organization has gone underground. We are also receiving an influx of Russians into our ranks."

If everything else that had happened seemed improbable, the latest was sufficient to convince me that I was enmeshed in the impossible. "There is no Zionist Liberation Army," I said. "I would have heard of it."

"You're not the only one privy to secrets" was her smug reply.

"Are you a Zionist now?" I asked my daughter, thinking that nothing else would astound me. I was wrong again.

"No," she answered. "I don't support statism of any kind. I'm an anarchist."

"But, Hilda," came a voice from the rear. There was no reason not to use her name. "You admitted the possibility of anarcho-Zionism."

"Yes," she said without losing a beat, "theoretically. But you have admitted it is by no means the mainstream."

"When I suggested it to my mother," said a pretty young woman to my left, "she threatened to sit *shiva* for me. She thinks all anarchists are crazy bomb throwers and can't imagine that sort of violence in the Zionist movement."

The serious-faced young man standing next to Hilda held up a hand and said: "Be glad you still have a mother to make threats." Several nodded at this.

As they began to discuss the ramifications of applying pacifism to anarchy, I wondered if Mabuse was playing another trick on me. Had he injected me with an hallucinogenic drug? I certainly didn't have a cylinder attached to my head to account for these fantasies involving my daughter. I returned to reality with a shock: I had not pocketed one of the micro-Tesla coils when I had the opportunity. Damn it!

A large Negro with a beard took it on himself to edify me: "There is only one requirement to be in this army, Nazi. You must oppose National Socialism, German or Burgundian. As for myself, I'd be satisfied to have a European government that respected rights, the same as they have in America." He had a French accent, wouldn't you know it?

Hilda took it from there. "After growing up in your family, Father, I don't trust any government not to become a tyranny; but I respect the American Dream."

If I had to listen to much more of this, I would regret not having joined Hitler in the flames. Flesh of my flesh, blood of my blood, Hilda had her ruthless side. Next, she told me: "We have Marxists here. We don't trust them, but we will not turn them away. If we are victorious, we won't give them the chance to do to us what they did to the anarchists in Spain, or what Lenin did to his own radicals."

"Don't forget the anarcho-Marxists," came the exact same voice that had mentioned anarcho-Zionism. Did he do nothing but hyphenate words? What was next? Anarcho-Nazism? I couldn't take it.

"You and your dirty Party are responsible for everything," my daughter said. "The small wars Hitler kept waging well into the 1950s, always pushing deeper into Russia, made more converts to Marx than you realize."

"But you hate communism, daughter. You've told me so ever since you were a teenager and began thinking about politics." In retrospect, it was not prudent for me to say this in such company, but I no longer cared. I was emotionally exhausted, numb, empty.

She took the bait, but I was unable to reel her in. "I hate all dictatorships," she said, a breeze stirring her hair on cue, and every male eye admiring her convictions. "In the battle of the moment, I must take what *comrades* I can get. You taught me that."

I could not stop myself from trying to reach her. I had lost Helmuth, and it was in the cards that Hilda was next. "The Bolsheviks were worst statists than we ever were. Surely the war crimes trials we held at the end of hostilities taught you that, even if you wouldn't learn it from your own father."

She raised her voice: "I know the evil that was done. What else would you expect from your darling princess than I can still recite the names of the Russian death camps: Vorkuta, Karaganda, Dalstroi, Magadan, Norilsk, Bamlag, and Solovki. But it has only lately dawned on me that there is something hypocritical about the victors trying the vanquished. You didn't even try to find judges from neutral countries."

"What do you expect from Nazis?" added the Negro.

My daughter reminded me of myself, as she continued to lecture all of us, captors and captives alike: "The first step on the road to anarchy is to realize that all war is a crime, and that the cause is statism." Before I could get a word in edgewise, other members of the group began arguing among themselves. I was in the hands of real radicals, all right. The early days of the Party were like this. And whether Hilda was an anarchist or not, it was clear that the leader of this ad-hoc army—enough of a state for me—was the thin, dark-haired Jew.

He leaned into my face and vomited up the following: "Your daughter's personal loyalty prevents her from accepting the evidence we have gathered about your involvement in the mass murder of Jews. You're as bad as Stalin."

I don't remember the other words he spoke. Perhaps the tape recorder I carried in my head had become demagnetized because of Mabuse. But I do remember the pain that came off my captor like a wave. He had known nothing but violence his entire life. His parents had died at Auschwitz. He had become a "pirate" while still a child. He had seen most of his friends killed or driven mad, some quiet as the grave, some chattering like a machine gun, before they threw themselves to their deaths before the steel treads of the Reich. He had been forged in a hundred night missions where the flashing lights of artillery fire, like strobe lights in a nightclub, had hypnotized him and made him an automaton of a killer. I had never thought a

Jew could have the qualities we worked so hard to program into our soldiers.

I do remember him saying, "You know what you are, Reichsminister Goebbels? You're the pig who complained about how ghetto Jews were unclean, and then helped to put them in the most unsanitary conditions imaginable. You're a conductor of hatred. You *are* hatred!"

My dear sweet daughter couldn't believe the worst of me. Not she! Reaching out to embrace her and to escape my accuser, I not only caused several guns to be leveled on my person, but received a rebuff from her. She slapped me! Her words were acid as she said, "Fealty only goes so far. Whatever your part in the killing of innocent civilians, the rest of your career is an open book. You are an evil man. I can't lie to myself about it any longer."

So it was over between us. I regarded my new enemy, who had just risked her life to rescue me. There was no room for anger. No room left for anything but a hunger for security. I was ready to happily consign my entire family to Hitler's funeral pyre, if by so doing I could return home to New Berlin. The demeanor of these free-lance terrorists suggested that they bore me no will that was good. Having just escaped death, it was a less exciting prospect the second time.

Hilda must have read my thoughts. "They are going to release you for now, as a favor to me. We agreed in advance that Burgundy was the priority. Everything else had to take a back seat, including waking up about my . . . parents."

"When may I leave?"

"We're near the Burgundian border. My friends will disappear, until a later date when you *may* see them again. I don't care what happens. As for me, I'm leaving Europe for good."

"Where will you go?" I didn't expect an answer.

"To the American Republic. My radical credentials are an asset over there."

"America," I said listlessly. "Why?"

"Just make believe you are concocting another of your ideological speeches. Do this one about individual rights and you'll have your answer. They may not be an anarchist utopia, but they are paradise compared to your Europe."

"Daughter, they have a terrible society. Don't you realize that you can legally will your body to a necrophiliac to raise money for your family? There has never been a country so monstrous in history as to allow that."

"In other words, they have the first free society. The only crimes are force and fraud, murder and theft, kidnapping and rape . . . crimes where you have a victim. And you, one of the supreme criminals of history, choose one unsavory example of what it means to live free and . . . oh, why do I bother? Fuck you."

So that was that. I was blindfolded again. Despite mixed feelings, I was grateful to be alive. The last I saw my daughter was her angry face in the twilight, surrounded by other young faces, all of them impractical and naive; none of them mature enough to live by Bismarck's profound insight that politics is only the science of the possible. Civilization cannot survive without hypocrisy; and to whatever extent possible, murder and kidnapping and all those other activities must be a monopoly of the state.

They released me at the great oak tree I had observed when flying into Burgundy. As I removed the blindfold, I heard the helicopter take off. My eyes focused on the plaque nailed to the tree that showed how SS men had ripped up the railway and transplanted this tremendous oak to block that evidence of the modern world. It had taken a lot of manpower.

How easily manpower can be reduced to dead flesh.

Turning around, I saw the flowing green hills of a world I had never fully understood stretching to the horizon. With a shudder, I looked away, walked around the tree, and began following the rusty track on the other side. It would lead to the old station where I would put in a call to home . . . to what I thought was home.

Postscript by Hilda Goebbels

January 1975

In a few months, I will place these pages in the hands of an American editor. But, first, I will enjoy the most exquisite pleasure of my life and type the following words:

PAUL JOSEPH GOEBBELS
BORN OCTOBER 29, 1897
DIED MARCH 15, 1970

For half a decade I tried to get my hands on the final entries. I didn't know for certain that they existed until a few years ago. But I'd had my suspicions that Father recorded everything. He was a remarkable diarist. It was the only place where he could allow himself to be honest.

He must have recorded his Burgundian experiences shortly after returning to New Berlin. I make this deduction because all entries dated past this point are incoherent. He had a mental breakdown, a most convenient development for Reich officials. It must have been galling to Father when they assigned psychiatric help.

Hypocrisy was their watchword as much as it was his. Even while treating him as a lunatic, they sent in a full strike force to clean out Burgundy. I doubt they got them all. The top Burgundians who survived the attack to which I made my contribution had more than enough time to regroup. The real issue boils down to one man: Richard Dietrich.

I saw white-coated lab technicians escaping from the castle before the explosives went off, sending the virus and Dietrich's other monsters to kingdom come. If they could get away, surely the greatest genius in the world could have escaped. I never saw the man in person, but there were photographs. I knew the danger he posed before reading my father's account. But after translating these pages, Dietrich seems to have taken on new life for me. Until I know that he's dead, I live in dread. One man could eliminate mankind. If he survived, why is the world still around? Was he injured? Did he run out of funds? Or did he simply lose interest? If the latter, what new project could engage his attention. Mother of Jesus, I do not want to think about this.

The Greater Reich also came down hard on the underground. The concentration camp population needed infusion of new blood, I suppose. No more favoritism for the children of the well-to-do. That was the policy for a little while at least. It appears that nothing stays the same in this mad world. Only yesterday I heard that the Reich intends to liberalize itself and set prisoners free, so as to curry favor with the West over some new business enterprise involving Africa. I don't want to think about this either.

Sometimes I try to decode Father's final entries, scrawled out in the last year of his life. He was a broken man in 1970, unhinged by the Burgundian affair, afraid of reprisals from the underground (which never happened), and to the bitter end unable to fathom why his favorite child hated him so. His last comment about me suggests that he was suffering senility on top of everything else. He goes into a rage about what a cruel and faithless daughter I am because of something I did as a child that I can't even remember. It seems that Hitler had given Father an ornate Swastika that was made of fine, hand-blown Austrian crystal. While playing in the study, I had accidentally broken this symbol of Hitler's high regard for a subordinate. Despite everything else that happened, I didn't believe Father was so petty as to harbor a grudge over something like that.

There is a consistent pattern in his last writings, and it is that his recurring nightmare of the Teutonic Knights had been displaced by a Jewish terror: an army of Golems concocted by Dietrich. Father was also convinced that the doppelgänger visited him late at night. The manner in which he determined that it was the double instead of the man who had "entertained" him in the laboratory was because this white-haired phantom entered and exited through the walls.

Yet even in his madness, Father never questioned the wicked beliefs that had twisted his life; and that is part of the madness. Not until I read the diary did I realize what a moral lesson Father could have learned in Burgundy. If he is to be believed, he even had a brief moment in which he could recognize Dietrich's evil. Why could he not see the black heart in himself?

His cynical and murderous outlook never softened. He remained what he was. Fortunately, he was in such a decrepit state, and his influence so eroded, that he was in no position to cause any more harm in the world. His talents in this regard could have added more suffering very easily. According to his final scribblings, he regretted not being able to finish a work he'd been doing to foment unrest in the Middle East, as if that tragic region didn't have more than its fair share of sorrow already. He had intended to foist off on the public a forgery of his entitled *The Protocols of the Elders of Islam*. Thank God he wasn't able to do to the Arabs what he did to the Jews.

Images that crop up in these sad pages include a landscape of broken buildings, empty mausoleums, bones, and other wreckage that shows he never got over his obsession with the war. As for Mother leaving him at long last, he makes no comment but *das Nichts*. To the end he retained the habits of a literary German.

Mother's last criticism of him had nothing to do with his philandering. It was a charge that could be laid against me, but not with as much justification. She felt that Father's tendencies to self-dramatize had been given undue reinforcement by his work with the film industry. In effect, she disbelieved his recounting of the Burgundian affair because she said it was too much like a movie! She was reminded of how he used to inspire his listeners by suggesting they were starring in an imaginary Technicolor film, and if they showed cowardice in the face of the enemy, an equally imaginary audience would boo. He had simply imagined the events in Burgundy. And as I was no longer available to corroborate the story, and Helmuth had died in a "hunting accident," there was little he could do on that front.

What probably was the straw breaking mother's back was when he made a scene in front of Hitler's tomb, demanding to be let inside where he would prove that the body behind the glass was a double that had been substituted for the real Fuehrer. It didn't help his case that he wasn't confusing film and real life, when later he asked Magda to accompany him to Nuremberg, where he could make a public spectacle of himself again by proving that the Spear of Longinus had also been replaced. When he told her that he suspected Stefan Schellenberg was involved, *a movie director,* Mother had all the evidence she needed that he was beyond recovery. If there had been any real love between them, she would have stayed. But their marriage had been more a matter of politics than anything else, a favor to Hitler; and ghosts of the past no longer had a claim on her.

The examples of my father's alienation are drawn from an almost infinite supply. How did he get through the day? One moment he takes pleasure from the "heart attack" suffered by Himmler on the eve of Father's return—and there are comments here about how Rosenberg has finally been avenged, the "unluckiest Nazi of them all," to quote directly. This material is interspersed with grocery bills from the days of the Great Inflation, problems he had with raising money for the Party in the mid-thirties, and a tirade against Hörbiger. Before I can make heads or tails of this, he's off on a tangent about Nazis who believed in the hollow earth, and pages of minute details about Hitler's diet.

I am a woman of the world, and I know that what I am placing before the world will be subjected to the most intense scrutiny. The only hard evidence I have about Richard Dietrich has been in the hands of American scientists these past five years. Yet it's only a small part of what was to be found in that laboratory; and it is a wonder I was able to lay my hands on one of the complete genetics files. They do not prove the rest, but if the only way to prove it all was to destroy the world, then I'll live with readers having doubts.

As for the critics who will heap abuse on my head, some will operate from sincere motives; but many will take a page from Hitler's own book. It was well known in 1943 and 1944 that the Fuehrer punished the bearers of bad news. Many were the clever manipulations to avoid the personal dishonor of telling him what he did not want to hear. As one who has survived in the blast furnace of Hitler himself, I will be little bothered by the slings and arrows of historians and critics who will question everything up to, and including, the ink used by my father when he penned these mind-numbing pages.

The world must be told the truth, no matter what the cost!

CHAPTER NINETEEN

I believe that all government is evil, in that all government must necessarily make war upon liberty; and that the democratic form is at least as bad as any of the other forms.

—H. L. Mencken,
Living Philosophies

NEW YORK

Alan Whittmore's hands were trembling as he put down the pages he had been reading with such intense concentration that he had a crimp in his neck. Hilda and Baerwald were talking. He leaned back and listened, not to the content of their words, but to the sound. They were two brave and happy people. They were free. Life was a challenge to them instead of a nightmare.

How, how could a majority of Germans have supported the government of Adolf Hitler? But this wasn't the real question. Before this day, Alan had wondered why the majority of people at all times in history had advocated tyranny. The Founding Fathers of the American Republic had feared the mob as much as the return of a king. Nobody said that freedom was going to be a picnic. But who would choose hell over freedom? The statists throughout history promised security, but didn't deliver it. Well, freedom didn't deliver it either . . . because there was no such thing as security in the first place. What mattered was that in America they couldn't shoot your rights down, and they couldn't vote them away. If Alan had any religion, it was to be found in those two words of Jefferson: "inalienable rights."

The first time he'd seen Hilda Goebbels on television, she was standing in front of an American flag (she wasn't fetishistic about her anarchy), and she was saying bright, clean words for the camera: "Private property to the people!" The circumlocutions and obliqui-

210

ties of an unfriendly television interviewer had done nothing but make her look better and better. She would not be tarnished by her family name; but neither would she give in to blackmail by people who believed in Voodoo. She would not change her name.

Sure, he'd had a moment of unease when he first saw the name GOEBBELS on a letterhead addressed to him. But inside was a fan letter from an already famous woman who had read his article on how the first recipients of the Roosevelt administration's socialized largesse had been filthy-rich tycoons. The idea that capitalism was the best hope for the poor had almost been wiped out during the red decade of the 1930s. But the truth could not be buried forever, and the very magazine that Alan so proudly edited had been one of the first voices saying that governments had caused the Depression, just as governments created monopolies and almost every other ill except, maybe, Dutch elm blight. Hilda had about a million footnotes to add, taken from her inside view of what happens when nationalism and socialism get together.

Before he could say negative financing, they were engaged in an enriching correspondence. They talked about how Woodrow Wilson tried to export freedom when liberty was endangered at home. They talked about Bismarck and the first modern welfare state. They talked about what kind of world it might be if the primary threat to freedom were communism instead of fascism, and the rhetoric of collectivism relied on class instead of race. And he learned from her about alternate histories and a peculiar genre of entertainment called science fiction (which he had thought was restricted to invasions-from-outer-space stories).

It was to be a fulfillment, his coming here today and reading her manuscripts. He had expected yet another ringing denunciation of the Nazi system, and this she had given him in spades. What he had in no way been prepared for was the rest of it: his sense of reality and logic was shaken to the core. He wasn't sure that he wanted to live in a world that had a Richard Dietrich in it.

The morbid contemplation kept him occupied until he realized that Hilda had been watching him for an indeterminate length of time. Baerwald was in the bathroom. "I'm sorry," said Alan, "I've been in never-never land."

"You've finished," she said. "Thank you for reading it straight through without asking questions."

"I wouldn't know what to ask."

"Would you like something more to drink?"

"No thanks. I've had enough."

Night had fallen, and the city had become an insect hive of lights drifting to and fro, traffic flowing beneath the penthouse window in the busiest part of town. Alan watched the flickering lights—a medley of traffic signals and automobile headlights turning off here, turning on there. He'd heard that lightning bugs were used in genetic research because the on/off mechanism of their illumination was one of nature's more generous clues for those who would penetrate her mysteries.

Baerwald was returning to his seat when someone knocked on the door. Hilda tensed slightly, and Alan felt his heart stop. Harry Baerwald remained nonchalant as he opened the door and let in the young Russian waiter who had brought them their dinner. Hilda and the waiter knew each other and exchanged pleasantries in Russian, before she gave him a good tip and sent him on his way.

"You probably think I'm being ridiculous with all these precautions," she said. "I only want to eat food prepared by people I know personally, at least for the immediate future."

"I don't question it at all, Hilda, after reading your father's diary. And there is something I have to tell you. I couldn't let myself believe it at first, but as I read the manuscript I became convinced I'd have to share my experience with you."

He told them about the man in the Horch limousine. He described the face in detail . . . and admitted why Baerwald had startled him at first. Neither of his listeners seemed surprised or skeptical, a very bad sign for someone wanting to be put at ease. He even mentioned the mysterious phone call.

"It's not possible, is it?" asked Alan Whittmore. "This Dietrich person couldn't still be alive, and following you?"

The young editor might not want a refill, but Hilda poured herself a stiff one before resuming her seat and answering him. Their dinners remained untouched under the steam covers on the cart the Russian had wheeled into the room. "As you read in my postscript, I have doubts about whether or not he perished in the explosion. Toward the end, my father referred alternately to Dietrich's döppelganger and to an immortal 'Mabuse.' He had it all mixed together, and I doubt that he really saw him again."

"What about the man I saw?"

"It could be a coincidence. It could be someone playing a joke on us."

"With the diary a secret, who would know enough about Dietrich to be able to fool us?"

"Burgundians," said Baerwald in the tone of voice one uses for expletives. "They'd be more likely to harass us with stupid phone calls. That's not Dietrich's style."

"I wouldn't worry too much about the phone call," said Hilda. "There's a science fiction convention going on downstairs. Quite a remarkable phenomenon, really. There's nothing like it in the Reich. They'd be arrested for the jokes they're telling if this were back home. The call may have been a prank or a wrong number."

"You don't seem very concerned that we might be under surveillance from the scientist," said Alan, a bit let down.

"To tell you the truth, Alan, my precautions have been against the Burgundians. The Death's Head SS has been reduced in power and wealth, but it still has what is left of a whole country as a base of operations. They will give us trouble when we bring out the book. If nothing else, they will see to it that the final testament of my father is banned in Europe. Any Reich official who is foolhardy enough to give the book a certificate of approval will be in hot water with them."

"You're not worried about Dietrich?" asked Alan in confusion.

"There are limits to what we can do," said Baerwald. "During the war, I was frightened by what I learned concerning biological weapons being developed by the Reich. When I arrived in America, I met a man to whom I'd been sending intelligence. I learned that of the data I'd provided, all of it that was of any value came from one man—this Dietrich. I thought it was the result of a whole team of researchers."

Hilda was ruthlessly logical: "If he lived, he's had time to improve on his virus, or find something else. What if the means to destroy humanity could be had for the price of a few chemicals and some secondhand equipment? What if he's gotten it down to where he can afford to finish the project on his own?"

No one spoke for several minutes. Any doubts he might have had concerning the authenticity of what he'd read were long gone. Alan understood the rumors of Hilda stopping World War III. She had been involved with preventing something compared to which a world war was a sane enterprise. "So the fact we are still here," said Alan, "proves that either Dietrich is dead, or he is out there somewhere, still working on the virus."

"There is a third possibility," said Baerwald. "He may be alive, but no longer interested. Kaufmann died. No one may have offered him a renewal of the contract." Hilda and Alan stared with horror at the survivor of a concentration camp. "You must bear in mind that this man is completely mad. Although a genius, he thinks like a petulant child. He took the words of Adolf Hitler literally and extrapolated from there. Unlike the usual demented follower, the rank and file of the Nazi Party, this man was in a position to do something about the odious principles of the *Übermensch.*"

"I don't agree with you," said Hilda. "Nietzsche's Overman is a noble ideal that was completely twisted by the Nazis, and by Dietrich as well. The superior man would have no reason to enslave anyone. He would be a creator, not a destroyer. The Nazis put uniforms and shiny boots on street thugs and called that the Superman. Nietzsche warned against German nationalism. He condemned Wagner for racism."

"All very true," said Baerwald, "but you must also consider—"

"How can you sit there and debate history?" Alan cried out. "Our lives may be endangered at this very moment."

"Young man," answered Baerwald in a kindly voice, "nobody gets out of here alive. I learned that in the camp. I wouldn't let the Nazis degrade me in my own mind. I refused to feel shame. But there was a price: I became philosophical about death. Modern man has been very quick to give up religion, but he hasn't put anything in its place to help him face the truth. Man is mortal."

"What about the religions of the SS?" asked Alan, still reeling from his journey through a mental landscape he could hardly credit.

"A perversion, Mr. Whittmore. The religions of antiquity were not a concoction of mad ravings. Wise old pagans would be as horrified by what goes on in Burgundy as the rabbi who instructed me."

"Or the pope. Or any minister of the gospel," said Hilda.

"OK, OK, but what about Dietrich? Isn't there some way to find out what happened to him?"

"Let's say he's dead," said Baerwald. "We dance around his grave. But his discoveries are not secret. Science gives its fruit to anyone who plucks the vine. Others will learn what he learned. How would that be different from living under the threat of nuclear annihilation? You seem able to live with that."

Hilda came to the rescue. "Don't pick on Alan. I am especially bothered by Dietrich and would take personal offense to die at his hand."

"Yes, but no death is preferable. If he crosses our path again, we will fight him. I would kill him if I could. But I will not waste my life thinking about him. There are limits. Vengeance is mine, saith the Lord. An 'eye for an eye' was an accounting for God, not for man."

"I envy your faith," said Alan.

"Mine is not an exceptional case. I choose not to live as if I were a Nazi. I prefer the hard path of love to the easy path of hatred."

Hilda leaned over and kissed Baerwald on the cheek. Alan embarrassed himself by remembering he had intended to ask her frankly impertinent questions about her sex life. The answers to those questions seemed irrelevant now.

"I have a splendid idea," said Hilda. "Let's eat our dinners before they get cold."

And they did. The food was unexceptional, but with every bite, Alan felt a lessening of tension. He couldn't help noticing the almost painful formality with which Hilda dined, her back straight, the silverware used with a studied correctness. At first, no one spoke, and there was only the sound of cutlery tapping and scraping on the plates, and the labored breathing of Baerwald, who was old, but still strong beneath his weathered frame. Raising his gray head from contemplation of a brussels sprout, the man known to the world as H. Freedman said, "I dread someday to learn that Total Evil and innocence are one and the same, but a man such as Dietrich cannot be innocent, can he?"

Catching Hilda's glance, Alan could see that she was as perplexed as himself. There was tenderness in her voice. "Harry, what are you saying?"

"My brief experience of Nazi hospitality is something that stays with me, spoils little things for me. There is a point where physical horror crosses over into the spiritual. The flesh takes on new meanings. I never eat a meal that I don't recall the hungry faces of the other internees, who had been there longer, so much longer than I, even in what was officially a temporary holding area. I saw a man I knew from before, but I didn't recognize him until he spoke. He'd changed that much. He was very thin. I think that he was a Lutheran, but I'm not sure. He was a Berliner, though. He'd been quite cosmopolitan before."

Alan and Hilda looked to each other once again. Baerwald was drifting in memory, his words coming farther apart, eyes focused on the wall that was a blank screen for the past. Alan felt a spark jump the distance between Hilda and himself—a sudden empathy seeming to suggest that all the facts and theories with which they had been wrestling were nothing in the face of existential experience. A man like Baerwald was shaped by his suffering, but he had refused to relinquish his identity to that suffering.

The sad witness continued: "I think they selected certain recalcitrant individuals to starve to death. What did your father say, Hilda? Wasn't it that the disruption of transport by Allied bombing was why so many starved? Yet some ate. I ate. I shared, but I was caught and punished. Still, they fed me. They made up categories, you know, and we couldn't change their rules for them. Only they could make the changes. They didn't seem very scientific, not these men. I only remember cruelty. But, then, Dietrich was both scientific and cruel, wasn't he? We only have our memories in the end. I remember the face of that young man. I held him in my arms and saw that he was beyond anger and hatred. That may be why his words stay with me. He said a phrase I'd always abhorred when he whispered, 'Forgive them, Father, for they know not what they do.' I answered him too quickly, in a voice much too loud for that place: 'Do *not* forgive them, for they know what they do.' With a last tired smile, he spoke in a voice much firmer than before: 'But evil *never* knows.' And he died. I wanted to embrace him, but I also wanted to cast him away. I'd have called him a fool, but he was no longer with me. Then another internee told me that I should not draw attention to myself and quickly moved away to demonstrate that he was himself an apt pupil of these hard lessons. But I sat on the floor, next to the corpse, until the ones who never knew about anything came to take us away."

There were tears when he finished, but they weren't from his solemn eyes still transfixed on the wall. Hilda was crying. And Alan, looking at her the whole time, began to cry as well. "Oh, what have I done?" asked Baerwald, his voice completely different and attention returned to the Isabel Paterson Hotel. "You must forgive an old man," he said.

216

"It's as if I've lived a whole year in the course of one evening," said Alan, passing a handkerchief to Hilda.

"I think that I should leave and let you two talk business," said Baerwald.

"Not tonight," said Hilda. "As far as business is concerned, I have a headache."

Inopportunely and irritatingly, the phone rang. "I hope it's not the convention downstairs," said Hilda, "asking us to keep the weeping down."

"Puts a real damper on parties," chimed in Alan.

Baerwald said something in German, and while Alan was working out its meaning about the penalties awaiting punsters in hell, Hilda took care of the call. She had returned the phone to its cradle for some moments before Alan noticed that she was just standing there, a statue.

"Hilda, what's the matter?" he asked.

"Someone just asked if my name was Goebbels. When I said it was, he said the phrase *Yom Hashoah,* then hung up."

Baerwald half shouted, "That's Yiddish for 'the Night of Fire'!"

"I know," said Hilda, as Alan was already running for the door. She called after him but he was already in the hallway, headed for the elevator. It had to be him! The white-haired man he'd confused with Baerwald earlier! Could it really be Richard Dietrich? He was certain that the man had been following him. Maybe he had called from the lobby.

The elevator doors were closing as he rounded the corner, and without even looking pressed the OPEN button and slid between the doors before they reversed direction. He bumped into a woman standing dead center and she fell against the wall. "Hey," she began, but her outrage lacked conviction. With her beehive hairdo and red leotard, she was in the regulation outfit of an "elevator operator."

"Excuse me," he said, already pushing LOBBY and trying to mentally speed them on their way.

"I wasn't sure there was anybody on this floor, it's so dead up here."

"You're not supposed to be here, are you?"

"You're kind of cute" was her entirely professional response. "Besides, I've paid the hotel dick for the rest of the week, and I do mean pay."

217

He had no time for this. But the special elevator, with no stops on the way, was still taking forever and then some to descend. "I guess this isn't your night," he replied.

"Oh, jeez, you're not with that convention are you? They're all kids, and nobody pays. The old guys have these young girls hanging around them for free. Don't they know that free enterprise built this great country?"

"Old? How old?" He was finally looking at her, and she wasn't half bad. She must have retired from the street trade before it was too late.

"Search me, puh-leeeeze. One really old gootch seemed to be giving me the once over, and I was charitable enough to make contact, but he had such a crazy grin that it gave me the creeps and I moved on. Now you—"

"How old?" Alan had her by the arm, but the funny thing was that he didn't remember reaching for her.

"Ancient."

"Where?"

"Toward the bar up by the phones but . . . oh, jeez, now you're running away. Don't you like my perfume?" They had arrived.

Alan was sprinting across the lobby, driven to reach the man sidling over to the revolving door that led to the street, the man from the Horch limousine. Adrenaline rushing through his system, Alan's body became one uninterrupted motion—all his violence channeled into reaching the target. The grinning-skull face maddened him with its awful sneer.

He could kill the mysterious old man if he weren't careful. This is what brought him up short. Here was not the body of the Superman. Why, if Joseph Goebbels had been prescient in his worst imaginings, then Richard Dietrich would appear younger today than he was at the time of the Burgundian affair. He wouldn't be this tottering wreck of a man shaking in front of him. None of these infirmities had been evident from the window of the car.

But the damned sneer was still there on the huge head with the shock of white hair, and the malign intelligence must still be reckoned with. If final proof of his guilt were required, he was attempting to escape. "Hold it right there," said Alan, and as the man paid no heed, the young embraced the old, one strong arm behind a stooped back, the other in front of a fallen chest. The elderly body was trembling as Alan released the pressure. "You've got some explaining to do," said Alan, himself out of breath. "Why have you been following me? Why did you make that call?" Even now, with the quarry firmly in hand, he couldn't bring himself to ask what was really on his mind: *Who are you?*

It was a relatively simple matter to move his prisoner back toward the elevator. The man was offering no resistance. Alan's immediate concern was to think of a semiplausible explanation should someone inquire as to why he had kidnapped a seemingly harmless old man. He was certainly not prepared for the booming voice of Harold Baerwald emanating from the elevator that had since ascended and returned with its new passenger: "Oh, my God, I don't believe what I'm seeing. It can't be, and yet it is, it is. I'd know that face anywhere."

"Dietrich?" asked Alan, heedless of the curious onlookers.

"No," said Baerwald, in a softer voice. "He's my brother."

Back in the penthouse apartment, old affections were rekindled as best they could be, and small mysteries were solved. Hilda had ordered coffee brought up, and she complimented Alan on his quick, diplomatic recovery. As an agitated hotel manager approached them, Alan's hold on the old man had transformed into a friendly patting on the back. The lost brother would not speak at first, which provided some difficulties, but at least he didn't contradict anyone.

Poor, long-lost Herman, the older brother of Harold, not seen since the war. It did not take long to ascertain that he was to some degree demented. Baerwald was so thrilled over finding his absent sibling that he could not be put off by the the eccentric circumstances of the reunion; or, as he wisely observed to Alan, "Don't fret, my boy. It's all for the best. And one does expect a certain lassitude from the elderly, rather than high-spirited skullduggery."

It was such a close thing. Alan was still concerned that he might have done serious damage to his prisoner. His right hand shook when he thought about it and spilled coffee in his saucer. Hilda watched his every move.

Encouraging Herman to speak was a bit like extracting gold from an unstable mine. But Harold was persistent. It was learned that the Horch limousine and chauffeur had been rented for the day. Herman seemed to find it difficult to speak, even after he accepted that this was indeed his brother and that he could trust him. A contributing factor to the man's unease was physical. The sneer that had so inflamed Alan was a permanent scar from the war. It was a sobering experience to confuse two Baerwalds with the ghostly presence of Dr. Dietrich, and this in one day. No need for doppelgängers around here.

But how could such a family separation have lasted for so many decades, especially when Harold had become world famous? The pseudonym was not the explanation, as biographical material was in all the Freedman books and his photograph was well publicized. The answer seemed to be amnesia. In that great human wake of wartime refugees, the addled Herman had been swept up and deposited in an institution where he was all too common a case. And so he had adjusted. Hitler had stolen his past.

The flood of newspaper reports about Baerwald and Goebbels and the *American Mercury* had triggered something in the deeper currents of memory that had driven half-mad Herman to make contact with these people. He sat near the window, trying desperately to communicate something of this. When asked questions, he would adopt the mannerisms and gestures of response, moving his shoulders, nodding his head, but the words rarely came except in spurts. He had not seen the name Baerwald since the war, according to him; although it was more likely that he had and simply failed to recognize it.

"What name have you been using?" asked Alan, the first to wonder.

"I'm . . . I've been Raymond."

"I'm sorry that I attacked you, Raymond."

"You did?"

For a very long time, the Baerwalds spoke together, and pieces of the past were reconstructed, or invented to fill in the spaces. Hilda and Alan observed the past come alive. Then, at length, the night passed into memory. Outside, the dawn began to paint the sky with a mixture of pink and dark blue. A bird was singing somewhere below their window, but still high above the soon to be crowded streets.

Alan felt stiff in every joint and was delighted when Hilda—too wound up to sleep—suggested that they go out to breakfast. As they took a last glance at the disheveled form being embraced by Harold

Baerwald, Hilda whispered, "I was ready to believe he was our mad scientist as well." They shared in equal portions of relief.

"There won't be time for you to sleep before the television interview we've arranged," he reminded her as they hit the street.

"I'll be fine. Just slap some makeup on me so I won't dissolve under the lights."

He reached out for her hand. She held it tightly.

They met in dark places but they brought their own light. They were banished from their own country and left muttering curses at the sallow-faced youngsters who now sat on their old thrones of power, humbly following orders from New Berlin. But these last of the true Burgundians were not beaten. Not while old ideas bubbled just below complacent surfaces. Not while the young eagerly sought out the old for guidance. These angry ones would not let the flame of vengeance be extinguished.

There had been no word from Herr Doktor Dietrich, but neither had they found his body. If he rejoined them, all the better; but if his services were forever denied them, they would simply have to improvise. There was still a good crop of Hitler youth waiting to be harvested—and their numbers would grow, the longer the secret masters bided their time.

Each month brought reports of new outrages, as self-proclaimed Nazis discovered the practical benefits of compromise and expediency. This was not the Das Tausendjährige *Reich that Hitler had intended. To strike now would be futile, and so the Burgundians camouflaged themselves, pretending conformity to that which they most despised; but only in the daylight were they bourgeoise New Europeans. Under cover of darkness they came alive.*

A crisis had arisen in their diminished ranks when the initial space missions did not disturb the Eternal Ice. But the orthodox may always be relied on to explain away discrepancies when the Sacred Articles of Faith do not quite fulfill expectations. It was suggested that there would be a cumulative effect. Too much activity in outer space would bring down the wrath of the gods, later if not sooner. They would wait out the years.

The miserable failure of an attempt to sabotage a German rocket launching taught them the strategy of patience, and the tactical necessity of a more significant target. Against the audacious plans for industrialization in space must be brought the most daring attack, and to win the favor of the gods, the sin must be large and complete before it was punished. Only then would the Burgundian schemers believe that they might win the favor of all the gods, who were known to quarrel among themselves. What the gods really needed was a proper Fuehrer, a role that Odin did not completely satisfy.

And so they planned for the future, as did their enemies. A decisive blow must be struck against the false dream of progress. To achieve this lofty purpose, hundreds must be prepared, tested, screened, and distilled into one special individual. He would have a technical aptitude unhampered by any convictions about the skills he would acquire. They would train him and condition him and lie to him. And when the time drew near, they would take him out under the night sky of Burgundy and point out the star he must destroy.

Their ceremonies always ended at dawn.

CHAPTER TWENTY

The dead can be more dangerous than the living.

—H. R. Trevor-Roper,
quoted in *Imagining Hitler*

Mein Führer, I can walk.

—Peter Sellers in
*Dr. Strangelove, or: How I Learned to Stop
Worrying and Love the Bomb*

Alan and Hilda's first week in New York had been a hectic one. There is nothing quite like an American audience, composed as it is of volatile contradictions—Puritanism colliding against hedonism, while self-absorption vies with rhetorical high-mindedness. Hilda was a magnet to draw the expected guest but also the peculiar, the sincere alongside the antagonistic and the ignorant. She had thrived in the electric atmosphere at first. With a woman's eye for detail, she found delight in the *outré* costumes parading in front of her that seemed to be playfully mocking her old-world tastes. New York was the first place she'd ever seen a zoot suit, which Alan helpfully explained was making a comeback among the literati. She signed hundreds of autographs and wore unusual hats. She made new friends; but there was also the requisite number of enemies.

Hilda had been surprised by the abuse she received in some quarters. It was one thing to face an honorable opponent who challenged her assumptions, but quite another to be roundly denounced by a total stranger employing the sort of personal terms she didn't expect to hear outside a family circle. But always Alan was there to help. "This is America," he told her. "Remember that we threw out the libel laws for running contrary to the spirit of the First Amendment. In this country, the only opinions that matter are the ones you choose to accept. It's not nearly so easy to destroy a reputation as

223

it used to be. For every fool, there is an intelligent person who makes up his own mind."

After the life she'd led, Hilda was nothing if not adaptable. Although she was committed to theoretical anarchy, the American Republic was still the freest society she had ever experienced. She even picked up the uniquely American trait of making light of impertinence. "It's just that under National Socialism," she recalled, "character assassination is performed at the institutional level . . . with literal results."

"We do a lot of forgiving over here," said Alan. "We have to."

He enjoyed coaching her. Where she would answer difficult questions at considerable length, he advised the succinct response. A few grillings on television and radio brought her around to his persuasion. The decisive encounter was on Alexei Tierni's aptly named show "The Inquisition Box." This former Bible salesman had a national audience, but most of his subscribers were in what he himself called the boondocks. Guests were warned to expect a hardhitting interview on the "Box," which weekly ordeal Tierni quite predictably touted as a family program. But when a guest struck his fancy, he could be nice.

"So, Hilda Goebbels," he began in the tone of voice he reserved for passing judgment, "why should we believe this little book of yours?" Sitting in the green room, watching her on the monitor, Alan could see Hilda brace herself. Until that moment, neither of them had known if they'd be in for the hard or soft treatment. If Tierni was going to be a bastard about it, Alan could only hope that the practice sessions he'd insisted on would pay off. He was spending more time on Hilda than on his wife or the magazine.

"What would you like documented?" she asked without allowing the pause that is deathly in broadcasting.

"You speak English well, I'll give you that." When all else failed, Alexei relied on the non sequitur.

Her eyes kept drifting to the quite remarkable wig the host carried on his head, a black spread of oil that seemed in danger of sliding off at any moment. Also the lights were too bright. Was this a plot to make her squint into the camera? At least the studio audience seemed divided in its sympathies.

Tierni appealed to the disenchanted who wanted the return to a more vigorous nation-state. Even so, his religious zealotry limited his practical influence within this group. And a large part of his audience simply enjoyed the circus. Alan had warned Hilda of the problems, but she insisted on going after the publicity anyway. She'd be a good American, yet.

"I don't know what's worse," intoned Alexei, "our libertine liberty lovers here—and I do mean lovers—or the Nazis over there who at least show a little public decorum."

"I've lived there and I know what's worse," Hilda shot back. She garnered a few random bits of applause for that. So far, so good.

Alexei made the mistake of returning to her facility with languages, an unsubtle way of reminding the viewers not to trust a damned foreigner. She remembered that Baerwald had told her of how Jews who had come to America to escape persecution in Germany all too often found themselves the victims of prejudice for being Germans! Times had changed a lot since then, and the kind of demagoguery she was experiencing was no longer the norm. In some ways, she found the Yankee style of hate mongering almost quaint, compared to the Nazi variety.

"Do you want to know if I'm grammatical in every language I speak?" Smiling sweetly, she continued: "How about you? I understand that you lapse into 'Tongues' when you worship. When yours is the voice, does the Holy Ghost speak grammatically or not?"

"How the hell would you know about that?" he shouted, unaware that the research was courtesy of Mencken's good old magazine, ever vigilant. Tierni didn't want to play up his religion currently (despite the oath to witness for the faith). The Lord's Laborers, the sect to which he belonged, was currently in hot water because some of its most vocal members were being prosecuted for violating two of the laws that the libertarian republic actually enforced. The leader had mistakenly thought that decentralization of powers meant that the Bill of Rights did not apply to local matters, such as the regulation of sin. The right reverend gentleman was duly informed that the Fourteenth Amendment was still on the books, much to the dismay of a constabulary made up almost entirely of members of the Lord's Laborer's who had imprisoned pornographers and burned a bookstore. These officials were themselves now up on criminal charges. Property rights were taken seriously in the republic.

"Well, Hilda Goebbels," stammered Alexei, "if you're going to get personal, I ain't . . . I'm not going to stoop to your level." Alan

225

silently applauded as the interview moved on and noted that the audience was laughing with Hilda.

The flustered host went back on the offensive: "If you're a repentant Nazi, like you say, then why haven't you changed your name?"

"First, I never joined the Party. Contrary to popular belief, you're not born into it. Oddly enough, Father never insisted. I turned down an invitation to join the *Reichsschrifttumskammer,* their writer's organization. I wanted no part of it. Second, I don't believe in Voodoo."

"Huh?"

"Guilt by association is bad enough. Guilt by name is so primitive an idea that I'm shocked it has seeped into our civilization. In fact, there is no reason why the greatest enemy of Hitler couldn't be named Hitler himself!"

Shifting in his seat, leaning toward her menacingly, the host lamented, "Obviously you don't care about the feelings of the people."

"Are we concerned with form or substance?" she asked. "The feelings that matter are not isolated from thought, for heaven's sake. From the earliest age, German children are taught that there is no injustice so great that it cannot be cured by more injustice. The Nazis are very concerned with the people's feelings, take it from me. The only way to fight that is with clear thought." This won her murmurs of approval out there beyond the stage lights, and Alan marveled at how the cadences of her speech were adjusting to TV talk. In private, she spoke slowly, accumulating pauses with the unconscious certainty that her listeners would bear with her. She wasted no seconds now. She finished her hymn to reason by suggesting that if the Allies had been reasonable at Versailles, the world would have been spared the worst monstrosities of the century.

When sensing a sea change in the studio audience's prejudices, Alexei Tierni could always be relied on to plumb the depths. "Well, Miss Goebbels, isn't it true that the SS is full of homosexuals?"

"I can't believe you'd ask a question like that in America!"

"Hey, we have free speech here. Maybe you don't appreciate how much inquiring minds want to know."

She shrugged. "You're confusing the SA with the SS. National Socialist Germany is homophobic, in case your inquiring mind missed that detail." Tiring of the boor sitting across from her, Hilda wondered if she shouldn't have heeded Alan's suggestion to pass on this one. But if her new home was to be the country devoted to the teachings of the Profits, then she did not want to pass up a potential market, even one so unsophisticated as the subscribers to this benighted program. Rather than discuss her views on sex, she preferred putting the inquisitor on the defensive. "Why are you so interested in . . ." She committed her first pregnant pause as she struggled to recall her American slang, confused for a moment by the British slang for cigarette. ". . . the fags, Mr. Tierni? Is it from tender concern over some of Hitler's victims?"

He used his down-home, simple-boy voice: "I just want Mom and Pop to know that Nazis are all sexual degenerates and Europe is perverted."

It was becoming a worse spectacle than Alan had anticipated. In his self-adopted role as Hilda's manager, he wanted to reach out and pull her off the stage. His admiration for her grew as she weathered the storm, a woman of the old world with elegant vices and staunch virtues. While she wanted to tell America how Germany was pursuing the siren call of empire, and turning its people into dupes and corpses in the bargain, this amateurish demagogue with the phony hair was less interested in what came out of a leader's head than his loins. Alexei Tierni seemed a whole lot less quaint all of a sudden.

Having caught his drift, she made it abundantly clear that she would not answer questions about her sex life, or her father's or mother's, or Hitler's, or even Hitler's dog. Chuckles from the audience reminded her how silly it all was. There was no point in losing her temper, apparently the only reason this man had guests. He'd probe and prod and insult until he struck angst. The trick was to make yourself calm and avoid the traps.

At which moment, the man in the "Box" became the first interviewer to raise the specter: "What about this Dietrich feeb, this lunatic in the lab, huh? You can't expect Mom and Pop to believe someone like that really exists."

Oh, hell, thought Alan.

The mere mention of the dreaded name was like a trickle of cold water dampening Hilda's high spirits of the earlier moment. To her it was as if Tierni had asked for proof that there had been an Isaac Newton. She explained: "Someone did the work that's led to the new vaccines, hormones, and drugs. And that's only the tip of the recombinant DNA iceberg. However, these facts don't mean that Dietrich is still living. We have the fruits of his brilliant mind, but hopefully he has taken his evil soul with him to the grave."

"Pretty poetic. Sounds like you're quoting from your book. But how do we know that a whole bunch of guys didn't do this work you claim is Dietrich's."

This segued nicely into a plug, which opportunity she was not about to miss. "For the answer to that, you should read my book!"

Before the time ran out, Alexei had one last inanity he'd been saving. He actually asked if there shouldn't be limits on technology. Without missing a beat, she suggested that any medical technology that might prolong the life of rude television hosts should be withheld by all means. The studio audience liked her, a good indication of how she was received by the home viewers. The thunderous applause caught Tierni by surprise. Every now and then this happened, but he couldn't let that discourage him. He was all set to torment his next guest: a Nordic cult believer who was planning an expedition to reach the hollow interior of the earth. This was one of his theme programs.

Alan had planned their escape route beforehand, and a limo was waiting for them. (He'd made sure it wasn't a Horch!) Hilda was laughing as they sped off into the night. She wanted to be angry, but she couldn't quite manage it. There are limitations to righteous indignation when the inquisitor is a clown. Alan began rattling off a list of advantages and disadvantages to accrue from the broadcast, but she didn't want to hear it. "My good friend," she said, "you have a tendency toward an overbearing solicitude that is fortunately offset by a paranoia to match my own."

"Hilda Goebbels," he replied, mimicking the style of the unlamented program, "you sure are a writer, and you use English real good."

"You warned me that this 'gentleman' with the living wig has the right to, what was the term, bleep me?"

"Yeah, he'll bleep the word *fag,* for instance."

"That's terrible. Didn't I use the right word?"

"It fit."

"Why am I to be . . . bleeped?"

"It offends the morality of the show, says he."

"I'm surprised that kind of censorship can happen in America."

"He's not the government, Hilda. Don't forget you signed his contract, and when he says 'family program,' he means *his* family. Alexei is the kind of guy who is afraid of his own imagination. Your other interviews didn't allow any bleeps. Contracts are sacred."

"Let's not do any more shows like 'The Inquisition Box.' I've learned my lesson. To tell the truth, I'd just as soon not make any more appearances for a while. I need a rest."

He moved closer to her, and she pleased him by putting her head on his shoulder. Now was the time to ask if she'd let him show her the town. She nodded. He gave instructions to the driver.

"Alan, where do you find so much time for me?"

"I manufacture it."

"You'll have to teach me how to do that."

He'd never seen her vulnerable before, or so relaxed. They parked just outside a pedestrian zone and went to a Bohemian restaurant that specialized in soft lighting and good wine. When they had finished, he suggested that they once again face the hazards of motorized traffic so as to reach an entertainment ghetto and take in a show. This they did, and the chauffeur, waiting for them a second time, thanked Alan for the generosity of his tips.

Perhaps the Teutonic gods were in a capricious mood, because the first notable entertainment that caught their attention was a Sturm und Drang concert, the vibrations of which could be felt for blocks ... and the musicians were only warming up. She was drawn to find out what this could be and Alan had a morbid fascination as well. His music reviewer on the *American Mercury* had referred to this stuff as the secret weapon of German *Kultur*. The only musical taste he was certain he shared with Hilda was a fondness for the German Richards: Strauss and Wagner. (But theirs was reputed to be quiet music next to an S&D concert.)

As if they were two children, accepting each other's dares, they waded into the steam pouring out the doors, money held out in front of them as if to propitiate demons. They never made it to seats. The sound was a physical force blocking them in the aisles, but judging from the collection of frenzied Townies (probably looped on Speck) in the auditorium, standing was an appealing proposition. It was impossible to understand what language was being sung, but each word had the force of a blow to the head.

Alan saw Hilda's lips move, but no smaller sounds could be heard over the cacophony. Realizing this, she pointed with some amusement to the lead singer, whose attire was nothing to talk about. He was shaved bare all over, covered in neon paint, and his sole attire consisted of shiny black boots that came up to his knees. While marveling at his various bodily imperfections, Alan and Hilda were rewarded by the incomparable sight of a Townie in the front row throwing an entire mug of beer on the lead singer.

This was not a smart move. Having successfully avoided electrocution from his electric violin, the singer-screamer silenced the fellow members of his band and began shouting at the Townie in a most recognizable American idiom: "Hey, this piece of slime in the front row threw a beer on me. Do you hear me, loyal fans? He could've killed me. Now why don't you take this slime outside and turn him into ashes, man. *Kill him for me!*"

They went for him. They held up in the air this one Townie begging for mercy over the fever throbbing of the mob, and suddenly Alan felt Hilda trembling up against him, and she was dry heaving. There was no rush for the exits. The rush was in the other direction, down toward the stage where they could get a better view. The security guards were shouting into their walkie-talkies and trying to figure out what they could do.

Alan got Hilda out of there fast, and when they were back on the street she threw up. He hustled her back to the limo as fast as he could, and the driver, who was good, didn't talk but knew a quiet place to go when Alan asked.

They took a walk, not far from the car but far enough. "I can't stand it, Alan. I'm in the concert, hating it, sensing how much it's like a Party rally, but telling myself it's not really the same thing, not really. And then *that* happens. And it comes back, it all comes back. I don't want to listen to the filthy rhetoric here, not here. I don't want to hear about killing slime and ashes and . . . not here, not here. And then to see them, that killing fury. First the chaos, then impose order. That is how Hitler did it."

She sat on the ground, exhausted. He joined her, arm at her waist. They rocked together like that until she was ready to go home.

The publication of Hilda's books changed Alan Whittmore's life. There were rough times in the beginning, but the rewards made it all worthwhile. Dr. Evans came out of the woodwork long enough to try proving that the diaries were fake, but the Bipartisan party provided him with less than adequate experts. The general public bought the book in droves. And then they bought the books arguing about the book. As Alan said to Evans on the occasion of their last meeting, "The most money you've ever made was from debunking the Goebbels Diary." Evans couldn't argue with that. The public preferred reading about Nazis over the definitive study of the New Deal.

The kooks had a field day. Hundreds of phone calls and letters and telegrams purported to be threats from "Doctor Mabuse." It got to the point where Hilda and Alan agreed that the real mad scientist would need to provide his bona fides before anyone would take the next end-of-the-world threat seriously.

The SS behaved in Europe as Hilda had predicted. They ignored the book. Within a few months of the diaries being published, Baerwald sent one of his best bottles of wine to Hilda in celebration of the fact that no acts of terror had been committed against them for her exposé. They all hoped that SS bravado had been dealt a mortal blow. (Baerwald wasn't about to miss the diary bandwagon. He wrote an introduction and helped with the considerable documentation. Hilda said that he was invaluable; and to repay the compliment he used his real name.)

Harold Baerwald died in 1984, and Hilda and Alan attended the funeral in New York, where the author of the Freedman books had finished his life. The next day, Alan introduced Hilda to Oscar, who now had a chain of restaurants; and an autographing party ensued for Hilda, on condition that a complete set of Harry's works be auctioned off to raise money for his family.

"So when are you going to give me your autobiography to publish?" asked Alan.

"You were pushy when you were solely an editor. Now that you've become your own publisher, you're in danger of terminal megalomania."

"Got bills to pay."

"You don't need more money, do you?" she asked cheerfully. "Success has gone to your head." She pointed to the golden dollar sign he wore on his cheek. "You used to abhor tattoos and face illustration."

"They like it for the talk shows," he said apologetically. "But why are you wasting a talent like yours on translating German science fiction when you're famous? Any political book with your name on it will sell a million copies right off the bat."

"It's the fault of our mad scientist, Dietrich. I've come to see that we live in a science fiction world. Nothing is certain. There have been more changes in the last century than, oh, God, how many millennia before? The First World War finished off the old world and left humanity high and dry, without purpose or direction. Then World War II created a new world, an incredible world that we don't really understand, but we must embrace. We've unlocked powers that will either send us to the stars or turn the whole planet into a death trap where everyone is a victim. We have no guarantee that there won't be another Hitler, with a man like my father orchestrating his followers, and a Dietrich giving him new weapons of destruction. Let's spread out and make ourselves a more difficult target."

"Go to space, young man; go to space," said Oscar, ever the eavesdropper in his own establishment. "That's what I told my son when he graduated. He's up there on temporary, but he's signed up for permanent residence when a berth is available. He sent me back to school. I wouldn't have done it for anyone but my son."

"Business has been good?" asked Alan.

"The best with my chain opened up, and with my son's winning a choice contract on the station, I didn't have any excuse not to go to college. He wants me to move spaceward eventually, but I don't know about that."

"I'm going," said Hilda.

"You are?" asked Alan. "But what about—"

"Writing is allowed in space, Alan. They haven't outlawed it. I only regret that Harry won't be coming with me."

As they parted at the curb, Alan thought back to a rainy day when he and a sour old man had exchanged words on the same piece of pavement, and Alan was about to enter the Isabel Paterson Hotel and a new life. "I'll make you a deal," said Hilda. "I'll give you a finished copy of the autobiography, for what it's worth, if you come to a convention at which I'll be a guest next month."

"I'm game."

"Here." She passed him a flyer. "The Free Tribes of South Africa are hosting the World Science Fiction Convention at the Laissez-Faire Center in Capetown. This will be the first convention where artists from the Reich will attend in company with us lucky stiffs from the Free World."

"I'm surprised the Reich will let them attend."

"It's the latest attempt at good public relations. We'll be on the outlook for Gestapo agents shadowing the German guests. Want to bet there will be defections? The writers with subversive tendencies gravitate to science fiction. The Reich is not exactly the utopia they've been promising their wretched populace year after year. And the authorities didn't predict the future of Africa with any success."

"Maybe the Reich is disappointed over its attempt to forge the tribes into miniature National Socialisms. When apartheid collapsed, the last hope for the Nazis to colonize that region collapsed."

"They're stuck, and they know it. Without American and African capital, they'll never finish the world's largest autobahn. Let them learn the limitations of empire! Let them learn that racism doesn't work!"

"You've mapped out quite an educational program there."

"You said it. *Ciao,* honey." He continued talking to her in his mind long after the cab was gone. It was a long month to wait.

On the flight to Africa, Alan considered the postcard Hilda had mailed. The picture was of the partially completed space habitat that she intended to make her home. The mineral resources of South Africa would contribute significantly to the celestial city. She wrote about how important it was to mine the moon for the many future environments that were planned. She started to say a few words about the resources of terrestrial oceans, but she ran out of space.

During the trip, he watched the moon grow brighter with the fall of night, as if it fed upon the day to become an unblinking eye to guide the plane. The hours passed peacefully. He slept. When he opened his eyes again, they were coming in at a low altitude, and the city was spread out like ladies' fine jewelry on black velvet. There were stars above and stars below. A young black man was waiting for him at the gate. "Hello, Mr. Whittmore. I'm David."

"Oscar's boy! Welcome back to Earth. I've always wanted to meet you."

"Hilda asked if I'd take you to the hotel."

"How long have you known each other?"

"Since yesterday, but she comes highly recommended by my father. And there is the little matter that I'm a fan of her books."

"The science fiction?"

"And your book, Alan. May I call you Alan?"

"If you want me for company, you better!"

She was waiting for them in the bar, the center of attention for well-groomed young men, self-conscious in their formal attire, escorting very proper, willowy ladies in white evening gowns. The waitresses were every bit as elegant as the guests. He'd never experienced an atmosphere so full of grace and etiquette, a small, polished, discreet echo of the old colonialism that had been preserved by the New Africa. Hilda took his arm and walked him out onto a spotlessly clean veranda overlooking a waterfall.

"Won't you miss Earth?" he asked.

"I will see all of it every day," she answered. "From space."

"Will you be harder to pester about deadlines up there?"

"Not if you're nice about it. Why don't we discuss the matter at PAXCON tomorrow?"

"What's that?"

"The name of this year's world science fiction convention, of course. If we're going to have world peace, this is a good place to begin."

He got her to admit that the seed of her complicated plot went back to the choice of hotel where they had first met. She must have had her eye on the teenage eccentrics and their fantasies all the time, but Africa was a safer place to meet than the Wild East. Yes, it was all a vast conspiracy to bring him halfway around the world to watch her deliver a prospace speech to Martians and monsters, as if he didn't have enough troubles.

Twenty-four hours later, he understood. She had done this so he would better appreciate her impending change of address. And he enjoyed himself immensely at PAXCON.

Where but a convention like this, in a country recently torn by civil war but now enjoying the prosperity and camaraderie that only comes from the profit motive, where else, he asked himself, could be found on the same stage, in 1984, as co-guests of honor, the aged figures of Fritz Lang and Thea von Harbou? Lang, who had declined the odious offer from Joseph Goebbels to join in the symphony of hate and instead taken his directorial skills to Hollywood; von Harbou, who had remained loyal to the Third Reich but without a degeneration in her talent as a writer and scenarist—the husband-and-wife team who had presented the world with *Metropolis, Frau im Mond* (Woman in the Moon), *Die Nibelungen* (based on *The Ring of the Nibelungen*) . . . and introduced a sinister character to the

cinema screens in *Dr. Mabuse der Spieler!* Futuristic medical technologies they had dreamed in their fiction came true for them. Advanced eye surgery had returned to Lang his precious sight after he'd
suffered the dark night of blindness; other medical advances had kept
von Harbou alive.

Through the auspices of an American science fiction enthusiast
named Forrest J Ackerman, the impossible had been accomplished.
The couple had been reunited at PAXCON. (An earlier convention in
Los Angeles had used the name in reference to the Pacific Ocean, but
the title had been resuscitated for the first SF convention to capitalize
on détente and hopes for world peace.) Lang's most recent film was
premiered, finished since the recovery of his vision: *Tomorrow,*
shown on a double bill with the H. G. Wells picture of 1936 that
predicted World War II, *Things to Come.* The prediction of *Tomorrow* was: *No more war!*

Hilda introduced Alan to virtually everyone, and he was pleased
that the Dietrich matter was not broached in Lang's presence. He
had the impression that the venerable director had not read the final
entries of Joseph Goebbels's diaries, and this was just as well. No real
Mabuse hovered over the shoulder of this man.

Alan enjoyed meeting Ackerman and his wife, Wendayne Mon-
delle. The high point of the convention was when Ackerman led a
toast, first in English, then in Esperanto, in honor of departed writers
of fantasy and science fiction. There was a special remembrance for
H. G. Wells and C. S. Lewis, who both died in the nuclear destruction of London. Nothing better illustrated the waste and stupidity of
war than the loss of these two inventive and imaginative minds.
(Afterward, Alan learned that Lewis had come down from Oxford
to debate with Wells on the day that became a holocaust. The subject: Is There an Afterlife? The Christian apologist and atheist lecturer found out the answer, all right, but the world was denied future
works by two of the century's finest writers. The loss in talent and
ability would never be calculated from Hitler's revenge on the British.)

When Alan got his autographed copy from Thea von Harbou of
her *Erdtunnel Nr. 1 Antwortet Nicht* (Earth-Tube No. 1 Does Not
Reply), there was a *Jugend Spräche* band in the background, playing
music banned in the Greater Reich. He wondered how a talented
artist, no matter what her political beliefs, could live in a country that

stifled creativity and enslaved the mind. He mentioned Baerwald to her, but got no response. Was that a Gestapo man watching them over by the bar? Alan thanked liberty that civilization did not belong entirely to the killers and slavers. The hope for world peace lay in the dignity of man.

He couldn't sleep that night. The convention was showing a movie series until dawn. He didn't know what to expect until he was comfortably in his seat and watching an all-night Mabuse retrospective. A Mexican version was playing, and the first closeup he saw was of an actor who was the spitting image of Herman, who had frightened him so badly. Alan's Spanish was only rudimentary at best, but the subtitles were in English. "Nothing in the world will save you from my vengeance," the villain was telling an unseen victim. "I will kill you, kill you, kill you." The hair was white, the face a skull.

For the first time since the man in the Horch limousine stared with mad eyes in his direction, Alan could laugh about it. A young boy sitting in front turned around and hissed out a long "Shhhhhhhhhhhhhhh." He smiled to the boy and nodded.

If a lone madman was threatening the world, the guy was certainly taking his own sweet time about letting the axe fall. It was corny, actually. And what was the worst that could happen? Alan wouldn't have to put up with any more Townies. Meanwhile, he had his life to live, and Hilda Goebbels's autobiography to publish.

CHAPTER TWENTY-ONE

*Under a tyranny, most friends are a liability. One
quarter of them turn "reasonable" and become your
enemies, one quarter are afraid to stop and speak and one
quarter are killed and you die with them. But the blessed
final quarter keep you alive.*

—Sinclair Lewis,
It Can't Happen Here

LETTER TO ALAN WHITTMORE FROM HILDA GOEBBELS
**The Charles A. Lindbergh Experimental Orbital Community,
September 1, 2000**

Dear Alan:

Don't send the marines. This is not Nicaragua. Seriously, we are
all right up here. Nobody died. But it was a close call, I'm not about
to deny that. The reports of my heroism are greatly exaggerated, I
regret to say. But I did perceive the danger first, my only gift I
sometimes think.

Will we never be free of Burgundy? The new computer technicians
had arrived, and it was only by a fluke that I even saw Fritz—that's
his name. There were plenty of other Germans in the crew, but there
was something about him that bothered me. Next you'll be saying
I have telepathy!

He had undergone security clearance, but when you believe in
freedom, you only take a probe so far. Fritz was on the Greiman
System team. You know that's how our weather is controlled. We
live inside a cylinder that if Father had lived to see, he would certainly compare to one of those micro-Tesla coils. The solar collectors
do look a bit like suction cups, now that I notice. At least the German
colony is being developed along similar lines instead of a swastika!
But you want to hear about Fritz.

He was working on the code for the system that governs the
climate-control unit. The Greiman system, in case you're not famil-

237

iar with it, is a method by which the length of the day is controlled by large mirrors on the outside of the colony. The mirrors reflect the sun onto the landscape. They are rotated about a pivot attached to the end of our habitat. This is how, by a clever reflection, we have the impression of the sun crossing our sky once a day. But when anyone feels like being a space cadet, there are many viewing areas allowing unobstructed communion with the earth and the moon and the stars.

The Greiman system regulates the colony's environment. It is a giant air conditioning unit. Through solar power, the air can be heated or cooled according to taste. Most of the time we have temperate climate, but on special holidays arrangements are made for changes. We have snow for Christmas.

The climate-control device is huge, and it makes use of an endless flow of information. That's one of the reasons we have room for more computer people. Now, when someone like Fritz is hired, the main concern is that he be familiar with the solid-state digital computers we use instead of the unwieldy liquid-helium-cooled analog computers on which the Reich has wasted so much effort. He did fine on the tests. There was no reason to suspect he was a Burgundian. Why would one of them even come up here, in direct violation of their religious tenets?

Anyway, part of the weather system controls air circulation—what I used to call the wind before I started reading technical manuals in place of poetry. The wind blows because of energy from the sunlight that is reflected by the mirrors into the *Lindbergh*. Heated air rises here, the same as anywhere else, and we are subject to the "coriolis force." This is a real place, you know. A moving parcel of air is affected by the rotation of the colony.

The security officers blame themselves for not recognizing the degree of danger that could come from this quarter. Too many years on earth gave them what you might call a "bomb mentality." We almost lost our lives because of a thin wafer of software, but we would have entered eternity secure in the knowledge that no explosives were detonated inside our home.

Fritz had been well prepared for his assignment. The accelerated air currents resulting from the heated air move toward or away from the axis of rotation. The nearer to the axis, the slower is the air parcel's velocity. New streams of air enter the system at about 100 mph, where they encounter slower masses of air. But as the parcel retains its inertia, it cannot help but pass the slower-moving air; and there are no traffic cops to pull it over. The result, as Fritz knew, is that air spirals toward the center.

After interrogation, it was evident that Fritz wasn't smart enough to make the calculations he used. But he was a good soldier. The calculations had been made beforehand by his masters, who had all the data they needed from our own press releases. The plot was to alter the angles of solar collection so as to direct a concentration of energy inside the *Lindbergh*. The air would be superheated, and the resulting turbulence would create a hurricane of ever-increasing magnitude until that moment when our correspondence would of necessity be terminated.

I don't mean to make light (is that a pun?) about what almost happened, but I'm the sort who would rather laugh than cry. The changes were gradual, and that gave us time to act . . . but there would have come that moment when there was no turning back. Fritz was prepared to sacrifice his life, and he had other programs to seal off the computer section and prevent overrides in the short run. Nobody died, and I will take credit for sounding the alarm.

What gave Fritz away? I saw him in one of the *Lindbergh*'s nightclubs. And to think Mother looked down her nose at cabarets. The Lazy Fairy employs the full spectrum of light in its floor shows, including a touch of infrared. Oscar's boy, David, is invariably outgoing with new people who come to work here. He's always trying to get them to immigrate. There's nothing like closed borders here to people with skills who want to work. And as for the land question, we keep making more of it; and new colonies are flowering in the sky. Well, David can be very inspiring. So we were talking to Fritz when the infrared bathed his forehead for a brief moment.

The letters and diagrams had been washed from his forehead, but they had been written in something that left its signature, a concoction of blood and ink, I suspect. I recognized the five- and six-sided polygons; I recognized what the SS purports to be the lost letters of Arya. This in itself did not prove him to be a poor, deluded Hörbigerian. And even if he was, that's not the same as evidence we had a Burgundian saboteur in our midst.

I respect other people's rights even when my life is in danger. I'm not a Gandhi, but I also don't jump the gun. The evidence justified a thorough investigation of his work, and that's how the scheme was uncovered. The hard-core members of security suggested that Fritz be summarily executed by spacing him out an airlock, as had been done with our last murderer; but I defended him on the grounds that, thanks to my timely intervention, he had not managed to kill anyone, himself included. I'm a softy in my old age. I was also curious.

Obviously Fritz had been brainwashed. The first step was to communicate with the part of him that didn't belong to Burgundy. He was earnest and amusing. Often, he would interrupt himself to comment on his comments, a sort of metaconversation. But when he would comment on the comment on the comment, an oral footnoting, he risked sliding into an uncomputable recursive function. Just about the time he'd put David to sleep, and bored our friends from security right out of their violent impulses, I found the key I needed. He had the ideal personality to be sucked into a cult. His mind was a series of disparate subjects linked together, but without a discriminator to tell him what was important and what was trivial. Because he had no true beliefs of his own, he was the perfect zombie for an evil master. I broke the chain. He had been programmed to come up here and destroy the colony. My death was to be a bonus, but not the main object of the mission. I knew the Burgundian mantra, and I could ask him in a fashion he could not ignore the question of why he had been sent to destroy us. As I suspected, his answer was that our habitat violated the Eternal Ice. I asked why the Eternal Ice had not destroyed us itself. He'd never thought of that. I asked him how the mechanics of his scheme against us made any sense if Hörbiger was correct. He hadn't thought of that either. Like all cultists, he only echoed the beliefs of others, but had no beliefs of his own. His mind was so compartmentalized that the orders he was following had no referent to the data he would pick up on the mission, the very facts of physics and meteorology he would have to employ to finish his task.

They'd used drugs on him, too. At least he wasn't suffering from that poison the Townies of New York use. Speck is applied natural selection, but let each man go to hell in his own way. Fritz didn't mind being rescued, so he was worth the trouble. The physiological side of his problem was easier to fight than the psychological. Only he could do something about the latter if we weren't to brainwash him all over again. Because he wasn't sent to his grave in the vacuum, he had the opportunity to learn a few facts about space.

Cynics think Fritz is exploiting my kindness, and that his reform is not genuine. As I have no intention of reforming him, I don't care about that. I'm introducing him to the universe. He has no argument against the nonaggression principle, which is the contract and bond between free men. He is not committed to force. When his facade collapsed, and he was crying in my arms, he told how they conditioned him in Burgundy. He recounted every detail of the last night of his training. They whipped him. They used Dietrich's dreadful mind-control cylinders on him. That is why I do not regret that we haven't been able to recreate the technology of those coils. I'm convinced they do more than inform or entertain; I think they alter the structure of the brain. I wouldn't be at all surprised to learn that exposure to two of the coils in quick succession contributed to Father's mental breakdown. Another reason to find this Burgundian cult—as if we need it—is to get our hands on those coils and take them out of circulation.

Yes, Alan, I will cover all this in the second volume of the autobiography, but after I submit the manuscript you must agree that whatever remains of my life is private. Deal?

Fritz also provided an opportunity to find out if Dietrich is still involved with Burgundy. You will be relieved to learn that our amateur in the art of sabotage never encountered anyone with Mabuse-like characteristics during his time with the enemy. This does not prove that Dietrich is dead, but it increases my conviction that the alliance between electromagnetic biology and the SS feudalists is at an end. Alan, let us agree that Dietrich died in the explosion. Say it with me. Believe it with me.

David wants me to ask you if you'd consider a book from him contrasting the difference in the German and American space programs. This is a case of blowing our own horn, as the Reich is shifting its approach. They are probably envious of the new hydrogen-fueled hypersonic spaceplane traveling at twenty-five times the speed of sound. This will certainly facilitate travel between the colonies and Earth. Consider how much quicker it will be to get from Earth to the intermediary stations en route to the celestial cities. Everything tried in this line by the Reich was a flat bust. Maybe they'll learn.

Where would we be without leaks from the sieve of New Berlin? The impetus behind David's suggestion is the information smuggled out about the incredible stupidity of the German side in the moon race. Typical! Did you know they wiped out their entire ground crew at liftoff? Then again, this might not have been accidental. The ground crew was largely Hungarian, and some creep in authority might have decided that in the name of national security, the men should be told to move to shelters only half the distance from actual safety. When considering the Nazis, one must always be suspicious.

The only benefit of the doubt I'm willing to extend is because of the nature of the *Hitler,* their appropriately named boondoggle. Despite protests from Wernher von Braun, they did not follow the approach America used: multistage chemical rockets, and a space platform from which to launch for massive savings in payload to gladden a capitalist's heart. No, they insisted on building a colosseum-sized disk, with a diameter of half a kilometer, and powered by hundreds of small atomic bombs. The shielding for the ship alone could bankrupt most countries. What's your gut instinct about the blast area? Was it a miscalculation, or did they really put the bunkers within the destructive radius? However you slice it, this was an entirely characteristic Nazi project. Well, at least they had the sense to confront the Hörbigerians with the facts about what the moon is made of when they got back home.

I will always delight in the fact that without leaving a trail of bodies in its wake, the American Republic got to the moon first. You're a good minarchist, Alan, and you believe in a limited government; but as an anarchist, I'm pleased that the businessmen who first set foot on Luna did not erect a flag, but declared it an open range, for the use and development of whoever gets there. Nobody owns the moon. Wouldn't you know it that when their turn came, the National Socialists claimed the entire satellite as theirs? But of course that is common knowledge. There are twice as many non-Reich explorers on the moon right now as Teutonic imperialists; but it annoys me to see the Swastika in the German zones. Am I the only person to notice that socialists were the first to try and turn a new frontier into, well, a private preserve of their own, a monopoly?

Now, about your question. I don't see what more I can add to my father's diaries, even with the new editions. Will you make it available to the micronet? I have one of the carry-all books with me currently. It's strange to open a plastic box in the shape of a book and see a display screen that can bring up any text available in the library to which it is keyed. I'm a traditionalist at heart; I like the smell of glue and paper.

You are so insistent when you want something! You won't let me forget my father, will you? After all these years, it is a strange feeling to look at the diary pages again. He accurately described me as the young and headstrong girl I was, although I wonder if he realized that I was firmly in the underground by the time I was warning him about Burgundy. In one sense we were using him; but in another sense I hoped to save his life . . . then. What finally pushed me over the edge I can't rightly say. It was cumulative. I wonder what my father, my enemy, would say if he could see the crotchety old woman I have become.

I regret not speaking to him on his deathbed, as he did with Hitler. The question I would have asked would be how he thought Reich officials would ever allow his diaries, from 1965 on, to appear in Europe? The early, famous entries, from 1933 to 1963, had been published as part of the official German record. The entries beginning with 1965 would have to be buried, and buried *deep,* by any dictatorship. Father's idea that no censorship applied to the privileged class—of his supposedly classless society—did not take into account sensitive state documents, such as his record of the Burgundy affair, or his highly sensitive discussion with Hitler. If the real *Final Entries* had not been smuggled out of Europe as one of the last acts of the underground, and delivered to me, I would never have been in a position to come to terms with memories of my father. Nor would I have had the book that secured my reputation. I'm honest enough to admit it. Americans love hearing about Nazi secrets.

As I begin a new life of semiretirement in America's first space city, haunted by equal portions of earthlight and moonlight, I'm willing to reconsider this period of history, but I would like to find something new to say. Yesterday, they had me speak to an audience of five hundred about my life as a writer. Only one questioner had a morbid curiosity about the details of my tenure as a soldier. Who was it who said that hell hath no fury like a noncombatant?

Most of them wanted to know how much research I had put into the series about postwar Japan and China. They wanted to know how

I deal with writer's block. But most of all, they wanted to hear about Nazis, Nazis, Nazis.

A handsome young Japanese man saved me by asking what I considered the greatest moment of my life. I told him it was that I had been a successful thief. Once the audience of dedicated free-enterprisers had stopped gasping like fish out of water, I explained. The specter of cancer was put to rest because of work derived from original research by our old friend Richard Dietrich. There's no denying it. But why should we? The most pleasant irony I've ever tasted was that his final achievement was for life instead of death. I made it possible. It was I who brought his papers to human beings. If a flesh-and-blood Dietrich, or a ghost, intends to punish me for this good deed, it has yet to happen. Farewell to shadows, I say.

As the presentation was entirely in English, I wrapped it up with a pun that I think most of the Japanese had sufficient command of the language to appreciate, but they are so unfailingly polite that you can't help but wonder if there would be the slightest difference no matter what was said. The matter of German philosophy had been brought up, not without cause, and I was expected to give my opinion on the Big Names. I hit them with: "Nietzsche sustains my interest but Immanuel Kant!" My pleasant young man's groan seemed real enough.

I must take repeated breaks in dictating this addendum. My back gives nothing but trouble, and I spend at least three times a day in zero-g therapy. How Hitler would have loved that. After the last bomb attempt on him, his central concern became the damage to his *Seig Heiling* arm, and his most characteristic feature—his ass. To think my father virtually worshiped that man! I guess if Napoleon had succeeded in unifying Europe, he'd be just as popular.

Now I'm reclining on a yellow couch in Observation 10A. There is a breathtaking view of Europe spread out to my right, although I can't make out Germany. The Fatherland is hidden beneath a patch of clouds. What I can see of the continent is cleaner than any map. Do you know what is missing? You can't see any borders. You can't see any districts. All there is is land and lakes and enough *Lebens-raum* for everyone.

I hate to think what sort of person I might have become if I had been a good little girl and done my duty. One of my prides is that I never betrayed a friend. My hope is to live to see Europe free once more. I'm not holding my breath, but I see small signs, small hopes. I am the last person in the world to suffer from wishful thinking, Alan, so you can take any optimism on my part as carefully considered.

How did it feel in the old days when I lived in the bowels of Hitler's monster, and will I ever forget when engaging in contemporary analysis? The bitter taste will never leave. There were more victims of the Nazis than only those who wore the patches. For me, it was as if I existed in a glass hothouse for the care of sickly plants in which I was the primary specimen. Instead of the refreshing aroma of sweet flowers, there was the cloying odor that comes from ripeness and decay. And the soil, although having the darkness associated with fertile earth, was a carpet of blood. I spent the empty hours listening to the howling of the wind outside those thin glass walls.

I do not miss the dangerous people, guarded conversations, and nameless dread. If a gauleiter failed to return a phone call, that was ample cause for the Asphalt Man to prowl the landscape of my dreams. No matter how high on the ladder, there was never a sense of the morrow assured. In fact, the greater the altitude, the more painful was the nibbling fear, for high above the ground is no good place to hide.

Every social engagement was cause for anxiety. If not the inexplicable frown, then the smile withheld would do the trick. Those who imagine Nazi Germany to have been an unsubtle place are right for the open victims of its policy; but for the rest of us, there were other infiltrations of the soul.

Can I put all this in context when attempting honest analysis today? My answer is that Harry Baerwald could. The emotional scars I wear from the Goebbels family cannot compare to his physical scars. He is my inspiration. I will be as objective as humanly possible. You have helped free me of my past as much as anyone could, Alan, and I will always be grateful.

Who could have predicted the ultimate consequences of Hitler's war? Certainly not myself. I recognized what Nazi Germany was because I grew up there, but that's not the same as seeing to the heart of things. It was an organization in the most modern meaning of the word. It was a conveyor belt. Hitler's ideology was the excuse for operating the controls, but the mechanism had a life of its own. Horrors were born of that machine, but so were fruits. Medals and barbed wire, diplomas and death sentences—they were all the same to the machine. The monster seemed unstoppable. In the belly of such a state, it was easy to become an anarchist. The next step was obvious: join a gang of your own, to fight the gang you hate. None of us on any side—not the Burgundians, not the underground, not the Reich itself—could see what was really happening. Only a few pacifists grasped the point.

Adolf Hitler achieved the exact opposite of all his long-term goals, and he did this by winning World War II. Economic reality subverted National Socialism.

The average German used to defend Hitler by saying that he got us out of the Depression, without bothering to note that the way the glorious Fuehrer paid off all the classes of Germany was by looting foreigners. This was not the friendliest method for undoing the harm of Versailles. But as Europe began to remove age-old barriers to commerce, economic benefits began to spread. A thriving black market insured that all would benefit from the new plenty, and ideology be damned. While the Burgundians actually tried to implement Hitlerian ideals, the rest of Europe began to enjoy a new prosperity.

Father was intelligent enough to notice this trend, but he avoided drawing the obvious conclusion: Nazi Germany was becoming less National Socialist with every passing decade. For all the talk of Race Destiny, it was the technical mind of Albert Speer and his successors at the controls of the German Empire. Ideology would surface long enough to slow down the machine, or cause it problems, but in the end technical management would reassert itself.

The side-show bigots provided decoration. Their rationale was not the class fantasies of Marx or dreams of the Common Man during the most fascistic period of the democracies, but the myth of race. Whatever bleak form the rituals of self-delusion may take, the motivation remains to build an illusion of personal power in the age of impersonal bureaucracy.

Adolf Hitler was going to achieve permanent race segregation when it's not even clear what constitutes a race. He couldn't be bothered by details. His New Order lasted only long enough to knock down the barriers of ethnic and national separation. Economics did the rest. Today there is more racial intermarriage than ever, thanks to Adolf Hitler. The theories of Isabel Paterson rise over the wreckage of *Mein Kampf.* She had told us all along that it is through the mixing of cultures that the long circuit of economic energy is maintained. But I doubt that any Nazis have read her book *The God of the Machine,* even though it explains what is happening to them.

Judging from your last letter, you accept the Great Man theory of history. I know you have moved back and forth on this. As for me, I believe in the Inexorable Event. Is it my age speaking? But what really matters is the outcome, the world we live in. That is what should concern us.

Another cause for hope is that today we see an outbreak of historical revisionists within Germany itself. Although they choose their words with care, the message comes through: they show Hitler's feet of clay. They are asking why Germany used a nuclear weapon against a civilian population, while President Dewey restricted his atomic bombs to Japanese military targets in the open sea. Even a thickheaded German may get the point after a while. The Reich's youth protests against the treatment of Russians by the Rosenberg Cultural Bureaus, and they are no longer shot, no longer arrested . . . and who knows but that they may accomplish something. If this keeps up, maybe my books, including *Final Entries of Dr. Joseph Goebbels,* will become available in the open market, instead of merely being black-market best-sellers already. America is still the only completely uncensored society.

More than anything else, I am encouraged by what happens when German and American scientists and engineers work together. The autobahns of Africa are finally finished, and they have the trade to justify it. But nothing is more beautiful than the space colonies: the American and German complexes, the Japanese one (only half finished but potentially the most efficient), and finally, Israel.

When I was extended an invitation by President Levi ben Sherot to attend, I asked if I could bring Fritz along. The last stage of the lad's cure should be to walk among hundreds of Jews and discover that he has nothing to fear. The noxious fantasies that were poured into his head are almost gone, but this should be the litmus test.

Personally, I look forward to setting foot inside a colony that proves *Der Jude* could not be stopped by a mere Fuehrer. I'm promised a full tour, including the smaller attached colonies, or *kibbutzim,* in which most of the farming is done. I understand that bananas grow very well in space. The most notable feature is the location of the Israeli colony. They have returned to their Holy Land, but at an unexpected altitude.

What would Father make of this sane new world? His final testament was the torment of a soul that has seen his victory become something alien and unconcerned with its architects. His life was melodrama, but his death a cheap farce. They didn't even know what to say at his funeral, he, the great orator of National Socialism. Without his guiding hand, they could not give him a Wagnerian exit.

The final joke was on him, and its practitioner was a man in a laboratory. Father sincerely believed that, in Adolf Hitler, the long-awaited Zarathustra, the New Man, had descended from the mountain. This, above all the rest, was the greatest lie of Paul Joseph Goebbels's life.

The New Man will ascend from the test tube. Nothing can stop his coming. I pray that he will be wiser than his parents.

Comparative Environmental Risk Assessment

Comparative
Environmental Risk
Assessment

Edited by
C. Richard Cothern

LEWIS PUBLISHERS
Boca Raton   Ann Arbor   London   Tokyo

Library of Congress Cataloging-in-Publication Data

Comparative environmental risk assessment / edited by C. Richard
  Cothern.
      p.   cm.
  Includes bibliographical references and index.
  ISBN 0-87371-605-1
  1. Pollution — Risk assessment — Congresses.   I. Cothern, C.
Richard.
TD193.5.C66   1992
363.7 — dc20   92-2389
                                                                        CIP

ISBN 0-87371-605-1
COPYRIGHT © 1993 by LEWIS PUBLISHERS
ALL RIGHTS RESERVED

PRINTED IN THE UNITED STATES
1 2 3 4 5 6 7 8 9 0

Printed on acid-free paper

This volume is based on the symposium "The Quantitative Ranking of Environmental Problems According to Risk: What Must We Yet Know to Accomplish This Task?" held on Wednesday, August 28, 1991, as part of the program of the 4th Chemical Congress of North America and the 202nd American Chemical Society National Meeting in New York City. The chapters here are the presentations from that symposium with a few additions to round out the subject.

The organizers of this symposium were all participants in the production of the report *Reducing Risk* by the U.S. Environmental Protection Agency's Science Advisory Board. The symposium is a follow-up of the report and is intended to be a step in the implementation of the recommendations of the report. The symposium was organized by: William Cooper, Richard Cothern, Paul Deisler, and Morton Lippmann.

A wide audience will find this volume interesting, useful, and thought provoking. Included are those who desire or need an overview of the health and value of quantitative risk assessment including: environmentalists, regulators, educators, students, planners, scientists, and industrialists. This volume can be used as a supplementary textbook for courses and discussion groups in quantitative risk assessment.

The main objective of the symposium and this volume is to determine what data are missing from those needed to determine the relative quantitative risk for all different environmental problems. A second objective is to provide information to be used in explaining to the general public and Congress the rationale for environmental regulations. A third objective is to determine which missing information is the most important in terms of its relative value in establishing comparative risk. With limited resources, all information about all environmental problems cannot be collected simultaneously. A fourth objective is to indicate what methodology, protocol, quality assurance, analytical techniques and analysis methods will be needed to collect the missing information.

The goals of the symposium and this volume are fourfold: (A) What data are needed to complete a quantitative risk estimate for the environmental and public health consequences in the many different areas of the environment, especially those deemed high in the Science Advisory Board's *Relative Risk* report. (B) Are there other areas which might also be high in risk and for which there are insufficient data for risk assessment? Or is it important to establish for sure that some of these might be low risks? (C) How accurate does a quantitative risk estimate have to be? What are the acceptable range of uncertainties for regulatory purposes? How confident does the risk assessor need to be in presenting the risk estimates to the decision maker? (D) In any given environmental problem area there are insufficient data to precisely,

---

* The thoughts and ideas expressed here are those of the editor and are not necessarily those of the U.S. Environmental Protection Agency.

completely, and with perfect accuracy estimate the risk. In some areas the needed information is entirely missing and in other areas it is so skimpy as to make its use questionable. Can we characterize the data in terms of: essential, important, helpful, nice but not really needed? Finally, the methods and research needed to collect the missing data need to be described in terms of methodology, scope, and cost.

C. Richard Cothern
Washington, D.C.

C. Richard Cothern, Ph.D. is presently with the U.S. Environmental Protection Agency's Center For Environmental Statistics Development Staff. He has served as the Executive Secretary of the Science Advisory Board at the USEPA as well as their National Expert on Radioactivity and Risk Assessment in the Office of Drinking Water. In addition he is an Associate Professorial Lecturer in the Chemistry Department of the George Washington University. Dr. Cothern has authored over 70 scientific articles including many related to public health, the environment and risk assessment. He has written and edited ten books involving such diverse topics as: science and society, energy and the environment, trace substances in environmental health, lead bioavailability, risk assessment, radon and radionuclides in drinking water. He received his B.A. from Miami University (Ohio), his M.S. from Yale University and his Ph.D. from the University of Manitoba.

LIST OF AUTHORS

Roy E. Albert, Department of Environmental Health, Medical Center, University of Cincinnati, Cincinnati, Ohio 45221

Bruce N. Ames, Division of Biochemistry and Molecular Biology, University of California, Berkeley, California 94720

Jeffrey Arnold, School of Public Health, University of North Carolina, Chapel Hill, North Carolina 27514

John Bachmann, Assistant Director, Office of Air Quality Planning and Standards, USEPA, Research Triangle Park, North Carolina 27711

Douglas J. Crawford-Brown, School of Public Health, University of North Carolina, Chapel Hill, North Carolina 27514

Harlal Choudhury, U.S. Environmental Protection Agency, Cincinnati, Ohio 45268

William Cooper, Department of Zoology, Michigan State University, East Lansing, Michigan 48824

Rob Coppock, National Academy of Sciences, Washington, D.C. 20418

C. Richard Cothern, Center for Environmental Statistics Development Staff, USEPA, Washington, D.C. 20460

Rosalie R. Day, U.S. Environmental Protection Agency, Region V, Chicago, Illinois 60604

Paul F. Deisler, Jr., Private Consultant, Houston, Texas 77024

Christopher T. DeRosa, ATSDR, Atlanta, Georgia 30333

Michael Dourson, U.S. Environmental Protection Agency, Cincinnati, Ohio 45268

William Farland, Director, Office of Health and Environmental Assessment, USEPA, Washington, D.C. 20460

William V. Garetz, Center for Environmental Statistics Development Staff, USEPA, Washington, D.C. 20460

Chuck P. Gerba, Department of Microbiology and Immunology, University of Arizona, Tucson, Arizona 85721

Lois Swirsky Gold, Life Sciences Division, Lawrence Berkeley Laboratory, Berkeley, California 94720

Art Gregory, 220 Ash Road, Sterling, Virginia 22170

Nancy K. Kim, Division of Environmental Health Assessment, New York State Department of Health, Albany, New York 12202-3313

Morton Lippmann, Professor of Environmental Medicine, New York University, Tuxedo, New York 10987

Neela B. Manley, Division of Biochemistry and Molecular Biology, University of California, Berkeley, California 94720

D. McKean, U.S. Environmental Protection Agency, Cincinnati, Ohio 45268

Moiz Mumtaz, U.S. Environmental Protection Agency, Cincinnati, Ohio 45268

David Policansky, National Academy of Sciences, Washington, D.C. 20418

Palma Risler, U.S. Environmental Protection Agency, Region II, New York, New York 10278

Joan B. Rose, Department of Environmental and Occupational Health, College of Public Health, University of South Florida, Tampa, Florida 33612

Rakesh Shukla, Department of Environmental Health, University of Cincinnati Medical Center, Cincinnati, Ohio 45221

Ellen K. Silbergeld, Toxicology Program, University of Maryland, Baltimore, Maryland 21201

Thomas H. Slone, Cell and Molecular Biology Division, Lawrence Berkeley Laboratory, Berkeley, California 94720

Bonnie R. Stern, Life Sciences Division, Lawrence Berkeley Laboratory, Berkeley, California 94720

James D. Wilson, Monsanto Chemical Company, St. Louis, Missouri 63167

CONTENTS

Overview

Ecological Health Risks

Human Health Risks

Quantitative Risk Assessment Problem Areas and Issues

Thoughts for the Future

---

* This chapter is based on the presentation made at a symposium of the American Chemical Society on August 28, 1991 entitled "The Quantitative Ranking of Environmental Problems According to Risk: What Must We Yet Know to Accomplish This Task?".

Overview

CHAPTER 1

Introduction and Overview of Difficulties Encountered in Developing Comparative Rankings of Environmental Problems*

C. Richard Cothern

The symposium "The Quantitative Ranking of Environmental Problems According to Risk: What Must We Yet Know to Accomplish This Task?" was held as part of the National Meeting of the American Chemical Society August 28, 1991. This volume includes presentations from the symposium plus a few extra chapters. This chapter is an introduction and overview of the symposium, highlighting the topics discussed and adding some more detail concerning the scope of the problem and its place in the emerging area of quantitative risk assessment.

INTRODUCTION

Quantitative risk assessment is a new, emerging, and potentially useful method for comparing the risks to human health and environmental degradation due to natural and anthropogenic contamination. Although assumptions have to be made in such an assessment and the resulting quantitation may have a large range of uncertainty, it can be useful in determining a rank order or comparative risk between different environmental problems and different solutions. One of the main impediments to the development and use of quantitative risk assessment is the lack of complete information and data as input to this process. It is the goal of the present symposium/volume to examine some of these gaps and deficiencies and determine how they might be filled. The present symposium/volume is not intended to be a complete analysis of all the missing elements, but is intended to give some idea of the breadth and depth of this problem and thus provide direction for solutions.

Support for the idea of determining the number of human lives involved and impact of environmental contamination on ecosystems in the form of

---

* The thoughts and ideas expressed in this chapter are those of the author and are not necessarily those of the U.S. Environmental Protection Agency.

quantitative risk assessment in the development of plans, budgets, and research directions was given recently by the U.S. Environmental Protection Agency's Science Advisory Board (SAB). Their report *Reducing Risk* made several recommendations, including some that are directly relevant to the current symposium/book (USEPA, 1990). These recommendations are directed towards EPA, but are equally applicable to state, local, and other environmental groups that are involved in regulatory, policy, and mitigation activities. First the SAB recommended that "EPA should target its environmental protection efforts on the basis of opportunities for the greatest risk reduction". Here it is recognized that the country has addressed the most obvious environmental problems first (e.g., those easily detected by human senses) and now should use several criteria to determine the future direction including quantitative risk assessment (other criteria include economic, social, and political concerns as well as feasibility and timing, to mention some). Secondly, "EPA should improve the data and analytical methodologies that support the assessment, comparison, and reduction of different environmental risks". As pointed out here this is a major deficiency in the current process and has many facets and dimensions that will be discussed in this symposium/book. Third, "EPA should reflect risk-based priorities in its strategic planning process". These risks should include those already prevented and those that could be prevented by future actions. Fourth, "EPA should reflect risk-based priorities in its budget process". The legislation determines the priorities to a large degree; however, some discretion is available and in the long run the public and hence Congress should develop a new direction that minimizes the health and ecological consequences of environmental degradation. This broader mandate is more clearly seen in the next two recommendations. Fifth, "EPA — and the nation as a whole — should make greater use of all the tools available to reduce risk". In order to use these tools the concept of quantitative risk needs to be more completely understood throughout our society. Sixth, "EPA should work to improve public understanding of environmental risks and train a professional workforce to help reduce them". An important aspect of this process is risk communication. Some problems in this area will be discussed later.

The symposium and this volume are organized around the following general themes, in order: ecological risks — what do we need to know?, health risks — what do we need to know?, quantitative risk assessment problem areas, and issues and thoughts for the future.

This chapter gives some background thoughts and ideas concerning some of the issues, problem areas, and an overview of the data and information that are missing for a comparative risk assessment of environmental problems. The connection to the chapters in the entire book are indicated in the context of this chapter. The topics discussed here in order are data needs, comparing different kinds of risks, confounding factors, risk communication concepts, and strategies for the future.

SOME OF THE GAPS AND NEEDS BEYOND EXISTING KNOWLEDGE AND INFORMATION

Examples of some of the problem areas where information and data are missing or very sparse are discussed here. The list is admittedly incomplete as this is a vast and complex problem.

Entire Areas Missing

In some cases the data are so skimpy or nonexistent that even educated guesses are not possible in order to provide the input information for quantitative risk assessment (see, for example, chapters by Day, Reisler, and Silbergeld). Exposure data are a good example of large areas of missing information and data (see, for example, the chapter by Kim). Often the existing data are anecdotal and does not include temporal or spatial variation. Another complication is that exposure to a contaminant is not exposure of the organ or body part that is susceptible, since the chemical structure can be metabolized or changed after it enters the human or other living things. Only in a few cases do baseline data exist, thus it is difficult to determine whether the data are from a new source or have been there for a long time. Another complication that is seldom addressed in exposure data is its multichemical and multimedia character (see, for example, the chapter by DeRosa et al.). An environmental contaminant can be transported in the air, water, soil, food, and dust and enter humans by ingestion, inhalation, and dermal routes. Data for all these variables are seldom available. Two variables that are too often missing in exposure data are the temporal and spatial character (see, for example, the chapter by Bachmann). Some contaminants have constant levels for centuries and some only exist for seconds. Seasonal variations are often important and even day-night variations can be important and are often missing. Often, contaminants exist only locally and sometimes the global concentrations are important. As examples, industrial pollution is often localized and stratospheric ozone depleters are global in character.

There are on the order of 50,000 man-made contaminants. Exposure and health-effects data exist for only a few of these. These data are expensive to collect and clearly not all of them will ever be collected. Developing a priority list of which ones to monitor will be a continuing problem.

There is clear information that there are some synergisms between environmental contaminants. Examples of synergisms are SO_2 and particulates, tobacco smoke and asbestos or radon, and a few others. It is not clear what other synergisms or antagonisms exist, although it seems likely that many are present.

In the area of ecotoxicity the loss of species, communities, and systems is not clear due to lack of data. In most cases the information involves estimates by experts and no "hard" data. Another area, habitat destruction, is difficult to measure and it is difficult to determine the baseline data (see, for example, the chapter by Policanski).

In the area of microbiological contaminants in water, especially drinking water, some new contaminants have been discovered, such as legionella and cryptosporidium, for which little data concerning occurrence, health effects, or possible mitigation techniques exist (see, for example, the chapter by Gerba and Rose). Since it is possible that a single microbiological contaminant can cause an illness, current monitoring practices may be inadequate to serve as input for the quantitative risk-assessment process.

There is currently at EPA a major effort to reassess the methods for disinfection. This was motivated by the revelation that chlorinating drinking water introduced the carcinogen chloroform and other trihalomethanes. Although the tradeoff between disease from not chlorinating and cancer from trihalomethanes seems to favor chlorination, EPA is investigating alternatives that may not have the cancer consequence. Other methods being investigated include: ozonation, chloramination, and the use of chlorine dioxide. There are not enough occurrence or health effects data concerning the consequences of these three processes (not to mention other possibilities) to be able to rank them according to quantitative risk.

Areas Where the Data Could Be Improved

In some cases environmental information and data exist and can be used for quantitative risk assessment. However, if data were improved the assessment would become clearer. As discussed in the chapter by Wilson, the existing data can be used in making comparative quantitative risk assessments.

Most scientists agree that putting carbon dioxide into the atmosphere leads to an increase in the temperature of the earth (see, for example, the chapter by Coppock). However, when viewed from the perspective of global climate this only one of the phenomena that can affect global temperature. Most agree that the overall effect of current anthropogenic practices is a temperature increase, but the situation is far from clear and requires more and better information.

Data for hazardous waste sites are largely anecdotal and little or no baseline data exist. The existing data are enough to make some quantitative estimates; however, better data would improve the situation.

Other areas where data exist, but could be improved include: indoor air radon, lead, stratospheric ozone depleters, and pesticides. In each of these cases data exist that can be used in developing quantitative risk assessments, but better data would make the situation clearer.

COMPARING DIFFERENT KINDS OF RISK — OR APPLES AND ORANGES

A number of problems occur in comparing risks due to different environmental contaminants. One of these problems is that the things that are being compared are so different in character hat it seems they cannot be compared, or there are major contaminants that are ignored (see, for example, the chapter by Gold and Ames). Can an apple be compared to an orange? Of course, it can in many respects, but perhaps not exactly all. One example of this problem in comparative risk assessment is comparing two contaminants, one of which has a cancer endpoint and the other has a noncancer endpoint. For example, compare the risk from inhaling radon, which can cause lung cancer, and ingesting lead, which causes neurotoxicological effects, such as lowering the IQ. Is early death equal to a lowered IQ? Can early death be compared in any way to a lowered IQ? Can a weighting factor be used to estimate their comparative risk? Methods exist for these intercomparisons and one is described in the chapter by Deisler. A further discussion of this topic is contained in the chapter by Farland and Dourson.

Another comparison that presents problems is that of human health vs. ecological health. Which is more important, a human being or a bird, fish, or forest? An interesting example of the interrelationship between human and ecological health is the treatment of drinking water. Some drinking water supplies are treated whereby the resulting sludge is dumped into the river. It is common to remove iron, copper, and zinc as part of the process, although they are relatively harmless to humans. However, the latter two are rather deadly to other forms of life in the river. How should the relative importance of these two areas be weighed? (see, for example, the chapter by Policanski).

In the area of human health, a problem in comparative risk arises between mortality and morbidity. In the earlier example of chlorinating water, the chlorine significantly reduces morbidity, but causes mortality due to the cancer caused by the resulting trihalomethanes. How can mortality (early death) and morbidity be compared?

Other factors that are important include whether the contaminant is natural or man made. It has been shown that our society generally accepts a risk ten times higher for a natural contaminant than for a man-made contaminant (Latai et al., 1983).

CONFOUNDING FACTORS AND OTHER PROBLEMS

A number of factors tend to confound epidemiology as well as animal toxicology studies. Some of these factors include smoking history, the transient nature of our population, the multiplicity of causes for each endpoint, the lack of good exposure data, the imprecise knowledge of how much of the contaminant actually reaches the organ affected, and so on. In addition, there are other problems that make intercomparison of risks difficult.

Very few health effect studies have the statistical power needed to make statistically valid statements and draw statistically valid conclusions. For perspective remember that it took 20 years and millions of rats, mice, and humans to show statistically that cigarette smoking causes lung cancer. Realize that to study a compound that causes ten times less risk than cigarette smoking (a 10% lifetime individual risk) requires 100 times more subjects in the study, 100 times less requires 10,000 times more subjects, and so on (a quadratic relationship). It is unlikely that environmental contaminants that have risk levels of 1 in 10,000 or less will ever be demonstrated to have statistically relatable cause and effect — there simply are not that many people. Another approach to the question of statistical limits is discussed in the chapter by Albert and Shukla.

Another health effect problem is that there is a wide range of sensitivities among human beings. Regulators use the most sensitive person for predictions of health effects. These should not be confused with most probable case predictions or most likely calculations. The range of susceptibilities needs to be included in analyses of comparative risk.

Consistency is a general problem. Not all environmental measurements are made in the same way, follow the same protocol, or use the same methodology, and thus intercomparisons are subject to erroneous conclusions unless the user is most careful (see, for example, the chapter by Gregory). Even with care there are questions about comparing data from different measurements. In addition, models are used to predict the transport of contaminants through the environment and to extrapolate dose-response data for animals at high doses to humans at low doses. There are many different models and their conclusions are in general quite different. Unless the data are collected in the same way and analyzed in the same way or the differences are compensated for, the conclusions about comparative risk can be confounded and in error.

RISK COMMUNICATION CONCEPTS

One of the largest gaps in the comparative risk assessment field is the methodology to communicate the results to decision makers and the public. As seen in the Reducing Risk Report (Appendix C, pp. 127 to 128) there is a disparity between the judgment of scientists concerning the comparative risk between environmental problems and the perception of the public. If the approach of basing the development of priorities in the environmental area on factors such as comparative risk, the methodology of risk communication must be developed.

Several aspects that make risk communication difficult with decision makers and the public are becoming more clear. One problem is the vast range of numbers involved. In order to understand the ranges of environmental risk involved, several orders of magnitude of quantitation must be considered. However, most of the general public does not understand the concept of order of magnitude. This concept is rooted in the idea of logarithms — a subject few hear about, let alone master. In general, scientists think logarithmically and the public thinks linearly. Thus to the public 50 parts per thousand, 50 parts per million, and 50 parts per billion all sound like the same number. The concept of orders of magnitude is not that difficult and could be easily introduced earlier in the mathematical curriculum.

An important component of risk communication that is not only poorly understood, but often avoided is that of probability. This concept seems to be ignored by the public — likely because they have no training for this concept and have little use for it in their daily lives.

Another quantitative concept that is a stumbling block to the understanding of comparative risk is that of error or range of uncertainty. Scientists realize that giving a number that results from a measurement or estimate alone is dangerous. All have some quantitative uncertainty that reflects the methodology used to arive at the number. This plus or minus quantity is common in scientific data, but almost nonexistent in the popular literature. Thus the public sees the inclusion of a range of numbers as admitting that the actual value is not known rather than a reflection of the methodology. This confusion is carried further in that most in the public think that if the radon levels in their houses are less than the suggested guidance level of 4 pCi/L level, they are safe. They ignore the reality that there is error in this measurement and also ignore that this level represents a roughly 2% per lifetime risk of dying early from lung cancer.

Although there are many considerations that need to be dealt with in the area of risk communication, one final one that needs to be further analyzed is that of language. For example, instead of range of uncertainty, why not range of certainty? Risk communication usually involves negative words such as absolutely, chronic, fear, hazard, poisonous, probability, risk, toxic, and uncertainty, rather than such positive words as assurance, benefit, certainty, confidence, health, prevention, safety, and trust.

STRATEGIES FOR THE FUTURE

There is a clear need to include comparative risk, along with other considerations, in the processes of planning, budgeting, and research efforts in environmental endeavors at all levels of government, in the private sector, and among environmental groups (see, for example, the chapter by Garetz). This is an idea whose time has come with the development of quantitative risk assessment. One of the most significant impediments to this effort is the lack of information and data. These gaps need to be filled before a complete estimate of the comparative quantitative risk can be accomplished. In addition, there are other areas that need to be considered in this development.

There are several cross-cutting issues that are important in the development of comparative quantitative risk assessment. For example, environmental contaminants can exist in several media (air — indoors and outdoors, water, soil, food) and can be transferred from one to the other, thus potentially changing the relative risk. Other cross-cutting issues involve the artificial division among Federal, state, and local governments that make cooperation in addressing a single environmental contaminant difficult, differential time scales in the flow of environmental contaminants, and the relative importance of an individual contaminant in the areas of human health and ecological health.

The results of a comparative quantitative risk assessment must be communicated to decision makers and the public or it will have little value. However, little attention has been given to risk communication both at the formal educational level and the general public level. More effort will clearly be needed here as more information and data become available for comparative quantitative risk assessments. The focus here should be on the language used and the mathematical concepts needed, such as order of magnitude, probability, and uncertainty.

The estimates of risk need to be tested against reality (see, for example, the chapter by Crawford-Brown and Arnold). Our transient society with the myriad pollutant exposures and diversity of susceptibility make direct measures difficult, but every effort needs to be made to bring quantitative risk assessment into direct proof.

Two points here can help put this effort into context. First, comparative risk assessments are only one of several considerations in dealing with environmental problems. They need to be considered along with economic, political, social, and psychological aspects of the problems. However, after all the details are gathered there will be some uncertainty and the decision maker will have to make use of judgment born of experience to make the final decisions.

REFERENCES

D. Latai, D. D. Lanning, and N. C. Rasmussen, "The Public Perception of Risk," in *The Analysis of Actual versus Perceived Risks*, V. T. Covello, W. G. Flamm, J. A. Roderick, and R. G. Tardiff, Eds., Plenum Press, New York, 1983.

U.S. Environmental Protection Agency, Reducing Risk: Setting Priorities And Strategies For Environmental Protection, SAB-EC-90-021, Washington, D.C., 20460, 1990.

Current Concerns Regarding the Implementation of Risk-Based Management: How Real Are They?*

William V. Garetz

Although there is widespread support for the concept of risk-based management "in theory", there are many individuals who feel that practical problems in implementing such a system are so severe that no such system can in fact be put in place any time in the near future. In essence, they agree that such a system should be put in place "someday", but believe that it would be impossible or unwise to put it in place "now".

In this chapter I will first describe and discuss what appear to be the seven mostly widely held concerns that have caused doubts about the ability to implement such a system. I will then describe and discuss ten additional concerns that I believe need to be addressed in any such system. In a later chapter (see the last section of this book) I will present a specific proposed system for risk-based priority setting and resource allocation that could be used in the short term.

The context for the present discussion is that documented in two reports from the U.S. Environmental Protection Agency, viz., *Unfinished Business* and *Reducing Risk*. The first of these two reports proposes a ranking of 31 areas of environmental concern within the Agency. The second report is a re-examination of some of the principles in the first and contains some recommendations for future efforts.

THE SEVEN MOST WIDELY HELD CONCERNS

I begin by listing seven widely heard concerns regarding the implementation any time soon of a system of risk-based management. I will first describe each of these concerns. I will then discuss the merits of each.

---

* The thoughts and ideas expressed in this chapter are those of the author and are not necessarily those of the U.S. Environmental Protection Agency.

The seven most often heard concerns are

Concern #1. The risk information currently available is *incomplete*.

What is the Concern? Because risk information is incomplete (i.e., there are some unknown elements of risk and there are other elements of risk that are not fully known), the resulting resource allocation will be flawed and therefore should not be conducted.

Discussion: It is not so much the *incompleteness* of risk information that is a potential problem, but the fact that it is *differentially incomplete*. If the degree of incompleteness were uniform across all environmental threats, then the incompleteness of the data would have no skewing impact on the resource allocation. However, we know that risk information *is* differentially incomplete. There are some kinds of environmental threats for which we believe our current risk estimates to be much more complete than for other environmental threats. This differential incompleteness will indeed result in a skewed resource allocation as compared with that which would result from use of the "true" risk values.

If, however, we look at this situation from another point of view, we see that for each case in which an environmental threat "gets short changed" in the resource allocation, it is because there is differentially less complete risk information for that threat. Since, in fact, it is programs and program managers (and not the environmental threats per se) that will get use of the allocated resources, that means that the program and program manager that gets less than its/his/her fair share of the resources is one who is less "on top of" the true extent of the environmental threat he/she is addressing. Looked at this way, it is only fair that they should get differentially less of the resources — they haven't done as adequate a job of identifying the risks. Conversely, there will always be a strong incentive in a system of risk-based priority setting to more fully identify the risks associated with each environmental threat (in order to increase that program's or manager's share of the resources to be allocated).

Thus, rather than seeing the skewed allocations resulting from differentially incomplete risk information as being a disadvantage of such a system, we might instead more productively see it as an *advantage* to such a system. This is so since that very skewing provides a strong incentive to those getting the "short end of the skew" to take the appropriate action (socially beneficial in itself) of more fully characterizing the risks associated with the environmental threat addressed by that program and manager.

Conclusion: At best, this concern has little or no merit as a reason for postponing implementation of a risk-based approach for priority setting.

Concern #2. The risk information currently available is *uncertain*.

What is the Concern? At first glance, this concern is very similar to that just discussed regarding the incompleteness of data. Uncertainty is different, though, in that we could (theoretically) be confident that our risks data were complete (i.e., that no components of risk [i.e., undesirable endpoints of exposure] had been omitted), and yet have a high degree of uncertainty as to the magnitude of the risk associated with each component. The concern here is that because risk estimates often have large uncertainty bands around them, the resulting resource allocation will be flawed and therefore should not be conducted.

Discussion: As with incompleteness, it is not so much the uncertainty per se within risk estimates that is a potential problem, but the fact that the degree of uncertainty differs so greatly from one environmental threat to another. If the degree of uncertainty were uniform across all environmental threats, then the uncertainty of the risk estimates would have no skewing impact on the resource allocation. However, risk estimates *do* differ in the extent of the associated uncertainty. There are some kinds of environmental threats for which we believe our current risk estimates to be much more precise than for other environmental threats. Depending on how any specific system for generating a risk-based resource allocation handles uncertainty may result in a skewed resource allocation as compared with that which would result from use of the "true" risk values. However, unlike with incompleteness in the risk data, differential uncertainty in the risk estimates could cut in either of two ways, depending on how the uncertain component of each risk estimate is handled. If "full credit" is given for the uncertain portion of a risk estimate (i.e., the *uncertain* portion of the risk estimate is treated exactly the same as the *undisputed* portion of that same risk estimate), then there is no incentive to resolve the uncertainty. Indeed, there will be a positive incentive *not* to resolve the uncertainty.

If, on the other hand, "no credit" is given for the uncertain portion of the risk estimate, or if relatively little credit is given, then there is a strong positive incentive to resolve the uncertainty. In either case, the "skewing" of the resource allocation due to differences in the extent of the uncertainty will produce a strong incentive to resolve the uncertainty. This is so since if the program gets "no credit" for the uncertainty, then there is nothing to be lost and possibly much to be gained by resolving the uncertainty. The incentive is nearly as strong if only "little credit" is given for the uncertainty. Such an incentive to resolve the uncertainty would not be a disadvantage, but rather an *advantage* of a risk-based approach to resource allocation. Those programs and managers who successfully resolve (i.e., reduce) the uncertainty in risk estimates for environmental threats for which they are responsible will, on average, achieve proportionately higher resource allocations. Since it is socially desirable to resolve such uncertainties, this is a desirable feature of well-designed systems for risk-based resource allocation.

Concern #3. The risk information currently available is *noncomparable*.

What is the Concern? Risk estimates for different environmental threats have often been developed based on different risk estimation procedures or at different times, often using different assumptions.

(1) *Noncomparability of risk estimation procedures:* an example of this class of noncomparability is that some human health risks have been determined based on direct human epidemiological evidence. Others are based on human epidemiology, but rely on extrapolation from high human doses to low doses (e.g., estimates of the risks of exposure to low doses of radiation based on the epidemiology of uranium miners exposed to very high doses). Other health risk estimates are based on animal studies in which both a high-dose to low-dose and a species-to-species extrapolation were required. These different approaches for estimating (in this case) human health risk are clearly "noncomparable". Despite the best efforts of technical experts, it may be very difficult to place estimates derived from such highly disparate sources on a single risk scale.

(2) *Noncomparability of the assumptions or models used in making two different risk estimates:* even if the kind of data used to make risk estimates for two different environmental threats is the same (e.g., both are based on extrapolation from animal data to humans, which required both high-dose to low-dose and species-to-species extrapolation), there may still be differences due to the fact that (e.g.) different high-dose to low-dose extrapolation models were used.

(3) *Noncomparability of the time at which the risk estimates were made:* a risk estimate made for one environmental threat in 1978 will almost certainly be different (and noncomparable with) another made for that same environmental threat in 1986 — because the baseline data are almost certainly from a different year or set of years. Similarly, risk estimates for *two different* environmental threats conducted in different years are almost certainly noncomparable for the same reason.

Discussion:

(1) *Noncomparability due to use of different risk estimation procedures:* this concern is widely held for health risk estimates. It may not be so widely held for ecological risk, but if so, only because there has been much less effort to develop "comparable" risk estimates for different kinds of ecological risks. In fact, this concern is likely to be at least as great if not greater for ecological risks. It may also be great for welfare risks, even though it is generally agreed that welfare risks should all be put on a single scale using dollar value as the common metric. (For example, if the welfare risk to be evaluated is the accelerated deterioration of the Parthenon in Athens due to air pollution, how can a dollar value be assigned to the loss of a unique structure of such great historical and cultural value? And should the attempt even be made?)

(2,3) *Noncomparability due to use of data from different baseline years or due to use of different assumptions or models:* such sources of noncomparability can be quite significant. A procedure is therefore needed in any proposed system of risk-based management to adjust risk estimates to account for such differences. One such approach or procedure would be to convene an expert panel to adjust the estimates to a standard baseline year or period and to adjust to a standard set of assumptions. Use of such a panel would help ensure reasonable comparability in the different risk estimates provided for different environmental risks. Furthermore, for certain classes of risk estimates (e.g., high-dose to low-dose extrapolation of cancer risks), EPA has taken steps in recent years through (for example) issuance of the *Guidelines* for Cancer Risk Assessment to promote much greater comparability in newly generated risk estimates. Further initiatives to develop such guidelines should be strongly encouraged.

In general: it is suggested that noncomparability be dealt with by converting it to an equivalent (differential) degree of uncertainty. Any proposed system that does so in this manner should then be evaluated in terms of the likely effectiveness of the procedure or mechanism it establishes to achieve this conversion. (See, in particular, the procedures contained in the proposed system presented in my later chapter.)

Concern #4. Risk-based management is biased against *future* as compared with *present* risks.

What is the Concern? The risk estimates developed in the *Unfinished Business* effort and somewhat less so in the *Reducing Risk* effort tended to focus on current, as-yet unmitigated risk. The focus was on current environmental risks that are currently resulting in harm due to current or past exposure or are likely to result in future harm due to current exposure. Due to (for example) the latency periods known to be associated with the development of cancer, current exposure may not result in an adverse effect until some point in the future. This "future harm associated with current exposure" was fully considered to the best of the ability of the two separate panels to do so. Much less fully considered was "the future harm likely to result from future risk" (i.e., from anticipated future releases or exposures that have not yet occurred). Although such "future risks" that have not yet occurred were not explicitly eliminated from consideration in the *Unfinished Business* effort, much less effort was devoted to consideration of them than to the harm associated with "current risks". This concern is most frequently expressed by those associated with two programs developed to prevent potential future exposures to toxic substances: the Superfund Program and the Hazardous Waste (RCRA) Program. For both programs, it is generally acknowledged that very little such exposure has yet occurred. Each of these two programs is intended, they remind us, to help make sure that it never does.

Discussion: Harm associated with future risks that have not yet occurred are necessarily based primarily on projections rather than on current measurements. They are therefore inherently less certain in virtually all respects: there is uncertainty (1) with regard to the likelihood and extent of occurrence, (2) with regard to the magnitude of the associated releases, (3) with regard to the exposures likely to result from these releases, and (4) with regard to the harm likely to result from these exposures. Nevertheless, where there is compelling evidence in the form of plausible projections that such risks are likely to occur, they *should be included* in any system of risk-based management.

Because of the unusually great uncertainties associated with such future risks, such a system can best accommodate them if it explicitly allows for wide uncertainty bands for the risks associated with each environmental threat included within the system.

Concern #5. How can we add health, ecological, and welfare risks to come up with a single consolidated risk estimate and ranking?

What is the Concern? Different kinds of environmental stress result in different effect "endpoints" (e.g., lung cancer, neurotoxicity, congenital deformities, interference with the spawning of a certain fish species, eggshell thinning in certain bird species, hardening of certain materials, discoloration of other materials, decreased yields of certain crops, etc.). Since it is difficult, if not impossible, to put these different endpoints on a single uniform risk scale, it will not be possible to come up with a single undisputed ranking of different environmental threats based on risk. Any effort to come up with such a ranking anyway will inevitably be artificial and subject to great dispute. It is therefore pointless to try to develop such a system.

Discussion: What we have at present, coming out of the *Unfinished Business* and the *Reducing Risk* efforts, is not one set of rankings of environmental problems based on risks, but instead three separate rankings, one each based on health, ecological, and welfare risks. How can we move forward given that we have three rankings rather than one? Ideally, if we are to be able to develop a single unified set of risk-based priorities and if we are to conduct a single risk-based resource-allocation process, then we would want somehow to consolidate these three separate risk-based rankings into one combined ranking. One way to do this would be to develop a "universal risk metric" or "uniform risk unit" to which each of the three distinct kinds of risk could be converted. Once this conversion to this "universal risk metric" has been completed, the three separate kinds of risks could then be summed for each of the identified environmental threats and we would have a "total environmental risk" for each of the identified threats. What are the chances of developing such a metric that would receive wide support? Not likely — at least not in the next decade or two. That doesn't mean that we shouldn't begin working towards the development of such a universal risk metric. We should. Instead, it means that our immediate efforts to design and implement a system of risk-based management should *not* be predicated on the existence of such a metric.

If we are unlikely to have a widely supported universal risk metric anytime in the near or intermediate future, then what else can we do? An alternative possible approach that could be implemented fairly quickly would involve setting up the three risk rankings as parallel scales and then expanding or shrinking the length of two of the scales until (for example) a broad-based technical panel with no vested interests in any one kind of environmental risk or in any one environmental concern or program can agree that the three scales are properly "pegged" to each other. This pegging process might reasonably be repeated every 5 to 10 years to reflect any significant new information about environmental risks developed in the meantime and also to reflect any significant changes in underlying values that occur over time. To work well and to be widely accepted, such a panel should probably represent a broad cross section of concerns and views and should, if possible, include only individuals with broad-based knowledge about and interest in the environment. It should contain no one with a vested interest in any one kind or subset of environmental risks, threats, or programs. Another alternative *short-term approach* that could *very quickly* be implemented would take a wholly different tack. It would consist of taking the entire "pot" of resources to be invested and dividing it into three smaller pots: one each to address health risks, ecological risks, and welfare risks. A separate resource allocation could then be conducted with each of these separate "pots" of resources. I believe that this is the only approach that is available to us in the short term.*

Concern #6. The breakout of total environmental risk into specific environmental threats to be ranked "was not done right".

What is the Concern? In the *Unfinished Business* effort, the full array of environmental threats was divided into 31 distinct threats or concerns that were separately evaluated as to the associated environmental risk. There were some concerns expressed (by, among others, the panelists in the *Reducing Risk* effort) that the 31 environmental threats identified were "not the right ones". There were several different bases for this criticism. One was that some of the 31 environmental threats are overlapping, thus introducing the potential for (or certainty of) double counting of certain risks. Another concern was that the 31 categories were selected primarily to line up with current EPA

---

* Editor's note: A semiquantitative approach to combining cancer and noncancer risks is discussed in the chapter in this volume by Deisler.

program lines, rather than to line up with "logical" or "natural" groupings in the environment. Most of the panels in both the *Unfinished Business* and the *Reducing Risk* efforts felt strongly enough on this point that they unilaterally made adjustments in the numbers of categories or in the definitions of the categories. Some even deleted entire categories or groups of categories and created different new categories to replace them.

Discussion: In general, every person approaching the problem of how to break the environment into distinct environmental threats (i.e., categories) to be addressed in a system of risk-based management will have different thoughts regarding the best breakout to use. In fact, there are a number of different approaches that can be used to do this which can be used separately or in combination with each other. These approaches include: (1) breakout by the substance released (or the nature of the change in habitat produced); (2) breakout by the nature of the endpoint produced (e.g., lung cancer, neurotoxicity, congenital deformities, interference with the spawning of a certain fish species, eggshell thinning in certain bird species, hardening of certain materials, discoloration of other materials, decreased yields of certain crops, etc.); (3) breakout by the source of the release; (4) breakout by the medium through which the released substance is transported; (5) breakout by the receptor (i.e., human beings, fish, trees, man-made structures, etc.) exposed to the released substance (or affected by the change in habitat); (6) breakout by the specific geographic areas in which the adverse effects will occur; (7) breakout by the type of actions likely to be effective in eliminating or mitigating the release, exposure, or effects; (8) breakout by the responsible program or agency, etc.

No one approach for accomplishing the breakout is inherently any better or worse than any other. It is simply that some breakouts are more useful for certain purposes and others are more useful for other purposes.

Where a mixed approach is used (e.g., breakout by substance released for certain environmental threats, breakout by the medium through which the substances are transported for the others), there *is* great potential for overlap and for double counting. Specific steps should be taken in such cases to draw the lines carefully between categories to eliminate any such double counting. As long as such steps are taken (to eliminate double counting), *any* approach or combination of approaches can be used for the needed breakouts.

Clearly, *some* approach must be used to generate the needed breakouts. And the likelihood of a breakout being found that everyone is happy with is probably nil. So a more or less arbitrary choice must be made among the many possibilities.

Making an arbitrary selection of the breakout procedure to be used is a more workable approach than it might at first seem. This is so because experience has shown that the strongest reservations tend to be expressed by individuals when they are *first* exposed to a particular breakout. Once they have worked with it for a while and have struggled a bit to come up with a better alternative (and have found that it is not so easy to do and that even if done, it is even less easy to get general agreement to), their reservations tend to diminish quickly.

In any case, the best way to deal with these continuing concerns is to build the risk estimates for each category up in such a way that they can be disaggregated and then reaggregated fairly readily into whatever other different breakout categories may be selected for use in the future. As a practical matter, any breakout to be used should probably have at least 15 categories in it in order to be useful for meaningful priority setting and resource allocation, and should probably not have more than 40 to 50 categories in it (at most) in order not to produce results that are too fragmented and confusing.

Concern #7. Any method used to achieve risk-based resource allocations will inevitably be too rigid and mechanical.

What is the Concern? There is concern among some individuals that any system for risk-based management, and especially any system that allocates resources based on relative risk, will be too rigid and will result in significant misallocations because of its inability to take into account special circumstances surrounding specific classes of environmental threats or the programs needed to address them.

Discussion: This concern would be valid if the actual distribution of resources were in fact to be assigned to a computer-based algorithm which served as the sole and final decision-making authority, from which there is no appeal. In fact, in the real world, there will be human beings reviewing the results of any algorithm used and checking it for balance and consistency. Furthermore, the program managers with strong knowledge of and interest in any program that "has not been dealt with fairly" will be able to identify any imbalances or inconsistencies in the results, explain how it was they came about (i.e., point out the significant factor that was not considered or was not given proper weight), and suggest what adjustments might be appropriate. There will then be ample opportunity in the budget formulation process within the Federal Executive Branch for appropriate adjustments to be made. Finally, Congress together with the President will have the final say (through the process of adopting and signing an appropriation bill) in determining the final allocation of resources among different EPA programs for the coming year. I think it safe to predict that neither the President nor the Congressional Appropriation Committees are likely to delegate their decision-making responsibilities in this key area to a computer algorithm. In any case, any concerns in this direction can be alleviated by making it explicit that the risk-based resource-allocation procedure to be used is an *advisory* one, to be used to develop an *initial, preliminary* allocation for the consideration of the EPA Administrator, and that it is expected that appropriate adjustments will be made in that initial allocation as compelling arguments are presented for doing so.

Nevertheless, it should be urged that whenever anomalous features are found in the preliminary allocation, efforts be made subsequently (1) to discover what has not been fully or not appropriately considered within the algorithm and (2) to modify the algorithm appropriately prior to the next year's implementation of the (revised) algorithm. If these steps are taken each year, the extent of the need to adjust the preliminary results derived from using the algorithm should continue to diminish, and significantly so, over time.

TEN ADDITIONAL CONCERNS THAT SHOULD BE ADDRESSED IN DESIGNING ANY SYSTEM FOR RISK-BASED MANAGEMENT

In addition to the seven widely held concerns presented and discussed above, there are a number of other factors that should be of concern in designing a system of risk-based management for EPA. I will now describe each of these additional concerns and discuss its significance. For an example of the application of these criteria to a specific system for risk-based priority setting and resource allocation, please see my later chapter in the final section of this volume.

Concern #8. Any method used to achieve risk-based resource allocation has the potential to be biased against controlled as compared with uncontrolled risks.

What is the Concern? The *Unfinished Business* effort and the *Reducing Risk* effort both focused primarily on current risks and secondarily on potential future risks. Those on the panels for each of these two efforts were explicitly instructed to disregard any environmental risk deemed already to be adequately controlled or mitigated. It was further stated in the final reports from both efforts that both were intended to identify how best to allocate resources among remaining (residual) risks and that it was assumed that the resources then already being devoted to risks already adequately mitigated would continue to be applied to those mitigation efforts. Thus, the focus was on allocating resources "on the margin" in order most effectively to address as yet unmitigated risks.

As a consequence, by design, the associated panels did not address the question of how to allocate resources between efforts to operate ongoing programs that "have already done their job" of mitigating risks (i.e., "maintenance programs") and efforts to reduce as yet unmitigated risks (i.e., "new abatement programs" and "new prevention-oriented programs"). There is some concern that if any system of risk-based management were to be applied to all programs EPA-wide, it may fail to assign the appropriate level of resources to maintenance programs.

Discussion: We define a "maintenance program" to be a program that continues to operate in order to maintain a reduction in environmental risk that was achieved previously as the result of prior successful risk reduction (i.e., abatement or prevention) programs.

The crucial question is this: is there any way to incorporate maintenance programs explicitly in the functioning of a process for achieving risk-based management? The answer is yes.

One way to look at the situation is this: a maintenance program is a program intended to *prevent* the reappearance of an environmental risk that had once been prevalent, but that has since been mitigated. Viewed in this way, a *maintenance* program is simply a *prevention* program. It should therefore be dealt with in the same way that other prevention programs are addressed. (See discussion above under Concern #4.) The one difference is this: while prevention programs to prevent risks that have never previously occurred are likely to have wide bands of uncertainty in the associated risk estimates, the opposite will often be true for maintenance programs.

Because the risk being prevented through the effective operation of a maintenance program is a risk that has actually previously occurred on a widespread basis, it should be possible to quantify the associated risks with a considerable amount of precision. As a result, the associated risk bands should be fairly narrow when compared with those for other prevention programs.

Concern #9. What is to be allocated? Federal dollars only? Or total public and private expenditure for environmental protection and management?

What is the Concern? In the *Reducing Risk* report, it is sometimes suggested that only Federal expenditures are to be allocated using any new system for risk-based resource allocation. At other times, however, it is acknowledged that it is the effective use of *all* resources devoted to environmental protection that is of concern. In the latter case, it is the total public and private expenditure for environmental management that should be addressed by any new system of risk-based resource allocation.

Discussion: The total public and private expenditure for environmental protection in the U.S. is estimated to be about $100 billion per year. EPA itself spends about $6 billion each year, of which the EPA Administrator currently has significant discretion (subject of the approval of the President and the Congress) for about $1.5 billion. If an elaborate new system of risk-based resource allocation were to be developed and applied only to the current discretionary $1.5 billion, we would find ourselves in a situation in which we (to use a homey example) are painstakingly maintaining the porch, while neglecting the rest of the house and just kind of hoping everything will turn out okay back there. That's silly. What's important is to see to it that we make the best possible use of the full $100 billion currently devoted to environmental protection. It is not unreasonable to strive to do so. After all, the expenditure of the entire $100 billion is directed or influenced by EPA through its rulemaking, through its enforcement presence, and through its interaction with its counterpart agencies at the state and local levels. It is therefore both desirable and appropriate that any new system of risk-based resource allocation be applied to the entire $100 billion expended.

Concern #10. What is risk-based management? There seem to be several different notions about this, which, on the face of it, are inconsistent with each other.

What is the Concern? One problem in moving forward to actual implementation of a system for risk-based environmental management is that the very meaning of the phrase "risk-based management" has remained somewhat fuzzy. Some have talked more specifically of "risk-based priority setting" and of "risk-based resource allocation". What do we mean by these things? Unfortunately, this also is unclear. At certain points in *Unfinished Business* and in *Reducing Risk*, the intent of a system of risk-based management is stated to be risk-based priority setting; at others the intent is clearly risk-based resource allocation. Yet there is no clear discussion in either *Unfinished Business* or in *Reducing Risk* of what the relationship is between risk-based priority setting and risk-based resource allocation. Any specific system of risk-based management must clearly define these two terms and state which of the two it is intended to accomplish; if it is intended to accomplish both, it must clearly indicate how it will achieve each.

Discussion: The concern about the confusion as to what is meant by "risk-based management" can easily be resolved by adopting a single, clear set of definitions. Any proposed system can then be measured against these definitions to see what that particular system actually accomplishes. The following definitions are offered as candidates for achieving this purpose:

- *Risk-based priority setting* means determining how big one environment problem is when compared to others as a contributor to the total environmental risk from all classes of environmental threats and challenges. It means determining how big each problem is as a percentage or slice of the full environmental risk pie. It is also an indication of how much we would be *willing* to invest in addressing each environmental threat, "all else being equal". I propose that it be expressed as:
  "Environmental Threat A (or B or C . . .) is responsible for 9% of the total environmental risk we face."
  and
  "All else being equal, we would be willing to invest 9% of our total environmental management resources to the elimination or mitigation of Environmental Threat A."
- *Risk-based resource allocation* is a process for determining how much it is appropriate to spend on each of these distinct environmental problems given

that we live in the real world in which "not all else is equal". To be more specific, there are certain environmental threats for which we have not yet developed effective responses. Investing an amount on these threats proportional to their contribution to total environmental risk would be a poor investment. It would constitute "throwing money at the problem" rather than investing wisely to reduce or eliminate it. For such problems we should instead focus for now on developing more effective abatement and prevention *strategies* including, where appropriate, more effective abatement and prevention *technologies*. Sensible risk-based resource allocation must consider not only the magnitude of each environmental threat in terms of the amount it contributes to total environmental risk, but must also consider the relative effectiveness of the responses now available to us to invest in to reduce or eliminate these threats. Such an allocation would be expressed as:

"The recommended investment for the response to Environmental Threat A in Fiscal Year 1993 is $37,700,000."

Concern #11. If a risk-based resource allocation is to be achieved, what is to be the basis for the allocation? The total cost of control/prevention? Or the marginal cost?

What is the Concern? In certain points in the *Reducing Risk* report, the panel appears to be thinking in terms of achieving proportionality between the *total* national (or the *total* Federal) expenditure for a given environmental threat and the *total* risk associated with that threat. At other points, the panel made it clear that it is the *marginal* expenditure of resources that should be made proportional to the *marginal* risk reduction to be achieved through use of those resources.

Discussion: As discussed in part in conjunction with Concern #10 immediately above, I think it most useful for the *"priority"* assigned to an environmental threat to be proportional to the *total risk* it presents, but for *the resources* to be devoted to a given set of risk-reduction activities (abatement and prevention activities) to be assigned based on the amount of *risk reduction* to be achieved *per dollar expended* (or, as I prefer to say, per dollar "invested"). The latter amounts to resource allocation for risk reduction on the basis of the *marginal* risk reduction to be achieved per (*marginal*) dollar spent. A system that allocates resources based on marginal cost effectiveness (i.e., marginal risk reduction achieved for a given marginal investment) results in a risk-based allocation of resources that considers not only the magnitude of that portion of total environmental risk associated with that environmental threat, but also the potential effectiveness of the various responses currently available to us to deal with these various threats.

Concern #12. Will a given approach for resource allocation be useful in guiding the allocation of dollars for: Research on Health Effects? Research on Ecological Effects? Development of Needed New Control Technology? Development of Needed New Management Strategies?

What is the Concern? Most attention until now on the development of a risk-based system for resource allocation has focused the allocation of resources among risk-reduction (i.e., abatement and prevention) activities. The question is, will any specific system for risk-based allocation of resources address only such risk-reduction activities or will it also address how best to allocate resources among such critical adjunct activities as (1) the development of new control technology (i.e., risk-reduction technology) and the conduct of such activities as (2) health effects research and (3) ecological effects research? The latter (health effects research and ecological effects research) may be critical for reducing current uncertainty regarding the magnitude of the environmental risk associated with a given environmental threat.

Discussion: While it is essential that any proposed system give guidance on the allocation of resources among risk-reduction activities, it would also be highly desirable for it to provide guidance on the allocation of resources among critical adjunct activities like those discussed above.

Concern #13. There is no *central repository* for environmental risk data.

What is the Concern? With the exception of certain limited classes of environmental risk data, there is no central repository within EPA for such data. Without such a central repository, it will be difficult to establish and operate a system of risk-based resource allocation.

Discussion: There is at present only one EPA-wide repository of risk information: the Integrated Risk Information System (IRIS) maintained by the Office of Health and Environmental Assessment within the EPA Office of Research and Development. Furthermore, IRIS contains only information relevant to cancer risks and certain acute risks.

I fully agree with this concern. I believe that any specific proposal to establish a system for risk-based priority setting and resource allocation *must address* the need for a centrally maintained repository of risk information (and of information on the projected cost and projected effectiveness of each risk-reduction option proposed for each category of risk).

Concern #14. There is no on-going process for routinely supplementing incomplete risk data.

What is the Concern? All of the panels convened to support the *Unfinished Business* and *Reducing Risk* efforts have noted that the available risk information is quite incomplete. Unless there is some on-going process for making this risk information increasingly more complete, there will be continued reservations about the merits of any system of risk-based resource allocation.

Discussion: If a proposed system of risk-based resource allocation creates sufficient incentives to fill gaps in available risk information and provides a mechanism to accept this new information and a repository to contain it, then this concern will be greatly alleviated.

Concern #15. There is no on-going process for routinely improving risk data for which there are large current uncertainties.

What is the Concern? All of the panels convened have also noted the extent of the uncertainty as to the magnitude of the risk even for those components of risk that have been clearly identified. Many of the panelists have expressed strong concerns about the magnitude of this uncertainty and would like to see vigorous action to reduce the magnitude of those components of known risks for which there is significant uncertainty.

Discussion: If a proposed system of risk-based resource allocation creates sufficient incentives to reduce the extent of the uncertainty in current risk estimates for known risks, and provides a mechanism to accept this new information and a repository to contain it, then this concern will be greatly alleviated.

Concern #16. There is no on-going process for updating risk data to incorporate newly developed data and findings.

What is the Concern? This concern is essentially the same as that for Concerns #13 and #14 above, except that, in this case, the concern is with *unanticipated new components of risk* associated with existing or newly identified environmental threats.

Discussion: If a proposed system of risk-based resource allocation creates sufficient incentives to capture and make use of risk information on newly identified components of environmental risk, and provides a mechanism to accept this new information and a repository to contain it, then this concern will be greatly alleviated.

Concern #17. There is no on-going process for comparing risk numbers with expenditures.

What is the Concern? A systematic process for comparing risk estimates for individual environmental threats with the associated current expenditures is needed. Without it, EPA will never fully know the extent to which current expenditures in the U.S. for environmental protection are commensurate with the associated risks.

Discussion: I fully agree with this concern. I would add that to be effective, such comparisons should be conducted annually and should be conducted on a consistent, comprehensive basis for all environmental threats of concern to EPA.

We have now addressed ten other major concerns that must be adequately addressed by any system put forward for risk-based priority setting and resource allocation. Before we conclude, we must still address one remaining concern of critical significance.

ONE FINAL CONCERN OF OVERRIDING IMPORTANCE: WHAT IS THE APPROPRIATE BASIC DESIGN OF SUCH A SYSTEM — FULLY QUANTITATIVE, SEMIQUANTITATIVE, OR QUALITATIVE?

We now address one final concern that is of such critical importance that responding inappropriately will guarantee that a newly established system for risk-based priority setting and resource allocation will self-destruct within 3 to 4 years no matter how strong the initial commitment to it.

The basic question is, what is the appropriate design for such a system — fully quantitative, semiquantitative, or qualitative? Due to the peculiar institutional dynamics that have already been seen to occur when applying qualitative and semiquantitative approaches to risk-based management, and the consistently destructive outcome of these dynamics on previous attempts to establish risk-based priority setting and resource allocation at EPA, the treatment of this final concern is much more detailed than that of the previous 17 concerns.

In the discussion below, it is argued that only a fully quantitative system can function equitably and can continue to obtain the necessary internal support to continue to function indefinitely. It draws on recent experience within EPA to show that semiquantitative and qualitative systems are inherently inequitable and contain within them the seeds of their self-destruction. It points out that recent history shows that such self-destruction occurs within 3 to 4 years of the initial launching of a less than fully quantitative system.

Here now is the final, overriding concern:

Concern #18. There is insufficient commitment to continuing and building on an explicitly *quantitative* approach for risk-based priority setting and resource allocation.

What is the Concern? Explicitly quantitative approaches to risk-based management are quite distinct from semiquantitative and qualitative approaches. There has been a strong inclination in the past to be satisfied with qualitative approaches "guided by" or "informed by" quantitative risk information as contrasted with explicitly and fully quantitative approaches. Such approaches have consistently broken down in practice due to certain persistent institutional dynamics. Strictly quantitative approaches seem to have the potential to resist such breakdown. Despite the strongly contrasting dynamics associated with these different basic designs, qualitative and semiquantitative approaches *continue* to be put forward as "reasonable" proxies for a purely quantitative approach.

Discussion: A strictly quantitative approach to risk-based resource allocation has two essential features: (1) it contains *numerical* estimates of risk and (2) it allocates resources in a manner *proportional* to the estimated risk. As a consequence, any environmental threat for which there is an identified positive risk, no matter how small, will have a certain portion of the available resources allocated to it. For example, even if a given environmental threat is found to account for only one tenth of 1% (0.1%) of the total environmental risk we face, it will still receive a (preliminary) allocation of resources equal to one one-thousandth (0.1% = 1/1000) of those available. Given that the total U.S. expenditure for environmental protection and management is $100 billion, that would mean that this one "very small" environmental threat would get an allocation of $100 billion/1000 = $100 million, a significant amount of resources.

Similarly, even if it were decided to apply the allocation process only to discretionary EPA resources, we would get a comparable result. Specifically, given that EPA has a discretionary budget of $1.5 billion, that would mean that this one "very small" environmental threat would get an allocation of $1.5 billion/1000 = $1.5 million of EPA discretionary funds, again a not insignificant amount of resources for a "very small" threat.

By contrast, semiquantitative and qualitative approaches to risk assessment operate quite differently. A number of such approaches have been implemented within EPA since the early 1970s, so we have considerable practical experience with them.

The most rigorous of such approaches are the *semiquantitative approaches,* which seek to put the environmental threats to be addressed in strict rank order (i.e., first, second, third, fourth, etc.). We find that with this first step we already encounter serious operational problems, as we discovered when we sought such ordinal ranking in both the *Unfinished Business* and the *Reducing Risk* exercises. The difficulty arises as a result of the uncertainties in the risk estimates. Where the risk bands for two or more environmental threats overlap, there can be legitimate questions about which of the two ranks higher in terms of risk, especially so if there is significant opinion that one threat is likely to fall near the upper end of its risk range and another risk is likely to fall near the lower end of its range.

Once the environmental threats are put in ordinal rankings by risk (in the few cases where this can be achieved), or grouped, these approaches then operates as follows. Resources are now identified as "what is necessary" to address effectively each of the ranked environmental threats. In each case, it is a single resource figure that is provided for each environmental threat.

The available resources are then assigned in order to the highest-ranked environmental threat, then to the second highest-ranked threat, then to the third-ranked threat, and so on, until all of the available resources are assigned. Once this point is reached, all lower-ranked threats then (theoretically) go without any resources at all — since they are "below the line" of what is fundable. The result is the theoretically "ideal" allocation of resources under this semi-quantitative or qualitative approach". In general, under such an approach, numerous environmental threats for which there are appreciable risks end up "falling below" the "funding line" and being zeroed out" in terms of resources.

In practice, however, these approaches are never operated strictly as described above. Instead, once the rankings or groupings are completed and the positioning of the "funding line" is determined, resources then tend to get allocated on an "incremental basis". The intent is to move "incrementally" towards the "ideal" funding arrangement initially determined. The reason for moving incrementally is to minimize disruption to on-going programs slated for reduction by having phased reductions over several years, with the reduction limited to no more than (generally) 5% in any one year for any one program.

The incremental adjustments toward the qualitative ideal are made as follows. The highest-ranking threats are slated for large positive increments; those not ranking so high, but still above the funding line are slated for smaller positive increments. For an environmental threat falling below the line, where there is an existing program to address that threat, the threat is slated for a small incremental decrease (e.g., 5%). If there is no existing program to address an environmental threat falling below the line, that threat is assigned zero resources (i.e., no new program is ever initiated to address it).

What I have just described is the "incremental implementation" of a rigorous qualitative approach. As was suggested above, experience has shown that it is never possible to sustain a rigorous qualitative system, not even one with incremental implementation. Instead, the following evolution inevitably occurs.

First, due to the dynamics described earlier, the threats are arranged into groups of environmental threats that are deemed to present risks of comparable magnitude. When grouped by technical experts or staff, there tend to be five or six such "risk groups" or "categories" at first. When grouped by administrative or policy staff, they tend to be assembled into three categories: one each for "high-risk", "medium-risk", and "low-risk" environmental threats.

I will now focus on the dynamics that develop in the implementation of a qualitative system starting with three categories. I will do so since all of the practical experience at EPA has been with such "three-category" systems.

What happens now, once a three-category system has been established, is that "skirmishes begin to be fought" on the boundaries. To understand what this means, let's look at a manager responsible for responding to a threat that is near the boundary between the medium-risk and the high-risk categories. If the threat for which this manager is responsible was initially placed in the medium-risk category, he or she is likely to make an argument for moving it into the higher category. Similarly, arguments are made for threats near the boundary of the medium- and low-risk categories. Through the normal process of bureaucratic accommodation, some of those arguing most insistently will prevail. What then results is "category inflation": a general shift upward in the categories in which specific threats are placed.

For a number of reasons, significant inequities result from this process of category inflation. For one thing, there are differences in the willingness of program managers to engage in "self-sacrifice for the common good" (i.e., to acquiesce in placement of their programs in any group lower than the highest one). For this reason, some self-sacrificing managers will not even make the effort to "move up" the threat for which they are responsible. Beyond this, among those not willing to "self-sacrifice" and who therefore lobby vigorously to "move their programs up", because of the differential bureaucratic clout or effectiveness of different program managers, some of these managers will not be effective. That is, they will not be successful in moving up the environmental threats for which they are responsible. Others will be.

In general, the effectiveness of any given manager in this lobbying has not been highly correlated with the true relative risk associated with the threat being addressed by his or her program. Instead, it is correlated more with how much he or she is "owed" by the pertinent decision maker, by his or her general level of influence, and by his or her degree of insistence/relentlessness in demanding the upward shift.

As a consequence of these various dynamics, some threats that are generally perceived to present less risk will end up in a higher category than other threats generally perceived to present greater risks.

At this point, those willing to go along with a rigorous system — even one that reduces the resources assigned to their own program — as long as the system is fair, will decide that politics have taken over and will stop being willing to go along. Everyone will now either seek to move the threats of concern to their program up or else withdraw their support for the system as a whole, or both. At the same time that the above dynamics are taking place, concerns are raised about the "labels" associated with the various categories. In particular, it is argued that "low risk" sounds too much like "no risk". Through the same process of bureaucratic accommodation, it is agreed to assign new and grander names to each category.

As the result of the "boundary skirmishes" described earlier, together with the label change just described, so many threats will have "moved up" that there soon aren't enough environmental threats left in the lowest category to justify keeping it, so the number of categories is reduced to two: "high risk" (the lower of the two) and "very high risk" (the higher of the two). At this point, the two categories begin to sound so much alike and many individuals are so puzzled trying to figure out what the difference is between them, that the process has become pointless and is soon abandoned.

Although the evolution just described may sound comical and in a sense is, it is no fantasy: this exact course of evolution has actually occurred at two separate periods in the last 15 years in which qualitative systems have been implemented at EPA. The entire course of evolution in each case took 3 to 4 years. The EPA experience has shown that the qualitative approach inevitably self-destructs in a relatively short period of time.

In conclusion, we have two distinct approaches to allocating resources based on relative risk.

(1)   A strictly *quantitative approach*. Although such an approach can be ma-
      nipulated somewhat by "shading" the risk estimates used, there are
      "laugh test" limits as well as technical limits on the amount of "shad-
      ing" that can be accomplished. This is so because the need to justify
      the proposed risk estimates must be in some way grounded in reality.
      There must be some evidence from the real world to back up the numbers
      proposed. The quantitative approach will therefore always be anchored
      in the range of credible risk numbers that can be assembled for each
      environmental risk that is to be addressed. The respective positions of
      different environmental threats can therefore not be shifted indiscrimi-
      nately. Furthermore, the strict quantitative approach is a relatively eq-
      uitable one, in that every environmental threat for which there is a
      positive risk will get *some* resources.

(2)   A *semiquantitative approach* or a *qualitative approach*. The basic design
      of such approaches is inherently inequitable in that many very real
      environmental threats, for which there are very real and appreciable
      risks, will fall below the line and (if newly identified) will never receive
      any resources. Furthermore, for qualitative systems, its very qualita-
      tiveness and lack of rigorous anchoring in reality gives it a "squishiness"
      that results in a predictable course of evolution into total triviality and
      pointless, at which point it is abandoned as useless. Semiquantitative
      systems are not long sustainable as such and quickly devolve into qual-
      itative systems, at which point they suffer the same fate as systems that
      started off with a qualitative design.

Thus, although the quantitative approach is not immune from all manipulation, there are fairly reasonable natural limits to the extent of the possible
"shading" of the risk estimates used. And it is therefore reasonably equitable.
The qualitative approaches (and its close relative the semiquantitative system,
which soon devolves into a purely qualitative system) has no limits to the
manipulation possible and has been found on two separate occasions within
EPA to collapse within 3 to 4 years after being initiated. Furthermore, even
when it is "working well", the result produced using a qualitative system is
quite inequitable.

CONCLUDING REMARKS

As this chapter has endeavored to show, all but one of the identified
concerns regarding the ability to construct and operate an equitable system
for risk-based priority setting and resource allocation is valid. With that one
exception, none can be ignored or disregarded. (The one exception is Concern
#1, which does not in fact appear to be valid.) At the same time, this chapter
has endeavored to show that none of the listed concerns reflects a fundamental
"fatal flaw" that would prevent the design of an equitable system for this

purpose. Indeed, a specific system has already been developed (the "Quick-Start System", presented in my later chapter), which appears to perform well against all the concerns presented in this chapter.

REFERENCES

U.S. Environmental Protection Agency, *Unfinished Business: a Comparative Assessment of Environmental Problems, Office of Policy, Planning and Evaluation,* Washington, D.C. (February 1987).

U.S. Environmental Protection Agency, *Reducing Risk: Setting Priorities and Strategies for Environmental Protection,* Science Advisory Board, Washington, D.C., SAB-EC-90-021 (September 1990).

Ecological Health Risks

Introduction

William Cooper

Little has been done, until recently, to develop a methodology to analyze and estimate quantitative risk due to natural and anthropogenic ecological phenomena except for the effects on humans. Thus, the current efforts outside human health endpoints are not prejudiced by previous work. Following the EPA Science Advisory Board, we will here identify the two areas as human health and ecological health for convenience, although this is an artificial separation. In the area of human quantitative risk many estimates have been made, particularly for the cancer endpoints. However, to date, no adequate theoretical or philosophical basis has been developed in the area of ecological risk assessment. Ecological quantitative risk assessment is being developed in a systematic way, starting with a careful examination of the questions being asked and those that should be asked. Once the concepts are developed, ecological quantitative risk assessment should develop rapidly. The development of ecological quantitative risk assessment is still in its early stages, and many gaps and potential gaps for data and information are being found and some are discussed in the next chapters.

An important question that will be discussed is whether or not the current state of science is good enough. A pragmatic response to this question is to ask what is the alternative. The alternative is to use judgment to fill in the gaps, and I favor scientists supplying this need. It may be semiquantitative guessing, but it is better than nothing. This approach will naturally involve scientists in risk management which I think is essential. You just cannot hand the decision makers an endpoint and some probability and walk away.

Often we don't even use one tenth of the existing data. This is due to the poor quality of much of the data that had been collected. Much of the existing data are anecdotal, of unknown quality, and collected by a variety of methods, all making comparisons difficult if not impossible. Little attention has been focused on planning monitoring exercises to be statistically meaningful and in only a few cases has there been any attention to determining the quality of the data.

Human health models are based on predicting the effect on an individual life, while the individual is expendable in ecological matters. The mechanism of natural selection achieves quality control in nature. The outliers in a gene pool form a distribution, and perhaps as much as 10% can be outliers and are eliminated. If 10% of a group of humans were to be lost, the media would be headlining it the next day.

Although some pollution effects such as species extinction are irreversible, most are reversible. A good example is the kepone pollution of the James River. Over 60,000 pounds of this chemical that has almost no half-life and

0-87371-605-1/93/$0.00 + $.50
© 1993 by Lewis Publishers

is highly toxic affected various kinds of biota in the river. Today the river is open again and the striped bass populations are larger than ever. The oysters, blue crabs, and all the previous populations are back.

The presence of a pollutant is not automatically an indication of a problem. The point here is that you may not have a risk just because some pollutant is present. There has to be a mechanism of uptake and exposure or it isn't a hazard.

Sustainability is an essential prerequisite for a healthy environment. The time required for maintaining human health and achieving sustainable agriculture can be decades and centuries. Public health and ecological phenomena are not competing with each other for importance. It is not possible to achieve a high level of public health without maintaining a certain level of quality of the environment.

The following chapters address some of the essential aspects in the development of a methodology and estimates of quantitative risk due to ecological phenomena.

Application of Ecological Knowledge to Environmental Problems: Ecological Risk Assessment

David Policansky

INTRODUCTION

Although "ecological risk assessment" is a new term — even "risk assessment" has been in use for only about 20 years — people have been doing things that are similar to ecological risk assessment for a much longer time. The general idea is to apply a logical system to identifying the hazard and risk to (ecological) systems from various human activities. In this chapter, I discuss a recent National Research Council (NRC) report as an example of a discussion of ecological risk assessment and comment on some differences and similarities between ecological risk assessment and health risk assessment.

BACKGROUND

In 1986, the NRC published a report called *Ecological Knowledge and Environmental Problem-Solving: Concepts and Case Studies* (NRC, 1986). When that report was prepared, interest in ecological risk assessment was not as widespread as it is today, both in and out of federal government agencies. The Environmental Protection Agency (EPA) is 21 years old this year, and it was not the first federal agency to be involved in environmental protection. But today the growing interest in risk assessment — whether it is called that or not — has many manifestations. EPA's Science Advisory Board has published a major set of reports on reducing (environmental) risk (EPA Science Advisory Board, 1988a, b; 1990a, b, c, d) and EPA is planning to spend tens (perhaps hundreds) of millions of dollars a year on its Environmental Monitoring and Assessment Program (EMAP). Other federal agencies are also following the trend. The National Park Service is re-evaluating its science programs; the Department of the Interior's Minerals Management Service is spending tens of millions of dollars a year on environmental studies designed to provide information to predict and manage the effects of oil and gas activities on the U.S. outer continental shelf. The Fish and Wildlife Service, the National Oceanographic and Atmospheric Administration, the Department of Energy, the Bureau of Land Management, the Department of Defense, and the Department of Agriculture are also spending large amounts on environmental protection and environmental research. And Congress is considering the establishment of national institutes for environmental research and for environmental statistics.

Some of the increasing interest in environmental issues among federal, state, and private agencies, Congress, and the public stems from perceptions that there are increasing threats to the environment. Among these threats are "greenhouse warming" (Chapter 4), ozone depletion and other changes in the stratosphere, pollution of air and water, loss of wetlands, and so on. But people have worried about environmental degradation for many years. When I was a child in South Africa in the 1950s, soil erosion was a major concern; coal smoke in industrialized areas was a major concern when my father was a child; and in 1376, a petition was presented to the English Parliament by persons concerned that fishing with a "wondyrchoum" (a type of trawl) would devastate fish populations "to the great damage of the whole commons of the kingdom" (March, 1970).

What, then, is new? It appears that the current emphases on natural ecosystems and ecological risk assessment are new (although some far-sighted individuals had expressed these concerns many years previously). In 1376, people were worried that their supply of fish would be destroyed; in the 1930s, people worried about the conservation of wildlife; in recent decades, in addition to such concerns, people have begun to worry about "ecosystem health", "environmental integrity", and related concepts. The idea of risk assessment is also relatively new, and its application to ecosystems seems to be newer — less than 10 years old, to my knowledge.

TERMINOLOGY

Most of the terms pertaining to risk assessment and risk analysis are widely used, but they are not always used in the same way, and sometimes they are poorly defined.

Risk — "Risk" is defined by Merriam-Webster's Ninth New Collegiate Dictionary (1988) as the possibility or probability of injury or loss. Usually in risk assessment, and always in this chapter, "risk" refers to the *probability* of an adverse outcome or event.

Hazard — Dictionary definitions of "hazard" are almost interchangeable with their definitions of "risk". There is the element of chance in all their definitions. But that is not how it is usually used in risk assessment. Thus, Corhsson and Covello (1989) wrote "In the growing body of risk-assessment literature, the term *hazard* typically refers to the source of a risk. The likelihood of harm from exposure distinguishes risk from hazard. Risk is created by a hazard. For example, a toxic chemical that is a hazard to human health does not constitute a risk unless humans are exposed to it." As another example, being killed by a train is a potential hazard, but is not a risk if you stay away from railway lines. In its much-discussed report on risk assessment, the NRC (1983) wrote: "[Hazard identification] is defined here as the process of determining whether exposure to an agent can cause an increase in the incidence of a health condition (cancer, birth defect, etc.). It involves characterizing the nature and strength of the evidence of causation." In other words, it is an attempt to answer the question "Is there an adverse outcome from exposure to this agent?"

The way "hazard" is used in risk assessment is logical, but it is not quite constant or consistent with the normal English meaning of the word. Therefore, I avoid the term and use "adverse outcome" or "outcome" instead.

Risk assessment — For some (e.g., NRC, 1982), this is the formal process of estimating the likelihood of adverse outcome from a particular exposure. For others, it is the entire process of estimating the risk and evaluating the costs and benefits of various management options. In its more recent report, the NRC (1983), defined (health) risk assessment to include hazard identification, dose-response assessment, exposure assessment, and risk characterization. For ecological risk assessment, I restrict its use here to the identification of potential adverse outcomes due to various exposures and the estimation of the likelihood of their occurrence.

Risk analysis — This term is sometimes used to mean risk assessment plus policy analysis based on that risk assessment (e.g., Corhsson and Covello, 1989). Sometimes, however, it is synonymous with risk assessment. It is not used in this chapter.

Risk or hazard evaluation — The term, not used in this chapter, refers to putting a value judgment on a risk or adverse outcome. Its practice is of great interest, but is beyond the scope of this chapter. I mention it here because it should be clearly distinguished from risk assessment, even though one depends on the other. An example of a risk-evaluation question is asking whether or not the damage caused by a chemical spill in the Potomac River is an acceptable adverse outcome if its likelihood (risk) is 1% per year. How much money would it be worth to reduce the risk to 0.1% per year? The policy makers who do this kind of evaluation need a scientifically sound risk assessment on which to base their judgments.

THE 1986 REPORT OF THE NRC

The NRC Committee on the Applications of Ecological Theory to Environmental Problems (Gordon Orians was the chair and I was the project director) had an evolving view of its task, as indicated by the difference

between its name and that of its report (*Ecological Knowledge and Environmental Problem-Solving: Concepts and Case Studies*). The committee was
motivated by the recognition that environmental problems often are *ecological*
problems and require ecological knowledge to solve them. The committee
members also recognized that much academic ecological research, although
potentially valuable, was not being applied to environmental problem solving
and they wanted to examine the degree to which it could be applied. Finally,
the committee was strongly influenced by a Canadian publication, *An Ecological Framework for Environmental Impact Assessment in Canada* (Beanlands and Duinker, 1983). Thus, it proceeded to address the question "To
what degree can basic ecology be applied to useful environmental problem-
solving?" It illustrated its analysis of that question with 13 case studies.

The committee addressed various levels of ecological organization, from
populations to ecosystems. For each level, it considered how current knowledge could be usefully applied to the solving of environmental problems. The
committee then considered a variety of procedures and kinds of knowledge
that are common to most environmental problems. Its recommendations were
quite practical and were made concrete by the 13 case studies, which dealt
with such diverse topics as management of Pacific halibut, biological control
of California red scale, restoring derelict lands in Britain, and control of
eutrophication in Lake Washington. Rather than discuss the chapters dealing
with various levels of ecological organization here, I focus on five chapters
that seem relevant to this symposium: Chapter 6, Analog, Generic, and Pilot
Studies and Treatment of a Project as an Experiment; Chapter 7, Indicator
Species and Biological Monitoring; and Chapter 8, Dealing with Uncertainty.
Chapter 9, The Special Problem of Cumulative Effects, and especially Chapter
10, A Scientific Framework for Environmental Problem-Solving, come close
to outlining a risk-assessment approach, although the term was never explicitly
used in the report.

Analog, Generic, and Pilot Studies and Treatment of a Project as an Experiment

Analog studies — Analog studies deal with things that are similar to the
problem at hand. Thus, one might use a study of a power plant in Maryland
to improve understanding of the effects of a power plant in Virginia. Implicit
in any discussion of the value of analog studies is the notion that projects be
designed so that they might become analog studies for other projects or
situations. In other words, the project should be set up so that useful data
can be collected.

Generic studies — A generic study is one designed to increase knowledge
of the physical, chemical, and biological phenomena common to a group of
environmental problems. An example might be a study of the effects of oil

pollution on intertidal plants or on beach animals. The committee pointed out that the distinction between analog and generic studies was not always clear. It also had a major caveat about analog and generic studies: "a major question concerning [their] usefulness is the extent to which their results can be applied to a particular site and problem". Practically, the committee noted, generic studies are usually known to scientists, while analog studies are often buried in "gray literature".

Pilot studies — Pilot studies are small-scale models of a projected or predicted perturbation. They often provide useful ecological information. Their major limitation is the degree to which a small-scale study can replicate effects of a large-scale project. For example, a well-known case of such a limitation is the inability of a small-scale simulation to replicate the calculated effects of a large-scale nuclear war on atmospheric cooling. Similarly, the effects of overpopulation, destruction of biodiversity on a global scale, large-scale hydroelectric projects, use of internal combustion engines, and many others are difficult or impossible to simulate on a small scale. In addition, it is sometimes difficult or impossible to get permission to do the study legally, because it may involve a prohibited activity or be unacceptable to the public, such as deliberate small oil spills or deliberate contamination of a river. Some, such as the limited introduction of an exotic species, might be too unpredictable to perform. But it is usually possible to simulate some of the individual effects and learn something — if not enough — of the potential effects of a large perturbation.

Treating projects as experiments — Many projects go forward even without a complete understanding of their effects. Because complete information is never available and decisions on actions cannot wait indefinitely, proceeding with only partial information makes some social and economic sense. However, it does not make sense to undertake large projects without learning from them. Many engineering and construction projects and other large-scale activities amount to experiments that no research agency could afford to fund. Examples include the construction of large dams, the cutting of the Suez and Panama canals, the building of large highways, various aspects of forest and fishery management, dredging projects, beach renourishment, and even pollution controls. Most such projects require some form of environmental impact statement (EIS), and most EISs explicitly or implicitly contain scientific hypotheses or predictions. In many cases, an EIS could be slightly modified to include a research proposal that could be completed at a small marginal cost. Treating projects as experiments — *incorporating into them a way to learn from them* — is one readily available tool for ecological risk assessment that will certainly work in the medium term and one that should be adopted much more often and more thoughtfully.

Indicator Species and Biological Monitoring

This chapter anticipated perhaps the largest current ecological risk assessment — EPA's Environmental Monitoring and Assessment Program (EMAP). The report discussed the choice of organisms to use for monitoring, the different types of monitoring, and the relationship between monitoring and the treatment of projects as experiments. It is important to be able to identify the monitored organisms; this is sometimes a nontrivial taxonomic problem. The committee concluded that monitoring is most useful when "the functional relationships between perturbation and response are understood", although it could have value even when causal relationships are obscure (i.e., statistical associations can be useful, even if no causal relationship is known).

Indicators, of course, need not be whole organisms; they can range from molecules to landscapes. A great deal of attention is being focused on indicators by EPA. It has sponsored workshops and has received advice from the NRC on indicators or biological markers of pollution damage in forests (NRC, 1989a) and human health (e.g., NRC, 1989b). A major component of EMAP addresses indicators of ecosystem condition, exposure (to human perturbations), and response (EPA, 1991). The usefulness of indicators depends on their appropriateness to the question being asked and to the adverse outcomes that might occur. In choosing indicators it is necessary to take into account the biological, temporal, and spatial scales being considered and the relevance of the indicators to various processes. Finding useful indicators is a challenging task (NRC, 1986; 1989a).

Dealing with Uncertainty

The sources of uncertainty include the complexity of natural systems, natural variability in space and time, random variation, errors of measurement, and lack of information. The uncertainties discussed by Coppock in assessing climate change (Chapter 4) are due to all the items listed above. The chapter in the 1986 report dealt with the difficulties of managing in the face of uncertainty, including the difficulty of establishing a baseline or reference point and predicting the outcome of management actions. The report recommended that managers be conservative (e.g., fishery biologists should build in a margin for error in estimates of fishing pressure or fish populations, as discussed by Beddington [1984]), that they use adaptive environmental management (i.e., frequently test the effects of their management and be ready to modify it accordingly, e.g., Holling, 1978; Hilborn et al., 1980), that they use models, and that their models include error and sensitivity analyses.

Ecologists must not retreat behind the shield of uncertainty ("I can't tell you what to do; I don't know enough".) when asked for their advice. Someone is going to make a decision with or without their advice, and if ecologists' advice on ecological problems is not at least somewhat useful, then it is difficult to justify public support of their activities.

Cumulative Effects

Ecological risk assessment is usually based on single occurrences or sources of environmental effects, but often an ecological system is subject to multiple occurrences or sources of effects. Cumulative effects are increasingly part of environmental assessment. Yet they remain difficult to deal with (Beanlands et al., 1986). The NRC report identified different types of cumulative effects (adding perturbations; incremental reduction or destruction of habitats or resources, called "nibbing"; different things acting together; and so on). In general, the most troublesome cases arise from a mismatch between the scales or jurisdiction of assessment and management and the scales or jurisdictions of the phenomena involved or their effects. Thus, air-pollution and fisheries-management problems are caused by sources acting locally, although they can be extremely numerous (e.g., point sources of air pollution, individual nets or boats causing fishing mortality). The impacts (polluted air, reduced fish populations), however, are often spread over wide areas, often distant from the sources and covering multiple jurisdictions. These institutional and jurisdictional issues are extremely difficult to deal with, although the occasional success story (e.g., the establishment of the International Pacific Halibut Commission to address multi-jurisdictional and cumulative effects of fishing [Policansky, 1986]) proves that it is sometimes possible and worth the effort.

One recommendation in particular seems relevant to the present discussion. The committee recommended that agreements between decision makers, managers, and scientists about the appropriate time and space boundaries for dealing with cumulative effects be documented. This would "force clear thinking about important issues and provide a record so that process could be improved".

A Scientific Framework for Environmental Problem Solving

In this chapter, the committee set forth a scheme that has all the elements of an ecological risk assessment. The six main points of the scheme, which was based in part on a somewhat similar proposal by Beanlands and Duinker (1983), are the following:

- Define environmental goals and scientific questions.
- Scope the problem.
  Identify valued ecosystem components.
  Identify potential problems and difficulties.
  Make models if necessary.
- Establish study boundaries.
- Develop and test hypotheses.
- Specify predictions and determine the expected significance of effects.
- Monitor.

This scheme outlines a logical, comprehensive, and general approach to environmental problem solving and is applicable to a particular kind of environmental problem solving, namely, ecological risk assessment.

RELEVANCE OF THE 1986 STUDY TO ECOLOGICAL RISK ASSESSMENT

The study outlined principles for environmental problem solving, identified many practical problems and practical approaches to solutions, and — we hope — had a role in convincing academic ecologists of the need to apply their knowledge to real-world problems and that such is a respectable and intellectually challenging activity. We also hope that it informed environmental managers and policy makers. The report set forth an approach that seems sound and consistent with what people now call ecological risk assessment. Finally, it provided a set of good, illustrative case studies.

The study did not attempt to be exhaustive. The coverage of ecosystem ecology — especially in the case studies — was much less than the coverage of the ecology of one or two species at a time. The study also focused mainly on case studies from North America (with one each from Britain, Latin America, and West Africa), largely because it was easier to commission reports on North American cases given the constraints of time and resources available.

Ecosystem Health and Human Health

Ecological risk assessment has adopted some ideas and procedures from human health risk assessment. In particular, it has adopted the idea of a formal procedure for identifying and estimating the risk of damage to something of value. Although human health risk assessment usually focuses on a specific disease, usually cancer, the "something of value" is, of course, human health. It is much less clear what the ecological "something of value" is. In basing ecological risk assessment on human health risk assessment, there is a natural temptation to extend the analogy to include the idea of "ecosystem health". Although the concept of ecosystem health appears to have increased people's awareness of environmental deterioration and motivated them to make efforts to ameliorate it, the concept may actually hinder the careful scientific analysis that is needed for successful ecological risk assessment. The reason is that any definition of "ecosystem health" is an implicit value judgment. The challenge, therefore, is to arrive at an operational definition of the "something of value" that explicitly separates the value judgments from the scientific assessments. The issue is controversial, and merits a discussion at some length.

The 1986 study did discuss value judgments, but it did not deal much with the difficulty of separating value judgments from scientific ones in assessing ecosystem health. Indeed, the problem of defining ecosystem health has not been solved, despite recent attempts (e.g., Kutchenberg, 1985; Rapport, 1989; Schaeffer et al., 1988). There is, naturally, a temptation to base a concept of ecosystem health on human health, but this approach is full of difficulties. One reason for the difficulty is that an individual human is a single organism, more analogous to a spruce tree or a red fox than to an ecosystem. Epidemiology, of course, deals with human populations, but endpoints are defined in terms of an individual's health. Although defining human health is not a trivial challenge, and although human-health workers sometimes find difficulties with it, it is a useful concept and it has at least some objective reality. We all know when we feel sick and the relationships between sickness and various physiological conditions are well established. Similarly, the health of a spruce tree or a red fox has some objective reality and an arborist or a veterinarian can usually say whether a tree or a fox is healthy or not.

But although it might appear easy to identify a ravaged or unhealthy ecosystem, ecosystem health is difficult to separate from the aggregate health of the individuals in it. This is true even if the death of an individual or species in an ecosystem results from something that is likely to harm many individuals or species. Does a forest whose spruce trees are dying represent an ecosystem in trouble or an ecosystem with one species in trouble? Or is it somewhere in between: an ecosystem with one large species and several associated smaller species in trouble? If all the spruce trees died, would the ecosystem die? Certainly, some of the organisms in it would survive; would one then have a new ecosystem? If so, what does the death of an ecosystem mean? What is the normative ("healthy") condition of an ecosystem? (As a real example, do eastern deciduous forests represent a new ecosystem since the chestnut trees died? If not, is the ecosystem less healthy than it was?) Does all human-induced change in an ecosystem represent a loss of "health"? Does the presence of one or more introduced (exotic) species represent a loss of "health"? Is "loss of health" the same as an "adverse outcome"? Who decides? As Levin (1988) said, "some agreed-upon surrogate for ecosystem health is essential in transforming a socioeconomic battle into a quasi-scientific debate".

Yet another difficulty is defining the reference point against which the "loss of health" or change is to be measured. As individual species evolve and as climate and other aspects of the environment change, ecosystems also change. Should one compare the ecosystem to its state last year, in 1900, when European settlers arrived, when aboriginal settlers crossed the land-bridge from Asia, or in the period immediately preceding the mass extinctions during the late Cretaceous? What should be measured? Several approaches have been suggested, each related to a specific purpose, but to date, no single approach has been completely satisfactory. Even for specific purposes, the concept of ecosystem health often is more confusing than enlightening.

The difficulties carry over into restoration ecology. The 1986 report has a case study on restoring "derelict" land in Britain (Wathern, 1986). The example seems uncontroversial; derelict lands have depauperate vegetation; sometimes they are completely barren. But what should the land be restored to? If you cannot restore the entire ecosystem to some earlier state, either because of ignorance of that state or because it would be too difficult and expensive, then what part of the ecosystem should be restored? Should a particular function be chosen, or an overall visual appearance? Or is one species perhaps critical? Whose values should be taken into account in setting the goal? The case study addresses some of the options. In the case discussed, one of the goals was "to produce vegetation that would be self-regenerating once established, so that costly maintenance would not need to be continued for long periods". A species-rich system was also desired. Indeed, the goals were more sophisticated than merely producing "something pretty and green". Jared Diamond, both an ecologist and a physiologist who has worked in a school of medicine, has thoughtfully analyzed the difficulties of setting goals for restoration (Diamond, 1987). In particular, he pointed out that the goals involve implicit value judgments and that different segments of the population often hold different values. A recent NRC committee has reported on the restoration of aquatic ecosystems and its report (NRC, 1992) provides specific examples of restoration goals in its interesting case studies.

If one recognizes the inextricable intertwining of value judgments with science in defining ecosystem health, does that mean that ecological risk assessment is useless? Of course it does not. The appropriate approach is to develop descriptors and indicators of ecosystem structure and function and to develop operational definitions of ecosystem health in terms of explicit value judgments about desirable features of ecosystems. There are many ecological indicators that can alert one to undesirable changes in some ecosystems: they include the appearance of blue-green algae in lakes, warning of eutrophication (e.g., Lehman, 1986); the loss of species diversity or a change in the species composition of streams, warning perhaps of chemical pollution or thermal changes (e.g., Karr, 1991). Indeed, the recent research manifesto of the Ecological Society of America (Lubchenco et al., 1991) provides an eminently thoughtful, careful, and *useful* ecological research agenda designed to understand and ameliorate "the rapidly deteriorating state of the environment and to enhance its capacity to sustain the needs of the world's population" without mentioning "ecosystem health" or even introducing such a concept. Instead, the authors talk of "indicators of ecological responses to stress", which include functional measurements of ecological processes and structural properties of ecosystems. And they make their value judgments explicit and clear: they favor sustainability and biotic diversity. This, I believe, is a much more productive approach to ecological risk assessment. It avoids the temptation to make too close an analogy with human-health risk assessment and encourages a more rational, explicit discussion of adverse outcomes.

CONCLUSIONS: WHERE DO WE GO FROM HERE?

We are witnessing an encouraging and increasing focus on ecological problem solving. Many federal agencies, the Congress, states, and the public in this country are paying more and more attention to ecological issues, and similar trends are apparent in other parts of the world. It appears that the new discipline of ecological risk assessment is developing on a sound footing, with a great deal of scientific participation and agency support.

The Welcome New Focus on Ecosystems

The new focus on ecosystems in ecological risk assessment is a welcome development. A species-by-species approach, although necessary, is insufficient by itself in light of the seriousness of human impacts on the world environment. Although their functioning is not completely understood, ecosystems clearly are more than random aggregations of species. But ecological risk assessment will not be easy, and therefore, a sound, thoughtful, scientific approach is needed. The NRC's 1986 report provided guidance for the development of such an approach; a somewhat different, but certainly compatible approach is being developed by another NRC committee on ecological risk assessment (the Committee on Risk Assessment Methodology). The point is that the details are probably less important than the approach, which must be logical and comprehensive.

The Focus on Individual Species Must Also Be Retained

Welcome and essential as a focus on ecosystems is, it is not always required for ecological risk assessment. There are cases — several of them discussed in the 1986 report — where the risk assessment (although it was not called that) focused on one or two species and resulted in the development of a successful management strategy. It is essential to the scoping process to determine what level of ecological organization to focus on. If the problem is really an ecosystem one, focusing on an individual species might not reveal the true nature of the problem until it is too late. But focusing on an ecosystem when only one or two species (or populations) are at risk can dissipate resources and also lead to a failure of management.

Human Health Is Not an Exact Analog with Ecosystem Health

Applying the concept of health to ecosystems has been useful in some ways. Looking at the nonhuman world in terms of its "health" has allowed many people to develop a less anthropocentric outlook and made them more willing to give up goods to obtain or maintain a "healthy environment". But there is danger in carrying the analogy too far; scientists and policy makers need to distinguish clearly between value judgments and scientific assessments. For this reason, scientifically based ecological risk assessment should not be distracted by questions of ecosystem health, but should instead focus on understanding ecosystem structure and function, predicting the way that human impacts can change them, and developing indicators. It is important to note that performing a health risk assessment for an organism is not the same as performing an ecological risk assessment. Thus, it might be desirable to assess the risk of a chemical pollutant to the health of rainbow trout in a stream, and such an assessment might even be an essential part of an ecological risk assessment, but it should not be a *substitute* for an ecological risk assessment.

Treat Projects as Experiments

In discussing the value of restoration ecology, Diamond (1987) writes "There is no doubt that the controlled experiment with preselected perturbations and randomized experimental design is the most powerful tool of ecology, just as it is the most powerful tool of the other sciences. In ecology, however, most of the perturbations that would yield far-reaching insights are either immoral, illegal, or impractical. . . . Think, for example, how much faster community ecology would progress if you graduate students here today weren't restricted to the minuscule field experiments that are now in far, but if each of you were permitted to select and burn some part of the city of Madison twice a year; or if you could reintroduce wolves into an area of your choice, exterminate the local population of a select species, or dredge and flood a Wisconsin farm and convert it into a marsh. In fact, there is only one way that you get to carry out big manipulations of this sort, and that's by getting involved in restoration projects and taking advantage of the opportunities they offer."

As usual, Diamond raises an excellent point (although I hope he is not allowed to turn his graduate students loose on southern Wisconsin). But there is another way to carry out such big manipulations, and that is to take advantage of engineering and construction projects and accidents. Building highways, airports, shopping centers, and dams destroys many organisms and their habitats. Large spills, fires, and explosions are also much larger perturbations than most ecologists can perform experimentally. Agriculture, forestry, and fishing also can and should be viewed as experiments. These and other activities will continue whether or not they are set up to provide ecological information. For planned activities, despite the difficulties involved, ecologists should take advantage of the perturbation wherever possible to learn from the experience.

ACKNOWLEDGMENTS

Many people have contributed to the ideas in this chapter through their writings and discussions, including some who have disagreed with me. In particular, I thank L. Barnthouse, W. Cooper, J. Hobbie, J. Lubchenco, G. Orians, and J. Reisa. I am also grateful to G. Orians and an anonymous reviewer for their critical reviews of the manuscript.

REFERENCES

Beanlands, G. E. and P. N. Duinker. 1983. An Ecological Framework for Environmental Impact Assessment in Canada. Institute for Resource and Environmental Studies, Dalhousie University, Halifax, Nova Scotia, and Federal Environmental Assessment Review Office, Ottawa, Ontario.

Beanlands, G. E., W. J., Erckmann, G. H. Orians, J. O'Riordan, D. Policansky, M. H. Sadar, and B. Sadler. 1986. Cumulative Environmental Effects: a Binational Perspective. Canadian Environmental Assessment Research Council, Ottawa, Ontario, and National Research Council, Washington, D.C.

Beddington, J. R., Rapporteur. 1984. Management under uncertainty. Group report. Pp. 227–244 in R. M. May, Ed., *Exploitation of Marine Communities*. Dahlem Konferenzen. Springer-Verlag, Berlin.

Corhsson, J. J. and V. T. Covello. 1989. Risk Analysis: a Guide to Principles and Methods for Analyzing Health and Environmental Risks. U.S. Council on Environmental Quality, Executive Office of the President, Washington, D.C.

Diamond, J. 1987. Goals: Theory and practice in restoration ecology. Pp. 329–336 in W. R. Jordan, M. E. Gilpin, and J. D. Aber, Eds. *Restoration Ecology: a Synthetic Approach to Ecological Research*. Cambridge University Press, New York.

EPA Science Advisory Board. 1988a. Future Risk: Research Strategies of the 1990s. SAB-EC-88-040. Science Advisory Board, U.S. Environmental Protection Agency, Washington, D.C.

EPA Science Advisory Board. 1988b. Future Risk: Research Strategies of the 1990s. Appendix C. Strategies for Ecological Effects Research. SAB-EC-88–040C. Science Advisory Board, U.S. Environmental Protection Agency, Washington, D.C.

EPA Science Advisory Board. 1990a. Reducing Risk: Setting Priorities and Strategies for Environmental Protection. Report of the Science Advisory Board's Relative Risk Reduction Strategies Committee. EPA SAB-EC-90-021. U.S. Environmental Protection Agency, Washington, D.C.

EPA Science Advisory Board. 1990b. Reducing Risk. Appendix A. Report of the Ecology and Welfare Subcommittee. EPA SAB-EC-90-021A. U.S. Environmental Protection Agency, Washington, D.C.

EPA Science Advisory Board. 1990c. Reducing Risk. Appendix B. Report of the Human Health Subcommittee. EPA SAB-EC-90-021B. U.S. Environmental Protection Agency, Washington, D.C.

EPA Science Advisory Board. 1990a. Reducing Risk. Appendix C. Report of the Strategic Options Subcommittee. EPA SAB-EC-90-021. U.S. Environmental Protection Agency, Washington, D.C.

EPA. 1991. An overview of the Environmental Monitoring and Assessment Program. EMAP Monitor, January 1991. EPA-600/M-90/022. U.S. Environmental Protection Agency, Office of Research and Development, Washington, D.C.

Hilborn, R., C. S. Holling, and C. J. Walters. 1980. Managing the unknown: approaches to ecological policy design. Pp. 103–113 in *Biological Evaluation of Environmental Impacts*. FWS/OBS-80/26. President's Council on Environmental Quality and Fish and Wildlife Service, U.S. Department of the Interior, Washington, D.C.

Holling, C. S., Ed. 1978. *Adaptive Environmental Assessment and Management*. Int. Ser. on Applied Systems Analysis 3, International Institute for Applied Systems Analysis. John Wiley & Sons, Toronto.

Karr, J. R. 1991. Biological integrity: a long-neglected aspect of water resource management. *Ecol. Appl.,* 1:66–84.

Kutchenberg, T. C. 1985. Measuring the health of the ecosystem. *Environment,* 27:32–37.

Lehman, J. T. 1986. Control of eutrophication in Lake Washington. Pp. 301–315 (including comments by the NRC committee) in NRC, 1986. *Ecological Knowledge and Environmental Problem-Solving: Concepts and Case Studies*. National Academy Press, Washington, D.C.

Levin, S. A. 1988. Sea Otters and Nearshore Benthic Communities: a Theoretical Perspective. Pp. 202–209 in G. R. VanBlaricom and J. A. Estes, Eds. *The Community Ecology of Sea Otters*. Ecology Study Series 65. Springer-Verlag, Berlin.

Lubchenco, J.,A. M. Olson, L. B. Brubaker, S. R. Carpenter, M. M. Holland, S. P. Hubbell, S. A. Levin, J. A. MacMahon, P. A. Matson, J. M. Melillo, H. A. Mooney, C. H. Peterson, H. Ronald Pulliam, L. A., Real, P. J., Regal, and P. G. Risser. 1991. The sustainable biosphere initiative: an ecological research agenda. *Ecology,* 72:371–412.

March, E. M. 1970. *Sailing Trawlers* (new edition). David & Charles, Newton Abbot, Devon, U.K.

National Research Council (NRC). 1982. *Risk and Decision Making: Perspectives in Research*. National Academy Press, Washington, D.C.

National Research Council (NRC). 1983. *Risk Assessment in the Federal Government: Managing the Process*. National Academy Press, Washington, D.C.

National Research Council (NRC). 1986. *Ecological Knowledge and Environmental Problem-Solving: Concepts and Case Studies*. National Academy Press, Washington, D.C.

National Research Council (NRC). 1989a. *Biologic Markers of Air-Pollutant Stress and Damage in Forests*. National Academy Press, Washington, D.C.

National Research Council (NRC). 1989b. *Biologic Markers in Reproductive Toxicology*. National Academy Press, Washington, D.C.

National Research Council (NRC). 1992. *Restoration of Aquatic Ecosystems: Science, Technology, and Public Policy*. National Academy Press, Washington, D.C.

Policansky, D. 1986. North Pacific halibut fishery management. Pp. 137–150 (including comments by the NCR committee) in National Research Council (NRC). 1986. *Ecological Knowledge and Environmental Problem-Solving: Concepts and Case Studies*. National Academy Press, Washington, D.C.

Rapport, D. J. 1989. What constitutes ecosystem health? *Perspect. Biol. Med.*, 33:120–132.

Schaeffer, D. J., E. E. Herricks, and H. W. Kerster. 1988. Ecosystem health. 1. Measuring ecosystem health. *Environ. Manag.*, 12:445–455.

Wathern, P. 1986. Restoring derelict lands in Great Britain. Pp. 248–274 (including comments by the NRC committee) in NRC, 1986. *Ecological Knowledge and Environmental Problem-Solving: Concepts and Case Studies*. National Academy Press, Washington, D.C.

CHAPTER 4

The Threat of Greenhouse Warming

Rob Coppock*

Greenhouse warming has been called the most important environmental issue of the next several decades. The threat is extremely difficult to evaluate, however, for several reasons. It involves global phenomena. We do not have much experience analyzing such problems. The principal impacts may not emerge for 40 years or more. We have a very hard time planning over such time horizons. But perhaps most important, the planetary system is extremely complex. We have only a partial understanding of key components. The climate system has complex feedback mechanisms, which may play out in ways that reduce or enhance global warming. We cannot be sure. Human systems like agriculture and natural systems of plants and animals both react and adjust to changes in weather patterns. Such adjustments need to be allowed for in the analysis.

These and other factors make the assessment of greenhouse warming exceedingly difficult. Nevertheless, it is currently high on the national and international agendas. The National Academy of Sciences, National Academy of Engineering, and Institute of Medicine recently released a report on the subject called "Policy Implications of Greenhouse Warming". The report, prepared by a blue-ribbon panel under the chairmanship of former U.S. Senator Daniel J. Evans, took a careful and thorough look at the problem and what can be done. It concluded that the threat of greenhouse warming warrants action now. Most important, however, the report showed that U.S. emissions of greenhouse gases could be substantially reduced at relatively low cost.

Congress requested the study and asked for a comprehensive assessment, a task requiring an extraordinary breadth of knowledge. The study was conducted by four panels involving nearly 50 experts. They were asked to examine the full range of the ways to mitigate greenhouse warming, and to catalog the possible impacts and adaptive measures. This broad scope meant two things. First, the panels had to examine some areas where available knowledge is much more limited than for most Academy studies. Second, it required the

---

* The opinions expressed in this paper are those of the author, and do not necessarily reflect the position of the National Academy of Sciences, the National Academy of Engineering, the Institute of Medicine, or any parts of those organizations.

panels to develop an approach that placed this wide range of topics in perspective.

Daniel J. Evans, as a former U.S. Senator and Governor of the State of Washington, knows what it means to make difficult policy choices on the basis of uncertain evidence. As a registered civil engineer and former president of The Evergreen State College, he recognizes that empirical data are needed to temper judgment. But the other members of the Synthesis Panel, who authored the report containing the principal findings and recommendations, were equally qualified for the task. Three-quarters of them have held high appointed office in either federal or state government. At the same time, half of them are members of either the National Academy of Sciences or the National Academy of Engineering. This was a unique group of individuals competent to reach judgments about both the science and the policy choices involved.

The four panels worked in parallel, but with considerable exchange of information and some overlap in membership. The Effects Panel examined what is known about changing climatic conditions and related effects. The Mitigation Panel looked at options for reducing or reversing the onset of potential global warming. The Adaptation Panel assessed the impacts of possible climate change on human and ecologic systems and policies that could help them adapt to those changes. The Synthesis Panel, as mentioned earlier, developed overall findings and recommendations. They did so on the basis of the analyses of the other panels, of other scientific and technical reports, and of testimony from invited experts.

This study attempted a comprehensive, balanced assessment of the overall problem confronting the nation. No other study in this country, and several have appeared during 1991, has produced a similar analysis. Only the report of the Intergovernmental Panel on Climate Change (IPCC) had similar scope. The Academy study, however, included a more quantitative assessment of policy options than did the IPCC report.

ASSESSING RESPONSES TO GREENHOUSE WARMING

Several interrelated topics must be examined in assessing how to respond to the threat of greenhouse warming. First, it is necessary to examine the basic phenomena which affect the climatic system. Second, the events or conditions producing stress on the system need to be considered. These two components combine in the projection of climatic effects, which are the third element. Fourth, the consequences of these changes in climatic conditions and events for human and natural systems need to be assessed. These are the impacts of greenhouse warming. Finally, the costs of either reducing the rate of change of warming (mitigation actions) or assisting human and natural systems to adjust (adaptation actions) must be compared to the damages that would accrue if greenhouse warming were allowed to run its course without intervention. Each of these topics involves estimation and speculation, which must be reflected in the final judgments.

The Evans study presented a first-cut at this assessment. It assessed the scientific base, and concluded that the threat of greenhouse warming justifies action now. The study examined impacts on the U.S., and concluded that although the population should be able to adjust to the expected changes, the effort could involve considerable cost. Moreover, it concluded that natural ecosystems will be altered, although the ecosystem services currently associated with a given tract of land may be provided by different species in the future. Poor countries, or those with fewer climatic zones, would have more difficulty adjusting. The study produced a thorough cost-effectiveness assessment of mitigation options, and concluded that substantial reduction in emissions could be accomplished at relatively low cost.

The Evans study concluded that there are cost-effective mitigation actions that should be undertaken now, and produced a ranking of preferred options. It also recommended adopting some adaptation policies. It did not, however, conclude how much should be spent on the greenhouse warming problem at this time. That judgment requires comparing the cost effectiveness of actions in the area of greenhouse warming with the cost effectiveness of actions addressing other societal concerns.

The rest of this paper describes briefly the analysis presented in the Evans study.

THE GREENHOUSE EFFECT AND GREENHOUSE WARMING

There is consensus in the relevant scientific community that greenhouse gases trap energy. This is not necessarily bad. Without the naturally occurring greenhouse gases, mostly water vapor, carbon dioxide, and methane, the planet would be about 33°C colder than it is.

There also is consensus among scientists that atmospheric concentrations of greenhouse gases are increasing. This may be bad. It raises the possibility that increasing concentrations of greenhouse gases could increase temperatures to levels that would be detrimental for people and natural ecosystems.

There is widespread, but not unanimous, agreement that the global mean temperature has risen 0.3 to 0.6°C over the last 100 years. Measurements from earlier than 1900 are not very reliable, since the adjustments necessary to make them comparable to current measurements are larger than the observed differences in temperature. Most of the disagreements about the amount of observed temperature increase focus on whether or not the following kinds of problems have been adequately treated in the data.

- Adjustments for different measurement technologies (e.g., canvas buckets vs. wooden buckets vs. manifold intake for sea-surface temperature; mercury vs. electric vs. digital air temperature sensors)
- Adjustments for urban "heat islands" (i.e., observed temperatures increase as heat-generating urban areas grew up around traditional measurement sites)
- Adjustments of sea-surface measurements near coastlines (land masses warm and cool faster than bodies of water, so coastal measurements are not accurate indicators of sea-surface temperature)

There is contentious debate, however, about whether or not this global average temperature rise can be attributed to atmospheric concentrations of greenhouse gases. The principal disagreements address the following issues.

- The baseline of solar radiation (i.e., there may be a long-term trend in the incoming solar radiation; but there is theoretically no way to know, since we do not have empirical measurements of solar radiation from 100 years ago)
- The role of clouds (water vapor is a greenhouse gas, so high convective clouds function as greenhouse gases, enhancing warming, yet clouds also reflect sunlight; warmer air can hold more water, implying more clouds, but current cloud physics and chemistry is inadequate to determine whether the net change will enhance or reduce global warming)
- The role of water vapor (water vapor is *the* most important greenhouse gas, yet it is also the medium for mechanical dispersal of latent heat in the atmosphere; recent satellite observations suggest that the latter mechanism may provide an upper limit on sea-surface temperature, thereby providing a strong potential negative feedback on greenhouse warming)
- The carbon cycle (current understanding of carbon flows is unable to account for more than 40% of the CO_2 emitted into the atmosphere — the capacity of this "missing" sink is unknown, as is whether or not it will continue to absorb a constant portion of the CO_2 emitted into the atmosphere)
- The temperature lag of the oceans (the time lag for the oceans to reach temperature equilibrium is estimated at between 15 and 120 years — which results in a substantial difference between the committed, or equilibrium, temperature and the observed, or realized, temperature at any given time)

Thus, while much is known about greenhouse warming phenomena, there remain great uncertainties. Nevertheless, virtually the entire scientific community agrees that we have at least the sign of the change right for greenhouse warming. Continued release of greenhouse gases into the atmosphere will lead to a rise in global average temperature. How rapidly temperatures will change, however, we cannot say with precision.

Table 1
Key Greenhouse Gases Influenced by Human Activity

	CO_2	CH_4	CFC-11	CFC-12	N_2O
Preindustrial atmospheric concentration	280 ppmv	0.8 ppmv	0	0	288 ppbv
Current atmospheric concentration (1990)[a]	353 ppmv	1.72 ppmv	280 pptv	484 pptv	310 ppbv
Current rate of annual atmospheric accumulation[b]	1.8 ppmv (0.5%)	0.015 ppmv (0.9%)	9.5 pptv (4%)	17 pptv (4%)	0.8 ppbv (0.25%)
Atmospheric lifetime (years)[c]	(50–200)	10	65	130	150

Note: Ozone has not been included in the table because of lack of precise data. Here ppmv = parts per million by volume, ppbv = parts per billion by volume, and pptv = parts per trillion by volume.

[a] The 1990 concentrations have been estimated on the basis of an extrapolation of measurements reported for earlier years, assuming that the recent trends remained approximately constant.

[b] Net annual emissions of CO_2 from the biosphere not affected by human activity, such as volcanic emissions, are assumed to be small. Estimates of human-induced emissions from the biosphere are controversial.

[c] For each gas in the table, except CO_2, the "lifetime" is defined as the ratio of the atmospheric concentration to the total rate of removal. This time scale also characterizes the rate of adjustment of the atmospheric concentrations if the emission rates are changed abruptly. CO_2 is a special case because it is merely circulated among various reservoirs (atmosphere, ocean, biota). The "lifetime" of CO_2 given in the table is a rough indication of the time it would take for the CO_2 concentration to adjust to changes in the emissions.

From World Meterorological Organization. 1990. *Climate Change, the IPCC Scientific Assessment.* Cambridge University Press: Cambridge, United Kingdom. Table 1.1. Reprinted by permission of Cambridge University Press.

CURRENT EMISSIONS AND THEIR EFFECTS

Expressed as the equivalent of carbon dioxide — which is the common way to compare them — current concentrations of greenhouse gases are about 50% greater than before the industrial revolution. But the gases also remain effective in the atmosphere for different amounts of time. Table 1 summarizes current concentrations, emission accumulation rates, and atmospheric lifetimes of key gases.

Atmospheric concentrations of greenhouse gases are affected by most human activities. Table 2 shows estimated global greenhouse gas emissions from a variety of human activities for 1985. Emissions are shown both in totals for each gas, and as CO_2-equivalent amounts. It should be noted that not all chlorofluorocarbons (CFC) are included in the table, so that the percentage totals would probably change slightly with more complete data.

Table 3 shows CO_2 emissions per unit of economic activity for 1988/89. Note that the largest emitters in terms of total emissions are the U.S. (4804

Table 2
Estimated 1985 Global Greenhouse Gas Emissions from Human Activity

	Greenhouse gas emissions (Mt/year)	CO_2-equivalent emissions[a] (Mt/year)
CO_2 emissions		
Commercial energy	18,800	18,800 (57)
Tropical deforestation	2,600	2,600 (8)
Other	400	400 (1)
Total	21,800	21,800 (66)
CH_4 emissions		
Fuel production	60	1,300 (4)
Enteric fermentation	70	1,500 (5)
Rice cultivation	110	2,300 (7)
Landfills	30	600 (2)
Tropical deforestation	20	400 (1)
Other	30	600 (2)
Total	320	6,700 (20)[b]
CFC-11 and CFC-12 emissions		
Total	0.6	3,200 (10)
N_2O emissions		
Coal combustion	1	290 (>1)
Fertilizer use	1.5	440 (1)
Gain of cultivated land	0.4	120 (>1)
Tropical deforestation	0.5	150 (>1)
Fuel wood and industrial biomass	0.2	60 (>1)
Agricultural wastes	0.4	120 (>1)
Total	4	1,180 (4)
Total		32,880 (100)

Note: Mt/year = million (10^6) metric tons (t) per year. All entries are rounded because the exact values are controversial.

[a] CO_2-equivalent emissions are calculated from the Greenhouse Gas Emissions column by using the following multipliers:
CO_2 1
CH_4 21
CFC-11 and -12   5,400
N_2O 290
   Numbers in parentheses are percentages of total.
[b]   Total does not sum due to rounding errors.

Adapted from U.S. Department of Energy. 1990. *The Economics of Long-Term Global Climate Change: A Preliminary Assessment — Report of an Interagency Task Force.* National Technical Information Service: Springfield, VA.

million tons), the Soviet Union (3682 million tons), and China (2236 million tons). But in terms of emissions per unit of economic activity, the highest ranking countries are all less-developed or eastern-bloc nations. This indicates that there are possibilities for slowing greenhouse warming in virtually all countries.

Since greenhouse gases have different atmospheric lifetimes, it is necessary to consider their effect over time. Figure 1 presents a simplified extrapolation of current atmospheric transformation rates. The curves show emissions in

Table 3
Carbon Dioxide Emission Estimates

	1960		1970		1980		1988	
	Total	Per capita	Total	Per capita	Total	Per capita	Total	Per capita
East Germany	263.6	15.4	160.6	15.8	306.9	18.3	327.4	19.8
United States	2858.2	16.1	4273.5	20.9	4617.4	20.2	4804.1	19.4
Canada	193.2	10.6	333.3	15.4	424.6	17.6	437.8	16.9
Czechoslovakia	129.8	9.5	199.1	13.9	242.4	15.8	233.6	15.0
Australia	88.4	8.4	142.6	11.4	202.8	13.9	241.3	14.7
USSR	1452.4	6.6	2303.4	9.5	3283.5	12.5	3982.0	13.9
Poland	201.7	7.0	303.6	9.2	459.8	12.8	459.4	12.1
West Germany	544.9	9.9	736.6	12.1	762.7	12.5	669.9	11.0
United Kingdom	589.6	11.4	643.1	11.4	588.9	10.3	559.2	9.9
Romania	53.5	2.9	119.5	5.9	199.8	9.2	220.7	9.5
South Africa	98.6	5.5	149.6	6.6	213.4	7.7	284.2	8.4
Japan	234.3	2.6	742.1	7.3	934.6	8.1	989.3	8.1
Italy	110.4	2.2	286.0	5.5	372.5	6.6	359.7	6.2
France	274.3	5.9	426.1	8.4	484.4	9.2	320.1	5.9
Korea	49.1	0.4	52.1	1.5	125.8	3.3	204.6	4.8
Spain	12.8	1.5	110.7	3.3	198.7	5.5	187.7	4.8
Mexico	63.1	1.8	106.0	1.8	260.3	3.7	306.9	3.7
People's Republic of China	789.4	1.2	775.9	1.0	1490.1	1.5	2236.3	2.1
Brazil	46.9	0.7	86.5	0.7	176.7	1.5	202.4	1.5
India	121.7	0.4	195.4	0.4	350.2	0.4	600.6	0.7

Note: Emission estimates are rounded and expressed in million tons of CO_2; per capita estimates are rounded and expressed in tons of CO_2. All tons are metric.

Adapted from Thomas A. Boden, Paul Kanciruk, and Michael P. Farrell. 1990. *Trends '90: A Compendium of Data on Global Change.* Oak Ridge National Laboratory: Oak Ridge, TN.

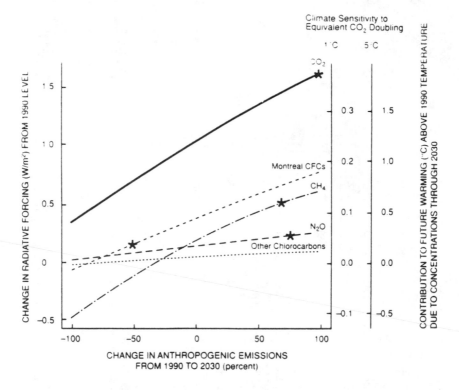

FIGURE 1. Commitment to future warming. An incremental change in radiative forcing between 1990 and 2030 due to emissions of greenhouse gases implies a change in global average equilibrium temperature (see text). The scales on the right-hand side show two ranges of global average temperature responses. The first corresponds to a climate whose temperature response to an equivalent of doubling of the preindustrial level of CO_2 is 1°C; the second corresponds to a rise of 5°C for an equivalent doubling of CO_2. These scales indicate the equilibrium commitment to future warming caused by emissions from 1990 through 2030.

To determine equilibrium warming in 2030 due to continued emissions of CO_2 at the 1990 level, find the point on the curve labeled "CO_2" that is vertically above 0 percent change on the bottom scale. The equilibrium warming on the right-hand scales is about 0.23°C (0.4°F) for a climate system with 1° sensitivity and about 1.2°C (2.2°F) for a system with 5° sensitivity. For CH_4 emissions continuing at 1990 levels through 2030, the equilibrium warming would be about 0.04°C (0.07°F) at 1° sensitivity and about 0.25°C (0.5°F) at 5° sensitivity. These steps must be repeated for each gas. Total warming associated with 1990-level emissions of the gases shown until 2030 would be about 0.41°C (0.7°F) at 1° sensitivity and about 2.2°C (4°F) at 5° sensitivity.

Scenarios of changes in committed future warming accompanying different greenhouse gas emission rates can be constructed by repeating this process for given emission rates and adding up the results. (From National Academy of Sciences, National Academy of Engineering, and Institute of Medicine. 1991. *Policy Implications of Greenhouse Warming.* Washington, D.C.: National Academy Press. With permission.)

2030 as percentages of 1990 levels (assuming linear changes from 1990 to 2030). The "stars" indicate the "business-as-usual" projections developed by the IPCC. The left-hand vertical scale shows the incremental changes in energy absorption that would accompany various emissions levels for each gas. The energy absorption is given in watts per square meter. Change in absorption is called "radiative forcing". The right-hand vertical scales indicate committed equilibrium warming. One scale shows the commitment to future warming for a "low" (1°C) and the other a "high" (5°C) degree of climate response to greenhouse gas concentrations. The total committed warming can be determined by adding the temperatures derived for the projected concentration of each gas.

Analytic techniques of this type need further development. The simplified approach in Figure 1, for example, does not account for chemical interactions among these trace gases in the atmosphere. Nevertheless, it can be used to produce first-approximation estimates for various emissions scenarios.

PROJECTING CLIMATE CHANGE

The best tools for projecting overall climate change are called general circulation models (GCMs). They are huge computer-simulation models with hundreds of thousands of equations and dozens of variables. They attempt to account not only for atmospheric concentrations of greenhouse gases, but for feedback mechanisms such as those involving clouds, for ocean lags, and for other relevant phenomena. There are about a half-dozen different GCMs. Although GCMs project global mean *equilibrium* temperature increases of between 1.8 and 5.2°C, there is no scientific way to be sure that this range includes the actual temperature increase that would accompany a doubling of preindustrial CO_2 concentrations. However, the GCMs do replicate many attributes of the global weather system (e.g., diurnal and seasonal variations, and atmospheric phenomena like jet streams and tropical cell intrusions). This suggests that they must replicate at least some relevant attributes of the system.

The Evans study concluded that the sensitivity of the climate system is such that the equivalent of doubling the preindustrial level of CO_2 could ultimately increase the average global temperature by somewhere between 1 and 5°C. This is a larger range than used in many other studies. The panel believes that prudence dictates a larger allowance for uncertainty when drawing policy conclusions.

POSSIBLE IMPACTS OF GREENHOUSE WARMING

Because of the uncertainties, and because of the relatively wide range of possible temperature rise, the Evans study looked at the sensitivity of the affected human and ecologic systems to the range of projected changes. We assessed key sectors of the U.S. economy and "unmanaged" ecosystems. On this basis the panel recommended actions that would help human and natural systems adapt to future climate change. We also examined the technical potential of various actions to slow or offset emissions of greenhouse gases and recommend several mitigation actions.

Our study focused on the U.S. We attempted to assess impacts on sectors of the domestic economy and on unmanaged ecosystems in this country. We drew a few comparisons to other geographic regions where these were obvious, but performed no systematic analysis of other regions.

People in the U.S. will likely have no more difficulty adapting to gradual climate changes than to severe climatic conditions in the past, such as the Dust Bowl. Needless to say, adjustments will involve some cost. There also may be substantial geographic differences in the impacts, with some regions winning and others losing. The overall net for the nation as a whole, however, should balance out. Some members of the panel thought our analysis may underestimate some of the adjustment costs because it did not include interactions among sectors or of the economy with natural systems.

Other countries are likely to have more difficulty adjusting to the projected changes, especially poor countries or those with fewer climate zones. They may face greater hardship in adapting, or have more difficulty taking advantage of favorable changes.

Many natural systems of plants and animals will change. Although key "ecosystem services" (e.g., absorption of CO_2 by plants) may be maintained on any given tract of land by replacement species, ecosystems will almost certainly be altered. Some people may find such changes unacceptable. The stronger this is felt, the greater the motivation to slow greenhouse warming.

We did not find credible assessments of major, sudden transformations with large consequences. For example, greenhouse warming conceivably could alter major ocean currents and thus regional climate, and change precipitation in the far north. This could affect surface reflectivity and energy absorption, or release trapped methane from melting tundra and inject an additional surge of greenhouse gas. No one knows, however, just what might initiate such transformations or how they might proceed once started. There is no way to analyze their likelihood or impacts. The panel combined the possibility that they might occur combined with the other uncertainties. It concluded that investments to slow greenhouse warming would be good "insurance" against the threat of greenhouse warming, including possible surprises.

MITIGATION OF GREENHOUSE WARMING

The Evans study examination of options for slowing, or mitigating, the onset of greenhouse warming used a different approach than found in other studies. We developed a cost-effectiveness ranking in terms of reduction in current emissions of CO_2 (or the equivalent in other gases, enhancement of CO_2 sinks, etc.). The approach calculates emissions reductions over the expected lifetime of each option, dividing by the years involved to produce a reduction in annual emissions. This is compared to the present value of the cost of that option to produce the cost effectiveness of that option. This approach has several advantages and disadvantages worth highlighting.

First, it is a method that enables widely different options to be compared. Improvements in fuel efficiency in automobiles that last 10 years can be compared with combined cycle electricity-generating plants that last 25 or 30 years. Replacement of incandescent light bulbs by high-efficiency fluorescent tubes can be compared with reforestation of marginal land. This breadth of applicability is essential for a comprehensive approach.

Second, the priority ranking of options is based on current conditions. The ranking may not be the same in, say, 2015. For example, among the most cost-effective options today are energy conservation in residential and commercial buildings. Further down the list are power plant heat-rate improvements, and further still, electricity supply options. The full implementation of energy conservation measures, however, might well change electricity demand such that the cost-effectiveness ranking of energy supply options would be different by 2015. We made no attempt to analyze such interactions among options in our analysis, however.

Third, the reductions of greenhouse gas emissions are expressed in terms of 1990 emissions. We did not estimate how much implementing these options might reduce emissions at any future point in time. We believe future emissions are highly dependent on economic conditions, technological progress, and success in implementing mitigation options. None of these can be predicted credibly. So our analysis does not give projections about the amount of reductions that could be achieved in, say, 2010. Rather, we estimate how much current annual emissions could be reduced if the decision were made now to implement these options. Putting the most cost-effective options in place, however, would be the wisest course of action whether future emissions follow a high or a low trajectory. The high-priority options would be high priority under either scenario.

Fourth, the fact that this approach produces a ranking of options under current conditions only implies that the analysis should be repeated on a regular basis. After 5 years, or perhaps 10, costs and mitigation potentials may be sufficiently different to alter the rankings. If the most efficient options are to be used on the scale of decades involved in greenhouse warming, it would be necessary to repeat the analysis on a regular basis.

Fifth, the mitigation options are ranked in the study according to their cost effectiveness, but their overall potential is also considered. Those achieving a given reduction in emissions of carbon dioxide or its equivalent most cheaply rank highest. Hydroelectric dams, for example, may be very cost effective, but there may be few locations remaining where they could be utilized.

The cost-effectiveness ranking of the most attractive options from the Evans study can be found in Table 3. If the "low-cost" mitigation actions were implemented, the technical envelope of emissions reduction would be between a little more than 10% of 1990 U.S. greenhouse gas emissions for pessimistic assumptions about implementation to slightly less than 40% for more optimistic assumptions. Our analysis showed these reductions could be achieved at low cost, or even at a net savings if proper policies were implemented. Determining the costs of achieving the recommendations with any degree of precision, however, is extremely difficult. Thus, the Evans study cannot be considered definitive. It is, however, a careful first cut. A substantial reduction in greenhouse gas emissions can be accomplished at low cost, or even a net savings to the nation if proper policies were implemented.

RECOMMENDATIONS

The Synthesis Panel concluded that, "despite the great uncertainties, greenhouse warming is a potential threat sufficient to justify action now". It went on to point out that there are a number of effective and low-cost options available to the U.S.

The panel developed recommendations in five areas: reducing or offsetting emissions of greenhouse gases, enhancing adaptation to greenhouse warming, improving knowledge for future decisions, evaluating geoengineering options, and exercising international leadership.

Three topics dominated recommendations to reduce or offset emissions: eliminating emission of halocarbons (principally CFCs), changing energy policy, and forest offsets. Although the international agreements on ozone depletion mandate elimination of many halocarbon emissions, if they are not implemented the concentrations of greenhouse gases will be much worse. In the area of energy policy, the panel recommended moving toward full-cost pricing of energy. It also recommended substantial improvements in energy conservation and efficiency, and significantly reducing emissions from energy supply, conversion, and end use. The panel recommended reducing global deforestation and exploring reforestation programs.

The great uncertainties surrounding virtually every aspect of policy concerning greenhouse warming puts information for future decisions at a premium. Policy decisions could be improved by careful gathering of data and targeted research in several areas: field research on effects of carbon dioxide enhancement, data of all kinds on climate change, improved weather forecasts, climate feedback mechanisms, and social and economic interactions with climate change.

The panel also recommended research into what we called geoengineering options. These are ways of blocking incident radiation, enhancing natural sinks for greenhouse gases, or altering the surface reflectivity of the earth.

Research and development projects should be undertaken to improve understanding of both the potential of such geoengineering options to offset global warming and their possible side effects. Preliminary assessment of these options suggests that they have large potential to mitigate greenhouse warming and are comparatively cost effective. However, their feasibility and especially the side effects associated with them should be carefully examined before action is taken to implement them.

Finally, the U.S. should resume full participation in international programs to slow population growth and contribute its share to their financial and other support. The U.S. should participate fully and at an appropriate level in international agreements and programs to address greenhouse warming.

GREENHOUSE WARMING AND OTHER PROBLEMS

This paper makes no attempt to evaluate policies for responding to the threat of greenhouse warming in comparison to other problems facing society. Such an evaluation is neither simple nor straightforward. Even though the U.S. emits more greenhouse gases than any other nation, unilateral action by this country alone would have little overall effect. Other countries, especially poorer countries, may well choose to focus on short-term problems of health and nutrition rather than long-term problems of climate change. There are similar trade-offs among societal goals within our own country as well. This paper does not address these choices. Rather, it tries to summarize what we know about the threat of greenhouse warming, about its likely impacts on human and natural systems, and about the costs of making a difference. As such it hopefully contributes to the broader debate about such priorities.

Human Health Risks

Introduction

Paul F. Deisler, Jr.

All that might be said on the topic of what we need to know about human health risks to make it possible to use risk assessment in setting priorities for risk reduction actions cannot be compressed into a handful of chapters. I hope no reader expects this. Possibly if the well-known experts represented in this section could have worked together to prepare a single chapter on the subject they might have met such an expectation — or perhaps not, given the very different vantage points of each and the variety of opinions expressed.

The readers of this section should therefore not set out with the idea of finding an orderly catalog of what is needed; rather, they should look for a set of expert perspectives on not only what we need to know, but on what we need to do. While the readers will not encounter a catalog, they will receive valuable insights from expert members of the risk assessment and management community.

In most of the views presented, current risk assessment methods are accepted in principle, prioritization is considered useful, and the writers seek to set forth what we need to know to improve the methods, to fill the gaps in our knowledge, and so to make risk-based prioritization more reliable. One writer objects to the intense focus on cancer and points to the need to consider other types of health risks, particularly in the case of the work of the U.S. Environmental Protection Agency; this same writer at one point challenges the idea that prioritization is needed, asking whether or not resources are really so limited after all.

Another writer concludes that while the current systems are inadequate for the assessment of absolute risks, they — or elements of them — are adequate for relative risk ranking, that in making risk comparisons the uncertainties tend to cancel; thus, in this instance, it is judged possible to get on, right now, with the business of prioritizing according to risk. This same writer warns against allowing value judgments into the assessment of risk, a scientific process.

In these chapters readers will find the subject of this section addressed in very specific terms by one writer: what is needed by the U.S. Environmental Protection Agency for the realistic estimation of residual risk under Section 112 of the Clean Air Act for the 189 substances or classes of substances whose regulation is therein prescribed. Better use of mechanistic data, of alternative, realistic approaches to risk assessment, of better epidemiological data and of the means to utilize it, and better comparative risk methodologies are advocated. Readers will further find explained in considerable detail, by another author, that research is now actively underway within the U.S. Environmental Protection Agency to provide better methods for assessments of noncancer health risks, methods which, while tending to do a better job of assessments and even of making such assessments more compatible with those for cancer risks, nonetheless tend to expand the data requirements considerably over the present ones — not good news.

In another expression of viewpoint of a less specific, more general type, readers are told that the biggest gaps in data and information which prevent us from doing the quality of cancer risk assessments which make relative or comparative risk ranking a more useful part of the priority-setting mechanism are some of the well-known, old, traditional ones: high-to-low dose, chronic-to-acute, route-to-route, and cross-species extrapolation. Of these, we are told, the one in greatest need of attention is cross-species extrapolation. The suggestion is made that the National Toxicology Program is deficient, and has been for some time, in that animal studies should be made — and could have been made — using positive carcinogenic controls, using known human carcinogens in such control tests, as a first step in learning more, directly, about cross-species (animal-to-human) extrapolation. Using physiologically based pharmacokinetics (PBPK) to estimate internal doses, we are told, is all very well, but until cross-species extrapolation is better mastered than it is, PBPK will give more the appearance than the reality of doing better risk assessments.

Although most of the writers accept, generally, the so-called National Research Council "paradigm" — or process — for risk assessment, seeking improvement in the area of data acquisition and interpretation, one writer, the same one who questioned the need for prioritization, concludes that this process and the way it is implemented constitute a barrier to setting true priorities and to reducing risk: data requirements are very great, quantitative risk assessment as now practiced is too rigid, the methods now used lack adequate means to escape from the default assumptions, and the results are neither understood nor accepted by the public. The alternative method of prioritization offered is one in which what is called a "public health" approach, an approach of "preventing the preventible", is taken. In this approach one needs to know which diseases are most prevalent; of these, which nonhost factors are most important; of these, further, for which does the U.S. Environmental Protection Agency have opportunities for prevention; and, finally, what long-term changes in incidence or prevalence would the U.S. Environmental Protection Agency's investment in prevention make. The reader is invited to decide whether or not this proposal is, indeed, more feasible and less controversial than existing methods, more understandable to the public, and whether its data requirements are more or less onerous.

All but one author address risks to health posed by chemical agents; in a refreshing change, this one author addresses the risks of infection, of illness, and of death, from exposures to microorganisms. One gets the impression that the data base is unusually rich in information compared with that for nonliving chemical substances, and that risk assessment in this field has few major gaps if any. There may be a major question of what models to use for extrapolation, just as is the case for the other types of risks discussed by others in this section, since the models presented have no particular mechanistic basis, but consist, generally, of well-known fitting functions. Extrapolations with such models could well lead to erroneous estimates of risk. The readers will have to bring their own understanding to this question.

The chapters in this section clearly contain a variety of views, assertions, proposals, and ideas on what we need to know — and do — about human health risks to make it possible to use risk assessment in setting priorities for risk-reduction actions. The ideas range from making specific suggestions on data needs for specific purposes to the throwing out of current methodologies and the adoption of a completely new and different one. While not providing a complete catalog of what needs to be known and why, they provide a set of provocative, creative, and useful insights, thoughts, and proposals. Readers interested in ideas and in advancing the art of risk assessment and its uses should find real interest in these chapters.

Revising the Risk Assessment Paradigm: Limits on the Quantitative Ranking of Environmental Problems

Ellen K. Silbergeld

The policy innovation proposed by EPA, to evaluate and prioritize its activities within the broad rubric of reducing risk has attracted considerable attention. While it is in principle an attractive goal to bring a purportedly objective analysis to the many activities required by statute of this agency, there are obvious and less obvious controversies in this particular approach to implementation. EPA has attempted to justify the need for a new paradigm in two recent exercises in self-examination: the *Unfinished Business* report, which ranked EPA's activities by priority; and the *Relative Risk Reduction Strategies Committee,* which reviewed this first effort and explored further the information required to revise EPA's strategic planning.

In both these projects it has been assumed by EPA policymakers, without much critical analysis, that risk assessment is a valid and useful metric for prioritizing the portfolio of issues in environmental protection. This paper challenges that assumption. In addition, a deeper critique of EPA's proclivities towards self-analysis and prioritization could be made. I shall only raise the following questions:

- Does EPA need to reconsider and reorganize its priorities, or are the much-discussed problems of this agency (see Landy, et al., *The EPA: Asking the Wrong Questions,* Oxford 1990) more a result of its *failures* to act rather than *inappropriate* actions?
- How necessary is prioritization; that is, how limited are the resources available for environmental protection? While EPA's budget is relatively large and total expenditures on environmental protection are considerable, have we actually reached a limit on available resources, or has a limit been self-imposed by this Administration, for political reasons, on the extent of environmental protection?

The major focus of this paper is on the dangers of using risk assessment, specifically quantitative risk assessment (QRA), for purposes of prioritizing issues in environmental health. "Risk" in environmental health is an inadequate operational concept for analysis and it remains a poorly realized tool in practice. The conceptual and practical problems in risk assessment have

0-87371-605-1/93/$0.00 + $.50
© 1993 by Lewis Publishers

not been resolved in the 10 years that risk assessment has been an important policy instrument (e.g., since the IRLG-proposed guidelines, published in 1979). Rather, scientific and methodological problems have accumulated over time and now burden the science and policy of environmental health such that the former is distorted and the latter follows a backwards approach to prioritization that is often at war with some obvious needs in public health. As an example, none of EPA's prioritizations and risk assessment-based analyses have identified lead poisoning as the most important preventable disease of environmental origin, as recognized by the Centers for Disease Control and other health authorities.

Risk assessment can be defined in general terms as the objective evaluation of the outcomes of human exposures to hazards; in these terms, its use is unobjectionable in public policy. However, this definition is nonoperational in terms of policy analysis. The formulation of risk assessment dogma by the National Research Council in the 1980s has resulted in considerable rigidity of approach and a general downgrading of epidemiologic, as opposed to toxicology, data (see below).

Since 1979, risk assessment in environmental policy has taken on a more specific meaning and a set of statistically based analytic methods to develop quantitative estimates of the associations between exposure and outcome. These methods of QRA are the base upon which EPA proposes to build its new structure of risk reduction.

Conceptual Limits to QRA

In concept, QRA remains limited as an instrument for analyzing environmental health issues. First, it supports an almost exclusive focus on one health outcome, cancer, and by inference one set of environmental hazards, carcinogens. The methods for QRA of noncarcinogens are primitive and nonspecific with respect to the biology of target organ systems. Most guidelines for assessing risks of all noncarcinogens follow the same "quantitative" methodology: establish a lowest or no observed adverse effect level, and divide by some *a priori* safety or uncertainty factor, almost always a multiple of ten. The State of California has been developing more science-based methods to assess risks of reproductive toxicants as part of Proposition 65, but these follow the same basic approach. Second, over time, the models utilized in QRA have become more and more inflexible as default assumptions have become inference rules. The criteria for escaping the default assumptions have never been made explicit; attempts to do so — such as EPA's novel approaches to thyroid and kidney carcinogens — are based on a controversial interpretation of scientific data. Third, and related to the above, the data needs for QRA are very great in three respects: to satisfy the models, to reduce uncertainty (decrease variance), and to escape the default assumptions. These data needs have escalated the costs of hazard identification (testing) and subsequent regulation, to the point of virtual paralysis (see below). Fourth, with a few exceptions (such as the comparison of the results of the NIOSH dioxin registry study of cancer risks with the EPA's original dioxin risk assessment of 1985, see Goldman et al. (1991), *N. Engl. J. Med.* 324: 1811), it has not been possible to validate QRA through epidemiological research; moreover, the uncertainties of many QRA make most validation exercises meaningless since their range would exceed that of any meaningful excess risk calculation (odds ratio or relative risk). Fifth, QRA cannot handle complex mixtures or complex exposure scenarios or chemicals whose risks may vary with dose:rate or timing of exposure. Sixth, QRA does not distinguish between preventable (potential) and reducible (actual) risks. EPA seems to have staked out only the latter as its arena for action, yet public health philosophy places a high premium upon the former.

Practical Limits on QRA

In addition to the conceptual limits on QRA, the practical limitations to this approach are considerable. The data needs for resolving uncertainty are very great, leaving the decision maker with a conundrum of choice between making decisions with a high degree of uncertainty or refusing to decide (which is a decision, in most cases) until a large amount of data become available. The present circumstances related to dioxin risk assessment exemplify this situation. Current QRA for the cancer risks of dioxin contains considerable uncertainty, particularly with respect to compounds other than 2,3,7,8-tetrachlorodibenzo-*p*-dioxin. Abdicating decision making until further scientific research fully reveals the molecular mechanisms of dioxin toxicity and its incorporation into QRA may defer those decisions for decades.

Second, risk assessment is not fully accepted as a policy tool by the public. It must continue to be a source of concern for those who support the American tradition of Jeffersonian democracy that the electorate remains suspicious of a major method of justifying public policy. Whatever the inherent values of QRA (which are debatable), the lack of public endorsement after a decade of proselytizing by a technological elite must be considered more seriously than repeated lamentations over the public's alleged scientific illiteracy. Many in the public may be scientifically illiterate (as are most of their representatives), but they — and their representatives — are politically astute.

Third, QRA does not provide a method for comparing risks on a practical basis. The "infinite risk" paradox of such assessments tends to distort comparisons at the extreme (e.g., how to assess a risk of high probability, but low magnitude with one of low probability and great magnitude). For the more general range of risks, while they may be compared in terms of probability, a numerical comparison does not give critical information on the qualitative value attached to different risks and the broader context of (for instance) intellectual impairment induced by lead as compared to arsenic-induced skin cancer that may be treatable if access to treatment were equitably distributed in the U.S. population. This limitation is a serious impediment to the use of QRA for EPA's purposes of prioritization.

Distortions of Science and Public Policy

The broad uses proposed for QRA by EPA in its new analyses represent the triumph of toxicology at the expense of epidemiology and public health. While the toxicological perspective is attractive as prevention in the case of evaluating new chemicals prior to human exposure, it tends to distort human experience of existing chemicals and environmental exposures. The most obvious consequence of this distortion is the discounting of exposure as a factor in final risk assessment. Although risk is posited as a function of all three elements — hazard identification, dose-response analyses, and exposure assessment — information on exposure is usually so limited that it plays a relatively minor role in risk assessment. Exposure data, including surveillance programs such as the National Human Adipose Tissue Survey, are very limited in scope and reliability. Little is being done to improve this situation. As a consequence, exposure assessment cannot really influence the final QRA. The clearest example of the dominance of toxicology is in EPA's generation of $Q*$ data, or slopes for cancer potency. These $Q*$ numbers, which do not reflect exposure assessment, have tended to influence unduly risk-management decisions. For instance, the carcinogen formaldehyde has a relatively low $Q*$ (incremental risk per increment in dose), while dioxin has one of the highest $Q*$ values (steepest slope). Arguably, the EPA has done only a little more to actually reduce human exposures to dioxin as compared to formaldehyde, but all regulations on source control of formaldehyde have been stalled for nearly a decade.

The risk assessment model, as developed by the NRC, is driven by hazard assessment and dose-response analyses. These functions are almost always dependent upon toxicological research and as such are shaped by available testing protocols that define the nature of hazard and the general shape of dose-response relationships. Testing programs have become in some cases nearly mindless, and the nature of a hazard is defined by the test protocol. This is exemplified in the circular definition of carcinogens as mutagens by means of the Ames-type *in vitro* revertant mutation test, such that chemicals are not found positive in such tests are argued to be noncarcinogens (or carcinogens of considerably lesser importance).

The Public Health Perspective

In contrast to the risk assessment paradigm, the public health perspective is embedded in the public health tradition of preventing diseases in real populations. Prevention includes primary intervention to interdict or eradicate the causes of disease; secondary intervention or early identification and reduction of exposures to these causes; and tertiary interventions to treat or remediate exposed persons or contaminated environments. While the certainty of cause-effect relations increases as the situation progresses to overt disease, the costs of prevention also escalate and the efficacy of prevention decreases. The public health perspective draws upon an understanding of the incidence and prevalence of disease (mortality, morbidity, disability) in real populations in which cofactors, susceptibilities, and other contributing events are also distributed.

A prioritization strategy based upon public health would require information on the following:

- What are the most prevalent diseases in the U.S. population, and for which ones are incidences changing?
- Of these, for which is a nongenetic (nonhost factor) etiology likely as a major causal or contributory factor (this recognizes the interaction of gene and environment and the practical advantages of modifying environment rather than genome in most situations)?
- Of these, for which does EPA have opportunities for preventive action to reduce risks (e.g., EPA cannot escape its particular set of statutory authorities, which are quite broad, by claiming that smoking and diet are the only significant causes of disease in the U.S. population)?
- What changes in *long-term* disease prevalence or incidence would an investment in prevention of exposure, using EPA's tools, make the greatest difference (in case numbers, costs, quality of life, or whatever indicators are most appropriate)?

The major difference in this approach from EPA's proposals in the relative risk reduction strategy documents is the emphasis on preventing preventable risks to human health through environmental interventions. The prevention, or public health approach, provides an interesting parallel to the strategy proposed by the ecological effects subcommittee, and one which the health community could consider. Such an approach would free the EPA from the tyranny of current toxicology-driven data and limited endpoint models towards a more broad approach of health promotion. Clearly, it would extend the Agency's health-related activities and perspective beyond a narrowing focus on cancer and carcinogens. I would predict that the analytic approach proposed above would identify as major opportunities for disease prevention such conditions as low birth weight, pulmonary and respiratory disease and disability, infertility and subfertility, neurodevelopmental disorders, and dementing disorders of the elderly. These are all conditions that impact upon the health and productivity of Americans; they exert very large direct and indirect costs on society; and because of their prevalence, small reductions in risk through environmental interventions are likely to have major benefits for our national health and wellbeing.

CHAPTER 6

It Is Possible to Do Quantitative Assessment of Relative Risk

James D. Wilson

ABSTRACT

Since some risks can be at least approximately quantified, it is obvious that when such risks are being considered quantitative assessments of the relative risks among different scenarios provide useful input for priority setting. EPA's present problem with choosing from among the many different potential risks to human health and the environment stems from the fact that most of those within its jurisdiction are small and roughly equal. The uncertainty in estimating the risks to real or hypothetical individuals is substantial, large enough to obscure differences among them. The uncertainty in the differences among risks inferred from toxicologic data can be reduced by a population-based method: estimating the number of individuals likely to be exposed above some response level such as an ED_{05}. However, risk comparisons are not an adequate sole criterion for priority setting; values must also be considered, and brought in through the normal political process. Properly applied, risk assessment can serve to bring into the process the relevant scientific information, thus allowing the political decisions to be made in greater clarity.

INTRODUCTION

The symposium presented here is devoted to examining the use of risk assessment for regulatory decision making, particularly as advocated recently by EPA's Science Advisory Board[1]. This essay was commissioned to argue the affirmative against criticism that such use is inappropriate, essentially because the uncertainties are so large as to make comparisons meaningless. In fact it is both possible and appropriate, although estimations of relative risk cannot be used as the sole input for such decision making.

0-87371-605-1/93/$0.00 + $.50

RISK ASSESSMENT IS A TOOL FOR HELPING TO MAKE DECISIONS THAT ALLOWS QUANTITATIVE COMPARISON AMONG ALTERNATIVES

On its face, any argument that risk assessment cannot be used for priority setting seems absurd. The term "risk assessment" describes a process for developing information on the possible adverse effects, or losses, that may occur as a consequence of an action (including absence of action) and the likelihood of such losses ("risk"). Critics of EPA's use of risk assessment must either define this term differently, or not understand that they — and all of us — unconsciously use this process virtually every day.

Some of the criticism seems to stem from EPA's own misuse of the phrase. For some years the Agency incorrectly used "quantitative risk assessment" to describe their process for arriving at exposure standards, or "unit risk values" to substances eliciting a carcinogenic response in test animals. The considerable uncertainty inherent in the calculations used in this process[2] lends supports to the conclusion that using risk assessment in priority setting would be an exercise of doubtful utility.

However, "risk assessment" refers to much more than the specialized techniques used to regulate exposure to carcinogens. We advocate use of the term in its broader sense, as a tool to facilitate comparison of risks from decision alternatives. Many definitions of "risk assessment" have been published; each includes the elements of "hazard", "exposure", and probability that exposure to the hazard will occur. For example, the recent National Academy Committee on Risk Perception and Communication described these key terms in this paragraph:

> "For this kind of analysis, some conceptual distinctions are useful. The most basic of these is between 'hazard' and 'risk'. *An act or phenomenon is said to pose a hazard when it has the potential to produce harm or other undesirable consequences to some person or thing.* The magnitude of the hazard is the amount of harm that may result, including the number of people or things exposed and the severity of the consequence. *The concept of risk further quantifies hazards by attaching the probability of being realized to each level of potential harm."* (Italics in the original.)[3]

Many of the risks we commonly face can be estimated with sufficient accuracy and precision to allow their direct use in decision making. For instance, rich data are available concerning rates of accidental death during use of various kinds of public transport; thus one can use these data directly in making the decision to travel, for instance, from New York City to Washington, D.C. by commercial airline, train, private car, or private plane — or even bicycle.

For this class of hazard, the likelihood of occurrence dominates the risk; both the loss and exposure functions are well defined.

Some risks to human health and the environment can be just as well characterized. For instance, consider the risk of contracting AIDS from a dental procedure or the risk of altering the ecology of a northern prairie glacial lake by harvesting the timber from its watershed. In both of these instances the hazard and exposure are well known, and the determinants of likelihood understood. (In addition, the utility functions can be described with some precision.) The decisions on whether or not to have a broken tooth treated or a logging permit granted can confidently be made taking these risks into account. Perhaps more importantly, we know enough to know how to *manage* these risks — make sure the dentist wears rubber gloves, leave a corridor of uncut vegetation along the tributary streams.

Many "natural" risks to individuals fall into this category, such as being killed by lightning while watching a golf tournament or being engulfed in volcanic ash while closely studying active volcanoes.

Other risks are less conveniently quantified. Crossing a busy street in front of a bus, for instance, is a risk frequently taken, seldom quantified. One cannot conveniently quantify such important variables as the reaction time of the bus driver, the likelihood that the risk-taker will stumble or slip in hurrying across the street, etc. Nevertheless, we seem to possess a "hard-wired" capability to compare our ability to traverse a distance in time to be safely out of the way before the hazard crosses our path — even though we, collectively, are wrong often enough that these acts are usually banned!

No controversy attends the general proposition that quantitative estimates of some kinds of risks can be made and comparisons of the estimated risks from different decisions can illuminate those decisions. The controversy concerns a very limited subset of all approximately quantifiable risks: those for which the benefits are either not easily described or for which the assessment of benefits is strongly influenced by value differences, and thus in dispute. The last two decades have seen many arguments framed in terms of human or environmental risk that really were about profound value differences. (One example: design and siting of the facilities required to manage trash in the New York City area.) It is profoundly wrong to disguise value-based arguments in this way. It is incumbent upon us in the risk-assessment profession to understand and communicate the limits on our results, in order to make best use of the information we possess, incomplete as it may be. When our calculus does not allow us to distinguish the risks from different choices, that should be made clear. That may frequently be the case, but if the choices and potential risks are appropriately described, it should happen less frequently than those opposed to use of risk assessment have claimed.

PRIORITY SETTING IS ONE KIND OF DECISION MAKING

This symposium is taking place because the Environmental Protection Agency's Science Advisory Board has recommended that the Agency use relative risks to establish priorities for regulatory action.[1] They suggest that the bigger risks should receive higher priorities for action. This recommendation has received criticism on three grounds. First, it is said not to be possible. As we have just seen, that conclusion cannot be sustained in the general case; I will show below that it will not usually be true for a subset of health risks of concern to the Agency. Second, it has been criticized (by Senator Durenburger, among others) for leading to neglect of important societal values in regulatory decision making. There is merit in this view, although as I will also discuss below, proper use of risk assessment methods should allow the political process to focus on exactly these other values, and not be distracted by argument over health and environmental risks. Finally, Finkel[4] has recently argued that strict application of the ''worst risks first'' paradigm would represent a departure from more than a century of public health practice, in which both magnitude and practicality of reducing risk is considered. I agree. In fact, his suggested approach is consistent with the spirit of the Science Advisory Board's recommendations, and provides a more realistic guidance for a regulatory agency.

The setting of priorities is one of several kinds of decisions a regulatory agency needs to make. While these priority-setting decisions must be at bottom political, as with all agency decisions, the most important political consideration is that serious risks cannot be ignored. It is only when risks appear to be roughly equal, or small, that setting priorities becomes difficult. I would suggest that there is now a large number of decisions before the Agency for which exactly this situation prevails. The number of easily measurable, imminent risks to human health and the environment regulable by, but not yet adequately regulated by EPA can be counted on the fingers of one hand. First on this short list are the related hazards caused by exceeding the carrying capacity of the lower atmosphere: acid deposition and ozone. (One can argue that the public has not demonstrated its willingness to reduce these risks to the negligible level.) Congress has not delegated to the Agency authority to regulate our most serious health hazards, cigarettes and poverty. Radon seeping into homes from the earth is not regulatable. EPA is left with a large number of small, diverse, and uncertain risks. It has received little guidance from Congress (or anyone else) about how to discriminate among these.

A POPULATION-BASED CRITERION CAN BE USED FOR RANKING

We commonly think of risk in terms of the likelihood of occurrence of some adverse consequence — airplane crash, cancer death, fish kill, whatever. This means of expression can provide relatively clear communication within the technical community because of the intuitiveness of the concept. (Outside of this community, communication of risks expressed in exponential notation is much less successful.)

For the kinds of risks identified just above — those that are small and comparable in magnitude — large uncertainties associated with the calculation of individual risks makes this approach problematic if distinctions need to be made among the different kinds of hazard.

Regulatory proceedings often use a related expression of risk, that estimated to be borne by a representative individual from a population, under some typical exposure scenario. (In some circumstances a hypothetical "most heavily exposed" individual — a "gluttonous consumer" — is used instead of a representative individual.) This approach allows use of statistical techniques to calculate and characterize risk, including distributions and simulations. It is better suited for use in priority setting than any attempt to focus on true individual risks. Proponents of EPA's using risks for priority setting seemingly have this approach in mind.

However, there remain significant problems of uncertainty and of variability that limit its usefulness, especially if it is necessary to estimate responses at exposures far from the observable range.

Individual risk is not the only means of expressing risk. The public health profession has traditionally focused on populations, on measures to improve the health of the population as a whole. Looking at risk this way suggests an alternate means of setting priorities. It would involve estimating the number of people (or other organisms) likely to suffer harm from a particular exposure.

In this mode, one would use dose-response data to identify some low-response exposure, for example, the dose at which 1% responds (ED_{01}) or a "no observed adverse effect level" (NOAEL). Using modern methods to estimate exposure, which provide reasonably reliable frequency distributions, it would then be possible to estimate the number of people in a population that would have an exposure greater than the ED_{01} criterion. If the adverse effects in two scenarios are comparably weighted, then the scenario with the higher number of people exposed above the criterion would be the "riskier".

For example, one could estimate the number of people in the U.S. exposed to more than 0.1 mg/l of arsenic in their drinking water and compare that to the number estimated to exhibit more than 10 $\mu g/dl$ lead in serum as a result of exposure to lead-based paints. These two measures of harm are not exactly commensurate, since the toxicological consequences differ, but each implies that injury is likely to follow. Using this population-based criterion, if there were more people drinking water above 0.1 mg/l than people with more than 10 $\mu g/dl$ lead in serum, reducing arsenic in drinking water would be assigned the higher priority.

In practice it would be more effective to use an estimate of the exposure level at which some small fraction of the population responds, such as an ED_{01} or ED_{05} than a NOAEL. The fractional response value can be reliably estimated from the kinds of toxicologic data commonly available; compared to the toxicologist's NOAEL it has the advantage of not being dependent on the exposures that happen to have been chosen for testing, and being less dependent on sample size for reliability.

A similar approach could be used for effects on nonhuman organisms. To compare human and environmental risks directly using this kind of methodology one would have to address the different values held — saving a tree vs. saving a person, for example. Since comparing values is and should be a political decision and not a technical one, I suggest that it would be more useful to rank the human and environmental risks separately. The highest-priority problems from each sphere could be ranked through the political process, if needed.

Note that under this approach, the Agency would not purport to estimate a risk, or the number of injuries that might occur in the absence of corrective action. If the data used to derive the comparison criterion in any particular case were animal data, the criterion would include an implicit assumption that the level of exposure causing injury in animals meaningfully relates somehow to a response in humans. But since it would be acknowledged to be an arbitrary criterion, useful only for planning purposes, the Agency could credibly deny any forecast of impact on real individuals.

FOR EPA, VALUES OTHER THAN HEALTH AND ENVIRONMENTAL RISK MUST BE CONSIDERED IN MAKING REGULATORY DECISIONS. HOWEVER, PROPER USE OF RISK ASSESSMENT METHODOLOGY ALLOWS THESE OTHER VALUES TO BE ADDRESSED EXPLICITLY

The Science Advisory Board's recommendation has one serious flaw: it neglects the important issue of differing values. Using a technically based criterion for priority setting is fine as long as no value differences exist among members of the set to be prioritized. Yet as yet noted above, in the arena under discussion there is not agreement on values. Resolving differences in values is a task that belongs in the political arena; our task, as professional risk accessors, is to resolve technical issues to the extent possible in order that these value differences can be cleanly addressed.

In the example used above, comparing the number of people who might be harmed by exposure to arsenic in drinking water with those exposed to lead from paint, there are some value-based issues to consider, such as the fact that the lead exposures occur mainly in children and may affect mental capacity. These issues need to be raised in any characterization of the two kinds of risk, but they are small enough to permit the relative ranking to proceed.

It should also be noted that other kinds of technical information can help illuminate priorities where endpoints are different. Different adverse effects do have different, and approximately measurable, economic costs. Economists are beginning to explore ways to use these costs as input to regulatory decisions (e.g., see Reference 5).

Risk assessment provides a publicly accessible framework for identifying the information important to identifying possible risks to health and the environment, and a process for analyzing that information. While this framework and process cannot be said to be totally value-free, there seems to be very broad agreement in our society on those values *necessary* to risk assessment. Virtually all of us acknowledge that risk assessment provides a useful way to address certain kinds of decisions. As long as we are careful not to subsume value differences in the technical analysis of risk, we can clearly create a quantitative ranking of risks for prioritization.

REFERENCES

1. U.S. EPA Science Advisory Board, *Reducing Risk: Setting Priorities and Strategies for Environmental Protection*. Report SAB-EC-90-021; U.S. Environmental Protection Agency: Washington, D.C., 1990. (Available from the National Technical Information Service as document PB91-155242).
2. A. M. Finkel, *Confronting Uncertainty in Risk Management: a Guide for Decision-Makers,* Resources for the Future — Center for Risk Management, Washington, D.C., 1990.
3. National Research Council, *Improving Risk Communication*. National Academy Press, Washington, D.C., 1989, p. 32.
4. A. M. Finkel, "Risk reduction policy". *Environment,* 33:2–4 (1991).
5. J. A. Mauskopf and M. T. French, "Estimating the value of avoiding morbidity and mortality from foodborne illnesses". *Risk Anal.,* 11:619–632 (1991).

CHAPTER 7

Noncancer Health Endpoints: Approaches to Quantitative Risk Assessment*

William Farland and Michael Dourson

ABSTRACT

Traditional approaches to health risk assessment for cancer and noncancer endpoints represent a dichotomy. Carcinogens have been treated as nonthreshold, intrinsically toxic compounds and incremental risk estimates have been calculated. Other health effects are generally thought to exhibit thresholds of response and substances producing these effects are thought to be situationally toxic. This perspective has led to the development of procedures for defining exposures (doses) for these substances at or below which no adverse effect is likely to occur. This so-called reference dose (RfD) is often used to indicate an exposure that is considered to be safe, i.e., without adverse effects, and therefore without risk. On the other hand, exposures above this level may represent a toxicological hazard with or without significant risk. Quantitative rankings of environmental problems would be improved by application of procedures to estimate risks for noncancer endpoints at exposures above the reference dose. No well-accepted approaches to this problem are currently available. Research to evaluate a number of statistically and/or biologically based methods for estimating risk under this situation will be described and implications for improved ranking of environmental toxicants will be discussed.

INTRODUCTION

Based in part on the seminal publication on risk assessment by the National Academy of Sciences (NAS, 1983), and in part on previous work in this area of science by the World Health Organization (WHO) and the U.S. Food and Drug Administration (FDA), the Environmental Protection Agency (EPA) has

---

* The views in this paper are those of the authors and do not necessarily reflect the views or policies of the U.S. Environmental Protection Agency.

been developing methods to clarify certain aspects of its risk assessments and to ensure consistent application of risk assessment principles across its programs. While hazard identification and risk characterization for both cancer and noncancer endpoints involve a similar weight of the evidence approach dose-response assessments have been handled differently. In the area of noncancer health risk, for example, the EPA has published reports on the reference dose (RfD) and reference concentration (RfC) as alternatives to the acceptable daily intake (ADI) (U.S. EPA, 1990a; Barnes and Dourson, 1988; Jarabek et al., 1989) and formed an RfD, RfC Work Group to review its dose-response assessments for noncancer effects. This risk information has been summarized and placed on the Agency's Integrated Risk Information System (IRIS) (U.S. EPA, 1990b). In addition, the Agency has developed several other quantitative approaches for assessing toxicological data, such as the benchmark dose (Crump, 1984; Dourson et al., 1985; Dourson, 1986; Kimmel and Gaylor, 1988; Kimmel 1990) and categorical regression (Hertzberg and Miller, 1985; Hertzberg, 1989).

The purpose of this manuscript is to describe some of the EPA's quantitative procedures in formulating judgments concerning the nature and magnitude of the noncancer hazard and risk, and to highlight new knowledge and new assessment methods. As new quantitative approaches are developed for noncancer endpoints, we also raise the question as to the usefulness of maintaining the dichotomy between the quantitative assessment of cancer and noncancer endpoints.

THE CONCEPT OF THRESHOLD

The common approach to assessing the risks associated with noncancer and nonmutagenic toxicity is generally different from that used to assess the potential risks associated with carcinogenicity or mutagenicity. It is most often assumed that a small number of molecular events can evoke carcinogenic and/or mutagenic changes in a single cell, which can lead to self-replicating damage. Traditionally, this approach has led to these endpoints being considered nonthreshold effects, since there is presumably no level of exposure that does not pose a small, but finite, probability of generating a response. It is most often assumed that noncarcinogenic and/or nonmutagenic effects have a threshold, that is, a dose level below which a response is implausible, because homeostatic, compensating, and adaptive mechanisms in the cell protect against toxic effects.

This threshold concept is important in many regulatory contexts. The individual threshold hypothesis holds that some exposures can be tolerated by an organism with essentially no chance for expression of a toxic effect. Further, risk management decisions frequently focus on protecting the more sensitive members of a population. In these cases efforts are made to keep exposures below the more sensitive subpopulation threshold, although it is recognized that hypersensitivity and chemical idiosyncrasy (i.e., genetically determined abnormal reactivity to a chemical) may exist at yet lower doses. This concept and focus have resulted in the development of quantitative risk assessment models (or approaches) that estimate subthreshold doses, such as ADI, RfD, and RfC. The scientific community has identified certain limits on some of these approaches: these models cannot make fuller use of available toxicity data in order to estimate possible health risks at doses higher than the RfD, for example, because they generally focus only on the no observed adverse effect level (NOAEL) of the critical effect. As a result, several quantitative procedures have been developed by EPA scientists and others, two of which are described in this paper. These procedures do not obviate the threshold concept, but rather make fuller use of the available toxicity data in estimating low adverse effect levels. In this capacity, these models might be useful to estimate the potential health risk for chemicals that cause cancer by overcoming homeostatic control on biological processes that leads to irreversible events in the multiple process which leads to tumor formation (see, for example, Hill et al., 1989). In addition, these methods also offer the flexibility to estimate the noncancer health risk for chemicals that may not exhibit a threshold. In both capacities, the dichotomy in the quantitative procedures for cancer and noncancer endpoints lessens.

HAZARD IDENTIFICATION

Hazard identification is a necessary first step in the risk assessment of a chemical. Hazard identification involves an evaluation of (1) the appropriateness, nature, quality, and relevance of scientific data on the specific chemical; (2) the characteristics and relevance of the experimental routes of exposure; and (3) the nature and significance to human health of the observed effects. The Agency has developed guidelines that explain the process of hazard identification for developmental (U.S. EPA, 1986, 1991) and reproductive (U.S. EPA, 1988a, b) health effects.

Much of the Agency's hazard identification process for noncancer toxicity depends in part on professional judgment as to whether or not an effect or collection of effects observed at any given dose of a chemical constitutes an adverse response. Such judgment may not be easily rendered, and requires experts trained in the area.

In addition, a chemical often elicits more than one toxic effect, even in a single species, or in tests of the same or different duration or dose. After assessing the quality of each study, identifying the biological and statistical significance of observed effects, and distinguishing between reversible and irreversible endpoints, the Agency often identifies the critical effects as another part of its hazard identification. The critical effects are the first adverse effects or their known precursors (such as mottling of teeth by fluoride as a precursor to pitting and tooth loss) that occur as dose rate increases.

Current dose-response methods described in this text and elsewhere often use the distinction of adverse/nonadverse effects and the choice of critical effects as a basis for the dose-response assessment. The judgment of whether an effect is adverse or critical may change among toxicity studies of different durations, may be influenced by toxicity in other organs or pharmacokinetics, and may differ depending on the availability of data or the shape of the dose-response curve. For example, increased liver weight due to a proliferation of smooth endoplasmic reticulum (SER) in response to an oral administration of a chemical, might be judged as *not* adverse if the parent chemical is the toxic moiety and such an increase in SER is likely to quicken its metabolism. The same increase in SER, however, might be judged as an adverse effect if a metabolite is the toxic moiety.

DOSE-RESPONSE ASSESSMENT

Empirical observation reveals that as the dosage of a chemical is increased, the toxic response generally increases. This increase occurs in both severity of the response (e.g., with new and more serious effects being observed) and intensity of the response (i.e., the magnification of an effect of given severity), and in the percent of the population affected. Such dose-response relationships are well founded in the theory and practice of toxicology and pharmacology.

Dose-response assessment follows hazard identification in the risk assessment process as defined by the NAS (1983). Dose-response assessment involves the quantitative evaluation of toxicity data to determine the likely incidence of the associated effects in humans. The information available for dose-response assessment ranges from well-conducted and controlled studies on human exposures, epidemiology studies with large numbers of subjects and well-characterized exposures, and supportive studies in several animal species, to a lack of human and animal toxicity data with only structure-activity relationships to guide the evaluation.

In any case, the Agency considers all pertinent studies in this process. However, only data of sufficient quality are used in the dose-response assessment of a chemical. Because we often must model animal data, the models themselves may not be good predictors of *human* risk. Assumptions can be made *a priori* or after modeling to enable the extrapolation to human risk from animal data. This aspect of dose-response modeling, however, will be problematic for the foreseeable future.

THE CHRONIC REFERENCE DOSE (RfD), REFERENCE CONCENTRATION (RfC), AND DEVELOPMENTAL TOXICITY RfD

Given at least a moderate amount of toxicity data, one risk assessment goal is to determine a level of daily exposure that is likely to be without an appreciable risk of deleterious effects during a lifetime. The Agency's oral RfD and inhalation RfC approaches strive to include scientific considerations in their determination. The history and rationale for the change in terminology and practice from ADI to RfD are described in detail in documentation supporting the Agency's Integrated Risk Information System (IRIS) (U.S. EPA 1990b; Barnes and Dourson, 1988).

The Agency defines the oral RfD as an estimate (with uncertainty spanning perhaps an order of magnitude) of a daily exposure to the human population (including sensitive subgroups) that is likely to be without an appreciable risk of deleterious effects during a lifetime (Barnes and Dourson, 1988). The oral RfD is determined by use of the following equation:

$$RfD = NOAEL \text{ or } LOAEL/(UF \times MF)$$

where

NOAEL = No observed adverse effect level. An exposure level at which there are no statistically or biologically significant increases in the frequency or severity of adverse effects between the exposed population and its appropriate control; *some effects may be produced at this level, but they are not considered as adverse, nor precursors to specific adverse effects.* In an experiment with several NOAELs, the regulatory focus is primarily on the NOAEL seen at the highest dose. This leads to the common usage of the term NOAEL to mean the highest exposure without adverse effect.

LOAEL = Lowest observed adverse effect level. The lowest exposure level at which there are statistically or biologically significant increases in frequency or severity of adverse effects between the exposed population and its appropriate control group.

UF = Uncertainty factor. One of several, generally tenfold, factors used in operationally deriving the RfD from experimental data.

MF = Modifying factor. An uncertainty factor to account for scientific uncertainties not covered with the traditional factors. The value of the MF is greater than zero and less than or equal to ten; the default value for the MF is one.

The Agency is also using this model for inhalation exposures and similarly defines an inhalation RfC. Interim methods for development of inhalation reference concentrations (U.S. EPA, 1990a; Jarabek et al., 1989) require the conversion of experimental exposure NOAEL to human equivalent concentrations (e.g., to a NOAEL [HEC]) before the critical study and species are identified. The conversion is specific both to the type of inhaled agent (particle or gas) and to the observed effect (respiratory or systemic) and adjusts for the dosimetric differences between various experimental species and humans. Once the NOAEL(HEC) is identified, the same equation is used to estimate the inhalation RfC with the application of similar, although not identical, uncertainty factors.

A reference dose for developmental toxicity (RfD_{DT}) has also been proposed (U.S. EPA, 1991). The RfD_{DT} is based upon NOAEL from short durations of exposure as are typically used in developmental toxicity studies. The term RfD_{DT} is used to distinguish from the oral RfD and inhalation RfC which refer to chronic exposure situations. Uncertainty factors for developmental toxicity generally include a tenfold factor for interspecies variation and a tenfold factor for intraspecies variation; in general an uncertainty factor is not applied to account for duration of exposure. In some cases, additional factors may be applied due to a variety of uncertainties that exist in the data base. For example, the standard study design for a developmental toxicity study calls for a low dose that demonstrates a NOAEL, but there may be circumstances where a risk assessment must be based on the results of a study in which a NOAEL for developmental toxicity was not identified. Rather, the lowest dose administered caused significant effect(s) and was identified as the LOAEL. In circumstances where only a LOAEL is available, questions relative to the sensitivity of endpoints reported, adequacy of dose levels tested, or confidence in the LOAEL reported may require the use of an additional uncertainty factor of 10. The total uncertainty factor selected is then divided into the NOAEL or LOAEL for the most sensitive endpoint from the most appropriate and/or sensitive mammalian species to determine the RfD_{DT}.

The RfD, RfC, and RfD_{DT} are useful as reference points for gauging the potential effects of other doses. Doses at the RfD or less are not likely to be associated with any health risks, and are therefore assumed likely to be of little regulatory concern. In contrast, as the amount and frequency of exposures exceeding the RfD increase, the probability that adverse effects may be observed in a human population also increases. However, the conclusion that all doses below the RfD are acceptable and that all doses in excess of the RfD are unacceptable cannot be categorically stated because these models cannot effectively predict the likelihood of particular effects above the RfD, RfC, or RfD_{DT}. This is because the assumption — that the effect observed in the experimental animal species is relevant to human — may not be correct. Moreover, the precision of these estimates depends in part on the overall magnitude of the composite uncertainty and modifying factors used in their calculation. The precision at best is probably one significant figure and more generally an order of magnitude. As the magnitude of the composite uncertainty factor increases, these estimates become even less precise.

Another risk assessment goal is to determine or estimate the likely human response to various exposure levels above the RfD/RfC of a particular contaminant. In most cases a dose-response model is appropriate if sufficient data exist. In the context of risk assessment, dose-response models for non-cancer endpoints are just now starting to be used. This paper highlights two new procedures and gives examples: benchmark dose and categorical regression.

The Benchmark Dose

Several limitations in the use of the RfD model have been described (Gaylor, 1983; Crump, 1984; Dourson et al., 1985; Dourson, 1986; Kimmel and Gaylor, 1988; Kimmel, 1990; Brown and Erdreich, 1989); for example, use of the NOAEL focuses only on the dose that is the NOAEL and does not incorporate information on the slope of the dose-response curve at higher doses where effects are observed, or the variability in the data. Since data variability is not taken into account, the NOAEL from a study with few animals will likely be higher than the NOAEL from a similar study, but with more animals in the same species. Additionally, the NOAEL is usually one of the experimental doses, and the number and spacing of doses in a study can influence the dose that is chosen for the NOAEL. Since the NOAEL is defined as a dose that does not produce an observable change in adverse responses from control levels and is dependent on the power of the study, theoretically, the risk associated with it may fall anywhere between zero and an incidence just below that detectable from control levels (usually in the range of 7 to 10% for quantal data). Crump (1984) and Gaylor (1989) have estimated the 95% upper confidence limit on developmental risk at the NOAEL for several data sets to be 2 to 6%.

The benchmark dose is a model-derived estimate of the lower confidence limit on the effective dose that produces a certain increase in incidence above control levels, such as 1, 5, or 10%. Most toxicity studies are designed to detect changes from control on the order of 10%. Some studies are so well designed they can detect yet smaller derivations from control, on the order of 5 or even 1%. Thus, in theory the use of a benchmark dose associated with a 10, 5, or 1% increased incidence over controls is congruent with the expected toxicity data. Because the application of the model is to derive an estimate of dose for a given incidence that is likely to fall within the experimental dose range and does not require extrapolation to estimates far below the experimental dose range, the uncertainty in the estimates is lessened.

The benchmark dose is derived by modeling the data in the observed range, calculating the upper confidence limit on the dose-response curve, and selecting the point on the upper confidence curve corresponding to a 10% increase in incidence of an effect, for example. Using this approach, a benchmark dose is calculated for each response that has adequate data. In some cases, the data may be adequate to also estimate benchmark doses at lower incidences, incidence levels which may be closer to a true no effect dose. As for the choice of the appropriate model to use in deriving a benchmark dose, various mathematical approaches have been proposed for modeling toxicity data (e.g., Crump, 1984; Kimmel and Gaylor, 1988; Rai and Van Ryzin, 1985; Faustman et al., 1989). Such models may be used to calculate the benchmark dose, and choice of the model may not be critical since estimation is within the observed dose range. Thus, any model which fits the empirical data well is likely to provide a similar estimate of the benchmark dose, although if there is some biological reason to incorporate particular factors in the model (e.g., intralitter correlation for developmental toxicity data), these should be included to account as much as possible for variability in the data. The Agency is currently supporting studies to evaluate the application of several models to data sets for calculating the benchmark dose.

To illustrate and compare the benchmark dose approach with the standard RfD/RfC method, benchmark doses were estimated for five chemicals listed on EPA's IRIS (U.S. EPA, 1990b) using a linearized multistage model. These benchmark doses were compared to the NOAEL and LOAEL of the critical effect on IRIS, as shown in Table 1. For each chemical, the oral RfD on IRIS was developed from a chronic animal study using an uncertainty factor of 100, and benchmark doses were calculated for all effects that were characterized by adequate dose responses in the critical study and other studies. Benchmark doses in this evaluation were considered as the dose associated with the 95% upper confidence limit on the response at 10%. Other values are possible. The choice of 10% here is used only as an example.

Ratios of the benchmark dose (95% upper confidence limit on the response at 10%) to the NOAEL for alachlor, hexachlorobenzene, and paraquat are nearly all within an order of magnitude of the NOAEL — where a ratio of 1 indicates identical values and an order of magnitude range is defined on a log 10 basis (i.e., 3 to 0.3). Ratios of the benchmark dose to the NOAEL for pentachlorophenol all fall within two orders of magnitude of the NOAEL (i.e., between 30 and 0.03) with many values falling within one order of magnitude. Ratios of the benchmark dose to the NOAEL for dichlorvos are uniformly two or three orders of magnitude higher than the ratio of 1 (i.e., 30 to 300) with one value yet higher. The benchmark doses estimated for dichlorvos are based on a study not used to estimate the RfD because the critical study for dichlorvos did not have sufficient quantitative data in order to estimate a benchmark dose. Thus, the benchmark dose to NOAEL ratios for dichlorvos may be misleading.

Ratios of the benchmark dose to the LOAEL were also calculated. Ratios of the benchmark doses to the LOAEL for alachlor and hexachlorobenzene are all within an order of magnitude of the LOAEL. Ratios of the benchmark dose to the LOAEL for paraquat and pentachlorophenol nearly all fall within two orders of magnitude of the NOAEL with many values falling within one order of magnitude. Ratios of the benchmark dose to the NOAEL for dichlorvos are uniformly one to two orders of magnitude higher than the ratio of 1 with one value yet higher.

Categorical Regression

The evaluation of toxicity data by categorical regression is a rather new application of an established statistical method. As described more extensively in Hertzberg (1989, 1991), "The underlying assumption for regression on ordered categories is that the response variable is distributed across the response categories according to a multinomial distribution, with different distributional parameters for each dose (McCullagh and Nelder, 1983)." For risk assessment, the response categories are progressive toxic effects, and the explanatory variables are usually dose (or exposure level) and duration of exposure. The probabilistic output of such a model is to estimate the risk of an effect worse than a given category, given a particular dose and duration. Several publications describe results with this model (Guth et al., 1991; Hertzberg and Wymer, 1991; Knauf and Hertzberg, 1990). In this example, the logistic model is used to estimate the probabilities. Other models could be used as well.

In this method toxicological responses are translated into four ordered categories of progressive effects: no effects, nonadverse effects, mild-to-moderate adverse effects, and severe or lethal effects. This set of categories resembles the dose categories used in setting the RfC (Jarabek et al., 1989) or RfD (Barnes and Dourson, 1988), namely, the no observed effect level (NOEL), NOAEL, LOAEL, and frank effect level (FEL), respectively. However, since all of the data are used in the regression, there is no need to specify a LOAEL, i.e., the lowest dose showing "mild-to-moderate" adverse effects. Thus, the more general term adverse effect level (AEL) is introduced.

To illustrate categorical regression, human toxicity data for arsenic (Tseng et al., 1968; Tseng, 1977) were summarized into categories as above (Table 2). These categories were regressed on the logarithms of exposure and duration; both parameters were statistically significant. The mathematical model used in this example is nonthreshold, but the extrapolation has been truncated at the oral RfD for arsenic of 3×10^{-4} mg/kg/d, since this value is considered by many to be a subthreshold dose for keratosis, the critical effect as defined by EPA (1990b).

Some difficulty exists with the interpretation of the Tseng (1977) and Tseng et al. (1968) toxicity data. For example, Tseng et al. (1968) did not show all necessary data for categorical regression; thus, some data have been estimated. Likewise, these authors maintained that blackfoot disease was attributed to arsenic exposure, but a recent publication disputes this (Lu, 1990). However, this data set is only used to illustrate the concept of categorical regression.

Table 1
Comparison of Estimated Benchmark Doses with Current IRIS No Observed Adverse Effect Level (NOAEL)

Chemical (CAS No.)	IRIS NOAEL and LOAEL[a] (mg/kg/d) and effect(s)	Study, species, sex and modeled effect[b]	Benchmark dose[c] (mg/kg/d)	Ratio of benchmark dose/NOAEL	Ratio of benchmark dose/LOAEL
Alachlor (15972-60-8)	1.0 and 3.0; hemosiderosis, hemolytic anemia (Monsanto Company, 1984)	Monsanto Co., 1984; D; M; kidney-hemosiderosis	0.86	0.9	0.3
		Monsanto Co., 1984; D; M; liver-hemosiderosis	1.9	2	0.6
		Monsanto Co., 1984; D; M; spleen-hemosiderosis	1.1	1	0.3
Dichlorvos (62-73-7)	0.08 and 0.8; increased liver weight and enlarged liver cells (Shell Chemical Co., 1967)	NCI, 1977; R; M; bile duct hyperplasia	2.2	30	3
		NCI, 1977; R; F; bile duct hyperplasia	2.3	30	3
		NCI, 1977; R; M; prostrate supportive inflammation	5.8	70	7
		NCI, 1977; R; L; liver-fatty metamorphosis	5.4	70	7
		NCI, 1977; R; F; bile duct inflammation	8.9	100	10
		NCI, 1977; R; F; pancreas-fibrosis	11	100	10
		NCI, 1977; R; M; pancreas-acinal atrophy	8.4	100	10
		NCI, 1977; R; F; pancreas-acinal atrophy	4.5	60	6
		NCI, 1977; M; M; endometrial cystic hyperplasia	11	100	10
		NCI, 1977; M; M; kidney-chronic inflammation	12	200	20
		NCI, 1977; M; F; kidney-chronic inflammation	20	300	30

Chemical	Note	Reference; effect			
Hexachlorobenzene (118-74-1)		NCI, 1977; M; F; liver-chronic focal inflammation	49	600	60
		NCI, 1977; M; F; endometrial cystic hyperplasia	7.1	90	90
	0.08 and 0.29; liver effects (Arnold et al., 1985)	Arnold et al., 1985; R; M; liver-centrilobular basophilic chromogenesis	0.11	1	0.4
		Arnold et al., 1985; R; F; liver-centrilobular basophilic chromogenesis	0.08	1	0.3
		Arnold et al., 1985; R; M; kidney-chronic nephrosis	0.16	2	0.6
Paraquat (1910-42-5)	0.45 and 0.93; chronic pneumonitis (Chevron Chemical Company, 1983)	Chevron Chem. Co., 1983; D; M; lung-chronic pneumonitis	0.16	0.4	0.2
		Chevron Chem. Co., D; F; lung-chronic pneumonitis	0.36	0.8	0.4
		Chevron Chem. Co., D; M; lung-hyperpnea	0.37	0.8	0.4
		Chevron Chem. Co., 1983; D; F; lung-hyperpnea	0.14	0.3	0.2
		Chevron Chem. Co., 1983; D; F; lung-increased vesicular sound	0.11	0.2	0.1
Pentachlorophenol (87-86-5)	3 and 10; liver and kidney pathology (Schwetz et al., 1978)	Schwetz et al., 1978; R; M; liver-brown pigment, etc.	28	9	3
		Schwetz et al., 1978; R; F; liver-brown pigment, etc.	3.0	1	0.3
		Schwetz et al., 1978; R; F; kidney-brown pigment, etc.	3.7	1	0.4
		NTP, 1989; M; M; liver-clear cell focus	11	4	1
		NTP, 1989; M; F; liver-clear cell focus	14	5	1
		NTP, 1989; M; F; liver-basophilic focus	23	8	2

Table 1 (continued)
Comparison of Estimated Benchmark Doses with Current IRIS No Observed Adverse Effect Level (NOAEL)

Chemical (CAS No.)	IRIS NOAEL and LOAEL[a] (mg/kg/d) and effect(s)	Study, species, sex and modeled effect[b]	Benchmark dose[c] (mg/kg/d)	Ratio of benchmark dose/NOAEL	Ratio of benchmark dose/LOAEL
		NTP, 1989; M; M; liver-basophilic focus	24	8	2
		NTP, 1989; M; M; liver-hematopoietic cell proliferation	2.5	0.8	0.3
		NTP, 1989; M; M; liver-chronic active diffuse inflammation	0.55	0.2	0.06
		NTP, 1989; M; F; liver-chronic active diffuse inflammation	0.99	0.3	0.1
		NTP, 1989; M; M; liver-multifocal pigmentation	0.46	0.2	0.05
		NTP, 1989; M; F; liver-multifocal pigmentation	0.78	0.3	0.08
		NTP, 1989; M; F; liver-hepatocytomegaly, diffuse	0.22	0.07	0.02
		NTP, 1989; M; M; liver-bile duct, multifocal hyperplasia	1.6	0.5	0.2
		NTP, 1989; M; F; liver-bile duct, multifocal hyperplasia	26	9	3
		NTP, 1989; M; M; liver-hepatocyte necrosis	0.63	0.2	0.6
		NTP, 1989; M; F; liver-hepatocyte necrosis	0.60	0.2	0.06
		NTP, 1989; M; M; adrenal gland-medulla, hyperplasia	6.6	2	0.7
		NTP, 1989; M; M; seminal vesicle dilation	1.0	0.3	0.1
		NTP, 1989; M; F; mammary gland-cystic hyperplasia	3.5	1	0.4

a   As on the Integrated Risk Information System (IRIS) as of 07/20/91 for the verified RfD. Note values since then may have changed.
b   Effects modeled are from the critical study as on IRIS, and/or other studies on IRIS. When information on both sexes (M = male, F = female) and different species (R = rat, M = mouse, D = dog) are available, separate benchmark doses have been estimated.
c   The dose associated with the 95% upper confidence limit on the response at 10%.

Table 2
As an Example of Categorical Regression, This Table Shows Arsenic Exposure and Resulting Toxicity from the Tseng et al. (1968) and Tseng (1977) Studies. Some Data Have Been Estimated. See Text for Discussion

| Age (years) | Number of people | Dose[a] (μg/kg/d) | Effect and its severity and prevalence[b] per 1000 | | |
			Hyperpigmentation (NOAEL)	Keratosis (AEL)	Blackfoot disease (FEL)
20–39	1561	0.8	0	0	0
		13	90	40	4.5
	9499	⎰37	250	120	13
		⎱49	270	120	14
40–59	955	0.8	0	0	0
		13	140	80	11
	6104	⎰37	420	230	32
		⎱49	600	340	47
60+	278	0.8	0	0	0
		13	250	140	20
	2021	⎰37	390	220	32
		⎱49	600[c]	340[c]	61

[a] Estimations of dose are based on Abernathy et al. (1989). Assumptions include the consumption of 4.5 l of water per day, arsenic from sweet potatoes and rice (which do not significantly contribute to the estimated dose), and a body weight of 55 kg. Arithmetic averages of well arsenic concentrations are used as a starting point of these estimated doses.

[b] All prevalence values have been rounded to two digits. Neither Tseng et al. (1968) nor Tseng (1977) give dose-specific prevalence rates for hyperpigmentation or keratosis. Thus, the prevalence rates for hyperpigmentation and keratosis with dose have been estimated based first on the averages across dose for these endpoints at each age given by Tseng et al. (1968) (Figures 5 and 6). These averages were modified first by assuming that the rate of blackfoot disease by dose and age (given in Tseng, 1977, page 113) could be used to build dose-specific rates for hyperpigmentation and keratosis. The resulting values were modified again to avoid the double-counting inherent in the Tseng et al. (1968) study as shown in their Table 2. We are attempting to get the raw data from Tseng et al. (1968).

[c] In this categorical regression method the prevalence per category is exclusive. Thus, the prevalence rates per 1000 of hyperpigmentation, plus keratosis, plus blackfoot disease cannot exceed 1000 (rounded). These values were reduced from 750 and 430, respectively.

Definitive conclusions on the toxicity of arsenic at levels above the RfD should not be drawn from this example.

Figure 1 shows the observed proportion of AEL or FEL (e.g., keratosis and/or blackfoot disease) in each of the dose and age groups listed in Table 2. This proportion is given by both age in years and dose in micrograms of arsenic per kilogram of body weight per day. This proportion has not been adjusted by mathematical manipulation. In this example, an increasing and sometimes erratic trend in a higher proportion of adverse and frank effects is seen with dose and duration.

Figure 2 shows the estimated probability of keratosis after 70 years of exposure using data from Table 2. The model shows an increasing probability of adverse effects with dose at doses at excess of the verified RfD. In this

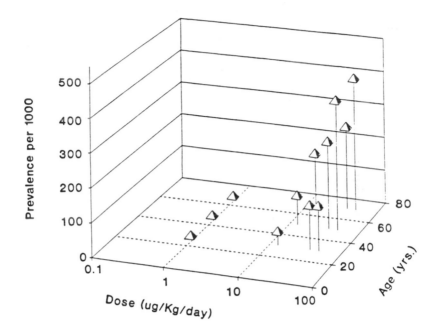

FIGURE 1.   The prevalence per 1000 people of keratosis and/or blackfoot disease with both dose (μg/kg/d) and age (years). Data are from Tseng et al. (1968) and Tseng (1977). This analysis is only used as an example of categorical regression. Some values have been estimated; see text for discussion and caveats.

example, at three- and tenfold of the RfD (that is at 0.9 and 3 μg/kg/d, respectively), the risk of adverse effects (i.e., keratosis) is estimated to be 7 and 28 per 1000, respectively. Both of these estimations lie between the NOAEL of 0.8 μg/kg/d and LOAEL of 13 μg/kg/d shown in Table 2.

DISCUSSION

EPA, FDA, WHO, and others have developed useful approaches for defining exposures that are likely to be without appreciable risks of deleterious effects during a lifetime (e.g., for EPA the oral RfD, inhalation RfC, and developmental RfD). These approaches involve a consensus process. Risk assessment information generated in EPA through this process is made available through an electronic data base (i.e., IRIS). However, unlike the traditional approach for carcinogens, estimates of incremental risk for the noncancer endpoints of concern (or disease states) are not generally possible with these approaches.

New methods for the analysis of noncancer data are being developed and tested on existing data. As shown in this paper, these methods have advantages

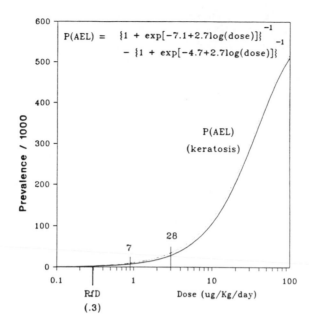

FIGURE 2. The prevalence per 1000 people of keratosis with both dose (μg/kg/d) at 70 years of age. Dashed line indicates upper 95% confidence limit. These values are estimated from data in Table 1 which are themselves estimated in part. This analysis is used only as an example of categorical regression. See text for caveats.

over existing approaches, but generally have requirements for larger and better data bases. Such requirements have not yet been worked out in detail, but in general would require incidence or continuous response data over several doses for the benchmark dose, and a sufficient number of dose groups in each of several categories of effect for the categorical regression approach. These models use more of the toxicity data, and thus, more information can be gleaned from their use — for example, risk above the oral RfD is possible. These methods might also be useful for evaluating carcinogenicity data where the mechanism of action appears to involve a threshold, e.g., homeostatic control.

In the example of benchmark dose in his paper, Table 1 is a comparison between the current NOAEL and LOAEL (as found on EPA's IRIS) and values obtained by the benchmark method. It is difficult to draw concrete conclusions from these comparisons. The current NOAEL and LOAEL are subject to a number of shortcomings as described earlier. As a result, the degree to which a benchmark dose does or does not agree is not a particularly good indicator of the performance of the new method. It could, in fact, be argued that the new method need not be totally consistent with the old one. If it were, then there would be no need for the new method. In addition, data sets were modeled for benchmark more on the basis of availability rather than from a close study of relevance to the particular critical effect as described on IRIS. While one might argue that this is a useful application of the model in that it accounts for adverse effects other than the critical effect, this has the result of increased variability in any resulting comparisons.

It is, however, useful to make the comparison in terms of orders of magnitude. For the data presented here, the estimation of benchmark dose reasonably predicts (i.e., within an order of magnitude) the NOAEL dose as found on IRIS in a majority of cases. From this limited analysis it also appears that ratios based on the LOAEL rather than the NOAEL lead to somewhat better predictions when the benchmark is restricted to a 10% response.

One limiting factor in this analysis is the small number of chemicals for which the toxicity data are dichotomous. IRIS was searched randomly for 40 chemicals and very few were found to have sufficient data on which to estimate benchmark doses. The fact that many toxicity data involve a continuous response variable (e.g., decrease in body weight) presents an obstacle that must be overcome before general application of the benchmark dose approach is feasible. Crump (1984) indicated that there has been little experience with using continuous response data with dose-response models, but that it would be possible to transform continuous data to dichotomous form by considering any animal with a value of the continuous response variable more extreme than some arbitrarily defined cut-off value to be a responder. His proposed alternative is based on a continuous linear regression model.

In the example of categorical regression in this paper, the RfD is assumed to be the threshold. However, the conclusion that all doses above the RfD are associated with risk or that all doses at or below these values are without risk cannot be unequivocally stated. As discussed in Barnes and Dourson (1988), as the frequency of exposures exceeding the RfD increases, the probability that adverse effects may be observed in the human population increases. Such an increase is not a certainty. It follows then, that the categorical model may overstate risk at doses near the RfD. For example, it will give estimates of risk at a dose just above the RfD, even though health scientists believe that an RfD is a subthreshold dose.

This model is quite useful when the risks above the RfD for multiple chemicals are compared for different regulatory actions because the slope of the dose-response curve is shown. For example, it can readily distinguish the chemical representing the more serious potential health risk among several, when the data for these chemicals are normalized on a scale, such as 10-fold, 100-fold, of the oral RfD. This model's usefulness for estimating a single chemical risk such as arsenic at exposures near the RfD is more limited, however, due in part to its assumption that the RfD is the threshold. Moreover, the data on arsenic that have been used to generate this analysis are themselves problematic. (Definitive conclusions regarding the likely health risk above the arsenic RfD should not be drawn from this work. Rather, this example is used to illustrate the concept of categorical regression.)

The most important principle in quantitative risk assessment consists of the knowledge and judgments of scientific assessors in the interpretation and integration of available information. Not all models described here apply at all times. In addition, statistical issues must be considered such as model significance, model fit as compared with the experimental data, and the testing of underlying mathematical assumptions for the model. For experts, these models should serve as an adjunct to organizing factors and scientific interpretations with which they are familiar. For others, these models should aid in the preparation or review of a dose-response assessment and of the issues to be discussed with experts. The available information when combined and used with one or more quantitative procedures generally represents a substantial, but not perfect data set. Thus, scientific judgment by experts is critical to a defensible quantitative risk evaluation.

EPA is in the process of developing guidance in the quantitative assessment of noncancer health effects. Several features of these guidelines, such as the oral RfD, inhalation RfC, or developmental RfD, have been published elsewhere. However, these guidelines also encourage the use and discussion of several of the newer approaches to this area of science.

ACKNOWLEDGMENTS

The authors acknowledge the comments of Linda Knauf in the preparation of this text and her guidance on several statistical issues. The authors are also thankful to Bette Zwayer for the typing of this manuscript.

BIBLIOGRAPHY

Abernathy, C. O., W. Marcus, C. Chen, H. Gibb, and P. White. 1989. Office of Drinking Water, Office of Research and Development. EPA memorandum to P. Cook, Office of Drinking Water and P. Preuss, Office of Regulatory Support and Scientific Management. Report on Arsenic (As) Work Group Meetings. February 23.

Anatra, M. 1985. A method for the estimation of incidence from continuous response data: proposed modification in health score evaluation. Prepared for American Management Systems, Inc. Federal Consulting Group, Arlington, VA.

Arnold, D. L., C. A. Moodie, S. M. Charbonneau et al. 1985. Long-term toxicity of hexachlorobenzene in the rat and the effect of dietary vitamin A. *Food Chem. Toxicol.* 23(9):779–793.

Barnes, D. G. and M. L. Dourson. 1988. Reference dose (RfD): description and use in health risk assessments. *Reg. Toxicol. Pharmacol.* 8:471–486.

Brown, K. G. and L. S. Erdreich. 1989. Statistical uncertainty in the no-observed-adverse-effect level. *Fund. Appl. Toxicol.* 13(2):235–244.

Chevron Chemical Co. 1983. MRID No. 00132474. Available from Environmental Protection Agency. Write to Freedom of Information, EPA, Washington, D.C. 20460.

Crump, K. S. 1984. A new method for determining allowable daily intakes. *Fund. Appl. Toxicol.* 4:854–871.

Dourson, M. L. 1986. New approaches in the derivation of acceptable daily intake (ADI). *Comments Toxicol.* 1(1):35–48.

Dourson, M. L., R. C. Hertzberg, R. Hartung, and K. Blackburn. 1985. Novel approaches for the estimation of acceptable daily intake. *Toxicol. Ind. Health.* 1(4):23–41.

Faustman, E. M., D. G. Wellington, W. P. Smith, and C. A. Kimmel. 1989. Characterization of a developmental toxicity dose-response model. *Environ. Health Perspect.* 79:229–241.

Gaylor, D. W. 1983. The use of safety factors for controlling risk. *J. Toxicol. Environ. Heath.* 11:329–336.

Gaylor, D. W. 1989. Quantitative risk analysis for quantal reproductive and developmental effects. *Environ. Health Perspect.* 79:243–246.

Guth, D. J., A. M. Jarabek, L. Symer, and R. C. Hertzberg. 1991. Evaluation of risk assessment methods for short-term inhalation exposure. Presented and published at the Annual Meeting of the Air & Waste Management Association, #91.173.2. June 1991, Vancouver, B.C.

Hertzberg, R. C. 1989. Fitting a model to categorical response data with application to species extrapolation of toxicity. *Health Phys.* 57:405–409.

Hertzberg, R. C. 1991. Quantitative extrapolation of toxicologic findings. in *Statistical in Toxicology,* D. Krewski and C. Franklin, Eds. Gordon and Breach, New York. 629–652.

Hertzberg, R. C. and M. E. Miller. 1985. A statistical model for species extrapolation using categorical response data. *Toxicol. Ind. Health.* 1(4):43–63.

Hertzberg, R. C. and L. Wymer. 1991. Modeling the severity of toxic effects. Presented and published at the Annual Meeting of the Air & Waste Management Association, #91.173.4. June 1991. Vancouver, B.C.

Hill, R. N., L. S. Erdreich, O. E. Paynter et al. 1989. Thyroid follicular cell carcinogenesis. *Fund. Appl. Toxicol.* 12:629–697.

Jarabek, A. M., M. G. Menach, J. H. Overton, M. L. Dourson, and F. J. Miller. 1989. Inhalation reference dose (RfD/i?): an application of interspecies dosimetry modeling for risk assessment of insoluble particles. *Health Phys.* 57:177–183.

Kimmel, C. A. 1990. Quantitative approaches to human risk assessment for noncancer health effects. *Neurotoxicology.* 11:189–198.

Kimmel, C. A. and D. W. Gaylor. 1988. Issues in qualitative and quantitative risk analysis for developmental toxicity. *Risk Anal.* 8(1):15–20.

Knauf, L. and R. C. Hertzberg. 1990. Statistical methods for estimating risk for exposure above the reference dose. EPA/600/8-90/065. NTIS/PB-90261504XSP. 104 p.

McCullagh, P. and J. Nelder. 1983. *Generalized Linear Models.* Chapman and Hill, New York.

Monsanto Co. 1984. MRID No. 00148923. Available from Environmental Protection Agency. Write to Freedom of Information, EPA, Washington, D.C. 20460.

NAS (National Academy of Sciences). 1983. *Risk Assessment in the Federal Government: Managing the Process.* National Academy Press, Washington, D.C.

NCI (National Cancer Institute). 1977. Bioassay of dichlorvos for possible carcinogenicity. NCI Tech. Rep. Ser. 10.

NTP (National Toxicology Program). 1989. Technical report on the toxicology and carcinogenesis studies of pentachlorophenol in B6C3F1 mice (feed studies). NTP Tech. Rep. No. 349. NIH Publ. No. 89-2804.

Rai, K. and J. Van Ryzin. 1985. A dose response model for teratological experiments involving quantal responses. *Biometrics.* 41:1–10.

Schwetz, B. A., J. F. Quast, P. A. Keeler et al. 1978. Results of 2-year toxicity and reproductive studies on pentachlorophenol in rats. in *Pentachlorophenol: Chemistry, Pharmacology, and Environmental Toxicology.* K. R. Rao, Ed. Plenum Press, New York. p. 301.

SRC (Syracuse Research Corporation). 1989. RfDs from dose response models. Contract No. 68-C8-0004. Prepared for the Environmental Criteria and Assessment Office, Cincinnati, OH. Project Officer: Carol Haynes. September 13.

Tseng, W. P. 1977. Effects and dose-response relationships of skin cancer and blackfoot disease with arsenic. *Environ. Health Perspect.* 19:109–119.

Tseng, W. P., H. M. Chu, S. W. How, J. M. Fong, C. S. Lin, and S. Yeh. 1968. Prevalence of skin cancer in an endemic area of chronic arsenicism in Taiwan. *J. Natl. Cancer Inst.* 40:453–463.

U.S. EPA. 1986. Guidelines for the health assessment of suspect developmental toxicants. *Fed. Regist.* 51:34028–34040. September 24.

U.S. EPA. 1988a. Proposed guidelines for assessing male reproductive risk and request for comments. *Fed. Regist.* 53:24850–24869. June 30.

U.S. EPA. 1988b. Proposed guidelines for assessing female reproductive risk and request for comments; notice. *Fed. Regist.* 53:24834–24847. June 30.

U.S. EPA. 1990a. Interim methods for development of inhalation reference doses. Office of Health and Environmental Assessment, Washington, D.C. EPA/600/8-90/066A. August.

U.S. EPA 1990b. The Integrated Risk Information System (IRIS). Online. Office of Health and Environmental Assessment, Environmental Criteria and Assessment Office, Cincinnati, OH.

U.S. EPA. 1991. Guidelines for the developmental toxicity risk assessment; final. *Fed. Regist.* 56:63798–63826. December 5.

CHAPTER 8

Gaps in Knowledge in Assessing the Risk of Cancer

Arthur Robert Gregory

ABSTRACT

Considerable scientific evidence has accumulated in the area of risk assessment. The use of physiologically based pharmacokinetic models and biologically based dose-response models gives the appearance that quite precise estimates of risk can be made. In cancer at least, such precise estimates are misleading to say the least.

The most gigantic gap in knowledge in cancer risk analysis today is cross-species extrapolation. It is indeed a pity that the most elaborate and largest cancer testing facility in the world continues to operate without the benefit of using known human carcinogen positive controls. Without such controls to gauge responses the risk accessor cannot possibly hope to quantitate cancer risk in man from the cancer risk determined in the model.

INTRODUCTION

There is increasing reliance on quantitative risk assessment when decisions in public health affairs are to be made. This is occurring in both regulatory bodies and industry. The advantages for this approach have been reviewed (NAS, 1983; U.S. DHHS, 1986; Clayson et al., 1985; and Cothern et al., 1988) and are now generally accepted (U.S. EPA Guidelines, 1986, 1988).

Nevertheless, the utility of risk assessment in risk management primarily resides in the reliability and applicability of the data base. Wherever data gaps occur, assumptions must be made before the risk assessment process can be completed. When these assumptions are unrealistic or eventually prove to be incorrect, the risk assessment supports an interpretation diametrically opposed to reality (Breslow et al., 1986; Weintrub et al., 1989).

Ideally, one would like to have only epidemiological data for the performance of risk assessments. Man is his own best experimental model. No cross-species extrapolation would be required. Unfortunately, epidemiological data are very expensive, often lack exact exposure measurements, and usually lack sufficient power to establish cause and effect.

Thus, on pragmatic as well as ethical grounds, carcinogenic potency must primarily be determined in experimental animals, preferably, short-lived animals. It is a fact of life that they are the best we have to work with. Nevertheless, unless animal data have realistic relevance to the human situation, they are of little value for establishing hazard for man (Gregory, 1988).

A major objective of the 1991 ACS meeting on Quantitative Risk Assessment is "to determine which information is the most important in terms of relative value in estimating relative risk". In the following paper I will demonstrate that the most important information that is missing is data on known human carcinogens in the model system used by the National Toxicology Program (NTP). If one does not know the relative response (sensitivity) from known human carcinogens in the model, one cannot begin to extrapolate an identical effect seen in that model back to man.

In the paper which follows, I discuss the relative importance of the various types of uncertainties encountered in risk assessment as it is practiced in 1992. I demonstrate that the largest gap in knowledge is in the area of species extrapolation. Finally, I present an initial obvious solution to the problem that has been ignored too long.

PHYSIOLOGICALLY BASED PHARMACOKINETICS (PB-PK) MODELS

The trend over the last few years has been to base quantitative risk assessments on the "delivered dose". This is the dose of proximate toxicant, whether the unchanged xenobiotic or its metabolite, or at the tissue site of toxic action, rather than the applied dose or ambient concentration. The determination of this delivered dose is in essence an extension of exposure assessment, in that the direct exposure of the actual target tissue is examined free of various physiological fate and transport processes by which the body absorbs, distributes, transforms, and modifies compounds taken in from its environment. Uncertainty can be reduced by further investigation into the effects of different conditions of exposure on the distribution pattern of the delivered dose using PB-PK models. For example, examination of delivered dose could prove very useful in comparing the toxic results of exposures by different routes of administration. In this way, extraneous factors such as different degrees or rates of absorption can be accounted for, resulting in more meaningful comparisons. The ability to estimate target-site doses also is necessary for further information on the mechanistic biological modeling of toxicity.

In risk assessment as often currently practiced, measurements of applied dose or exposure concentration are used merely as surrogates of the delivered dose since this frequently is unknown. The equivalencies among different conditions of exposure are mostly assumed and usually have little empirical support. This can represent a source of significant uncertainty (Conolly et al., 1988).

Among the more critical uncertainties associated with extrapolation from experimental to actual conditions are assumptions about:

- Route-to-route extrapolation, i.e., comparability of exposure by different routes of administration (by accounting for differences in absorption, bioavailability, and first-pass metabolism);
- Chronic-to-acute extrapolation, i.e., comparability of different regimes of exposure, such as the effect of repeated vs. single dosing on dose delivery; the equality of episodic, peak, and chronic exposures totalling the same cumulative dose remains to be examined in detail;
- High- to low-dose extrapolation, i.e., proportionality between external exposure level and the resulting delivered dose for high exposure studies, compared to lower levels typical of environmental exposure (by accounting for sources of nonproportionality such as saturation of metabolism, utilization of different pathways of biotransformation, and nonlinear binding); and
- Species-to-species extrapolation, i.e., scaling or translation of dose to determine, exposures yielding equivalent doses in different species, especially when extrapolating toxic effects in experimental animals to those expected in humans. Gregory (1988) has shown that in some cases the extrapolation cannot be made at all because of qualitative differences in species and strains.

One way to reduce the uncertainties related to scaling is to obtain data on doses at more biologically meaningful levels, i.e., delivered dose at the target issues. The examination of delivered dose still does not provide sufficient information for extrapolation in risk assessment, since the equivalency of effects across species is determined not only by relative dose delivery, but also by species differences in sensitivity to a given delivered dose (Moore et al., 1988). Similarly, the extrapolation of effects to low doses or from acute-to-chronic exposures depends not only on the delivered dose differences in these circumstances, but also on the relative toxicological effects of different levels and durations of tissue exposure to the proximate toxicant (OSTP, 19885; U.S. DHHS, 1986; Gaylor, 1989).

Even when there is the capability of establishing internal or delivered doses for particular tissue sites, mechanisms of action may take prominence in establishing level of risk. The delivered dose may not be the essential factor. The quantitation of DNA adducts or other carcinogen "markers" may not suffice (Moore et al., 1988). For different mechanisms of action, the oncogenic or other noxious response may be a function of the quantity of metabolite formed, the number of adducts or other covalent reactions produced with crucial cellular macromolecules, the extent of reversible binding to specific oncogeny receptors, or a requisite threshold toxicant concentration for a specific duration of time. The rate and fidelity of DNA repair must also be considered. These factors vary considerably among species, strains, sexes, previous histories of exposure, and physiological condition of the subjects (Oser, 1981; OSTP, 1985; Gregory, 1988). Although examination of delivered doses can remove a great deal of uncertainty from the various extrapolation processes in quantitative risk assessment, it should be considered a prerequisite and additional factors will also have to be considered. Nevertheless, it is clear that other biological factors cannot be addressed without first eliminating the confounding and obscuring effects of dose delivery and pharmacokinetics. Thus, further exploration in pharmacokinetics will be essential to performing more biologically rational risk assessments.

High- to low-dose extrapolation has been the source of major uncertainties. This is partially because of a paucity of pharmacokinetics and pharmacodynamic data. In quantitative risk assessment, extrapolation is often from the experimental chronic dose regimen used in an animal toxicological study to the expected human exposure. The doses must be compared not only on a total cumulative dose basis (the total mg/kg), but on a time scale as well. Both the dose rate of administration and the dose level can affect the pharmacokinetics of a compound and hence the amount delivered to the target site. High dose levels often include pathways that at lower dose levels do not contribute to metabolic conversions which are linked to the toxicity of the compound (Andersen et al., 1987).

Further research is also needed to verify certain of the assumptions used in route-to-route extrapolation. Information may be only available on the toxicological effects associated with a particular route of exposure. Assessors may be able to utilize, to some extent, such data for the exposure route of interest if models could be developed and verified. Very little work has been reported in this area and considerable effort will have to be expended if it is to be utilized in the future. A further discussion of the particular research needs in this area will be the subject of a subsequent paper.

BIOLOGICALLY BASED DOSE-RESPONSE (BB-DR) MODELS

In quantitative risk characterization both dose-response relationships and exposure estimates are required to calculate the incidence of a particular health effect at human exposure levels. Ideally, one would like to have human data available at the relevant exposure levels. But even when human data are available, confounding variables may make extrapolation of the results uncertain. In most cases, however, the data available are at higher exposures and based upon experiments in test species rather than obtained from human studies. As such, the risk assessor is required to select and apply an appropriate strategy (e.g., RfD or mathematical models) to perform a high- to low-dose extrapolation. One major uncertainty in quantitative risk assessment evolves from this often arbitrary selection process and a lack of testing for the bias that may guide selection. The final risk estimate may vary by orders of magnitude, depending on the approach (model) applied (Purchase, 1985).

The development and application of BB-DR models may substantially reduce the uncertainties in quantitative risk characterization. Under the BB-DR approach, the essential physiological elements and processes, as well as their interactions, are described. Utilization of such information may also assist in the selection of the most biologically plausible strategy relevant to the risk assessment process. Such models may assist in accounting for variation in any key element as it differs within and among species under varying exposure conditions. The integration of biologic/mechanistic relevance into the model process can also allow the risk assessor to examine the validity of some of the assumptions that are often applied in the risk assessment. The most noteworthy conclusion of a recent symposium on reducing uncertainty in risk assessment that was "the increased understanding of the underlying mechanisms . . . should be applied as fully as possible to the risk assessment process" (Kamrin, 1989). Thus, it is quite clear that risk assessors must learn to incorporate mechanistic data into dose-response models to more precisely predict human responses.

INTER/INTRASPECIES EXTRAPOLATION

A number of gaps exist regarding the factors responsible for differences in response within and across species. Work is desperately needed in this area to elucidate the critical physiologic and mechanistic factors that contribute to the health effects of concern in the risk assessment process. Such research is imperative if we are to be able to adjust for intra- and interspecies responsiveness in dose-response extrapolations. The extent to which effects observed in one species can be extrapolated to another is presently limited (Ames et al., 1987; Gold et al., 1989; Adamson and Sieber, 1983; OSTP, 1985; St. Hilaire, 1987; EPA Guidelines, 1986; Gaylor, 1986; Gregory, 1990). One of the key elements in attempting extrapolation is to determine whether effects in animals are analogous (i.e., superficially similar) or homologous (i.e., resulting from a common mechanism of action) to those in humans. Research emphasis should be placed on evaluating species similarities and differences in both the mechanism and the expression of a given outcome. For example, the species and strains used in the NTP bioassays have never been validated using known human carcinogens (Gregory, 1990). As such, these efforts may or may not confirm the existence of a homologous mechanism for inducing specific toxicities. The degree of homology in the expression of such disease (i.e., comparable outcome) could then lead to greater confidence in the risk characterization.

Theoretically, the use of pharmacokinetic models should lead to the determination of the effective dose at a given target site. However, given equivalent target doses, we are still left with questions regarding interspecies differences in sensitivity that need to be addressed independently. Recent research has revealed that interspecies extrapolation can be either very helpful or extremely misleading (Gregory, 1988; Reynolds et al., 1987; Spandidos and Anderson, 1989) since the oncogenes which suppress or enhance cancer are often species and/or strain specific (Spandidos and Anderson, 1989; Moore et al., 1988).

It is extremely important to note that while both low-dose extrapolation and cross-species extrapolation are the largest data gaps, only the latter is addressable experimentally in a relatively cost-effective manner.

There are relatively reliable quantitative data for seven human carcinogens. They are benzidine, benzene, amino biphenyl, arsenic, asbestos, bis chloromethyl ether, and vinyl chloride.

To fill a portion of the gap between specific rodent species risk and human risk assessments the NTP should drop the testing of seven of their more esoteric and exotic chemicals and instead get back to basics by testing at least these seven known human carcinogens. Only if this is done at one determine if the NTP program is relevant to human safety. At present, one simply does not know.

An increasing number of chemicals have been bioassayed by the NTP and have been found to have "Clear Evidence of Carcinogenicity, Some Evidence of Carcinogenicity, Equivocal Evidence of Carcinogenicity, or No Evidence of Carcinogenicity". A few cannot be considered valid for inclusion in any of the above categories, and are termed "Inadequate".

In the development of a new pharmaceutical, a good pharmacologist goes to great pains to utilize the particular test animal which most closely resembles man in physiological response. One does not use a worm or a rat to measure cardiac responses to a potential substitute for digitoxin, because the responses are quantitatively and qualitatively different. One does not use a rat to assay the physiologic responses to an aryl thiourea derivative, because these substances have unique edemagenic responses in the rat that are not present in man or higher mammals. Ben Oser was one of the first to call attention to the many unique differences in physiologic responses between man and rat. His publication, "Man Is Not a Big Rat", is a classic.

In some recent articles I have called attention to the futility of attempting to quantitatively estimate human risk from some of the specialized animal models used today in the field of oncology (Gregory, 1988). For example, cancer of the breast has been utilized as an endpoint of an assay in two very different strains of rats. In a highly sensitive strain (the Wistar-Furth rat) a single dose of dimethylbenzanthracene, acetyl aminofluorene, nitroso-methylurea, diethylstilbestrol, or radiation will all produce a 100% incidence of breast cancer in 170 to 180 d. In a different strain of rat (the Copenhagen) these same carcinogens do not produce any breast cancer under the same conditions, or when administered at the maximum tolerated dose over the lifetime of the rat. This site-specific resistance to breast cancer induction has been shown to be genetically determined, and is inherited as a dominant trait. Thus, while this strain of rat is very useful in attempting to elucidate oncogenic mechanisms, it is entirely useless in estimating oncogenic risk for humans. Since a risk would be estimated to be zero, no matter what substance was tested.

When NTP took over the National Cancer Institute bioassay program, some thought was given to the question of whether or not the best strains and species were being used. Dr. Rall convened a conference on alternative strains of mice.

No alternative strains or species could be decided upon, mainly because of lack of data. The final decision was to continue to use the Fischer rat and the B-6 hybrid mouse. The reason for this decision was mainly because of the accumulation of data on these two species over the years. The continuance was not because there was a good correlation between these strains and humans. In fact, the correlation could not be known because of the fact that known human carcinogens had not been tested in these particular rodents. There are at least 20 human carcinogens that have never been tested in the Fischer rat and the B-6 mouse, using the present protocols.

Every few months we see new rankings of the potencies of carcinogens (Allen et al., 1988; Gold et al., 1989). Christopher Portier comments on the species correlation presented by Allen et al. in the same issue. He points out the difference between correlation and predictiveness and examines one of the 55 cases presented by Allen. In this (the best) case, Portier describes how three compounds have near identical potencies in animals, but potencies varying from 17.9 to 0.04 in humans. This is a difference of over 447 times. Thus, trying to estimate human risk from animal risk, one could be in error by at least 44,700%.

To be really predictive, correlations must work both ways, no false positives, and no false negatives, and if the results are to be used in risk assessment in humans, the relative sensitivity must also be known. Of 26 probable human noncarcinogens reviewed by IARC (negative epidemiology), the Gold data reveal 25 are positive in at least one animal model. Only the substance methotrexate was negative in both animal model and man.

What good are the NTP bioassays if they do not predict safety for humans? Today, many journals will refuse to publish mutagenicity data if the investigator did not include a positive control in his study to verify that his system was performing correctly. But here we have a multibillion dollar program directed at giving us more data about more chemicals, but never having examined the animal model to determine if it gives us valid data in the first place. In some of the early carcinogenesis bioassays done under the auspices of the National Cancer Institute, a few antineoplastic agents and known animal carcinogens were used for quality control. NTP has not followed this procedure.

I propose a two-pronged attack on the problem. First, there should be a verification program to see if indeed the strains and species presently used by NTP are representative of human responses to chemicals. The first portion of this proposal will really cost nothing because known human carcinogens can be substituted for substances that even when bioassayed will still remain unknown as far as human response is concerned. Eventually, known human carcinogens and putative noncarcinogens will have to be tested. Of course, this will require a validation initiative never before attempted by any other institution in any country of the world. It will require effort, yes. But to continue the present course is to end up 20 years from now with a still larger list of chemicals that are of no use in risk assessment. Once the dose responses in the NTP rodents are known for these seven chemicals, they can be compared to the dose responses in man. Thus the risk assessor now has a translatable estimate of how similar compounds would be expected to act in man. Granted such comparisons would still be less than precise, but at present this gap in knowledge prevents any reliable estimate of the expected response from similar compounds.

Secondly, other short-lived species also should be examined to determine if other surrogates might better serve the final outcome. It is not enough to simply find out that a bioassay is nonpredictive if that turns out to be the case. We must have a bioassay that is truly predictive of what will happen in humans. Unfortunately, many regulatory agencies are already acting as if the NTP rodent assay is the *sine qua non* — the paradigm of human carcinogenicity, when the simple truth is that the system has never been verified. Unless we bridge this gap soon we will end up learning more and more about oncogenicity in rodents that is worth less and less in risk assessment for humans.

REFERENCES

Adamson, R. H. and Sieber, S. M. (1983). Chemical carcinogenesis studies in non-human primates, in *Organ and Species Specificity in Chemical Carcinogenesis: Basic Life Sciences,* R. Largenbach and S. Nesnow, Eds., Vol. 24, pp. 129–156, Plenum Press, New York.

Allen, B. C. et al. (1988). Correlation between carcinogenic potency of chemicals in animals and humans. *Risk Anal.* 8(4), 559–561.

Ames, B. M., Magraw, R., and Gold, L. (1987). Ranking possible carcinogenic hazards. *Science* 236, 271–280.

Andersen, M., Clewell, H., Garcias, M., Smith, F., and Reitz, R. (1987). Physiologically based pharmacokinetics and the risk assessment process for methylene chloride. *Toxicol. Appl. Pharmacol.* 87, 198–205.

Breslow, I., Brown, S., and Van Ryzin, J. (1986). Risk from exposure to asbestos (Letter). *Science* 234, 923.

Burns, L. A. (1985). Validation Methods for Chemical Exposure and Hazard Assessment Models. EPA/600/d-85/297, U.S. Environmental Protection Agency, Athens, GA.

Clayson, D. B., Krewski, D., Clewell, H. J., and Andersen, M. E. (1985). Biologically-structured models and computer simulation: application to chemical carcinogenesis. *Comments Toxicol.*, December.

Conolly, R. B., Reitz, R. H., Clewell, H. J., and Anderson, M. E. (1988). Biologically structured models and computer simulation: Application to chemical carcinogenesis. *Comments Toxicol.* (December).

Cothern, C. R., Mehlman, M. A., and Marcus, W. L., Eds. (1988). *Advances in Modern Environmental Toxicology*, Vol. XV. Risk Assessment and Risk Management of Industrial and Environmental Chemicals. Princeton Scientific Publishing, Princeton, NJ.

Gaylor, D. (1989). Preliminary estimates of the virtually safe dose for tumors obtained from the maximum tolerated dose. *Regul. Toxicol. Pharmacol.* 9, 101–108.

Gold, L. S., Bernstein, L., Magaw, R., and Slone, T. H. (1989). Interspecies extrapolation in carcinogenesis: prediction between rats and mice. *Environ. Health Perspect.* 81, 210–230.

Gregory, A. R. (1988). Species comparisons in evaluating carcinogenicity in humans. *Regul. Toxicol. Pharmacol.* 8, 160–190.

Gregory, A. R. (1990). Uncertainty in health risk assessments. *Regul. Toxicol. Pharmacol.* 11, 191–200.

Kamrin, M. A. (1989). Reducing uncertainty in risk assessment. *Regul. Toxicol. Pharmacol.* 10, 82–91.

Moore, C. J., Tricomi, W. A., and Gould, M. N. (1988). Comparisons of 7,12-dimethylbenz(a)anthracene metabolism and DNA binding in mammary epithelial cells from three rat strains with differing susceptibilities to mammary carcinogenesis. *Carcinogenesis* 9(11), 2099–2102.

National Academy of Sciences (NAS) (1983). Committee on the Institutional Means for Assessment of Risk to Public Health, Commission on Life Sciences, and National Research Council: Risk Assessment in the Federal Government: Managing the Process. National Academy Press, Washington, D.C.

Office of Science and Technology Policy (OSTP) (1985). Chemical carcinogens; a review of the science and its associated principles. *Fed. Regist.* 50, 10,371–10,442.

Oser, B. (1981). The rat as a model for human toxicological evaluation. *J. Toxicol. Environ. Health* 8, 521–542.

Portier, C. J. (1988). Species correlation of chemical carcinogens. *Risk Anal.* 8(4), 551–553.

Purchase, I. F. (1985). Carcinogenic risk assessment, a toxicologist view. in *Risk Quantitation and Regulatory Policy: Bambury Report 19* (D.C. Hoel, R. A. Merrill, and F. Perera, Eds.), pp. 175–186. Cold Spring Harbor Laboratory, Cold Spring Harbor, NY.

Reynolds, S. H., Stowers, S. J., Patterson, R. M., Maronpot, R. R., Aaronson, S. A., and Anderson, M. W. (1987). Activated oncogenes in B6C3F1 mouse liver tumors: implications for risk assessment. *Science* 237, 1309–1316.

St. Hilaire, C., Ed. (1987). *Review of Research Activities to Improve Risk Assessment for Carcinogens*. International Life Sciences Institute, Washington, D.C.

Spandidos, D. A. and Anderson, M. L. M. (1989). Oncogenes and oncosuppressor genes: their involvement in cancer. *J. Pathol.* 157, 1–10.

U.S. EPA Carcinogen Guidelines: Part II (Sept. 24, 1986). Environmental Protection Agency: guidelines for carcinogen risk assessment. *Fed. Regist.* 51(185), 33,992–34,054.

U.S. EPA Proposed Guidelines: Part IV (1988). Environmental Protection Agency: proposed guidelines for exposure-related measurements and request for comments: notice. *Fed. Regist.* 53(232), 48,830–48,850.

U.S. EPA, THERC (1989). Research needs in human exposure: a comprehensive 5-year assessment (1989–1993). Planning Document of the Total Human Exposure Research Council.

U.S. Department of Health and Human Services (U.S. DHHS) (1986). Task Force on Health Risk Assessment: *Determining Risks to Health: Federal Policy and Practice*. Auburn House Publishing Co., Dover, MA.

Wallace, I. A. (1987). The Total Exposure Assessment Methodology (TEAM) Study: Summary and Analysis, Vol. I. EPA/600/6-87/002a, U.S. Environmental Protection Agency, Office of Research and Development, Washington, D.C.

Weintrub, L. N., Taub, B. F., and Brown, D. R. (1989). Reassessment of formaldehyde exposures in homes insulated with urea-formaldehyde foam insulation. *Appl. Ind. Hyg.* 4(6), 147–152.

CHAPTER 9

Estimating Viral Disease Risk from Drinking Water

Charles P. Gerba and Joan B. Rose

INTRODUCTION

Water as a route of disease transmission has been well established for over a hundred years. The benefits of water treatment processes such as filtration and disinfection in the reduction of typhoid and enteric illness were shown by the dramatic reduction in the occurrence of these illnesses, when these practices were put into operation (Bull et al., 1990). However, waterborne illness continues to occur in the U.S. Outbreaks occur because of contamination of the drinking water with enteric pathogens. This may be due to a breakdown in treatment such as the inability of the treatment process to remove all of the pathogenic organisms present in the raw water, contamination after treatment, or no treatment of a contaminated supply (Craun, 1986).

Documented waterborne outbreaks usually occur when there has been an obvious and significant contamination of a water supply. However, the significance of exposure to low-level contamination is difficult to determine epidemiologically. This makes it difficult to estimate the impact on a community. Long-term exposure to such low-level contamination could have a significant impact on the health of individuals within the community. Risk assessment is an approach that allows such hazards to be defined in a more quantitative fashion. Risk assessment has been used for some time to evaluate risks associated from chemicals in our water supply (Hammond and Coppock, 1990), but has only recently been attempted for microorganisms (Haas, 1983; Gerba and Haas, 1988; Rose and Gerba, 1991a, b; Rose et al., 1991). This approach allows for a quantitation of risks and an assessment of cost/benefits of various control strategies. The object of this study was to review the factors that have to be considered in a viral risk assessment for drinking water, assess the existing data base, and estimate the risks from various concentrations of enteric viruses in drinking water.

0-87371-605-1/93/$0.00 + $.50
© 1993 by Lewis Publishers

Table 1
Human Enteric Viruses

Virus type	Illness
Enteroviruses	
Polio	Paralysis
Coxsackie A	Meningitis, fever, respiratory disease
Coxsackie B	Myocarditis, congenital heart disease, rash, fever, meningitis, pleurodynia, diabetes mellitus
Echo	Meningitis, encephalitis, rash, fever, gastroenteritis
Norwalk (probably a calicivirus)	Gastroenteritis
Astro	Gastroenteritis
Calici	Gastroenteritis
Snow Mountain agent (probably a calcivirus)	Gastroenteritis
Hepatitis A	Infectious hepatitis
Hepatitis E	Epidemic infectious hepatitis
Reo	Uncertain
Rota	Gastroenteritis
Adeno	Respiratory, eye infections, gastroenteritis

RISK ASSESSMENT

Risk assessment involves four basic steps: hazard identification, dose-response assessment, exposure assessment, and risk characterization (NRC, 1983). Enteric viruses have been known for some time to have a negative impact on human health, resulting in serious illness and sometimes death. Information on dose response is available for viruses from human feeding studies, so the probability of infection can be assessed from different levels of environmental exposure. The exposure of a population to viruses in the drinking water is dependent on the amount of contamination in the raw water supply and the amount of treatment it receives. Although the number of studies is limited, low-level contamination of potable waters with enteric viruses has been well documented (Rose and Gerba, 1986; Hurst, 1991). Finally, risk characterization can be accomplished using the information from the previous steps to develop a model to quantitatively assess the risks from exposure to viruses in drinking water via ingestion.

ENTERIC VIRAL ILLNESS

Currently there are over 120 different types of enteric viruses known. This list continues to grow as new types and strains of enteric viruses are discovered and as new methods and technology allow for their recognition. Table 1 lists the most common types of enteric viruses which infect humans. All of these agents are easily transmitted by the fecal-oral route. Exposure may occur from contaminated water, food, fomites, and direct contact with infected individuals. Enteroviruses represent the largest and best-characterized group of known human enteric viruses. Members of this group cause a wide variety of illnesses including paralysis, meningitis, myocarditis, and fever, which can be life threatening. However, this group is not a major cause of gastroenteritis. Hepatitis A and E are responsible for infectious hepatitis that may cause serious liver damage. Although hepatitis E has been shown to be responsible for large waterborne outbreaks in the developing world, no outbreaks have been documented in the U.S. (Gust and Purcell, 1987). Some types of adenovirus are associated only with gastroenteritis, while others may cause eye and respiratory infections. The other remaining enteric viruses cause gastroenteritis. The role of reovirus in human disease has never been clearly established. With the exception of reoviruses the host range of specific enteric viruses is restricted to humans and some primates. Lower animals are infected with viruses related to human rotaviruses, caliciviruses, and adenovirus. These viruses are antigenically distinct and are not believed to usually infect humans in nature. Human viruses may transitorily infect animals such as dogs and farm animals, but are not believed to cause illness (Clapper, 1970).

TRANSMISSION OF ENTERIC VIRAL ILLNESS BY DRINKING WATER

Documentation of waterborne disease outbreaks by microorganisms is difficult for a number of reasons. Investigation of possible outbreaks and reporting of such outbreaks are not required by any government agency in the U.S. and, until recent years, methods for detecting many of the agents in the water have not been generally available. Finally, the necessary epidemiological investigation is costly and results in a major commitment of resources at the local level. For these reasons, it is believed that the actual number of outbreaks documented each year represents a small number of those that actually occur.

Between 1971 and 1988, there were 564 outbreaks of waterborne disease and 138,247 cases of illness documented in the U.S. (Craun, 1986). Of the total number of outbreaks and cases of illness, almost 9% were shown to be associated with hepatitis A or viral gastroenteritis. However, in almost 50% (which classified as gastroenteritis) of the outbreaks no agent could be identified because of the lack of a field investigation or methods for identifying the agent. However, based on the nature and duration of the illness, many of these illnesses are believed to have a viral etiology (Kaplan et al., 1982).

Outbreaks of viral disease involving drinking water have been associated with echovirus, hepatitis A and E virus (Craun, 1986; Gust and Purcell, 1987), Norwalk virus (Kaplan et al., 1982), rotavirus (Craun, 1986), Snow Mountain agent (Madore et al., 1986), and astrovirus (Kurtz and Lee, 1987). In addition, outbreaks associated with recreational contact have been documented for

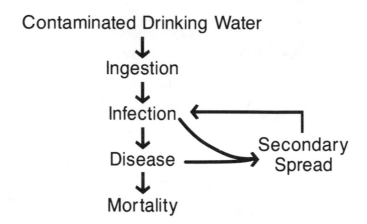

FIGURE 1.   Outcome of enteric viral exposure.

adenovirus, Coxsackie virus, and possibly poliovirus (Dufour, 1986). Although outbreaks of waterborne disease have not been clearly demonstrated for all of the enteric viruses, their presence in water represents a potential for infection in susceptible individuals.

DOSE RESPONSE

Important in any risk assessment is the degree of concentration of contaminant which affects health. In the case of enteric viruses, several outcomes are possible depending upon preexisting immunity, age, nutrition, ability to elicit an immune response, and nonspecific host factors. Not all individuals who become infected (i.e., replication or growth of the virus in the host) will develop clinical illness (Figure 1). The probability of developing clinical illness, at least for rotavirus, does not appear to be related to the dose an individual receives via ingestion (Ward et al., 1986). The likelihood of developing clinical illness will depend upon the type and strain of virus, host age, nonspecific host factors, and possibly preexisting immunity.

Poliovirus infections seldom result in obvious clinical symptoms. The percentage of individuals developing clinical illness may be less than one (Evans, 1982). However, other enteroviruses may exhibit a greater ratio of clinical to subclinical infection (Table 2). The incidence of clinical infection can vary from year to year for the same virus, depending on the emergence of new strains (Cherry, 1981). Age of the host can also play a major role. In the case of hepatitis A, clinical illness can vary from about 5% in children less than 5 years of age to 75% in adults (Lednar et al., 1985) (Figure 2). With rotavirus, children are more likely to develop gastroenteric disease than adults (Hry, 1987) (Table 2). Immunity is not believed to provide long-term pro-

Table 2
Ratio of Clinical to Subclinical Infections with
Enteric Viruses

Virus	Frequency of clinical illness
Polio 1	0.1–1
Coxsackie	
A16	50
B2	11–50
B3	29–96
B4	30–70
B5	5–40
Echo	
overall	50
9	15–60
18	Rare–20
20	33
25	30
30	50
Hepatitis A (adults)	75
Rota	
(adults)	56–60
(children)	28
Astro (adults)	12.5

From Cherry, 1981; Ward et al., 1986; CDC, 1985;
Wenman et al., 1979; Gurwith et al., 1981; Kurtz et
al., 1979.

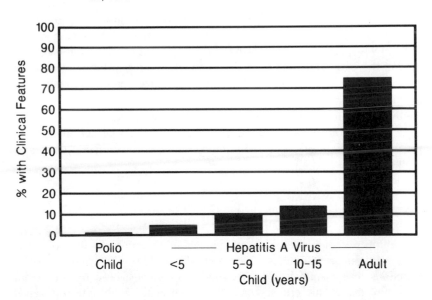

FIGURE 2. Incidence of clinical illness associated with polio and hepatitis A virus infections.

tection from reinfection for many of the enteric viruses that cause gastroenteritis, such as rotavirus or Norwalk virus (Ward et al., 1986). In the case of Norwalk virus, it also does not provide long-term protection against the development of clinical illness (Cukor et al., 1982). However, with most of the enteroviruses and hepatitis A, life-long immunity from reinfection is the case. Other undefined host factors may also control the odds of developing illness. For example, in the case of Norwalk virus it was found in human volunteers that those persons who did not become infected upon an initial exposure to the virus also did not respond to a second exposure (Cukor et al., 1982). In contrast, those volunteers who developed gastroenteritis upon the first exposure also developed illness after the second exposure.

MORTALITY

If the infection becomes serious enough, mortality can result with almost all illnesses caused by enteric viruses. The prospect of mortality will depend upon the same factors that control the chance of clinical illness developing. Mortality for hepatitis A and poliovirus is greater in adults than in children (CDC, 1985). In contrast, almost all mortality associated with rotavirus diarrhea is associated with children (Christensen, 1989). The very young and old and the immunocompromised are at the greatest risk of a fatal outcome of most illnesses. Reported mortality rates for North America and Europe for enterovirus infections range from less than 0.1% to 0.94% (Assaad and Borecka, 1977). Except for polioviruses, enteroviruses are not a reportable disease in the U.S. Thus, the mortality rates only represent hospitalized cases. In the case of hepatitis A, mortality of hospitalized cases is slightly more than double that of nonhospitalized cases (CDC, 1985). The difference is in the likelihood that a more serious case will be hospitalized. Mortality for this virus ranges from 0.3% for persons less than 39 years of age to 1.0% for persons over 40 (CDC, 1989). Mortality rates for some enteric viruses are shown in Table 3.

INFECTIOUS DOSE

A number of studies have been conducted on the infectious dose of enteric viruses in human volunteers (Ward and Akin, 1984). Determination of the infectious dose in animals and extrapolation to humans is usually not possible since humans are the primary or only known host. While infection can be induced by some of the enteric viruses such as poliovirus and Norwalk virus in laboratory-held primates, it is not known if the infectious dose data can be extrapolated to humans. Much of the existing data on infectious dose was done with attenuated vaccine viruses or avirulent laboratory grown strains so

Table 3
Mortality Rates for Enteric Viruses

Organism	Mortality rate (%)
Polio 1	0.90
Coxsackie	
A2	0.50
A4	0.50
A9	0.26
A16	0.12
Coxsackie B	0.59–0.94
Echo	
6	0.29
9	0.27
Hepatitis A	0.60
Rota	
(total)	0.01
(hospitalized)	0.12
Norwalk	0.0001
Adeno	0.01

From Assaad and Borecka, 1977; CDC, 1985;
Bennett et al., 1987.

that the likelihood of serious illness would be minimized. This could also result in a larger dose being required to cause infection. Finally, these studies were usually done with selected normal healthy individuals which could further reduce the likelihood of infection by low doses of virus.

Studies on infectious dose have been done with poliovirus, echovirus 12, and rotavirus (Ward and Akin, 1984; Schiff et al., 1984; Ward et al., 1986). Studies with poliovirus involved the use of vaccine strains usually administered to infants and young children. Koprowski et al. (1956) fed poliovirus 1 in gelatin capsules to adult volunteers and infected two of three subjects with two plaque-forming units (PFU) of the virus. Katz and Plotkin (1967) administered attenuated poliovirus 3 (Fox) by nasogastric tube to infants and infected two of three with 10 $TCID_{50}$ and three of ten with one $TCID_{50}$ of the virus. Minor et al. (1981) gave attenuated poliovirus 1 vaccine orally and infected three of six 2-month-old infants with 50 $TCID_{50}$.

All of the previous studies suffered from a limited number of subjects and did not involve actual exposure of the viruses through ingestion of drinking water. To overcome these deficiencies, Schiff et al. (1984) fed 149 healthy adults various doses of echovirus 12 in drinking water. Through statistical analysis of the data by probit transformation, a human-infectious dose of 17 PFU was predicted. These results were used in the second part of the study to determine the effect of previous infection on infectious dose. The results showed that the presence of serum antibody caused no significant change in the percentage of volunteers infected. This study and the previous study had used viruses that had been grown in tissue culture. Viruses grown in cell culture usually have a lower virulence and a different infectious dose than those isolated directly from human stools (Ward et al., 1986). In order to overcome this limitation, the same group of investigators evaluated the infectious dose of human rotavirus obtained directly from human stools. In addition, with this virus it was possible to measure both infection and clinical illness, something that had not been done in previous studies. In these studies different concentrations of the virus were administered via drinking water to 62 adults. The amount of virus required to cause infection (shedding of virus, seroconversion, or both) was comparable to the minimum detectable in cell cultures (i.e., one cell culture infectious dose). Approximately 56% of the subjects who became infectious developed gastroenteritis. The percentage of individuals who became ill was not found to be related to dose. Also, the concentration of preexisting serum antibody could not be correlated with protection from infection or illness.

From this review, it is obvious that low numbers of enteric viruses are capable of causing infection and illness in a susceptible host. To be useful for estimating risk from exposure to the low levels of enteric viruses likely to be present in drinking water, it is important to have models for extrapolating this experimental data to concentrations likely to be present.

The choice of the correct model is critical so that risks are not grossly over- or underestimated. Haas (1983) compared the simple exponential model, a modified exponential model (β), and the log-normal model with the existing experimental dose-response data. He concluded that the β model developed from the assumptions of random (Poisson) viral distribution and post-ingestion probability of viral infection, which has a β-distribution (Furumoto and Mickey, 1967), was superior at describing the data set. The only exception was for poliovirus type 1 for which the exponential model was found to be best (Regli et al., 1991). The probability of infection from a single exposure, P, can be described as follows:

$$P = 1 - (1 + N/\beta)^{-\alpha} \tag{1}$$

where N = number of organisms ingested per exposure, and α and β represent parameters characterizing the host-virus interaction (Haas, 1983). Values for α and β determined for enteric viruses from human studies are shown in Table 4.

SECONDARY SPREAD

Unlike risks associated with chemicals in water, individuals who do not actually consume or come into direct contact with the contaminated water may also be at risk. This is because viruses may be spread by person-to-person contact or subsequent contamination of fomites with which noninfected individuals may come into contact (Ward et al., 1991). The secondary attack

Table 4
Best Fit Dose-Response Parameters for Various Virus Ingestion Studies

Virus	Best model	Model parameters	Ref.
Echovirus 12	Beta-poisson	$\alpha = 0.374$ $\beta = 186.69$	Schiff et al., 1984
Rotavirus	Beta-poisson	$\alpha = 0.26$ $\beta = 0.42$	Ward et al., 1986
Poliovirus 1	Exponential	$r = 0.009102$	Minor et al., 1981
Poliovirus 1	Beta-poisson	$\alpha = 0.1097$ $\beta = 1524$	Lepow et al., 1982
Poliovirus 3	Beta-poisson	$\alpha = 0.409$ $\beta = 0.788$	Katz and Plotkin, 1967

Modified from Regli et al., 1991.

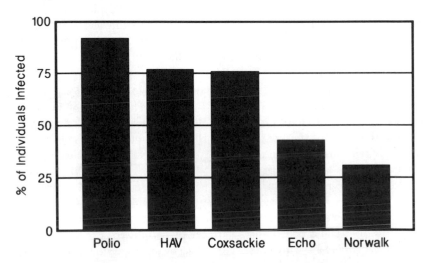

FIGURE 3. Secondary attack rates of enteric viruses.

rate for enteric viruses may range from greater than 90% for poliovirus to 30% for Norwalk virus (Figure 3). This secondary and tertiary spread of viruses has been well documented during waterborne outbreaks caused by Norwalk virus where the secondary attack rate was about 30% (Taylor et al., 1982; Kappus et al., 1982).

Table 5
Potential Routes of Virus Exposure

Ingestion
Bathing — showers, hand washing
Dishwashing
Laundering
Cleansing
Toilet flush (aerosol and surface)

EXPOSURE ASSESSMENT

Routes of Exposure

Ingestion is usually the only route considered in assessing risks of contracting illness from water containing enteric pathogens (Ward and Akin,
1984), but enteric viruses can be effectively transmitted by inhalation of
aerosols (Sattar and Ijaz, 1987) and contact of hands with water-contaminated
surfaces (Sattar et al., 1986). In fact, self-inoculation by placing the contaminated hand to the nose and mouth may be the most important transmission
mechanism of many viruses (Sattar et al., 1986).

Rotavirus and poliovirus may survive on household surfaces for more than
an hour (Keswick et al., 1983; Ward et al., 1991). Thus, washing household
surfaces, dishes, or clothes with contaminated water would likely serve as
additional routes of exposure (Table 5). Human volunteer studies have shown
that rotavirus can be transmitted after drying on surfaces and cause infection
if these surfaces are licked or touched (Ward et al., 1991). Bathing is also a
known route of transmission for many enteric viruses (Dufour, 1986). Aerosols created by showers, hand washing, and toilet flushing (Gerba et al.,
1975) are also potential sources of exposure. Microorganisms in these aerosols
due to fall-out could contaminate surfaces or be inhaled. Since enteric microorganisms can have a lower infectious dose by the respiratory route (Darlow
et al., 1961), the potential significance of this route should not be underestimated.

Occurrence of Viruses in Water

Human enteric viruses may originate in surface and ground waters. This
is due to the direct discharge of sewage effluents into rivers and lakes, sludge
disposal, septic tank discharges, leaking sewer lines, application of sewage
effluents to agricultural land, etc. The concentration and types of enteric
viruses in sewage will vary depending upon the time of year, incidence of
disease within the community, per capita use, and socioeconomic factors.
The concentration of enteric viruses in raw sewage in some parts of the world
have been reported to range from 100,000 to 1,000,000 per liter (Slade and
Ford, 1983).

Treatment of domestic sewage by activated sludge will reduce the number of viruses in the discharge, but not eliminate them even after disinfection as commonly practiced (Block, 1983). Virus concentrations have been reported to be as high as 9,000 PFU per liter in activated sludge effluents and from 0 to 750 PFU per liter for chlorinated effluents (Bitton et al., 1985). The actual concentration of viruses in treatment plant effluents will depend upon how well the plant is operated, the disinfectant concentration and contact time, type of treatment, etc.

It is important to recognize that almost all of our existing data are on enteroviruses with limited data on other enteric viruses, which could be transmitted by water. In addition, concentration and detection methods for enteric viruses are less than 100% efficient, usually being less than 50% (Gerba, 1987). The actual concentration of enteric viruses which have been observed, therefore, is probably at least an order of magnitude greater than what has been reported.

Data on the occurrence of enteric viruses in surface and ground waters is limited (Bitton et al., 1985). It has been estimated that the concentration of enteric viruses in polluted surface waters in the U.S. ranges from 10 to 100 PFU per liter (EPA, 1978). The highest concentration reported was 414 PFU per liter (Bitton et al., 1985). Hurst (1991) recently reviewed the published literature from 1980 to 1990 on the occurrence of enteric viruses in surface and ground waters. Most of the data were from North America and Europe. Almost half (47.2%) of the samples tested were positive for enteric viruses. The median values for the highest level and average level of viruses, including all negative samples, were 22.1 and 1.4 infectious (IU) per liter, respectively. Data on the prevalence of human enteric viruses in conventionally treated drinking water (i.e., coagulation, sedimentation, filtration, and postfiltration disinfection using chlorine/ozone) were also examined. Overall, 9% of the samples were positive for enteric viruses. The median efficiency of enteric virus removal for the entire treatment process was equal to or greater than 95%. Field and laboratory studies have indicated that at least 99.99% of the enteroviruses present in water can be removed by conventional treatment with proper disinfection (Rose and Gerba, 1986). Information on the efficiency of removal of other enteric viruses is limited and an area that requires more research.

RISK CHARACTERIZATION

The probability of becoming infected after ingestion of various concentrations of enteric viruses was estimated by Gerba and Haas (1988) using a modified exponential model. The modified exponential or β model had been previously shown to better represent the existing experimental viral data on dose response than a simple exponential model, or a log-normal model (log-probit) (Haas, 1983). The risk of acquiring a viral infection from consumption of contaminated drinking water containing various concentrations of enteric viruses can be determined from Equation 1. If we make the assumption that a person consumes 2 liters (l) of drinking water per day, we can estimate the probability of infection during that day. Annual and lifetime risks can be determined again assuming a Poisson distribution of the virus within the water consumed (assuming daily exposure to constant concentration of viral contamination).

annual risk of contracting one or more infections =

$$1 - (1 - P)^{365} \tag{2}$$

lifetime risk of contracting one or more infections =

$$1 - (1 - P)^{25550} \tag{3}$$

Risks of clinical illness and mortality can be determined by incorporating terms for the percentage of clinical illness and mortality associated with each particular virus.

$$\text{risk of clinical illness} = PI \tag{4}$$

$$\text{risk of mortality} = PIM \tag{5}$$

where I = percentage of infections which result in clinical illness and M = percentage of clinical cases which result in mortality.

Application of this model allows us to estimate the risks of becoming infected, development of clinical illness, and mortality for different levels of exposure (Table 6).

The estimated risk of infection from one rotavirus in 1000 l of drinking water (assuming ingestion of 2 l/d) would be almost 1:10,000 for a single day exposure. This risk would increase to approximately 1:3 on an annual basis. Risks of the development of clinical illness and mortality also appear to be significant for exposure to low levels of rotavirus and hepatitis A virus in drinking water. Exposure to drinking water containing one infectious hepatitis virus per 100 l could result in an annual risk of mortality of from 10^{-3} to 10^{-5}.

The U.S. Environmental Protection Agency has recently recommended that any drinking water treatment process should be designed to ensure that populations are not subject to risk of infection greater than 1:10,000 for a yearly exposure. To achieve this, it would appear from the data shown in Table 6 that the virus concentration in drinking water would have to be less than one per 1000 l. If the average concentration of enteric viruses in water is 1400/1000 l for polluted waters as reported by Hurst (1991), then treatment plants should be designed to remove at least 99.99% of the virus present in the rav·

Table 6
Risk of Infection, Disease, and Mortality for Rotavirus and Hepatitis A Virus (HAV)

Virus concentration per 100 l	Rotavirus[a]		HAV[b]		HAV[a]	
	Daily	Annual	Daily	Annual	Daily	Annual
Infection						
100	9.6×10^{-2}	1.0	1.8×10^{-3}	5.1×10^{-1}	9.6×10^{-2}	1.0
1	1.2×10^{-3}	3.6×10^{-1}	1.2×10^{-5}	4.4×10^{-3}	1.2×10^{-3}	3.6×10^{-1}
0.1	1.2×10^{-4}	4.4×10^{-2}	1.8×10^{-6}	6.6×10^{-4}	1.2×10^{-4}	4.4×10^{-2}
Disease						
100	5.3×10^{-2}	5.3×10^{-1}	1.4×10^{-3}	3.9×10^{-1}	7.3×10^{-2}	7.6×10^{-1}
1	6.6×10^{-4}	2.0×10^{-1}	9.0×10^{-6}	3.3×10^{-3}	9.1×10^{-4}	2.7×10^{-1}
0.1	6.6×10^{-5}	2.5×10^{-2}	1.4×10^{-6}	5.0×10^{-4}	9.1×10^{-5}	3.3×10^{-2}
Mortality						
100	5.3×10^{-6}	5.3×10^{-5}	8.4×10^{-5}	2.3×10^{-2}	4.4×10^{-4}	4.6×10^{-3}
1	6.6×10^{-8}	2.0×10^{-5}	5.4×10^{-8}	2.0×10^{-5}	5.5×10^{-6}	1.6×10^{-3}
0.1	6.6×10^{-9}	2.5×10^{-6}	8.4×10^{-9}	3.0×10^{-6}	5.5×10^{-8}	2.0×10^{-4}

a = infectivity data of Ward et al., 1986; b = infectivity data of Minor et al., 1981.

water. Treatment plants should be capable of greater removal of virus than this, since most of the existing data are only for enteroviruses, detection methods for even enteroviruses are usually less than 50%, and the impact of secondary spread has not been considered.

DISCUSSION

Pathogenic enteric viruses in drinking water continues to be a cause of illness among consumers in the U.S. Enteric viruses are present in many of the surface waters of the U.S. primarily because of sewage discharges and in groundwater due to septic tank discharges and leaking sewer lines. Information on the extent and concentrations of enteric viruses in these waters is limited because of the lack of any surveillance programs. In order to address the health risks posed by this contamination, a risk assessment-based conceptual framework and strategy must be developed. Such an approach could provide the basis for quantifying microbial risks relative to other risks in drinking water and aid in the development of control strategies.

Much of the information needed to characterize risks associated with enteric viruses in drinking water is available, but has not been organized systematically or placed in a framework for use in risk characterization. Microbial risk characterization differs in several aspects from that of chemicals. Data are available for infectious dose in humans for at least some agents and extrapolation from animal data is not needed. This greatly reduces the uncertainty with interspecies comparisons associated with toxicological data. Microbial risks must also be examined from the point of infection, illness, and mortality. Both human subject data and clinical data are available to make estimates without a great deal of uncertainty for these outcomes for many of the enteric viruses. In many cases data are available on factors such as age and socioeconomic conditions. Secondary spread is also another unique aspect whose impact on the health of a community should be included in any assessment of impact of exposure on a community.

Utilizing a risk assessment approach similar to that which has been used to characterize chemical risks in drinking water, we found that low levels of enteric viruses in drinking water can pose significant risks of infection, illness, and mortality. Acceptable risks of mortality over a lifetime of exposure have usually been defined in the range of 10^{-5} to 10^{-6} (Rodricks et al., 1987), but what might be acceptable levels of infection or illness has received little attention. Recently the U.S. Environmental Protection Agency suggested that a goal of water treatment should be the reduction of infection via drinking water to less than 10^{-4} per year (U.S. EPA, 1989). This level of risk was also suggested by others (IAWPRC, 1983). This is probably the most logical approach, since the outcome of infection is highly dependent on intrinsic host factors and will vary with the virulence of a particular type and strain of microorganism.

The impact of low-level infection in a community should not be underestimated. Recently, Payment et al. (1991) found that 35% of the gastrointestinal illness in a community receiving conventionally treated (i.e., flocculation, filtration, disinfection) drinking water was attributable to the consumption of the drinking water which met all current water quality standards. The costs of mild bacterial gastroenteritis have been estimated at $221 per case in 1987 dollars, while cases in which a physician was visited were estimated at $680 (Roberts, 1988). Costs for illness which require hospitalization may exceed $4350 per case. Such estimates for waterborne enteric viruses and information proved useful in cost benefit analysis of control strategies.

Microbial risk assessment is relatively new and there are many issues which need to be considered to better refine the risk analysis. For example, unlike chemicals, secondary and even tertiary spread of microorganisms occurs to individuals who do not become infected from directly consuming the contaminated water. Secondary spread rates for enteric microorganisms may range from 10 to over 90%. During waterborne outbreaks of Norwalk virus, secondary spread averaged about 30%.

What is an acceptable level of risk for microorganisms in water and over what time period of exposure should that risk be calculated? Risks from chemicals are usually determined on a lifetime basis. Should risks from microorganisms be assessed on a daily, monthly, yearly, or lifetime basis? Should an acceptable level of risk be determined by infection, clinical illness, or mortality? The U.S. Environmental Protection Agency in its recent Surface Treatment Rule stated that the goal of water treatment should be to reduce the risk of infection to no greater than 1:10,000 per year.

It is most likely that in a contaminated water supply persons consuming the water will be exposed to several types of infectious microorganisms. Should risks be added together if more than one agent is present in the water supply? Do synergistic effects occur between different types of microorganisms?

To reduce microbial risks, chemical disinfectants are added to drinking water which create chemical risks (i.e., trihalomethanes produced by chlorine). To ensure that we do not create a greater risk from toxic by-products of water treatment we must be able to compare chemical vs. microbial risks. Should this be done by costs associated with treatment of illness and loss of life, or are other approaches available?

Microbial risk assessment has many potential applications in risk management decisions involving the treatment and disposal of wastes containing pathogenic microorganisms such as sewage, sewage sludge, domestic and medical wastes, graywater, etc. For example, it can be used to evaluate treatment options and objectives, guidelines and standards, as well as cost-benefit analysis, and to compare competing risks.

REFERENCES

Assaad, F. and I. Borecka. "Nine-Year Study of WHO Virus Reports on Fatal Virus Infections," *Bull. W.H.O.* 55:445–453 (1977).

Bennett, J. V., S. D. Homberg, M. F. Rogers, and S. L. Solomon. "Infectious and Parasitic Diseases," *Am. J. Preventative Med.* 55:102–114 (1987).

Bitton, G., S. Farrah, C. Montague, M. W. Birford, P. R. Scheuerman, and A. Watson. "Survey of Virus Isolation Data from Environmental Samples," U.S. Environmental Protection Agency (1985).

Block, J. C. "Viruses in Environmental Waters," in *Viral Pollution of the Environment*, G. Berg, Ed. CRC Press, Boca Raton, FL (1983) pp. 117–145.

Bull, R. J., C. Gerba, and R. R. Trussell. "Evaluation of the Health Risks Associated with Disinfection," *CRC Crit. Rev. Environ. Contr.* 20:77–113 (1990).

Centers for Disease Control (CDC). "Hepatitis Surveillance," Report No. 49, Atlanta, GA. (1985).

Centers for Disease Control (CDC). "Hepatitis Surveillance," Report No. 52, Atlanta, GA. (1989).

Cherry, J. D. "Non-polio Enteroviruses: Coxsackieviruses, Echoviruses and Enteroviruses," in *Textbook of Pediatric Infectious Diseases*, R. D. Feigin and J. D. Cherry, Eds. W. B. Saunders, Philadelphia, PA (1981) pp. 1316–1365.

Christensen, M. L. "Human Viral Gastroenteritis," *Clin. Microbiol. Rev.* 2:51–89 (1989).

Clapper, W. E. "Comments on Viruses Recovered from Dogs." *J. Am. Vet. Med. Assoc.* 156:1678–1680 (1970).

Craun, G. F. *Waterborne Diseases in the United States.* CRC Press, Boca Raton, FL (1986).

Cukor, G., N. A. Nowak, and N. R. Blacklow. "Immunoglobulin M Response to the Norwalk Virus of Gastroenteritis," *Infect. Immun.* 37:463–468 (1982).

Darlow, H. M., W. R. Bale, and G. B. Carter. "Infection of Mice by the Respiratory Route with *Salmonella typhimurium*," *J. Hyg.* 59:303–308 (1961).

Dufour, A. P. "Diseases Caused by Water Contact," in *Waterborne Diseases in the United States*, G. F. Craun, Ed. CRC Press, Boca Raton, FL (1986) pp. 23–41.

Environmental Protection Agency (EPA). "Guidance for Planning the Location of Water Supply Intakes Downstream from Municipal Wastewater Treatment Facilities," Office of Drinking Water, Washington, D.C. (1978).

Evans, A. S. "Epidemiological Concepts and Methods," in *Viral Infections of Humans*, A. S. Evans, Ed. Plenum Press, New York (1982) pp. 3–13.

Furumoto, W. A. and R. Mickey. "A Mathematical Model for the Infectivity-Dilution Curve of Tobacco Mosaic Virus: Theoretical Considerations," *Virology* 32:216–223 (1967).

Gerba, C. P. "Recovering Viruses from Sewage, Effluents, and Water," in *Methods for Recovering Viruses from the Environment*, G. Berg, Ed. CRC Press, Boca Raton, FL (1987) pp. 1–23.

Gerba, C. P. and C. N. Haas. "Assessment of Risks Associated with Enteric Viruses in Contaminated Drinking Water," in *Chemical and Biological Characterization of Sludges, Sediments, Dredge Spoils, and Drilling Muds*, J. J. Lichtenberg, J. L. Winter, C. I. Weber, and L. Fradkin, Eds. American Society for Testing and Materials, Philadelphia, PA (1988) pp. 489–494.

Gerba, C. P., S. N. Singh, and J. B. Rose. "Waterborne Viral Gastroenteritis and Hepatitis," *CRC Crit. Rev. Environ. Contr.* 15:213–236 (1985).

Gerba, C. P., C. Wallis, and J. L. Melnick. "Microbiological Hazards of Household Toilets: Droplet Production and the Fate of Residual Organisms," *Appl. Microbiol.* 30:229–237 (1975).

Gurwith, M., W. Wenman, D. Hinde, S. Feltham, and H. A. Greenberg. "A Prospective Study of Rotavirus Infection in Infants and Young Children," *J. Infect. Dis.* 144:218–224 (1981).

Gust, I. G. and R. H. Purcell. "Report of a Workshop: Waterborne Non-A, Non-B Hepatitis," *J. Infect. Dis.* 156:630–635 (1987).

Haas, C. N. "Estimation of Risk Due to Low Doses of Microorganisms: a Comparison of Alternative Methodologies," *Am. J. Epidemiol.* 118:573–582 (1983).

Hammond, P. B. and R. Coppock. *Valuing Health Risks, Costs, and Benefits for Environmental Decision Making.* National Academy Press, Washington, D.C. (1990).

Hry, D. B. "Epidemiology of Rotaviral Infection in Adults," *Rev. Infect. Dis.* 9:461–469 (1987).

Hurst, C. J. "Presence of Enteric Viruses in Freshwater and their Removal by the Conventional Drinking Water Treatment Process," *Bull. W.H.O.* 69:113–119 (1991).

IAWPRC Study Group on Water Virology. "The Health Significance of Viruses in Water," *Water Res.* 17:121–132 (1983).

Kaplan, J. E., G. W. Gary, R. C. Baron, N. Singh, L. B. Schonberger, R. Fieldman, and H. B. Greenberg. Epidemiology of Norwalk Gastroenteritis and the Role of Norwalk Virus in Outbreaks of Acute Nonbacterial Gastroenteritis," *Ann. Intern. Med.* 96:757–761 (1982).

Kappus, K. D., J. Marks, R. C. Holman, J. K. Bryant, C. Baker, G. W. Gary, and H. B. Greenberg. "An Outbreak of Norwalk Gastroenteritis Associated with Swimming Pool and Secondary Person-to-Person Transmission," *Am. J. Epidemiol.* 116:834–839 (1982).

Katz, M. and S. A. Plotkin. "Minimal Infective Dose of Attenuated Poliovirus for Man," *Am. J. Public Health.* 57:1837–1840 (1967).

Keswick, B. H., H. L. Pickering, H. L. Dupont, and EW. E. Woodward. "Survival and Detection of Rotaviruses on Environmental Surfaces in Day-Care Centers," *Appl. Environ. Microbiol.* 46:813–816 (1983).

Koprowski, H., T. W. Norton, G. A. Jervis, T. L. Nelson, D. L. Chadwick, D. J. Nelson, and K. F. Meyer. "Clinical Investigations of Attenuated Strains of Poliomyelitis Virus: Use as a Method of Immunization of Children with Living Virus," *J. Am. Med. Assoc.* 160:954–966 (1956).

Kurtz, J. B. and T. W. Lee. "Astroviruses: Human and Animal," in *Novel Diarrhoea Viruses.* John Wiley & Sons, Chichester, England (1987) pp. 92–101.

Kurtz, J. B., T. W. Lee, and S. E. Reed. "Astrovirus Infection in Volunteers," *J. Med. Virol.* 3:221–230 (1979).

Lednar, W. M., S. M. Lemon, J. W. Kirkpatrick, R. R. Redfield, M. L. Fields, and P. W. Kelley. "Frequency of Illness Associated with Epidemic Hepatitis A Virus Infections in Adults," *Am. J. Epidemiol.* 122:226–233 (1985).

Lepow, M. L., R. J. Warren, V. G. Ingram, S. C. Daugherty, and F. C. Robbins. "Sabin Type 1 Oral Poliomyelitis Vaccine Effect of Dose Upon Drinking Water," *Am. J. Dis. Child.* 104:67–71 (1962).

Madore, H. P., J. J. Treanor, and R. Dolin. "Characterization of the Snow Mountain Agent of Viral Gastroenteritis," *J. Virol.* 58:487–492 (1986).

Minor, T. E., C. I. Allen, A. A. Tsiatis, D. B. Nelson, and D. J. D'Alessio. "Human Infective Dose Determination for Oral Poliovirus Type 1 Vaccine in Infants," *J. Clin. Microbiol.* 13:388–389 (1981).

National Research Council (NRC). *Risk Assessment in the Federal Government: Managing the Process* National Academy Press, Washington, D.C. (1983).

Payment, P., L. Rishardson, J. Siemiatycki, R. Dewar, M. Edwardes, and E. Franco. "A Randomized Trial to Evaluate the Risk of Gastrointestinal Disease due to Consumption of Drinking Water Meeting Current Microbiological Standards," *Am. J. Public Health.* 81:703–708 (1991).

Regli, S., J. B. Rose, C. N. Haas, and C. P. Gerba. "Modeling the Risk from Giardia and Viruses in Drinking Water," *J. Am. Water Works Assoc.* 83:76–84 (1991).

Rodricks, J. V., S. Brett, and G. Wrenn. *"Significant Risk Decisions in Federal Regulatory Agencies,"* Environ Corp., Washington, D.C. (1987).

Roberts, T. "Salmonellosis Control: Estimated Economic Costs," *Poultry Sci.* 67:936–943 (1988).

Rose, J. B. and C. P. Gerba. "A Review of Viruses in Treated Drinking Water," *Curr. Pract. Environ. Sci. Eng.* 2:119–141 (1986).

Rose, J. B. and C. P. Gerba. "Assessing Potential Health Risks from Viruses and Parasites in Reclaimed Water in Arizona and Florida," *Water Sci. Technol.* 23:2091–2098 (1991a).

Rose, J. B. and C. P. Gerba. "Use of Risk Assessment for Development of Microbial Standards," *Water Sci. Technol.* 24:29–34 (1991b).

Rose, J. B., C. N. Haas, and S. Regli. "Risk Assessment and Control of Waterborne Giardiasis," *Am. J. Public Health.* 81:709–713 (1991).

Sattar, S. A. and M. K. Ijaz. "Spread of Viral Disease by Aerosols," *CRC Crit. Rev. Environ. Contr.* 17:89–131 (1987).

Sattar, S. A., N. Lloyd-Evans, V. S. Springthorpe, and R. C. Nair. "Institutional Outbreaks of Rotavirus Diarrhea: Potential Role of Fomites and Environmental Surfaces as Vehicles for Virus Transmission," *J. Hyg.* 96:227–289 (1986).

Schiff, G. M., G. M. Stefanovic, E. C. Young, D. S. Sander, J. K. Pennekamo, and R. L. Ward. "Studies of Echovirus 12 in Volunteers: Determination of Minimal Infectious Dose and the Effect of Previous Infection on Infectious Dose," *J. Infect. Dis.* 150:858–866 (1984).

Slade, J. S. and B. J. Ford. "Discharge to the Environment of Viruses in Wastewater, Sludges, and Aerosols," in *Viral Pollution of the Environment,* G. Berg, Ed. CRC Press, Boca Raton, FL (1983) pp. 3–15.

Taylor, J. W., G. W. Gary, and H. B. Greenberg. "Norwalk-Related Viral Gastroenteritis due to Contaminated Drinking Water," *Am. J. Epidemiol.* 114:584–592 (1982).

U.S. Environmental Protection Agency (USEPA). "National Primary Drinking Water Regulations: Filtration Disinfection; Turbidity, *Giardia lamblia,* Viruses, Legionellia, and Heterotrophic Bacteria. Final Rule, 40 CFR parts 141 and 142," *Fed. Regist.,* June 29, 1989; 54:27486–27541 (1989).

Ward, R. L. and E. W. Akin. "Minimum Infectious Dose of Animal Viruses," *CRC Crit. Rev. Environ. Contr.* 14:297–310 (1984).

Ward, R. L., D. I. Bernstein, D. R. Knowlton, J. R. Sherwood, E. C. Young, T. M. Cusack, J. R. Rubino, and G. M. Schiff. "Prevention of Surface-to-Human Transmission of Rotaviruses by Treatment with Disinfectant Spray." 29:1991–1996 (1991).

Ward, R. L., D. I. Bernstein, and E. C. Young. "Human Rotavirus Studies in Volunteers of Infectious Dose and Serological Response to Infection," *J. Infect. Dis.* 154:871–877 (1986).

Quantitative Risk Assessment Problem Areas and Issues

Introduction

Morton Lippmann

OVERVIEW

The first two sessions of this symposium addressed the nature of ecological and health risks and how they were addressed and defined. In this session, attention turns to approaches for the quantification of risk, in order to provide a framework for the ranking of risks. A first order of business is to define the risks to be ranked. When they are defined in the manner used by *Unfinished Business* (UB),[1] i.e., according to EPA's programmatic and regulatory authorities, then it is virtually impossible to make quantitative distinctions among them. For example, some significant risks, such as environmental exposure to lead, cannot be identified within the list of 31 UB categories. Sources of exposure to lead come under various categories, e.g., criteria air pollutants; indoor air pollutants; drinking water; consumer products; worker exposure; waste sites; etc., along with myriad other chemicals of greater or lesser toxicity and levels. As described in *Reducing Risk*:[2]

"At this time EPA does not have an effective, consistent way of identifying environmental problems in a manner that neither fragments nor aggregates sources of risk to an extent that renders comparisons untenable. EPA's current framework of statutory mandates and program structure helps to maintain artificial distinctions among environmental problems, and those distinctions are conducive neither to sound evaluation of relative risk nor to selection of the most effective actions to risk."

The Science Advisory Board (SAB), in its report *Reducing Risk,*[2] concluded that:

"Improved methodologies for comparing different human health risks also are needed. A new approach to ranking risks, one that uses a matrix of data on sources, exposures, agents, and endpoints, is needed to help identify specific agents and mixtures for quantitative risk assessments. Risk rankings should be based on risk assessments for specific toxic agents, or definable mixtures of agents, and on the total human exposure to such agents. When possible, risks should be assigned to persons in target or more sensitive populations, as well as to the population as a whole."

0-87371-605-1/93/$0.00 + $.50
© 1993 by Lewis Publishers

ISSUES

Among the key issues that need to be addressed are the needs for and purposes of quantitative risk assessments, how quantitative they need to be, and how the risks to be assessed are to be described and addressed.

NEEDS AND PURPOSES

There are at least three different needs for risk assessments. One is for developers and manufacturers of new chemicals and products. They need risk assessments to help guide decisions about occupational exposures, labeling, and product liability, and have the luxury of dealing with one or, at most, a few chemicals at a time.

A second need is related to regulatory requirements. Legislation may mandate that either manufacturers and/or regulatory agencies conduct risk assessments, and may also require that they be reviewed by governmental personnel and/or advisory bodies. For example, the 1990 Clean Air Act (CAA) amendments mandate risk assessments for 189 "air toxics". It is difficult to imagine how EPA can effectively address the mandate without an enormous increase in staff and effort. If such an effort was undertaken it might well divert resources that could have achieved a greater risk reduction if committed elsewhere.

A third need is for research planning. The risk assessment framework can be used to identify critical gaps in knowledge as well as summarize available knowledge, and a compilation of critical knowledge gaps can provide valuable input into the research planning process.

LEVEL OF QUANTITATION NEEDED

For some regulatory purposes, such as premarketing approvals, where large safety factors (orders of magnitude) are applied, relatively large quantitative uncertainties are tolerable. On the other hand, for ubiquitous chemicals of natural as well as anthropogenic origin, such as lead, radon, and ozone, large safety factors cannot be built in, and margins of safety, if they exist, are much less than an order of magnitude. Thus, the level of quantitation needed is dependent on the purposes to which the risk assessment is applied.

KINDS OF RISKS ADDRESSED

The kinds of risks addressed can be broadly (poorly) defined, as in *Unfinished Business,* or they can be specific. In the latter case, the specificity can be according to chemical or physical class as recommended by the Science Advisory Board in *Reducing Risk* for health effects or, alternatively, by the risk to be prevented. The health risks could be by disease category, such as cancer, birth defects, asthmatic attacks, etc. The risks can also be specified by major impacts, such as habitat alteration, species extinction, or global warming, as recommended for ecological effects by the Science Advisory Board in *Reducing Risk*. When taking the risk to be prevented approach, it is important to explicitly address the contribution made by anthropogenic activity to the change in risk from that unusually present at a baseline level.

Thus, there are many and varied issues that need to be addressed in quantitating risks, and the papers that follow address the concepts and problems in ways that are interesting and innovative. They provide some valuable inputs for a topic of increasing importance in environmental protection.

REFERENCES

1. U.S. EPA. Unfinished Business: a Comparative Assessment of Environmental Problems. U.S. Environmental Protection Agency, Office of Policy, Planning and Evaluation, Washington, D.C. (1987).
2. Science Advisory Board (SAB): Reducing Risk: Setting Priorities and Strategies for Environmental Protection. SAB-EC-90-021, Science Advisory Board, U.S. EPA, Washington, D.C. 1990).

CHAPTER 10

Atmospheric Nitrogen Oxides: a Bridesmaid Revisited

John Bachmann

INTRODUCTION

The relative risk ranking in both the Environmental Protection Agency's *Unfinished Business* study[1] and the Science Advisory Board report, *Reducing Risk*[2] placed ambient air pollution among the highest priority environmental problems. The subjective judgments leading to this ranking almost certainly accorded great weight to the risk to public health and the environment from problems such as tropospheric ozone (smog), acid deposition, particulate matter, and airborne toxins. Few, however, would have listed nitrogen oxides as a high-risk, high-priority category of air pollution problems.

Indeed, air pollution control programs have tended to assign a lower priority to nitrogen oxides than to other prevalent air pollutants. The lack of impressive direct effects of nitrogen dioxide, the belief that volatile organic chemical controls were favored for ozone reductions, that sulfur oxides were more important in acidification, the role of nitrates as a beneficial nutrient for crops, and the relative high cost of significant control technology are all partly responsible for the lesser emphasis on nitrogen oxide control. The Clean Air Act Amendments of 1990, for example, call for a 10 million-ton reduction in emissions of sulfur oxides[3] and mandate controls that will reduce anthropogenic volatile organic chemicals by an equivalent amount.[4] Despite being far more aggressive with respect to nitrogen oxides than previous legislation, however, the controls specified in these amendments over the next 20 years would hardly offset projected emissions growth (see below). In loose terms, nitrogen oxide control seems to have been "always a bridesmaid".

It is only recently that nitrogen oxides or, more broadly, atmospheric nitrogen compounds, have begun to be recognized as a significant contributor to multiple environmental problems.[5] While past scientific assessments have catalogued potential effects and interactions,[6] quantitative assessments of combined multiple effects have been lacking. This paper attempts to take an integrated view of nitrogen oxides and related nitrogen compounds, beginning with an overview of the effects associated with nitrogen. The paper also outlines past and projected trends in nitrogen oxide emissions, taking into account the provisions of the Clean Air Act Amendments of 1990, and summarizes some of the key uncertainties that limit our ability to conduct an integrated assessment of cumulative risk and to develop alternative strategies for reducing those risks.

MULTIPLE ENVIRONMENTAL EFFECTS

Direct Effects of NO_2

Traditionally, the nitrogen species of concern in air pollution regulations are nitric oxide (NO) and nitrogen dioxide (NO_2).[6] These are formed and emitted during combustion of fuels. In the atmosphere, NO — the major component in emissions — is oxidized to NO_2, while NO_2 reacts with ozone to form NO. EPA has established a primary (health-based) National Ambient Air Quality Standard for NO_2 of 0.05 ppm (100 $\mu g/m^3$) annual mean.[7] Currently, this standard is violated only in the Los Angeles basin.

The NO_2 standard is based on scientific criteria as reviewed and revised through 1985. The major quantitative evidence suggesting the need for this standard comes from studies showing a relationship between NO_2 exposure in homes using natural gas and respiratory symptoms in children.[8] These and other studies suggest that single or repeated peak exposures of shorter duration are most likely to be responsible for these and other respiratory responses, but several studies raise doubts about the link between significant effects and NO_2 at levels prevalent in most U.S. cities. The most recent standard review found no basis in the direct environmental effects of NO_2 for a tighter secondary or welfare standard to protect vegetation, materials, or other values.[7]

Indirect Effects

By contrast, the indirect effects associated with nitrogen oxides and their transformation products are many and varied. A case can be made that, through atmospheric reactions, NO_x (to which we now add nitrous oxide, N_2O) plays at least a secondary role in all of the most important air pollution problems mentioned in *Reducing Risk*. A brief qualitative synopsis of the major pollutant/effects categories follows.

Tropospheric Ozone

Ozone and other photochemical oxidants form in the troposphere through reactions of nitrogen oxides and volatile organic compounds (VOCs) in the presence of sunlight and high temperature. On a local/urban scale, increased nitrogen oxides can actually *decrease* ozone concentrations, but at the expense of increased levels downwind. The choice of cost-effective control strategies is dependent on relative emissions and ambient concentrations of NO_x and VOC from anthropogenic and biogenic sources. Elevated exposures to ozone are widespread in major urban areas of the nation and much of the nonurban eastern U.S. Local and regional scale effects include both short- and long-term respiratory tract lung function and structure changes, and direct damage to forests, crops, other vegetation, and materials.[9]

Global Background Effect

Available evidence suggests that on a global scale, background levels of tropospheric ozone may have doubled since the turn of the century.[10] This increase may be linked to rising global emissions of NO_x or to growing methane emissions. Besides increasing the background upon which the regional and urban scale effects of ozone noted above may occur, on a global scale ozone is a greenhouse gas (although of uncertain significance).

Particulate Matter Effects

NO_x further transforms into particulate nitrate species. In several western cities, ammonium nitrate particles are a significant component of violations of the national particulate matter (PM-10) standard and related urban haze.[11]

Air Toxics/Acid Aerosols

NO_x reacts with organic species in the atmosphere, often increasing their toxicity. Peroxyacetyl nitrate, nitroarenes, and nitrosamines are examples. Addition of NO_x to a complex mix of VOC resulted in a significantly more mutagenic product than the original substances.[12] Nitric and nitrous acid contribute to the overall acidity of aerosols, with an associated increase in health risk.[13]

Eutrophication of Marine Coastal Areas

Primary productivity in estuaries and near coastal systems such as the Chesapeake Bay[14] and Albemarle/Pamlico[15] sounds are often nitrogen limited. In such cases, excess nitrate loadings may cause algal blooms, oxygen depletion, and associated effects on aquatic biota. There is a perception that noxious algal blooms, anoxic bottom waters, and fish kills are increasing in coastal marine areas around the world.[16,17] Estimates of the relative contribution of point sources, agricultural runoff, and other sources to the Chesapeake Bay indicate a range of 10 to 40% of the nitrogen budget comes from atmospheric deposition to the watershed.[18] An estimated 5 to 14% of the atmospheric nitrogen contribution is from ammonia, rather than NO_x. The Chesapeake Bay States have established a goal of reducing nitrogen loadings from all sources by 40% by the year 2000.[19]

Terrestrial Systems Changes

In many soils, nitrogen oxide-derived deposition serves as a fertilizer, increasing plant growth. This is most often viewed as a benefit in agriculture or silviculture, but may be harmful in some natural ecosystems. In some systems, soils and vegetation can become saturated with nitrogen, resulting in leaching to ground water and other aquatic systems.[20]

Acidification

NO_x is transformed into nitric acid vapor or aerosol, depending on atmospheric conditions. Deposition of nitric acid contributes to episodic acidification events in aquatic systems and buildup in snowpacks. In some cases, it may also contribute to long-term acidification of terrestrial and associated aquatic systems. Evidence suggesting that nitrate plays a role in surface water chemistry exists for many areas of the eastern U.S., including the Adirondacks, the Catskills, the West Virginia mountains, and some areas of Vermont.[21] Nitric acid also causes direct damage to materials.

Stratospheric Ozone Depletion

N_2O is linked to destruction of the stratospheric ozone layer and is also a greenhouse gas.[22] Anthropogenic nitrogen oxides and fertilizers increase nitrogen cycling in the biosphere, increasing the opportunity for denitrifying bacteria to form and emit nitrous oxide.

SOURCES, PATTERNS, AND TRENDS

Current Patterns and Trends

Figure 1 shows a breakdown of the major source categories and trends in U.S. NO_x emissions and ambient air concentrations of NO_2. Over the most recent 10-year period of record, both emissions and air quality show little change, with some suggestion of a small decline. This indicates that growth in vehicle use and fuel combustion in stationary sources have tended to offset the moderate improvement in controls during the period. Of the approximately 20 million tons emitted annually, mobile sources contribute about 40%, while major stationary point sources emit about 50%.[23]

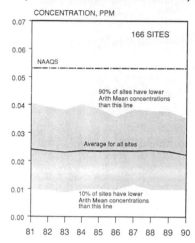

**NO2 TREND, 1981-1990
(ANNUAL ARITHMETIC MEAN)**

1981-90: 8% decrease
1989-90: 6% decrease

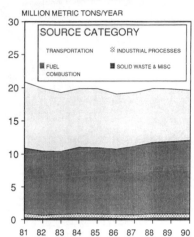

**NOX EMISSIONS TREND
1981-1990**

1981-90: 6% decrease
1989-90: 1% decrease

FIGURE 1. Trends in U.S. nitrogen oxides emissions and nitrogen dioxide air quality, 1981 to 1990.[23] Left: trends in annual mean nitrogen dioxide concentrations at 148 sites. Right: trends in emissions. Highway vehicle emissions decreased by 25% over the period, but this was largely offset by increases in stationary fuel combustion.

Figure 2, the spatial pattern of annual nitrate wet deposition, is a fair representation of the geographical distribution of NO_x emission sources. Heaviest deposition occurs in densely populated urban areas and generally in the Northeast region near both the northeast megalopolis and the midwestern power plants. Comparison of the deposition rates of the dominant atmospheric transformation products of NO_x in the east (nitric acid vapor) with that of sulfur oxides (sulfate aerosol), as well as the spatial distribution of deposition, suggest that while both SO_x and NO_x are clearly regional pollutants, the bulk of NO_x emissions tends to be deposited somewhat nearer source regions than are sulfur oxides.

In comparison to established and provisional effects guides, it is clear that NO_2 concentrations are well below the ambient standard. By contrast, nitrate deposition rates in much of the northeast exceed preliminary regional targets (termed critical loads) developed by some in the European Community[25] to protect sensitive terrestrial and aquatic ecosystems.

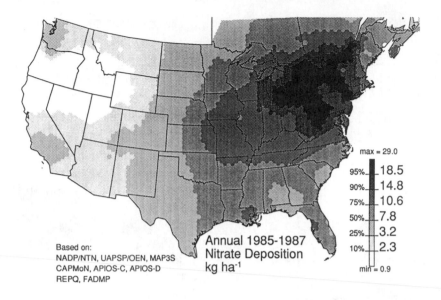

FIGURE 2.   The 1985 to 1987 spatial pattern of annual wet nitrate deposition.[24] The pattern is similar to that of the distribution of emissions sources.

Projected Effects of the Clean Air Act Amendments of 1990

The new Clean Air Act Amendments contain a number of significant new provisions that will result in major additional controls of NO_x from existing and new sources. Among the mandated controls are

- Title I — Reasonably available controls on major existing point sources and "lowest achievable" reductions on major new sources in ozone nonattainment areas and transport regions where such control results in air quality benefits
- Title II — A 60% reduction in tailpipe emissions from the current standard for light-duty vehicles (to 0.4 g/mi)
- Title IV — Mandated emission limits requiring low NO_x burner technology for all utilities affected by the acid-deposition program

An analysis of the net effect of these mandated controls when combined with projected growth through the next 2 decades is presented in Figure 3. The major reductions effected by mobile source controls level off after about 2005, with projected growth thereafter, while point sources show only a modest decrease between 1995 and 2000 with growth thereafter. Even given the uncertainties associated with such projections, the net effect of this set of controls for all sources over the period appears to be a continuation of NO_x emissions at about their current level for the foreseeable future.

NOx Emissions, 1980 to 2010

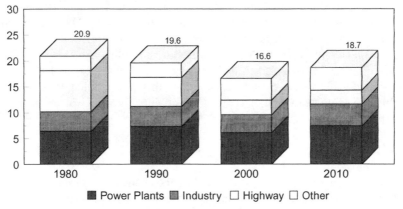

Assumes implementation of mandatory Clean Air
Act Amendment Program, excludes discretionary
programs, e.g. ozone attainment strategies

FIGURE 3. Projected trends in nitrogen oxides emissions assuming implementation of mandated reductions in the Clean Air Act Amendments of 1990.[26] Additional discretionary controls are possible.

This analysis omits a number of options and requirements in the Act that, if exercised, could result in significant reductions beyond those indicated in the figure. For example, states and local agencies will model VOC and NO_x reductions needed to meet the ozone standard and choose the most cost-effective approaches. Similarly, the Northeast Ozone Transport Commission will examine additional controls needed for standard attainment in that region. Initial results from regional modeling (ROMNET) suggest that significant new NO_x controls may well be a cost-effective approach for the northeast region. Additional mobile source controls may be required by various states (e.g., California), and an option exists for EPA to require tighter (Tier II) tailpipe standards nationwide.

TOWARDS AN INTEGRATED ASSESSMENT

A number of NO_x-related risk management decisions must be made over the next several years, on scales ranging from local air quality management, to regional inputs into Chesapeake Bay, to international concerns over regional nitrogen deposition and global warming. While judgments may be possible for particular decisions early on, it is desirable to move towards an integrated assessment of the present effects of atmospheric nitrogen oxides and the benefits of reductions. Despite the known and suspected role of nitrogen oxides in the problems outlined above, our ability to develop such an integrated assessment in support of future policy decisions would be greatly enhanced by further analyses and research in a number of key areas. The multimedia nature of many of these issues and complex biogeochemical cycling of nitrogen species further complicate assessment and policy decisions.

A complete list of research and assessment needs for each of the issues summarized above is beyond the scope of this paper; what follows is an outline of some of the major areas of uncertainty from a U.S. air programs perspective.

Emissions

Current emissions inventories (including those under development) for major known anthropogenic source categories of NO_x are considered reasonably good for assessing annual emissions. Spatial and temporal improvements for utilities can be expected as a result of CAAA requirements for continuous emissions monitors on these sources. Relatively little attention has been paid, however, to "quasinatural" sources of nitrogen oxides, including heavily fertilized soils and prescribed burning associated with silvicultural and agricultural activities. An integrated understanding of regional transport and effects will also require development of quality ammonia emissions inventories and improved VOC inventories, particularly for biogenic sources.

Atmospheric Chemistry and Transport

Regional and urban scale models for tropospheric ozone (e.g., ROM) exist and already are being used in policy assessment. More work on validation and mechanisms such as nighttime reactive nitrogen chemistry are warranted for predicting ozone. Model aggregation approaches should permit assessment of longer daily averaging times and other measures of chronic exposure of people and ecosystems to ozone. Further model development and testing is needed to validate predictive capabilities for nitrogen species-specific wet and dry deposition. An important near-term need is tools for assessing the geographical scale of influence of major NO_x sources for ozone formation and deposition. This is of importance in evaluating emissions offset policies and the extent of region-specific approaches, for example, in managing coastal resources.

Effects

Clearly, additional research is desirable on all of the direct and indirect effects noted above. Based on current information, the most critical include health and welfare effects of chronic ozone exposures, eutrophication of marine waters, terrestrial acidification/nutrient effects, and acidification of fresh waters. Research needs in the latter three areas are related and linked to assessment of land and water sources of nitrogen compounds. A better understanding is needed of system processes for nitrogen delivered by any media to forested ecosystems, agricultural, suburban, and urban landscapes, and subsequent release to surface and ground water. This would permit integration of these elements into models for specific regional assessments of atmospheric and other source contributions to watersheds of interest. Ultimately, it would be useful to develop region-specific models for assessing the beneficial and detrimental effects of atmospheric nitrogen loadings.

Strategies for Reducing Risk

Modest controls for nitrogen oxide emissions are considered to be cost effective. More substantial controls for existing sources can be significantly more expensive. Work to improve cost effectiveness of add-on controls should increase, as well as development of alternative approaches for heat and power generation. As with all combustion-related pollution, improved energy efficiency generally leads to reduced effective emissions.

Framework for Assessment

Integrated assessments form the link between scientific research and policy analyses for decision making. While qualitative summaries of multiple effects are useful in identifying problems, an integrated assessment framework should be developed to ensure relevant information is collected by scientific research programs. The current review of the nitrogen oxides National Ambient Air Quality Standards offers an opportunity for arraying the information, but the traditional standard assessment programs have not provided such a framework. The challenge will be to recognize and adjust current research and assessment to the emerging needs for multiple effects/media policy decision making over the next several years.

CONCLUSIONS

Atmospheric nitrogen oxides, or more broadly, nitrogen compounds, play a role in most or all of the major air pollution problems we face. Current programs will likely prevent increases in national NO_x emissions, with options for more substantial reductions available. Exercising these options in many cases would be served by a concerted effort over the next several years to develop an integrated assessment of the benefits and costs of alternative reduction programs.

REFERENCES

1. "Unfinished Business: A Comparative Assessment of Environmental Problems," U.S. Environmental Protection Agency, Washington, D.C. (1987).
2. Science Advisory Board Relative Risk Reduction Strategies Committee. "Reducing Risk: Setting Priorities and Strategies for Environmental Protection," SAB-EC-90-021 (September 1990).
3. "Clean Air Act Amendments of 1990," conference report to accompany S. 1630, House of Representatives Report 101-952 (October 26, 1990).
4. E. H. Pechan and Associates. "Ozone Nonattainment Analysis: a Comparison of Bills," Report Prepared for the U.S. Environmental Protection Agency, Office of Air and Radiation (January 1990).
5. Persson, G. "Nitrogen Has Many Faces," Acid/Enviro. 9:1 (1990).
6. "Air Quality Criteria for Nitrogen Oxides," Environmental Criteria and Assessment Office, Report #EPA-600/8-82-026F (1982).
7. Thomas, L. Fed. Regist. 50FR25532 (June 19, 1985).
8. "Review of the National Ambient Air Quality Standards for Nitrogen Oxides: Assessment of Scientific and Technical Information. OAQPS Staff Paper," Office of Air Quality Planning and Standards, Report #EPA-450/5-82-002 (August 1982).
9. "Review of the National Ambient Air Quality Standards for Ozone: Assessment of Scientific and Technical Information. OAQPS Staff Paper," Office of Air Quality Planning and Standards (June 1989).
10. Logan, J. "Tropospheric Ozone, Seasonal Behavior, Trends and Atmospheric Influence," J. Geophys. Res. 90:10463–10484 (1985).
11. Utah State Implementation Plan, Section 9, Control Strategy and Compliance Schedule, Utah Department of Health, Salt Lake City (September 1990).
12. Shepson, P. B., Kleindienst, T. E., Edney, E. O., Cupitt, L. T., and C. D. Claxton. "The Mutagenic Activity of the Products of Ozone Reaction with Propylene in the Presence and Absence of Nitrogen Dioxide," Environ. Sci. Technol. 19(11):1094–1098 (1985).
13. "An Acid Aerosols Issue Paper: Health Effects and Aerometrics," Office of Health and Environmental Assessments. Report #EPA-600/18-88-005F (April 1989).
14. D'Elia, C. F. "Nutrient Enrichment of the Chesapeake Bay: Too Much of a Good Thing," Environment 29:2 (1987).
15. Paerl, H. W. "Enhancement of Marine Primary Production by Nitrogen Enriched Acid Rain," Nature 315:747–749 (1985).

16. "Marine Eutrophication," *Ambio* 19:101–176 (1990).
17. Hagerall, B. "Coastal Seas Damaged Worldwide by Excess Nutrients," *Acid/Enviro* 9:18–21 (1990).
18. Fisher, D. C. and M. Oppenheimer, "Atmospheric Deposition and the Chesapeake Bay Estuary," *Ambio* 20:102–108 (1991).
19. Chesapeake Bay Agreement (December 1987).
20. Nihlgard, B. "Nitrogen Pollutants Seriously Stressing Europe's Forests," *Acid/Enviro* 9:22–24 (1990).
21. U.S. Critical Loads Program Demonstration Program (Draft). Office of Research and Development, U.S. Environmental Protection Agency, Washington, D.C. (November 1989).
22. Stordal, F. and I. S. A. Isaksen. "Ozone Perturbations Due to Increases in N_2O, CH_4, and Chlorocarbon: Two Dimensional Time-Dependent Calculations," in *Effects of Changes in Stratospheric Ozone and Global Climate Chapter*, pp. 83–119. U.S. Environmental Protection Agency, UNEP (August 1986).
23. "National Air Quality and Emissions Trends Report, 1990," Report #EPA-450/4-91-023, Office of Air Quality Planning and Standards, (November 1991).
24. Sisterson, D. L. et al. "Deposition Monitoring: Methods and Results." NAPAP State of This Science Report 6. National Acid Precipitation Assessment Program (November 1990).
25. Nilsson, J. and P. Grennfelt, "Critical Loads for Sulphur and Nitrogen." Report from a workshop held at Skokloster, Sweden (March 1988).
26. Wilson, J. "NO_x Emissions Projections," Report to Office of Air and Radiation, U.S. Environmental Protection Agency, Washington, D.C. (January 1991).
27. Possiel, N. C. et al. "Impacts of Regional Ozone Strategies on Ozone in the Northeastern United States," Air and Waste Management Association Annual Meeting, Pittsburgh, PA, paper 90–93.3 (1990).

CHAPTER 11

Temporal Variations in Exposure Data

Nancy K. Kim

INTRODUCTION

In 1987, the U.S. Environmental Protection Agency (EPA) issued a report on relative environmental risk entitled "Unfinished Business. A Comparative Assessment of Environmental Problems."[1] The report was produced by a group of EPA's senior career managers and was designed to provide information that would help individual EPA programs, the agency, and society identify how the Agency's resources should be used to address and minimize existing risks most effectively. The report was to provide a focus for public and governmental discussion of the range of policy options which were available for reducing risks.

In 1989, William Reilly, EPA Administrator, requested that the Science Advisory Board review the 1987 EPA report. One of the charges of the committee was to "develop a long term strategy for improving the methodology for assessing and ranking environmental risks." One of the findings from this review was "the lack of pertinent exposure data makes it extremely difficult to assess human health risks."[2] That finding naturally leads to one of the report's recommendations, that "EPA should improve the data and analytical methods that support the assessment, comparison and reduction of different environmental risks."[3] The recommendation specific to exposure data was that EPA should monitor chemicals in the environment and in human tissues much more systematically.

Two components of risk assessment are hazard identification and exposure assessment. Historically, we have focused on acquiring toxicological data for hazard identification with minimal emphasis on obtaining exposure data. Fortunately, that is changing and we are beginning to define average exposures using national surveys. However, we still have very little understanding about how daily and yearly exposure variations affect us and how to identify and address the risks of those individuals who are exposed significantly more than the average person.

Although there is little information on the temporal variation of exposure, there are indications that this variation can be significant. This is particularly true when evaluating exposures from air emissions.

Table 1
Outdoor Air Concentrations (μg/m³)

Compound	Number of points	Average	Median	Quartile Lower	Quartile Upper
Acetone	17	16	2.2	0	6.7
Methylene chloride	798	5.6	2.7	1.1	6.3
Tetrachloroethene	3226	5.8	2.4	0.8	5.9

Source: Adapted from Shah, J. J. and E. K. Heyerdahl. 1988. National Ambient
Volatile Organic Compounds Data Base, Update. U.S.E.P.A. Research
Triangle Park, N.C. PB 88–195631.

Table 2
Team Study Tetrachloroethene (μg/m³)

	No. of samples	Average	Upper quartile	99 percent	Range
Indoor night					
New Jersey	346	11.3	12.0	70	0.08–250
Devil's Lake, ND	23	11.9	20.0		0.25–45
Outdoor					
New Jersey night	81	3.7	4.1	23	0.06–27
New Jersey day	86	8.3	13	57	0.11–57

Source: Adapted from Pellizzari, E. D. et al. 1987. Total Exposure Assessment Methodology (TEAM) Study, Vol. II. U.S.E.P.A, Research Triangle Park, NC., EPA/
600/6–87/002b.

The total exposure assessment methodology, or TEAM study, and the
National Ambient Volatile Organic Compounds data base provide some information on indoor and ambient air concentrations for many organic compounds. Table 1 contains data from the National Ambient Volatile Organic
Compounds data base.[4] Using these data alone, the concentrations of acetone,
methylene chloride, and tetrachloroethene do not seem to vary greatly by
location or by time. Data from the TEAM studies shown in Table 2 provide
some indication that the concentrations of tetrachloroethene are likely to vary
from location to location and over time (maximum concentration is relatively
high).[5] However, recent data suggest that this variation is much greater than
indicated by these two studies.

TEMPORAL VARIATIONS IN VOC CONCENTRATIONS

Recently, New York State has investigated exposure to several organic
solvents around the Eastman Kodak Company's Kodak Park manufacturing
complex in Rochester (see Figure 1).[6,7] Early in 1989, indoor air samples
were taken in a school beside Kodak Park for 8 h a day for 21 d. Ambient
air samples were collected concurrently on the school roof and in the school

FIGURE 1. Kodak park area of Rochester, NY.

yard. The samples were analyzed for methylene chloride, acetone, and cyclohexane. Concentrations ranged from nondetect, with a detection limit of about 5 to 355 $\mu g/m^3$.

Figure 2 shows the variation in methylene chloride concentrations in ambient air, in the school crawl space, and in the school rooms (average of all

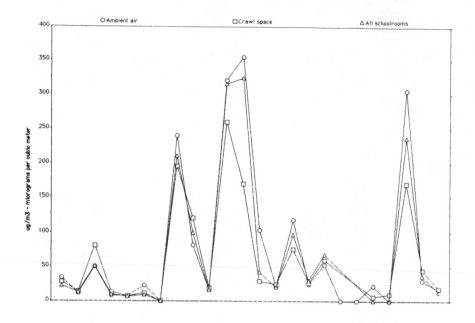

FIGURE 2.   School 41: methylene chloride.

rooms). The indoor air and crawl space concentrations correspond well with the ambient air concentration over the sampling period. The correlation coefficients ranged between 0.85 and 0.97 for linear regressions between the data for ambient air sampling locations and the fixed room sampling location. The high correlation between methylene chloride levels indoors and outdoors suggests that Kodak Park is the source of the methylene chloride levels in the school.

The chemical levels are dependent on the wind direction. On days when the wind is from the northeast and east (i.e., the winds were blowing from Kodak Park toward the school), the air concentrations are much higher than on other days (see Figure 3). These data show that a temporal variation of two to three orders of magnitude in the concentration of an air contaminant is not unusual around this facility. How we should use these data or even describe them in a risk assessment is uncertain.

One way to use data with large variations is to consider average exposure. The average exposure levels could be used to evaluate chronic risks and the maximum level (or 95th percentile) could be used to evaluate acute risks. Another approach would be to use a pharmacokinetic model to determine if an average target organ concentration could be estimated to evaluate chronic exposure.

Table 3 contains average concentrations of both methylene chloride and acetone in ambient air and in one of the rooms in the school beside Kodak

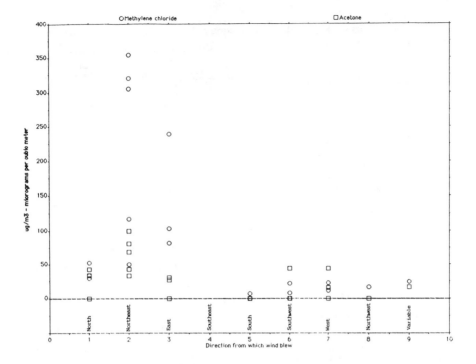

FIGURE 3.   School 41: ambient concentration vs. wind direction.

Table 3
Methylene Chloride and Acetone Concentrations in Air
(μg/m³)

	Average	Range	Number of days	
			Total	Not detected
Methylene chloride				
School 41:				
Ambient	78	ND–355	24	4
Room 322	72	ND–340	22	3
School 44:				
Ambient	7	ND–19	20	17
Room 113	7	ND–20	17	16
Acetone				
School 41:				
Ambient	33	ND–100	24	10
Room 322	29	ND–160	22	11
School 44:				
Ambient	15	ND–32	20	15
Room 113	176	ND–740	19	6

ND = Not detected.

Table 4
Loving Care Dry Cleaners Mahopac-Putnam County Tetrachloroethene (μg/m³)

Location	Sampling dates/results)		
	10/18/89	11/06/89	12/01/89
Family "A" (now vacant)	197,000	14,500	
(Baby's bedroom)		41,200	5,700
(Apt 1E — 2nd Floor)			
Family "B" (now vacant)			
(Apt 1C — 2nd Floor)	5,300	3,370	5,030
Outdoor (window ledge)	1,900	1,780	5,605
First-floor apartment	—	40	—
Third-floor apartment (vacant)	—	36	7,215
Lakeside rooming house (control)	1,500	11	340
Field trip blank	0.137	0.024	0.2
Wind direction and speed (mph)	NNE, 12	Calm	NW, 5–10

Park (School 41) and a control school (School 44) about 4 miles southwest of Kodak Park. .The average indoor and ambient concentrations of acetone and methylene chloride at School 41 are as much as an order of magnitude higher than both the average and upper quartile levels in the National Ambient Volatile Organic Compounds data base.

Apartments above or beside a dry cleaning establishment provide another example of homes which may be heavily impacted by air emissions from nearby sources. Recently, following a complaint, we investigated tetrachloroethene levels in an apartment above a dry cleaners.[8] Table 4 shows analytical results from three different sampling events. In this particular situation, one bedroom contained an average tetrachloroethene value for a 3-h sampling period that was greater than the OSHA 8-h standard of 170 mg/m³. The control house that was selected and thought to be distant from any tetrachloroethene source was also found to be impacted, primarily from a nearby tailor (see Figure 4).

The Health Department also surveyed dry cleaners in the Albany, NY, area to determine how frequently homes or apartments could be impacted.[9] An initial survey was conducted from July 25 to August 7, 1990, of the 102 facilities listed in the NYNEX Capital District yellow pages under "Cleaners". The investigators telephoned each facility and asked whether "dry cleaning" was performed on the premises. Those operators indicating no dry cleaning were asked whether or not dry-cleaned goods were pressed on the premises. Exterior inspections of these 67 facilities were also conducted to determine, among other items, the building construction (masonry, wood frame, steel, or other), the number of stories, other uses of the building (dwelling units, offices, etc.), and whether or not they were dwelling units in separate buildings within an approximate 50-foot radius.

The survey results are summarized in Table 5. Of the 67 facilities with cleaning or pressing on the premises, 14 had dwelling units above in the same

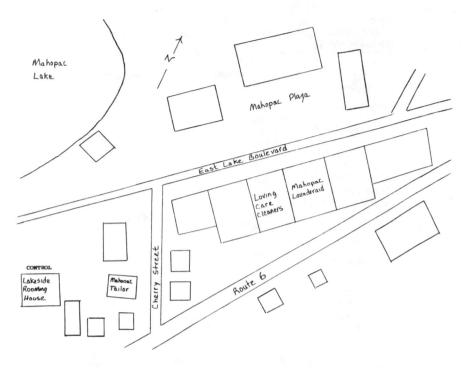

FIGURE 4. Area near the Loving Care dry cleaners, Mahopac, NY.

Table 5
Capital District Dry Cleaners Survey Summary of Findings
July 25 to August 7, 1990

| Facility onsite process | Facilities with proximate dwelling units | | Facilities with no proximate dwelling units | Facility totals |
	Same building	Separate building		
Dry cleaning	12	14	37	63
Pressing only	2	1	1	4
No dry cleaning or pressing on premises	xx	xx	xx	35
				102

building and 15 other facilities were within 50 feet of other buildings with dwelling units. Thus, 43% (29 out of 67) of Albany-area dry cleaners surveyed who clean or press on the premises are proximate to dwelling units.

After the initial survey, we measured tetrachloroethene levels in apartments directly above a dry cleaning facility.[10] Of the 14 dry cleaners that clean or press clothes on the premises, 6 were eliminated because the apartments above them were either vacant or used for storage. One facility was eliminated

Table 6
Tetrachloroethene Concentrations for Study and Control Residences ($\mu g/m^3$)

Residence	Tetrachloroethene indoor		Tetrachloroethene outdoor	
	AM	PM	AM	PM
Study homes				
Residence 1 (O)	55,000	36,500	2,600	360
Residence 2 (T)	17,000	14,000	1,400	1,400
Residence 3 (T)	3,850	8,380	530	812
Residence 4 (T)	1,730	1,350	1,110	441
Residence 5 (D)	440	160	195	66
Residence 6 (D)	300	100	300	400
Control homes				
Residence C1	<6.7	<6.7	<6.7	<6.7
Residence C2	103	77	21	<6.7
Residence C3	<6.7	<6.7	<6.7	<6.7
Residence C4	<6.7	<6.7	<6.7	<6.7
Residence C5	44	56	<6.7	<6.7
Residence C6	9.7	22	16	6.9

Study residence above dry cleaner using:
O = old dry-to-dry unit
D = dry-to-dry unit
T = transfer unit

because it didn't use tetrachloroethene and another was eliminated because it only pressed clothes. Thus, of the 102 dry cleaners only 6 (6%) remained for further study. The air sampling results are given in Table 6. They confirm the finding from the first apartment investigated by the Department of Health, that people in apartments directly above a dry cleaner can be exposed to significantly elevated levels of tetrachloroethene, levels that can be more than three orders of magnitude greater than average indoor levels reported in the National Ambient VOC Data base and the TEAM study reports.

CONCLUSIONS

These two studies of air contaminant exposure in a school and in apartments demonstrate that there may be significant temporal variation in exposure. In addition, average population exposure levels do not adequately characterize exposure. Some individuals are being exposed at much higher levels than the average.

Characterizing human health risks from chemical exposure requires consideration of both exposure and toxicity data. Exposure assessments have improved. The New York State Department of Health, with cooperation from the New York State Department of Environmental Conservation, which regulates air contaminant emissions from dry cleaners, is continuing to study tetrachloroethene exposure of individuals who live above or near dry cleaners.

Although such studies are time consuming and costly (about $2000 analytical costs and 2 person-days for sample collection to sample one apartment, a control, and the ambient air), there is no alternative to sampling to establish exposure ranges for individuals affected by air contamination sources. As the exposure data improve, additional methods of combining the exposure and toxicologic data, e.g., pharmacokinetic modeling, will have to be developed to estimate the effects of highly variable exposure data.

REFERENCES

1. U.S. Environmental Protection Agency. 1987. Unfinished Business: a Comparative Assessment of Environmental Problems. Office of Policy Analysis, February 1987.
2. U.S. Environmental Protection Agency. 1990. Reducing Risk: Setting Priorities for Environmental Protection. Science Advisory Board. SAB-EC090-021. September 1990.
3. U.S. Environmental Protection Agency. 1990. Reducing Risk: Setting Priorities for Environmental Protection. Science Advisory Board. SAB-EC090-021. September 1990.
4. Nero and Associates, Inc. 1988. National Ambient Volatile Organic Compounds (VOCs) Data Base Update, Documentation, prepared for Environmental Protection Agency, March 1988.
5. Pellizzari, E. D. et al. 1987. Total Exposure Assessment Methodology (TEAM Study) Final Report. U.S. Environmental Protection Agency, Office of Research and Development. EPA/600/6-87. June 1987.
6. New York State Department of Health. 1989. Indoor Air Investigation Public School 41, Rochester, New York. Bureau of Toxic Substance Assessment, New York State Department of Health, Albany.
7. New York State Department of Health. 1990. Groundwater/Indoor Air Investigation in a Neighborhood South of Kodak Park. New York State Department of Health, Monroe County Health Department, August 1990.
8. Putnam County Health Department, New York State Department of Environmental Conservation, New York State Department of Health. 1990. Investigation of Tetrachloroethene in the Mahopac Business District. New York State Department of Health, Albany.
9. Harding, Rose and Bettsy Prohonic. 1990. A Survey of Capital District Dry Cleaning Facilities. Conducted July 25, 1990 to August 7, 1990. Bureau of Toxic Substance Assessment, New York State Department of Health, Albany.
10. New York State Department of Health. 1991. Report on an Investigation of Indoor Air Contamination in Residences above Dry Cleaners. Bureau of Toxic Substances Assessment, Division of Environmental Health Assessment, New York State Department of Health, Albany.

CHAPTER 12

An Integrated Approach to Risk Characterization of Multiple Pathway Chemical Exposures*

Christopher T. DeRosa, M. M. Mumtaz, Harlal Choudhury, and D. L. McKean

ABSTRACT

Human and other biotic components of the environment are typically exposed to hazardous materials by a wide range of potential pathways. Exposures may occur via multiple routes and media. Risk assessments based on such exposure scenarios are conducted on different levels, depending on the goals of the assessment efforts available, associated level of refinement of the risk assessment tools, and data availability. Several methods have been developed that include screening, prioritization, protection, or prediction of the human health risk as a result of exposure to hazardous chemicals. The data requirement for each of these methods varies significantly. Most often, the criteria for the application of a method or a tool will be dictated by data availability as illustrated in this paper through two multiroute, multimedia case studies, namely, incinerator emissions and lead risk assessment.

Approaches currently available for the characterization of such exposures are limited by their ability to integrate multiroute scenarios. Lead is a unique toxicant for which there is a lack of empirical evidence for a physiological threshold. Since there exists a robust data base on this chemical, a predictive model has been developed that integrates its exposure and pharmacokinetics. This model is flexible and illustrates a useful approach for integrated site- and situation-specific risk assessment using empirical data and/or default assumptions for a wide range of physiological and exposure parameters.

* Presented at the 4th Chemical Congress of North America and 202nd ACS National Meeting, New York, NY, August 25–30, 1991. The views expressed in this paper are those of the authors and do not necessarily reflect the views or policies of the U.S. Environmental Protection Agency. The U.S. government has the right to retain a nonexclusive royalty-free license in and to any copyright covering this paper.

165

INTRODUCTION

Humans and the other biotic components of the environment are typically exposed to potentially hazardous materials by means that diverge significantly from the controlled exposures used in toxicologic studies. The majority of laboratory studies include controlled exposures for a specified period of time to a single agent by a single route. Typical ambient exposures, however, are better characterized as "complex"; that is, exposures involving multiple agents, multiple pathways, and variable temporal patterns.

Currently, most risk assessments are done on a chemical-by-chemical basis. In order for risk assessors and managers to make reasonable decisions on the extent of potential exposure-specific risks or the possible hazards associated with remediation or a control technology, they must rely on tools that are, in turn, often contingent on default assumptions. For example, the 1986 Guidelines for the Health Risk Assessment of Chemical Mixtures (U.S. EPA, 1986a) offer guidance for the evaluation of available health data on mixtures for use in hazard identification or dose-response assessment. These Guidelines describe procedures for using data on individual components of a mixture based on assumptions of dose or response additivity. Risk assessment procedures have also been based on similarity of activity (comparative potency) (Lewtas, 1985) or special instances of dose additivity (toxicity equivalency factor approaches) (U.S. EPA, 1989a).

Environmental issues encountered by federal agencies frequently extend beyond a chemical-specific, dichotomous (safe vs. nonsafe) decision. Complex problems confront these agencies as episodic events, such as accidental spills, or exposures associated with hazardous waste sites that present multichemical, multiple pathways and multimedia hazards. These types of environmental problems require risk assessment protocols that synthesize knowledge as well as judgment from a wide range of disciplines.

As a means of organizing the information necessary to evaluate the impact of an exposure to the human population, the approach developed by the National Academy of Sciences (NRC, 1983) has been followed by the various federal agencies. This approach highlights four major components of evaluation as listed below:

1. Hazard identification — characterization of the adverse effects that the agent can produce
2. Dose-response assessment — quantification of the relationship between the dose and the consequent predicted incidence of the disease in the human population
3. Exposure assessment — the intensity, frequency, and duration of exposures that are currently experienced or anticipated under different conditions
4. Risk characterization — integration of the information and uncertainties in the previous three steps to predict the health risk of an exposure to the human population

As described above, steps 1 to 3 of the NAS approach address the acquisition, organization, and interpretation of information. Consequently, research in these areas tends to reflect an approach derived, in part, from the basic sciences. This orientation emphasizes chemical-specific hazard and risk assessment. While this is clearly a useful approach as a means to impart a disciplinary focus and thereby organize information, excessive reliance on a rigidly defined linear progression of information can restrict interactions between disciplines.

The goals of risk characterization are categorically different than those of the other three steps. This process is distinguished by an emphasis on articulating what needs to be known to define a context-specific problem and delineate risk management options in contrast with a more generic identification and description of a chemical-specific hazard. Traditionally, risk characterizations have been tailored to reflect a scenario-specific need. However, this is undergoing a fundamental shift and more formal guidance is being considered to serve this purpose. This requires a synthesis of disciplines to define assessment methods that transcend the characteristic study designs used within relevant disciplinary fields.

With the rapidly growing emphasis on risk-based management decisions linked to pollution prevention and risk reduction, a broad range of activities have been initiated intended to support the development of corresponding research activities to strengthen the technical premise of biologically based inference and extrapolation.

Risk Assessment Approaches

Risk assessments are conducted on many different levels, depending on the goals and associated level of refinement of the assessment effort. Since each situation requiring an assessment dictates a certain level of sophistication, each type of risk assessment calls for differing amounts and types of data about the toxicity/carcinogenicity of the chemical(s) in question. Thus, each of these types of risk assessments has its own unique utility.

Screening tools, such as *in vitro* screening tests or structure activity relationship models, can be used when virtually no data exist in a certain category for a particular chemical. These types of methods can be validated for certain applications; for example, a structure activity relationship model for absorptivity, or an *in vitro* screening test for teratogenicity. The results of these models can then be compared with results from chemicals of known toxicity to project baseline estimates of relative risk.

Prioritization approaches can be used to rank chemicals based on a nominal amount of data from different types of studies. Comparative potencies can be developed on whole mixtures and can be used for determining priorities for expenditure of resources.

Protective methods are those such as the reference dose and health advisory or the quantitative carcinogenic risk estimates such as maximum likelihood estimate or slope factor (q_1*, estimated upper bound). These methods employ data from chemicals of interest and apply data selection criteria and mathematic models to estimate levels of exposure for which risk is generally viewed as *de minimis*.

Predictive methods are generally more data intensive. For example, the model used to characterize lead exposure and attendant effects utilizes blood lead as an index of exposure and to predict the likelihood of general toxicity, expressed as incidence of adverse or frank effects.

Case Study — Incinerator Emissions

Exposure to pollutants in incinerator emissions may occur by direct and indirect exposure pathways. Direct exposure pathways are those such as inhalation in which humans come in contact with the pollutants before any deposition or transfer between media has occurred. In contrast, indirect pathways are those in which pollutants are deposited and transferred through the terrestrial and aquatic food chains and through residuals (for example, ash) to other media. Exposure by indirect pathways can occur from contact with or ingestion of soil, vegetation, meat and dairy products, water, and fish. There is strong scientific evidence that human exposures and risks from incineration sources through indirect exposures are at least as significant as, and potentially much more significant than, direct inhalation exposure. For example, recently conducted incinerator risk assessments estimate the direct and indirect exposures of a typical individual who has lived for 30 years (from childhood) within 5 km of a hazardous waste incinerator that has been in operation for 60 years (scenario B) (Figure 1 and Table 1). The results indicated that 99.95% of total benzo(a)pyrene (a product of organic material combustion) exposure and 98.4% of total cadmium exposure could be attributed to indirect exposure as opposed to direct exposure (inhalation). The contrasting scenarios A and C demonstrate the significance of the variable duration of exposure; properly characterized complex exposures will reflect less-than-lifetime as well as lifetime risk. Were human exposures limited to a point source of a single chemical pathway or temporal pattern of exposure, the exposure-response scenario would be dramatically different. This example illustrates, however, that credible risk characterization of such scenarios precludes the broad application of default assumptions to the extent that risk characterizations remain as a single-pathway, single-chemical event over a lifetime of exposure treated as a time-weighted average.

Case Study — Lead

A viable risk assessment methodology that is to be of significant utility in making regulatory decisions or for developing site-specific abatement strategies must be flexible enough to incorporate site-specific information on

SCENARIO A

Goal: To represent a most likely occurence for exposure.

Length of Incinerator Operation: 30 yrs   Concentration of Pollutant in Air and
Soil: Ave for 50 km

Individual Age: Adult   Location: Within 50 km radius   Years at Location: 16

Food Production: Some food produced in small home garden (percentage for
central city dweller); remainder produced outside the 50 km
radius from source.

Milk Production: 50% produced within the 50 km radius from source

Food, Water, and Fish Consumption Rate: Ave (50th Percentile) for US population

Source of Water and Fish: Lake within 50 km radius   Soil Ingestion Rate: Ave for
adult

SCENARIO B

Goal: To represent an intermediate between Scenarios A and C.

Length of Incinerator Operation: 60 yrs   Concentration of Pollutant in Air and
Soil: Ave for 5 km

Individual Age: 1–30 yrs   Location: Within 5 km radius   Years at Location: 30

Food Production: More food produced in home garden (percentage for suburban
dweller); remainder produced outside the 50 km radius from
source.

Milk Production: Very small fraction produced at home (percentage for suburban
dweller); remainder up to 50% produced commercially within 50
km radius from source.

Food, Water, and Fish Consumption Rate: 70–75th percentile for US population

Source of Water and Fish: Lake within 50 km radius   Soil Ingestion Rate: Upper
end average for child and
adult

SCENARIO C

Goal: Maximize all variables so highest potential exposure can be determined

Length of Incinerator Operation: 100 yrs   Concentration of Pollutant in Air and
Soil: Ave for 5 km

Individual Age: 1–70 yrs   Location: Within 5 km radius   Years at Location: 70

Food Production: Large part of food produced at home (percentage for
non-metropolitan dweller); remainder produced outside the 50 km
radius from source.

Milk Production: Small fraction produced at home (percentage for non-metropolitan
dweller); remainder up to 50% produced commercially within 50
km radius from source.

Food, Water, and Fish Consumption Rate: 90–95th percentile for US population

Source of Water: Residential Cistern   Soil Ingestion Rate: High end range for
child and adult

Source of Fish: Farm pond

FIGURE 1.   Multipathway exposure scenarios.

Table 1
Percent Contribution of Different Pathways to Total Exposure for a Hazardous Waste Incinerator

Exposure pathway	Scenario A		Scenario B		Scenario C	
	B(a)P	Cadmium	B(a)P	Cadmium	B(a)P	Cadmium
Inhalation	0.12	5.70	0.05	1.60	0.02	0.04
Soil ingestion	0.001	1.2	0.003	2.5	0.007	1.6
Crops	90	41	98	65	97	88
Animal products	9.60	7.80	2.00	2.40	2.40	0.49
Water ingestion	0.06	33.0	0.07	14.0	0.10	4.8
Fish ingestion	0.01	11.0	0.02	8.9	0.06	5.1
Total exposure	99.80	94.30	99.95	98.40	99.98	99.96

exposure sources and demographic data. Lead serves as an example of such a multimedia integrated risk assessment approach.

The purpose of any risk characterization effort is to integrate the information of concern to risk managers and characterize risk in a fashion that reflects the complexity of the exposure scenario of concern. This requires not only more robust tools for exposure assessment, but also more informed use of biomarkers and pharmacokinetics data and a tighter linkage of the components of the risk assessment paradigm throughout its application. Integrated assessment of the toxicity of a chemical also requires an understanding of the short- and long-term consequences of the interaction of the specific pollutant both within a particular medium and across various media in order to estimate the toxic dose in the target organ tissue(s). This, in turn, necessitates approaches that integrate information from physical, chemical, and biologically based models of the processes leading from exposure to expression of toxicity.

The lead model developed by the Office of Air Quality Planning and Standards (OAQPS) (U.S. EPA, 1989b) and New York University (Harley and Kneip, 1985) estimates age-specific blood lead levels associated with levels of continuous exposure to air, diet, drinking water, dust/soil, and paint lead sources. The uptake model accepts site-specific data or default values for lead levels in each medium. This information is combined with assumptions regarding behavioral and physiologic parameters that determine intake and absorption of lead from each medium to yield estimated rates of lead uptake into the blood. Behavioral and physiologic parameters are adjusted for different ages and include such items as time spent indoors and outdoors; time spent sleeping; diet; dust/soil ingestion rates; daily breathing volumes; deposition efficiency in the respiratory tract; and absorption efficiency in the respiratory and gastrointestinal tracts. The model incorporates default assumptions regarding rate constants for transfers between blood and bone, kidney, liver, and gastrointestinal (GI) tract. Transfers from blood to urine, liver to GI tract, and mother to fetus are also considered. These assumptions include adjustments that reflect age-related changes in metabolism and physiology that affect the distribution and excretion of lead (e.g., bone turnover rates). The uptake/biokinetic model sums predicted uptakes over time to yield

Table 2
Lead Intake and Uptake in 2- to 3-Year-Old Children

Parameters		Default values (μg/d)
Air lead:	Intake	0.5
	Uptake	0.2
Diet lead:	Intake	6.8
	Uptake	3.4
Soil/dust lead:	Intake	200.0
Soil/dust lead:	Uptake	6.0
Drinking water lead:	Intake	2.0
	Uptake	1.0
Total lead uptake		10.6

estimates of blood lead levels associated with continuous uptakes over the lifespan. The default assumptions and values on which uptake rate and blood lead calculations are based can be replaced with site-specific data or revised defaults. Thus, the model can be updated as new information on exposure level, intake, and uptake parameters become available. This can be used to project the impact of future trends in environmental lead levels as a result of potential regulatory decisions.

The *OAQPS version of the model* has been extended in several directions, based on recent data, to develop *the current version of the uptake/biokinetic model (UBK)*. These extensions include: additional compartmentalization of the blood and bone lead pools, kinetic nonlinearity in the uptake of lead by red blood cells at high concentrations, transfer of lead from the mother to fetus (Marcus, 1985).

This model predicts mean blood lead levels associated with defined multimedia exposure levels. However, to assess the risks associated with such exposures in a given population and evaluate potential effects of regulatory or abatement decisions, the frequency distribution for the population blood lead levels is a more useful parameter than population means. The fraction of the population with the highest blood lead levels could then be the focus of regulatory and abatement decisions.

Based on the National Health Assessment and Nutritional Evaluation Survey II data (U.S. EPA, 1986b), the model assumes a geometric standard deviation (GSD) of 1.42 as a default. This value, however, pertains to fairly homogeneous populations exposed to similar mean levels of lead from the same sources. Other distributions and levels of variability may be encountered in populations having subgroups exposed to very different soil or air lead concentrations. Table 2 presents the intake/uptake parameters used in this model. Maternal blood lead was assumed to be 7.5 μg/dl (U.S. EPA, 1990).

The probability distribution of blood lead levels in 2- to 3-year-old children as predicted by the model is presented in Figure 2. The model predicted a mean blood lead level of 2.98 μg/dl; and that 0.02% of the children will have

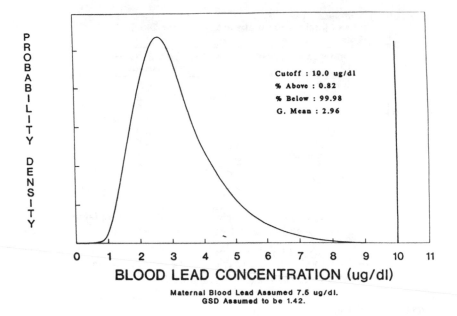

FIGURE 2. Probability distribution of blood lead levels in 2- to 3-year-old children as predicted by the lead uptake/biokinetic model. A value of 1.42 was assumed for the GSD.

blood lead levels higher than 10 µg/dl, the low end of the range of concern for adverse health effects (i.e., 10 to 15 µg/dl, or possibly lower).

U.S. EPA (1989b) discusses several validation exercises undertaken to test the performance of the UBK for predicting mean blood lead levels and distributions in human populations. Results of the most extensive evaluation are shown in Figures 3 and 4. The UBK model was used to predict blood lead levels in 299 children living in the vicinity of a lead smelter. The frequency distribution of the predicted blood lead in individual children was compared with the observed distribution. Using site-specific data for air, dust, and soil lead in the model, predicted and observed mean blood lead levels and distributions were essentially observed to be identical up to the 90th percentile (see Figure 3). Above the 90th percentile, the model slightly underpredicted blood lead levels. Using default estimates of dust and soil lead in the model, predicted mean blood lead levels were within 2% of those observed; however, the model again slightly underpredicted blood lead levels at the highest percentile (see Figure 4).

SUMMARY AND CONCLUSIONS

Humans are exposed to chemicals from a variety of media; the determination of relative contribution of each medium to total uptake is important and could

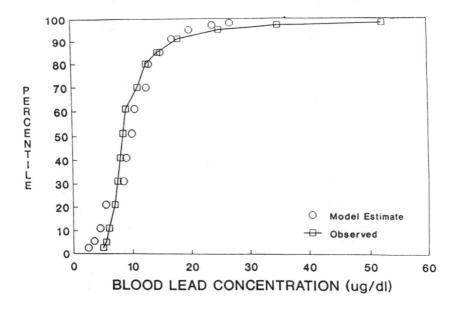

FIGURE 3. Comparison of distribution of measured blood levels in children 1 to 5 years of age, living within 2.25 miles of a lead smelter with levels predicted from the uptake/biokinetic model. Measured dust and soil lead levels were included in the input parameters to the model (U.S. EPA, 1989).

play a critical role in determining human exposures. The case study of incineration emissions that demonstrates the significance of consideration of all relevant, direct and indirect, pathways and temporal patterns of exposure to environmental pollutants.

Multimedia exposure analysis coupled with predictive biokinetic models can provide powerful tools for developing risk assessment strategies. It is currently feasible to utilize biokinetic models to provide predictions of blood lead levels that will result from any given range of route-independent lead uptake rates and vice versa (U.S. EPA, 1989b). These models allow benchmark blood lead levels to be related quantitatively to route-independent uptake rates and can provide estimates of frequency distributions of blood lead levels associated with any given uptake rate. Site-specific data or plausible default assumptions regarding exposure scenarios and absorption efficiency for lead intake from various media have been incorporated into existing multimedia exposure analysis methods to yield estimates of the relative contributions of air, dietary, and soil lead to any given estimated lead uptake.

Outputs from such multimedia analyses can be used to define the implications of regulatory decisions and abatement strategies on the distribution of blood lead levels in relevant human populations. The type and quantity of data available for lead is not available for most chemical exposure situations.

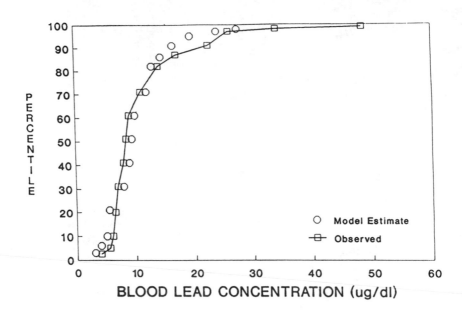

FIGURE 4. Comparison of distribution of measured blood lead levels in children, 1 to 5 years of age, living within 2.25 miles of a lead smelter with levels predicted from the uptake/biokinetic model. Dust and soil lead levels were estimated using default calculations (U.S. EPA, 1989).

However, the example of the UBK illustrates the potential utility derived from an informed integration and application of information on biomarkers, pharmacokinetics, and predictive models.

The limitations of currently available risk assessment methods makes the characterization of risk to environmental pollutants somewhat difficult. In order to enhance the merit of risk assessment as a credible adjunct in decision making, risk characterization issues must be addressed systematically within each stage of the risk assessment paradigm (i.e., hazard identification, dose-response assessment, and exposure assessment). The unique challenges presented by risk characterization underscore the need for a coordinated multidisciplinary approach to the risk characterization research of complex exposures. If the overall goal is to improve environmental protection, research must also facilitate the development and/or application of more plausible risk assessment methods.

Risk assessment has emerged as a major factor that "drives" clean-ups, local decision making, regulation, and even legislation. Risk assessment guidelines are a means by which to interpret and integrate knowledge concerning the potential health impacts of chemical exposures. New data generated by researchers is of more use to risk assessors when it is tied into a set of procedures for their consistent application in specific environmental problems.

ACKNOWLEDGMENTS

The authors wish to acknowledge the editorial contributions of Ms. Judy Olsen, the typing assistance of Ms. Sandra Malcom and Ms. Bette Zwayer, and the assistance of Mr. Terry Meranda in the preparation of graphics.

REFERENCES

Harley, N. H. and Kneip, T. H. (1985). An integrated metabolic model for lead in humans of all ages. Final report to the U.S. Environmental Protection Agency, Contract No. B44899. Office of Air Quality, Planning and Standards, Research Triangle Park, NC 27711. January, 1985.

Lewtas, J. (1985). Development of a comparative potency method for cancer risk assessment of complex mixtures using short-term *in vivo* and *in vitro* bioassays. *Toxicol. Ind. Health* 1(4):193–203.

Marcus, A. H. (1985). Multicompartment kinetic model for lead. III. Lead in blood plasma and erythrocytes. *Environ. Res.* 36:473–489.

NRC (National Research Council). (1983) *Risk Assessment in the Federal Government: Managing the Process.* National Academy Press, Washington, D.C.

U.S. EPA (1986a). Guidelines for the health risk assessment of chemical mixtures. *Fed. Regist.* 51:34006–34012 September 24.

U.S. EPA (1986b). Air Quality Criteria for Lead. June, 1986 and Addendum, September, 1986. Office of Research and Development, Office of Health and Environmental Assessment, Environmental Criteria and Assessment Office, Research Triangle Park, NC. EPA 600/8-83-028AF, BF, CF, DF. EPA/602/8-83/028A.

U.S. EPA (1988). Interim Report: Risk Characterization for Chemical Mixtures. Prepared by the Office of Health and Environmental Assessment, Environmental Criteria and Assessment Office, Cincinnati, OH for the Office of Emergency and Remedial Response, Washington, D.C.

U.S. EPA (1989). Review of the National Ambient Air Quality Standards for Lead: Exposure Analysis Methodology and Validation. Final Draft. Office of Air Quality Planning and Standards, Research Triangle Park, NC.

U.S. EPA (1989a). Interim Procedures for Estimating Risks Associated with Exposures to Mixture of Chlorinated Dibenzo-p-dioxins and -dibenzofurans (CDDs and CDFs) and 1989 Update. EPA/625/3-89/016.

U.S. EPA (1989b). Review of the National Ambient Air Quality Standards for Lead: Exposure Analysis Methodology and Validation. Final Draft. Office of Air Quality Planning and Standards, Air Quality Management Division, Research Triangle Park, NC.

U.S. EPA (1990). Air Quality Criteria for Lead: Supplement to the 1986 Addendum. Office of Research and Development, Office of Health and Environmental Assessment, Environmental Criteria and Assessment Office, Research Triangle Park, NC. EPA/600/8-89/049F.

A Method for Obtaining Guidance for the Combination of Qualitative Rankings by Cancer and Noncancer Risks into a Single, Qualitative Health Risk Ranking

Paul F. Deisler, Jr.

INTRODUCTION

In a major study,[1] herein called the UBR (for "Unfinished Business" Report), the U.S. Environmental Protection Agency ranked its 31 major problem areas (Table 1) in four ways: by *cancer risk, noncancer health risk, ecological risk,* and *welfare risk.* The problems cover the Agency's immediate and primary regulatory responsibilities, such as *criteria pollutants from mobile and stationary sources* or *inactive (Superfund) waste sites;* other areas where the Agency has less direct or secondary regulatory interest, such as *worker exposure to chemicals;* and areas it is evaluating, but not regulating, such as *indoor radon* or *global warming.* The rankings were qualitative since the data do not support quantitative ranking, although quantified information was used when available to help form the *judgments* as to the rankings of the problems relative to each other.

A second study,[2] herein called the RRR (for "Reducing Risk" Report), make by the Agency's Science Advisory Board at the Administrator's request, evaluates the UBR and advises the Agency on following it up. During this study the author was asked how to produce a single *health risk* ranking of the Agency's problems since such a ranking would be useful in resource allocation and planning. This chapter discusses quantitative health risk ranking in general, some serious obstacles to doing such ranking, and the author's early response to the question addressed to him plus some further progress, namely, the derivation of some new principles and guidelines, based on principles of *quantitative* ranking, for merging two *qualitative* rankings.

The principles derived in this chapter do not solve the major problems of direct health risk ranking directly; rather, they offer a way to simplify and facilitate the decision making involved in merging separate, qualitative rankings by suggesting which specific problems or groups of problems need to be compared, and which need not be, to arrive at a single, proposed, merged, health risk ranking.

Table 1
U.S. EPA's 31 Principal Problems

Number	Problem description
1.	Criteria air pollutants from mobile and stationary sources (includes acid precipitation)
2.	Hazardous/toxic air pollutants
3.	Other air pollutants (includes fluorides, total reduced sulfur, substances not included above that emit odors)
4.	Radon — indoor air only
5.	Indoor air pollutants — other than radon
6.	Radiation — other than radon
7.	Substances suspected of depleting the stratospheric ozone layer — CFCs, etc.
8.	CO_2 and global warming
9.	Direct point source discharges (industrial, etc.) to surface water
10.	Indirect point source discharges (POTWs) to surface water
11.	Nonpoint source discharges to surface water
12.	Contaminated sludge (includes municipal and scrubber sludge)
13.	Pollutants to estuaries, coastal waters, and oceans from all sources
14.	Pollutants to wetlands from all sources
15.	Exposure to pollution from drinking water as it arrives at the tap (includes chemicals, lead from pipes, biological contaminants, radiation, etc.)
16.	Hazardous waste sites — active (includes hazardous waste tanks) — (groundwater and other media)
17.	Hazardous waste sites — inactive (Superfund) — (groundwater and other media)
18.	Nonhazardous waste sites — municipal (groundwater and other media)
19.	Nonhazardous waste sites — industrial (includes utilities) — (groundwater and other media)
20.	Mining waste (includes oil- and gas-extraction wastes)
21.	Accidental releases — toxics (includes all media)
22.	Accidental releases — oil spills
23.	Releases from storage tanks (includes product and petroleum tanks — above, on, or underground)
24.	Other groundwater contamination (includes septic systems, road salt, injection wells, etc.)
25.	Pesticide residues on foods eaten by humans and wildlife
26.	Application of pesticides (risks to applicators, which includes workers who mix, load, as well as apply, and also consumers who apply pesticides)
27.	Other pesticide risks, including leaching and runoff of pesticides and agricultural chemicals, air deposition from spraying, etc.
28.	New toxic chemicals
29.	Biotechnology (environmental releases of genetically altered materials)
30.	Consumer product exposure
31.	Worker exposure to chemicals

DESCRIPTION OF THE RANK-MERGING PROBLEM AND THE GENERAL APPROACH TAKEN

A set of items (or "problems" as in Table 1) ranked qualitatively according to two different criteria — cancer risk and noncancer adverse health effects risk, here — may be plotted in a square array as in Figure 1 to yield the three-by-three array of nine cells shown. The risk rankings of the problems in Figure 1 (H = high, M = medium, and L = low) are from the UBR as

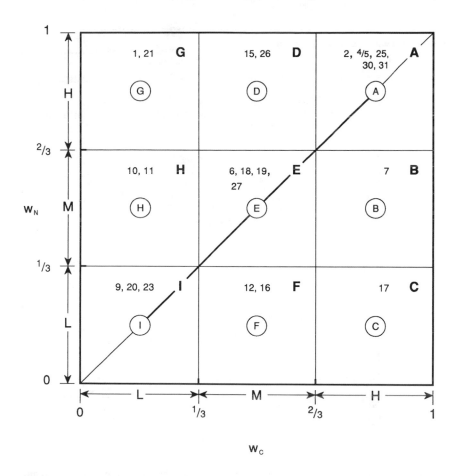

FIGURE 1. Three-by-three, symmetrical, linear array (problems plotted in appropriate cells).

summarized in the RRR (Appendix B, Table 5.4, page 63), but with Problems 4 and 5 combined into a single problem, denoted 4/5, as recommended in the RRR. The problems are simply listed within the appropriate cells, their exact positions within their cells not being shown since the rankings are qualitative. Some problems are not plotted because not all problems were ranked, in the UBR, for both cancer and noncancer adverse health effects risks.

The rankings of the problems within three of the cells (A, E, and I) are already clearly merged where the merged rankings by overall health risk are as follows: the problems in cell A rank above those in cell E, which rank above those in cell I, or A > E > I; this is true since the three cells lie on the primary diagonal of the array and do not overlap (an upward sloping diagonal is called the primary diagonal in this chapter; a downward sloping

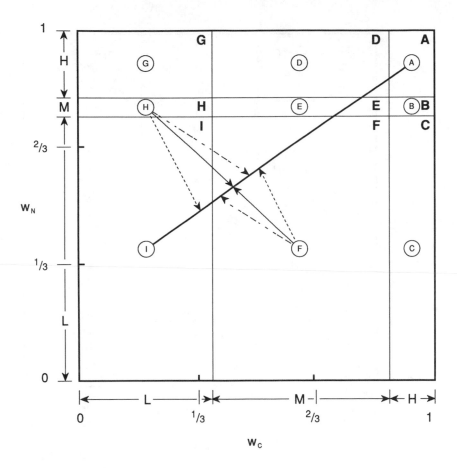

FIGURE 2.   Three-by-three, unsymmetrical, nonlinear array (highly irregular cell boundary spacing).

one, the secondary diagonal). Intuitively, to rank the problems in the remaining cells against those in the three already ranked, one would like to have a way to "project" the unranked problems (or, perhaps, the problems in a cell as a group) onto the primary diagonal with the thought that the relative positions of the projections on the primary diagonal might define the relative merged ranks.

In Figure 1 the boundaries between cells are shown evenly spaced on a scale of relative quantitative risk ranging from zero to one. Where the boundaries would really be located if the problems had been quantitatively ranked is not known; conceivably, they could be unevenly spaced as illustrated in Figure 2. Projection turns out to be possible, as shown in this chapter, not only for three-by-three arrays like the one in Figure 1, but for others with more or fewer cells or with evenly or unevenly spaced cell boundaries. Moreover, because such projections are possible, a set of simple principles can be derived which offer guidance for selecting those problems or groups of problems which need to be compared, and those which do not, to merge two qualitative rankings. The approach taken to derive the projection method, the principles, and the guidance they offer, is to consider, first, how to rank items or problems quantitatively if the necessary data were available to do so.

QUANTITATIVE HEALTH RISK RANKING AND ITS DIFFICULTIES

To rank a set of problems quantitatively according to environmental health risk, information one might wish to have includes, at least, the numbers of people exposed in each problem situation, the totality of agents to which these people might be exposed, the totality of adverse health effects that can result from exposures, the level of response or fraction of the exposed population that exhibits each adverse health effect as caused by each agent associated with each problem exposure situation, and the relative severities of each of the adverse health effects. The adverse health effects must be carefully defined, for different levels and durations of exposure if necessary. The weights which determine the rankings of the problems will be proportional to these factors (or to monotonic functions of them if so desired). It is also necessary to specify the weight to be given to individual risk relative to population risk if both types of risk are to be considered.

If all this information were available, then a quantitative weight for ranking purposes for each problem could be calculated straightforwardly from the following equation, the rank order of each problem being determined by the value of its overall weight, W_j:

$$W_j = N_j \sum_{i=1}^{E} \sum_{k=1}^{A} S_i (1 + U_{ijk}) f_{ijk} \tag{1}$$

(See NOMENCLATURE for definitions of all terms). Other factors can be included if relevant to the problem at hand, such as increased weight for sensitive members of the populations or how to allocate joint severity between adverse health effects in fractions of the population affected by more than one health effect. Factors such as synergism or antagonism between agents are already inherently included in Equation 1. Note that for $N_j > 1$ *and* U_{ijk} = 0 or a constant, W_j is the weight considering population risk, alone, whereas for $N_j = 1$ *and* $U_{ijk} = 0$ or a constant, W_j is the weight considering individual risk, alone.

For a ranking effort as large as the one undertaken in the UBR, information is often lacking on objectively measurable factors, and where it exists it is of highly uneven completeness and quality; even good data involve great uncertainties. The list of agents present is usually far from complete, and health-effects data are often only available for a fraction of them, making the use of assumed surrogates and educated guesses necessary for the remainder. Estimating the number of people exposed, for the broad types of problems listed in Table 1, involves making judgments, assumptions, and guesses. In estimating the fraction of the population affected, the well-known problems with epidemiological and animal test data, and with low-dose extrapolation, all arise; and the question of interpreting exposure information (levels, durations, time patterns, and effects on response) from measurements or modeling calculations (or from assumptions) adds further uncertainty. These objective factors need to be pursued and knowledge of them greatly improved before quantitative health risk ranking of items of similar severity can be practiced with any confidence.

While it is obvious that there are differences in the severities of adverse health effects, there are no generally agreed severity scales. It may only prove possible to develop such scales in very specific, narrow cases; even then, controversy is likely since many key judgments needed to establish them are subjective, personal, societal, and ethical in character. The severities tentatively suggested by the Agency in the UBR for noncancer health risk ranking were highly controversial and were not confidently subscribed to by the team doing the ranking.

Relative weighting of individual vs. population risk also involves subjective, personal, societal, and ethical factors. Population risk was used for ranking in the UBR, though in at least one instance individual risk was also given unspecified weight; therefore, it is included in Equation 1.

Given the above problems, a direct, quantitative health risk ranking of the U.S. EPA's 31 problems is not now possible. Conceivably, a merging of two preexisting rankings could be achieved by trial-and-error, hunt-and-peck comparisons of pairs of problems; the numbers of comparisons could be large, the process long and difficult, and there is no assurance that the result would be in keeping with general principles of quantitative ranking. Even making a single pair of comparisons of the information about two problems for both cancer and noncancer risks is very difficult, as will be seen later on, so that reducing the number of key comparisons that need to be made can be of considerable help. An organized approach is proposed which is applicable, also, to merging rankings of other types of items ranked on other bases (e.g., types of industrial processes by cancer and by safety risks; ecological and welfare problems; consumer product preferences), provided one or more connecting factors equivalent to severity exist, at least in theory (for example, economic, aesthetic, or other types of factors) and provided the general, direct, ranking equation in each case is of a form similar to Equation 1, namely, that it consists of the sum of weights of individual contributions to the weight of the item being ranked. The approach hinges on the fact that for two rankings of the same items by discrete, qualitative categories of two different ranking criteria, one can derive a set of *possible* merged rankings of defined groupings of the items which can then be compared with available information to select the possible ranking which is in greatest conformity with the information. This is itself a largely qualitative kind of comparison.

DERIVATION OF THE RANK-MERGING PRINCIPLES

Breaking Equation 1 into two portions, one for total cancer risk weight W_{Cj} and another for total noncancer risk weight W_{Nj}, yields

$$W_{cj} = N_j \sum_{i=1}^{C} \sum_{k=1}^{A} S_i (1 + U_{ijk}) f_{ijk} \qquad (2)$$

and

$$W_{Nj} = N_j \sum_{i=C+1}^{E} \sum_{k=1}^{A} S_i (1 + U_{ijk}) f_{ijk} \qquad (3)$$

Equation 1 then becomes

$$W_j = W_{cj} + W_{Nj} \qquad (4)$$

Introducing the relative weights w_j, w_{Cj}, and w_{Nj} into Equation 4, where the latter two are normalized to lie between zero and one, corresponding to the coordinates of Figures 1 and 2, the relationship of the relative quantitative weights of the problems for cancer, only, and for noncancer health effects, only, to a combined, merged weight for both is

$$w_j = w_{cj} + v w_{Nj} \qquad (5)$$

The coefficient v is constant for a particular set of items being ranked, and

$$v = W_{NH}/W_{CH} \qquad (6)$$

Referring to Figures 1 and 2, it is the sets of items (or problems) in each of the cells that constitute the defined groupings referred to above for which allowable rankings can be derived. Since the locations of the problems within the cells are not known in actual fact, the prior distribution of points within a cell may be assumed uniform over the area of the cell (including those cells which have upper boundaries, expressed in nonrelative terms, corresponding to W_{CH} and W_{NH}, provided these boundaries have been defined as in the NOMENCLATURE) and the prior mean location of the points in a cell is therefore the centroid of the cell (plotted as a circular node with the same letter designating it as the cell containing it in the figures).

Since the two right-hand terms in Equation 5, w_{Cj} and w_{Nj}, refer to the coordinates of points within the array measured along the w_C and the w_N axes, then any two points having different coordinates, but the same values of w_j are of equal merged rank. With w_j constant, solving Equation 5 for w_{Nj} gives the equation for a line on which all points have the same merged weight and therefore rank:

$$w_{Nj} = w_j/v - (1/v) w_{cj} \tag{7}$$

This line is called the projection trajectory in this chapter, and the intersection of a projection trajectory with any other line (or curve), such as the primary diagonal, is therefore a projection of any point on the projection trajectory onto the line (or curve). Equation 5 thus supplies the means for thinking about projecting off-diagonal points — problems, if we knew their actual locations, the centroids of cells which are definable for any particular configuration of cells, or any other points — onto the primary diagonal, for any value of v.

The slope of the projection trajectory is seen to be $-1/v$; that is, all projection trajectories are parallel and of slope no greater than zero. Considering this fact and Figures 1 and 2, geometrically, leads to the following conclusions and principles:

1. Any point in an array to the left and/or below any other point in the array ranks below that other point.
2. The order, from right to left, of projections of points in an array onto any line (or monotonic curve), whatever its slope or location, is always the same for a given v and is their merged rank order from highest to lowest.
3. Since any line (or monotonic curve), not just the primary diagonal, may be selected as the line onto which points are projected to determine their merged rank orders according to conclusion (2), then one is free to choose the most convenient line or curve as the line or curve onto which projections are made.
4. The most convenient line or curve onto which to project cell centroids in an array is the primary diagonal of the array, since all projections of off-diagonal centroids must lie on the diagonal within its boundaries.
5. Assuming different values of v is equivalent to rotating all projection vectors simultaneously and in parallel, thus shifting the relative positions of projected points to create different, discrete rankings of the points as v changes (see in Figure 2 the projections of centroids F and H with three values of v).

DERIVATION OF POSSIBLE CELL RANKINGS

The projection of an entire cell onto the primary diagonal is a line segment lying on the primary diagonal (and extensions of it, as needed) between the projections of the upper right and lower left vertices of the cell, since the projections of any or all points within the cell must lie between the projections of those two points. The projections of cells thus overlap, sometimes extensively, making the definition of the position of the projection of one cell relative to another, on the basis of the projections of the cells, inconclusive.

With the prior assumption mentioned earlier that the probability distribution of points (or problems) is uniform over the area of any cell, the value of the probability density function of projected points at any projected point is proportional to the length of the projection trajectory which lies within the cell of that projected point; the resultant probability density function of the projections of all points in a cell is thus symmetrical about the expectation of the probability distribution of projections which, in turn, is just the projection of the centroid of the cell (the shapes of these symmetrical probability density distributions are triangular, trapezoidal, or rectangular, depending on the value of v). So, though the lines which are the projections of cells may overlap, the relative average positions of the cell projections on the primary diagonal, and therefore of the merged rankings of their corresponding cells, are well characterized by the positions of the projections of the centroids of the cells. In determining the possible merged cell rankings for a particular configuration of cell boundaries (or of cells) for different values of v, one need only consider the arrays of the centroids and the projections of the centroids of the cells on the primary diagonal.

With the projections of the centroids of cells taken as the best descriptors of the relative positions of cell projections, rotating centroid projection vectors, as in principle number 5, generates the full set of rank orders of cells possible for any and all values of v for a given set of cell boundary configurations. While extremely unsymmetrical arrays as in Figure 2 may be unlikely to occur, there is no way of knowing, when attempting to generate possible merged qualitative rankings, either what the quantitative cell boundaries or what the value of v might be. In developing possible rankings, all possibilities must therefore be considered.

The advantage of selecting the diagonal from centroid A to centroid I as the primary diagonal for three-by-three arrays for any cell configuration now becomes especially apparent: all centroid projections lie on this primary diagonal between centroids A and I, making the geometrical determination of the ranking of cells for any v easy to visualize. For example, projection trajectories for three values of v are shown in Figure 2, projecting centroids F and H onto the primary diagonal; the merged rank orders of the two cells as v rotates from its highest to its lowest value are H ranks higher than F, or $H > F$; F and H are of equal rank, or (FH); and F ranks higher than H, or $F > H$. Allowing v to take on all possible values in Figure 2 yields the full set of possible merged rank orders of cells (see Table 2).

For comparison, the set for the array of Figure 1 is shown in Table 3, and for a two-by-two array (Figure 3) only one set of possible rankings exists

Table 2
Rankings Possible for the Nonlinear, Unsymmetrical, Three-by-Three Array Shown in Figure 2

For	The ranking is
$v = \infty$	(ADG) > (BEH) > (CFI)
$v > v_o$	A > D > G > B > E > H > C > F > I
"	A > D > (BG) > E > H > C > F > I
"	A > D > B > G > E > H > C > F > I
"	A > D > B > (EG) > H > C > F > I
"	A > D > B > E > G > H > C > F > I
"	A > (BD) > E > G > H > C > F > I
"	A > B > D > E > G > H > C > F > I
"	A > B > D > E > G > (CH) > F > I
"	A > B > D > E > G > C > H > F > I
$v = v_o$	A > B > D > E > (CG) > H > F > I
$v < v_o$	A > B > D > E < C > G > H > F > I
"	A > B > D > E > C > G > (FH) > I
"	A > B > D > E > C > G > F > H > I
"	A > B > D > E > C > (FG) > H > I
"	A > B > D > E > C > F > G > H > I
"	A > B > D > (CE) > F > G > H > I
"	A > B > D > C > E > F > G > H > I
"	A > B > (CD) > E > F > G > H > I
"	A > B > C > D > E > F > G > H > I
$v = 0$	(ABC) > (DEF) > (GHI)

Table 3
Rankings Possible for the Linear, Symmetrical, Three-by-Three Array Shown in Figure 1

For	The ranking is
$v = \infty$	(ADG) > (BEH) > (CFI)
$v > v_o$	A > D > G > B > E > H > C > F > I
"	A > D > (BG) > E > (CH) > F > I
"	A > D > B > G > E > C > H > F > I
$v = v_o = 1$	A > (BD) > (CEG) > (FH) > I
$v < v_o$	A > B > D > C > E > G > F > H > I
"	A > B > (CD) > E > (FG) > H > I
"	A > B > C > D > E > F > G > H > I
$v = 0$	(ABC) > (DEF) > (GHI)

(see Table 4) since, whatever the cell boundaries might be, the four centroids can only form a square.

Following the geometrical technique described above, different sets of rankings can be derived for different cell configurations for all values of v for three-by-three arrays; whereas for two-by-two arrays there is only 1 short set, for three-by-three arrays there are 95 sets of which the one in Table 3 is the shortest and simplest. Four-by-four and higher arrays have not been explored, but the number of sets clearly increases rapidly with array order.

For three-by-three arrays, the same rankings can occur in more than one set (four rankings always do), which somewhat alleviates the problem of finding a ranking most in keeping with information associated with the prob-

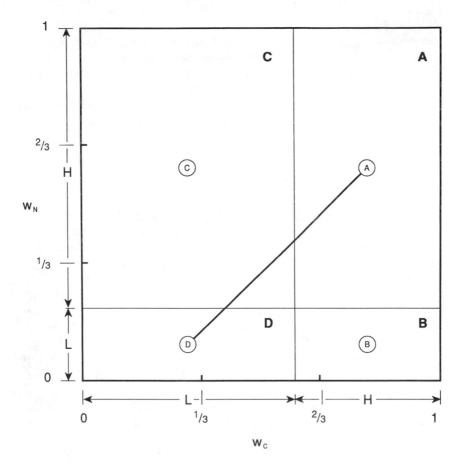

FIGURE 3.   Two-by-two, unsymmetrical, nonlinear array.

Table 4
Rankings Possible for Any Two-by-Two Array

For	The ranking is
$v = \infty$	(AC) > (BD)
$v > 1$	A > C > B > D
$v = 1$	A > (BC) > D
$v < 1$	A > B > C > D
$v = 0$	(AB) > (CD)

lems within the cells. Although rules are easily derived to help focus the search for a best ranking on only a part of full list of rankings, even for the three-by-three case a simpler approach is highly desirable; extension of the approach to higher-order arrays becomes rapidly more cumbersome, making a simpler approach even more desirable.

In the RRR report (Appendix B, Sections 6.3.3 and 8.2), a process of rank merging was used, involving guessing which kinds of cell configurations should be considered in searching for an appropriate ranking. In the illustrative example it was supposed that symmetrical configurations might be more likely to occur than others and, as it happened, the simple, linear symmetrical configuration of Figure 1 produced a suitable ranking (sheer good luck, in retrospect!). A general method is proposed here which does not depend on luck.

A PROCESS FOR SELECTING A MERGED CELL RANK ORDER

In the rest of this chapter rankings for $v = 0$ and $v = \infty$ will not be considered, since in any practical merged ranking case the first implies that the merged ranking is just the cancer-only ranking and the second implies that the merged ranking is just the noncancer-only ranking; such eventualities should be easily and immediately recognized from the raw information, obviating the need to use a merging process to obtain merged rankings. With this in mind, a result of principle number 1 is, for any three-by-three array at all, that the following rankings must inherently occur: (1) $A > D > G > H > I$ and (2) $A > B > C > F > I$. If in any case these rankings are violated, then the following possibilities must be investigated before reaching a conclusion: the original rankings are faulty, the data used in making the comparisons are inadequate to the task, or the overlap of projections of cells leads to individual problem rankings inconsistent with the cell rankings. It is also possible that a quantitative ranking equation not reducible to an equation of the form of Equation 4, and also not yielding the same ranking sets, underlies the case. What such an equation might be cannot be said in general. Some equations involving such exotic terms as the cross product $W_{Cj}W_{Nj}$ which do not yield Equation 5 with constant v nonetheless can yield the same ranking sets as in the case of Equation 5.

The method proposed here involves the use, as guides, of the above two *inherent* rankings and the fact that a three-by-three array may be visualized as containing four overlapping two-by-two arrays. Referring to Figure 1 or 2, the four two-by-two arrays are composed of the following cells: ABDE, EFHI, BCEF, and DEGH. Table 5 shows these four ranking sets omitting the ones for $v = 0$ and $v = \infty$. The first two arrays straddle the primary diagonal of a three-by-three array and are of primary utility in what follows, and the second two are of secondary utility: all four arrays contain cell (or, centroid-projection) E, but for the two primary arrays cell E provides the link between them so that if appropriate rankings can be selected from each of the two primary two-by-two arrays they can be merged into a single ranking with cell E as the juncture (this is true even if cell E contains no problems according to principle number 1). If any one of the four two-by-two arrays

Table 5
Ranking Sets for the Four Linked Two-by-Two Arrays Within any Three-by-Three Array

(A) The basic two-by-two arrays			
Primary		**Secondary**	
ABDE	**EFHI**	**BCEF**	**DEGH**
A > D > B > E	E > H > F > I	B > E > C > F	D > G > E > H
A > (BD) > E	E > (FH) > I	B > (CE) > F	D > (EG) > H
A > B > D > E	E > F > H > I	B > C > E > F	D > E > G > H

(B) Inherent rankings, three-by-three array
(1) A > D > G > H > I
(2) A > B > C > F > I

is removed from the three-by-three array the four cells will not form a square unless the three-by-three array happens to be like that in Figure 1. The coordinates w_C and w_N of such a two-by-two array may be renormalized so as to range from zero to one for that array; the four cells will then form a square and, though the consequence of this renormalization will be to change the actual numerical values of the merged weights, w_j, their numerical order and therefore the ranking of the cells of the new two-by-two array will be unchanged from the unrenormalized one. Thus, the possible rankings shown in Table 4 apply to each of the four two-by-two arrays regardless of their shape; substituting the appropriate letters for each array leads to the primary and secondary array rankings shown in Table 5. The two inherent rankings given earlier are also shown in Table 5.

In Table 5 it is seen that to consider which ranking might agree best with the information it is only necessary, to start with, to consider the ranking relations of one pair in each set: deciding the relative ranking of B and D in array ABDE is all that is needed, for that set, to select a ranking for cells A, B, D, and E. Further, if the proper ranking is similarly selected from each of the two primary arrays, then a ranking of seven cells is automatically selected, since, as explained earlier, the two selected rankings have E as a common cell and principle 1 applies. Having selected an appropriate seven-cell ranking, the ranking of the seven cells should be compared with the two inherent rankings to determine which pairs of cells need to be considered to locate C and G within the ranking of seven already in hand and so to provide a qualitative ranking of all nine cells in keeping with the principles of quantitative ranking. Empty cells are no barrier to completing the ranking selection as explained further on. The secondary rankings in Table 5 can be used to check the conclusions reached or to help resolve difficulties that might arise.

This general method is extendable to four-by-four and higher arrays as well as to lopsided arrays (e.g., two-by-three).

Table 6a
Summary of Information Highlights, Cell B

Problem #7 Cancer: Ranked 7th for cancer risk, would rank higher if uncertainty of future risk projections lower. Steady increase in nonmelanoma (basal and squamous) and melanoma skin cancer deaths, together, is projected, reaching 10,000 per year by year 2100 (double today's rate). Agent(s) considered: increased UV radiation (related to CFCs and other O_3-depleting gases, gases that buffer O_3 depletion, and projections of future emissions). Population growth, age, race, and sex and U.S. regional effects considered in estimating exposure. (For more detail and references see UBR, Appendix I, pp. B-28 to B-33).

Noncancer: Ranked MEDIUM for noncancer risk. Increased risk: moderately serious eye damage (e.g., cataracts) to the entire population; 1% O_3 depletion estimated to increase incidence of senile cataracts by 10,000 to 30,000 per year. Possible effects on immune system, but not considered. Agent(s) considered: increased UV radiation (as for problem 7, above). Little additional detail given in UBR, Appendix II except as to general ranking methodology.

ILLUSTRATION OF THE USE OF THE PROPOSED METHOD

Tables 6a and 6b summarize the chief points of information available for cells B and D. Cell B contains only one problem, #7, and cell D contains only two problems, #15 and #26 (information in Tables 6a and 6b is abstracted from the UBR, Table 1 in Appendix I and Table 1 in Appendix II). If there were no problems in one of a critical pair of cells, such as B, all rankings for array ABDE would reduce to A > D > E and the relative ranking of F and H would determine which ranking from array EFHI would merge with this curtailed ranking. The rest of the process would then proceed as before. Similar logic yields an appropriate answer if other cells contain no problems.

With the guidance for selecting possible cell rankings established, the most difficult task of all must be addressed: weighing the actual information so as to *decide* on the relative qualitative ranking of the selected cells. In comparing information, it is necessary to remember that it is the merged rank order of the *cells*, not of the *problems* within the cells, that is first sought. The information on the problems should be viewed from the perspective of answering the questions: "Does the available information on the problems in one cell give more support than not, on balance and despite uncertainty, to the idea that it is a cell containing problems of generally higher rank than another? If not, is the reverse possibly supported or are the cells possibly not distinguishable?" Despite the uncertainty and paucity, even the sketchiness, of the information, answers must be selected if qualitative rank merging is to be done, just as was true in making the original qualitative rankings. This is not a statistically based exercise (not can it be), but rather one of *best qualitative judgment:* one should commit to making the best judgment possible, with the fundamental premise that the few problems available are to

Table 6b
Summary of Information Highlights, Cell D

Problem #15 Cancer: Ranked 9th for cancer risk. Current estimate: 400 to 1,000 excess cases per year, basis home surveys of public water systems, half of samples selected at random, half because of known contamination. Most estimated cases due to radon and trihalomethanes; possible double counting (problems 4, 5, and several problems related to contaminated ground water). Agent(s) considered: ingestion and/or inhalation of 23 substances subject to regulation (VOCs, other synthetic organic chemicals including pesticides, and radionuclides). (For more detail and references see UBR, Appendix I, pp. B-43 to B-45.)

Noncancer: Ranked HIGH for noncancer risk. Generally very large exposed population and serious health effects (neurotoxicity, mortality) are possible, but exposures not often far above levels of concern. Primary concerns were over disinfection by-products, lead, and pathogens. Agents considered: lead, pathogens, legionella, nitrates, chlorine disinfectants. Little additional detail given in UBR, Appendix II except as to general ranking methodology.

Problem #26 Cancer: Ranked 10th for cancer risk. Approximately 100 cancers per year estimated by methods analogous to those used for residues on food. Small population exposed, but high individual risks. Agent(s) considered: 1 herbicide, 3 fungicides, 1 insecticide, 1 growth regulator (note: about 200 pesticide chemicals are considered to be oncogenic). Variable exposures, high potential for exposure, protective measures considered. 40 years of exposure out of a 70-year lifetime assumed. Estimated lifetime risks to agents considered were extrapolated to the 200 oncogens. (For more detail and references see UBR, Appendix I, pp. B-46 to B-48.)

Noncancer: Ranked HIGH for noncancer risk. Modest applicator populations exposed (10,000 to 250,000). Potentially very serious health effects (acute poisoning, fetotoxicity, teratogenicity). Exposures often above levels of concern. Substantial incidence estimates: 350 annual poisonings for ethyl parathion, 100 from paraquat. Little additional detail given in UBR, Appendix II except as to general ranking methodology.

be taken as *representative of their cells* so as to produce a merged ranking of cells as a first step.

Before attempting qualitative ranking, of problems or of cells, the objective of the ranking must be recalled so as to set ranking criteria. In general, the use to which a ranking is to be put must be considered in setting up appropriate ranking criteria. Here, supposing that the purpose of ranking is to assist in deciding which actions will best reduce risks in the future (the only time period in which risks can, in fact, be reduced) in keeping with the thrust of the RRR, the *potential for future risk,* as opposed to the *estimate of current risk,* is to be considered, with current regulations, controls, and trends continuing in place. Different rankings might very well be obtained by considering current risk. Also, the information on individual problems as contained in the UBR, unmodified by the critiques of the RRR, were used for consistency in the illustrative ranking exercise given as an example, below, an exercise carried out solely by the author to illustrate what a committed group of diverse experts might have done. Qualitative ranking is best done by such a group, following well-defined and agreed upon ground rules and not, in any real case, by a single individual. Judgments as to ranking as made in the UBR were also accepted, with minor modifications made in the RRR where these apply.

Referring to Tables 6a and 6b, and as discussed below, the potential for future risk, cancer and noncancer risks considered together, appeared in the view of the author to be higher for problem #7 in cell B when compared with either problem #15 or problem #26 in cell D; the main points considered in reaching this *judgment* are described further on. Taking the problems as indicative of the levels of risk represented in general by their respective cells, this would lead to the judgment not that B = D or that D > B, but that, on balance, B > D. In drawing such cell-ranking judgments it should be noted that individual cross comparisons of individual problems is done to gain an idea of where the problems in one cell seem to lie with respect to risk, qualitatively, in comparison with those in another; that is, generally above, the same, or below. The fact that there are more problems in one cell than in another is to be given no weight, since it is a matter of happenstance as to how many problems may lie in any one cell; no "average" is to be struck, and no "variance" can or should be calculated in these qualitative comparisons.

Considering cancer, first, in problems 7 and 15, #7 exhibits little current risk compared to #15, but, taking the figures at face value, potential future risk may well be a different matter. In either case there will be geographic, seasonal, and other differences in exposure, but the total exposed population can be taken as large, roughly that of the U.S. Assuming a steady increase in death rate in #7 and a constant one in #15, in only about half a generation or less the excess death rate in #7 would overtake that in #15, considering the expressed uncertainties, and cumulative deaths would do so in about a generation or less. Given on the one hand the persistence of CFCs with their half-lives of several generations, the global distribution of their discharges into the atmosphere, and the real difficulty of achieving true global regulation of these discharges over time, and given, on the other hand, the continuing and expanding role of current U.S. regulation and control (reducing individual risk) and the possibility of overestimation of deaths by double counting, the potential for future cancer risk seems substantially higher for #7 than for #15 even if the estimated death rate in #7 is not achieved as rapidly as estimated. Considering potential future noncarcinogenic risk, the severity of effect appears greater for #15 than for #7, the main effect in #7 being one which appears in old age, by and large, and which is correctable in most instances; both were ranked HIGH by the UBR ranking team, however, possibly because in each case the exposures are large despite the fact that, in the case of #15, the "levels of concern" are not "often" exceeded. A further factor weighing in the author's mind in placing #7 ahead of #15 for merged, future risk ranking is the fact that the number of cancer deaths is, for these types of cancers, only a small percentage of total skin cancers; while many skin cancers are not considered serious, they do have impact on the quality of life, they are a real medical problem for the victims, and in some cases they can lead to serious disfigurement. Weighing this factor into the total, especially considering it as a growing, "generally nonlethal" effect impacting several hundred thousand individuals, adds considerable weight to #7 and offsets a decrease in weight, if any exists, brought about by relative consideration of the noncancer effects. The principal consideration in this comparison was population risk.

If problems 7 and 26 were considered in terms of the future population risk, #26 would rank far below both #7 and #15. In fact, heavy weight was given to individual risk in the UBR in #26 such that it ranked only one place below #15 and three places below #7 for cancer risk and was ranked HIGH for noncancer risk. Accepting the information and judgment in the UBR, and the apparent weight given to individual risk, it appeared to the author that #26 must be judged to be of similar (or perhaps slightly lower) merged weight to #15 and therefore below #7. Problem #26 may rank somewhat lower still, since the extrapolation of risks estimated from a few agents to some 200 agents may overestimate risk; this would only increase the weight of the judgment in favor of $B > D$, however.

Returning to the guidance in Table 5, if $B > D$, then $A > B > D > E$. Similarly, the same kind of rankings of pairs of problems made in the RRR (Appendix B, page 150 ff), yields $F > H$ so that $E > F > H > I$. Accepting these for purposes of illustration, seven of the nine cells therefore rank as follows: $A > B > D > E > F > H > I$.

Referring again to the RRR for purposes of this illustration, the UBR data indicate $C > G$; also, the two inherent rankings, compared to the seven-cell ranking, above, show that it is necessary to compare C with D, C with E, E with G, and F with G to locate C and G (the secondary rankings confirm this). Also in the RRR, it was concluded that (CD) and (FG) are most sustainable. Thus, finally, the most fitting ranking of the nine cells, in this example, becomes:

$$A > B > (CD) > E > (FG) > H > I$$

Since projections of cells are lines which can overlap at least partially with other such projections, individual problems, first within and then between cells, need to be compared with each other to allow for the possibility that the merged ranking of some problems within different cells may differ from

Table 7
Illustrative Rank-Merging Results

Number	Problem name	Cancer rank	Noncancer rank	Merged rank
2	Haz. tox. air pollutants	H	H	H
4/5	Indoor air: radon, other	H	H	H
7	Ozone depletion	H	M	H
25	Pesticides, on food	H	H	H
30	Consumer products	H	H	H
31	Worker exposure	H	H	H
1	Criteria air pollutants	L	H	M
6	Nonradon radiation	M	M	M
12	Contaminated sludge	M	L	M
15	Drinking water at tap	M	H	M
16	Haz. waste sites, active	M	L	M
17	Haz. waste sites, inactive	H	L	M
18	Nonhaz. wst. sts., ind.	M	M	M
19	Nonhaz. wst. sts., muni.	M	M	M
21	Accidental releases	L	H	M
26	Pesticide application	M	H	M
27	Other pesticide risks	M	M	M
9	Dir. pt. dis. srf. wat.	L	L	L
10	Indir. pt. dis. srf. wat.	L	M	L
11	Nonpt. dis. srf. wat.	L	M	L
20	Mining waste (+oil and gas)	L	L	L
23	Stor. tnk. releases (all)	L	L	L

the ranking of their cells and/or that the problems are not, in fact, representative of their cells. This first ranking of cells thus does not provide "the answer"; rather, it provides a base from which to make more intimate problem-to-problem comparisons. The details of this process are described in the RRR, Appendix B, Section 8.2.9, and the result is given in Table 8.2.9.2 in the same section. As emphasized repeatedly, *this ranking is only illustrative;* it was done in that sense by the author and not, as stated, by an appropriately diverse expert panel as recommended. For comparison purposes, the above result is reported here not as given in the RRR, but divided into H, M, and L categories, consistent with the information as used in this chapter. Examining the information in the UBR indicates that a reasonable grouping is cells A and B rank High, cells H and I rank Low, and the rest rank Medium. Table 7 shows this result in column 3 compared to the initial rankings in columns 1 and 2.

CONCLUDING REMARKS

The method provides guidance and a flexible framework for an organized decision process for selecting cell rankings which are in keeping with simple, quantitative ranking principles derived from Equation 4 and with available information; it does so by indicating which specific pairs of cells, with their contained problems, must be compared to arrive at a merged ranking. It is not a ranking "formula", since judgment, not calculation, must be used to decide, in the light of stated ranking criteria, what the relative rankings of the indicated cells might be based on qualitative information on the problems within the cells. Strong discipline is necessary to exercise such judgment consistently and constructively.

The method marries quantitative and qualitative ranking concepts and gives comfort that a quantitatively *possible* ranking has been achieved and not an impossible one. Further, the method permits the qualitative, localized consideration of severity (or another connecting variable), since it depends on considering the specific cases of the few problems in the compared pairs of cells and does not depend on deriving a general, highly controversial severity scale, a task that may be impossible; it therefore offers a deliberate, alternative route to deriving combined rankings of items of different severities. There is a high degree of generality in the method, too: any two rankings of the same set of items for which there exists, at least in theory, a connecting variable is amenable to this treatment even if that variable cannot be quantified.

Finally, the difficulties in making ranking judgments should serve as a warning to risk managers and planners that qualitative rankings, especially merged rankings, are to be used as "soft" inputs; in any case, it must always be remembered that a risk ranking is not, by itself, a priority list for action.

NOMENCLATURE

A:
The total number of all possible agents which might be found in any and/or all exposure situations (when used in an equation; otherwise, A denotes cell number A).

C:
The total number of types of cancer among the E adverse health effects of all types (when used in an equation; otherwise, C denotes cell number C).

E:
The total number of all possible adverse health effects that can result from any and/or all agents present in any and/or all exposure situations (when used in an equation; otherwise, E denotes cell number E).

f_{ijk}:
The measured or estimated level of response for, or the fraction of the exposed population that exhibits, the ith adverse health effect as caused by the kth agent in the exposure situations associated with the jth problem or item being ranked.

i:
A subscript ranging from $i = 1$ to $i = E$, designating a particular one of the possible E adverse health effects.

J:
The total number of problems or items being ranked.

j:
A subscript ranging from $j = 1$ to $j = J$, designating a particular one of the J problems or items being ranked.

k:
A subscript ranging from $k = 1$ to $k = A$, designating a particular one of the possible A agents.

N:
The number of individuals exposed.

N_j:
The number of individuals exposed to agents in the exposure situations associated with the jth problem of the J problems being ranked.

$N_j U_{ijk}$:
The weight to be given to individual risk relative to population risk if both types of risk are to be considered. This weight is conveniently defined as the product of N_j and the weighting factor U_{ijk}: N_j to bring the two risks to the same scale, and U_{ijk} to indicate the relative weight to be given, where $0 \leq U_{ijk} \leq \infty$.

S_i:
The severity of the ith of the E adverse health effects relative to the severities of the remaining adverse health effects.

v:
A constant for the particular set of J items being ranked; v is defined by Equation 6.

v_o:
The value of v corresponding to the slope of the secondary diagonal.

U_{ijk}:
See $N_j U_{ijk}$.

W_{CH} and W_{NH}:
Weights selected to represent the uppermost ends of the weight ranges for cancer and noncancer effects, respectively, in setting up separate, relative, quantitative scales for each of the two kinds of effects; they cannot be less than the highest actual such

weights (the highest values of W_{Cj} and W_{Nj} regardless of the value of j in each case) for a given set of items and should be no higher than physically attainable values of the weights in either case.

W_{Cj}:   The total cancer weight of the jth problem or item (see Equations 2 and 4.

w_{Cj}:   The normalized total cancer weight of the jth problem or item; $w_{Cj} = W_{Cj}/W_{CH}$.

W_{Nj}:   The total noncancer adverse health effects weight of the jth problem or item (see Equations 3 and 4).

w_{Nj}:   The normalized total noncancer adverse health effects weight of the jth problem or item; $w_{Nj} = W_{Nj}/W_{NH}$.

W_j: The overall adverse health effects weight of the jth problem or item (see Equations 1 and 4).

w_j: The "normalized" overall adverse health effects weight of the jth problem or item; $w_j = W_j/W_{CH}$.

REFERENCES

1. *"Unfinished Business: a Comparative Assessment of Environmental Problems"*, Office of Policy Analysis, Office of Policy, Planning and Evaluation, U.S. Environmental Protection Agency (February 1987).
2. *"Reducing Risk: Setting Priorities and Strategies for Environmental Protection"*, Science Advisory Board (A-101), U.S. EPA Report-SAB-EC-90-021 (September 1990).

The Use of Statistical Insignificance in the Formulation of Risk-Based Standards for Carcinogens

Roy E. Albert and Rakesh Shukla

Environmental health deals with the identification and control of chemical and physical agents that cause disease or disability. It is also involved with the interaction of these agents with other influences in the environment that produce the same effects, e.g., biological, nutritional, or socioeconomic factors. A basic approach used in the field of environmental health is the reduction of exposures, by regulatory controls, to levels that either produce no toxicant effects or produce effects at acceptable levels of risk.

The field of health risk assessment began in the U.S. Environmental Protection Agency in the mid-1970s with an initial focus on environmental chemical and physical carcinogens.[1-3] Risk assessment was called into being because of the need for a rigorous and impartial display and analysis of the evidence on toxicants. However, risk assessment does not go further than a characterization of the qualitative and quantitative aspects of health risk. It does not tell the risk manager, i.e., the regulator, how to deal with its output. This uncertainty about how to use risk assessment in regulation has contributed to the slowness of the regulatory process.

The setting of permissible standards of exposure for toxic agents in the environment has its historical roots in the workplace, where exposure standards seek to control the toxic effects of the individual agent to negligible levels without regard to other factors or agents that cause the same toxic endpoints. Traditionally, the formulation of occupational exposure standards has been done by applying safety factors to the highest no-effect dose level in test animals. Given the assumption of dose-effect thresholds for toxic effects, the exposure standards were considered to entail zero risk.

The evolution of standard setting in the U.S. Environmental Protection Agency has taken the same approach of dealing with agents on a one-by-one basis without reference to other causes of the same toxic effects. With agents such as carcinogens, particularly if they are genotoxic, there is no basis for assuming a threshold dose-effect pattern. The currently used linear nonthreshold dose-response model implies that large populations exposed to even very small doses can have calculable increases in cancer mortality. This consideration has led to vigorous public resistance to carcinogen exposure, particularly from industrial sources in instances where there are no attendant benefits. Regulatory agencies, both Federal and state, have responded by setting *de minimis* exposure standards, i.e., standards entailing vanishingly small levels of risk such as the 10^{-6} lifetime excess cancer risk for hazardous waste cleanup. There are two problems with the use of risk-based *de minimis* standards: there is no solid rationale for the selection of the standard, and the approach does not necessarily make for a balanced use of resources. If an agent is a minor cause of a particular disease in relationship to a variety of dominant causes, then large expenditures of resources in the reduction of exposure to that particular environmental agent will have little impact on the public health burden of the disease, and the regulatory effort may be excessive in relation to the benefits.

In this paper we develop and apply the concept of statistical insignificance. The rationale for statistical insignificance is analogous to that of statistical significance. If we do not know whether or not a drug produces an effect, we test it; the larger the difference between the test and control groups, the more likely we are to think that the drug has a real effect. The judgement of significance is heavily dependent on the variability of the control and test groups. In the case of low-level exposure to an environmental carcinogen, we also do not know whether or not the carcinogen has an effect. We have to estimate the effect on the basis of extrapolation models, because the response is far below any level which can be measured directly with either animal or human studies. Our approach is to select an estimated response such that if it were true, we would never know it because the response would be so small in relation to the background variability that the odds of the responding population being different from the background population (without the carcinogen exposure) would be exceedingly small. Statistical insignificance is related to the idea of the detectability of a signal in relation to background noise. Cancer rates have inherent variability. We can consider the effect of a carcinogen as insignificant when its effect is small in relation to the random forces that both increase and decrease the occurrence of cancer and account for its variability. We explore the use of statistical insignificance in two ways: (1) as an alternative to the use of *de minimis* risk-based standards in which the regulation of carcinogens is dealt with as one component of a program to reduce the public health burden of cancer from all controllable causes of cancer. The objective is to find the most effective allocation of resources to achieve the greatest reduction in cancer. Statistical insignificance is used as a target for control instead of absolute risk estimates, e.g., 10^{-6}, because insignificance, as proposed, is a better measure of the triviality of a response, i.e., its *de minimis* character. The absolute risk estimates may be useful as a common endpoint of response, but there is nothing in such numbers that inherently relates to their importance or lack of it. (2) The second application is a reinterpretation of the 10^{-6} *de minimis* standard in terms of insignificance. Here, the standard is based on the idea that if a carcinogen effect were real, the effect would be so small as to involve a million-to-one odds in favor of a zero effect. This approach has the advantage that the size of the exposed population is an inherent part of the standard.

The idea of background variability has been advanced by others as an approach to formulating *de minimis* risk-based standards.[4,5] For example, Adler and Weinberg[5] suggested that one standard deviation in the background levels of ionizing radiation could be an appropriate *de minimis* standard because no ill effects of ionizing radiation have been noted at such incremental exposures. This level of incremental exposure is equivalent to a *de minimis* cancer risk of 10^{-4}. The same approach was extended by Travis to environmental chemicals. However, we are not assuming that there are no health effects, which is impossible to demonstrate. Our position is that if there were, they would be trivial in magnitude.

LIKELIHOOD RATIO METHOD FOR INSIGNIFICANCE

Conventionally, the likelihood ratio is used to estimate the relative plausibility that a given data set is consistent with one or another population distribution.[6] In this case we begin with a background distribution of a toxic effect, e.g., cancer, in the absence of exposure to a toxicant in question. We then estimate the effect of a given dose of the toxicant based on a dose-response model. On the assumption that the dose-response model and its estimate are correct, we have the equivalent of the set of data used in the likelihood ratio method. We then estimate the likelihood that these "data" belong to the background population or to a new population with the estimated increment as its mean. Figure 1 illustrates the likelihood ratio. Population A, with its mean, m, is the frequency distribution of the toxic effect in the absence of the toxicant in question. We estimate a low-dose increment to m assuming a dose-response model. Given the assumed correctness of the model, we expect to see Population B with its mean at V because it is equally likely that the response is larger or smaller than V. We assume that the two populations have the same variability. We evaluate the odds that V represents a zero toxicant effect. The odds that the Population A and Population B are the same is given by the ratio of the heights of the intercepts on the two frequency distribution curves, i.e., a/b. For small reductions in a/b, namely, w, in the vicinity of the maximum of Population A, the insignificance level is 100 $(1 - w)\%$, and $(2w)^{1/2}$ is the corresponding fraction of the standard error.[7] For example, for w = 0.01, which is an insignificance level of 99%, the corresponding fraction of the standard error is $(2 \times 0.01)^{1/2}$, which is 0.14.

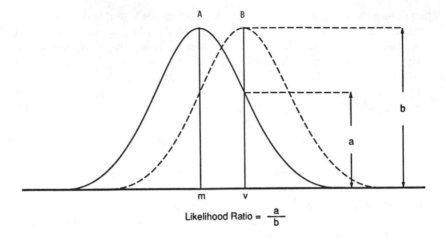

Likelihood Ratio = $\dfrac{a}{b}$

FIGURE 1. The likelihood ratio.

Population A can be viewed as representing the background cancer death rate and Population B as the estimated cancer death rate from background causes plus the calculated effect of a permissible carcinogen exposure. The compliment of the likelihood ratio, $1 - a/b$, represents the loss of confidence that the carcinogen exposure has no effect on the background cancer death rate. The value of V is expressed in Table 1 as the fraction of the standard error of the mean, which is shown together with the loss of confidence in a zero toxicant effect, and the level of insignificance. For example, a fractional standard error of 0.32 corresponds to a 5% loss of confidence in a zero effect and a 95% level of insignificance.

APPLICATION OF INSIGNIFICANCE TO RISK APPORTIONMENT AND ABATEMENT

Cancer is caused by a variety of factors, including genetic defects, man-made and naturally occurring environmental chemicals and physical agents, and biological organisms, such as parasites, bacteria, and viruses. An overall public health strategy involves addressing those factors that can be controlled. To evaluate the costs of controlling cancer causes, one needs a dose-response relationship pegged at some measurable level of effect and modelled at doses which extend down into the unmeasurable effect levels. One can compare the costs of reducing the impact of controlling different causes on the basis of common levels of residual risk or in terms of comparable levels of insignificance. We are suggesting the utility of the insignificance approach because it gives an appreciation of the likely detectability of the carcinogenic response, if, in fact, it does occur, in relation to noise of the background variability in

Table 1
The Relationship Between the Likelihood Ratio and the Standard Error Fraction

Standard error fraction	0.14	0.32	0.46	0.63	0.68	0.71	0.77	1.00	1.38
Likelihood ratio (insignificance)	0.99	0.95	0.90	0.80	0.77	0.75	0.71	0.50	0.05
% Confidence loss	1	5	10	20	23	25	29	50	95

the occurrence of cancer. We illustrate the application of the insignificance approach with the example of one class of cancer-causing agents, namely genotoxic carcinogens, that are released into the environment by human activities and can therefore be controlled by regulatory action. We have chosen the genotoxic carcinogens because the commonly used linear nonthreshold dose-response relationship is more likely to be applicable to these agents than nongenotoxic carcinogens. We illustrate with a calculation based on only one level of insignificance with the understanding that calculations would have to be done for a series of insignificance levels as a basis for determining cost-insignificance relationships. Essentially all of these agents involve relatively low exposures with long latent periods, and many have been introduced more recently than the likely duration of the latent period. However, we assume that they are all causing cancer at the predicted rate after being in the environment for many decades. We need to have some estimate of the total number of genotoxic carcinogens that are likely to be regulated because we are looking at the cost of controlling the aggregate cancer impact of the group in relation to costs. We have turned to the EPA's registry of carcinogens for this information.[8] It has 200 putative carcinogens. The registry has not been analyzed for the number of carcinogens which are genotoxic, so we assume for purposes of illustration that there are 100 genotoxic carcinogens.

The fractional standard error of the background cancer rate for the U.S. for the 20-year period 1950 to 1969 was estimated geographically and temporally.[9,10] The fractional standard error is the standard error divided by the mean. The geographic variability was estimated on the basis of state cancer mortality data; the fractional standard error was essentially the same for men and women and averaged 2.0×10^{-3}. The temporal variability was estimated by linear regression over the 20-year period. The fractional standard error, ignoring the trend in the data, was 1.6×10^{-3}. The two approaches to variability had an average fractional standard error of 1.8×10^{-3}.

We selected, as the illustrative basis for an insignificance calculation, a 50% loss of confidence in a zero carcinogen effect; this corresponds to one standard error in the background variability (Table 1). The aggregate carcinogen risk from the 100 carcinogens is calculated to be 4×10^{-4}. This is the product of one standard error (unity), and the fractional standard error of the cancer rate (1.8×10^{-3}) and the lifetime probability of dying of cancer (0.22). The risk from each of the 100 carcinogens is therefore 4×10^{-6}/F, where F is the proportion of the population of the U.S. exposed to the carcinogen. The factor F has to be introduced because we are dealing with the impact of the aggregate of the 100 carcinogens on the amount of cancer being produced in the country. If it happened to turn out that the appropriate use of resources involved regulating genotoxic carcinogens at the 50% level of insignificance, the exposure standards would have to be formulated for each carcinogen on the basis of its risk standard using the appropriate value for the carcinogenic potency. For example, if a given genotoxic carcinogen exposed only one tenth of the U.S. population, the risk standard would be 4 × 10^{-6}/F, where F would equal 0.1 and the risk standard would be 4 × 10^{-5}. If the only exposure were by inhalation, and the potency of the agent, using the linear nonthreshold extrapolation model, were an excess lifetime cancer risk of 4 × 10^{-5} per lifetime exposure to an average of 1 μg of the carcinogen per cubic meter of air, the exposure standard would be 1 μg/m³ of the carcinogen in air. If there were several routes of exposure the risk standard for that carcinogen would have to be apportioned to each route of exposure.

One can make a ballpark estimate for the effectiveness of regulatory effort that involves reduction of the risks to a 50% insignificance level. In their unregulated form, the number of cancers produced by these 100 carcinogens is in the domain of 15,000 per year. This figure is based on a crude estimate that an average carcinogen causes in the order of 150 cancer deaths per year.[11] These 15,000 cancer deaths caused by the 100 genotoxic carcinogens represent about 3% of the annual cancer death rate in the U.S., which is about 500,000 per year. When regulated to the above standard, there would be an estimated 476 cancer deaths per year which, if achieved, would represent an efficiency of 97% in the regulatory effort. The figure of 476 cancer deaths per year is the product of 4 × 10^{-4} (aggregate genotoxic carcinogen risk) × 250 million (U.S. population) × 1/3 (rough proportion of the population exposed to individual carcinogens)[11] × 1/75 (reciprocal of the human life span).

APPLICATION OF INSIGNIFICANCE TO THE FORMULATION OF A ONE-IN-A-MILLION RISK-BASED CARCINOGEN STANDARD

The notion that one-in-a-million is rare is a part of our folklore. By inference, a million-to-one-odds is almost certainty. If we apply such overwhelming odds to the proposition that a carcinogen effect is zero, we can calculate an insignificant risk-based standard. The standard error, expressed as a fraction, of the value of w, a/b, equal to 10^{-6}, is $(2 \times 10^{-6})^{-1/2}$. This equals 1.4 × 10^{-3}. When multiplied by the fractional standard error of the cancer rate (1.8 × 10^{-3}) and the cancer death rate (0.22), the insignificant risk standard equals 5.5 × 10^{-6}/F, where F is the proportion of the population exposed to the given carcinogen. The factor F is necessary since the insignificance relates to the cancer rate for the entire country. For example, if a carcinogen exposed 10 million people, which is 4% of the population, the risk standard would be 5.5 × 10^{-7}/4 × 10^{-2}, or 1.4 × 10^{-5}. It is evident that some minimal value of F is necessary.

NEEDS FOR FURTHER DEVELOPMENT OF THE APPROACH TO STATISTICAL INSIGNIFICANCE

Since the statistical approach to insignificance depends on the background variability, we need to know more about the nature of variability. In the case of cancer, we need to know how variability is affected by the size of the population, as for example, in terms of county, state, and national data. Variability might be estimated in other countries, which have contrasting levels of medical care to determine how the accuracy of death reporting affects variability. Year-to-year variability might be examined by comparing mortality data from death certificates with incidence data from tumor registries. Further insight might be obtained by comparing the variability of specific tumor types in states, counties, and the country as a whole and from year to year.

In the illustration given above, we have assumed that the variability in background has a normal distribution, but this needs to be examined in some detail. From a statistical standpoint we need the methodology for determining confidence limits on our measures of insignificance.

FUTURE DEVELOPMENTS FOR RISK APPORTIONMENT AND ABATEMENT

The above approach could be extended to other toxicants as the basis for a comprehensive public health regulatory strategy. For example, it would be useful to try the above approach with a single regulatable environmental chemical, such as nonoccupational lead exposure in relation to other possibly controllable causes of retarded growth and development. Body length at birth might be a suitable indicator of developmental lead toxicity. Substantial background information exists on this parameter and its variability. A dose-response model for body length at birth in relation to lead toxicity would have to be selected and the risk standard apportioned to the various routes of exposure to give a subset of standards. The costs of achieving the standards having different levels of insignificance would then be evaluated in terms of the importance of lead with respect to other major causes of the same effect, for example, alcohol, cigarette smoking, and poor nutrition. Such an exercise would be helpful in uncovering the generic issues associated with the methodologic approach, as well as the specific issues related to the formulation of an insignificant-risk standard for lead exposure.

The criteria for judging the acceptability of a particular risk standard involves the interaction of four factors: (1) the chosen level of insignificance to be achieved, (2) the costs of regulation to the given level of insignificance, (3) the efficiency of the regulatory effort as a disease prevention program, and (4) the magnitude of the health problem posed by the candidate agents in relation to other causes of the same diseases or deleterious health effects.

These same criteria can be applied to the more general issue of formulating an overall control strategy by apportionment and abatement of risks from the known environmental factors that cause a given deleterious health effect. To illustrate, let us suppose that there are two causes of a given deleterious health effect: A and B. We estimate the contribution of A and B individually to the combined effect, A + B. We also estimate the societal costs (SC) of A + B. We consider the regulation of A and B each to various levels of insignificance, A' or B'. The effectiveness of the regulatory effort for cause A is 1 − A'/A, and the same true for B. We estimate the societal savings (SS) = SC(1 − A' + B'/A + B), and the total regulatory costs (RC_T) of achieving the various regulated levels of A' and B'. We look for the combination of A' and B' that will make the difference between total regulatory costs and societal savings as close to zero or less, as possible: $RC_T − SS \leq 0$.

The importance of this form of analysis is that it would introduce the concept of evaluating, in a quantitative way, the known and controllable (by regulatory action or otherwise) causes of a particular disability or disease. It would analyze the resources needed to reduce the causal factors to a level of acceptable insignificance with the aim of having an overall prevention strategy that would give the greatest return for the investment. Risk apportionment and abatement is a logical follow-on to health risk assessment because it involves quantitative approaches to risk management. The formulation of overall regulatory strategies to minimize disabilities and diseases that have important environmental contributions would help to minimize the dichotomy that currently exists in the control of environmental chemicals and physical agents by regulatory agencies from the control of other causes of the same effects that are of public health importance.

REFERENCES

1. Albert, R. E., R. E. Train, and E. Anderson. Rationale developed by the Environmental Protection Agency for the assessment of carcinogenic risks. *J. Natl. Cancer Inst.* 58(5):1537–1541 (May, 1977).
2. U.S. Environmental Protection Agency (U.S. EPA). (1976) Interim procedures and guidelines for health risk and economic impact assessments of suspected carcinogens. *Fed. Regist.* 41:21402.
3. Albert, R. E. U.S. Environmental Protection Agency revised interim guidelines for the health assessment of suspect carcinogens. in *Banbury Report 19: Risk Quantitation and Regulatory Policy,* Cold Spring Harbor Laboratory, Cold Spring Harbor, NY (1985) pp. 307–329.
4. Travis, C. C. and S. A. Richter. On Defining a De Minimis Risk Level for Carcinogens. *De Minimis Risk,* Contemporary Issues in Risk Analysis, Vol. 2, 1987.

5. Adler, H. I. and A. M. Weinberg, "An Approach to Setting Radiation Standards," *Health Phys.* 34:719–720 (June 1978).
6. Goodman, S. M. and R. Royall, "Evidence and Scientific Research." *Am. J. Public Health* 78, 1568–1574 (1988).
7. Edwards, A. W. F. *Likelihood,* Cambridge University Press, New York (1976).
8. IRIS, U.S. EPA, ECAO, Cincinnati, OH (1991).
9. U.S. Cancer Mortality by County: 1950–1969. U.S. Department of Health, Education, and Welfare. (PHS) T. J. Mason and F. W. McKay. DHEW Publication No. (NIH) 74-615.
10. Cancer Mortality in the United States: 1950–77. NCI Monograph 59, U.S. Department of Health and Human Services. PHS-NIH.
11. Travis, C. C., S. A. Richter, E. A. C. Crouch, R. Wilson, and E. D. Klema (1987). Cancer risk management. *Environ. Sci. Technol.* 21(5).

Possible Carcinogenic Hazards from Natural and Synthetic Chemicals: Setting Priorities

Lois Swirsky Gold, Thomas H. Slone, Bonnie R. Stern, Neela B. Manley, and Bruce N. Ames

SUMMARY

In order to set priorities for laboratory research, epidemiological research, and regulatory policy, a broad perspective on the chemicals to which humans are exposed is necessary. However, the enormous background of natural chemicals in the diet, such as plant pesticides and the products of cooking, has not been a focus of carcinogenicity testing. One reasonable strategy for gaining a broadened perspective is to use a rough index to compare and rank possible carcinogenic hazards from a wide variety of chemical exposures at levels that humans typically receive, and then to focus on those that rank highest. This paper presents a ranking of possible carcinogenic hazards from 80 typical daily exposures to rodent carcinogens from a variety of sources. The ranking uses an index, Human Exposure/Rodent Potency (HERP), that relates human exposure to a chemical to its carcinogenic potency in rodents; a similar rank ordering would be expected using standard risk assessment methodology for the same exposure values.

The data indicate that when viewed against the large background of naturally occurring chemicals in typical portions of common foods, the residues of synthetic pesticides or environmental pollutants rank low in possible carcinogenic hazard. In a separate ranking of 32 *average* daily exposures to natural pesticides and synthetic pesticide residues in the diet, the synthetic pesticides are all at the bottom. Although one cannot say whether the ranked exposures are likely to be of major or minor importance in human cancer, it is not prudent to focus attention on the possible hazards at the bottom of a ranking if, using the same methodology, there are numerous common human exposures with much greater possible hazards.

INTRODUCTION

Cancer prevention strategies that are aimed at chemical exposures as potential causes of human cancer routinely use the results of standard rodent bioassays in risk assessment. There is accumulating evidence, however, that carcinogenesis bioassays do not provide sufficient information to assess carcinogenic risk at the low doses of most human exposures.[1,2] In current risk assessment methodology, an estimate of the upper bound on risk is obtained by multiplying the human exposure to a chemical by the potency in a rodent bioassay. Recent analyses indicate that measures of carcinogenic potency from rodent tests are restricted to a narrow range about the high dose tested, the maximum tolerated dose (MTD),[1,3,4] and that a "risk" can be approximated just by knowing the bioassay dose. It has been shown that routine estimates of "one-in-a-million risk" can be approximated merely by dividing the high dose in a positive experiment by 380,000.[5] This strikingly simple extrapolation emphasizes the point that animal cancer tests were not designed to determine low-dose risks and that using them for such a purpose requires an enormous toxicological leap in the dark. Extrapolation should, instead, be based on an understanding of the mechanisms of carcinogenesis.

Whereas linear extrapolation has been the dominant assumption in regulatory policy, we have postulated that administration of the MTD in rodent bioassays can increase mitogenesis, which in turn increases rates of mutagenesis and thus carcinogenesis.[2,6,7] To the extent that increases in tumor incidence in rodent studies are due to the secondary effects of administering high doses, then *any* chemical that increases mitogenesis (e.g., by chronic cell killing and cell replacement or by suppression of intercellular communication) is a likely rodent carcinogen; thus, one would expect that a high proportion of chemicals tested at the MTD would be positive. The animal data in our Carcinogenic Potency Data Base (CPDB)*[8-12] are consistent with this hypothesized mechanism, because about half of all chemicals tested are indeed rodent carcinogens and about 40% of the positives are not detectably mutagenic.[2,14,15] If mitogenesis is a dominant factor in carcinogenesis at the

---

*   References to, and analyses of, individual cancer tests are in the Carcinogenic Potency Data Base papers.[8-12] Our analyses are based on this data base, which reports only results of chronic, long-term bioassays that are adequate to detect a carcinogenic effect or lack of effect and to estimate potency. More than 4400 experiments met the inclusion criteria of the data base, but thousands of others did not: e.g., tests that lack a control group, that are too short or include too few animals to detect an effect, that use routes of administration not likely to result in whole-body exposure (like skin painting or subcutaneous administration), cocarcinogenesis studies, and bioassays of particulate or fibrous matters.

One third of the chemicals in the data base have been tested by the National Cancer Institute/National Toxicology Program, using standard protocols with tests in two species at the MTD.[13] About half of the chemicals in the data base, however, have been tested in only one species. Positivity rates and prediction between species have been analyzed.[1,14]

In this analysis, we classify the results of an experiment as either positive or negative on the basis of the author's opinion in the published paper and classify a chemical as positive if it has been evaluated as positive by the author of at least one experiment. We use the author's opinion to determine positivity because it often takes into account more information than statistical significance alone, such as historical control rates for particular sites, survival and latency, and/or dose response. Generally, this designation by author's opinion corresponds well with the results of statistical reanalysis of the significance of the dose-response effect.[14]

MTD, then at low doses where mitogenesis is not generally induced, the hazards to humans of rodent carcinogens may be much lower than commonly assumed. As more theory is developed and more evidence is produced about the mechanisms of carcinogenesis, assessments of human risk can be improved by taking into account mechanistic information on a given chemical as well as shape of the dose-response curve and mutagenesis. Currently, however, it is better to acknowledge the serious limitations of risk assessment methodology and to educate the public that what we call a one-in-a-million "risk estimate" is a linear extrapolation that represents a fraction of the MTD administered to rodents; the true risk at low dose is not known and may be zero.[16] It is also clear that the mechanisms of action for all rodent carcinogens are not the same, and that one cannot use a simple linearized risk assessment model for all of them.

WHY IT IS IMPORTANT TO RANK POSSIBLE CARCINOGENIC HAZARDS

Given the gap in scientific knowledge about mechanisms and shape of the dose response, what should be done if the goal is to try to prevent human cancers that may be due to chemical exposures? In several papers we have emphasized that it is important to gain some perspective about the vast number of chemicals to which humans are exposed. One reasonable strategy is to use a rough index to *compare* and *rank* possible carcinogenic hazards from a wide variety of chemical exposures at levels that humans typically receive, and then to focus on those that rank highest.[17,18] Ranking is a critical first step that can help to set priorities when selecting chemicals for chronic bioassay or mechanistic studies, for epidemiological research, and for regulatory policy. The emphasis in such work is to compare possible hazards rather than to provide direct estimates of risk. Although one cannot say whether the ranked chemical exposures are likely to be of major or minor importance in human cancer, it is not prudent to focus attention on the possible hazards at the bottom of a ranking if, using the same methodology, there are numerous common human exposures with much greater possible hazards. Our earlier evaluation of possible hazards from known rodent carcinogens[17] was based on the HERP index. In this paper we expand the earlier analysis to include many common exposures to rodent carcinogens that occur naturally in food, as well as several synthetic pesticide residues. In general, we would expect a similar rank order of "risk estimates" using current regulatory risk assessment methodology for the same exposures, since linear extrapolation from the TD_{50} generally leads to low dose slope estimates similar to those based on the linearized multistage model.[4]

WHICH CHEMICALS SHOULD BE RANKED BY POSSIBLE CARCINOGENIC HAZARD?

What chemical exposures should be included in a ranking if the goal is to gain perspective about exposures that may be potential causes of human cancer? Toxicological examination of synthetic chemicals such as pesticides and industrial pollutants, without similar examination of chemicals that occur naturally, has resulted in an imbalance in both data and perception about chemical carcinogens. Three points that we have discussed[17,19,20] indicate that comparisons should be made using natural as well as synthetic chemicals, despite the fact that natural chemicals have not been a focus of attention:

1. The vast proportion of chemicals that humans are exposed to occur naturally. Yet the public tends to view *chemicals* as being only synthetic and to think of synthetic chemicals as toxic; however, every natural chemical is also toxic at some dose. We estimate that the daily average American exposure to burnt material in the diet is about 2000 mg, and to natural pesticides (the chemicals that plants produce to defend themselves) about 1500 mg.[19] In comparison, the total daily exposure to all synthetic pesticide residues combined is about 0.09 mg based on the sum of residues reported by the FDA in their study of the 200 synthetic pesticide residues thought to be of greatest concern.[21] We estimate that humans ingest roughly 5,000 to 10,000 different natural pesticides and their breakdown products.[19] Despite this enormously greater exposure to natural chemicals, among the chemicals tested for carcinogenicity in rats and mice, 79% (378/479) are synthetic (i.e., do not occur naturally).[12]

2. It has often been assumed that humans have evolved defenses against natural chemicals that will not protect against synthetic chemicals. However, defenses that animals have evolved are mostly general rather than specific for particular chemicals (e.g., continuous shedding of surface cells that are exposed to toxins in the skin, colon, stomach, and mouth). Additionally, general detoxifying mechanisms are inducible and therefore protect well at low dose against both synthetic and natural chemicals.[20]

3. Since the toxicology of natural and synthetic chemicals is similar, one expects, and finds, a similar positivity rate for carcinogenicity among synthetic and natural chemicals. Among chemicals tested in rats and mice in our CPDB,[8-12] about half of the natural chemicals are positive as are half of all chemicals tested. Therefore, since humans are exposed to so many more natural than synthetic chemicals (by weight and by number), humans are probably living in a sea of natural rodent carcinogens as defined by high-dose rodent tests. We have shown that even though only a tiny proportion of natural pesticides in plant foods have been tested, among the 57 tested, the 29 that are rodent carcinogens occur in more than 50 common plant foods.[19] It is probable that almost every fruit and vegetable in the supermarket contains natural pesticides that are rodent carcinogens.

It is unlikely that the high positivity rate in rodent studies is due simply to selection of suspicious chemical structures: most chemicals were selected because of their use as industrial compounds, pesticides, drugs, or food additives. Moreover, historically the knowledge to predict carcinogenicity has been inadequate.[14]

Coffee is one example of the background of natural chemicals to which humans are chronically exposed. A cup of coffee contains more than 1000 chemicals. Only 26 have been tested for carcinogenicity, and 19 of these are positive in at least one test totaling at least 10 mg of rodent carcinogens per cup.*[22-25] The average American consumption of coffee is about 13 g per day.[27] Among the rodent carcinogens in coffee are the plant pesticides caffeic acid (present at 1800 ppm)[22] and catechol (present at 100 ppm).[28,29] Two other plant pesticides, chlorogenic acid and neochlorogenic acid (present at 21,600 and 11,600 ppm, respectively[22] are metabolized to caffeic acid and catechol, but have not been tested for carcinogenicity. Chlorogenic acid and caffeic acid are mutagenic[30-32] and clastogenic.[33,34] For another plant pesticide in coffee, d-limonene, data are available on the mechanism of carcinogenicity that suggest the rodent results are not relevant to humans because carcinogenicity in the male rat kidney is associated with a urinary protein that humans do not excrete.[35] Some other rodent carcinogens in coffee are products of cooking, e.g., furfural, benzo(a)pyrene, and MeIQ.

The point here is not to indicate that rodent data necessarily implicate coffee as a risk factor for human cancer, but rather to illustrate that there is an enormous background of chemicals in the diet that are natural and that have not been a focus of attention for carcinogenicity testing.** Among the natural chemicals that have been tested at high dose, the proportions that are positive are as high as they are for other chemicals. These results emphasize that a chemical pollutant should not be a high priority of concern with respect to carcinogenicity if, when ranked by the same methods as natural chemicals, its possible carcinogenic hazard appears to be far below that of many common food items.

HERP RANKING OF NATURAL AND SYNTHETIC CHEMICALS

In an earlier paper[17] we compared possible hazards from several different exposures to rodent carcinogens by HERP. HERP indicates what percentage

---

* The 19 rodent carcinogens in coffee are acetaldehyde, benzaldehyde, benzene, benzofuran, benzo(a)pyrene, caffeic acid, catechol, 1,2,5,6-dibenzanthracene, ethanol, ethylbenzene, formaldehyde, furan, furfural, hydrogen peroxide, hydroquinone, limonene, MeIQ, styrene, and toluene. The chemicals that have been tested and are not positive are: acrolein, biphenyl, eugenol, nicotinic acid, phenol, and piperidine. The carcinogenicity of caffeine is uncertain.[26]

** The epidemiological evidence on coffee and human health has been recently reviewed, and the evidence to date is not sufficient to show that coffee is a risk factor for cancer in humans.[22,36,37] of the rodent potency (mg/kg/d) a human receives (mg/kg/d) from a given exposure. The measure of rodent potency, reported in our CPDB, is the TD_{50}: the daily lifetime dose rate estimated to halve the proportion of tumor-free animals by the end of a standard lifetime.[38,39] The range of TD_{50} values among rodent carcinogens varies more than 10 million fold.

Criteria for Inclusion in HERP Ranking

In this paper we more than double the number of HERP values that we reported earlier[17] by adding exposures to each rodent carcinogen in the CPDB that occurs naturally in the diet and for which reliable data are available on concentrations in food. We have also added dietary exposures to each rodent carcinogen in the CPDB that is a synthetic pesticide currently in use, and for which the FDA reports residues.*[40]

It should be noted that in the HERP rankings of rodent carcinogens in Tables 1 and 2, dietary exposures to natural chemicals are markedly under-represented compared to synthetic pesticide residues because few natural chemicals have been tested for carcinogenicity. In addition, HERP values for natural chemicals are underestimated compared to synthetic pesticide residues: the daily exposures for synthetic pesticides are for all foods combined, whereas for nearly all natural chemicals the concentrations are reported for a single food even though the chemical may occur in several common foods. Importantly, for each plant listed, there are about 50 additional untested natural pesticides. The HERP values for the natural exposures in Table 1 are for typical portions of individual foods. For natural pesticides, Table 2 uses average U.S. daily exposures to each food rather than typical portions; for synthetic pesticides Tables 1 and 2 use average daily residues for all foods combined. Table 2 compares only natural pesticides in plant foods and residues for synthetic pesticides, whereas Table 1 includes many other exposures to natural and synthetic chemicals. Methodological details for both tables are given in Table 1.

Caution is necessary in interpreting the implications of the occurrence in the diet of natural chemicals that are rodent carcinogens. It is not argued here that these dietary exposures are necessarily of much relevance to human cancer. Indeed, with respect to natural pesticides in plant foods, a diet rich in fruits and vegetables is associated with lower cancer rates.[37,41] This may

---

* The average daily exposure value for each synthetic pesticide is for residues on all foods combined as determined by the FDA's Total Diet Study. Additionally, three currently used synthetic pesticides (captan, chlorothalonil, and folpet) are included that do not have recent positive results in the CPDB, but for which we were able to obtain unpublished positive bioassay results from EPA. These three were selected because residues are reported by FDA, because EPA currently evaluates them as probable human carcinogens (category B_2), and because each was evaluated in a study by the National Research Council as being of relatively high risk to humans.

Table 1
Ranking Possible Carcinogenic Hazards from Natural and Synthetic Chemicals (Natural Chemicals in the Diet are in Bold)

Possible hazard: HERP (%)	Daily human exposure	Human dose of rodent carcinogen	Potency of carcinogen: TD_{50} (mg/kg)		Ref.
			Rats	Mice	
140	EDB: workers' daily intake (high exposure)	Ethylene dibromide, 150 mg (before 1977)	1.5	(7.44)	43, 44[a]
17	Clofibrate (average daily dose)	Clofibrate, 2 g	169	(?)	45[a]
16	Phenobarbital, 1 sleeping pill	Phenobarbital, 60 mg	(+)	5.5	46[a]
[14]	Isoniazid pill (prophylactic dose)	Isoniazid, 300 mg	(150)	30	47[a]
6.2	Comfrey-pepsin tablets, 9 daily	**Comfrey root, 2.7 g**	626	(?)	48, 49[a]
[5,6]	Metronidazole (therapeutic dose)	Metronidazole, 2 g	(542)	506	47[a]
4.7	**Wine (250 ml)**	**Ethyl alcohol[b], 30 ml**	9110	(–)	50[a]
4.0[c]	Formaldehyde: workers' average daily intake	Formaldehyde, 6.1 mg	2.19	(44)	51[a]
2.8	**Beer (12 ounces; 354 ml)**	**Ethyl alcohol[b], 18 ml**	9110	(–)	50[a]
1.4[c]	Mobile home air (14 hours/day)	Formaldehyde, 2.2 mg	2.19	(44)	52[a]
1.3	Comfrey-pepsin tablets, 9 daily	**Symphytine, 1.8 mg[d]**	1.91	(?)	48, 49[a]
0.4[c]	Conventional home air (14 hours/day)	Formaldehyde, 598 µg	2.19	(44)	53[a]
[0.3]	Phenacetin pill (average dose)	Phenacetin[b], 300 mg	1246	(2137)	54[a]
0.3	**Lettuce, 1/8 head (125 g)**	**Caffeic acid, 66.3 mg[d]**	284	(4970)	55–57
0.2	Natural root beer (12 ounces; 354 ml)	**Safrole, 6.6 mg (now banned)[d]**	(436)	56	58, 59[a]
0.1	**Apple, 1 whole (230 g)**	**Caffeic acid, 24.4 mg[d]**	284	(4970)	56, 57, 60
0.1	**1 Mushroom (*Agaricus bisporus* 15 g)**	**Mixture of hydrazines, and so forth[d]**	(?)	20,300	61[a]
0.1	**Basil (1 g of dried leaf)**	**Estragole, 3.8 mg[d]**	(?)	52	58, 62[a]
0.07	**Mango, 1 whole (245 g; pitted)**	**d-Limonene, 9.8 mg[d]**	204	(–)	63, 64
0.07	**Pear, 1 whole (200 g)**	**Caffeic acid, 14.6 mg[d]**	284	(4970)	56, 57, 60
0.07	**Brown mustard (5 g)**	**Allyl isothiocyanate, 4.6 mg[d]**	96	(?)	65[a]
0.06	Diet cola (12 ounces; 354 ml)	Saccharin, 95 mg	2143	(–)	66[a]
0.06	**Parsnip, 1/4 (40 g)**	**8-Methoxypsoralen, 1.28 mg[d]**	32	(?)	67
0.04	**Orange juice (6 ounces; 177 ml)**	**d-Limonene, 5.49 mg[d]**	204	(–)	63, 68
0.04	**Coffee, 1 cup (from 4 g)**	**Caffeic acid, 7.2 mg[d]**	284	(4970)	22, 56, 57
0.03	**Plum, 1 whole (50 g)**	**Caffeic acid, 6.9 mg[d]**	284	(4970)	56, 57, 60

Table 1 (continued)
Ranking Possible Carcinogenic Hazards from Natural and Synthetic Chemicals (Natural Chemicals in the Diet are in Bold)

Possible hazard: HERP (%)	Daily human exposure	Human dose of rodent carcinogen	Potency of carcinogen: TD$_{50}$ (mg/kg)		Ref.
			Rats	Mice	
0.03	Safrole: U.S. average from spices	Safrole, 1.2 mg[d]	(436)	56.2	69
0.03	Peanut butter (32 g; one sandwich)	Aflatoxin[b], 64 ng (U.S. average, 2 ppb)	0.003	(+)	70, 71[a]
0.03	Comfrey herb tea (1.5 g)	Symphytine, 38 µg[d]	1.91	(?)	49[a]
0.03	Celery, 1 stalk (50 g)	Caffeic acid, 5.4 mg[d]	284	(4970)	56, 57, 72
0.03	Carrot, 1 whole (100 g)	Caffeic acid, 5.16 mg[d]	284	(4970)	56, 57, 72
0.03	Pepper, black: U.S. average (446 mg)	d-Limonene, 3.57 mg[d]	204	(−)	27, 63, 73
0.02	Potato, 1 (225 g; peeled)	Caffeic acid, 3.56 mg[d]	284	(4970)	56, 57, 74
0.008	Swimming pool, 1 hour (for child)	Chloroform, 250 µg	(262)[c]	90	75[a]
0.008	Beer, before 1979 (12 ounces; 354 ml)	Dimethylnitrosamine, 1 µg	(0.2)	0.2	76, 77
0.006	Bacon, cooked (100 g)	Diethylnitrosamine, 0.1 µg	0.02	(+)	78[a]
0.006[c]	Well water, 1 liter contaminated (worst in Silicon Valley, CA)	Trichloroethylene, 2.8 mg	668	(830)	79[a]
0.005	Coffee, 1 cup (from 4 g)	Furfural, 630 µg	(679)	197	27, 80
0.004	Bacon, pan fried (100 g)	n-Nitrosopyrrolidine, 1.7 µg	(1.05)	0.679	81[a]
0.003	Nutmeg: U.S. average (27.4 mg)	d-Limonene, 466 µg[d]	204	(−)	27, 63, 82
0.003	1 Mushroom (Agaricus bisporus 15 g)	Glutamyl p-hydrazinobenzoate, 630 µg[d]	(?)	277	83
0.003[c]	Conventional home air (14 hours/day)	Benzene[b], 155 µg	(169)	77.5	53[a]
0.003	Sake (250 ml)	Urethane, 43 µg	(41.3)	22.1	84[a]
0.003	Bacon, cooked (100 g)	Dimethylnitrosamine, 300 ng	(0.2)	0.2	78[a]
0.002	White bread, 2 slices (45 g)	Furfural, 333 µg	(679)	197	27, 80
0.002	Apple juice (6 ounces; 177 ml)	UDMH, 5.89 µg (from Alar, 1988)	(−)	3.94	85–87
0.002	Coffee, 1 cup (from 4 g)	Hydroquinone, 100 µg	82.8	(225)	28, 88, 89
0.002	Coffee, 1 cup (from 4 g)	Catechol, 400 µg[d]	336	(−)	28, 29, 90
0.002	DDT: daily dietary intake	DDT, 13.8 µg (U.S. average 1970: before 1972 ban)	(84.7)	12.3	91
0.001	Celery, 1 stalk (50 g)	8-Methoxypsoralen, 30.5 µg[d]	32	(?)	92
0.001	Tap water, 1 liter	Chloroform, 83 µg (U.S. average)	(262)[c]	90	93[a]

0.001	Heated sesame oil (15 g) — **Sesamol, 1.13 mg**[d]	1540	(4490)	90, 94
0.0008	DDE: daily dietary intake — DDE, 6.91 μg (U.S. average 1970; before 1972 ban)	(—)	12.5	91
0.0006[c]	Well water, 1 liter contaminated (Woburn, MA) — Trichloroethylene, 267 μg	668	(830)	95[a]
0.0005	1 Mushroom (Agaricus bisporus 15 g) — **p-Hydrazinobenzoate, 165 μg**[d]	(?)	454[e]	96
0.0005	Hamburger, pan fried (3 ounces; 85 g) — **PhIP, 1.28 μg**	3.74[e]	(28.6)	97–99
0.0005	Jasmine tea, 1 cup (2 g) — **Benzyl acetate, 460 μg**[d]	(—)	1440	100
0.0005	Salmon, pan fried (3 ounces; 85 g) — **PhIP, 1.18 μg**	3.74[e]	(28.6)	98, 99, 101
0.0004	EDB: daily dietary intake — Ethylene dibromide, 420 ng (U.S. average from grain; before 1984 ban)	1.5	(7.44)	102[a]
0.0004	Beer (12 ounces; 354 ml) — **Furfural, 54.9 μg**	(672)	197	27, 80
0.0003	Well water, 1 liter contaminated (Woburn, MA) — Tetrachloroethylene, 21 μg	101	(126)	95[a]
0.0003	Carbaryl: daily dietary intake — Carbaryl, 2.6 μg (U.S. average 1990)[f]	14.1	(—)	40
0.0002	Apple, 1 whole (230 g) — UDMH, 598 ng (from Alar, 1988)	(—)	4.01	85–87
0.0002	Parsley, fresh (1 g) — **8-Methoxypsoralen, 3.6 μg**[d]	32	(?)	103
0.0002	Toxaphene: daily dietary intake — Toxaphene, 595 ng (U.S. average 1990)[f]	(—)	5.57	40
0.00008	Hamburger, pan fried (3 ounces; 85 g) — **MeIQx, 111 ng**	1.99	(24.3)	104–106
0.00008	DDE/DDT: daily dietary intake[g] — DDE, 659 ng (U.S. average 1990)[f]	(—)	12.5	40
0.00003	Whole wheat toast, 2 slices (45 g) — **Urethane, 540 ng**	(41.3)	22.1	107
0.00002	Dicofol: daily dietary intake — Dicofol, 544 ng (U.S. average 1990)[f]	(—)	32.9	40
0.00002	Cocoa (4 g) — **α-Methylbenzyl alcohol, 5.2 μg**[d]	458	(—)	27, 108
0.00001	Lager beer (12 ounces; 354 ml) — **Urethane, 159 ng**	(41.3)	22.1	107
0.000008	Hamburger, pan fried (3 ounces; 85 g) — IQ, 23.4 ng	4.0[e]	22.1	105, 109
0.000001	Lindane: daily dietary intake — Lindane, 32 ng (U.S. average 1990)[f]	(—)	30.7	40
0.0000004	PCNB: daily dietary intake — PCNB (Quintozene), 19.2 ng (U.S. average 1990)[f]	(?)	71.1	40
0.0000001	Hamburger, pan fried (3 ounces, 85 g) — **MeIQ, 1.28 ng**	(?)	12.3	110
0.0000001	Chlorobenzilate: daily dietary intake — Chlorobenzilate, 6.4 ng[f] (U.S. average 1989)[f]	(—)	93.9	40
<0.00000001	Chlorothalonil: daily dietary intake — Chlorothalonil, <6.4 ng[f] (U.S. average 1990)[f]	828	(—)	40, 11
0.000000008	Folpet: daily dietary intake — Folpet, 12.8 ng (U.S. average 1990)[f]	(?)	2280	40, 112
0.000000007	Coffee, 1 cup (from 4 g) — **MeIQ, 0.064 ng**	(?)	12.3	25
0.000000006	Captan: daily dietary intake — Captan, 11.5 ng (U.S. average 1990)[f]	2690	(2730)	40, 113

Table 1 (continued)
Ranking Possible Carcinogenic Hazards from Natural and Synthetic Chemicals (Natural Chemicals in the Diet are in Bold)

Note: Potency of carcinogens: A number in parentheses indicates a TD_{50} value not used in HERP calculation because it is the less sensitive species; $(-)$ = negative in cancer test. $(+)$ = positive for carcinogenicity in test(s) not suitable for calculating a TD_{50}. $(?)$ = is not adequately tested for carcinogenicity.[8-12] TD_{50} values shown are averages calculated by taking the harmonic mean of the TD_{50} of the positive tests in that species from the Carcinogenic Potency Data Base. Results are similar if the lowest TD_{50} value (most potent) is used instead. For each test the target site with the lowest TD_{50} value has been used. The average TD_{50} has been calculated separately for rats and mice, and the more sensitive species is used for calculating the possible hazard. The data base, with references to the source of the cancer tests, is complete for tests published through 1988 and for the National Toxicology Program bioassays through 1989.[8-12,39] We have not indicated the route of exposure or target sites or other particulars of each test, although these are reported in the data base. *Daily human exposure:* We have tried to use reasonable daily intakes to facilitate comparisons. The calculations assume a daily dose for a lifetime; where drugs are normally taken for only a short period we have bracketed the HERP value. *Possible hazard:* The amount of rodent carcinogen indicated under dose is divided by 70 kg to give a milligram per kilogram of human exposure, and this human dose is given as the percentage of the TD_{50} dose in the rodent (in milligram per kilogram) to calculate the Human Exposure/Rodent Potency index (HERP).

a   Additional information reported in our earlier HERP paper.[17]
b   The IARC has evaluated as human carcinogens: alcoholic beverages, aflatoxin, benzene, and analgesic mixtures containing phenacetin (but not phenacetin alone).
c   The value differs from that reported in our earlier HERP paper[17] due to more recent experimental results in the CPDB.
d   The chemical is a naturally occurring pesticide.
e   The CPDB includes experiments on the hydrochloride salt. The TD_{50} value reported is expressed as the free base.
f   Estimate is based on 60 to 65 year old females, the only adult group reported for 1990. Because of the agricultural usage of these chemicals and the prominence of fruits and vegetables in the diet of older Americans, the residues are generally slightly higher than for other adult age groups.
g   Total DDT, of which >90% is DDE, the main metabolite of DDT present in food products of animal origin.

Table 2
Comparison of Average Exposures to Natural and Synthetic Pesticides: Ranking Possible Carcinogenic Hazards (Natural Pesticides Are in Bold)

Possible hazard: HERP (%)	Average daily human exposure	Human dose of rodent carcinogen	Average Exposure Ref.
0.1	**Coffee (from 13.3 g)**	**Caffeic acid, 23.9 mg**	27
0.04	**Lettuce (14.9 g)**	**Caffeic acid, 7.90 mg**	120
0.03	**Safrole in spices**	**Safrole, 1.2 mg**	69
0.03	**Orange juice (138 g)**	**d-Limonene, 4.28 mg**	120
0.03	**Pepper, black (446 mg)**	**d-Limonene, 3.57 mg**	27
0.02	**Mushroom (Agaricus bisporus 2.55 g)**	**Mixture of hydrazines, and so forth**	27
0.02	**Apple (32.0 g)**	**Caffeic acid, 3.40 mg**	85
0.01	**Celery, (21.6 g)**	**Caffeic acid, 2.33 mg**	121
0.006	**Coffee (13.3 g)**	**Catechol, 1.33 mg**	27
0.004	**Potato (54.9 g; peeled)**	**Caffeic acid, 867 µg**	120
0.003	**Nutmeg (27.4 mg)**	**d-Limonene, 466 µg**	27
0.003	**Carrot (12.1 g)**	**Caffeic acid, 624 µg**	120
0.002	[DDT: daily dietary avg]	[DDT, 13.8 µg (before 1972 ban)]	91
0.002	[Apple juice (6 oz; 177 ml)]	[UDMH, 5.89 µg (from Alar, 1988)]	85–87
0.001	**Plum (1.86 g)**	**Caffeic acid, 257 µg**	122
0.001	**Pear (3.29 g)**	**Caffeic acid, 240 µg**	27
0.0009	**Brown mustard (68.4 mg)**	**Allyl isothiocyanate, 62.9 µg**	27
0.0008	[DDE: daily dietary avg]	[DDE, 6.91 µg (before 1972 ban)]	91
0.0006	**Celery (21.6 g)**	**8-Methoxypsoralen, 13.2 µg**	121
0.0006	**Mushroom (Agaricus bisporus 2.55 g)**	**Glutamyl-p-hydrazinobenzoate, 107 µg**	27
0.0005	**Jasmine tea (2.19 g)**	**Benzyl acetate, 504 µg**	27
0.0004	[EDB: Daily dietary avg]	EDB, 420 ng (before 1984 ban)	102
0.0003	Carbaryl: daily dietary intake	Carbaryl, 2.6 µg (1990)	40
0.0002	Toxaphene: daily dietary intake	Toxaphene, 595 ng (1990)	40
0.0002	[Apple, 1 whole (230 g)]	[UDMH, 598 ng (from Alar, 1988)]	85–87
0.0001	**Mango (522 mg)**	**d-Limonene, 20.9 µg**	122
0.00009	**Mushroom (Agaricus bisporus 2.55 g)**	**p-Hydrazinobenzoate, 28 µg**	27
0.00007	**Parsnip (54.0 mg)**	**8-Methoxypsoralen, 1.57 µg**	123

Table 2 (continued)
Comparison of Average Exposures to Natural and Synthetic Pesticides: Ranking Possible Carcinogenic Hazards
(Natural Pesticides Are in Bold)

Possible hazard: HERP (%)	Average daily human exposure	Human dose of rodent carcinogen	Average Exposure Ref.
0.00005	**Parsley, fresh (324 mg)**	**8-Methoxypsoralen, 1.17 µg**	123
0.00002	Dicofol: daily dietary intake	Dicofol, 544 ng (1990)	40
0.00001	**Cocoa (3.34 g)**	**α-Methylbenzyl alcohol, 4.3 µg**	27
0.000001	Lindane: daily dietary intake	Lindane, 32 ng (1990)	40
0.0000004	PCNB: daily dietary intake	PCNB (Quintozene), 19.2 ng (1990)	40
0.0000001	Chlorobenzilate: daily dietary intake	Chlorobenzilate, 6.4 ng (1989)	40
<0.00000001	Chlorothalonil: daily dietary intake	Chlorothalonil, <6.4 ng (1990)	40
0.000000008	Folpet: daily dietary intake	Folpet, 12.8 ng (1990)	40
0.000000006	Captan: daily dietary intake	Captan, 11.5 ng (1990)	40

be because many anticarcinogenic vitamins and antioxidants come from plants.[37,41,42] What is important in our analysis is that widespread exposures to naturally occurring rodent carcinogens may cast doubt on the relevance to human cancer of far lower levels of exposures to synthetic rodent carcinogens.

Overview of HERP Ranking in Table 1

The exposures in Table 1 are ordered by possible carcinogenic hazard (HERP), and exposures to natural chemicals in food are printed in bold. A convenient reference point is the HERP of 0.001% for the average U.S. exposure to chloroform in a liter of tap water. Chloroform is a by-product of water chlorination, which protects humans against pathogenic viruses and bacteria. The rank order in Table 1 supports the findings we reported earlier:[17] when the same HERP index is used for natural and synthetic chemicals, carcinogenic hazards to humans from current levels of pesticide residues or water pollution are likely to be of minimal concern relative to the background levels of natural substances.

A general overview of the ranking indicates that current synthetic pesticide residues rank near the bottom. Even among those synthetic pesticides that are no longer in use (EDB, DDE/DDT, and UDMH from Alar), the HERP values for residues are not above the median value for the table: 0.003%. Contaminated water, even for trichloroethylene in the most severely polluted well in Silicon Valley, ranks just above the median and below many natural chemicals in food. If average U.S. exposure to trichloroethylene in drinking water[114,115] were used rather than the worst-case exposure, the HERP value would rank near the bottom.

Historically, exposures in the workplace have sometimes been high, and the HERP values for those that we report rank at or near the top. Some pharmaceutical drugs are also clustered near the top; however, since most drugs are used for only short periods while the HERP is an index for a lifetime exposure, the possible carcinogenic hazards would usually be markedly lower than indicated in the table. Some indoor air pollutants rank above the median. HERP values for natural chemicals in foods occur throughout the ranking: alcoholic beverages are near the top, and several exposures to natural pesticides and mold toxins rank in the top half. These include rodent carcinogens in such common foods as coffee, lettuce, mushroom, spices, and common fruits. Many other natural chemicals in food, including those produced by cooking or fermentation, rank at the median or below the median, e.g., furfural (bread, coffee, beer), heterocyclic amines (beef, salmon), and nitrosamines (bacon, beer).

In our earlier ranking paper[17] we discussed in detail several categories of exposure; below we concentrate on natural chemicals in the diet and synthetic pesticide residues that have been added to the HERP ranking since the earlier paper.

Natural Pesticides

Natural pesticides are an important subset of natural chemicals in the diet. Plants produce these toxins to defend themselves against fungi, insects, and other predators. Although tens of thousands have been discovered, only 57 have been adequately tested in carcinogenesis bioassays. We estimate that by weight, the daily American intake of natural pesticides is 10,000 times greater than the intake of synthetic pesticide residues.[19] Concentrations of natural pesticides are usually measured in parts per thousand or parts per million rather than in parts per billion — the concentration range for most pollutants or synthetic pesticides.[19] In Table 1 many plant pesticide rodent carcinogens in common foods rank above the median, ranging from a HERP of 0.3 to 0.02%. These include caffeic acid (lettuce, apple, pear, coffee, plum, celery, carrot, potato); estragole (basil); allyl isothiocyanate (mustard); d-limonene (mango, orange juice, black pepper); 8-methoxypsoralen (parsnip); safrole (in spices); and symphytine (comfrey herb tea). Other natural pesticide exposures rank near the bottom, e.g., α-methylbenzyl alcohol in cocoa. Caffeic acid is more widespread in plant species than other natural pesticides.

Synthetic Pesticides

Synthetic pesticides currently in use that are rodent carcinogens and found by FDA as residues in food are all included in Table 1; exposures are reported for the most recent estimates. They are all at or near the bottom of the HERP ranking. For pesticides no longer in use, (EDB, DDE/DDT, and UDMH from Alar), average daily intakes in Table 1 are from years before they were discontinued. None of these formerly used pesticides rank above the median, and all are below many natural chemicals in the diet. Because the uses for some current synthetic pesticides have been restricted by EPA, we investigated whether or not the low HERP values may be due to reduced usage. We examined the residue values reported by FDA for the Total Diet Study in the past 10 years,[21,40,116-119] and found that the HERP rankings of synthetic pesticides in Table 1 change only marginally and are still at the bottom even if the highest past residues are used instead of the most recent.

Since the exposures in Table 1 for natural pesticides are for typical portions while those for synthetic pesticides are for average daily intake, we examined whether or not the relative rankings of these two groups of chemicals would be changed if average consumption of each plant food was the basis for the HERP values of natural pesticides (Table 2). Generally, the average daily intake is within a factor of 5 of the typical portions reported in Table 1, although some of the less common foods vary by more than a factor of 10, e.g., mango and parsnip. For coffee, the average daily consumption is about 3 cups, compared to the 1 cup portion in Table 1. Table 2 reports all exposures to natural pesticides and synthetic pesticides from Table 1, for which average consumption data are available; the natural pesticides are reported in bold. Strikingly, all HERP values that rank in the top third of Table 2 are for natural pesticides. Thus, while synthetic pesticides have been a major focus of scientific and regulatory attention, the data strongly indicate that there is a large background of natural pesticides in the diet that are rodent carcinogens and that rank higher in possible carcinogenic hazard when the same methodology is applied. Using average daily exposures to the natural rodent carcinogens rather than typical portion sizes does not alter this finding.

Cooking and Preparation of Food

Cooking and food preparation can also produce chemicals that are rodent carcinogens. The HERP values in Table 1 for alcohol in wine and beer rank high, 4.7 and 2.8%, respectively. These values are enormous relative to those for synthetic pesticide residues. The carcinogenic potency of alcohol is among the weakest in our data base, but the human intake is high, about 18 g per beer. Another rodent carcinogen in prepared food is urethane, which is present in tiny amounts in both alcoholic beverages and bread. The HERP values rank low in Table 1 for urethane in whole-wheat toast (2 slices) and in one beer; the value for toast is slightly higher. Furfural, a chemical formed naturally when sugars are heated, is one of the most widely distributed constituents of food flavor.[23,124,125] It is found in coffee (1 cup) and white bread (2 slices) at concentrations that give HERP values of 0.005 and 0.002%, respectively. The average U.S. exposure to furfural in food is 2.7 mg per day.[27]

A variety of mutagenic and carcinogenic heterocyclic amines formed during cooking are also included in Table 1. Exposure in Table 2 is from intake of beef and salmon. The individual HERP values range from 0.0005 to 0.000000007%.

Occupational Exposures

Occupational exposures to some chemicals have been high, and most of the single chemical agents or industrial processes evaluated as human carcinogens have been identified by high-dose exposures in the workplace.[126] The HERP values for exposure to EDB and formaldehyde are at or near the top of the ranking, 140 and 4.0%, respectively. The U.S. OSHA still permits worker exposure to EDB at levels above the TD_{50} in rodents; in contrast, the EPA banned the use of EDB for fumigation because of the residue levels found in grain, HERP = 0.0004%.

For occupational exposures with very high HERP values, little quantitative extrapolation is required from the high (MTD) doses used in rodent bioassays to the doses for workers; therefore, mechanistic assumptions about extrapolation are less important than for the large extrapolations required for low-dose exposures of the general population to pesticide residues or water pollution. For formaldehyde, the tumorigenic dose response is clearly nonlinear close to the MTD, and recent work on mechanism in the rat indicates that this may be because mitogenesis shows a threshold at that level.[127-129]

In a separate analysis, we have calculated an index (PERP) similar to HERP for permitted exposures in the workplace.[18] PERP is the ratio of the U.S. OSHA Permissible Exposure Level (PEL) (mg/kg/d) to the rodent TD_{50} (mg/kg/d), expressed as a percentage. Recently, OSHA lowered the PEL for many chemicals, and we have updated our PERP analysis. We find that among 76 rodent carcinogens with PELs, 9 have PERP values greater than 10%, and 36 have PERP values greater than 1%. For some chemicals, workplace exposures are close to the PEL[18,130] and therefore should be a priority for further attention.

DISCUSSION

The HERP rankings in this paper indicate that there is an enormous background of human exposure to rodent carcinogens in the diet. Some perspective is clearly needed when setting priorities for research and regulatory policy concerning chemical carcinogens and human cancer. The possible hazards to the general population from pollutants and synthetic pesticide residues are of minimal concern when considered against the background of possible hazards to natural chemicals. Our ranking is not a ranking of risks to humans, but is only a way of setting priorities for concern, and one cannot say whether these natural exposures are likely to be of major or minor importance in human cancer. What one can say, is that when ranked on an index that compares human exposure to rodent potency, the synthetic pesticides and water pollutants rank at the bottom. A similar result is expected if the ranking were to use the potency values obtained by the usual regulatory risk assessment methodology.

Because of the mechanistic considerations we have discussed above and elsewhere,[6] carcinogenic effects at the low doses of most human exposures are likely to be much lower than a linear model would predict. This would be the case for both natural and synthetic chemicals. To the extent that increases in tumor incidence in rodent studies are due to the secondary effects of administering high doses, then *any* chemical that increases mitogenesis is a likely rodent carcinogen. High-dose tests are relevant for some occupational or medicinal exposures that can be at high doses.[17,18] With mutagens there is some theoretical justification for thinking that low doses may have an effect, although the complexities of inducible protection systems may well produce a dose-response threshold, or even protective effects at very low doses, e.g., radiation.[131,132] The high endogenous DNA damage rate is also relevant.[6] Our results suggest that an important contribution that animal studies can offer is insight into possible mechanisms of carcinogenesis (e.g., more studies on mitogenesis).

It is by no means clear that many significant risk factors for human cancer will be single chemicals that will be discovered by screening assays.[133] Epidemiological studies do not implicate low-level exposures to synthetic pollutants or pesticide residues as significant risk factors for human cancer.[134] The major preventable risk factors for cancer that have been identified thus far are tobacco, dietary imbalances,[37,41,42,135-139] hormones,[140,141] and chronic infections.[140-148] High-dose exposures, often to complex mixtures, in an occupational setting[18,149] may also contribute to a few percent of human cancer.[134,150] It would be a mistake to interpret the results of this paper as suggesting that natural pesticides in plant foods and chemicals formed by cooking food are necessarily risk factors for human cancer. Eating more fruits and vegetables may be a practical way to lower cancer rates.[42] Strong epidemiological evidence indicates that low intake of fruits and vegetables doubles the risk of most types of cancer compared to high intake.[37,41] This is likely to be due in good part to anticarcinogenic antioxidants and vitamins in fruits and vegetables.[37,42] Since only 9% of adult Americans[41] eat the recommended 5 servings of fruits and vegetables per day,[37] we should be eating more of them not less. Additionally, individual natural pesticides can be bred out of plants, and cooking methods can be modified if further mechanistic or epidemiological studies indicate that it is important to do so.

We need to take a broader view of the chemical world, and try to identify the greatest potential carcinogenic hazards, whether natural or synthetic. One strategy for choosing chemicals to investigate is to prioritize chemicals according to how they might rank in possible hazard *if* they were to be identified as rodent carcinogens. A useful first approximation is the analogous ratio of Human Exposure/Rodent Toxicity (HERT). HERT would use readily available LD_{50} values (acute toxicity) rather than the TD_{50} (carcinogenic potency) values used in HERP. We have compared the ranking by HERP in this paper to a ranking of the same exposures by HERT, and as expected the rank order is similar. This indicates that it would be useful to perform HERT rankings for chemical exposures that are high and with attention to the number of people exposed. Chemicals with high HERT values could then be investigated in more detail as to mutagenicity, mitogenicity, pharmacokinetics, etc.

The arguments in this paper thus undermine many assumptions of current regulatory policy and necessitate a rethinking of policy designed to reduce human cancer. Regulatory agencies have an important educational role to play with respect to the public perceptions about chemicals and cancer. EPA risk assessment guidelines indicate methodological difficulties in quantitative risk assessment and state that the risk estimates are an upper bound on risk and that the true risk at low dose may be zero.[16] The public might be well served if each risk assessment for a particular chemical were to include such a caveat. Additionally, it would be useful for risk assessments to be presented as comparisons to similar estimates done for cups of coffee, beer, and other natural dietary exposures. This would put risk estimates into perspective and is necessary because of the enormous natural background of potential rodent carcinogens and the fact that those of investigated generally rank higher in possible carcinogenic hazard than synthetic environmental pollutants or pesticide residues. In any case, there should be a threshold of attention for hypothetical cancer risks that are low compared to background risks, or else resources are diverted from important risks.

ACKNOWLEDGMENT

This work was supported through the Lawrence Berkeley Laboratory by the U.S. Department of Energy, Contract DE-AC-03-76SF00098 and the U.S. Environmental Protection Agency, Agreement R-815619-01-0, and through the University of California, Berkeley, by the National Institute of Environmental Health Sciences Center Grant ESO1896, and by the National Cancer Institute Outstanding Investigator Grant CA39910. We thank E. L. Gunderson, J. S. Felton, and G. A. Gross for advice on exposure assessment and B. Peterson and C. Chaisson for food consumption data. We thank Leah Slyder and Lars Rohrbach for technical assistance. This paper is adapted from L. S. Gold, T. H. Slone, B. R. Stern, N. B. Manley, and B. N. Ames, Rodent Carcinogens: Setting Priorities, *Science,* 258, in press.

REFERENCES

1. Gold, L. S., Manley, N. B., and Ames, B. N., Extrapolation of carcinogenicity between species: qualitative and quantitative factors, *Risk Anal.* in press.
2. Ames, B. N. and Gold, L. S. Perspective: too many rodent carcinogens: mitogenesis increases mutagenesis. *Science.* 249:970–971 (1990). Letters: 250:1498 (1990); 250:1645–1646 (1990); 251:12–13 (1991); 251:606–608 (1991); 252:902 (1991).
3. Bernstein, L., Gold, L. S., Ames, B. N., Pike, M. C., and Hoel, D. G. Some tautologous aspects of the comparison of carcinogenic potency in rats and mice. *Fund. Appl. Toxicol.* 5:79–86 (1985).
4. Krewski, D., Szyszkowicz, M., and Rosenkranz, H. Quantitative factors in chemical carcinogenesis: variation in carcinogenic potency. *Regul. Toxicol. Pharmacol.* 12:13–29 (1990).
5. Gaylor, D. W. Preliminary estimates of the virtually safe dose for tumors obtained from the maximum tolerated dose. *Regul. Toxicol. Pharmacol.* 9:101–108 (1989).
6. Ames, B. N. and Gold, L. S. Chemical carcinogenesis: too many rodent carcinogens. *Proc. Natl. Acad. Sci. U.S.A.* 87:7772–7776 (1990).
7. Ames, B. N. and Gold, L. S. Endogenous mutagens and the causes of aging and cancer. *Mut. Res.* 250:3–16 (1991).

8. Gold, L. S., Sawyer, C. B., Magaw, R., Backman, G. M., de Veciana, M., Levinson, R., Hooper, N. K., Havender, W. R., Bernstein, L., Peto, R., Pike, M. C., and Ames, B. N. A Carcinogenic Potency Database of the standardized results of animal bioassays. *Environ. Health Perspect.* 58:9–319 (1984).

9. Gold, L. S., de Veciana, M., Backman, G. M., Magaw, R., Lopipero, P., Smith, M., Blumenthal, M., Levinson, R., Bernstein, L., and Ames, B. N. Chronological supplement to the Carcinogenic Potency Database: standardized results of animal bioassays published through December 1982. *Environ. Health Perspect.* 67:161–200 (1986).

10. Gold, L. S., Slone, T. H., Backman, G. M., Magaw, R., Da Costa, M., Lopipero, P., Blumenthal, M., and Ames, B. N. Second chronological supplement to the Carcinogenic Potency Database: Standardized results of animal bioassays published through December 1984 and by the National Toxicology Program through May 1986. *Environ. Health Perspect.* 74:237–329 (1987).

11. Gold, L. S., Slone, T. H., Backman, G. M., Eisenberg, S., Da Costa, M., Wong, M., Manley, N. B., Rohrbach, L., and Ames, B. N. Third chronological supplement to the Carcinogenic Potency Database: standardized results of animal bioassays published through December 1986 and by the National Toxicology Program through June 1987. *Environ. Health Perspect.* 84:215–286 (1990).

12. Gold, L. S., Manley, N. B., Slone, T. H., Garfinkel, G. B., Rohrbach, L., and Ames, B. N. The fifth plot of the Carcinogenic Potency Database: results of animal bioassays published in the general literature through 1988 and by the National Toxicology Program through 1989. *Environ. Health Perspect.* 100 (in press).

13. Haseman, J. K. Issues in carcinogenicity testing: dose selection. *Fund. Appl. Toxicol.* 5:66–78 (1985).

14. Gold, L. S., Bernstein, L., Magaw, R., and Slone, T. H. Interspecies extrapolation in carcinogenesis: prediction between rats and mice. *Environ. Health Perspect.* 81:211–219 (1989).

15. Gold, L. S., Slone, T. H., Manley, N. B., Garfinkel, G. B., Hudes, E. S., Rohrbach, L., and Ames, B. N. The Carcinogenic Potency Database: analyses of 4000 chronic animal cancer experiments published in the general literature and by the U.S. National Cancer Institute/National Toxicology Program. *Environ. Health Perspect.* 96:11–15 (1991).

16. U.S. Environmental Protection Agency (EPA). Guidelines for carcinogen risk assessment. *Fed. Regis.* 51:33997–33998 (1986).

17. Ames, B. N., Magaw, R., and Gold, L. S. Ranking possible carcinogenic hazards. *Science.* 236:271–280 (1987). Letters: 237:235 (1987); 237:1283–1284 (1987); 237:1399–1400 (1987); 238:1633–1634 (1987); 240:1043–1047 (1988).

18. Gold, L. S., Backman, G. M., Hooper, K., and Peto, R. Ranking the potential carcinogenic hazards to workers from exposures to chemicals that are tumorigenic in rodents. *Environ. Health Perspect.* 76:211–219 (1987).

19. Ames, B. N., Profet, M., and Gold, L. S. Dietary pesticides (99.99% all natural). *Proc. Natl. Acad. Sci. U.S.A.* 87:7777–7781 (1990).

20. Ames, B. N., Profet, M., and Gold, L. S. Nature's chemicals and synthetic chemicals: comparative toxicology. *Proc. Natl. Acad. Sci. U.S.A.* 87:7782–7786 (1990).
21. Gartrell, M. J., Craun, J. C., Podrebarac, D. S., and Gunderson, E. L. Pesticides, selected elements, and other chemicals in adult total diet samples. *J. Assoc. Off. Anal. Chem.*, 69:146–161 (1986).
22. Clarke, R. J. and Macrae, R., Eds. *Coffee.* Vol. 1–3. Elsevier, New York (1988).
23. Maarse, H. and Visscher, C. A., Eds. *Volatile Compounds in Foods. Qualitative and Quantitative Data.* TNO-CIVO Food Analysis Institute, Zeist, The Netherlands (1989).
24. Fujita, Y., Wakabayashi, K., Nagao, M., and Sugimura, T. Implication of hydrogen peroxide in the mutagenicity of coffee. *Mutat. Res.* 144:227–230 (1985).
25. Kikugawa, K., Kato, T., and Takahashi, S. Possible presence of 2-amino-3,4-dimethyl-imidazo[4,5-*f*]quinoline and other heterocyclic amine-like mutagens in roasted coffee beans. *J. Agric. Food Chem.* 37:881–886 (1989).
26. Yamagami, T., Handa, H., Takeuchi, J., Munemitsu, H., Aoki, M., and Kato, Y. Rat pituitary adenoma and hyperplasia induced by caffeine administration. *Surg. Neurol.* 20:323–331 (1983).
27. Stofberg, J. and Grundschober, F. Consumption ratio and food predominance of flavoring materials. Second cumulative series. *Perfum. Flavor.* 12:27–56 (1987).
28. Tressl, R., Bahri, D., Köppler, H., and Jensen, A. Diphenole und Caramel-komponenten in Röstkaffees verschiedener Sorten. II. *Z. Lebensm. Unters. Forsch.* 167:111–114 (1978).
29. Rahn, W. and König, W. A. GC/MS investigations of the constituents in a diethyl ether extract of an acidified roast coffee infusion. *J. High Resolution Chromatogr. Chromatogr. Commun.* 1002:69–71 (1978).
30. Ariza, R. R., Dorado, G., Barbanch, M., and Pueyo, C. Study of the causes of direct-acting mutagenicity in coffee and tea using the Ara test in *Salmonella typhimurium. Mut. Res.* 201:89–96 (1988).
31. Fung, V. A., Cameron, T. P., Hughes, T. J., Kirby, P. E., and Dunkel, V. C. Mutagenic activity of some coffee flavor ingredients. *Mut. Res.* 204:219–228 (1988).
32. Hanham, A. F., Dunn, B. P., and Stich, H. F. Clastogenic activity of caffeic acid and its relationship to hydrogen peroxide generated during autooxidation. *Mut. Res.* 116:333–339 (1983).
33. Stich, H. F., Rosin, M. P., Wu, C. H., and Powrie, W. D. A comparative genotoxicity study of chlorogenic acid (3-O-caffeoylquinic acid). *Mut. Res.* 90:201–212 (1981).
34. Ishidate, M., Jr., Harnois, M. C., and Sofuni, T. A comparative analysis of data on the clastogenicity of 951 chemical substances tested in mammalian cell cultures. *Mut. Res.* 201:89–96 (1988).
35. Dietrich, D. R. and Swenberg, J. A. The presence of α_{2u}-globulin is necessary for *d*-limonene promotion of male rat kidney tumors. *Cancer Res.* 51:3512–3521 (1991).

36. International Agency for Research on Cancer. *Coffee, Tea, Mate, Methylxanthines and Methylglyoxal.* Vol. 51. Lyon, France: IARC, 1991. (IARC Monographs on the Evaluation of Carcinogenic Risk of Chemicals to Humans.)

37. National Research Council. *Diet and Health, Implications for Reducing Chronic Disease Risk.* National Academy Press, Washington, D.C. (1989).

38. Sawyer, C., Peto, R., Bernstein, L., and Pike, M. C. Calculation of carcinogenic potency from long-term animal carcinogenesis experiments. *Biometrics.* 40:27–40 (1984).

39. Peto, R., Pike, M. C., Bernstein, L., Gold, L. S., and Ames, B. N. The TD_{50}: a proposed general convention for the numerical description of the carcinogenic potency of chemicals in chronic-exposure animal experiments. *Environ. Health Perspect.* 58:1–8 (1984).

40. U.S. Food and Drug Administration (FDA). FDA pesticide program: residues in foods 1990. *J. Assoc. Off. Anal. Chem.,* 74:121A–141A (1991).

41. Block, A. G., Patterson, A. B., and Subar, A. A. Fruit, vegetables, and cancer prevention: a review of the epidemiologic evidence. *Nutr. Cancer.* 18:1–29 (1992).

42. Bendich, A. and Butterworth, C. E., Jr., Eds. *Micronutrients in Health and in Disease Prevention.* Marcel Dekker, New York (1991).

43. Ott, M. G., Scharnweber, H. C., and Langner, R. R. Mortality experience of 161 employees exposed to ethylene dibromide in two production units. *Br. J. Ind. Med.* 37:163–168 (1980).

44. Ramsey, J. C., Park, C. N., Ott, M. G., and Gehring, P. J. Carcinogenic risk assessment: ethylene dibromide. *Toxicol. Appl. Pharmacol.* 47:411–414 (1978).

45. Havel, R. J. and Kane, J. P. Therapy of hyperlipidemic states. *Annu. Rev. Med.* 33:417 (1982).

46. American Medical Association (AMA) Division of Drugs. *AMA Drug Evaluations,* 5th ed. AMA, Chicago, IL (1983), pp. 201–202.

47. American Medical Association (AMA) Division of Drugs. *AMA Drug Evaluations,* 5th ed. AMA, Chicago, IL (1983), pp. 1717, 1766–1777, 1802.

48. Hirono, I., Mori, H., and Haga, M. Carcinogenic activity of *Symphytum officinale, J. Natl. Cancer Inst.* 61:865–868 (1978).

49. Culvenor, C. C. J., Clarke, M., Edgar, J. A., Frahn, J. L., Jago, M. V., Peterson, J. E., and Smith, L. W. Structure and toxicity of the alkaloids of Russian comfrey (*Symphytum × Uplandicum nyman*), a medicinal herb and item of human diet. *Experientia.* 36:377–379 (1980).

50. Ethyl alcohol is assumed to be present at 12% in wine and 5% in beer.

51. Siegal, D. M., Frankos, V. H., and Schneiderman, M. Formaldehyde risk assessment for occupationally exposed workers. *Reg. Toxicol. Pharm.* 3:355–371 (1983).

52. Connor, T. H., Theiss, J. C., Hanna, H. A., Monteith, D. K., and Matney, T. S. Genotoxicity of organic chemicals frequently found in the air of mobile homes. *Toxicol. Lett.* 25:33–40 (1985).

53. McCann, J., Horn, L., Girman, J., and Nero, A. V. Potential risks from exposure to organic carcinogens in indoor air. in Sanbhu, S. S., de Marini, D. M., Mass, M. J., Moore, M. M., and Mumford, J. S., Eds. *Short-Term Bioassays in the Analysis of Complex Environmental Mixtures.* Plenum Press, New York (1987).

54. Piper, J. M., Tonascia, J., and Matanoski, G. M. Heavy phenacetin use and bladder cancer in women aged 20 to 49 years. *N. Engl. J. Med.* 313:292–295 (1985).
55. Herrmann, K. Review on nonessential constituents of vegetables. III. Carrots, celery, parsnips, beets, spinach, lettuce, endives, chicory, rhubarb, and artichokes. *Z. Lebensm. Unters. Forsch.* 167:262–273 (1978).
56. Hagiwara, A., Hirose, M., Takahashi, S., Ogawa, K., Shirai, T., and Ito, N. Forestomach and kidney carcinogenicity of caffeic acid in F344 rats and C57BL/6N × C3H/HeN F_1 mice. *Cancer Res.* 51:5655–5660 (1991).
57. Hagiwara, A. Personal communication.
58. Leung, A. Y. *Encyclopedia of Common Natural Ingredients Used in Food, Drugs and Cosmetics.* John Wiley & Sons, New York (1980).
59. Wilson, J. B. Determination of safrole and methyl salicylate in soft drinks. *J. Assoc. Off. Anal. Chem.* 42:696–698 (1959).
60. Mosel, H. D. and Herrmann, K. The phenolics of fruits. III. The contents of catechins and hydroxycinnamic acids in pome and stone fruits. *Z. Lebensm. Unters. Forsch.* 154:6–11 (1974).
61. Toth, B. and Erickson, J. Cancer induction in mice by feeding of the uncooked cultivated mushroom of commerce *Agaricus bisporus. Cancer Res.* 46:4007–4011 (1986). *Agaricus bisporus* is the most commonly eaten mushroom in the U.S. The TD_{50}, based on a study that fed raw mushrooms to mice, is expressed as dry weight so as to be comparable to other TD_{50} values in Table 2; 90% of a mushroom is assumed to be water.
62. Heath, H. B. *Source Book of Flavors.* AVI Publishing, Westport, CT (1981).
63. National Toxicology Program (NTP). Toxicology and Carcinogenesis Studies of d-Limonene (CAS no. 5989-27-5) in F344/N Rats and $B6C3F_1$ Mice (Gavage Studies). (NTP Tech. Rep. Ser. No. 347) Research Triangle Park, NC (1990).
64. Engel, K. H. and Tressl, R. Studies on the volatile components of two mango varieties. *J. Agric. Food Chem.* 31:796–801 (1983).
65. Carlson, D. G., Daxenbichler, M. E., VanEtten, C. H., Kwolek, W. F., and Williams, P. H. Glucosinolates in crucifer vegetables: broccoli, Brussels sprouts, cauliflower, collards, kale, mustard greens, and kohlrabi. *J. Am. Soc. Hort. Sci.* 112:173–178 (1987).
66. Diet cola available in a local market in 1986 contained 7.9 mg of sodium saccharin per fluid ounce.
67. Ivie, G. W., Holt, D. L., and Ivey, M. Natural toxicants in human foods: psoralens in raw and cooked parsnip root. *Science.* 213:909–910 (1981).
68. Schreier P., Drawert, F., and Heindze, I., Über die quantitative Zusammensetzung natürlicher und technologish veränderter pflanzlicher Aromen. *Chem. Mikrobiol. Technol. Lebensm.* 6:78–83 (1979).
69. Hall, R. L., Henry, S. H., Scheuplein, R. J., Dull, B. J. and Rulis, A. M. Comparison of the carcinogenic risks of naturally occurring and adventitious substances in food. in Taylor, S. L. and Scanlon, R. A., Eds. *Food Toxicology: a Perspective on the Relative Risks.* Marcel Dekker, New York (1989) p. 205.
70. Stoloff, L. Aflatoxin control: past and present. *J. Assoc. Off. Anal. Chem.* 63:1067–1073 (1980).

71. Busby, W. F., Jr. and Wogan, G. N. Aflatoxins. in Searle, C. E., Ed. *Chemical Carcinogens,* 2nd ed., Vol. 2. (ACS Monograph 182) American Chemical Society, Washington, D.C. (1984) pp. 944–1136.

72. Stöhr, H. and Herrmann, K. On the phenolic acids of vegetables. III. Hydroxycinnamic acids and hydroxybenzoic acids of root vegetables. *Z. Lebensm. Unters. Forsch.* 159:219–224 (1975).

73. Hasselstrom, T., Hewitt, E. J., Konigsbacher, K. S., and Ritter, J. J. Composition of volatile oil of black pepper. *Agric. Food Chem.* 5:53–55 (1957).

74. Schmidtlein, H. and Herrmann, K. Über die Phenolsäuren des Gemüses. IV. Hydroxyzimtsäuren und Hydroxybenzösäuren weiterer Gemüsearten und der Kartoffeln. *Z. Lebensm. Unters. Forsch.* 159:255–263 (1975).

75. Beech, J. A. Estimated worst case trihalomethane body burden of a child using a swimming pool. *Med. Hypotheses.* 6:303–307 (1980). Exposure is for absorption by a 37-kg child in an average pool (134 µg/l).

76. Fazio, T., Havery, D. C., and Howard, J. W., Determination of volatile N-nitrosamines in foodstuffs. I. A new clean-up technique for confirmation by GLC-MS. II. A continued survey of foods and beverages. in Walker, E. A., Griciute, L., Castegnaro, M., and Borzsonyi, M., Eds. *N-Nitroso Compounds: Analysis, Formation and Occurrence.* International Agency for Research on Cancer, Lyon, France (1980) pp. 419–435. (IARC Scientific Pub. No. 31).

77. Preussmann, R. and Eisenbrand, G. N-Nitroso carcinogens in the environment. in Searle, C. E., Ed. *Chemical Carcinogens,* 2nd ed., Vol. 2. American Chemical Society, Washington, D.C., (1984) pp. 829–868. (ACS Monograph 182).

78. Sen, N. P., Seaman, S., and Miles, W. F. Volatile nitrosamines in various cured meat products: effect of cooking and recent trends. *J. Agric. Food Chem.* 27:1354–1357 (1979).

79. California Regional Water Quality Control Board #2, Santa Clara County Public Health Department, Santa Clara Valley Water District, Environmental Protection Agency. Ground Water and Drinking Water in the Santa Clara Valley: a White Paper. Table 8. 1984.

80. National Toxicology Program (NTP). Toxicology and Carcinogenesis Studies of Furfural (CAS no. 98-01-1) in F344/N Rats and B6C3F$_1$ Mice (Gavage Studies). (NTP Tech. Rep. Ser. No. 382) Research Triangle Park, NC (1990).

81. Tricker, A. R. and Preussmann, R. Carcinogenic N-nitrosamines in the diet: occurrence, formation, mechanisms and carcinogenic potential. *Mut. Res.* 259:277–289 (1991).

82. Bejnarowicz, E. A. and Kirch, E. R. Gas chromatographic analysis of oil of nutmeg. *J. Pharm. Sci.* 52:988–993 (1963).

83. Chauhan, Y., Nagel, D., Gross, M., Cerny, R., and Toth, B. Isolation of N^2-[γ-L-(+)-glutamyl]-4-carboxyphenylhydrazine in the cultivated mushroom *Agaricus bisporus. J. Agric. Food Chem.* 33:817–820 (1985).

84. Ough, C. S. Ethyl carbamate in fermented beverages and foods. I. Naturally occurring ethylcarbamate. *J. Agric. Food Chem.* 24:323–328 (1976).

85. U.S. Environmental Protection Agency (EPA). Daminozide special review. Crop field trials. Supplemental daminozide and UDMH residue data for apples, cherries, peanuts, pears, and tomatoes. February 21, 1989 (memo from L. Cheng to M. Boodée).

86. Goldenthal, E. I. Two year oncogenicity study in rats. International Research and Development Corporation (IRDC), Mattawan, MI (1989). IRDC Report Number 399-062 in UDMH.

87. Goldenthal, E. I. Two year oncogenicity study in mice. International Research and Development Corporation (IRDC), Mattawan, MI (1990). IRDC Report Number 399-065 in UDMH.

88. Henrich, L. and Baltes, W. Über die Bestimmung von Phenolen im Kaffeegetränk. Z. Lebensm. Unters. Forsch. 185:362–365 (1987).

89. Shibata, M., Hirose, M., Tanaka, H., Asakawa, E., Shirai, T., and Ito, N. Induction of renal cell tumors in rats and mice, and enhancement of hepatocellular tumor development in mice after long-term hydroquinone treatment. Jpn. J. Cancer Res. 82:1211–1219 (1991).

90. Hirose, M., Fukushima, S., Shirai, T., Hasegawa, R., Kato, T., Tanaka, H., Asakawa, E., and Ito, N. Stomach carcinogenicity of caffeic acid, sesamol and catechol in rats and mice. Gann. 81:207–212 (1990).

91. Duggan, R. E. and Corneliussen, P. E. Dietary intake of pesticide chemicals in the United States (III), June 1968–April 1970. Pestic. Monit. J. 5:331–341 (1972).

92. Beier, R. C., Ivie, G. W., Oertli, E. H., and Holt, D. L. HPLC analysis of linear furocoumarins (psoralens) in healthy celery Apium graveolens. Food Chem. Toxicol. 21:163–165 (1983).

93. Williamson, S. J. Epidemiological studies on cancer and organic compounds in US drinking waters, Sci. Total Environ. 18:187–203 (1981).

94. Fukuda, Y., Nagata, M., Osawa, T., and Namiki, M. Chemical aspects of the antioxidative activity of roasted sesame seed oil, and the effect of using the oil for frying. Agric. Biol. Chem. 50:857–862 (1986).

95. Lagakos, S. W., Wessen, B. J., and Zelen, N. An analysis of contaminated well water and health effects in Woburn, Massachusetts. J. Am. Stat. Assoc. 81:583 (1986).

96. Chauhan, Y., Nagel, D., Issenberg, P., and Toth, B. Identification of p-hydrazinobenzoic acid in the commercial mushroom Agaricus bisporus. J. Agric. Food Chem. 32:1067–1069 (1984).

97. Felton, J. S., Knize, M. G., Shen, N. H., Lewis, P. R., Andresen, B. D., Happe, J., and Hatch, F. T. The isolation and identification of a new mutagen from fried ground beef: 2-amino-1-methyl-6-phenylimidazo[4,5-b]pyridine (PhIP). Carcinogenesis. 7:1081–1086 (1986).

98. Ito, N., Hasegawa, R., Sano, M., Tamano, S., Esumi, H., Takayama, S., and Sugimura, T. A new colon and mammary carcinogen in cooked food, 2-amino-1-methyl-6-phenylimidazo[4,5-b]pyridine (PhIP). Carcinogenesis. 12:1503–1506 (1991).

99. Esumi, H., Ohgaki, H., Kohzen, E., Takayama, S., and Sugimura, T. Induction of lymphoma in CDF$_1$ mice by the food mutagen, 2-amino-1-methyl-6-phenylimidazo[4,5-b]pyridine. Jpn. J. Cancer Res. 80:1176–1178 (1989).

100. Luo, S., Guo, W., and Fu, H., Correlation between aroma and quality grade of Chinese jasmine tea. Dev. Food Sci. 17:191–199 (1988).

101. Gross, G. A. and Grüter, A. Quantitation of mutagenic/carcinogenic heterocyclic aromatic amines in food products. J. Chromatogr. 592:271–278 (1992).

102. U.S. Environmental Protection Agency (EPA). Ethylene Dibromide (EDB) Scientific Support and Decision Document for Grain and Grain Milling Fumigation Uses. February 8, 1984.

103. Chaudhary, S. K., Ceska, O., Tétu, C., Warrington, P. J., Ashwood-Smith, M. J., and Poulton, G. A. Oxypeucedanin, a major furocoumarin in parsley, *Petroselinum crispum. Planta Med.* 6:462–464 (1986).

104. Hargraves, W. A. and Pariza, M. W. Purification and mass spectral characterization of bacterial mutagens from commercial beef extract. *Cancer Res.* 43:1467–1472 (1983).

105. Felton, J. S., Knize, M. G., Wood, C., Wuebbles, B. J., Healy, S. K., Stuermer, D. H., Bjeldanes, L. F., Kimble, B. J., and Hatch, F. T. Isolation and characterization of new mutagens from fried ground beef. *Carcinogenesis.* 5:95–102 (1984).

106. Murray, S., Gooderham, N. J., Boobis, A. R., and Davis, D. S. Measurement of MeIQx and DiMeIQx in fried beef by capillary column gas chromatography electron capture negative ion chemical ionisation mass spectrometry. *Carcinogenesis.* 9:321–325 (1988).

107. Canas, B. J., Havery, D. C., Robinson, L. R., Sullivan, M. P., Joe, F. L., Jr., and Diachenko, G. W. Chemical contaminants monitoring: ethyl carbamate levels in selected fermented foods and beverages. *J. Assoc. Off. Anal. Chem.* 72:873–876 (1989).

108. National Toxicology Program (NTP). Toxicology and Carcinogenesis Studies of α-Methylbenzyl Alcohol (CAS no. 98-85-1) in F344/N Rats and B6C3F$_1$ Mice (NTP Tech. Rep. Ser. No. 369) (Gavage Studies). Research Triangle Park, NC (1990).

109. Barnes, W. S., Maher, J. C., and Weisburger, J. H. High-pressure liquid chromatographic method for the analysis of 2-amino-3-methylimidazo[4,5-*f*]quinoline, a mutagen formed during the cooking of food. *J. Agric. Food Chem.* 31:883–886 (1983).

110. Felton, J. S., Knize, M. G., Shen, N. H., Andresen, B. D., Bjeldanes, L. F., and Hatch, F. T. Identification of the mutagens in cooked beef. *Environ. Health Perspect.* 67:17–24 (1986).

111. U.S. Environmental Protection Agency (EPA). *Peer Review of Chlorothalonil.* Office of Pesticides and Toxic Substances, Washington, D.C. (1987). Review found in Health Effect Division Document No. 007718. The TD$_{50}$ value is a harmonic mean of values from this study and studies in the CPDB.

112. U.S. Environmental Protection Agency (EPA). *Integrated Risk Information System (IRIS).* Office of Health and Environmental Assessment, Environmental Criteria and Assessment Office, Cincinnati, OH (1991).

113. U.S. Environmental Protection Agency (EPA). *Peer Review of Captan.* Office of Pesticides and Toxic Substances, Washington, D.C. (1986). Review found in Health Effect Division Document No. 007715.

114. U.S. Environmental Protection Agency (EPA). Health Assessment Document for Trichloroethylene. 1986.

115. Bogen, K. T., Hall, L. C., Perry, L., Fish, R., McKone, T. E., Dowd, P., Patton, S. E., and Mallon, B., *Health Risk Assessment of Trichloroethylene (TCE) in California Drinking Water.* California Public Health Foundation, Berkeley (1988).

116. Gunderson, E. L. Chemical contaminants monitoring: FDA Total Diet Study, April 1982–April 1984, dietary intakes of pesticides, selected elements, and other chemicals. *J. Assoc. Off. Anal. Chem.* 71:1200–1209 (1988).

117. U.S. Food and Drug Administration (FDA). FDA Pesticide Program: residues in foods 1987. *J. Assoc. Off. Anal. Chem.* 71:156A–174A (1988).

118. U.S. Food and Drug Administration (FDA). FDA Pesticide Program: residues in foods 1988. *J. Assoc. Off. Anal. Chem.* 72:133A–152A (1989).

119. U.S. Food and Drug Administration (FDA). FDA Pesticide Program: residues in foods 1989. *J. Assoc. Off. Anal. Chem.* 73:127A–146A (1990).

120. Technical Assessment Systems (TAS). Exposure 1 Software Package. Washington, D.C. (1989). Provided by Barbara Petersen.

121. Economic Research Service (ERS). *Vegetables and Specialities Situation and Outlook Yearbook.* U.S. Department of Agriculture, Washington, D.C. (1990).

122. Economic Research Service (ERS). *Fruit and Tree Nuts Situation and Outlook Yearbook.* U.S. Department of Agriculture, Washington, D.C. (1990).

123. United Fresh Fruit and Vegetable Association (UFFVA). Supply Guide: Monthly Availability of Fresh Fruit and Vegetables. Alexandria, VA (1989).

124. Maarse, H. and Visscher, C. A., Eds. *Volatile Compounds in Foods. Qualitative and Quantitative Data. Supplement 1 and Cumulative Index.* TNO-CIVO Food Analysis Institute, Zeist, The Netherlands (1990).

125. Flament, I. Coffee, cocoa, and tea. in Maarse, H., Ed. *Volatile Compounds in Foods and Beverages.* Marcel Dekker, New York (1991) pp. 617–669.

126. Tomatis, L., Aitio, A., Wilbourn, J., and Shuker, L. Human carcinogens so far identified. *Jpn. J. Cancer Res.* 80:795–807 (1989).

127. Butterworth, B. E., Slaga, T. J., Farland, W., and McClain, M., Eds. *Chemically Induced Cell Proliferation: Implications for Risk Assessment.* Wiley-Liss, New York (1991).

128. Butterworth, B. E. Consideration of both genotoxic and nongenotoxic mechanisms in predicting carcinogenic potential. *Mut. Res.* 239:117–132 (1990).

129. Swenberg, J. A., Richardson, F. C., Boucheron, J. A., Deal, F. H., Belinsky, S. A., Charbonneau, M., and Short, B. G. High- to low-dose extrapolation: critical determinants involved in the dose response of carcinogenic substances. *Environ. Health Perspect.* 76:57–63 (1987).

130. Roach, S. A. and Rappaport, S. M. But they are not thresholds: a critical analysis of the documentation of Threshold Limit Values. *Am. J. Ind. Med.* 17:727–753 (1990).

131. Kelsey, K. T., Memisoglu, A., Frenkel, D., and Liber, H. L. Human lymphocytes exposed to low doses of X-rays are less susceptible to radiation-induced mutagenesis. *Mut. Res.* 263:197–201 (1991).

132. Ootsuyama, A. and Tanooka, H., Threshold-like dose of local beta irradiation repeated throughout the life span of mice for induction of skin and bone tumors. *Radiat. Res.* 125:98–101 (1991).

133. Peto, R. Epidemiological reservations about risk assessment. in Woodhead, A. D., Shellabarger, C. J., Pond, V., and Hollaender, A., Eds. *Assessment of Risk from Low-Level Exposure to Radiation and Chemicals.* Plenum Press, New York (1985) pp. 16–30.

134. Doll, R. and Peto, R. *The Causes of Cancer.* Oxford University Press, New York (1981).

135. Joossens, J. V., Hill, M. J., and Geboers, J., Eds. *Diet and Human Carcinogenesis*. Elsevier, New York (1985).
136. Lipkin, M. Biomarkers of increased susceptibility to gastrointestinal cancer: new application to studies of cancer prevention in human subjects. *Cancer Res*. 48:235–245 (1988).
137. Yang, C. S. and Newmark, H. L. The role of micronutrient deficiency in carcinogenesis. *CRC Crit. Rev. Oncol*. 7:267–287 (1987).
138. Pence, B. C. and Buddingh, F. Inhibition of dietary fat-promoted colon carcinogenesis in rats by supplemental calcium or vitamin D$_3$. *Carcinogenesis*. 9:187–190 (1988).
139. Reddy, B. S. and Cohen, L. A., Eds. *Diet, Nutrition, and Cancer: A Critical Evaluation*. CRC Press, Boca Raton, FL (1986).
140. Preston-Martin, S., Pike, M. C., Ross, R. K., and Jones, P. A. Increased cell division as a cause of human cancer. *Cancer Res*. 50:7415–7421 (1990).
141. Henderson, B. E., Ross, R., and Bernstein, L. Estrogens as a cause of human cancer: the Richard and Hinda Rosenthal Foundation Award Lecture. *Cancer Res*. 48:246–253 (1988).
142. Yeh, F., Mo, C., Luo, S., Henderson, B. E., Tong, M. J., and Yu, M. C. A seriological case-control study of primary hepatocellular carcinoma in Guangxi, China. *Cancer Res*. 45:872–873 (1985).
143. Wu, T. C., Tong, M. J., Hwang, B., Lee, S. D., and Hu, M. M. Primary hepatocellular carcinoma and hepatitis B infection during childhood. *Hepatology*. 7:46–48 (1987).
144. Peto, R. and zur Hausen, H., Eds. *Viral Etiology of Cervical Cancer. Banbury Report 21*. Cold Spring Harbor Laboratory, Cold Spring Harbor, NY (1986).
145. Inoue, J., Seiki, M., Taniguchi, T., Tsuru, S., and Yoshida, M. Induction of interleukin 2 receptor gene expression by p40x encoded by human T-cell leukemia virus type. *EMBO J*. 5:2883–2888 (1986).
146. Taniguchi, T., Yamada, G., Shibuya, H., Maruyama, M., Haradu, H., Hatakeyama, M., and Fujita, T. Regulation of the interleukin-2 system and T cell neoplasm. in Kakunaga, T., Sugimura, T., Tomatis, L., and Yamasaki, H., Eds. *Cell Differentiation, Genes and Cancer*. Vol. 92. International Agency for Research on Cancer, Lyon, France (1988) pp. 181–184.
147. Rathbone, B. J. and Heatley, R. V., Eds. *Campylobacter pylori and Gastroduodenal Disease*. Blackwell Scientific, Oxford (1989).
148. Blaser, M. J., Ed. *Campylobacter pylori in Gastritis and Peptic Ulcer Disease*. Igaku-Shoin, New York (1989).
149. International Agency for Research on Cancer (IARC). *Overall Evaluations of Carcinogenicity* (Suppl. 7). IARC, Lyon, France (1987).
150. Henderson, B. E., Ross, R. K., and Pike, M. C. Towards the primary prevention of cancer. *Science*. 254:1131–1138 (1991).

The Impact of Data Gaps in EPA's Regional Comparative Risk Projects

Rosalie R. Day

REGIONAL PROJECTS

All ten U.S. Environmental Protection Agency (EPA) Regional Offices have completed risk analysis and ranking of environmental problems as the foundation for risk-based strategic planning. Each Region conducted a comparative risk project examining the residual risks (the risk that remains after consideration of the present controls and regulations) associated with 24 or more environmental problem areas. The analysis estimated the intensities and magnitudes of the threats to ecological systems and human health within the Region's geographic boundary.* Most Regions also analyzed the economic impacts of threats to the environment. The assessment provides a broad snapshot of the current environmental status of each EPA Region.

The results of the analysis provided the basis for ranking the environmental problem areas relative to one another with respect to the current threats posed to ecological systems, human health and economic welfare, respectively. Not all problem areas were determined to pose risks within all three categories.

The projects provided semiquantitative descriptions of relative risks facing EPA Regions at a policy level of precision and accuracy. The analysis and rankings were used in combination with risk management factors, such as statutory authority and technical feasibility, to determine the most effective strategies for managing the environment. The level of certainty of the analyses and the broad resolution of the information provided by the projects allowed the Regions to allocate resources on the margin to target reduction of currently uncontrolled risks and promoted efforts to build capability to further quantify risks. The prioritization of pollution control activities using the risk reduction criteria is captured in 1- to 4-year strategic plans.

The environmental problem areas analyzed were designated based on existing EPA program activities, and include sources, receptors, media, specific

---

* Transregional impacts were accounted for differently across projects. Generally, the lack of data prohibited their inclusion in the ranking process.

chemicals, and a few environmental problems not specified within the Agency's statutory authority, such as physical degradation of ecosystems* and indoor air quality. This scheme of defining the fields of inquiry was useful for the risk management/planning aspects of the risk-based strategic planning process as the areas mostly conform to current programmatic budget and workplan development. However, the aggregation and disaggregation of information that was often necessary to determine risk for the problem areas, as they were defined, increased uncertainty in the analysis already introduced by limited appropriate data.

Lack of data characterizing the state of the landscape and impacts of specific stressors on its ecosystem components as well as magnitudes of human exposures for many of the defined problem areas prohibited strictly quantitative analyses. In addition, lack of infrastructure needed to manipulate large amounts of incompatible or disparate data often did not allow assessment within the time constraints. These data problems were especially apparent with respect to individual stressors and evidence of their impacts and exposures for estimating risk to specific ecological systems.** Therefore, the relative risks either incorporated, or were supported by, a variety of qualitative information.***

However, similar risk rankings of particular problem areas across Regions resulted from different methodologies and data sources. This consistency indicated that the level of analysis was sufficient for the broad planning uses for which it was intended. Given the inexact science of policy making, the common results, combined with reasonable internal consistency, allowed for a credible risk-based Regional prioritization. In addition, the planning exercise following the analysis allowed Regions to identify the most significant data gaps and initiate the building of a risk information and methodology infrastructure to facilitate development of new risk management approaches and measures of progress.

IMPACT OF DATA GAPS ON REGIONAL RESULTS

Given the state of the practice of broadly targeted risk management, greater precision or accuracy in the analysis would probably not have altered the

---

* The National Environmental Policy Act (NEPA) defines EPA's role loosely as "steward" of the environment. However, only federal facilities or projects with federal funding requiring review in the environmental impact statement process provide EPA opportunity to directly impact physical degradation of ecosystems. However, enforcement is limited to action by the Council on Environmental Quality.

** As the dose-response-type relationship of ecological systems are not fully understood, quality and magnitude trends data were used where available to estimate current risk and, by some Regions, to predict future risks resulting from current actions. Available trends information tended to exist only at a very broad level of resolution.

***Qualitative information was often converted to a point scale and incorporated into the quantitative analysis. In addition, qualitative description was used to enhance the risk characterization and to ameliorate uncertainty in the analysis resulting from the quantitative estimates.

Regional priorities that emerged in the process. However, the risk reduction approaches developed to address the priority problems could benefit significantly from additional information on specific stressors, impacts, exposures, and trends.

The lack of existing data collected (by EPA or externally) for the purpose of risk characterization was the most significant contribution of uncertainty to the analysis, ranking, and management targeting in the Regional projects. The amount and quality of data necessary to quantify relative risk for human health, ecological systems, and costs to society, respectively, varied by information type and geographic location. Much of the data collected by the Regions in fulfilment of Agency statutory responsibilities are administrative, compliance records, permitting documents, and numbers of activities accomplished, rather than environmental indicators. (Environmental indicators are the parameters that provide the ability to assess the quality of the environment.) While existing data collected for purposes other than risk characterization were used extensively, it was often too time consuming or resource intensive to access and manipulate into useful information for the Regional analyses.

Due to the nature of existing statutory obligations, Regional regulatory programs generally collect minimal data on exposures and extent and intensity of stressor impacts. Data routinely collected includes magnitudes of emissions for major sources, through the permitting processes, and some ambient concentrations for the media programs. While some national programs have conducted substantial robust modeling to determine human health exposures and satisfactory Region-specific extrapolation is plausible, in others, application of national estimates to a particular Region relies on inappropriate assumptions. In the economic risk analysis, national parameters were used more frequently (for estimating pecuniary damages) than in other risk categories. Often extrapolation to a particular Region did not yield useful or appropriate results.

The aggregation and disaggregation of information necessary to rank the problem areas as defined exacerbated uncertainties due to the other data problems. Often, risk assessment based on robust data was combined out of necessity with estimates from primarily professional judgment, weakening the quantitative intent of the analysis for many problem areas. The resulting degree of uncertainty depended on both the type of qualitative information incorporated and its importance to the overall risk calculation. The analytical weaknesses that may have emerged due to disaggregation, required by some problem area definitions, were particularly apparent in the analyses of discharges to surface waters. Impacts from nonpoint sources and industrial and municipal point sources were overlapping and often indistinguishable. The respective impacts were estimated through partitioning based on professional judgment. The stage in the analysis at which the impacts were partitioned varied across Regions.

In addition, aggregation of cancer and noncancer risks, ecological threats from a particular stressor across ecosystem types, and impacts of numerous stressors on a particular ecosystem type often mixed the robust quantitative analysis with less well-supported information. In many cases, the risk calculated was generally driven by the components for which the best data existed. Some Regions conducted a partitioned analysis of impacts allowing for a more sophisticated summation of impacts where the quality or quantity of data varied significantly. These approaches generally yielded results that tended to be skewed consistently within Regions, allowing decision makers to adequately rank the risks for internal policy use.

The lack of data, especially where little qualitative information was available, often resulted in lower risk rankings.* This is likely to have occurred in some waste problem areas. Data on risk from the low-ranked municipal and industrial waste sites were often limited to the number of sites in the Region without indication of fugitive emissions or extent of physical degradation. Professional judgment combined with a few existing studies identified types of stressors likely to be present and their potential impacts on a hypothetical exposure radius or groundwater plume. For example, the primary ecological risk cited was an unquantified reference to habitat destruction from landfill and access route construction.

In the groundwater analysis, only current human health risk from well water was considered. There were no data on exposure to ecosystems through possible groundwater recharge to surface waters. Due to the "snapshot" nature of the analysis, no resource-based analysis was undertaken. Therefore, impacts that will occur once there is exposure (contaminated groundwater becomes a drinking water or irrigation source) were generally not captured in estimates of residual risk. Also, current residual risk analysis often did not capture the threat where controls in place have predicted life spans posing threats to groundwater in the foreseeable, but uncertain, future. As a result, the risk to groundwater may have ranked lower than if it were analyzed as a long-term natural resource.

Exceptions to the lower risk ranking of problem areas due to impacts occurring in the future (not technically captured in current residual risk) emerged where the impacts were global in scope. Despite the considerable uncertainty, producing wide ranges of risk estimates for global warming and stratospheric ozone depletion, the maximum impacts predicted in the modeled ranges usually compelled high rankings across Regions. As the stressors remain in place and causes of the potential impacts are unmitigated (similarly to the contamination of groundwater not currently pumped), the Regions

---

* Uncertainty was incorporated in the rankings differently across Regions. Qualitative information was often included to support the ranking. Uncertainty was typically scored and presented to decision makers together with the analysis.

generally included these global risks in their rankings despite the lack of fit in the residual framework.

ACCESS TO EXISTING DATA

The information needs that were revealed in the Regional process identified the lack of access to existing useful data (given time and resource constraints) in addition to the lack of data, gathered specifically for risk analysis or sufficient to quantitatively analyze environmental impacts. Often the collection and interpretation of data in fulfillment of the same delegated program requirement differed across states within a Region. Aggregation of these risks calculated for each state introduces further uncertainty in the analysis. Additionally, information on certain waste facility types regulated by states largely exists in hardcopy in inactive files. Other state program data are submitted to the Regions in summary, not intended or suitable for risk analysis nor useful for trend analysis due to inconsistent sampling methods. Neither Regions nor states had the resources to devote to the data search required for obtaining risk information possibly in state possession.

Time and resource constraints prohibited exhaustive inventorying of federal data sets, collected and maintained in other agencies.* Due to the commonly slow pace of digitization much of the accessible data are outdated. Federal data sets were utilized for comparative risk analysis in isolated instances, primarily Census, Geological Survey, and Soil Conservation Service data. Most often this information was used to determine past trends and project future trends. Other federal data bases, such as the U.S. Fish and Wildlife's National Wetlands Inventory, were effectively inaccessible due to the status of the digitization efforts.

ECOLOGICAL DATA

The severe lack of Agency terrestrial ecology data in most Regions, not only for estimating risk, but also for characterizing the current magnitude, location, and status of ecosystems, presented a formidable challenge in the comparative risk process. There were somewhat more data on the causes and extent of degradation to aquatic ecosystems. Superfund had limited information on site-specific impacts collected to assess risk at National Priority List sites. No other EPA-collected data, gathered regularly in the course of

---

* Very little of the useful data collected and maintained by private and not-for-profit organizations were accessible due to time and resource constraints.

program activities, specifically document impacts to terrestrial ecological health.* Isolated studies estimate or predict impacts to agricultural crops.

Routine monitoring of the ecological environment occurs in aquatic ecosystems. While individual states may gather data for various indices of biotic integrity, the indicator species information was generally not available to Regions for use in risk analysis. The summary reports on water quality submitted for designated use determinations for stream segments and control of toxic effluents (Sections 305b and 304l, respectively, of the Clean Water Act [CWA]) are not suited for time-series analysis due to incomplete sampling coverage, varying sampling methodologies, and different underlying water quality criteria. While ambient concentration information was available for certain chemical pollutants in particular waterbody segments, including from air deposition, causal links to ecosystem impacts were unquantifiable, if not dubious.

Staying the physical degradation of ecosystems, both terrestrial and wetland/aquatic, is not explicit in legislatively mandated EPA activities. Because wetlands protection has recently emerged as an Agency priority, slightly more information on its status were available. Regional Offices have acquired wetlands acreage data through the permitting of dredged or fill material through the Army Corps of Engineers (CWA Section 404 program) and some qualitative information in the course of executing NEPA responsibilities. Urban sprawl and widespread development and the supporting activities present the most significant physical threat to wetland ecosystems. Acres of wetlands were often estimated by areas of potential wetland vegetation less those areas currently identified as having a different land cover/use. Wetlands lost was the potential acreage less the estimated remaining area. Most other documentation was anecdotal. The ecological risk calculated was based on such variables as extent of impact, reversibility of impact, and required a significant amount of professional judgment to make assessments given the limitations of the data. With greater than 80% of National Wetlands Inventory data not yet digitized, very little locational information was available that could be associated with risk due to specific development occurring presently or projected in the short term.

Development, road construction, conversion to cropland, recreation, and most other human-induced impacts threaten ecosystems of all types in each Region. The geographic extent and location of even those ecosystems valued for species diversity and/or scarcity was not usually ascertainable. Therefore,

---

* Until risk becomes the common criteria across environmental or land management agencies, data gathered specifically sufficient to characterize ecological risk may not occur outside EPA. However, data useful for characterizing trends, if not specifically stressors and impacts, currently exist in federal and state data sets as well as in environmental foundations. Accessibility to this existing data, such as that from The Nature Conservancy, is being pursued as a result of the Regional comparative risk experiences.

estimates of exposure and intensity of impacts to these ecosystems were qualitative. The high risk ranking attributed to physical degradation resulted largely from the irreversible and progressive human encroachment on a largely irreplaceable resource. This information is sufficient for prioritization and strategic planning. However, only references to the concepts of habitat fragmentation or sustainability were plausible in the qualitative discussions on risk to ecosystems. These ecological data are needed to develop comprehensive and targeted approaches to managing ecological risks for long-term environmental protection.

DATA-CONSTRAINED IMPLEMENTATION OF REGIONAL PRIORITIES

Prioritization of risk reduction activities is credible on a broad scale based on Regional project results. Particular environmental problem areas and geographic areas emerged as relatively high risk. Consideration of other risk management factors, such as legislative authority, technical feasibility, and foreseeable marginal benefit given limited resources, was required to determine whether or not there were cost-effective risk reduction opportunities.

The level of analysis was less useful for developing specific risk reduction activities than for targeting particular environmental problems and identifying needs for further investigation. While the intent of the analysis and ranking was for this broad planning use, extrapolation to very specific planning activities would require greater resolution in the analysis in order to identify the most significant risk and its respective source(s), particularly in a relatively small geographic area. New risk management strategies that emerged from the project predominantly addressed the problem areas where outreach was the primary means of risk management and where little or no regulatory authority exists.

Lack of locational information on stressors often prohibited developing activity plans to directly implement risk reduction at the stressor or source level. The Toxic Release Inventory was a useful first indication of toxic chemicals emitted. For many other permitted sources no latitude or longitude data were available for directing pollution control efforts. Determining the exposures relevant to the stressors the Regions manage was equally difficult with existing information. For example, the location of public drinking water supply wells generally was either not available or not obtainable due to the project's resource constraints, though necessary for determining human exposure to groundwater contamination.

Elevating the Ecological Agenda

Ecological systems emerged as priority for every Region as a result of the projects and was confirmed by the Science Advisory Board's recommendations in Reducing Risk. Elevating ecological concerns on the Regional agenda and the Agency agenda requires sufficient information to develop and target activities to address impacts to specific ecosystem types from particular stressors, and a data infrastructure that will facilitate incorporation of ecosystem information into the daily activities of EPA programs. Currently, the environmental impact statement review is the only program implemented in the Regions will experience in considering impacts to ecosystems other than aquatic.

Waterbodies are routinely monitored in each state. While not risk focused, the data collected could provide information for developing ecological risk reduction approaches. Because the CWA allows states to choose what they monitor, and the methodologies used vary across states, aggregation to the Regional level effectively loses credibility for many stressors to aquatic ecosystems. Within state approaches may be developed using the information gathered. However, taken individually and compared for geographic targeting purposes, the state aquatic trends data available are not plausible due to the vast differences in the precision and accuracy derived from the sampling and data interpretation techniques used across states. A few obvious examples include location and frequency of sampling, how designated use is defined for each waterbody segment, and adjustment for seasonal variation.

EPA does not have regulatory authority to address many ecological problems. Effective strategies for ecosystem protection involve coordination with other parties and creating incentives for private sector and general public involvement. One risk-reduction tool that emerged in other problem areas where limited regulatory authority exists was outreach. This strategy requires the Regions to provide interested private partners with the information necessary to develop and target risk reduction efforts of their own. Lack of ecosystem stressor location data seriously hampers a Region's capability to target other private partners in their ecosystem protection efforts.

For Forest Service and U.S. Fish and Wildlife, among others, provide significant opportunities for risk reduction to terrestrial ecosystems within their own program activities. The ecological data collected by these agencies are determined by the classification schemes driven by their respective missions. It emerged once the process was underway that unless Regions adopted similar ecosystem classifications in their respective ecological analyses, these data were often not useful for quantitative analysis even had it been accessible. As a new priority, not secured by legislative mandate, EPA cannot yet adequately characterize the terrestrial ecological risk-related problems to be addressed. An assessment of how Regional efforts can compliment activities of other agencies is being undertaken as a result of this recognition.

Risk Perception and Public Support

Polls in the popular press have indicated that the risk most private citizens consider urgent is that associated with problem areas with significant health or economic impacts. However, public perception of these risks is often associated with sources determined relatively less significant by the Regional assessments. Many ecological risks are often overlooked or unrecognized by the general public.

While sufficient health information is available to support human health risk in the public forum, data on the costs of ecological degradation adequate for influencing public opinion and behavior are effectively nonexistent. For example, the failure of pricing to capture the externalities of carbon consumption disguises the social need to conserve energy. The public does not generally associate degradation of ecological resources as decrements to their own utilities, and indirectly (or directly) incomes (through use of societal resources to compensate), now and in the future. Credible data of this type were generally not available given the time and resource constraints and the relatively new emergence of these issues. Economic valuation data may capture for decisionmakers the importance of the functions that provide sustainability for ecological entities society values directly. This approach could facilitate the implementation of protection of ecological systems within context of the landscape and long-term needs, and provide incentives for modification of personal behavior affecting global environmental issues.

Public perception of risk is critical to legislative support and personal contributions (through behavior modification) to risk reduction. Information presented must be credible and comprehensible based on concrete examples. Altering the public perception to be based on science is the risk management tool, perhaps most valuable. However, risk-based public perception may also be the most difficult tool to implement due to lack of the data. Quantitative information could prove the means by which to capture its importance for the public. Quantitative information on the range of impacts may provide perspective for the layman, without comprehensive understanding of the complex relationships and uncertainties involved.

CONCLUSION

The Regional comparative risk projects ranked environmental problem areas in terms of the residual risk posed to human health, ecological systems and economic well-being. The comparative risk assessment will help the Agency determine the greatest environmental risk so its efforts can be targeted toward the greatest risk reduction opportunities. The Regional projects are incomplete and will remain incomplete as long as high levels of uncertainty remain in the assessment. The considerable gaps that exist in the necessary data sets, in exposure and toxicity models, and in established methodologies (adapted for use given information constraints) were documented in the Regional process. Methodologies with respect to the ecological and economic analyses are not as advanced as with human health assessment and precluded strictly consistent Regional assessments. As a result of the Regional analyses, many of these data and methodological issues are now being addressed.

The common risk rankings of particular problem areas with respect to human health, ecological systems, and economic impacts across Regions, even having used differing methodologies and data sets, indicate a level of analysis appropriate to the EPA planning process. Given the state of environmental policy making, the comparative risk rankings in combination with established Regional and national mandates allowed for a credible environmental risk-based prioritization. The process was critically important and successful in that Regions identified their data and methodology needs for future assessments of environmental trends and status.

This paper does not necessarily represent the views of the U.S. Environmental Protection Agency or Region 5.

The Use of Economic Data and Analysis in Comparative Risk Projects: Questions of Policy and Reliability

Palma Risler

INTRODUCTION

The concept of comparative risk projects is relatively simple — use the best available data combined with professional judgment to determine which environmental problems pose the greatest risk to our health, the environment, and our well-being. Throughout the last 2 decades there has been an explosion of information regarding dangers to the environment, and comparative risk projects are an attempt to make sense of this information by determining what are the worst environmental problems. Yet what should be the yardstick by which we determine the worst problems? Three types of problems caused by environmental pollution have been used — human health risk; ecological risk; and economic and social damages.

The appropriate use of economic data and analysis remains one of the least defined areas of comparative risk projects. In this paper, I discuss the rationale for including economic damages and attempt to clarify issues of defining what can be included in an economic and social damages ranging and why it is important to consider economic damages along with health and ecological risk. Finally, the most important data gaps within current welfare rankings are examined.

Comparative risk projects have already been completed both nationally and regionally. Even with their current levels of uncertainty (high) and sophistication (low), they provide decision makers with useful perspectives on the relative severity posed by the many environmental problems that confront EPA.

While there is basic agreement that both health risk and ecological damages should be used as criteria for setting priorities for the Environmental Protection Agency, no such consensus exists on the inclusion of a ranking on societal welfare/economic damages. Even the name of the criteria varies widely: societal welfare, economic damages, and economic welfare have all been used, reflecting the variety of opinions as to what should be included in a welfare ranking. While the debate is far from over, this paper argues that economic damages from pollution should be considered with a healthy regard for the opinions of those not immersed in the conventions and assumptions of economic analysis. Further, this paper argues that the two most important data gaps in current analyses are in evaluating the economic damages from contaminated ground water and destruction of complex ecosystems such as wetlands.

A brief review of the analyses conducted to date illustrates the variety of attitudes — from presumption to disinterest to rejection — towards the use of economic analysis in comparative risk projects. The original *Unfinished Business* report used economics as one type of problem caused by environmental pollution, but did not expound upon the rationale for using a separate welfare ranking, presumably because it was an obvious choice. Subsequently, the consensus on having societal welfare as a third, and distinct, ranking has been questioned.

The analyses conducted in the regional offices of the EPA have varied. Five of the ten regions completed an economic welfare analysis and used the results as part of strategic planning. These regions believe that the ranking adds an important element that is not captured by the health and ecological rankings. Several others conducted economic analyses, but they were not incorporated into a ranking or strategic planning process — largely due to lack of time and (possibly) interest. Several other regions did not invest time or resources into a welfare ranking at all. Possibly this was due to a lack of expertise and resources. This patchwork of acceptance and rejection of the use of welfare rankings illustrates the need for an expanded dialogue between the believers and agnostics.

The first direct questioning of the believability and usefulness of economic rankings was from the 1990 Science Advisory Board (SAB) report. The SAB was initially charged with combining the ecological and welfare rankings into an aggregate ranking, an idea the SAB seems to have endorsed with little discussion. The SAB rejected a separate welfare ranking for a variety of reasons. One overriding reason appears to be that no one on the SAB subcommittee was an economist and the ecologists had been historically annoyed by the use of economic analysis against environmental protection. However, the SAB rejection has not been the final word on completing a welfare ranking, primarily because it is such a general renunciation. Currently, the SAB is forming an environmental economics advisory committee. This committee will hopefully further the discussion of the limitations and utility of economic data and analysis in priority setting.

This paper outlines the current issues that need to be addressed by such a group and suggests a proper manner for completing a welfare ranking in the interim. Discussions on the use of a societal welfare ranking should be concerned with broad issues of policy, as well as the validity of current methodologies and data. Questions and assumptions on the usefulness and appropriateness of economic damages should be delineated, along with questions about what constitutes a welfare ranking.

WHAT WILL ECONOMIC ANALYSIS TELL US?

The most basic questions regarding economic data and analysis are (1) Why use it at all? and (2) Is it essential to priority setting? While it can be difficult for economists to take questioning of the basic utility and validity of economic analysis seriously, the lack of consensus surrounding the use of a welfare ranking exposes the need for these questions to be addressed directly.

The first challenge that needs to be tackled is whether or not the economic criteria captures something different than the health or ecological criteria. Many contend that economic criteria simply recapture health and ecological concerns in a different, and less believable, framework. But two factors dispute this contention. First, although many welfare concerns are related to health or ecological concerns, there are still substantial differences, and therefore welfare considerations deserve to be highlighted and counted. For example, particulate matter in ambient air causes health problems, increases cleaning costs, and damages buildings and industrial materials. Only looking at health and ecological concerns, while ignoring economic damages, underestimates the full range of effects of environmental degradation.

Second, there are some environmental problems that have small ecological or health effects, but large economic impacts. Specifically challenging the SAB's contention that welfare concerns can be safely subsumed in ecological concerns, it remains to be seen how natural resource use and enjoyment is always complimentary to ecological quality. Certainly, forestry and fisheries depend upon the health and quality of their ecological base. However, there can be trade-offs between ecological concerns and the economic use of natural resources (e.g., recreation near critical habitats or effect of forestry on diversity). While careful resource management may make these trade-offs minimal, the trade-offs are important in some cases. For example, the closings of the striped bass fishery in the Hudson River has not hurt the ecology of the striped bass; in fact there are many reports the number of fish have increased since the closure. The ban reduced the health risk caused by eating contaminated striped bass. Therefore, without an economic damages ranking, the priority of toxics in surface water would rank quite low without an economic welfare criteria. However, the economic loss to commercial and recreational fishing is an important component that must be considered and can be by including an economic welfare ranking.

Two other areas, groundwater contamination and beach closings, have virtually no ecological concerns and rank low for health risk because wells and beaches are monitored and closed whenever there is a threat to public health. But these same actions that eliminate health risk create an economic damage. A priority-setting project that did not include an economic damages component would be blind to the billion dollar damages that have been estimated for the year that beach closings were widespread in New York and New Jersey.

While examples of beach, fisheries, and well closings demonstrate that economic welfare concerns are distinct from health or ecological concerns and that decision makers should be aware of the differences, the question is, should EPA be concerned about these types of effects in setting priorities? The answer is clearly yes, based on history, law, and common sense.

Certainly, the political and legal history of the conservation and environmental movements have underlined the importance of economic welfare and protecting common resources. Lands in New York's Adirondack and Catskill mountains were set aside primarily to protect the watershed areas and the navigation of the Hudson. Early water pollution control regulations were concerned more about navigation impacts than ecological concerns. This is not to imply that welfare concerns are more important than health or ecological, or that they are in conflict, however, concern for the "general welfare" has a historical, legal, and most importantly, a logical place in the goals of the EPA.

Both the Clean Air Act and the Clean Water Act clearly state that the EPA should be concerned about the general societal welfare. The Clean Air Act's secondary national ambient air quality standards are intended to "to protect the public welfare from any known or anticipated adverse effects".[1] Effects on welfare are defined in the Act as including, "effects on soils, water, crops, vegetation, man-made materials, animals, wildlife, weather, visibility and climate and damage to and deterioration of property, and hazards to transportation, as well as effects on economic values and on personal comfort and well-being".[2] Congress included economic welfare concerns in the Clean Water Act's objective to "protect the public health or welfare . . . taking into consideration their use and value for public water supplies, propagation of fish and wildlife, recreational purposes, and agricultural, industrial and other purposes, and also taking into consideration their use and value for navigation".[3]

There are some related advantages to using economic data and analysis in comparative risk projects. Strategically, information on the economic damages from pollution can play well to audiences that may not be conversant with the intrinsic need for ecological protection. For example, protection of the watersheds surrounding New York City's reservoirs are estimated to save large amounts of public dollars in the future. Economic analysis can illustrate the tangible dividends of environmental protection. This type of information is a necessary counterpoint to the constant stream of information that EPA generates on the costs of pollution control.

While this appears to be a pragmatic approach, some fear the underlying values this may foster. To some, there is a real danger in promoting the use of economic analysis in assessing environmental problems because it may lead to buying into a paradigm favoring profit maximization over ecological protection. The SAB in objecting to the welfare ranking stated that "it has long been recognized that short-term profit maximization is a misguided objective".[4] While this type of critique may be more of a misunderstanding of how using economic analysis differs from promoting unrestrained avarice, a dialogue regarding this issue is needed.

METHODS OF ECONOMIC ANALYSIS AND RANKING

Separate from the question regarding the use of economic well-being as a criteria, is the issue of what constitutes a welfare ranking. The basic methods used in a welfare ranking are standard economic damages methods from environmental and natural resource economics. In addition, a variety of amendments to and criticisms of these basic methodologies have been suggested. Two different and useful dialogues are taking place. The first is a broad critique of economic analysis. The critique ranges from a needed airing of suspicions about, if not rejection of, economic analysis (especially from ecologists) to the embracing of economic data and analysis by some with a broader (or at least different) concept of "societal welfare". The second is a more specific critique aimed at determining which of the data and methods can be relied upon in policy decision making.

The SAB critiqued economic analysis because of the generally short time frame of economic analyses, use of discounting and the lack of data and methods to account for complex ecosystem functions. These are good critiques of the limitations of current economic analysis, however, the alternative developed by the SAB seems to take most currently accepted categories of welfare damages and reclassify them, but not use any of the data and methods. It is unclear what is gained from the reclassification, but it appears much information is lost. While certainly the critique is important and reflects the views of some economists, the critique is more appropriately thought of as a data gap for certain environmental problems rather than a fundamental flaw of economic analysis.

Expanding, rather than rejecting, the traditional economic damages approach has appealed to many. Suggestions of additions and adjustments to the traditional economic damages approach include: equity issues, reversibility, effects on local economies, size of the affected population, and theoretical vs. actual damages. Of special concern is equity. A very large analytic gap in current comparative risk projects is information on how evenly and fairly risks and damages are distributed. Some have suggested that these distributional or equity concerns might be captured in a true societal welfare ranking. However, there is a danger in ranking small unevenly distributed damages as a larger problem than large evenly distributed damages. One must take care to explain carefully to decision makers (and the public) the basis for the ranking or a disservice will be done because higher ranked problems may communicate large damages, rather than small, but unevenly distributed damages. Certainly equity concerns could be easily be taken care of in the actual priority setting and resource allocation (as current budget allotments suggest) but information on the distribution of impacts needs to be developed regardless of where it is used.

Analysts from Vermont have even suggested elevating nonmaterial issues such as ''sense of community'' and ''peace of mind'' as equal concerns with other more material economic damages. These types of nonmaterial concerns are intended to better reflect the full gamut of values suggested by the concept of societal welfare. While interesting and worth exploring further, these concerns are far afield from the original purpose of using data and science in priority setting.

While the criticisms and suggested innovations may appear to cast complete doubt on the usefulness of current economic welfare rankings, this is not intended. Making decisions based on uncertain data is necessary in any undertaking and comparative risk projects are no different. Certainly anyone who has participated in these types of projects would attest to their reliance upon a combination of quantitative and qualitative judgments. Yet current information and analyses are providing useful information.

LARGEST AREAS OF UNCERTAINTY IN CURRENT PROJECTS

Despite the broader issues discussed above, questions remain: where are our results most questionable? and, where are we so devoid of information that we could be making a large mistake in priorities? Our conclusions in two areas — evaluating damages to the ground water resource and evaluating complex and uncertain ecological damages — are the most unreliable.

Damages to Groundwater

A variety of rankings, mainly moderate/high or moderate/low, have been given to the economic losses from ground water contamination. While this may simply indicate that ground water contamination is more or less of a problem in different geographic areas, there are several methodological gaps that may be leading to the systematic undervaluing of damaged ground water resources.

Specifically, there is no clear understanding of how much of the resource has been lost for future use. Current methods of valuation concentrate on the replacement cost of water for valuing ground water resource damages. In addition to replacement costs not being a perfect indicator of economic damages, these analyses have generally found that the economic damages to the ground water resource are not large. A more serious problem with the analyses is that they do not take into account future use or situations of very limited quantities. When wells become contaminated, it is assumed they are either treated or a new source of water is obtained. Although water treatment is generally effective, some contaminants cannot be treated using current technologies. Ground water contamination is usually very localized, and at least in most places in the eastern United States, new wells can be drilled at fairly low cost or a surface water supply can be used. But evaluations of the resource damages have not looked closely at determining if and when these options are available or when the costs rise dramatically.

The failure to look or account for any situations of finite resource limits or the general impact of resource depletion needs addressing. We must better account for the current limited water resources and include future impacts based on water demand increases because of population increases and/or other development. Situations of limited water resources are not just a future concern; threats of economic disaster have accompanied the most recent drought years in the West. As surface water supplies continue to dwindle, ground water becomes more valuable and hence contaminated ground water more of an economic loss to society. Until we determine if the impacts from these realistic scenarios are large or small, we cannot have confidence in our judgment that ground water contamination is of only moderate concern economically.

Damages to Complex Ecosystems

Any current conclusions regarding the economic impact of damages to complex ecosystems such as wetlands is also suspect. Three regions ranked these problems in the highest category, while one region ranked wetlands destruction in the low category.

The economic methods for valuing loss of wetlands are not well developed. While replacement value is often used, it is theoretically unsatisfactory. Wetlands do contain undeniable ecological value and logically are rated the highest ecological concern in most rankings. However, tracing back economic benefits from wetlands remains an area of large uncertainty and belief that these economic benefits (to water purification, fisheries, recreation) are large is more a matter of assurances than proof. In addition, no one has attempted to account for the ongoing damages to fisheries, recreation, and water purification from the historic losses of wetlands. Such an accounting would provide insights into the current and future damages from loss of wetlands.

In addition to determining the size of easily recognized economic damages, economic analysis has not developed any methods of valuing diversity and intrinsic ecological values. However, limiting the economic ranking to more easily identified ecosystem services and recognizing that the ecological ranking takes ecological values into account is a logical method of proceeding.

In this manner, concrete data and methods on economic damages can be used without stretching economic analysis to encompass all values.

OTHER ISSUES

Other issues that have been mentioned as large concerns in a welfare ranking can also be tabled because they are adequately addressed in the health or ecological ranking. These issues include the estimation of nonuse values, intrinsic values, and any estimation of "value of a life". Not only are these taken into account in other criteria, but the push to estimate all societal values in monetary terms or use some totally numeric system for decision making can be so tenuous that it tends to cast doubt on the more appropriate use of economic data and analysis. For example, any monetarization of the value of a human life is not only offensive in concept, but unnecessary because the health risk criteria takes these concerns into account.

A related nonissue for comparative risk projects is the problem of the discount rate. There are many important discussions that need to take place about the discount rate in other contexts; however, discount rate issues are really not relevant in actual comparative risk projects because the information to support any differences is lacking. Given the data that exist (overwhelmingly order of magnitude yearly damages), all environmental problems will be discounted (or not discounted) in the same manner and therefore the comparative level of damages should not change. For discount rates to matter, one would need data on how different levels of damages change over time. Any attempt to claim that this type of data exists is difficult to believe.

CONCLUSION

In summary, economic data and analysis has a role in comparative risk projects. However, discussions are needed on broad questions concerning: why use economic data; why constitutes a welfare ranking; and what is the appropriate use of economic analysis in environmental priority setting? Critiques of specific methodological and data gaps by economists are needed, but the larger challenge is to take the suspicions and improvements of non-economists seriously. Only then will the information be believed by the variety of people involved in environmental priority setting.

REFERENCES

1. Clean Water Act, as amended by the Water Quality Act of 1987, Public Law 100-4, March 1988.
2. Clean Water Act, as amended by the Water Quality Act of 1987, Public Law 100-4, March 1988.
3. Clean Air Act as amended 1977.
4. *Reducing Risk: Setting Priorities and Strategies for Environmental Protection*, U.S. EPA, Science Advisory Board, September 1990, SAB-EC-90-021.

Thoughts for the Future

Introduction

C. Richard Cothern

The future development of the concept of comparative environmental quantitative risk assessment will take many different directions in the future. Many of these are clear from the preceding chapters and many of the ideas expressed in these chapters can and will be used as the basis of further developments in this field. In this last section two potential directions for future development are explored. These are not the only two possible and they are not mutually exclusive. In many respects these two endeavors can be pursued simultaneously.

One of the potential new directions is the development of a theory of quantitative risk assessment. This idea is discussed by Douglas Crawford-Brown and Jeffrey Arnold. Their chapter discusses theory testing and can be extrapolated to the idea of developing philosophical basis like that which exists now for other sciences.

Another thought that is receiving much attention is that of using the existing information and data, along with the needed assumptions to complete the development of risk-based management as is discussed in the chapter by William Garetz.

In a larger view the concepts discussed in this volume can be part of a systems approach. Consider overlaying the variables that are involved in risk management, the groups that use risk assessments, and the uses to which this analysis is put. The variables include: comparative quantitative risk, economics, politics, and the social and psychological impact. The groups involved include Congress, the public, environmental groups, regulatory agencies, industry, academe, and the news media. The uses include resource allocation, development of regulations, and research priorities. The interplay of these factors provides a broad view of environmental problems with an eye to their solution.

The Role of Evidential Reason and Epistemic Discourse in Establishing the Risk of Environmental Carcinogens

Douglas Crawford-Brown and Jeffrey Arnold

INTRODUCTION

The recent history of societal attempts to mitigate risks has been characterized by increasing reliance on risk analysis in general and quantified, ordered risk ranking in particular. Because risk analysts have constructed these ordered rankings of risk from fundamental and applied science data sets, they have co-opted the language of science for their analyses. Thus it is that risk analyses and rankings are couched in terms of "objective", "deductive", "logical", "rational", and "scientific". If science is understood to be the highest expression of rational thinking (as some philosophers and more scientists would claim), then there is a great deal to be gained in associating the quantitative practice of risk ranking with wider, more established scientific reasoning. These risk analysts could then warrant the use of quantitative, ordered rankings as the basis for public policy by simply claiming to have allowed the science to determine the risk estimate. Nothing, these analysts and managers might say, could be more "objective" and "rational".

Clearly this raises the issue of what it means to be rational, particularly in the sense of scientific rationality. We do not intend here to provide a formal framework for judging the rationality of specific examples of risk analysis. Rather, we present a philosophical discussion of the general epistemic issues on which any analyst invoking claims to scientific rationality must reflect prior to development of a particular formal procedure for quantifying and/or eliciting judgments of confidence. It is our contention that philosophical discourse must precede consideration of formal tools if use of those tools for risk ranking is to be deemed rational rather than simply procedural. Such an epistemic discussion incorporates reflection on the relationship between bodies of evidence, procedures for generating that evidence, principles of evidential reasoning, the testing of theories (where these are required), and the formation of confidence.

While we recognize the existence of competing approaches to formalizing mathematically the above relationship in terms of subjective probability, long-

0-87371-605-1/93/$0.00 + $.50
© 1993 by Lewis Publishers

term frequency or Bayesian measures of confidence, the focus of the present discussion is not on the assignment of numerical values of confidence. It is, instead, on the epistemic properties which form the foundation for any candidate approach to formalization of confidence in beliefs. The choice to focus on this transcendental aspect of rationality in belief formation stems from two primary considerations. First, this avoids the need to discuss details of specific procedures, which in any event are highly controversial in their relationship to views on rationality (unless rationality is conflated with logical consistency). Second, it is not the belief of the authors that such formal tools are either necessary or desirable in the pursuit of rationality. This is not to say that formal tools related to decision theory are inherently irrational or arational. Our contention, instead, is that philosophical discourse on epistemological foundations of risk analysis provides a framework for discussion against which formal procedures may be tested for "completeness of conception", rather than the other way around. The history of risk analysis has been dominated by discussion of procedures, as if issues of the philosophical foundations of risk and of the relationship of risk analysis to scientific practice already were resolved. This paper stems from the conviction that these issues are by no means resolved and that the future direction of risk analysis will be towards increasing philosophical reflection as such analyses are challenged in a scientific or legal setting.

We note also that the following discussion is applicable to all forms of risk analysis, whether the analysis is of environmental carcinogenesis, nuclear reactor failure, stability of bridges, etc. Some areas of risk analysis, particularly those of engineered systems, have a stronger empirical base than do analyses of carcinogenesis (the primary example used here). This stronger empirical base does not, however, remove the issues raised here. It simply suggests that scientific rationality may not play quite as strong of a role in warranting beliefs in those areas of risk analysis where direct human experience is plentiful. These nonscientific areas retain a claim to rationality if the end of the analysis is instrumental rather than explanatory, although there remain constraints on the claim to rationality where the influence of antecedent conditions is unconsidered and/or unknown. It is for this reason that claims to "knowing that" (scientific rationality) and "knowing how" (instrumental rationality) are distinguished in the text as separate bases for the rationality of belief. Still, it should be borne in mind that the present discussion is centered on claims to scientific rationality and the epistemic conditions that must be met to warrant such claims.

The invocation of science in support of risk rankings raises the issue of how the field of risk analysis is related both philosophically and practically to the scientific disciplines. Clearly, the conceptual basis of risk incorporates ideas of the frequency of effect in a population (the frequency of attributes within the elements of a set) and the value placed on those effects. As a start, then, to be elaborated upon in a later section, the risk imposed by the presence of some factor such as a chemical in the environment is described at the very least by the total decrement of value residing in the world as a result of that presence under prespecified antecedent conditions. Chemicals may, for instance, induce death, chronic irritation, susceptibility to infection, and liver dysfunction. All of these effects are part of the risk, and the risk increases if the frequency of any of the effects increases within the population. This increased frequency produces a decrement in the total state of human health. Since human health is valued, the chemicals produce a decrement in total value and, hence, risk. Both frequency under specified antecedent conditions and value are required for risk to be specified.

Note that this definition of risk requires provision of three components to become an operational term for purposes of decision. The first is the frequency with which each effect (attribute) occurs in a specified population. The second is the value placed on each effect. The third is the manner in which the above two components are to be combined in giving a composite (perhaps numerical) indicator of the magnitude of risk. A complete "theory of risk analysis" would include elucidation of each of these components. Science, however, is concerned strictly with the first of these components, with science theories being constituted to predict and explain frequencies of effect. At best, therefore, risk analysts might be said to incorporate science in estimating risk, but risk itself is more than a concept for science alone. Risk analysis is not synonymous with scientific analysis, but draws upon it in pursuit of distinct goals.

To avoid this complication in the following discussion of the use of science theories in constructing tables of risk, it is assumed here that such tables are intended only to compare the frequency of a single effect (fatal cancer) imposed by each carcinogen considered by the analyst. This circumvents the troubling issue of how basically incommensurable effects are to be united meaningfully into a single numerical risk estimate. In addition, it will be assumed that, conditional upon examination of a single category of effect, empirical risk (more on this term later) is related monotonically to the difference in frequency of effect in a well-specified population (where "specified" refers to antecedent conditions) under conditions of exposure and nonexposure. In this case, which is artificial but common in quantitative risk ranking, the ranking will be driven entirely by the estimates of frequency. Since such estimates employ statistical theories relating attributes of exposure and effect, such as appear in physics or biology, the task of risk analysis takes on a clear link to the sciences from which the causal theories derive. Risk analysis then becomes basically an application of science to decision problems.

One possible confusion raised by this definition of risk analysis as an application of science is the role of an existing set of scientific inquiries typically referred to loosely as risk analysis. These inquiries study the phenomena of biokinetics, metabolism, dosimetry, carcinogenesis; in other words, precisely those phenomena that govern the frequency of effect in populations exposed to environmental chemicals. This interdisciplinary field is a science, in the same manner than quantum chemistry (combining concepts from physics and chemistry) or biochemistry (combining concepts from biology and chemistry) are proper sciences. We wish, however, to distinguish this field of science from the act of risk analysis itself. The former is concerned with general principles of movement, transformation, and action of substances within biological systems. The latter is concerned with applying those principles, analyzing their implication, under heavily constrained sets of antecedent conditions. In a sense, the message of this paper is that the success of the former activity (the sciences associated with frequency of effect) does not ensure the success of the latter (the analysis of risks), even if both are called by the same name.

It is assumed further that the primary task of the risk analyst is to provide a rational basis for decisions concerning the frequency of cancer to be associated with exposure to various chemicals. In public policy, however, where risk analyses are invoked as warrants, the analysis is used to suggest the manner in which the frequency of cancer might be reduced. Since the use of risk analysis in public policy is the topic of this conference, some recognition of the application of risk analysis will be given here. What, then, is to be meant here by "rational"? A simplified definition might be the adoption of apt means to reach the highest ends. From the example here, the end is the reduction of the frequency of cancer in a population. The means to this end reside in the removal of various carcinogens from the environment, with these carcinogens being enumerated in the risk ranking. This leaves only the issue of what is to be meant by the term "apt". To begin the discussion, we assert only that "apt" means are taken in some sense to be means to which the analyst has attached a "reasonable" level of "confidence" that the adoption of those means will bring about the desired ends. If this confidence is to be said to be "scientific" in any sense, it must be the case that it is formed in the same manner that practicing scientists form confidence about their own theories and methods of practice. We restrict our discussion, therefore, to consideration only of the scientifically warranted confidence assigned to estimates of risk, and not to the broader question of the use of such estimates in setting policy (which will involve a broader range of ends). We contend that the end of the analyst is to produce an estimate of the frequency of effect and a depiction of the epistemic status of that estimate with respect to scientific rationality.

This introduces a fourth concept into the production of risk tables, namely the degree to which a given estimate of frequency of effect may be warranted by evidence and the manner in which such warrants result in confidence deemed reasonable. Since each estimate (for the different chemicals) will rest on different evidential bases, the rationality of decisions based on risk tables will ultimately be traceable to some notion of the evidential bases of those estimates. While it is beyond the range of this brief paper to resolve the philosophical issue of evidential reasoning, and its relationship to the formation of reasonable confidence, the claim is made that invocations of science as a warrant for confidence are meaningless without consideration of the state of development of evidence drawn from science in its existing historical state.

While the well-developed sciences have gained their predictive and explanatory success through the dialectic between data and theory, risk analysts have expended most of their effort tending data sets and constructing their statistical interpretations as tables of ordered risks. There is just now some evidence that science theory is beginning to increase in value with risk analysts as some of them move toward biologically based risk assessments for carcinogens.[1] Though even here the focus is not on science theories in themselves, but rather on the adjusting of frequencies of effect through the consideration of other empirical factors such as blood perfusion, body weight, and breathing rates.

The relatively higher importance of data to risk analysis has produced the widely held belief that special experiences exist which can reveal true estimates of risk with minimal intervention of contentious theories of etiology. Ideally, these experiences are taken to be controlled experiments, but often are available only as retrospective epidemiological studies. The science data sets to which statistical methods are applied in risk analysis represent for the analyst the most objective and rational, the least biased estimates of attribute occurrence frequencies. In this regard, risk analysts have reverted to the beliefs and defenses of the logical positivists of some 70 years ago, calling for analysis of the "critical experiment" from which rationally justified beliefs may be formed with confidence. The hope (which the authors believe to be unjustified) is that such experiments can yield meaningful measurements of attribute frequency even in the absence of causal understanding as to why the measured frequencies occur as they do.

This paper results from an attempt to understand the roles and uses of science data and theory within the field of risk analysis, in hopes of tying the two more securely together in current conception and future practice. A key claim we will make here is that science data cannot provide a rational basis for ranking risks from different sources unless intimately wedded to science theories. There are two reasons for making this claim. The first stems from our earlier comment that risk analysts hope to warrant the use of their quantitative risk estimates as a basis for public policy by harkening back to the empirical success of the science from which the data sets were drawn. We contend that the success of these sciences has been due to the active interplay between science theory and science data, and an equal if constantly changing valuation of the importance of both these parts. Such interplay and equal valuation does not, however, describe most of current risk analysis methodology. Second, it will be shown that the rationality of employing past data to make predictions of future risk under potentially changing antecedent conditions requires the explicit use of causal theories. These theories are the means by which rational confidence is formed through evidential reasoning.

If science data and theory are to be better joined for future risk analyses, and if judgments of the confidence attached to the science employed in generating risk estimates are to be incorporated into rational deliberations, then the following objectives must be examined:

1. The role theories play in the present state of risk order ranking
2. The ways in which science data may simultaneously support and be explained by theories
3. The requirements placed on the systematic collection of data and the design and execution of proper experiments if the data are to serve in their various potential roles

To make the discussion concrete, we will use here the example of ranking risks from environmental exposure to carcinogens, and will assert at the opening the possibly controversial claim that tables listing expectation values of the fraction of people dying after environmental exposure to various carcinogens do not necessarily provide a rational basis for making public policy decisions or even for summarizing the state of scientific understanding (taken here to be some measure of the predictive and explanatory success of existing theories). The tables of expectation values fail to provide a rational basis for risk decisions because they are not grounded with the philosophical roots of scientific rationality underlying the past successes either at applying science to human affairs or in judging a phenomenon scientifically explained. These roots have included explicit judgments of the epistemic status of predictions prior to any claims that the predictions deserve to enter the ranks of scientific knowledge.

THEORIES, DATA, AND RATIONAL CONFIDENCE

In the classical tradition of rationality,[2] decisions of how to achieve ends are based on a comparative ranking of the confidence assigned to the competing means. This confidence is a reflection of the state of belief of the agent, which is taken to be driven by the epistemic status of the evidence on which the belief is based. Translating this conception of rationality into the language of risk analysis, the "risk" imposed upon society by each carcinogen is determined using the "best" data (hopefully, prospective human epidemiological studies) interpreted through the "best" methodology (presumably science, ignoring for the moment the difficulty in determining what is to be meant by the scientific method). The idea here is that such an estimate is believed to possess the greatest potential for correspondence to the desired attribute frequency. This results in the best estimate of the risk characterized by the highest level of confidence residing in the analyst, given by such concepts as maximum likelihood estimator, judgment of the most highly qualified expert, etc. Rational decisions then are based on consideration of that estimate. Competing estimates play no further role in rational decisions since they have been judged less apt means for attaining the end of generating truthful statements about attribute frequencies. When risks are ranked, the above process presumably is repeated over each source of the risk, leading, for instance, to the tables of risks ranked by Cohen[3] and others. This is what the classically rational risk analyst produces.

This tradition of rationality contrasts with the more recent view of rationality offered by philosophers such as Rorty,[4] Ravetz,[5] or Maxwell.[6] These latter authors view the success of paradigmatically rational enterprises such as science as lying not in the simple application of forms of reason, but rather in a conception of crafting or pragmatic success. Their views are germane here since at least the APPLICATION of risk analysis (the subject of this conference) is to provide insights into the apt means for attaining the end of reduced frequencies of cancer. It is important here to distinguish between science as RESEARCH (with an eye towards future avenues of inquiry) and science as a basis for ACTION. In research, the appropriate means is to adopt a strategy of inquiry most likely to yield further truthful insights (increase truth content). Since theories structure the inquiry, the scientist is left with no option other than to adopt the best EXISTING theory as a basis for normal research. It becomes rational, therefore, to focus decisions onto the task of providing a relative ranking of research strategies (although, as Laudan[7] has shown, even this task is controversial, since theories display both existing success and "velocities" indicative of future possibilities for success).

With respect to selecting or justifying modes of action, however, the question of crafting arises. A theory then is a rational means for selecting or structuring action if it has been demonstrated to suggest actions characterized by a reproducible and reliable result. In this case, even the best theory may fail to provide a rational basis for designing action if it is poorly crafted. The resulting belief that the theory-structured action will yield the desired end may fail to possess MINIMAL EPISTEMIC STATUS. This does not, of course, imply that the theory is not a rational basis for continued research. It does, however, suggest that any meaningful judgment of the EXISTING epistemic status of a given science must include consideration of the degree to which that science WORKS in constructing experimental settings characterized by agreement between predictions and results.

But what is this epistemic status? It may be found in four primary purposes of a science theory as that theory is employed in estimating attribute frequency:

1. Theories provide causal explanations of how and why a given frequency arises from interaction between a given variable (such as chemical con-

centration) and a given set of antecedent conditions. This epistemic state characteristic of rationality is more commonly termed UNDERSTAND-ING.[8] It is a way of saying not only that such and such a frequency was observed, but that it is understood to be a necessary (analytic) consequence of a state of the world (with that state being a constant feature of that world). Without understanding, rationality must rest on faith where the future is concerned (as Hume suggested).

2. Theories provide PREDICTIONS of the future world under changes in the variable of interest or in antecedent conditions. In other words, the theory allows predictions to be generated as DEDUCTIVE CONSE-QUENCES. This requires of a theory used in risk analysis that it represent an analysis of the world which includes both the variable of interest to the analyst (such as the concentration of a chemical) and the antecedent conditions under which this variable expresses its nature. With respect to risk analysis, this is tantamount to a claim that there is no such thing as THE frequency of effect of a carcinogen, but rather different frequencies under different conditions. Another way of putting this is that attribute frequency arises from a causal constellation, with the entire constellation being the "cause".[9] The interaction of radon with cigarette smoke is a prime example, with the latter determining the effect of the former (as well as the inverse).

3. A theory structures the creation of experiences from which expert judgments may be formed. As Heidegger suggested,[10] properly constituted science experiments EMBODY a theory. They are the physical manifestations of the theory and therefore hold out the possibility of discovering new truths. Without the organizing properties of the theory, the experience available to the scientist would be too complex for the perception of patterns. It goes without saying that much of risk analysis relies on human judgments, either by individual experts or by groups. Is this judgment scientifically rational, having a quality sufficient to warrant inclusion in a process carrying claims to being scientific? The third function of theory answers in the affirmative only to the degree that such judgments spring from the contemplation of well-defined experiences constructed by the deliberate manipulation of variables and/or antecedent conditions.

4. A theory organizes seemingly disparate bodies of data, giving to each some relevance in the task of prediction.[11] By "relevance" we mean here simply the role played by a given body of data within the framework of a research program or predictive task. This function, in turn, has two purposes. The theory aids in bringing COHERENCE to bodies of data, as when the initiation-promotion theory of carcinogenesis is invoked to explain both the shape of the dose-response curve for formaldehyde and the data on hyperplasia.[12] This coherence represents a heightened degree of understanding by uniting varied experiences. The second (and related) organizational property allows these separate bodies of data to gain calculational RELEVANCE in the task of prediction. The theory then displays how frequencies of interest are compound probabilities decomposable into two or more distinct probabilities susceptible to experimental

study. Carcinogens simultaneously produce myriad effects such as cell death, DNA damage, and hyperplasia. These effects separately may push the judgment of carcinogenicity in conflicting directions. The theory acts, in a sense, to show the analyst how to "fold in" the various effect frequencies in making an overall judgment of carcinogenicity.

This fourth property of theories is particularly important in testing predictive theories through the use of data. As Popper[13] so forcefully argued, data do not really test a theory if the theory is so flexible that it would, even upon articulation, have fit essentially any set of data. Theories of carcinogenicity involving an arbitrary number of stages with unconstrained rate constants ARE highly flexible, and the available data on dose response are poor. As a result, almost any number of variants of dose-response equations can be fit to the data with equal statistical measures of confidence.

As shown by Crawford-Brown and Hofmann[14] in the case of theories of radiation carcinogenesis, prior constraints on parameter values can be obtained from experimental data on DNA damage, cell death, mitotic rates, etc. Once so constrained, the theory may be meaningfully tested by the composite dose-response data (although poor data negate even this hope). Without the theory, however the experimental data would have had no ability to constrain prior expectations. This is a particularly important point in judging the epistemic status of simple polynomial fits to data. Since the parameters in these fits have no physical significance, they are not susceptible to scientific explanation and cannot be constrained.

The above discussion of relevance skirts an important issue in the testing of theories, and this point must be raised here. Theories, in and of themselves, are not actually tested by data. The multistage theory of carcinogenesis is a CAUSAL theory, explaining WHY an event such as cancer occurs, but not the frequency or magnitude of the event. It is not tested by dose-response data alone since these arise from both physical laws (the topic of the theory) and material conditions specific to the experimental setting. Useful predictions in the sciences drawn upon by risk analysis require ARTICULATION[15] of a theory. The probabilities (cell death, mitosis, etc.) giving rise to the composite frequency (of death) must be obtained through measurement in a given experimental setting. They are properties of the setting, and not of the theory itself or of the general processes elucidated by the theory.

This process of collecting data during the attempt to articulate a theory with the physical world (the role of normal science) occurs PRIOR to the testing of the theory and the formation of confidence. Note that here data collected for articulation are separate from data collected for testing of a theory, but that one need not precede the other. They must be fully separate, however, to constitute an accurate test of a correctly constructed theory. A simple fitting of a dose-response equation without prior constraints on parameter values can yield a prediction CONDITIONAL UPON acceptance of the equation, but it does not provide a SCIENTIFICALLY rational basis for assigning confidence to the resulting prediction (although it may still be deemed unethical to ignore the prediction,[16] an issue unrelated to science).

What role can data play in placing prior constraints on predictions, thereby allowing meaningful tests required in the formation of confidence? Here, there are three roles that are evident. The data may show that one of the causal assumptions of the theory is correct or incorrect. For example, the location of oncogenes may support the assumption that damage to DNA is important for initiation, that such damage is an important analytical category under appropriate antecedent conditions. In this role, the data may be said to have ONTOLOGICAL RELEVANCE.[17] This may, in the case of multistage theories of carcinogenesis, allow prior constraints on the particular stages affected by a carcinogen.

The second form of relevance for data is FORMAL RELEVANCE. Data on mutation might be used both to support the ontological axiom that alpha radiation causes initiation (ontological relevance) and that it does so by a process with linear kinetics. Within a multistage theory, this places prior constraints on the number of substages involved in initiation (i.e., on the mathematical form of this stage of transition).

Finally, the data may be assigned NUMERICAL RELEVANCE. In this case, both the form of the kinetics and the numerical value of the transition rate constants are obtained from the data (as in the case of cell killing rate constants for radiation employed by Crawford-Brown and Hofmann[14,18] in developing a theory of radiation carcinogenesis).

Care must be taken in choosing the relevance assigned to a particular body of data. This may be seen most clearly in considering the role of antecedent conditions. Experimental data usually are obtained under antecedent conditions potentially quite different from those of interest to the risk analyst. If the antecedent conditions of the experiment alter the transition rate constants between stages of carcinogenesis (for example), perhaps through the presence of competitors for sites of action, then numerical relevance may be ruled out. More extreme is the case in which different antecedent conditions alter the form of an interaction. For example, it has been argued that certain cell lines are characterized by preexisting transitions not present in normal human cells. In this case, formal relevance might be rejected. It might even occur that an effect exists only because of the antecedent conditions, as in theories of emergent properties. The same pathway of action may not be present under other conditions. The presence of cancer of the zygote gland in rats is an obvious example, since the same gland does not exist in humans. This suggests that even ontological relevance may be suspect for a given body of data.

Consider the case in which a single "measurement" of the frequency of death following exposure to a substance such as environmental tobacco smoke (ETS) has been made (this is not, in fact, the case). Presumably, this particular frequency arose due both to ETS and the antecedent conditions of the exposed population. Estimates of the frequency of cancer in populations exposed to ETS may be conditional upon these conditions, being quite different under other antecedent conditions. The tobacco industry, for example, has argued against the use of epidemiological data from Greece and Japan. The claim is that these populations constitute different antecedent conditions, reducing the confidence that these data provide a rational basis for articulating cancer theories used in predicting frequency of cancer in the U.S.[19] This claim can be tested only through comparison of the frequencies under what are perceived to be different antecedent conditions.

Proper development of data sets for estimating attribute frequencies, therefore, requires consideration of sampling across antecedent conditions. Systems of risk estimation which fail to describe important antecedent conditions do not allow the analyst to determine *Which* antecedent conditions must be considered in sampling. In this case, the formation of confidence must rest on the observation that data were compared under a wide range of conditions (such as in as many countries in the case of ETS), with the measured frequencies being roughly constant. If a hard look at potential antecedent conditions has been taken, and IF the frequencies of effect have remained stable, a reasonable claim may be advanced for numerical relevance of the existing data. Where different conditions produce unexplained variation, the confidence in a particular attribute frequency within an unsampled population will decrease. This shows the importance of theory in determining how differences in antecedent conditions affect the judgment of relevance and structure the collection of data with a potential for relevance. Without the theory, there is a strong requirement of collecting data under many randomly selected conditions. Of course, without a causal theory, it may be impossible to support the claim (essential for judging epistemic status) that the existing samples constitute a reasonable sampling over potential antecedent conditions. There is no confidence that measured frequencies are a stable property of the world (stability of result being an important hallmark of well-developed science experiments).

The reference to Heidegger made previously deserves elaboration at this point in the discussion. To Heidegger, an experiment embodies a theory, which in turn expresses a way of living in (acting in) the world. This suggests a distinction between "mere" data and the results of a deliberate experiment. This difference is expressed in the distinction between KNOWING THAT and KNOWING HOW. True understanding in the Heideggerian sense is demonstrated through experiments in which prior predictions of a theory are borne out in subsequent experience. Claims to scientific understanding that removal of radon is an apt means for reducing cancer frequencies then are warranted by reference to deliberate experiments in which manipulation of one physical entity (radon concentration) yields a desired change (lowering the frequency of cancer in a population). This is particularly true in situations where the action of mitigation (which invariably involves physical manipulation of material resources) alters the antecedent conditions themselves (perhaps through the redistribution of wealth in society, with the associated effects on human welfare).

Does this imply that experimental results are always better in the formation of confidence than observational results unconnected to a deliberate experiment? The answer is yes, all things being equal and if a claim to SCIENTIFIC rationality is being made. But care must be taken here. Experiments that control, or even incorporate, the full range of antecedent conditions important in carcinogenesis are difficult (if not impossible) to conduct. Given this fact, the claim to knowing how provided by an experiment is contingent on the specific antecedent conditions of that experiment. If conditions important to the task of predicting attribute frequencies in a specific population are missing, and if these alter the causal link between physical effects of interest, then knowing how in a circumscribed experiment does not necessarily provide a more rational basis for statements of risk in the larger world of human affairs. It all hinges on the manner in which antecedent conditions missing from the experiment alter the relevance of the physical manipulations, and the degree to which a scientific warrant, rather than a simple observational warrant, is desired.

Where does the discussion to this point leave us? It suggests that a particular estimate of attribute frequency carries an epistemic status related to the degree of crafting represented by that estimate. Some of this status is quantitative and statistical, related solely to issues of sample size contingent on a particular theoretical framework of analysis. Another quantitative aspect is the degree to which the measured frequencies have been shown to be stable properties of the world (as when meta-analyses are performed). Much of the status of a prediction founded in science theories, however, is not quantitative, but still is an essential ingredient in judging rationality. It is given by the answer to questions such as:

1.   Is the cause of the data understood conceptually?
2.   Is there a predictive theory from which the properties of the observed data follow as a deductive consequence given proper articulation of the theory?
3.   Has the theory been properly articulated?
4.   Has the theory been tested by data in a way that involved potential falsification rather than mere curve fitting?
5.   Does the estimate of attribute frequency stem from coherent use of all relevant bodies of data?
6.   In which of the three senses are these bodies of data relevant (ontological, formal, numerical)?
7.   Are the data stable under the possible antecedent conditions in which use of the risk estimate for guiding mitigation might be attempted? This is not strictly the concern of the risk ANALYST, but it does suggest that a proper analysis must specify the antecedent conditions under which the estimates hold true.

8. Does the act of mitigation alter the antecedent conditions and, if it does, what does this say about the relevance of the existing data? The same comment as in number 7 applies here.

9. Have the data resulted from experimental manipulation through deliberate physical action, or are they simply collected by an observer "after the fact"?

10. Are the antecedent conditions that control the effect understood? If so, how do they compare in the setting from which data are collected and the setting of interest to the analyst?

Without distinct answers to these questions, and a judgment of the quality of such answers, rationality of accepting a given risk estimate cannot be fully assessed.

SOME CONCEPTIONS OF RISK

We return now to the original broader issue of how an analyst might construct tables of risk, thereby meeting the ends of indicating apt means for summarizing risk in a manner indicative of the status of the risk estimates. To see the difficulty in resolving this issue, we offer four possible conceptions of risk against which the "aptness" of a risk estimate may be judged through invocation of results from science. We assume here that the task of the analyst is only to produce statements meeting the requirements of the definitions of risk, thereby avoiding the complications introduced by consideration of HOW those statements will be used.

(1) The most completely empirical conception of risk, and the one towards which a complete science theory might be applied, we term RISK-1. This includes a description of all antecedent conditions in an individual life and how these affect the outcome of exposure to a carcinogen. The only residual (nonunity) probability then is due to the random nature of physical events, such as the random walk of carcinogenic molecules in a cell or the random interactions of radiation with biological molecules. Risk then is a monotonic function of the frequency of times cancer occurs under a fully specified set of antecedent conditions. If one follows Einstein in rejecting all sources of randomness, RISK-1 reverts to a completely determined phenomenon and the word "risk" itself probably is a misnomer.

There is, however, a conceptual problem with the scientific attainment of RISK-1 knowledge. Imagine that each individual constitutes a piece of datum, and that the totality of antecedent conditions differs between individuals (so that no individual set of antecedent conditions is totally repeated in another person). The data required by a covering law approach to science,[20] in which the same general laws are assumed to "cover" all individual cases, would therefore be impossible to obtain since an individual can die only once. Hopes of determining the underlying covering laws through multiple regression analysis on GROUPS would be feasible only if both numerical and formal relevance could be assumed to apply under all combinations of antecedent conditions. RISK-1, therefore, probably will remain epistemologically unreachable due to inherent limitations in the collection of data.

(2) The second level of risk we term RISK-2. It also is an empirical risk but applies to the frequency of effect in populations rather than to individuals. As a result, it skirts some of the issues in RISK-1. In this case, the goal of RISK-1 is dropped and some parameters in predictive equations are left either unexplained (despite the recognition that they contain hidden variables in the form of antecedent conditions from which explanations might be constructed), or are recognized as arising from distributions of the remaining antecedent conditions not appearing formally in the equations. The goal of the analyst simply is to determine the correct value of the unreduced parameters through direct measurement under specified antecedent conditions (or, more properly, distributions of conditions). The goal of the scientist, of course, remains explaining the parameter values by relating them to these distributions of conditions.

The problem of relevance remains when employing data to estimate RISK-2. Since the antecedent conditions on which the remaining parameters ultimately rest are not formally specified, it is impossible to justify from theory any claim that values measured in a sample were obtained under the proper distribution across the underlying conditions. All that can be done is to collect data under a wide range of situations (with the term "range" being theoretically unexplained) and HOPE that the conditions of interest to the analyst have been reproduced. In addition, since the form of the dose-response relationship for carcinogens can be driven strongly by variability of dose within a population,[21] the data from which parameters are estimated must be obtained under the desired dose distribution.

(3) Both RISK-1 and RISK-2 are empirical frequencies that exist independent of measurement techniques or human knowledge. They are the "reality" against which correspondence is to be judged in the classical theory of rationality on which maximization of expected utility (the justification of employing tables of expectation values in public policy) rests. The state of carcinogenesis research at the moment clearly precludes any claim that either of these conceptions of risk can be predicted with high epistemic status. In fact, most estimates of risk to date are obtained from simple curve fits to rather poor data, with little physical significance to the terms of the equation. Still, since these two conceptions of risk are empirical, it is possible to speak of the analysis in terms of THE risk, UNCERTAINTY in THE risk, the QUALITY of THE risk estimate, and so on.

RISK-3 is similar to RISK-2 with one exception. Like RISK-2, it refers to the frequency of effect in a population. It allows, however, that risk of a given magnitude exists if it is predicted by a combination of a causal science theory (the best available) and a parameter value obtained by analysis of data conditional on that theory. Since the parameter values are obtained by a sampling method with its own source of variability, variability in the measured parameters becomes part of the definition of the risk. In other words, a DISTRIBUTION of frequency of effect is obtained, with the properties of the distribution driven by the statistical properties of the sampling method. Since the resulting distribution recognizes only empirical sources of variation, RISK-3 may be considered a case of METHODOLOGICAL EMPIRICISM. Here, a state of affairs is risked if that frequency of effect is deduced from consideration of variability introduced by the act of measurement, as interpreted under a given theory.

The reader should note a crucial difference between RISK-2 and RISK-3. Whereas in RISK-2 it makes some sense (under the classical theory of rationality) for the analyst to provide only a best estimate in summarizing risk, RISK-3 makes such a summary profoundly irrational. It does so because the distribution of predicted frequencies within a mode of interpreted data IS the risk (even though only one of these frequencies in the distribution corresponds to the RISK-2 case). RISK-3 requires, therefore, data capable of revealing the correct distributional form of the sampling consideration, embodied in the accuracy and precision of the science measurements.

(4) The final, and most complete, conception of risk arises from an interaction of (1) variability in parameter values CONDITIONAL ON causal theories and (2) conceptual uncertainty as to the appropriate causal theory. A frequency of effect than is risked if it is an analytic consequence of the interaction of a theory and bodies of data. This level of risk, termed here RISK-4, is summarized by distributions of predicted frequencies taking into account confidence assigned to theories. In other words, confidence in a prediction can be decreased if the theory on which data are interpreted is judged of low quality. The distribution requires explicit weighting (not necessarily quantitative) of the strengths of theories appearing as candidates for the interpretation of data. The result is a cumulative confidence distribution using, for example, Bayesian tools[22] or belief functions. While RISK-1, RISK-2, and RISK-3 refer to frequency distributions which are empirical properties of a phenomenon (RISK-1 and RISK-2) or a process for measuring the phenomenon (RISK-3), RISK-4 is primarily PSYCHOLOGISTIC. There is no claim in RISK-4 that a given frequency of effect WILL occur in a certain fraction of instances, only that the available evidence lends weight to the belief that if MIGHT occur. This is a way of saying that an effect is risked if there is a minimally epistemic rational reason for deeming it possible in the face of existing evidence (both data and theories). This minimal epistemic status is taken here to be provided by a science theory that has undergone at least limited proper testing and scrutiny.

4. CONCLUDING REMARKS

Is there any hope for a purely empirical (atheoretical) basis for estimating risk, as seems to be indicated by current practice in risk analysis? Not if science is to be invoked as a warrant, and by science one means a discipline characterized by conceptual understanding, deductive success, and confidence in the crafting of solutions. Consider in these closing paragraphs the four sources of estimates of attribute frequency laid out by Crawford-Brown and Pearce[16] in a paper on evidential justification. A given estimate may spring from:

(1) A direct empirical claim to having observed the desired frequency in a body of data. At the very least, such claims hinge critically on the ability to identify the antecedent conditions on which the frequency depends; to determine that these are identical in the sample and in the world of interest to the analyst; that the frequency is stable in time rather than random or evolutionary in nature; that the act of mitigation itself doesn't alter important conditions; that the considered variable is a true cause rather than in common cause with the desired effect; that variability of dose in exposure groups doesn't affect the ability to predict; that physical adjustment of a variable is understood in the sense of KNOWING HOW; and so on.

(2) A risk estimate might spring from extrapolation of a semiempirical equation from high to low doses. Here, all of the factors in the direct empirical case apply to each of the data points on which extrapolation is based. In addition, some method for generating the extrapolation equation is required. This might be (2a) semiempirical sketching, in which a pattern is claimed to be observed in the data and followed to lower doses. This claim might well be made in the absence of a well-developed causal theory, although SOME theory obviously is present or the data would not have been obtained in a manner capable of revealing patterns. But data on which risk estimates are based usually fail to show patterns that are clearly and distinctly perceived. This approach would require a body of highly accurate and precise data outside the realm of feasibility at the moment. Even this possibility leaves aside the issue of the relevance of the patterns beyond the edges of the data and under different antecedent conditions. Directly observed patterns can't be ignored by the analyst, but their quality must be expressed truthfully and the lack of understanding of their cause admitted.

The extrapolation might also be based on (2b) theory-based extrapolation using a complete causal theory, introducing all of the difficulties of the section on Theories, Data, and Rational Confidence which arise in justifying a theory. Still, the approach at least carries a claim to conceptual understanding and allows the coherent use of those data deemed relevant by the theory. The spectre of RISK-4 lies waiting, however, as the analyst must admit to cases in which the predictive and explanatory success of a favorite theory is enjoyed by other theories as well. A rationally developed field of science continues to articulate and refine existing theories, but it also strives to uncover new theories which might resolve existing dilemmas. This is why data must be sufficiently precise to yield potential disagreement between predictions and the data.

Finally, risk estimates may spring from (3) strong theory, in which attribute frequencies are estimated entirely from the theory-driven combination of probabilities obtained from measurements of subeffects that unite to produce the effect of interest. This is clearly the strongest role of theory and carries the greatest burden of claims to understanding the role of antecedent conditions that might differ between the experimental settings in which the effects and subeffects are determined. While the role of "missing" variables is hidden within parameters measured by the other three approaches to risk estimation, they must be formally and DELIBERATELY incorporated in the case of strong theory. Otherwise, they will play no role at all (either deliberate or accidental) in the process of estimation.

Such an approach represents the highest ideal of science and, we would argue, the quest for its attainment is what has made scientific inquiry truly rational over the years. Strong theory is never completely attained, but the other three approaches have their own flaws. Rational confidence rests on a simultaneous consideration of the three modes of estimation. It rests on the deliberate dialectic between the collection of data and the generation of theories used to interpret those data. Both the theories and the data must be of high quality if the process of judging risk is to be warranted by claims to scientific rationality. The state of development of both must be considered in the rational ranking of risk, as humans strive to observe the world, to give relevance to those observations, and to confront the state of understanding within which human decisions and actions take place.

REFERENCES

1. See, e.g., *Cancer Risk Assessment,* C. Travis and E. Anderson, Eds., Plenum Press, New York, 1988.
2. K. Brown, *Rationality,* Kegan and Routledge, New York, 1990.
3. See, e.g., B. Cohen, "A Generic Probabilistic Risk Analysis for High Level Waste Repository," *Health Phys.,* 51, 519–528, 1986.
4. R. Rorty, *Philosophy and the Mirror of Nature,* Princeton University Press, Princeton, NJ, 1980.
5. J. Raetz, *Scientific Knowledge and Its Social Problems,* Oxford University Press, Oxford, 1971.
6. N. Maxwell, *From Knowledge to Wisdom,* Basil Blackwell, Oxford.
7. L. Laudan, *Progress and Its Problems,* University of California Press, Berkeley, 1977.

8. S. Toulmin, *Foresight and Understanding,* Indiana University Press, Bloomington, 1961.

9. H. Checkoway, N. Pearce, and D. Crawford-Brown, *Occupational Epidemiology,* Oxford University Press, Oxford, 1989.

10. See, e.g., the discussion of Heidegger in R. Rorty, *Essay on Heidegger and Others,* Cambridge University Press, Cambridge, 1991.

11. H. Longino, *Science as Social Knowledge,* Princeton University Press, Princeton, NJ, 1990.

12. J. Graham, L. Green, and M. Roberts, *In Search of Safety: Chemicals and Cancer Risk,* Harvard University Press, Cambridge, MA, 1990.

13. K. Popper, *The Logic of Scientific Discovery,* Basic Books, New York, 1959.

14. D. Crawford-Brown and W. Hofmann, "The Role of Variability of Dose in Dose-Response Relationships for Alpha Emitting Radionuclides," *Radiat. Prot. Dosimetry,* 29, 293, 1989.

15. T. Kuhn, *The Structure of Scientific Revolutions,* University of Chicago Press, Chicago, 1964.

16. D. Crawford-Brown and N. Pearce, "Sufficient Proof in the Scientific Justification of Environmental Actions," *Environ. Ethics,* Summer, 153–167, 1989.

17. D. Crawford-Brown, *Analyzing Risk in a Shared Environment,* Oxford University Press, submitted.

18. D. Crawford-Brown and W. Hofmann, "A Generalized State-Vector Model for Radiation Induced Cellular Transformation," *Int. J. Radiat. Biol.,* 57, 407–423, 1990.

19. D. Crawford-Brown and J. Holmes, "Regulatory Science and the Value of Coherence," Science, Technology and Human Values, submitted.

20. R. Miller, *Fact and Method,* Princeton University Press, Princeton, NJ, 1987.

21. D. Crawford-Brown, "The Role of Dose Inhomogeneity in Biological Models of Dose-response," in *Low Dose Radiation: Biological Bases of Risk Assessment,* K. Baverstock and J. Stather, Eds., Taylor and Francis, 1989, 155–161.

22. D. Crawford-Brown, "The Price of Confidence: the Rationality of Radium Removal from Drinking Water," in *Radon, Radium and Uranium in Drinking Water,* C. Cothern and P. Rebers, Eds., Lewis Publishers, MI, 1990, 213–223.

CHAPTER 19

How to Move Quickly to Risk-Based Environmental Management: a Specific Proposal*

William V. Garetz

The current effort to establish the basis for risk-based management at the U.S. Environmental Protection Agency has been underway for some time now. The initial thinking and proposals that led subsequently to preparation of the *Unfinished Business* report in 1987 and the *Reducing Risk* report in 1990 originated in 1984, 7 years ago. EPA has not yet reached its 21st anniversay as an independent Federal agency. That means that efforts towards establishing a risk-based approach to Agency management have now been underway for more than one third of EPA's existence as an Agency. And yet no specific risk-based procedures for priority setting or for resource allocation have yet been developed and put forward, not to mention implemented, within EPA.

The chapters presented so far in this book have focused on the current completeness and quality of the environmental risk information that is needed to drive risk-based management at EPA. Many of the papers have identified remaining gaps and shortcomings in these data. Clearly, efforts must continue to improve the completeness and quality of this risk information.

At the same time, it seems reasonable to ask: when will we finally get on with the job of beginning to use risk-based information explicitly in the management of EPA? If the answer is, "not till we have perfect risk information!" then the last 7 years of effort have been wasted since we will *never* have perfect risk information. But an alternative answer is, "as soon as we have good enough risk information to make better management decisions than we would make without it!" I'm convinced that the second answer is the appropriate one. If so, then I believe that we already meet that criterion, and the time to begin is now. That is the point of view of this paper: we have good enough risk information so that if we now begin to carry out a sensibly

---

* The thoughts and ideas expressed in this chapter are those of the author and are not necessarily those of the U.S. Environmental Protection Agency.

designed process of risk-based decision making, our management decisions will be better than they would have been without such a process.

What I will therefore do is present a specific proposal for what such a risk-based decision-making process might look like — a "strawman" proposal, if you like. I will then test it against the various concerns (presented in my earlier chapter) that have been expressed about moving "too quickly" to launch a system of risk-based management to see how it stands up against these various concerns. I hope in this way to help launch a discussion regarding what the "best" initial design of such a system might be and when we might prudently begin to use it. As I will make clear in this chapter, I believe the "strawman" I am putting forward is a *reasonable initial system* and that it could be implemented *exactly as presented here* with very good results, and that the time to begin using such a system is *now*.

WHAT IS RISK-BASED ENVIRONMENTAL MANAGEMENT?

One problem in moving forward to actual implementation of a system for risk-based environmental management is that the very meaning of the phrase "risk-based management" has remained somewhat fuzzy. Some have talked more specifically of "risk-based priority setting" and of "risk-based resource allocation". What do we mean by these things? Unfortunately, this also is unclear. I therefore propose the following clarifications:

- *Risk-based priority setting* means determining how big one environment problem is when compared to others as a contributor to the total environmental risk from all classes of environmental threats and challenges. It means determining how big each problem is as a percentage or slice of the full environmental risk pie. It is also an indication of how much we would be *willing* to invest in addressing each environmental threat, "all else being equal". I propose that it be expressed as:
  "Environmental Threat A (or B or C . . .) is responsible for 9% of the total environmental risk we face" and "All else being equal, we would be willing to invest 9% of our total environmental management resources to the elimination or mitigation of Environmental Threat A."
- *Risk-based resource allocation* is a process for determining how much is appropriate to spend on each of these distinct environmental problems given that we live in the real world in which "not all else is equal". To be more specific, there are certain environmental threats for which we have not yet developed effective responses. Investing an amount on these threats proportional to their contribution to total environmental risk would therefore be a poor investment. It would constitute "throwing money at the problem" rather than investing wisely to reduce or eliminate it. For such problems we should instead focus for now on developing more effective abatement

and prevention *strategies* including, where appropriate, more effective abatement and prevention *technologies*. Sensible risk-based resource allocation must consider not only the magnitude of each environment threat in terms of the amount it contributes to total environmental risk, but must also consider the relative effectiveness of the responses now available to us to reduce or eliminate these threats. Such an allocation would be expressed as: "The recommended investment for the response to Environmental Threat A in Fiscal Year 1993 is $37,700,000".

The system proposed below will accomplish both of these purposes: it will result in risk-based priority setting by showing the relative contribution of each distinct environmental threat to total environmental risk. It will also result in a risk-based allocation of resources that considers not only the magnitude of that portion of total environmental risk associated with that environmental threat, but also the potential effectiveness of the various responses currently available to us to deal with each of these threats.

DESIGN CRITERIA

Before I present the proposed system, let me first set forth the design criteria I have sought to adhere to in developing it.

1. The system must fully acknowledge the uncertainty in the environmental risk information that is currently available to us.
2. The system must provide strong incentives to Agency managers to continue to take effective action to reduce the incompleteness and the uncertainty in the risk information now available to us.
3. The system must result in a sensible allocation of resources among the various responses (i.e., risk reduction options) currently available to us to reduce the current and future risk associated with each identified environmental threat.
4. It would also be highly desirable for the system also to result in a sensible allocation of resources among various ancillary activities intended to result in more effective future responses or in more appropriate future priorities and allocations of resources. For example, it would be highly desirable for the system to indicate where investment is most needed in *new risk reduction strategies* (abatement strategies and prevention strategies) and in *new risk reduction technologies* (abatement technologies and prevention technologies). It would also be highly desirable for the system to indicate where investment is most needed in activities that will result in *improved environment risk information*. Such activities include: research on environmental health effects, and research on the ecological effects of environmental pollution and disturbance. Such ac-

tivities also include: development and implementation of improved monitoring technologies and monitoring programs, improved exposure monitoring and assessment programs, and improved methodologies for assessing available information on environmental hazards, exposures, and risks.

DEALING WITH DIFFERENT KINDS OF RISK

I am now almost ready to present the "strawman" proposal, but there is one more basic issue that must first be addressed. This is the question of how to deal with the fact that we have at least three very different kinds of environmental risk that we are dealing with. They are health risks, ecological risks, and welfare risks.

What we have at present, coming out of the *Unfinished Business* and the *Reducing Risk* efforts, is not one set of rankings of environmental problems based on risks, but instead three separate rankings, one each based on health, ecological, and welfare risks. How can we move forward given that we have three rankings rather than one?

Ideally, if we are to be able to develop a single unified set of risk-based priorities and if we are to conduct a single risk-based resource allocation process, then we would want somehow to consolidate these three separate risk-based rankings into one combined ranking.

In the discussion of Concern #5 in my earlier chapter, three alternative approaches are presented for developing such a combined ranking. The approach identified as the one that is immediately implementable is the one that consists of taking the entire "pot" of resources to be invested and dividing it into three smaller pots: one each to address health risks, ecological risks, and welfare risks. A separate resource allocation could then be conducted with each of these separate "pots" of resources. I believe that this is the only approach that is available to us in the short term, so this is the one that I urge be adopted and used at least for the first 1 or 2 years until a suitable panel can be convened to do the pegging necessary to implement the "intermediate approach" described in Concern #5 in my earlier chapter.

For the short-term approach, there is still one key question that must be answered: how much of the total resources available should go into each pot? Here's one suggestion. It has been said frequently in the last year or two that we have not devoted enough attention to the ecological impacts associated with the various environmental threats and challenges facing us. Indeed, it has been said that we should devote as much attention and effort to addressing the ecological impacts as the health impacts. It would be consistent with this perspective to propose devoting as much to ecological risks as to health risks. As for welfare risks, these are generally acknowledged to be significant, but not nearly as large as the health and environmental risks. So for the sake of stimulating debate, I propose that the total available resources be divided as follows: 45% to health risks, 45% to ecological risks, and 10% to welfare risks. In order to carry out the proposed "strawman" approach employing the *short-term approach* described above, the process described in the strawman will have to be conducted three times, once for each of the three distinct kinds of risk (health, ecological, welfare).

THE STATUS OF THE PROPOSED APPROACH

I will now describe, step by step, a specific approach for using risk information to set priorities for and allocate resources among the various environmental threats facing us. I present this not as the ultimate or an ideal system, but as an initial "strawman". At the same time I believe it to be a full, complete, practical system that could be implemented with excellent results "as is". I offer it for use as the initial system, subject to adjustment over time as operating experience is obtained using it. However, even if it is not adopted for immediate implementation as is, I still believe it to be useful as a "strawman" to stimulate debate and help elicit alternative approaches intended for immediate implementation. If such alternatives are proposed, the various alternatives (with this strawman included among them) can be compared based on their anticipated performance and the one with the best performance can be selected as the initial system for immediate implementation.

PROPOSED APPROACH FOR RISK-BASED PRIORITY SETTING AND RESOURCE ALLOCATION

Here is the proposed system: (1) Begin by constructing, on one or more sheets of paper, the graphic display of risk information shown below (Figure 1). The "risk units" used in constructing this figure should be appropriate to the type of risk being addressed (e.g., "years of healthy life lost" for health risk, dollars lost for welfare risk, and some to-be-defined "ecological risk units" for ecological risk). Note that, for each environmental threat or concern, the point L is the "consensus lower bound" of the risk associated with that threat. This would be the *lowest* estimate of that risk agreed to by a panel of experts. Similarly, the point H is the "consensus upper bound" of the risk associated with that threat (the *highest* estimate of risk agreed to by the expert panel). Note that the lower value (L) reflects the *undisputed amount* of risk associated with that threat. And the band from L to H is the "uncertainty band" — it's the additional amount of risk that the experts determine *may possibly* be associated with that threat, but about which there

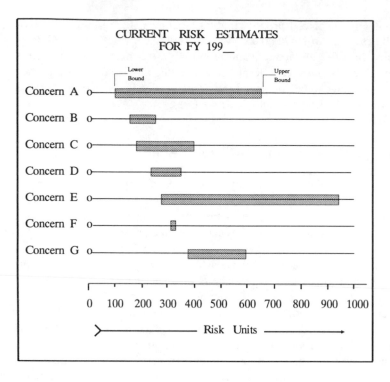

FIGURE 1.   Proposed standard method for arraying risk estimates and uncertainty bands.

is legitimate unresolved uncertainty. For simplicity in what follows, we define the uncertainty ban (U) for each environmental threat as follows:

$$U = H - L$$

(2) Determine the relative priority of each environmental threat or concern for that kind of risk (i.e., health risk, ecological risk, or welfare risk) as follows:

> (a) For each environmental threat, compute a risk score (S) as follows:

$$S = L + (20\% \times U)$$

> Note that this formula for computing the score (S) counts the full undisputed portion of the risk and gives credit for one-fifth of that portion of the risk about which there is unresolved uncertainty. The rationale for allowing credit for only a portion of the uncertain part of the risk is to ensure that there is a strong incentive to *"resolve the uncertainty"*. The formula also gives program managers a strong incentive to make the risk estimates for the environmental threats they deal with as *complete*

as possible, because obtaining and providing information on additional risks will push the L and H points to the left on the risk line (in Figure 1) and therefore increase the risk score (S).

(b) Set the priority (P) of each environmental threat equal to the percentage determined by dividing its risk score (S) by the sum total (T) of all the risk scores:

$$P = S/T$$

(3) For each environmental threat, multiply its priority (P) by the "total resources available for allocation for that class of risk" (R) to determine the total "willingness-to-pay" (W) — all else being equal — to address that environmental threat:

$$W = P \times R$$

"R" is the size in dollars of the "pot" of resources assigned to the class of risk (i.e., health, ecological, or welfare risk) for which the current allocation is being conducted. *Note that in steps (2) and (3) we have already accomplished what we set out to accomplish towards risk-based priority setting.* Also, see Appendix B for the (simple) derivation of an alternative form of the above equation which we will find useful below.

(4) Determine the "investment to be made in improved risk information" (I) for each environmental threat. The purpose of such investment is to *reduce the current uncertainty* in the *risk estimates* for that environmental threat. The amount that it is worth investing should therefore be proportional to the extent of the uncertainty. The following is proposed as the investment to be made in reducing the uncertainty for each environmental threat:

$$I = (5\% \times U) \times w$$

where

$$w = R/T$$

Note: w ("lower case w") is the "willingness to pay per unit of risk" (see Appendix B).

Thus it is proposed that, for each separate environmental threat, 5% of the resources that we would be *willing to pay* if the uncertain portion of the environmental risk were made certain be devoted to obtaining the improved risk information that will reduce that uncertainty.

(5) Determination of the amount of "willingness to pay" remaining.

For each environmental threat, the total initial willingness to pay was "W".

We have now allocated a portion of that ("I") to activities intended to improve risk information. The remaining "willingness to pay" (W_1) is

$$W_1 = W - I$$

Substituting:

$$W = w \times [L + (20\% \times U)]$$

(see Appendix B) and:

$$I = w \times (5\% \times U)$$

we obtain:

$$W_1 = [w \times (L + 20\% \times U)] - [w \times (5\% \times U)]$$

$$W_1 = w \times [L + (15\% \times U)]$$

Thus, the "remaining willingness to pay" is based on the full undisputed portion of the risk (L) and 15% of the portion of the risk about which there is uncertainty (U).

(6) It is proposed that for every environmental threat, a minimum amount be devoted each year to developing new risk reduction options for that threat. Some of these options may require the development of new risk reduction technology and others may involve development of new management strategies or strategic options that are nontechnological or utilize existing technology. It is proposed that, for every environmental threat, the following amount be the *initial allotment* (C_1) from the "remaining willingness to pay" *for the development of new risk reduction technologies and management strategies (strategic options):*

$$C_1 = 5\% \times W_1$$

That is, it is proposed that an initial allotment of 5% of the "remaining willingness to pay" be devoted to the development of new risk reduction technologies and new risk reduction management strategies (strategic options).

(7) The next step is to array all of the currently identified risk reduction options available for each of the environmental threats (see Figure 2). Note the scale at the bottom of Figure 2. Risk reduction options are arrayed in order of relative cost effectiveness, with the most cost-effective options to the left and the increasingly less cost-effective options to the right. Note also that the left-most risk reduction option for *each environmental threat* is labelled "Option 1"; the second most cost-effective option is labelled "Option 2," etc.

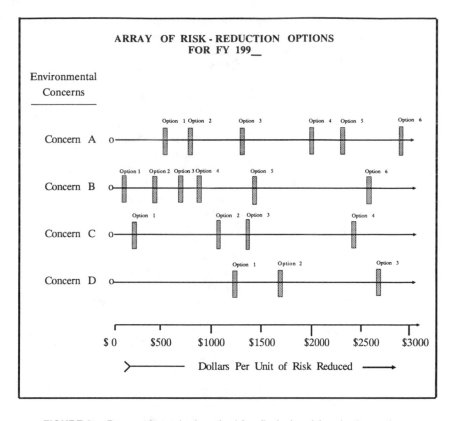

FIGURE 2. Proposed standard method for displaying risk reduction options.

(8) The following procedure is then proposed to select risk reduction options for implementation:

(a)   Scanning the full array of all Risk Reduction Options for all environmental threats/concerns as shown in Figure 2, select the left-most option in the array (i.e., select the most cost-effective option in the array). In Figure 2, the left-most option is Option 1 for Threat B. Place this option in the Response Plan for Threat B. Assign to Threat B the associated resources required and subtract these resources from the remaining willingness to pay for Threat B.

(b)   Scan the array again and select the left-most option in the array that has not yet been selected. In Figure 2, the left-most option remaining is now Option 1 for Threat C. Place this option in the Response Plan for Threat C. Assign to Threat C the resources required and subtract these resources from the "remaining willingness to pay" for Threat C.

(c)   In similar manner, proceed in successive steps to select at each step the left-most remaining option. In Figure 2, the next option to be selected will be Option 2 for Threat B. The next option to be selected after that will be Option 1 for Threat A. The next will be Option 3 for Threat B, and the next after that will be Option 2 for Threat A. For each option selected, take the additional actions called for in step (b) above. Continue in this manner until the next option to be selected will exceed the remaining willingness to pay for the Environmental Threat to which that option is directed. When such a situation arises, go to step (d) below.

(d)   When the next option to be selected exceeds the remaining willingness to pay for the Environmental Threat towards which that option is directed (e.g., in Figure 2, if the process proceeds to the point that Option 6 for Threat B is the left-most option remaining, but the resources required to implement Option 6 for Threat B exceed the remaining willingness to pay for Threat B), then take the following additional actions:

     (i)   Expand the "willingness to pay" for the associated Environmental Threat sufficiently to accommodate the option about to be selected.

     (ii)   Compensate for this expansion by shrinking the currently remaining willingness to pay for all of the other Environmental Threats by an equal amount. The amount of shrinkage in the willingness to pay for each of the others Threats will be proportional to the amount of willingness to pay remaining for that Threat as compared with the total remaining willingness to pay for all Environmental Threats. (As a consequence, Environmental Threats for which the initial willingness to pay has been fully allotted or which have had their willingness to pay expanded earlier will not shrink at all since their "remaining willingness to pay" will at this point be zero.)

     (iii)   For each Threat incurring shrinkage in its "remaining willingness to pay" as a result of step (B) above, allocate an amount of resources equal to the amount of shrinkage just incurred to "C", the amount to be invested in the development of new risk reduction technologies and in new management strategies for that Threat. The "remaining willingness to pay" for each Threat is now reduced by the amount of shrinkage determined in step (d) (ii) above plus the amount just allocated to "C" for that activity.

(e)   Repeat step (c) above (where necessary going to step (d) as well) until the "remaining willingness to pay" has reached zero for every Threat (i.e., until all resources available for risk reduction activities have been expended) or has reached such a low level that there is insufficient "remaining willingness to pay" to fund the left-most remaining option and also make the necessary contributions to "C". In the latter case, allocate all remaining "willingness to pay" for each Threat to "C" for that Concern.

When step (8) (e) is completed, we will have achieved our second objective — we will have developed a risk-based allocation of resources for each environmental threat.

See Appendix C for a relatively simple modification of the algorithm contained in steps 7 and 8 to accommodate multiple simultaneous cost constraints on the selection of risk reduction options.

(f)   Apportion the resources allocated to "development of new risk reduction
      strategies and technologies" among the two distinct activities: (1) "de-
      velopment of new (or revised) risk reduction strategies" and (2) "de-
      velopment of new risk reduction technologies". Although this appor-
      tionment should vary from threat to threat and, for each threat, should
      vary from year to year, it is suggested that in most years for most threats,
      at least 10% of these resources be apportioned to "development of new
      (or revised) risk reduction strategies".

OVERVIEW AND SUMMARY

The outcome of the process described (in steps 1 to 8 above) is as follows:

- Resources will in every case be allocated to the most cost effective remaining
  option not yet funded — until all resources are allocated.
- As a consequence, some Environmental Threats, for which there happen to
  be a large number of unusually cost-effective control options, will be
  assigned resources that exceed the initial ("all else being equal") willingness to pay (to reduce the risk associated with that Threat).
- Other Threats will receive resources for use in risk reduction that are *less
  than* the initial willingness to pay. All such Threats "losing resources" in
  this manner will also have assigned to them an amount equal to what was
  lost for use in developing new, more cost-effective risk reduction technologies and strategic options. The most extreme case would be a Threat
  for which there are *no* cost-effective options currently available. In such
  a case, (1) half of the resources available as "remaining willingness to
  pay" (W_1) for that Threat at the beginning of the allocation will have been
  reallocated to other Environmental Threats for which cost-effective options
  are currently available; (2) the other half will be devoted to the development
  of new risk reduction technologies and strategic options. Over time, these
  development activities should result in new, more cost-effective technologies and strategic options that will allow that Environmental Threat to
  fare better in future allocations.

OUTPUT OF THE PROCESS

The specific outputs of the Process as a whole (steps 1 to 8) are as follows:

- We have provided two critical, easily understood Graphical Displays (Figures
  1 and 2). The first presents on a *single sheet* of paper the environmental
  risk associated with *all current Environmental Threats* faced by the agency
  and the degree of uncertainty regarding the extent of that risk. The second
  presents *on a single sheet of paper* the number of Risk Reduction Options
  currently identified as available for *all current Environmental Threats* and

arrays them graphically in rank order, most cost effective first, second most cost effective second, etc. Also, the relative cost effectiveness of each available option is clearly apparent through a quick scan of this second Graphical Display.

- We have also developed a process in which:
  (a) Resources are assigned to activities *to improve the available risk information* associated with each Environmental Threat. The amount assigned to each Threat is proportional to the extent of remaining uncertainty regarding the risk associated with that Threat.
  (b) Resources are assigned *to the development of new risk reduction technologies and strategies.* Some resources are assigned in every case. More are assigned for those Environmental Threats for which few or no cost-effective risk reduction options are currently available. The greater the risk associated with an Environmental Threat, the greater the investment in developing cost-effective risk reduction technologies and strategic options if few or no cost-effectiveness technologies/strategies are currently available.
  (c) Resources are assigned *to currently available risk reduction options* based purely on the relative cost effectiveness of these options. By using this approach, we maximize the amount of risk reduction achieved for each risk-reduction dollar spent.
  (d) Where the risk associated with a given environmental threat (e.g., for Environmental Threat L) is high, we will have a high "willingness to pay" to reduce the risk associated with that Threat. If, however, there are few or no cost-effective options currently available for reducing that risk, then resources that we would have been willing to expend on Environmental Threat L will be transferred to other Environmental Threats and will be used to implement more cost-effective options available for these other threats. At the same time, an equal amount of resources will be invested in developing new risk reduction technologies and strategies for Environmental Threat L.

WORKSHEETS

Worksheets have been developed to capture the information needed to produce Figures 1 and 2 and to supply the information needed for steps 1 to 8 above. Figure 3 is the Risk Information Input Matrix. Only *one sheet* is needed to capture *all* the risk information needed to drive the above process. Figure 4 is the Risk Reduction Options Input Matrix. One copy of Figure 4 (a single sheet) is needed for *each* Environmental Threat included in the resource allocation process. Figure 5 is the Resource Allocation Output Matrix. The process will produce allocations for all of the Environmental Threats included in the process. All of the recommended allocations generated by this process will fit on a single sheet. Thus, the process proposed cannot in the least be considered paper intensive.

INPUT MATRIX FOR FY 199__				
	ESTIMATED RISK		CURRENT EXPENDITURES	
ENVIRONMENTAL CONCERN	LOWER BOUND	UPPER BOUND	TOTAL	FEDERAL SHARE
Concern A				
Concern B				
Concern C				
Concern D				
Concern E				
Concern F				
⋮				
Concern N				

FIGURE 3. Proposed input matrix, which captures the information needed to generate Figure 1 (and more).

	CONTROL OPTIONS LIST FOR ENVIRONMENTAL CONCERN __ FOR FY 199__						
Option	Description	Risk Reduced Per Dollar Spent	Average Total Public/Private Cost Per Year	Average Federal Share of Cost	Federal Cost In Year 1	Federal Cost In Year 2	Federal Cost In Year 3
Option 1							
Option 2							
Option 3							
Option 4							
Option 5							
⋮							
Option L							

FIGURE 4. Proposed format for the risk reduction options list for a given environmental concern.

OUTPUT MATRIX FOR FY 199_							
Environmental Concern	Total Willingness to Pay		Recommended Allocation for FY 199_				
			Total Public/Private Expenditure	Federal Expenditure			
	(%)	($)		Program Operations	Strategy Development	Health Research and Improved Risk Assessment	Prevention/ Control Technology Development
Concern A							
Concern B							
Concern C							
Concern D							
Concern E							
Concern F							
: : : : :							
Concern N							

FIGURE 5. Proposed output matrix, which displays the relative priority and resource allocation assigned to each environmental concern.

Additionally, due to the nature of the information provided on each of the input worksheets and captured on the two key graphical summaries (Figures 1 and 2), the input worksheets and graphical summaries will generally change very little from one year to the next. There will only be marginal changes to reflect additional risk reduction options developed and new or revised risk information or cost-effectiveness information obtained in the previous year.

Further, the process is simple enough to be set up as a very simple PC-based computer program.

OTHER FEATURES RECOMMENDED FOR THE PROPOSED SYSTEM

I have now described the specific algorithm and procedural steps to be included in the proposed system and the outputs that will be obtained. I will now describe the adjunct activities needed to make this process work smoothly and equitably.

The following are critical to the effective functioning of the above process:

1. Comparable lower bound and upper bound risk estimates for each environmental threat to be included in the process

2. Risk reduction options for each environmental threat — along with cred-
    ible and comparable estimates of risk reduction effectiveness and cost
    for each option

It is proposed that individual EPA program managers be assigned responsibility (1) for providing the initial estimates of risk for the environmental
threats for which they are responsible and (2) for developing and specifying
the risk reduction options for each of these environmental threats, together
with the associated estimates of risk reduction effectiveness and cost.

It is proposed that these estimates then be provided to two separate "Equalization Panels", one for Risk Estimates and the other for Risk Reduction
Options and Associated Estimates. I will now refer to these as the "Risk
Panel" and the "Options Panel". These panels would each be constituted as
described below.

The Risk Panel will consist of three independent subpanels — One each
will be responsible for human health risks, for ecological risks, and for welfare
risks. Each subpanel would consist of technical experts from academia; from
Federal, state, and local governments; from environmental advocacy organizations; and from industry. Each member would to the extent possible be
an individual with no bias towards or against any one kind of risk within the
area on which he or she is serving and with no bias towards or against any
one environmental threat or EPA program. Each subpanel will be charged
with (a) identifying the baseline year or period to be used for developing or
adjusting estimates, the standard assumptions to be used, where appropriate,
and the standard models to be used, where appropriate, and (b) adjusting the
estimates provided accordingly — where they were derived using different
baseline years, assumptions, or models. The subpanels will also be empowered
to make any other adjustments they deem appropriate, subject to the single
requirement that, in each case, they give the basis for or the justification they
relied on for making the adjustment.

The Options Panel would initially be a single panel with no subpanels
— The institutional composition of the Options Panel would be the same as
that of the Risk Subpanels except that the expertise represented would be
risk-reduction expertise, with a balance between those with expertise in technological options and those with expertise in nontechnological and low-tech-
nology risk reduction options. The role of this panel will be

1. To identify "overly amalgamated" options with too many disparate ele-
    ments that operate differently. The panel will be empowered to reject
    such options and require their resubmission by the program manager as
    separate options.
2. To identify options that are "too large". Again, the panel will reject such
    options and require the resubmission of multiple smaller options con-
    suming smaller increments of resources.

3.   To adjust estimates of projected risk reduction effectiveness and cost. The Panel will do so to increase consistency across options that use different risk reduction approaches. The panel (where appropriate) will also increase the consistency of cost estimates and risk reduction effectiveness estimates for each distinct risk reduction approach proposed for use to address different environmental threats. For example, if two different program managers are proposing to conduct public education campaigns, the panel will be responsible for ensuring that differences in the estimated risk reduction effectiveness are consistent with the differences in program design, differences in target audience, differences in the incentive or disincentive to take the steps recommended, etc., between these similar options as proposed for the different environmental threats.

ASSESSMENT OF THE PROPOSED STRAWMAN PROCESS AGAINST THE DESIGN CRITERIA

We now assess the extent to which the proposed system conforms to the design criteria initially set forth.

- Does the proposed system provide "risk-based priorities"?
  Yes. The "willingness to pay" value (W) and the priority score (S) both give a clear indication of the priority of each Environmental Threat as compared with other current Environmental Threats.
- Does the system result in a resource allocation that is based strongly on risk, but also considers the cost and the likely effectiveness of each proposed investment?
  Yes.

1.   Does the system fully acknowledge the extent of uncertainty about the risk estimates for each Environmental Threat?
     Yes. It not only acknowledges the uncertainty, it goes much further. It treats uncertainty as *useful information* that helps shape the allocation of resources.

2.   Does the system provide a strong incentive to reduce current uncertainties related to risk estimates?
     Yes. It does so in two ways: (1) by giving Agency managers "full credit" for that portion of risk that is undisputed and only "partial credit" for that portion about which there is reasonable doubt, it gives managers a strong incentive to resolve the uncertainty in order to increase the portion of the estimated risk that is not in dispute, thereby increasing the amount of resources that will available in future years to carry out the risk reduction activities associated with that program. (2) It allocates resources to the improvement of risk information in an amount proportional to the magnitude of that portion of the risk about which there is uncertainty.

3.   Does the system provide reasonable allocations among alternative risk reduction activities?
     Yes.

4.   Does the system provide suggested allocations of resources among such ancillary activities as (a) activities to improve risk information, and (b) activities to develop new risk reduction technologies and strategic options?
Yes. It produces explicit resources allocations for both (a) and (b).

AN ASSESSMENT OF THE PROPOSED "QUICK-START" SYSTEM AGAINST THE IDENTIFIED CONCERNS ABOUT SYSTEMS FOR ACHIEVING RISK-BASED MANAGEMENT (SEE CHAPTER 2)

Concern #1. The risk information currently available is *incomplete*.

Assessment of the Proposed System Against This Concern: As will be true of any such system, the proposed system provides very strong incentives to obtain the risk data needed to fill out a previously incomplete risk picture for each environmental threat. To the extent that there is an "undisputed component" of the additional risk for which information is obtained and provided as a result of these incentives, additional resources will be obtained proportional to the full amount of the increase in the amount of undisputed (lower bound) risk. To the extent that the additional risk information results in an increase in the amount of risk about which there is legitimate uncertainty, the increase in resources will be proportional to 20% of the increase in the disputed amount of risk (i.e., the resultant increase in the upper bound estimate of risk). So again, the incentives provided seem sound in that providing *any* additional credible risk information results in increased resources, but the amount of additional resources is smaller if it is only "squishy" (i.e., uncertain or questionable) new risk information that is provided while the amount of additional resources will be much greater if it is "solid" (i.e., undisputed) additional risk on which new information is provided.
Conclusion: At best, this concern has little or no merit as a reason for postponing implementation of a risk-based approach for priority setting. Even so, the proposed system performs extremely well against this concern due to the fact that it strongly differentiates between the weak new risk information and the solid new risk information that will both inevitably be produced as a result of the strong incentives for producing such new risk information provided by any system for risk-based resource allocation.

Concern #2. The risk information currently available is *uncertain*.

Assessment of the Proposed System Against This Concern: By giving relatively little credit in the resource allocation for the uncertain component of the risk estimate, the proposed system creates a strong positive incentive to programs and program managers to resolve the uncertainty in the risk estimates for the environmental threats that they are addressing. Thus, for the proposed system, uncertainty in the risk estimates results in strong incentives towards the (socially desirable) objective of reducing the extent of this uncertainty.

Conclusion: The system therefore performs well when measured against this concern. It is designed so that it creates strong positive incentives to resolve current uncertainty in risk estimates, which is a highly desirable outcome.

Concern #3. The risk information currently available is *noncomparable.*

Assessment of the Proposed System Against This Concern:

1. *Noncomparability due to use of different risk estimation procedures;* The proposed system performs no worse than any other when measured against this concern. It may in fact perform better than most since it allows a lower bound and upper bound risk estimate for each class of risk (health, ecological, welfare) associated with each environmental threat and it places no restrictions on the width of the resulting "uncertainty band". One way to address noncomparability would be to assign greater uncertainty bands (smaller lower bounds and, where appropriate, higher upper bounds) to those risks for which greater amounts of extrapolation were required and less for those risks for which less extrapolation or no extrapolation was required.

2,3. *Noncomparability due to use of data from different baseline years or due to use of different assumptions:* The proposed "Equalization Panel for Risk Estimates" would have the role of making appropriate adjustments to correct for noncomparability resulting from these factors.

Conclusion: The proposed system is able to respond to these concerns reasonably well. No other system has been proposed that performs better. No breakthroughs that are likely to result in greater comparability are likely to occur soon.

Concern #4. Risk-based management is biased against *future* as compared with *present* risks.

Assessment of the Proposed System Against This Concern: Because the proposed system allows for wide uncertainty bands within the risk estimates used, it can fully accommodate the incorporation of such projected "future risks". *Conclusion:* The proposed system has no inherent bias against projected "future risks". On the contrary, it has a design feature that allows it to incorporate such future risks appropriately into the full array of risk estimates used within the system.

Concern #5. How can we add health, ecological, and welfare risks to come up with a single consolidated risk estimate and ranking?

Assessment of the Proposed System Against This Concern: Three different approaches have been put forward in the proposed system for addressing this concern. One approach which finesses this concern in a manner that appears to be sensible and workable (the approach that entails dividing the "resource pot" into three separate pots) would allow the system to go forward at once. A second approach which addresses the concern more head-on (the approach that entails setting up three separate scales and convening an expert panel to establish peg points among these scales) would require some preliminary work and could not be implemented for possibly 6 to 8 months while the necessary procedures are agreed to and implemented. The third approach (which entails development of a universal metric for environmental risk) is not likely to be implementable any time in the foreseeable future. Both of the first two approaches appear to be fully satisfactory as immediate or near-term resolutions to this concern.
Conclusion: The proposed system includes two appropriate options for dealing quickly with this concern.

Concern #6. The breakout of total environmental risk into specific environmental threats to be ranked "was not done right".

Assessment of the Proposed System Against This Concern: The proposed system is not tied to any one set of breakouts. It will work well for any nonoverlapping set of categories. (At the same time, no system is likely to be developed that works well if there are significant overlaps among categories.)
Conclusion: The proposed system performs well when measured against this concern.

Concern #7. Any method used to achieve risk-based resource allocations will inevitably be too rigid and mechanical.

Assessment of the Proposed System Against This Concern: With the understanding (a) that the proposed system is to be advisory, (b) that it is to provide a preliminary initial allocation that will be adjusted where compelling arguments to do so are made and that such compelling arguments are considered a certainty, (c) that further appropriate revision will take place as the President's Budget is developed and as Congress and the Executive Branch engage in the annual appropriation process, and (d) that it is expected that adjustments will be made each year to reduce the number of imbalances likely in the next year's preliminary allocation, the proposed system should perform well against this concern.

Conclusion: The proposed system when operating in the decision making context described above will not be unnecessarily rigid or mechanical — there will be ample opportunity to adjust the results to correct any anomalies.

Conclusion: The proposed system has now been assessed against the most widely held concerns about the functioning of any system for risk-based priority setting. The proposed system has been found to perform well when measured against each of these concerns. No shortcomings are revealed that would argue against rapid implementation of the proposed system.

ASSESSMENT AGAINST THE TEN ADDITIONAL CONCERNS THAT SHOULD BE ADDRESSED IN DESIGNING ANY SYSTEM FOR RISK-BASED MANAGEMENT

As was discussed in my earlier chapter, in addition to the seven widely held concerns discussed above, there are a number of other factors that should be of concern in designing a system of risk-based management. I will now assess the proposed system in terms of its effectiveness in minimizing the impact of these additional concerns.

Concern #8. Any method used to achieve risk-based resource allocation has the potential to be biased against controlled as compared with uncontrolled risks.

Assessment of the Proposed System Against This Concern: For the reasons given above together with those given previously, the proposed system should perform well when considered in light of this concern.
Conclusion: As stated above, the proposed system should perform well when considered in light of this concern.

Concern #9. What is to be allocated? Federal dollars only? Or total public and private expenditure for environmental protection and management?

Assessment of the Proposed System Against This Concern: The proposed system can be applied *either* to the $1.5 billion of discretionary EPA resources or to the entire $100 billion of total public and private investment for environmental protection and management. It is strongly urged that it be applied to the entire $100 billion. Any option selected will have to fall *both* within the available total resources (i.e., total public and private resources) for that environmental threat *and* within the available discretionary EPA resources available for addressing that environmental threat. Modification of the algorithm presented in the proposed system to accommodate such "dual constraints" can easily be accomplished.

Conclusion: The proposed system will work well whichever frame of reference (discretionary EPA resources only or total public and private resources) is selected as the scope of operation of the new system. (See Appendix C.)

Concern #10. What is to be the basis for the allocation? The total cost of control/prevention? Or the marginal cost?

Assessment of the Proposed System Against This Concern: The proposed system appears to take a sensible approach for establishing priorities and for allocating resources. No other system has been proposed that performs better.
Conclusion: The proposed system performs well when measured against this concern.

Concern #11. Will a given approach for resource allocation be useful in guiding the allocation of dollars for: research on health effects? research on ecological effects? development of needed new control technology? development of needed new management strategies?

Assessment of the Proposed System Against This Concern: The proposed system provides suggested allocations not only for risk reduction activities, but also for virtually all of the critical adjunct activities, including all of those listed above.
Conclusion: The proposed system performs well when measured against this concern.

Concern #12. There is no *central repository* for environmental risk data.

Assessment of the Proposed System Against This Concern: Because of the way it is structured, the proposed system, in essence, helps force the creation of a central repository of risk information in the form of the Input Worksheets and the Graphical Summary of Risk Estimates. Furthermore, the proposed system would require the establishment of a small staff office to operate it and revise it each year. This staff office would inevitably then become a repository of risk information. It could also be officially designated to serve as such a repository. Ideally, it would do so under some formal arrangement with OHEA. (The small new staff office could serve as a repository of summary risk information, while OHEA could serve as the repository of the underlying studies and research data on which the summary risk data are based.)
Conclusion: The proposed approach would require the establishment of a small new staff office which would then serve as the repository of summary risk information. Thus, adoption of this proposed system would force the creation of such a repository. The proposed system therefore performs well against this concern.

Concern #13. There is no on-going process for routinely supplementing incomplete risk data.

Assessment of the Proposed System Against This Concern: As discussed under Concern #12 above, the proposed system contains all of the elements just discussed and therefore should work to reduce the force of this concern over time.

Conclusion: The proposed system performs well when assessed against this concern.

Concern #14. There is no on-going process for routinely improving risk data for which there are large current uncertainties.

Assessment of the Proposed System Against This Concern: As discussed under Concern #12 above, the proposed system contains all of the elements just discussed and therefore should work to reduce the force of this concern over time.

Conclusion: The proposed system performs well when assessed against this concern.

Concern #15. There is no on-going process for updating risk data to incorporate newly developed data and findings.

Assessment of the Proposed System Against This Concern: As discussed under Concern #12 above, the proposed system contains all of the elements just discussed and therefore should work to reduce the force of this concern over time.

Conclusion: The proposed system performs well when assessed against this concern.

Concern #16. There is no on-going process for comparing risk numbers with expenditures.

Assessment of the Proposed System Against This Concern: The proposed system does exactly this — on a consistent, comprehensive basis once each year.

Conclusion: The proposed system performs well when measured against this concern.

Concern #17. There is insufficient commitment to continuing and building on an explicitly *quantitative* approach for risk-based priority setting and resource allocation.

Assessment of the Proposed System Against This Concern: The proposed system is a "strictly quantitative" one as defined above. As a consequence:

(1) it is less subject to manipulation than even the best qualitative system, and (2) the resource allocation it produces will always be more equitable than that produced by even the best qualitative system.

Conclusion: The proposed system performs well when measured against this concern.

CONCLUDING REMARKS

It has been shown that one specific system already developed, the "Quick-Start" proposal presented in this chapter, does in fact perform well when measured against all of the concerns presented in my earlier chapter regarding the immediate implementation of a system of risk-based priority setting and resource allocation at EPA. I can therefore recommend implementation of the proposed "Quick-Start" system forthwith as being consistent with prudent acceptance of the validity of the concerns that have been put forward with regard to such a system.

APPENDIX A: PROPOSED "INTERMEDIATE-TERM" APPROACH FOR COMBINING HEALTH, ECOLOGICAL, AND WELFARE RISKS

The following approach could be carried out within 6 to 8 months and would give a single combined risk score for each environmental threat.

> *Step 1.* Rank each environmental threat separately on each of three separate risk scales (one each for health risks, ecological risks, and welfare risks). Have each scale go from 0 to 100, with the score of 100 being assigned to the specific environmental threat that ranks highest *for that kind of risk* (see Figure A-1).
>
> *Step 2.* Convene an expert panel whose members have broad environmental expertise and concerns and with no known bias towards or against (1) any particular kind of risk, (2) any particular environmental threat, or (3) any particular environmental program. Have this expert panel peg one point on each scale as representing "equivalent risks" for each pair of the scales developed in Step 1 (see Figure A-2). Note in Figure A-2 that Environmental Threat H with a score of 76 on the health risk scale is pegged as representing a health risk approximately comparable in magnitude to that of the ecological risk presented by Environmental Threat E (which has a score of 62 on the Ecological Risk scale).
>
> *Step 3.* Expand or shrink two of the three scales as necessary so that the pairs of peg points identified in Step 2 above "line up" (see Figure A-3).

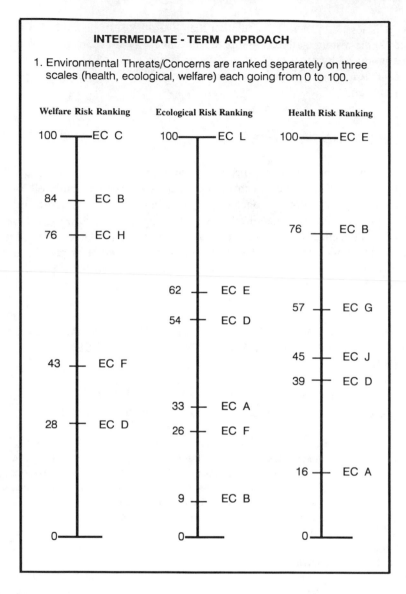

INTERMEDIATE - TERM APPROACH

1. Environmental Threats/Concerns are ranked separately on three scales (health, ecological, welfare) each going from 0 to 100.

FIGURE A1. Starting point for the proposed intermediate-term approach for developing a "common risk metric".

> *Step 4.* The scales are now "calibrated" against each other and each type of risk (health, ecological, and welfare) and can now be converted to its equivalent on the other two scales. Any one of these scales (e.g., the health risk scale or the ecological risk scale) can now be used as the interim "common risk metric".

INTERMEDIATE - TERM APPROACH (Continued)

2. An expert panel pegs one point on each pair of scales as representing "equivalent risks".

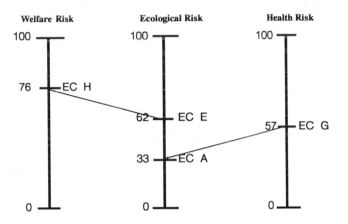

3. The scales are shrunk/expanded as necessary so the peg points "align up".

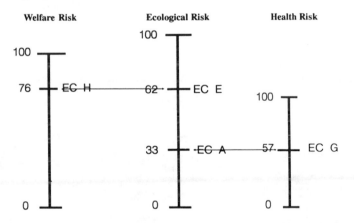

4. The scales are now "calibrated" against each other and each type of risk unit (ecological, health, welfare) can now be converted to its equivalent on the other two risk scales. Any one of the scales (e.g. the ecological risk scale or the heallth risk scale) can then be used as the interim "common risk metric."

FIGURES A2 and A3.   Steps 2 and 3 of the proposed intermediate-term approach for developing a "common risk metric".

APPENDIX B: ALTERNATIVE FORMULATION OF THE "WILLINGNESS TO PAY" EQUATION

The "willingness to pay" equation derived above is, for each distinct environmental threat,

$$W = P \times R \tag{1}$$

We now develop an alternative formula for this equation that will be useful later.

Note that:

$$P = S/T \tag{2}$$

If we substitute the values for P in formula (2) into formula (1) above, we obtain:

$$W = P \times R$$
$$= (S/T) \times R$$
$$= S \times (R/T)$$
$$= w \times S$$

where $w = R/T$

w ("lower case w") is "willingness to pay per unit of risk"

We therefore have for each environmental threat:

$$W = w \times S \tag{3}$$

Since:

$$S = L + (25\% \times U) \tag{4}$$

we also have:

$$W = w \times [L + (25\% \times U)] \tag{5}$$

APPENDIX C: CLARIFICATION OF HOW TO USE THE PROPOSED SYSTEM TO ALLOCATE TOTAL (RATHER THAN JUST FEDERAL) EXPENDITURES FOR ENVIRONMENTAL PROTECTION

In this attachment I elaborate how the procedures in steps 1 through 8 would work when there are two constraints to be met: total dollars available to address each environmental threat and total discretionary Federal dollars available to address each environmental threat.

In Step 3, establish two separate "preliminary allocations": (1) one for total dollars (i.e., total public and private dollars), (2) another for total EPA dollars.

Set up the Graphical Display of the Risk Reduction Options using "total cost (i.e., total public and private cost) divided by the amount of risk to be reduced" as the number to be used for placing each option on the table. But have three numbers associated with each option: total dollars per year, total EPA dollars in an average year, and total EPA dollars in the first year.

Go through the process, using the "preliminary allocation" based on total cost as the basis for the allocations. At the same time, at each stage in the process, keep track of the total of "the average EPA dollars" assigned, and the "first year EPA dollars" assigned. Take the process through to the end, without stopping, even if the total available EPA dollars is exceeded. At the end of the process, if the total of the average EPA dollars does not exceed the projected total EPA dollars in a typical year and if the total of the "first year EPA dollars" does not exceed the EPA dollars projected to be available for the year being budgeting, then stop. The allocation already developed is the allocation to be used.

If, however, either of the "total EPA dollars" totals exceeds the number of EPA dollars actually available, then add the following additional steps:

9. Calculate the total risk reduction ("total risk reduced") that would be achieved under the allocation already developed (which we will refer to as the "initial allocation of resources".

10. Start substituting the left-most unselected options for options already selected in such a way that the smallest possible decrease in "total risk reduced" is achieved while the ratio of Federal dollars to total dollars is reduced to the point that they are in balance with the actual number of dollars of each kind that are available (approximately 1.5 "Federal dollars" for every 100 "total dollars"). The result is the "revised allocation of resources" (to bring total dollars and EPA dollars in balance). (A specific numerical algorithm comparable to those presented earlier will be developed to carry out this procedure in an equitable fashion.)

11. Calculate the decrease in "total risk reduced" from that achieved in the "initial allocation of resources" (which was generated at the end of step 8) and the "revised allocation of resources" (which was generated at the end of step 10). Note the specific areas where risk reduction opportunities were lost due to the need to throw out previously selected options to bring EPA dollars and total dollars in balance. (That is, note which specific options for which specific Environmental Threats were eliminated in moving from the "initial allocation of resources to "the revised allocation of resources".

12. Adjust the algorithm for use in the next year (and subsequent years) to provide an additional incentive to decrease the ratio of Federal to total

dollars for *all* options in order to reduce (and hopefully eventually eliminate) the need to go through the additional steps (steps 9 through 11) described above. Make the magnitude of this incentive proportionate to the amount of reduction in the Federal-dollar-to-total-dollar ratio that is needed. (That is, if a small reduction is needed, make it a relatively small incentive. If a large reduction is needed, make it a larger incentive.)

REFERENCES

U.S. Environmental Protection Agency, *Unfinished Business: a Comparative Assessment of Environmental Problems,* Office of Policy, Planning and Evaluation, Washington, D.C., February 1987.

U.S. Environmental Protection Agency, *Reducing Risk: Setting Priorities and Strategies for Environmental Protection,* Science Advisory Board, Washington, D.C., SAB-EC-90-021, September 1990.

Index

Index